I0650799

ForkBraid

III

Just Rewards

By Michael Robert von Blucher-Altona

30-June-2024

Copyright @ 2024 by Michael Robert von Blucher-Altona

Library of Congress Control Number: 2023920897

ISBN: Hardback   978-0-6459906-8-3
       Paperback   978-0-6459906-7-6
       Kindle   978-0-6459906-6-9

All rights reserved. No part of this book may be reproduced or transmitted in any from or by any means, electronic or mechanical, including photocopying, recording, or by any information storage and retrieval system, without permission in writing from the copyright owner:

This is a work of fiction. Names, characters, places and incidents either are the product of the author's imagination or are used fictitiously, and any resemblance to any actual persons, living or dead, events, or locales is entirely coincidental.

First published 2024

Books by Michael Robert von Blucher-Altona
ForkBraid
Book 1: ForkBraid   – The Price of Peace
Book 2: ForkBraid II – The Cost of War
Book 3: ForkBraid III – Just Rewards

Table of Contents

1. Straighten out the Record..5
2. Cattle on Mars..14
3. Medallions..33
4. Horridious Horridians..42
5. Follow the Money..64
6. Places to Hide..88
7. Hunters and Collectors..102
8. Homeward Bound..126
9. Family Dynamics..141
10. The Grey Council..157
11. The Blood Nut..172
12. In the News Weekly Hot Takes..198
13. Flies on the Wall..212
14. First Contact..227
15. Io Prime..245
16. Io - Lagrangian Point Four..265
17. Reactions..285
18. The Fall of Venusville..305
19. Aftermath..315
20. The Fall of Patroclus..328
21. Our Dear Sister..343
22. The Belters be Pissed..353
23. The Day of the Dreadnoughts..362
24. The Fall of Hector..372
25. Heavy is the Loss..387
26. Callisto - Lagrangian Point Four..395
27. Europa - Lagrangian Point Four..405
28. Aphrodite's Revenge..411
29. Plan B - We have No Rabbits..427
30. Ganymede - Lagrangian Point Four..437
31. Ganymede - Lagrangian Point One..445
32. The High Prince..456
33. Elysium..471

What goes around, comes around.

That which ye sow, so shall ye reap.

That which you send out, you shall receive back.

Thrice here, thrice from above and thrice from below.

The Good and the bad.

These things are always the same.

They do not change!

For those who have performed evils deeds.

Beware your Just Rewards!

Lord Folcrom Tafazah. Winter Solstice 2028.

1. Straighten out the Record

President Banyan walked down the corridor to the news conference room, his secretary Tanya close behind. General Stanton, Captain Carmichael and Adjutant Lieutenant Blixen followed closely behind them.

Recently, the Captain and Crew of the Martian space ship Solstice had been awarded medals of honour and gallantry in a ceremony aboard their ship for services performed in the defence of the L5 colonies. The battle of L5. This medal ceremony had been recorded and later released to the public via the various news services and their associated networks. This had occurred very recently.

This was quickly followed by the release of a wanted, reward video by the Jovian High Council. The wanted video called those very same crew members Pirates and accusing them of heinous crimes, including mass homicide. The video posted rewards for each and every crew member. Rewards in the millions of Jovian golden credits. President Banyan's communications office had since been inundated with calls wanting answers.

As they approached the news conference room door, President Banyan turned around briefly and told the others, "Let's straighten out the record, shall we", then they entered the room.

President Banyan walked across to the podium that stood upon the stage. His entourage lined up on either side of him.

"Ladies and Gentlemen", President Banyan greeted the people gathered before him, "You all know who I am. I have with me General Arch Stanton of the Earth Defence Forces and Fleet Captain Bartholomew Carmichael of the Colonial Fleet, along with Lieutenant Adjutant Blixen and my own Secretary Tanya. We all know why we are here, so please ask your questions."

The first question was then quickly shouted out, "Mr President. Leticia Jonquil of the Colonial News Services. Are the crew of the Solstice Heroes or Pirates? Exactly what are they?"

"Well Ms Jonquil, the crew of the Solstice are most definitely Heroes. The wanted video that was released by the Jovian High Council was just pure propaganda. Nothing more", President Banyan replied.

"What makes them Heroes Mr President?", asked another reporter, who added, "Martin Aragon of the Inner System News."

"That would be the highly illegal and unprovoked attack, launched against the Earth, Mars and our own L5", President Banyan replied, then added, "I will let Fleet Captain Carmichael of the Colonial Fleet give you all the relevant details."

Captain Carmichael stepped slightly forward, "The Horridian Dynasty of the Jovian Realms launched a decapitation attempt against the Earth, Mars and L5. Those attacks consisted of twenty two hundred missiles, each one containing ten cold fusion warheads with two megaton yields. In addition to the missile attack, the Jovian Realms also sent Trojan occupation forces to both Mars and our own L5."

Ms Jonquil stepped back in and asked, "How do the crew of the Solstice fit into these attacks?"

Captain Carmichael continued, "The crew of the Solstice destroyed those missiles that were en-route to Mars. They later fought the Trojan occupation forces that landed on Mar, in the Battle of the Elysium Plains. After defeating the Trojans, they then convinced them to leave Mars and return home to the Aft Trojan Colonies. They did not stop there either."

Captain Carmichael paused and then continued, "After saving Mars, the Solstice then flew to the Earth and L5. They destroyed a third of the missiles headed our way. They did this by making three highly dangerous sorties inside the missile swarm. Then after the missile's warheads were launched, they chased them down and destroyed as many warheads as they could, that were targeting L5. The crew of the Solstice were absolutely crucial during the Battle of L5. Absolutely crucial."

President Banyan stepped in, "We lost over sixty five thousand colonists that day. We would have lost Lord knows how many more had the crew of the Solstice had not stepped in. If that doesn't make them Heroes, then what does?"

The was a silent pause for a few moments before another reporter spoke up.

"Pauline Quinn, Cis-lunar news. General Stanton. How does the Earth feel about the crew of the Solstice?", another reporter asked.

General Stanton quickly answered, "As you are all aware, the Earth lost four cities across Europe and somewhere in excess of two and a half million souls. We are still counting the dead. If not for the actions of the Solstice's crew, there is no telling how many more cities would have been lost. How many more souls might have perished. The Earth, most definitely considers the crew of the Solstice to be Heroes. They were crucial to our defence as well. They saved untold millions."

"Then why hasn't the Earth given them medals like L5 did?", Pauline Quinn asked.

General Stanton cocked an eye brow and replied, "Ms Quinn. We have suffered horrendous losses and have been doing our level best to deal with them. Our emergency services have been busy around the clock since the attacks. The crew of the Solstice will be awarded the appropriate medals in the due course of time. We, however, are just a little busy at the moment."

"General. Bob Thomas, Interplanetary News. General. What medals will the crew of the Solstice be awarded with?"

"When time comes Mr Thomas. The crew of the Solstice will receive the Earth's Medal of Honour", the General replied, he then added, "There was also a combined fleet of Earth Defence Force and Colonial Fleet ships, that flew two sorties into that same missile swarm. Their crews will also be receiving Medals of Honour. Thirty three of those ships were destroyed during those missions. So we will also be awarding both Medals of Honour and Purple Hearts to the crews of those thirty three ships, who made the ultimate sacrifice."

"Colleen Turner. Venusian Times. What about the unprovoked and unjustified mass homicide of those one hundred and twenty five thousand Trojan troops?", another reporter asked.

Captain Carmichael quickly answered that question, "That never happened. That is a Jovian lie."

"In what way Captain?", Ms Turner questioned.

Captain Carmichael replied, "The Trojan occupation forces that were en-route to the Earth and L5, were intercepted by both the Solstice and my own ship, the Spartan. The Captain of the Solstice informed General Trask, the commander of the Trojan occupation forces, that they were flying directly into the combined Earth Defence Force and Colonial Fleets. Captain Forkbraid convinced the General to bypass Cis-lunar space altogether and to return back to the Trojan asteroid colonies. This was done to avoid further loss of lives."

"And this actually happened?", Ms Turner pushed

"Ms Turner. I was there. My ship, the Spartan and the Solstice, we both escorted the Trojan occupation forces out of our territory. The last we saw of them, they were on their way home. Indeed, our surveillance facilities are still watching their progress in their long flight home.", Captain Carmichael informed her.

General Stanton stepped in, "There were a handful of Trojan ships, around twenty five that made a suicide run at L5. They were intercepted and destroyed by the Earth Defence Forces. That action was taken at my command. The Solstice took absolutely no part in that action. Just opposite in fact. The Captain and crew of the Solstice saved a good ninety eight percent of the Trojan occupation forces."

Ms Turner asked, "So everything the Jovian High Council say about the Trojan troops is a lie?Everything they've said about the Solstice's crew being responsible for those one hundred and twenty five thousand deaths is a lie?"

"Now you know the truth Ms Turner. There were maybe two and a half thousand dead Trojans at the most and the Solstice had absolutely nothing to do with that action. They attacked us and my ships intercepted them. That's the entire truth of the matter", General Stanton confirmed.

Captain Carmichael added, "The trajectory of the Trojan fleet is published online and freely available. If you really want you can purchase a telescope and track their progress for yourselves."

Martin Aragon commented, "Sounds to me like the Trojans should award them medals as well."

"Well, you'd think so. However, that is unlikely to happen Mr Aragon. It seems that the Jovian High Council decided to declare them Pirates instead. A seriously ungrateful bunch aren't they", Captain Carmichael replied.

President Banyan then informed the gathered reporters, "It is a moot point anyway. There is ancient agreement, called the Geneva Convention. It is a centuries old agreement. A convention that sets forth the protocols and laws pertaining to armed conflicts. Under that agreement, I think you will find that combatants in a time of war cannot simply be declare Pirates. All of the major colony groupings around our solar system are signatories to that agreement, including the Jovian Realms."

"So the crew of the Solstice are considered combatants amongst our allies?", another reporter asked, "Sid Tuckerson, Colonial Central Times."

"You will have noticed during the medal ceremony, that the crew of the Solstice were all in uniform. The uniform of the Martian Defence Forces I do believe", President Banyan replied, adding, "That makes them not only our allies, but also lawful combatants in this conflict."

"President Banyan Sir", Leticia Jonquil caught the President's attention, "A small fleet has been spotted heading out to Mars. What would that be about then?"

President Banyan turned to General Stanton, "I do believe that General Stanton should probably answer that question."

General Stanton informed Leticia, "That small fleet Ms Jonquil, was organised by myself and Captain Carmichael here. It is a combined Earth Defence Force and Colonial Fleet. We put in three destroyers and three frigates each. We also included three heavy cruisers, two from the Earth and one from L5. We have seconded that small fleet of fifteen ships to aid the Martian Defences."

Captain Carmichael added, "I am pleased to say that Earth Defence Force Admiral, Samantha Zumwalt has been placed in command of that fleet. The EDCF Martian Task Force. The Martian Defence Forces are quite small and will be requiring our assistance."

There were a few snickers around the news conference room and reporter Bob Thomas remarked, "It seems that we needed their assistance not too long ago."

"Yes, we certainly did Mr Thomas. The crew of the Solstice provided us not only with data and information, they helped to destroy a great many missiles and warheads. That is why they are Heroes and definitely not Pirates", President Banyan replied, closing the meeting with, "Now, if that answers all of your questions, we must get back to our usual duties."

"Before we do Mr President. What about the rewards being offered by the Jovian High Council?", asked Leticia Jonquil.

"I find those rewards to be abhorrent. What are they going to do next? Offer rewards for the Capture of my Colonial Fleet Captains? Our ship's crews. It is patently ridiculous", President Banyan replied.

Captain Carmichael stepped in, "To any would be bounty hunters out there thinking of collecting those rewards. Going after my comrades would be a huge mistake on your part. Do so at your own risk and always remember this. My comrades have the backing of the entire Colonial Fleet behind them. If you go after them, we will come after you!"

"And that's how we view the situation as well", General Stanton added, "We've got the crew of the Solstice's back. If you go after them, we will come after you, as well!"

"Well noted Captain Carmichael, General Stanton", the President remarked, then added, "Now. We really must get back to our duties. Good day to you all, Ladies and Gentlemen."

"Mr President! Mr President! One more question please", Colleen Turner shouted.

"Okay Ms Turner. One final question and then we really must go", President Banyon replied.

"After this unprovoked attack on the inner solar system by the Jovian Realms, how are the Earth Defence Forces and Colonial Fleets going to respond?", Ms Turner asked.

President Banyon responded, "Now Ms Turner. We aren't going to be telegraphing our moves to the Jovian High Council before we make them, are we now."

"That is correct Mr President", Captain Carmichael agreed, "There will be a response. Mark my words Ms Turner. There will definitely be a response. The Jovian High Council and the Horridian Dynasty will rue the day that they embarked on this unprovoked attack on our people."

General Stanton nodded his head and stated, "There will be a response and that response will be heading their way. They will pay for their heinous crimes."

"Now ladies and gentlemen. We really must get back to our duties. Good day to you all, Ladies and Gentlemen", President Banyon closed the meeting.

Lieutenant Adjutant Blixen had been recording everything throughout the meeting on his grip.

After gathering back in President Banyan's office, "Gentlemen. How about a glass of wine? Tanya, bring me a bottle from that new batch that came in from Mars."

"From Mars? New batch?", General Stanton queried.

"Yes. Martian red cherry wine", President Banyan informed them, "It was confiscated from some smugglers making an illegal run from Mars. It's from New Tortuga I believe. It is apparently very popular on Mars. We may have to make its importation official. It is actually very good."

President Banyan opened a bottle while Tanya passed around some glasses and they all sat down and partook of the Martian red cherry wine. They all agreed it was quite a good drop. General Stanton looked at the label on the bottle, it read *'From the CCF Orchards of New Tortuga'*.

"CCF Orchards, New Tortuga", the General enquired.

President Banyan turned to his secretary, "Tanya? CCF Orchards, New Tortuga?"

"Oh. Give me a second or two Mr President", Tanya replied as she quickly pressed a few keys on her virtual keyboard, "Cormac and Candice Farmer, New Tortuga. CCF is their moniker Sir."

"I'm going to have to contact Admiral Zumwalt. When Sam returns to cis-lunar space, maybe she can bring a few crates back with her", the General remarked.

"That shouldn't be too hard General", Captain Carmichael replied, informing him further, "Cormac and Candy are friends of Captain Forkbraid and his crew. We can make arrangements."

"That is good to know Captain", the General replied, "This is definitely a good drop."

Captain Carmichael remarked, "Mr President. You did make an incorrect statement during the press conference."

"Did I? What would that be Captain?", the President enquired.

"The Martian Defence Forces Sir", Captain Carmichael replied, informing him further, "There isn't actually any such organisation. There is no Martian Defence Forces Sir."

"Really? I just assumed they were a part of the Martian Defence Forces", President Banyon replied, before adding, "They were all in uniform after all. Just what are they then?"

"Mars doesn't currently have any Defence Forces. Each major colony has security forces and a militia. Nothing else", Captain Carmichael informed him, adding, "The crew of the Solstice are actually just private citizens Sir."

General Stanton commented. "That makes them privateers Captain."

"Yes I know General", the Captain replied.

"What does that mean gentlemen?", President Banyan queried.

Captain Carmichael replied bluntly, "As privateers, the Jovian High Council actually has every right to call the crew of the Solstice Pirates Sir."

"Well that is not a good thing Captain", the President replied, asking, "How do we fix this?"

Captain Carmichael turned to his Lieutenant Adjutant, "Blixen. Contact Governor Anderson at Chryce Colony. Tell him we need him to convene a meeting of the Colonial Governors. The Governors need to create a new Martian Defence Force. Make sure he understands what we need and how we need it done. You do understand the problem, don't you Blixen?"

"I believe I do Captain. Mars needs an official Defence Force on their books. It needs to cover certain personnel and they will need to back date everything appropriately. We still have those ten pilots and their atmo rated wisps on secondment to the Elysium Colony on Mars as well Captain. So with those and the Solstice, they can start with a small fleet of ships. I'll get the ball rolling Sir", Lieutenant Blixen replied.

"Good man Blixen", Captain Carmichael replied, then turning back to President Banyan, "Lieutenant Blixen thinks of everything. We've got this covered Mr President."

"That should cover the crew of the Solstice Captain", General Stanton remarked, adding, "I'll contact Admiral Zumwalt about awarding those medals of honour, when the EDCF Task Force arrives in Martian orbit."

Captain Carmichael replied, "Another award ceremony for the crew of the Solstice. Have it all recorded and released to the news feeds, along with re-runs of the original award ceremony. That should cement those crew members, those personnel, as Heroes in the minds of the public."

"That and the fact that our personnel with the EDCF Martian Task Force can also aid in the setting up of the Martian Defence Forces", General Stanton commented.

"Yes General. Between your personnel and mine, I think the Martian Defence Forces will become a very capable little force", Captain Carmichael replied.

"How is that possible Captain Carmichael?", President Banyan questioned, "Aren't we starting the Martian Defence Forces pretty much from scratch?"

"Mr President. Eight colonies, each with their own militias and security services", the Captain pointed out, explaining, "So Mars has those, then there's the Solstice, its Crew and the ten Colonial Fleet Pilots on secondment to the Elysium colony and we have a very good start."

"It doesn't sound like much", President Banyan noted.

General Stanton replied, "It's a start. There will be recruitment to bring in new personnel as well. Before the years out, I bet they'll have something formidable."

"And we are forgetting something else Mr President", Captain Carmichael remarked.

"What would that be Captain?", the President asked.

"Varakhan Utana Mr President", Captain Carmichael replied.

"Varakhan Utana?", President Banyan queried.

Captain Carmichael replied, "He is the Solstice's chief engineer. He is also the reason why the Colonial and the Earth Defence Force Fleets are being upgraded with new technologies as we speak. His technology Mr President."

"I was kind of wondering where all those high tech goodies came from", the President admitted.

Captain Carmichael replied, "Yes Mr President. Varak's very own technological developments. All of them were his work. Varakhan Utana is the man who can build anything and he has all that lovely Trojan weapons scrap to work with. There is absolutely no telling what that man might come up with next."

2. Cattle on Mars

Jim Murphy flew his wives, Zuawalo and Zeealas south to the Elysium colony. Along with them came Jim's in laws Kwoth and Zyaliep, along with their Aunt Nyaliep and her husband Varak. The idea for the short trip came from Varak, who did need to take a short break from his duties. He also wanted to show the Pod family something that he had been working on in the background.

Jim's Hummer landed at the airfield and space port at the Elysium colony. As they had approached Elysium, they could see the tall steel and glass towers of the colony, intermixed and surrounded by large expanses of green grass lands and park lands. A great deal of the Elysium colony was actually underground and invisible from the surface.

"This is nothing like Chryce colony", Zeealas remarked, asking, "Where are all the buildings?"

"Yes", Zuawalo agreed, "In Chryce colony the city centre is all tall steel and glass towers, surrounded by very old shanty towns."

"When Lady Selene commissioned the Elysium colony, the design specification was for big open spaces. Park lands and grass lands, with not so many tall building embedded into the landscape", Varak informed them, adding, "Over ninety percent of the colony is underground. You cannot see it. It is all hidden."

"Like an ice berg. You only see the top ten percent", Jim commented.

"Yes Jim. Like an ice berg", Varak agreed.

"If most of the colony is underground, how did those Pirates cause so much damage?", Zuawalo enquired.

"They mostly hit the parts they could see", Jim replied.

"Yes. They hit the towers and the infrastructure around the perimeter of the colony", Varak agreed, adding, "We were very lucky. Much of what they hit, was empty at the time."

"True, but we still lost quite a few hundred people and some vital projects were halted", Jim informed everyone.

Zuawalo looked around and began pointing out to her family some of the damage that was still visible on the towering buildings that had not yet been repaired.

"Yes Zuawalo", Varak replied to her unspoken question, "It does take a lot of time to repair the damage. There are many areas we are still working on."

Jim passed Varak a belt, with a holstered pulse pistol, "Keep the women safe Varak."

As Jim put on his own belt with its pulse pistol, Varak replied, "I will Jim."

"Where is your Jim going my daughters?", Zyaliep asked Zuawalo and Zeealas.

Jim answered for his wives, "I have work to do Mother Zyaliep. With the possibility of bounty hunters turning up, I have to make sure that the Elysium security services are ready for anything."

"It is okay my Sister in law", Varak told Zyaliep, "Jim and I have discussed this. I will show you around the colony. Jim will sort out the colony security. We all meet up later at my apartment."

"And the pulse pistols?, asked Kwoth, Zyaliep's husband.

"Just a precaution Kwoth", Jim replied, "I don't expect we'll be needing them, but we have them just in case. Which reminds me. Girls, do you have your sheath knives?"

Both Zuawalo and Zeealas nodded and showed Jim their sheath knives. Their Mother Zyaliep and Aunt Nyaliep, also pulled out their sheath knives and showed Jim.

Jim was a just little surprised. "You too? You also have knives?", he had no idea.

Kwoth smiled, "Like Mother. Like Daughters. Our women know how to look after themselves."

"If we need you Jim. I'll message you with my grip", Varak noted.

"Good to hear Varak", Jim replied, adding, "I'll see you all tonight at Varak's apartment", he then headed off to a waiting transport.

Varak instructed an attending Android to have their luggage taken to his apartment, where they'd be staying during their visit. He then placed a large picnic basket and some picnic blankets into a nearby transport chariot and asked everyone to climb aboard.

"I will show you all around the park lands first, then we will stop for a picnic lunch", Varak informed the others.

Varak drove the chariot around the park lands. Young trees, only planted within the previous five years were reaching for the sky. Growing tall under the lower Martian gravity. Most of the trees had been planted for their aesthetics, although here and there, were the occasional fruiting trees.

Varak pointed out, "Here, if the tree has fruit, you can pick it and eat it."

"Anyone can pick and eat the fruit?", Zeealas queried.

"Of course Zeealas. That is why we planted them", Varak replied.

Lakes were abundant in the park lands as well.

Zeealas, always looking for a place to catch fish asked, "Are there fish in those lakes?"

"The largest lakes are stocked with brown trout, rainbow trout, golden perch and short finned eels. There are also yabbies in the lakes and fresh water mussels", Varak informed her.

"We can fish the lakes as well?", Zeealas questioned.

"Of course you can Zeealas. That is why they are stocked", Varak informed her.

Visible in the background, embedded in the park lands and grass lands, were the ever present tall, steel and glass towers of the colony.

"So few people. So many metal men", Zyaliep noted.

And Zyaliep was correct. The parks and gardens were managed by lower level Androids.

"Yes Zyaliep. The Androids manage these park lands", Varak informed her, "There are many people here, but they are mainly custodians and newer colonists. They tend to work underground."

"Do they ever come up?", Zyaliep queried.

"Of course they do", Varak answered, adding, "But there is a lot of work to be done. We are still fixing the damage caused by the Pirates and we are still in the process of building the colony."

"When will the colony be open?", Nyaliep asked.

"The Elysium colony is open Nyaliep", Varak informed his wife.

"Then why so few people?", Nyaliep questioned.

"When the Pirates attacked and they did attack twice, we lost well over three hundred people", Varak explained, adding, "A few ship loads of colonists arrived after that, but then the Jovian High Council declared war. So L5's Colonial Central Command stopped all Mars bound transports and no other colony vessels have arrived since then."

Zeealas noted, "That very bad man. He was responsible for those Pirate attacks."

Zuawalo replied, reminding everyone, "That very bad man was once Leroy McGuvan. He is no longer that very bad man. He has since been demolished by Gwek and he has been redeemed."

"So the war is holding back the colony?", Kwoth asked.

"Yes", Varak agreed, "If not for the stop on colony transports, the population would be triple what it is now. At the very least."

"Maybe people can come here from other places on Mars or perhaps from the colonies in High Martian orbit?", Kwoth enquired.

"That is a great idea Kwoth. Perhaps even some of your people might even come here to live", Varak replied, thinking, it would be nice for Nyaliep to have some family and friends nearby.

Varak then commented, "I will discuss this with Lady Selene when we get back to the academy."

Every now and then Varak would stop the chariot and let everyone out to stretch their legs and get a good look around the park lands. Zuawalo and Zeealas both waded out into one of the lakes at one point. The water was cool, but not cold and it was clean and fresh. They mentally noted the occasional fish swirls they could see in the water.

"The air here, it smells so nice. Almost like back home", Zuawalo remarked.

"Almost Sister, but not the same. Our air is more cool, more crisp", Zeealas noted.

"Our air is cold and crisp. It makes you strong", Nyaliep told everyone.

"Our Jim did not mention fish. We could have brought our rods with us", Zeealas commented.

Varak drove their chariot to a point roughly in the centre of the Elysium colony and parked under an immense, tall and broad Banyan tree. This Banyan was the oldest tree in the region and the colony had been built around it. Supporting prop roots had formed secondary trunks, combined with Mars's thirty eight percent gravity, allowing the tree to grow exceptionally broad.

The tall, steel and glass towers appeared to be built in concentric rings around the tree. That was of course in the design specification, lots of parks and open space, tall buildings in concentric rings. Everything else, including infrastructure was underground. This was to be the most beautiful colony on Mars and Varak had done his level best to make it so, despite the Pirate attacks.

Varak removed the picnic basket from the chariot and placed it on the ground under the shade of the banyan tree. Zyaliep and Nyaliep spread the picnic blankets around the basket and they all enjoyed their picnic lunch. Zuawalo and Zeealas could not help themselves and climbed high up into the Banyan tree. Around one o'clock they all packed up and continued on their tour.

Varak showed them a couple of the tall, steel and glass towers. These were mainly above ground living quarters, for those colonists who preferred living above ground, but also access points to the greater colony beneath. The current population of the Elysium colony was only a little more than five thousand people and this was far less than one percent of its intended population. It would take many, many years for the colony to develop into the thriving metropolis it was intended to be. Several decades perhaps.

"So many metal men", Zyaliep noted once more.

"Yes Zyaliep", Varak replied, "The colony is almost empty. The Androids are needed to keep everything clean and well maintained."

"It is still very beautiful Mother", Zeealas noted.

"Yes", Zuawalo agreed, "I could live here. At least until, it got too crowded."

Varak's heart dropped just a little, he was hoping to convince them all, how wonderful it would be to live in the Elysium colony. He had already convinced his wife Nyaliep, but he didn't want her to be all alone. Varak had hoped to convince her family and friends to join them.

After seeing more of the colony park lands and a few more of the tall towers, Varak drove their chariot into an underground parking garage beneath one of the southernmost towers, where he parked the vehicle. They all alighted the chariot and headed over to the centrally located elevator.

Once they were all in the elevator, Varak entered his key into the control slot and the elevator began its journey upward in the tower. The top floor highlighted in green and each floor lit up briefly in red as the elevator passed by. Eventually they stopped at the top floor and the doors opened automatically. They were on the one hundredth floor of the tower.

As they walked out onto the landing, they could see that only one apartment was accessible.

"It is the penthouse. As I am the architect of the Elysium colony and its builder, I was given the pick of any apartment in the colony. So I chose this one", Varak informed them, "You will be able to see why when we get inside."

Varak placed his key into the access slot and the door opened. They all walked into Varak's penthouse apartment and were greeted by the apartment's house Android.

"Metal men, even here", Zyaliep noted.

"My Android Toby. He keeps my apartment in order", Varak replied.

Toby greeted them, "Welcome guests. We have taken the liberty of placing your luggage in your intended rooms, as designated by Master Varak", to Zyaliep, Toby remarked, "Metal men? We are a hyper dynamics model three-o-three Android. We have the designation, Toby. You may call us metal man if you so wish."

Zyaliep scoffed, "It talks, but it has no soul. This metal man!"

Toby then recognised Nyaliep, having been shown photos of her and announced, "You are Nyaliep. You are the wife of Varak. You are the Lady of this House. Your room is the master bedroom over there", he then pointed to the master bedroom.

"Thank you Toby. That will be all. We will call you if we need your assistance", Varak replied.

Toby bowed and went about his usual daily routines.

Nyaliep looked around at the sumptuous apartment, "This is your home Varak? I thought you lived in your rooms in the construction hanger at the academy."

"This is our home Nyaliep. Those rooms in the construction hanger are also yours as well", Varak replied, adding, "It is a long commute from Elysium to the Academy, so I stay there more often than not."

"I did not know Varak. Why did you not tell me?", Nyaliep asked.

"I wanted it to be a pleasant surprise my Queen", Varak replied with what he considered to be the ultimate compliment.

Nyaliep held Varak very closely and hugged him tightly, pressing her face against his strong, muscled chest, "I think I chose my man very well", she told him.

Her Sister Zyaliep smiled, she was just happy that Nyaliep had finally chosen at all and was now happy with her choice.

Jim walked into the apartment. As the Elysium colony's head of security, he had access to every door across the entire colony. The ultimate master key. As soon as he entered the main room, Zuawalo and Zeealas rush up to him and they both hugged him tightly.

"I take it you guys had a great day", Jim greeted.

"It was very good. This colony is very big, very clean, very nice", Mother Zyaliep replied.

"It is also very empty and there are lots of metal men everywhere", Nyaliep added.

"And there are fish in all the big lakes", Zeealas commented.

"Has Varak shown you all the view?" Jim asked.

"Not yet Jim. We have only just arrived a little bit before you", Varak answered, "This way."

They all followed Varak to the apartment's southern balcony. Varak opened the sliding glass doors. The vista before them was fantastic.

To their south was a huge flooded crater called Lake Eddie. It was a shade short of ninety kilometres wide and as much as three kilometres deep. An island in its centre, Eddie Island, was formed by the impact that created the Eddie crater. The crater floor had rebounded following the impact, creating a mountain in the middle of the crater. Now the crater was flooded, this mountain formed a rather large and tall island.

A broad canal had been carved through the northern rim of the crater, towards the new Elysium colony. At the near end, the canal was formed into a large harbour for docking boats and ships. A much broader canal had been carved through the southern rim of the crater, connecting Lake Eddie to the somewhat shallower, yet quite broad Elysium Channel. The Eddie Cut.

The far coastline of the Elysium Channel, with its myriad of islands was almost visible in the distance nearly a thousand kilometres south of their vantage point.

Varak remarked, "On a good day, with clear skies and good weather, you can almost see the Isidis Gulf. Sometimes, I think I can actually see it."

The view was spectacular and Nyaliep held onto Varak's strong left arm tightly, "It is truly beautiful my Varak."

Kwoth noted, "I am at a loss. Which view is more beautiful? This view? Or the view of the Hummocks?"

His wife, Zyaliep replied, "Kwoth. I have seen both and truly, I can not say!"

"I thought they'd like the view Varak", Jim commented, adding, "I find it awe inspiring every time I see it. Now you have two muses. This beautiful view and your beautiful new wife, Nyaliep."

Nyaliep smiled a broad smile, "My nieces. Your Jim is ever so sweet!", then she turned to her Sister Zyaliep, "And you called their Jim, short and pale like a ghost."

"That was tradition Nyaliep. As their Mother, I am expected to pick faults", Zyaliep replied.

"Yet you called my Varak, very tall, very strong and very handsome", Nyaliep smiled.

"Yes I did. Varak was a very good choice for you Nyaliep and I wanted you to keep him", Zyaliep admitted.

Jim Murphy whispered to Varak, "You get use to it mate. Just go with the flow."

Nyaliep noted, "The view is here. The bedroom is right there. I can wake up to this view, every morning. At least when we stay here."

Once they had moved back into the penthouse apartment's main room, Jim informed everyone, "We've put procedures into place to prevent any bounty hunters coming through the Elysium colony. So that vector of attack has been nullified."

"How does that work Jim?", Varak asked.

"It's really quite simple Varak. Anyone who comes to the colony, comes through the airfield or space port. If they have valid business here, we check them out and if they are legit, they enter the Elysium colony. If on the other hand, they don't have any valid business here or they fail our checks, we boot them out and they're out of here", Jim explained.

"And what if they don't come through the airfield or space port?", Varak enquired.

"That's even simpler. We have Lieutenant Roberts up there on Phobos, watching over the Elysium subcontinent with his satellites. Those birds of his. Anyone trying to land, anywhere on the subcontinent, will be tracked down and we'll come after them and arrest them", Jim explained.

"That is good to know", Varak replied, "I do worry about my Nyaliep."

"Yes. I worry about my wives as well Varak", Jim replied.

"I copied these off of the news feeds earlier today", Jim informed them, adding, "It's a press conference from L5, with President Banyan, Captain Carmichael and General Stanton. You might find this very interesting."

They all listened to the press conference recording and at the end of it Jim noted, "Captain Carmichael and General Stanton have both stated very clearly, if any would be bounty hunters comes after us, they will both come after them."

"That definitely helps us", Varak replied, adding, "No one wants Colonial Fleet or Earth Defence Force Heavy Cruisers coming after them."

"Very true Varak, very true", Jim agreed.

Nyaliep noted, "The Earth wants to give us medals of honour."

"Yes Nyaliep", Jim confirmed, "Apparently they are. Although, it could be quite a while before they get around to it. They have a huge problem in Europe to deal with at the moment, with four nuked cities and all."

"President Banyon told the reporters you were all part of the Martian

Defence Forces", Kwoth commented.

"Yes Kwoth. That itself could be a problem", Jim replied, "As there is no such thing as the Martian Defence Forces. President Banyon must have made an incorrect assumption I think."

The discussion about the press conference continued until late into the night, at which point everyone went off to their rooms to get some sleep.

The next morning Nyaliep awoke to the incredible view to the south of their apartment. Nyaliep climbed out of bed and walked over to the balcony's sliding doors. Looking through the glass and smiling, thinking to herself, *"I think I can get use to this."*

Varak walked into their bedroom carrying a tray with their breakfast on it, "You are awake Nyaliep my love. I was bringing you breakfast in bed."

Nyaliep smiled and patted her pregnant belly lightly, it was still far too early to show, "We can still eat in bed. If you wish."

Commotion beyond their bedroom door indicated their guests were awake and moving about, "Perhaps another time my Queen. Our guests are already awake."

It was well past ten am when the group left Varak and Nyaliep's apartment and headed back down the elevator to continue their tour of the Elysium colony. The hardest part was pulling themselves away from the southern view across Lake Eddie and the Elysium Channel. Jim made sure he had some good photos, to have blown up and displayed on his wive's dormitory wall back at the New Flinders Psychic Academy.

The elevator travelled down past the parking garage which was designated by the number zero. Below this were the sub-levels, which were designated minus one through minus fifty. Each sub-level lit up in red as the elevator passed by, travelling all the way to the lowest level which was lit up in green as their destination.

"We are not so deep as the towers are tall, but the sight. You should find it spectacular", Varak informed everyone.

Jim had been here many times before and noted, "You have to see this from the base level to truly get an idea of the sheer size and scope of this colony. Seeing is believing."

When the elevator doors opened they all stepped out and walked down a short corridor. When they reached the end of the corridor, they found themselves at the southern edge of a huge underground cavern. It was enormous, oval shaped, longer than it was broad. The top of the cavern, some five hundred feet above them, was encased in what appeared to be a plasteel dome structure.

The entire colony had been dug out, the dome and all other supporting structures put in place and hermetically sealed, then the whole thing back-filled and covered over. After which, all the colony superstructure and infrastructure was constructed beneath the dome. The thousand foot plus tall, steel and glass towers, sky scrapers, were added last, as above ground living and access points.

The walls of the cavern had at least fifty levels, each with broad terraces, lined with safety barriers. Shops and stores were visible, Restaurants were visible. Corridors led off away from the cavern into underground apartment complexes and manufacturing, industrial zones.

There was a spire in the very centre of the cavern, a good distance away from their entrance point. It was fairly broad and was a good three hundred and fifty feet tall. Many, many offices were contained within it. That was the cavern's, centre of governance and communications centre, all centrally located at the middle of the cavern.

There were Androids, soulless metal men as Zyaliep called them, moving about as was common in the Elysium colony. All going about their business, maintaining and cleaning etc. However what caught their eyes were the colonists. There must have been ninety percent or more of the colony's population in this one cavern. All going about their daily work and duties.

"Nearly all the colonists live in this one suburb", Varak noted, adding, "Many of them have jobs locally, although quite a few have jobs elsewhere in the colony."

"Suburb?", Zyaliep queried.

"Yes Mother Zyaliep. This is just one of Elysium's suburbs", Varak replied.

Jim pointed to a terrace about ten levels up, "There's a nice cafe up there on level ten. That's where we'll probably have lunch. After we've had a good look around that is. And yes Zeealas my love, they do serve slork."

Zeealas was pleased to hear that and smiled accordingly, "Goody!"

Zuawalo snorted in disgust, "Zeealas. A slig is not a pig! Slork is not pork!"

Jim commented, "Zuawalo my love, they do serve pork as well. Real pork. It is very new."

"We can show you that later in the afternoon", Varak replied, "Another surprise for you."

"What is this place called?", Nyaliep asked.

"This suburb is called Elysium Alpha or simply Alpha for short", Varak informed her.

"How many people live here?", asked Zyaliep.

"At the moment, under five thousand people live here. There are some who prefer to live on the surface. They're mostly people from Earth. People from L5 prefer places like this", Jim replied.

"It looks so very big for so few people Jim", Zuawalo noted.

"Yes it does Zuawalo", Jim answered, informing her, "This one suburb my love, can easily house well over fifty thousand plus people. And that's without any need to expand it further."

"There are twenty five other suburbs just like this one in the colony", Varak informed them all.

That statement alone had them all in awe of the Elysium colony. The Elysium colony was huge and at the moment, so incredibly empty and underpopulated.

Varak informed them further, "All of the other suburbs, Beta through Omega are largely empty. Only Androids and maintenance crews go there."

The group spent the next three hours exploring the suburb, but its sheer size was enormous. They could have spent days just looking around. Eventually Jim and Varak led then to the cafe on the tenth level, where they all had their lunch. A happy Zeealas ordered the slork, as did her Aunt Nyaliep. Her older Sister Zuawalo, however, tried the pork.

After looking around the Elysium Alpha suburb for most of the afternoon, Varak led the group back to their original point of ingress. They all boarded the elevator of Varak's apartment tower and alighted at level zero, the underground car park. Everyone boarded the chariot and Varak drove further south to the Elysium Ports. Just north of the port was another complex of much lower buildings and Varak drove their chariot to another underground car park where they all alighted once more.

Varak led the group over to a very specific area of the complex. It was underground and they had to access the relevant department via an elevator.

After they all alighted from the elevator, Varak announced, "This is the Elysium colony's cryogenic storage facility."

"Cryogenic storage?", Nyaliep queried.

"Yes Nyaliep", Varak replied, adding, "Here we store DNA, embryos, seeds, life, anything the colony, all the colonies for that matter, might need to store for the future. These vaults are vast and this is probably the most important facility on the whole of Mars."

"That isn't the reason Varak brought us here though", Jim noted.

"Ah. Yes Jim", Varak agreed, then added, "Have a look around, just in this small section here. Look at these catalogues. They can be very enlightening."

The small group of visitors looked around at what was being stored in this immediate area of the Elysium cryogenic facility.

"Dolphins? Porpoises? Orca?", Zuawalo enquired.

"Yes Zuawalo", Varak confirmed, "We had plans to introduce dolphins and porpoises to Mars. Even the possibility of whales. Our seas need predators as well as schools of fish. Apex predators help to balance the ecosystem."

"That pork you tried for lunch Zuawalo", Jim began, then continued, "The pigs were gestated and matured from the embryos from this very facility. Those pigs were lucky. They survived the Pirate attacks and our pig herds continued to grow. We have quite a few now. All of them attended to by our metal men, Androids."

"There are cattle in here!", an excited Zyaliep noted loudly, as she searched through the catalogues, "Many different breeds of cattle. Nguni, Bora, even Watusi! Even wild varieties!"

Zeealas became equally excited and joined her Mother, reading through the catalogues, quickly absorbing the information they contained.

"Yes Mother Zyaliep", Jim confirmed, adding, "They were not so lucky. We originally did have cattle herds on the surface before the Pirates attacked. After the attacks, not so much. We lost the entire lot. There wasn't much left of them either. The Pirates were very indiscriminate."

"This facility is very deep underground. So it survived the attacks", Varak informed everyone.

Mother Zyaliep was still awfully excited. On the Earth, cattle were so important to her ancestors and even though her people had been on Mars for centuries now, the importance of cattle still showed.

"Varak. You can make more?", Zyaliep excitedly asked.

Nyaliep was also excited, "Yes. Yes. Varak! Please tell us you can make more cattle!"

Varak replied, "The Pirate attacks destroyed the gestation and maturation chambers and those are crucial for developing the embryos. That is why we have no cattle herds today."

Jim stepped in, "The facilities for gestation and maturation were surface facilities."

Zyaliep and Nyaliep both sighed in unison. It was catchy, Zuawalo and Zeealas also sighed. Kwoth, however, didn't sigh. Varak and Jim had let Kwoth in on their little secret.

"It is okay ladies", Varak noted, explaining, "We have rebuilt those gestation and maturation chambers and systems. All in a new facility, in a much safer location underground."

Jim chimed in with, "We will have a couple of new herds of cattle within a year. Assuming everything goes well, that is."

Kwoth who had been quietly informed of this earlier, the previous night added, "It gets even better ladies. You get to decide which cattle breeds. One for milking and one for meat."

An excited Zyaliep was so quick to answer, "For the milk, surely it must be the Watusi!"

Nyaliep, equally excited, was almost as quick, "For the meat, maybe, maybe we should choose the Angus!"

"Only two?", Zeealas questioned, "Why only two? Is not three better than two?"

"We have limits on what we can gestate and mature", Varak informed Zeealas.

Jim asked, "Do we actually have the capacity to develop a third breed, Varak?"

"Yes. Just barely. But when the herds are created, we will also need Androids to manage them", Varak replied, "That is the limiting factor."

Varak then checked on his grip and started pressing a few virtual key strokes, "Hmm. We can spare a few more Androids for this task. What breed of cattle would you like Zeealas?"

Zeealas, always the wild card, chose a breed that nobody would have considered. Especially as the particular breed she chose, was not a domestic cattle breed.

"I choose the Yak!", Zeealas decided.

"That is such an odd choice Zeealas", Mother Zyaliep noted, asking, "Are you sure? Why Yak?"

"Yes Mother. It is odd, but hear me out", Zeealas replied, explaining, "The Yak produces both milk and also meat. A Yak can also withstand very, very cold conditions, up to minus sixty degrees. It is a very good choice!"

"How do you know all of that?", Zeealas's Mother asked.

"It was in the information in the catalogues Mother. I read about it in there", Zeealas explained.

Zuawalo looked at the catalogue Zeealas was referring to and exclaimed, "It looks a big shaggy goat!", before starting to laugh.

Zeealas started to giggle.

"Zeealas does have a point Mother Zyaliep", Jim agreed, "Yaks are a very good choice."

"Maybe. If it can handle the high country winters, it is a good choice", Zyaliep responded.

"So be it!", Jim announced and Varak pressed a few more key strokes on his grip.

"There it is done!", Varak confirmed, informing them, "I have put the process into motion."

Zeealas the told her Mother Zyaliep excitedly, "There will be cattle on Mars Mother!"

It had been a tiring day exploring the Elysium Alpha suburb and after continuing their tour of the cryogenic storage facilities, they all headed back to Varak and Nyaliep's penthouse apartment.

When they arrived at the apartment, Toby the Android had already prepared food for them.

They entered the apartment and the table had already been set. Their food ready for serving.

"Mother. This Toby might have no soul, but he can cook", Zeealas noted after tasting the food.

"It Zeealas. It", Zyaliep corrected.

Varak commented, "We designate their names. We also designate their genders. Toby has been designated as male. He is an appropriate noun."

"Still no soul Varak. Still a metal man", Zyaliep replied.

"A useful metal man Mother", Zuawalo responded.

Later the women headed off to their rooms to get some rest. Jim, Varak and Kwoth stayed up a little later, having opened a bottle of Martian sweet cherry red wine. Zuawalo, Zeealas and Nyaliep all being pregnant, could not partake of the alcoholic beverage.

"I noticed a big problem, when I was looking over that beautiful view from the balcony there", Kwoth commented as he pointed to the south balcony.

"A problem Kwoth?", Jim asked.

"Your security Jim. It is all based on watching the skies and space", Kwoth replied.

"Yes Kwoth. We watch the sky, we watch space. Anything that is legit will land at the airfield or the space port. Anything that isn't, will try to bypass those and land somewhere else on the sub-continent", Jim confirmed.

"You are only watching the skies above the Elysium subcontinent Jim", Kwoth replied, as he walked over to the balcony and opened the sliding doors.

Jim and Varak followed Kwoth to the balcony.

Kwoth pointed to the lands across the Elysium Channel, "What if they land over there? In those places to the south? What if they approach by boat?"

Varak opened his grip and started taking notes.

Jim took note of that and replied, "We can have our security services watch for any boats coming across Kwoth."

"Yes, but what if those boats are under the water and they land over there or over there?", Kwoth replied, pointing to locations along Elysium's southern coast that could not be easily surveilled.

Varak took some further notes on his grip, then commented, "Kwoth has a point Jim. We cannot watch every possible approach vector."

"If they can get here and somehow get into this colony. There are twenty five very big, empty suburbs, in which they can hide", Kwoth explained, adding, "My daughters will not be safe here."

"If that comes to pass Kwoth, neither will my Nyaliep", Varak agreed, as all three had bounties on their heads.

"Noted. The safest place for Zuawalo, Zeealas and Nyaliep would be at the academy", Jim agreed, adding, "Bounty hunters will have a hard time getting past our psychics."

"Yes Jim", Kwoth agreed, commenting, "This is a beautiful place to live, truly. For the future yes. For the present, now not so safe. You both must keep my daughters and my sister in law safe."

"At the very least until those bounties are nullified", Jim agreed.

The next day the group left Varak and Nyaliep's penthouse apartment just after ten am. They took their chariot to the airfield and boarded Jim's Hummer. Their luggage had already been transferred and loaded into Jim's Hummer by Androids at the request of Varak. Jim had an improvised plan for the day. Instead of flying straight back to the academy, he instead flew the Hummer low and slow along the Southern Elysium coastline. They were taking the scenic route.

Jim took his Hummer as far to the west of the colony as he thought necessary and began flying eastward along the South Western Elysium coast. He made sure that everyone aboard had very good views of the coastline and made sure he took plenty of surveillance photos and videos as well. Jim was doing his level best to ensure that this was like a sight seeing flight, although he himself considered it a surveillance mission. An extremely important one at that.

Upon reaching Lake Eddie, Jim turned the Hummer north and flew it through the broad canal carved through Eddie Crater's southern rim. The Eddie Cut. After passing through the Eddie Cut and approaching Eddie Island in the middle of Lake Eddie, Jim landed his Hummer on a nice expanse of beach. His passengers alighted their Hummer and setup their picnic baskets and blankets on the soft Martian sand. Jim was in no hurry and after they all ate their picnic lunch, they stayed on the beach for around two hours, enjoying the cool waters of Lake Eddie.

This was a beautiful place that Jim could bring his family to anytime, to enjoy a pleasant day at the beach. Except of course for the bounty that was upon their heads. Five of their group, were faces on wanted videos issued by the Jovian High Council and in the coming weeks and months, this could become very dangerous. Just going to the beach for the day, could become an issue.

After three pm everyone boarded the Hummer once more. Jim flew his Hummer south through the Eddie Cut and turned his Hummer eastwards. Flying eastward, Jim ensured that everyone on board had excellent views of the South East Elysium coast. He of course, took plenty of surveillance photos and videos.

When their flight had gone as far east as Jim thought necessary, he then took his Hummer higher into the Martian skies and altered course to take them back to Lake Eddie. This time Jim flew his Hummer directly down into Eddie Crater from above. He flew his Hummer low above the deep waters of Lake Eddie and slowly circled Eddie Island, giving everyone aboard good views.

When they had circumnavigated Eddie Island, Jim changed course to the north and flew low along the Eddie Canal leading to the Elysium Ports. Jim took his Hummer so low above the waters of the canal, that it was almost like being in a boat, giving everyone board incredible views. When they reached the Elysium Port facilities Jim took his Hummer high into the Martian sky once more and made a bee line to the Elysium Airfields, where he landed.

"Jim. Are we going to stay another day?", Zuawalo enquired.

"I wish my love. I wish", Jim replied, then requested, "Please everyone. Wait here", before he stepped out their Hummer.

Varak informed the others, "For us. This was a pleasant few days. A little holiday. For Jim, not so much. He works very hard to keep us all safe. Always!"

A chariot was parked on the Airfield in front of their Hummer. Jim walked directly to the chariot and three men climbed out of it as he approached. All three of them wore long, dark trench coats, almost identical to the ones that Jim himself owned. These were some of Elysium's security personnel. Jim's subordinates. Probably his top three men in the Colony.

Jim talked to the three men for quite a while. Every now and again, they nodded, as if in agreement with what they were being told. Jim then passed a crystal memory strip to one of the three men. It was a copy of the surveillance photos and videos he had taken along the Elysium Southern coastline. After about ten minutes discussion, which seemed like much longer to the Hummer's passengers, Jim started walking back to the Hummer. The three men in trench coats climbed aboard their chariot and began driving back to the Elysium colony.

Jim Murphy climbed back aboard his Hummer and Zeealas asked, "Jim. What was that about?"

"Something your Father, Kwoth, noted last night Zeealas", Jim replied.

Zyaliep looked at her husband Kwoth and asked Jim, "What was that Jim?"

"Kwoth looked at the southern view from Varak's penthouse apartment and noted, that any bounty hunters might approach the Elysium colony by water, even under the water. From Hesperia Planum or Aeolis", Jim replied, explaining, "During today's little joy flight, I also took some detailed surveillance photos and videos of our southern coastline. I've just discussed the problem with some of my people and given them orders accordingly. My security personnel are now going to set up surveillance of our southern coastline. Even going so far as having regular surveillance overflights of the far coast of the Elysium Channel. That far coastline has so many islands, almost too many to count. It's not going to be easy to watch it all. I will be asking Lieutenant Roberts up at Phobos Port to place a satellite above those islands."

"You are keeping my Daughters and my Sister safe?", Zyaliep queried.

"Mother Zyaliep. My wives, your Sister, Varak, everyone. I fully intend to keep everyone safe. So if anyone has any useful suggestions, I will take them on board and action them", Jim informed her and everyone else.

Jim then flew his Hummer and its passengers back to the New Flinders Psychic Academy, to the north of the Elysium colony.

3. Medallions

The barbeque at the roof top gardens of the Appelbaum's and Neru's apartment had only just begun. Prince Leopold and his wife Princess Giselle had arrived with their son Prince Ulrick. The young Prince had been growing quickly and was playing with his nanny on a nearby picnic blanket.

The Neru girls, Lakshmi and Pavarti, were playing in one of the two roof top pools. The smaller one that had not been stocked with fish. Miriam, Rani and Giselle relaxed nearby on some deck chairs, chatting and taking in the reflected sun light from the northern end cap's redirection mirror. The deck chairs themselves, were positioned just outside the pool house in front of the pool where the Neru girls were playing.

The Prince's Butler and Confidant, Hubert was being extremely diligent in having the entire roof top screened for listening devices. He even went so far as to bring in and activate, a jamming device.

"Given the times, Hubert believes it's important to check for surveillance devices", Prince Leopold explained to everyone.

"You can never be to cautious Your Highness", Hubert remarked.

"Would you like to hear the latest news now or after we eat?", Prince Leopold asked.

"That would depend on what it is", Abram replied.

Rajsheev added, "Will the latest news spoil our lunch?"

"Probably not. It's just stuff that I'm privy to, that the general population isn't", Leopold replied.

Leopold led Abram and Rajsheev into the pool house and took a seat. Abram and Rajsheev sat in some chairs on either side of him. Their wives quickly moved from their deck chairs, to join them in the pool house.

Giselle commented, "My Leo. He really has no one else to talk to about these things."

Hubert checked the video screen for bugs and once he was certain it was clean, he then plugged in a memory strip, before passing Prince Leopold the remote control.

Prince Leopold played around with the remote control for a few seconds and an image appeared on the screen. It was a clear image of a ship of unknown design. It had a disk and sled style of construction and what looked like a plethora of weapons pods. At its rear were four thruster nozzles, set in an unusual, almost hidden, set back arrangement. Beneath the ship's wings, on either side of its main fuselage, were what appeared to be two nacelles with a completely unknown purpose.

"That my dear friends is what Captain Matthew Murphy of very our Jovian Armed Services, calls a Martian Solstice Class Gunship", Leo informed everyone, further explaining, "Martian because, well it comes from Mars. Solstice class, because that's its name and it is the first of its class. Gunship because, well Captain Murphy was able to count no fewer than thirty six weapons modules."

Abram stood up and approached the screen and looked closely at the image, "Impressive", he announced, then asked, "Where have I heard that name, Murphy before?"

"I'll get to that in a minute Abram", Leo promised, adding, "Impressive is an understatement. You all need to hear more about this ship."

Prince Leopold divulged what he knew about the Martian Gunship Solstice.

"The Solstice is ridiculously fast. We spot it in Mars orbit one day, then five days later it is in cis-lunar space. I kid you not!", Leo informed everyone, "That ship is almost impossible to observe with our optical surveillance network. We only have this image and others like it, because the Captain of that ship actually allowed it."

Prince Leopold then brought up other images of the ship that had been obtained by the Trojan Occupation Forces that had fled cis-lunar space.

"Leo. That sounds like something out of sheer fantasy", Rajsheev replied.

"That's exactly what my Brothers thought, but there you have it. We have the data", Leo replied, while pointing at the screen, "And it has my Brothers scared out of their wits!"

"Why Leo? It is only the one ship?", Abram asked.

"One ship yes, but it's so advanced. We have nothing at all, that even comes close to it and it's on the enemies side", Leo replied.

Leo went on the explain, "That ship, the Solstice, thwarted my Brother's missile attack on Mars. It then defeated our Trojan occupation forces on the ground at the Battle of the Elysium Plains and sent them packing. They are on their way home as we speak."

Leo stopped for a moment, then continued, "That was bad enough, but this is what frightens my Brothers the most. The Solstice flew from Mars to our missile swarm en-route to the Earth. It reached the swarm in three days, took out a ton of our missiles with impunity, then it continued on to L5. Reaching the Colonial Fleet two days later! "

"The Solstice then took two more forays into our missile swarm, again with impunity. After the missiles launched their warheads, that ship, the Solstice chased down as many warheads as it could. That one single ship, eliminated thirty percent of the missiles that my Brother Heinrich launched at the Earth and L5. He is absolutely livid. I've never seen Heinrich so angry", Leo told everyone.

"That one ship?", Abram queried.

"That one single ship Abram", Leo confirmed, adding, "It didn't stop their either. After helping defend the Earth and L5. The Captain of that ship, took it upon himself to convince our Trojan occupation forces, that they were heading into a death trap and he turned them around! Our Trojan Fleet bypassed cis-lunar space and headed for home. He saved ninety eight percent of the Trojans!"

Leo then added, "That's where we got these images from. The Trojans. It's not every day that an unknown class of ship just magically appears right in front of you."

"Magically?", Abram queried.

"Yep. Straight out of nowhere", Leo confirmed, "That ship just magically appeared."

"They saved their enemies?", Rani questioned.

"That is correct. They saved their enemies Rani", Leo confirmed.

"That is a good thing isn't it. A ship that powerful, that flies unseen and has a Captain willing to save his enemies?", Miriam questioned.

"May be. Potentially", Leo replied.

"I do have this other video from L5. Very few people in the Jovian Realms have seen it at all. Very, very few people. It is also the very reason that my Brothers issued a wanted video that's been repeating on the news feeds lately. Funnily enough, that wanted video is everywhere throughout the entire solar system. Except here in our Jovian Realms, our people don't get to see it in full. For us here, an entire section at the end of the video is missing. The Trojan colonies, everyone else, they get to see the full video", Leo told all of them before hitting play.

A medal award ceremony followed, in which each of the Solstice's crew received medals for their efforts in defending L5. One by one the crew members were listed out. Each receiving medals of the Battle of L5, medals of honour and medals of gallantry. Three of them had the same surnames. There was even a barely noticed brief moment where two of the crew members actually held hands.

"I do like those uniforms. Well tailored, well designed. Nice shades of blue", Rani remarked.

"Yes Rani. They are very nice uniforms", Leo replied, "Now I'm going to play what my Brothers did with that video. They created, the wanted video."

An image taken from the medal award ceremony appeared on the screen. Captions appeared. Wanted for Piracy above and then below it. The Crew of the Martian Pirate Ship Solstice. One by one, the crew of the Solstice were highlighted sequentially in popup windows. Each was labelled as a Pirate, their crew position and their names were listed, then underneath a reward posted in Jovian golden credits.

After the crew had completed cycling through, another person appeared on the screen. Leroy McGuvan. He was not a Pirate, instead listed as. Wanted for high treason against the Jovian Realms, with his reward posted underneath. Leroy McGuvan was listed as a traitor.

When the video finally stopped, it showed the entire crew of the Solstice once more, but on the left. Another caption had been added to the bottom. Wanted for the unprovoked and unjustifiable mass homicide of one hundred and twenty thousand trojan troops. On the right hand side was Leroy McGuvan's wanted posted.

Leo used a laser pointer to highlight Captain Folcrom Forkbraid, "The Captain of this ship, you might actually recognise him."

Miriam was quick to answer, "Yes. That's Lord Folcrom Forkbraid. He's the most powerful psychic on the Earth."

Both Miriam and Abram had emigrated from the Earth, so they knew.

"So now he's the Captain of a space ship?", Abram queried.

"Apparently Abram. A Martian space ship as well", Leo confirmed.

"No wonder they're offering a ten million Jovian golden credit reward", Miriam noted.

Abram pointed to the screen, "That one of the left, '*James Murphy*'. A coincidence?"

"Oh no. No coincidence Abram", Leo replied, explaining, "First officer, tactical and chief security officer James Murphy, is our very own Captain Matthew Murphy's first cousin."

"First cousins? Really?", Rajsheev queried.

"Yes. James and Matthew are apparently both from Colonial Central at L5. First cousins", Leo informed them all, then continued, "James Matthew was high up in the Colonial Central Security Services. He had the ear of the President or so I'm told. Matthew Murphy was trained as a Military Pilot by the Colonial Fleet. Somehow he became the Prophet's personal Pilot. He now works for us, in the Jovian Armed Services, with the brevet rank of Captain."

"Which is why James Murphy's reward is set at five million Jovian credits?", Abram speculated.

"Indeed. That is exactly why", Leo confirmed, adding, "My Brothers and the Generals all believe, he'll have an in depth knowledge of L5's security procedures. They want that information!"

Lakshmi and Pavarti walked into the pool room wrapped in towels and still dripping wet.

Pavarti pointed to the screen, "That guy on the right, they call him the Martyr."

"Yes they do, although now he's the Traitor", Leo confirmed, "He's also very interesting. He was the Prophets second in command and is supposed to have died in the rear guard action at the Battle of New Tortuga. The very rear guard action that enabled the Prophet to escape from Mars."

Lakshmi snickered, "He doesn't look very dead does he? What is he, a

Zombie?"

"Lakshmi!", Rani scolded.

"No. He's not dead and he's not a Zombie either", Leo replied, "He was captured at the end of the Battle of New Tortuga and apparently executed by Folcrom Forkbraid himself", again Leo highlighted Forkbraid with the laser pointer.

"Still not looking very dead for someone who's been executed", Lakshmi noted.

Prince Leopold continued, he highlighted security officer Zuawalo Pod, "Apparently that women, Zuawalo Pod, saved his life."

"At some point Leroy McGuvan flipped sides", Leroy informed them.

"He and Zuawalo Pod, along with this other one", he highlighted security officer Zeealas Pod, "Zeealas Pod, were instrumental in convincing the Aft Trojan Forces to leave Mars. And that was the end of the Martian Campaign. The Trojans left Mars and they're on their way home."

"Wait! No way! The Martyr flipped sides", Pavarti remarked, "Now that is news."

"Girls. Most of this information is not publicly available here. Very little of this information has been released to the public yet and it's very unlikely to be either. So treat all of it as confidential. Yes?", Hubert reminded them.

"Okay", both girls agreed.

"We do have plans in that regard, don't we Hubert?", Leo commented.

"Yes, there are plans in the works Your highness", Hubert simply replied.

"No wonder his bounty is so high", Lakshmi noted looking at rewards posted.

"Wait. Let me get this straight", Rani began, before continuing,"Leroy McGuvan, the Prophet's second in command, literally his right hand man, the Martyr, is now working with the same man who executed him, Folcrom Forkbraid. Leroy McGuvan's saviour and probably her sister as well, are now working on the crew of Folcrom Forkbraid's ship, the Solstice. Wait, is that other Pod women, Nyaliep Pod their Mother or another relative? Working on the same ship?"

Rani didn't wait for an answer and continued, "His first officer, his tactical officer on that ship, is the first cousin of the Prophet's Pilot, Captain Matthew Murphy of the Jovian Armed Services. Your Highness, had you not told us all of this yourself, I would never have believed it. It is just crazy!"

"I know right", Leo replied smiling, "It is just so damned ridiculous. Isn't it."

Giselle chuckled, "Leo has trouble believing it himself sometimes as well."

"Well it is, kind of hard to swallow", Rani commented in reply.

"There is more though", Leo told them as he put on the latest video, explaining, "This was a press conference held at Colonial Central Command at L5. President Banyan, a Captain Carmichael of the Colonial Fleet and a General Stanton of the Earth Defence Forces were present."

They all watched the video in which it was pretty clear that the Earth and L5 considered the Solstice and her crew to be Heroes, definitely not Pirates. More importantly, it appeared that they were active members of the Martian Defence Forces.

"This particular video has not been released to the Jovian or Trojan public yet and it probably never will be", Leo informed them, adding, "The fact that they're confirming, that they're Martian Defence Force personnel, has really irked my Brother Heinrich. My Brother is currently, actively ignoring, even denying that fact. That is exactly how I know it upsets him so much. Heinrich says that the Solstice's crew, is just too damn weird to be a professional military outfit! He's so pissed off about it, that my Brothers and I have been called into a special meeting on Ganymede Prime."

"It also confirms that the Captain of the Solstice, went out of his way to save Trojan lives", Giselle pointed out to them.

"It certainly shows that, that wanted video is a complete pack of lies as well", Abram noted.

"Yes it certainly does", Giselle agreed.

"It gets better my friends", Prince Leopold began, then continued, "I don't want that ship, the Solstice, coming here in anger. That would be terrible thing. I want them, to go out of their way to save Jovian lives. So, how do I contact Captain Folcrom Forkbraid? Any ideas?"

Everyone looked around at each other. No ideas were forth coming.

Giselle chuckled again, "Oh Leo. I did say that was an unanswerable question."

Abram looked at Giselle, "Actually Princess. Maybe it's not."

A curious look came over Giselle's face, "How's that?"

Abram pointed to the medallion Princess Giselle wore around her neck, it was a peace symbol.

Princess Giselle took her medallion in her fingers and rubbed it thoughtfully, "This thing?", she queried.

Prince Leo undid the top two buttons on his tunic and pulled out his medallion. It was identical to his wife's medallion. Again, a peace symbol.

"Oh Your Highness. That's even better", Abram commented, then asked, "When was the last time you had your family portraits taken?"

"It has been quite a while", Leopold replied.

"Then Leo, it's time you had a new family portrait taken", Abram announced, instructing, "Wear very casual clothing and make sure those medallions are clearly, clearly visible."

Prince Leopold stated, "I don't understand Abram."

"Convince your siblings of the need to have some new family portraits taken. Each Horridian Prince and Princess with their families and then a group photo of just the Horridian siblings. Make it sound urgent, so it happens very soon. Think of a very good reason for it. One that enhances their standing with the people perhaps", Abram advised.

"I don't see how that will contact Captain Folcrom Forkbraid", Giselle replied.

"The family portraits from Leo's siblings will be very official, very regal, very ostentatious" Abram explained, "Your family portrait will be very different. Much more casual, very casual, with those medallions clearly visible. When Leo sits for the Horridian family portrait, again keep his clothing much more casual than his siblings and again that medallion must be clearly visible. That's very important. I cannot stress that enough."

"I must agree with Giselle. I can't see how that's going to work", Prince Leopold remarked.

"Leo. Do your Brothers know you wear that medallion?", Abram asked.

"Yes. I always wear it. Giselle always wears hers as well. They all know it", Leo replied.

"Good then, your Brothers won't think twice about it", Abram noted.

"Abram. Exactly how is this going to contact Captain Folcrom Forkbraid?", Prince Leopold asked again, this time with more urgency.

"Subtleties Leo. Subtleties", Abram replied, explaining, "Once your portraits are completed. Those images will be posted everywhere, right across the entire solar system. Every single colony will see them. Your siblings all looking so officious and ostentatious in their absolute finest outfits. Then you and your family, looking so much more humble, a Prince and Princess for the people. It's that juxtaposition that's important. That and the fact that those medallions you're both wearing, are in fact peace symbols!"

"Peace symbols?", Leopold queried, "I chose this medallion years ago, back when my Father was still alive. This was actually my Father's medallion. My Father offered my Siblings and I some of his medallions. He told us all to choose one. We all chose the one we liked the most. Before I married Giselle, I had an identical one made for her."

"Even better. So all of your siblings will expect you to be wearing them", Abram replied, noting, "When the images of your portraits reach Mars and Captain Folcrom Forkbraid, he will notice the difference. He will see the pair of you looking deliberately humble and wearing peace symbols."

Giselle and Leopold were beginning to understand, "He's a powerful wizard. He'll see right through all the subtleties", Giselle noted.

"And the symbolism as well don't forget. He will see, that you are both different to the other Horridian siblings. He will also see, that you both want peace. Better yet, the caption underneath the portrait will be something like Prince Leopold and Princess Giselle von Horridian, Prince and Princess of Io", Abram explained, concluding, "He will even have your address. Contact made!"

"Oh my God Abram! That's genius!", Princess Giselle exclaimed.

"Excellent then. Let's get this barbeque going shall we", Abram replied, adding, "So Leo. How good are you with a hot plate and tongs?"

"Pretty good actually Abram. Pretty good indeed", Leo replied.

"Good then. Let's get cooking", Abram told everyone.

4. Horridious Horridians

High Prince Heinrich had convened a special meeting to discuss the latest issues cropping up in the Jovian Realms. The Princes Brothers were present. His Generals were present. His Sisters, being that they live in the Trojan Asteroid colonies, had representatives present. The Prophet and his Pilot, now a Captain Matthew Murphy in the Jovian Armed Forces were also present.

Heinrich greeted everyone one in the conference room and then began, "This latest bit of news from L5, has not yet been released to the public. In fact it won't be. There will be no official release of this information within our Realms. It is a press conference that was held at L5's Colonial Central Command colony by President Banyon."

The High Prince nodded to General Snide who then played the video for the room.

After the video finished, Prince Valdamar remarked, "Well then. That definitely can't be released to the public. It refutes everything we put out in our wanted video, about the crew of that damnable Martian gunship."

"You noticed that Brother", the High Prince replied, "I am more concerned about how it tells the truth about our Trojan occupation forces. Our wanted video says, that they were mercilessly slaughtered. A heinous crime. This press conferences creates a very different picture. That damned crew saved our occupation forces! Several of their news channels have even set up sites, where ordinary citizens can watch and track the Trojans on their journey back home! For fucks sake!"

"I hope our people don't have access to those news sites?", Prince Valdamar questioned.

"They don't Valdamar. We control what our news feeds show. You know that", the High Prince reminded his Brother.

"And Callthrope", the High Prince caught Princess Luisa's representative's attention and pointed to him, "Make sure my Sister, Luisa, fully understands. She is not to take any reprisals on those Trojan occupation forces returning from Mars. Their Martian campaign failed abysmally. We all know that, but her realm is simply far too unstable for her to behave like the blood thirsty bitch that she is. Make sure Luisa understands this."

Callthrope gulped, knowing very well the difficulty of that task and replied, "I will do my best Your Majesty."

"Good then Callthrope. Your failure is not an option here!", the High Prince reminded him, adding, "We are at war with the entire inner solar system, the last thing we need is a rebellion in our Aft Trojan Realm."

Prince Wulfric looked to his Brother Valdamar, before turning back to the High Prince, "Brother, as our Brother Valdamar noted, we will not be releasing that video to the public. So our people will never know of this."

"Really Wulfric. That cat is already out of the bag", the High Princes replied, glancing at two piles of reports, one red and one green, stacked at the centre of the table, before adding, "We'll get around to that little problem soon enough."

"We intended to drive up some bounty hunter activity, didn't we. Hence our wanted video and those extravagant bounties", High Prince Heinrich reminded everyone, "L5's President Banyan has declared that the crew of the Solstice are members of the Martian Defence Forces. Military personnel acting in a time of war cannot be declared as Pirates."

Matthew replied, "Your Majesty. I've never heard of the Martian Defence Forces."

"Thank you Captain Murphy. Neither have I", the High Prince replied, adding, "On the back of that one statement, the General in change of the Earth Defence Forces and the Captain of the Colonial Fleet have put their full weight and backing behind the Solstice and its crew. They've warned any bounty hunters off. If any bounty hunters go after that crew, the Armed Forces of both the Earth and L5 will go after them!"

The High Prince paused for a moment, then asked, "General Snide. Play the other video."

General Snide played the second video, then handed the remote control to the High Prince. It was a medal award ceremony.

"Your Majesty. Gentlemen. This video is the original medal award ceremony for the crew of the Solstice", General Snide informed them.

Everyone in the room knew of it and that it had not been released to the public.

The High Prince paused the video, "You see there. Those three women.

Zuawalo Pod, Zeealas Pod and Nyaliep Pod. We understand the first two are sisters. We do have information to that effect. That third one however?", he questioned, "Is she their Mother? their Aunt? another relative? perhaps a cousin? Seriously, if that's a military crew then I'm calling bullshit!"

General Tarzan stepped in with, "Your Majesty. It is extremely unlikely for a military organisation, to station three people from the same family on the one ship. It is not something we would do here. I doubt that any other military would either."

The High Prince pointed to General Tarzan, "My point exactly General. My point exactly. Now watch this next bit. Watch those two in particular. Watch their hands."

The High Prince replayed a section of the video, from before Communications officer Charlene Fewkes received her medals, to just after Helm and Navigation officer Marcus Greyhelm received his. Everyone in the room watched their hands.

Before Charlene was awarded her medals, both she and Marcus were holding hands. After Marcus was awarded his medals, the pair both recommenced holding hands.

The High Prince paused the video and placed the remote control on the table, he then clapped his hands together and proclaimed, "The hell that crew is a military crew. That is not a military ship! It's all complete bullshit! I refuse to believe any of it!"

Prince Leopold raised his right hand.

"Leopold. Little Brother. You don't need to raise your hand. Just say what's on your mind", the High Prince responded.

"Their uniforms Heinrich", Prince Leopold noted.

"Yes. Nice uniforms. What of them?", High Prince Heinrich asked.

"They're uniforms are too nice. They look like they've been specifically tailored for each crew member. It's almost like a fashion parade. Are they a the ship's crew or a line up of fashion models?", Prince Leopold questioned.

"What? Leo, are you telling me that this crew is too good looking to be military personnel?", the High Prince queried.

"No Heinrich. I'm saying that their uniforms are too good looking to be military issued", Prince Leopold corrected.

Matthew interjected, "Your Majesty. Prince Leopold has a very good point there. Those uniforms look like they were designed by a fashion designer. Most certainly they have been tailored."

Matthew stood up and held out his arms, "Your Majesty. As an example. To get a Captains uniform that fit me properly, I had to get a uniform from the Jovian Armed Forces stores, two sizes two big and then get it tailored to suit. No military goes out of its way to tailor uniforms for their personnel", having supported Prince Leopold's point, he then sat back down.

General Tarzan then stepped in, "Captain Murphy is absolutely correct Your Majesty. I actually gave Matthew that advice and the name of a good tailor. Otherwise our uniforms can be quite ill fitting and uncomfortable. I would expect exactly the same from any military outfit."

"Well there you have it. Three members of the crew from the same family. Unprofessional behaviour with Crew members holding hands and uniforms that were individually tailored to suit each crew member", the High Prince concluded, "Definitely not a military ship and definitely not a military crew. All agreed?"

Everyone in the room was in agreement with the High Prince.

"Good then. Let's get those bounty hunters back to work shall we", the High Prince commanded.

"Your Majesty", Matthew caught the High Prince's attention, "If I may."

"Yes Captain", the High Prince replied.

"Whether that ship and its crew are military or private, is really neither here nor there", Matthew told the room, "We call them Pirates. They call them Military. At the very least, they are Privateers."

"Privateers and Pirates are often the same thing Captain", General Snide noted.

"Yes. They are General, but that's not my point", Matthew replied, explaining, "It does not matter what we call them. That's not important. It is that ship, the Solstice, that is important. What do we really know about it? "

Matthew paused and then continued before anyone could answer his rhetorical question, "It has at least thirty six weapons systems Gentlemen. I know, I've counted them. That ship is wickedly fast. And it can hide, really hide, in plain sight. That ship can sit in front of an entire fleet of troop transports and not been seen or detected. Then bam! And just like that, there it is in plain sight, bold as brass! From out of nowhere!"

There were more than a few heads nodding in agreement with what he had just told them.

"Gentlemen. It is that ship that is important. We have no idea how it does what it does. Worse still, we don't know what other secrets, what other capabilities that ship has", Matthew concluded.

"The Captain has hit the nail of the head my Brothers", Prince Wulfric agreed, "We need to know more about that ship. The more intel we have on that ship, the better."

"General Tarzan. Work with Captain Murphy. Put together a team. We need to know more about that ship", the High Prince commanded.

"Yes Your Majesty. We'll start work on it today", the General replied, whispering across the table to Matthew and the Prophet, "Do you still have people on Mars?"

"Perhaps General. Perhaps", Matthew replied.

The High Prince pointed to a pile of red folders in the centre of the table and indicated that General Snide should distribute them around the table. General Snide passed the folders around. Everyone opened their copy and began reading through the report.

"This report contains some disturbing information Gentlemen", the High Prince informed everyone, "We block anything in the system-wide news feeds that we don't like, as you all know. That way our citizens only get to see what we want them to see."

"Oh yes. You did say the cat was out of the bag Brother", Prince Wulfric commented as he read.

"Yes Wulfric", the High Prince replied, remarking, "Somehow, that medal award ceremony video got loose and is now publicly available. Not just that medal ceremony either. The full version of the reward video, including our traitorous Mr McGuvan and that more recently posted press conference from L5's Colonial Central. All of the cats are now out of the bag and on the loose!"

"I haven't seen any of these in the news feeds Brother", Prince Valdamar noted.

"They're not in the news feeds Valdamar", the High Prince informed him, "We pick and choose what our news feeds show. Remember."

"Then how Brother?", Prince Valdamar queried.

High Prince Heinrich nodded to General Snide.

"We've found copies of these videos on our internal systems", General Snide informed everyone, adding, "We believe that the videos were uploaded to one of our networks share servers. One of the most popularly used ones and simply left there in plain sight."

"Uploaded?", Prince Valdamar questioned, "That would mean by someone who had access to the external data from the news feeds."

"And someone who knows how to upload to the internal server network without an account Your Highness", General Snide informed him.

"General. Everyone who accesses the share server network, has to have an account", Prince Valdamar reminded him.

"That's what I always thought too Your Highness", General Snide replied, adding, "However, with these initial uploads, there appears to have been no account. The metadata for each of the original files is simply not there."

"That should be impossible", Prince Wulfric commented.

"Apparently, it is not impossible Your Highness", General Snide replied.

"So General. What's the damage?", Prince Leopold questioned, even though he already knew.

"Your Highness. Those three videos were downloaded, shared and passed around. Then uploaded to the other servers and the cycle was repeated. Over and over. Over and over. They've basically gone viral", the General admitted, "If you read the report further, we believe that those videos have been seen by in excess of seventy five percent of our population. By the time it came to our attention, it was already too late. By the time these reports were put together, probably our entire Jovian citizenry will have seen them. There isn't even any point, in trying to remove them."

"And we have no idea how this was done?", Prince Leopold asked, himself knowing how it was.

"It should not be possible Your Highness", General Snide replied, explaining, "Everything that is uploaded and shared on our internal network servers, must be uploaded using an account. In these three cases however, there is absolutely nothing to indicate an account was used. The metadata that should be attached to the original file uploads is missing. Completely missing and that Gentlemen is completely impossible."

High Prince Heinrich stepped in, "To say I'm unhappy with this situation is an understatement. We need to know how this was done. I want the perpetrators caught. I want them executed!"

General Snide was quiet, as the High Prince's words sunk in, before continuing, "We have very purposely released nothing to our news feeds about any of this."

Matthew spoke up, "We can't leave things like that for very long General. We will have to make an official response at some point in time."

"We will Captain. We will", General Snide replied, informing him, "When the time comes, we are going to release to the news feeds, that these videos are propaganda spread by our enemy's spies, to destabilise the Jovian Realms. They are deep fakes is what we're going to tell them."

Matthew nodded, "That's probably the only thing we can do at the moment General, but I do recommend dealing with this sooner rather than later. We can find some way to spin all of this to our advantage at a later date."

Prince Leopold quickly commented before anyone could reply, "It looks to me, like it's time for us to issue some new official, Horridian family portraits."

"Little Brother. That seems to be just a little bit out of left field", the High Prince replied.

"Heinrich. It makes perfect sense", Prince Leopold told him.

The High Prince gestured for Leopold to continue.

"We are at war my Brothers. Our Martian campaign has failed. Our Earth and L5 campaigns did not pan out as well as we'd like. We are besieged by spies trying to destabilise our realms", Leopold began, then explained, "We need a distraction! A big distraction! One that shows the entire Jovian Realms, that the Horridian Dynasty is united and that a united Horridian Dynasty cannot and will not fail!"

Prince Valdamar stepped in, "And you think having our portraits taken and spread all over our news feeds will achieve that Little Brother?"

"It certainly can't hurt and what's the harm", Prince Leopold replied, "We need to remind our people, that the Horridian Dynasty is still in charge of the Jovian Realms and that we have got this!"

"Leopold my Little Brother", the High Prince smiled, adding, "You always come up with the oddest notions. How will these portraits work? Our Sisters are in the Trojan colonies after-all."

"That is actually the easy part Heinrich", Prince Leopold replied, explaining, "Each of our Horridian families, can have their own family portraits taken in their own realms. Then we four Brothers, can sit for our Family portrait here in Ganymede. Just us Horridians, together and united for the whole of the Jovian Realms to see."

"And our Sisters?", the High Prince asked.

"They can have their images sent to us, in any number of suitable poses and we can digitally add them into the family portrait later", Prince Leopold explained.

"My dear little brother", High Prince Heinrich began, "I like your idea. I really do. However, we have so many, much more pressing matters. Perhaps we can revisit this, concept at a later date."

"Heinrich. How long has it been since we issued our official portraits?", Prince Leopold asked.

Prince Wulfric broke in and spat out, "Long ago Brother, before you married that Slave whore of yours!"

Quick as flash, Prince Leopold was on his feet, with his Sabre in hand and its blade reaching across the table at Wulfric's throat, "Take that back!"

Prince Wulfric began to reach for his Sabre.

"Leopold!", the High Prince pointed to Prince Leopold and screamed, "Stand down! And you Wulfric! Do not make a move!"

Prince Leopold looked at Heinrich, gave an ever so slight nod and re-sheathed his Sabre, before sitting back down in his chair. A small trickle of blood was visible on Wulfric's throat. It trickled down to his nice, clean white collar. Wulfric gulped audibly.

The High Prince stood up from his chair and pointed to his Brother Wulfric, "You. Get over there now", he pointed to an ante room and he and his Brother slowly walked over to the room.

"What was that about?", the Prophet whispered.

Prince Valdamar looked to his younger brother Prince Leopold. The younger Prince, still embarrassed by his sudden outburst of anger and loss of control, nodded to Valdamar.

Valdamar stood up and walked around the table, before crouching down between the Prophet and Matthew, he whispered, "Our Father, when he was alive, gifted Leopold with a young Slave girl to do with as he pleased. I know, it sounds a bit off, but our Father was a bit off! Anyway, Leopold fell in love with her, which makes perfect sense. Giselle was and arguably still is, the most beautiful woman in the entire Jovian Realms."

"Anyway, to cut this long story short. Our Father died and Heinrich ascended to the Jovian High Throne. He then changed Giselle's status from that of a Slave to a free citizen, thus allowing Leopold and Giselle to marry. Nobody, absolutely nobody, is allowed to even mention Giselle's previous status, prior to her ascendance. Wulfric's lucky, very lucky! Leopold is the best swordsman in the Jovian Realms."

Matthew nodded in understanding, as did the Prophet. Prince Valdamar then got up and returned to his seat, touching his younger Brother gently on his shoulder as he did so.

Matthew caught Prince Leopold's eye and nodded to him. The Prince nodded in return.

Voices could be heard coming from the ante room, the High Prince's voice, "What the fuck was that Wulfric?", he didn't wait for an answer and continued, "You do remember my proclamation?"

Wulfric did not answer.

"Do you remember my proclamation?", the High Prince asked again.

"Yes", Prince Wulfric answered, his voice soft and stammering.

"Yes what?", High Prince Heinrich asked.

"Yes. Yes Your Majesty", Prince Wulfric replied, louder and clearer.

"Right then. What was my proclamation Wulfric?", the High Prince asked.

Wulfric answered, "That no one, absolutely no one, is to ever mention or bring up Princess Giselle's previous status as a Slave."

"And Wulfric, what is the penalty for breaking that proclamation?", the High Prince asked him.

Wulfric gulped and answered, "By penalty of death!", the fear was clear on his face.

"Wulfric. Brother, I have just saved your life", High Prince Heinrich told him, continuing, "Leopold could have taken your head! Right there! Right then! You are so damned lucky I stopped him when I did. How could you be so absolutely stupid, as to bait your Brother with that most sensitive of subjects? Seriously Wulfric. Do you have a death wish?"

Wulfric didn't answer, he just shrugged.

"Well my dim witted moron for a Brother. You've put me in an untenable situation", the High Prince informed him, "I had no right to save your life. You didn't just disobey my proclamation, you did so to Leopold's face. Leopold has every right to take your head. Every right! So you'd better hope, that he's in a very forgiving mood, because I can't help you. Not this time! Now get back in there and apologise and make it bloody good!"

Everyone in the conference room had heard the conversation. Leopold sat quietly in apparent embarrassment at his outburst of anger and loss of control.

Wulfric approached his seat. Across the table Leopold stood up, right hand on his Sabre's hilt.

Prince Wulfric bowed slightly and apologised, "I sincerely apologise for my words Leopold. I had absolutely no right to say them", then when Prince Leopold didn't respond, he urgently added, "Please Brother, please don't kill me!"

Nearly everyone at the table had shocked looks on their faces. There was a level of tension in the air that was palpable. Was this Prince Wulfric's end? Would Prince Leopold take his Brother's head? These were the thoughts running through the minds of those assembled at the table.

"No, I won't take your head today Wulfric, but next time, you might not be so lucky", Prince Leopold responded, "and besides, I have no wish to upset your wife and children."

"Thank you Leopold", a much more contrite Wulfric answered, "and again, I am so very sorry."

"Yes well. You can hardly have your family's portrait taken if I slice off your head, can you now?", Prince Leopold replied, adding in a half hearted, half morbid way, "It would not look good, to have your headless corpse in our family photo either, would it Brother? We need to show unity!"

Prince Wulfric involuntarily gulped audibly once more and sat himself down.

The High Prince was happy to see his Brother Wulfric was going to keep his head. He wasn't quite sure whether he could forgive Leopold, if he had beheaded him. Thankfully that moment had passed and things were much calmer now. Still quite tense, but becoming calmer by the second.

"Okay, since we have a much calmer room at the moment, General Tarzan could you pass around those green folders", the High Prince commanded.

General Tarzan passed around the green folders and began talking as he did so, "You might not know yet, but Captain Murphy and the Prophet have allowed us to have a good look a their space yacht, the Delilah. What's the point of that you might ask. Well, the Delilah is one of the most advance space yachts in the entire system. Indeed, I wish I had one myself. I'm jealous!"

"That is correct General", Matthew then took over, "We have handed over copies of the Delilah's blueprints and schematics. We have also allowed Jovian Defence Force technicians, access to all of the Delilah's systems. This was done so as to perform a comparative technological study between Jovian technology and L5's technology."

Wulfric wanted to asked a question, but given his previous behaviour remained silent.

Leopold noticed this and prompted him, "Brother, if you have questions. You should ask them."

A contrite Wulfric nodded to bis Brother Leopold and asked, "The Delilah is a space yacht. It's just a rich man's toy. It's not a warship. What can we possibly learn from it?"

"Ah. That is a great question Your Highness", Matthew answered, explaining,

"The Delilah was commissioned by none other than Clinton Usarian. He was the CEO of Hyper Dynamics Corporation and yes, he was a very rich prick. He was also an extremely clever one."

Matthew paused before continuing, "A lot of the systems on the Delilah, are in fact military grade systems. There are no weapons systems, absolutely none, but for a comparison based on non weapons technology, the Delilah is an excellent one. So please read the report."

"Captain Murphy. It says here that the Delilah is far more advanced than anything we have in our fleet", Prince Valdamar noted.

"Sadly Your Highness, that is the case. Your own technicians believe that Jovian technology is at least two, maybe even more decades behind the Earth and L5", Matthew replied.

"That's just crazy", Prince Valdamar remarked.

"Not really Your Highness. The estimate is at least two decades behind. Some of your technicians thinks it's closer to four or perhaps five decades behind", Matthew informed them all, "If you take away the weapons systems, there's nothing in your fleet that can match the Delilah. Let alone that Martian gunship, the Solstice. The hull of the Delilah is made of plasteel, your ship's hulls are still made of titanium alloys. That in itself says a lot."

"Sweet Mother of God Brothers, we're all fucked!", Prince Wulfric pronounced.

"No. Not really You Highness's", Matthew replied, allaying their fears by informing them,"The Earth and L5 are refurbishing their fleets before they set anything in motion. That gives us time to refurbish our fleet, using technological gleanings from the Delilah and its design specifications."

The room was quiet, "Your technicians are currently working hard as we speak, figuring out what technological advances can be copied from the Delilah and spliced into the Jovian Fleet", Matthew informed them, "You just have to have a little faith Gentlemen."

"What kinds of technologies are we talking about?", the High Prince enquired.

"I'm not across it all myself Your Majesty", Matthew admitted, "It's all there, in that initial report though. Mainly things like fusion and photon drive efficiencies. Power production and transmission techniques. Fuel systems, energy storage and so forth. Techniques and enhancements that have not been discovered out here in the Jovian Realms, but have long been discovered and implemented on the inner system worlds."

"Captain. How is it, that we have we fallen this far behind?", High Prince Heinrich asked.

"Your Majesty. If I speak openly and frankly, I'm likely to upset people", Matthew admitted.

"Captain Murphy. Matthew. We commissioned you into our armed forces, precisely for your frank and open opinions", the High Prince replied, adding, "So speak freely and openly."

Matthew goes out on a limb, "Your Majesty. Jovian Society has not yet struck the right balance between your religion and your sciences. A lot of the discoveries that have been missed or lost, have likely been tossed into the bin, because someone decided that they clashed with scriptures or the interpretations thereof."

The conference room was quiet, extraordinarily quiet. You could have heard a pin drop. The Prophet placed his head between his fingertips and began massaging his temples thinking to himself, *"Matthew what have you done!"*

Prince Leopold was the first to speak up, "Matthew is right my Brothers. If we keep going on like this, our society can never truly prosper. We'll end up becoming a technological backwater and eventually loose the capacity to maintain our own existence. This is an existential issue!"

"No Your Highness", Matthew replied, holding up his hand, "That kind of scenario is a very long way off. At this point, it is very highly unlikely. Especially as we are now openly discussing it."

"What do you suggest Matthew?", the High Prince was now addressing Matthew by his name once more, "Where do we go from here?"

"Your Majesty. We have to move forward by first looking backwards", Matthew replied, explaining, "Everything in science that has been banned by religion. We need teams of scientists to reopen all of those cases. Look at them cold and hard. What have we missed? What have we thrown out? Why was it thrown out? More importantly. What can we use? This really needs to be done."

The High Prince replied, "That could take quite a while Matthew."

"No doubts there Your Majesty", Matthew agreed, "but the quicker we all start, the better."

"Is it true, that there are no Slaves in Earth or L5 societies?", Prince Leopold asked, already knowing the answer to the question.

"Your Highness. The Earth has no Slaves. L5 has no Slaves. There are no Slaves at all, in the entire inner solar system", Matthew replied honestly.

"Then who does all the drudge work? How do you get things done?", Prince Wulfric asked.

"They use Androids. Robots. They are artificially intelligent, have no soul and are programmed to do what we tell them", Matthew informed them all, "They are even programmed to be safe and unable to complain or rebel. The Hyper Dynamics Corporation I mentioned earlier. It makes Androids. That is, it's main business."

"Androids! Robots!", Prince Wulfric repeated, then questioned, "Can we make those?"

"Your Highness. No. Again, it's another technology that the Jovian Realms simply does not have. Yet the inner solar system worlds have had Androids, I don't know, for over a century now!", Matthew replied.

Prince Leopold commented, "Heinrich. My Brother, we really need to adjust the narrative to get a better balance between our religion and the sciences."

"That won't be so easily done. We might find our bishops and clergy men getting upset, possibly even revolting", the High Prince considered.

Prince Leopold asked, "Heinrich. Who is the head of the Jovian High Church?"

"Little Brother, you know the answer to that question. I am", High Prince Heinrich replied.

Matthew caught on, "Your Majesty. When it comes to the Jovian High Church. It sounds like you're pretty much the Pope. If you decide to reform your church, shouldn't the clergy just agree with your reforms? You are after-all, effectively the voice of God."

High Prince Heinrich considered that idea, 'reform the church', then he answered forcefully, "I am the sovereign in all matters, Church and State! If the clergy disagree with me. I can have them frog marched to an airlock door and given a choice. Step back inside and reform or step outside and have faith in their God."

Prince Wulfric stepped in smiling, "Most people prefer to breath air than suck vacuum my Brother. I believe that reforms are in the air."

"Yes Brother", Prince Valdamar agreed, "Time for some reforms. We do control the narrative after-all. So it's time we made further use of it."

Prince Leopold looped back to the family portraits, "If we do this thing. Re-balance the narrative between religion and the sciences, we will need to show a united front. All Horridians united."

"You've brought us back to those family portraits again haven't you little Brother", the High Prince noted.

"Yes Heinrich. How better to show a united front", Prince Leopold admitted, "Individual Family portraits and a new Horridian Family portrait. Most especially if we're going to create theocratic disturbances with these church reforms."

The High Prince replied, "Agreed little Brother. Agreed. You have me hooked. Brothers! Family portraits are approved. Let's get them done!"

Matthew seeing an underlying pattern chimed in with, "It has the added advantage of showing to the inner solar system worlds, that the Horridian Dynasty is united. It will show them strength!"

The High Prince laughed, "Agreed Captain, but here's another idea. I'll put a motion before the Jovian High Council to annex Mars and everything in the Martian orbital zone, as a Jovian Realm. We can release that news with the family portraits. Let's show them both unity and purpose!"

High Prince Heinrich then asked, "Okay then. What about these reports and our current fleet deficiencies?"

"Play to your strengths Your Majesty", Matthew suggested, "Your missile technology is actually quite good. So that is a good starting point. Missiles, missiles and more missiles. Long range missiles to hold our enemies at bay. Shorter range missiles for when they get too close. If we can hold them at bay long enough, we buy more time to upgrade our fleet."

"While adding to and upgrading our fleet with whatever we can glean from the Delilah", Prince Valdamar replied, "That sounds like quite a plan."

"Your Highness. I'll add whatever engineering knowledge I have, such that it is, whenever I can", Matthew replied.

"Which reminds me Leopold. You have been making some reforms in the Ionian Realm of your own", the High Prince remarked, adding, "Not making the children of Slaves, automatically Slaves themselves. That seems to be skating on very fine ice Brother."

"Yes Heinrich it is, however, it's all within the constitutionals guide lines for such matters", Prince Leopold replied.

"How so Little Brother?", the High Prince queried.

"All immigrants that enter our Jovian Realms, are given the choice", Prince Leopold replied, reminding him further, "If they are Christian or they are non-Christian but willing to convert to Christianity, then they become are free citizens. If they are non-Christian and unwilling to convert to Christianity, they become Slaves."

"Yes Little Brother, that is well known to all of us", the High Prince replied.

"The children of Slaves have never been given that choice my Brother", Prince Leopold replied.

The High Prince considered that for a moment, as his other Brothers, Prince Valdamar and Prince Wulfric protested at how ridiculous Prince Leopold's statement sounded.

"This is something I have never really thought about before, never considered, Little Brother", the High Prince admitted, then asked, "What are your plans?"

"The reforms are actually quite simple Heinrich", Prince Leopold informed him, explaining, "If a Slave couple, willingly gives up their child or their children for adoption and those children are adopted by Christian families and raised as Christians. Then so long as those children continue through their religious sacraments and are confirmed as Christians. Then they simply cannot become Slaves. I simply want to give those children the choice."

The High Prince sat back in his chair. He was in quiet contemplation for several minutes before sitting forward once more with his determination.

"You do have a very valid point there Little Brother", the High Prince replied, "As I noted earlier, you come up with the most unusual notions and this one is very poignant."

"I thought it might strike a chord with you Heinrich", Prince Leopold admitted

In reply High Prince Heinrich announced, "You may continue with these reforms Little Brother, but only in the Ionian Realm. We will see how they pan out. If things go to plan and it greatly benefits your realm, then we may decide to implement these reforms across all the Jovian Realms."

The meeting had been long and after it broke up, the Prophet and Matthew headed back to their apartment building.

During their pod ride, the Prophet remarked, "That would have to be the strangest meeting we've had with them so far. I've seem them get argumentative before, but I've never seen one of them lose control like Prince Leopold did."

"Yes. That was certainly different My Lord", Matthew agreed, adding, "At the insult that Prince Wulfric levelled, I can fully understand it. However, it was the most controlled loss of control, that I have ever witnessed."

"I'm not sure I understand you, Matthew", the Prophet queried.

"To get that angry and lose control to that extent. Then pull out a sabre with lightning speed, only to hold it back right at his Brothers throat, just close enough to nick his flesh. For a loss of control, that shows a huge amount of control don't you think?", Matthew explained, adding, "It was quick, clean and very precise."

"I hadn't really noticed", the Prophet admitted.

"There's more My Lord", Matthew remarked, then added, "The High Prince so easily talked Prince Leopold down. Again, very, very controlled."

"And what about all this talk of their portraits?", Matthew questioned.

"I don't know Matthew", the Prophet replied, querying, "What's your take on that?"

"I haven't figure that one out yet. Sure portraits are important for propaganda purposes. A good show of solidarity, but Prince Leopold was very insistent. He came back to the discussion about portraits a couple of times. It shows that their portraits are very important to him, personally", Matthew replied, adding, "That meeting, was not going to end until Prince Leopold had the High Prince's approval."

"Prince Leopold managed to get approval on three things that he wanted. Those Horridian Family portraits. His Ionian Slave reforms for the children of Slaves and the realignment of the balance between their religion and their sciences. That last one, just happened to be aligned with what I wanted. We need the Jovian Realms to step their game scientifically speaking", Matthew explained to the Prophet, adding, "There's a lot more going on here beneath the surface."

"More questions than answers it seems", the Prophet noted.

"Oh. My Lord. I did get some answers. Really, I did", Matthew replied, adding, "Horridian family dynamics."

"How so?", the Prophet queried.

"The High Prince keeps his Sisters at bay, in the Trojan asteroid colonies", Matthew began, adding, "Apparently he doesn't trust them one bit. They're ambitious, dangerous and untrustworthy. From what I've heard elsewhere on the grapevine, they're also psychopaths. Poisoners I've heard."

"I knew that they were sent to the Trojan asteroid colonies for a reason Matthew, I just didn't know what it was", the Prophet replied.

"There's a lot more going on there as a well. I've heard a lot more since joining the Jovian Armed Forces", Matthew admitted, "Remember the Aft Trojan rebellion of twenty three fifty six."

"Yes. They mentioned that in an earlier meeting, but never really explained it", replied the Prophet, "Their narrative blames it on L5 and calls it the L5 plot."

"It had nothing to do with L5. It was all about greed", Matthew replied, explaining, "In each Jovian Realm, citizens pay a sovereign tax of twenty percent and a church tithe of ten percent. All the Horridian siblings and their 'churches' get that. Heinrich however, is the High Prince. So he gets the taxes from Ganymede's colonies, but he also gets twenty percent of the taxes from the other Jovian Realms as well. That's what they call their 'fealty' tax. The High Church on Ganymede Prime also gets ten percent of the other Jovian Realm's church tithes, their 'primacy' tax."

"Yes. I am aware of that Matthew", the Prophet replied, "Their taxes on bended knee."

"Well my Lord, in the Aft Trojan colonies, prior to the Aft Trojan rebellion, Princess Luisa decide to 'recover' the fealty and primacy taxes, by making the Aft Trojans pay more", Matthew informed the Prophet, explaining, "Princess Luisa put the sovereign tax up to thirty percent and the churches tax up to twenty percent. So half of all the Aft Trojan peoples earnings went on taxes. The Princess wasn't even satisfied with that either and slapped a thirty percent tax on food."

"No wonder they had a rebellion", the Prophet remarked.

"Worse than that. All taxes are set by the High Prince", Matthew replied, adding,"None of this had been cleared by High Prince Heinrich."

Matthew continued, "We know that the rebellion was put down by General Verne. It was a short, very bloody rebellion. When it was over, the perpetrators, were literally beheaded in public executions by guillotine."

"So that's why the High Prince described his Sister as a blood thirsty bitch", the Prophet noted.

"Far worse actually My Lord. Princess Luisa rounded up the families of all of the perpetrators. You know, husbands, wives, children, siblings and parents. Three whole generations all tarred with the same brush. They were all guillotined. A lot of people were publicly executed", Matthew informed him, adding, "And Princess Luisa, she took it upon herself to guillotine the families of the rebellion's leaders herself."

"Even the children?", the Prophet questioned.

"Right down to the babies apparently", Matthew replied.

"The High Prince would never have agreed to that. I'm sure", the Prophet protested.

"He didn't even know. The High Prince spies on his own siblings. When he found out, he was furious to say the least", Matthew responded, adding, "The High Prince's first actions were to rescind all of Princess Luisa's tax hikes, each and every one of them. Then he personally berated her in front of his siblings. He tore strips off her for endangering the stability of her Realm. Princess Luisa has basically been told, never again and been given her first and final warning."

"I had no idea it was that bad", the Prophet commented, "What about Princess Sophia?"

"I haven't heard much about her, but what I have heard doesn't bode well", Matthew replied, adding, "Princess Sophia is apparently cruel, calculating and very, very smart. She is also in a more powerful position than her Sister Luisa. Mainly because the Fore Trojan asteroid field has larger asteroids and therefore more resources. It also has a lot more colonies."

"That explains why the High Prince keeps his Sisters at arms length", the Prophet noted.

"Then there's Prince Wulfric and Prince Valdamar. The High Prince keeps them both very close and in the military. The outer and inner Jovian Defences, which ostensibly they control, except they really don't, do they. The High Prince controls the whole shebang! Not the brightest sparks those two My Lord. They are just useful idiots. That's how High Prince Heinrich treats them both."

Matthew continued, "The two most powerful men in that conference room were High Prince Heinrich and Prince Leopold. Prince Wulfric and Prince Valdamar treat him like he's simple, much to their own detriment I suspect. The High Prince however, not so much. He has installed his youngest Brother as the Prince of Io, deep inside of Jupiter's Galilean moon system. He did that for a reason and I want to know why."

Prince Leopold does have direct control and access to both the Amalthean and Ionian mines", the Prophet suggested.

"Yes My Lord, but nothing, nothing military. The High Prince put his useful idiot Brothers in charge of the military, which they don't really control", Matthew pondered, "but then he put his smartest sibling in charge of those mines."

"The High Prince calls him Little Brother. Perhaps he's the High Prince's favourite?", the Prophet speculated.

"Maybe, but there has to be more to it than that and I want to know what that is", Matthew replied as the transport pod pulled into their apartment building's underground garage.

"Here's the thing. You'd think that the Ionian orbital zone would be the most dangerous, with the intensity of Jupiter's radiation belts in that region", Matthew commented before stepping out of the transport pod, "but it's not. Jovian radiation shielding is some of their greatest, most effective technology. So the High Prince has effectively placed his youngest Brother, Prince Leopold, in the safest possible place within the entire Jovian Realms. Again why? I want know. We need to know a lot more about the High Prince and Prince Leopold. There's something very odd going on there."

As Matthew and the Prophet reached the apartment building's level where their apartment were, Matthew's communicator buzzed. Matthew checked the message that appeared on its small screen.

"We need to contact General Tarzan", Matthew informed the Prophet.

"We'll make the call in your apartment", the Prophet suggested.

The pair entered Matthew's apartment and Matthew initiated the call to General Tarzan.

General Tarzan answered the call and was quickly on the screen.

"Excellent. You got my message", General Tarzan greeted.

"Yes General. What can we do for you?", Matthew asked.

"About the meeting", General Tarzan began, adding, "What a meeting! That was one of the more exciting ones to say the least."

"Yes. It was certainly different", Matthew agreed.

"Yes it was, but getting down to the reason I need to talk to you both. Do we still have people on Mars?", the General enquired.

The Prophet replied, "We did have people on Deimos, Pirates and we had people embedded on Phobos. Then of course we had people in all the main Martian colonies, except Elysium."

Matthew added in, "Many of our people from the main colonies came across to New Tortuga during our transit from L5 to Mars. Our people on Deimos and Phobos joined us in New Tortuga after we arrived."

"Of course we lost the Battle of New Tortuga, so we lost all of our people there", the Prophet continued, adding, "Before that, our people at the Aurorae colony ran afoul of that damnable Wizard and those that survived were rounded up and arrested by the Aurorae security services."

"Then what's left?", General Tarzan asked.

"We should have people, assets, in the other six main colonies", the Prophet replied, adding, "Those people that didn't join us in New Tortuga perhaps."

"We can't really be sure my Lord", Matthew replied, explaining, "When we fled Mars after our loss in the Battle of New Tortuga, there will have been a crack down across all the Martian colonies. What people we did have will have gone into hiding. They could be difficult to contact."

"Can we contact them Matthew? That's the question", General Tarzan enquired.

"We can try General. We can try", Matthew replied, "But I can't make any guarantees."

"So Matthew. What's the plan?", the General asked.

"The same deal as when we were at L5", Matthew replied, informing the General, "We post something into the news feeds with an embedded coded message."

"And that works?", the General queried.

"Yeah. Sure does. Our people have equipment that scans the news feeds for our coded messages in real time", Matthew explained.

"So how does this work?", the General asked.

"Well General. I'll put together a message with a series of instructions", Matthew began, adding, "Then I'll encode and embed the messages into the wanted reward video that we sent into the news feeds previously. We can then reissue that to the news feeds again and no one will suspect it has embedded messages in it. Assuming we still have people on Mars and they are still scanning for our messages, we should get a response."

"What instructions would you send Matthew?", a curious Prophet asked.

Matthew thought for a moment, "First, tell our assets to check in with us here at Ganymede Prime, so we know what assets we have. Next, take all necessary actions to gather intelligence on the Martian Gunship Solstice. Then finally, we want the crew of the Solstice. Capture them and collect their bounties. That last one should be an incentive."

General Tarzan considered the planned message, "Sounds good to me. How long will it be before we hear back?"

"General. That I cannot predict. Depending on what's left of our Assets, we may or may not even hear back. We'll just have to wait and see", Matthew informed him.

"Get the process started Matthew. I want to know what assets we still have on Mars", the General ordered.

5. Follow the Money

Earth Defence Force Admiral, Samantha (Sam) Zumwalt, watched her ship's main screen on the bridge of her Heavy Cruiser, the Vanguard. The Planet Mars was rapidly approaching ahead of them and the EDCF Martian Defence Task Force would soon arrive at Mars.

Captain Hart noted questioningly, "Admiral. We are detecting a magnetic field?"

"Mars doesn't have a global magnetic field Hart", the Admiral replied.

"Admiral. Apparently it does now. Quite a strong magnetic field in fact", Captain Hart replied.

"Have an analysis done", Admiral Zumwalt ordered, "We can look into the magnetic field later."

"Aye Admiral", Captain Hart replied before signalling to his Lieutenant Adjutant to arrange a analysis of the strange Martian magnetic field.

Admiral Sam Zumwalt continued to watch the main screen with great curiosity, she had never see Mars close up in it's terraformed state. The Planet loomed larger as they quickly approached.

"Captain Hart", Admiral Zumwalt caught the Captain of the Vanguard's attention, before ordering, "I want the heavy cruisers high above each pole. The Ptarmigan to the north and the Apollo to the south. Stationary well above high Martian orbit."

"Aye Admiral", Captain Hart replied before signalling to his Lieutenant Adjutant, Lieutenant Small, to get the orders out to the two heavy cruisers.

Admiral Zumwalt continued, "Defensive ring number one. Place all destroyers in a hexagonal arrangement in high Martian orbit. Dauntless, the Defiant and Dark-star north of the equator and the Hermes, Hephaestus and Hera south of the equator."

"Aye Admiral", again Captain Hart replied, before signalling Lieutenant Adjutant Small, this time to get the orders out to their six destroyers.

Admiral Zumwalt issued yet more orders, "Defensive ring number two. Place all frigates in a hexagonal arrangement in medium Martian orbit. The London, Anchorage and Melbourne north of the equator and the Dionysus, Erebus and Eos south of the equator."

"Aye Admiral", Captain Hart replied, then signalled his Lieutenant Adjutant once more, in order to get the orders out to their six frigates.

"Okay then!", Admiral Samantha Zumwalt remarked as she clapped her hands together, then stated, "We have our two watchers. We have our two rings of steel. Captain Hart. Take the Vanguard down into low Martian equatorial orbit."

"Aye Admiral", Captain Hart replied, the ordered, "Helm. Low Martian equatorial orbit."

Within a matter of minutes, all fifteen ships of the combined EDCF Martian Defence Task Force were dispersing into a defensive posture around the Planet Mars.

"Captain Hart", Admiral Zumwalt caught the Captain's attention once more, "Our orders are simple. If the Jovian Armed Forces attack Mars. Nothing, nothing at all gets past us. Pass that on."

"Aye Admiral", Captain Hart replied, adding, "I'll ensure that all the Captains understand that", as he signalled his Lieutenant Adjutant to make it so.

"Captain Hart. What can you tell me about Phobos?", Admiral Zumwalt asked.

"Admiral. Phobos, more specifically, Port Phobos, is an L5 operation. It's run by one Lieutenant Ira Roberts", Captain Hart informed the Admiral, adding, "He's been in command of Port Phobos for quite some time. Years in fact. Almost a fixture I'd say."

"An L5 operation", Admiral Zumwalt replied, commanding, "Good then. Contact the Apollo. Have them arrange recon and liaison teams to take up position at Phobos Port. Two teams, on fortnightly rotations."

"Aye Admiral", Captain Hart replied, then he signalled to his Lieutenant Adjutant to relay the orders to Captain Morris of the Heavy Cruiser Apollo to make the necessary arrangements.

"Okay. Next on the list. What do we know abut Deimos?", Admiral Zumwalt asked.

"Admiral. Deimos has an old abandoned L5 military base. It has been abandoned for eighty, maybe ninety years", Captain Hart began, informing the Admiral further, "According to our information from the L5 Cruiser Spartan, it has been ransacked and stripped of any valuable equipment over the years. There are even sections that have collapsed and are quite unsafe."

"Yes Captain, I've read those reports, but what about the base's fuel tanks? You know. How many tanks? Storage capacity? Current levels? That sort of thing", the Admiral requested.

"That we don't know Admiral. We do know that there are quite large fuel tanks and they do contain copious quantities of fuel. How much though is anyone's guess. We also know for certain that the refuelling stations work and that ships have recently refuelled there. The Spartan, the Ptolemy just to name a couple. From what I understand the fuel base stored, Hydrogen, Helium 3, Nitrogen, Oxygen and Argon.", Captain Hart replied.

"Okay Captain. Contact the Ptarmigan. Have them arrange recon and engineering teams. I want them to take up positions at the Deimosian base and I want a full report on everything that base has and what it needs. Two teams, fortnightly rotations. That base is going to be fully refurbished and recommissioned. So I want reports coming across my desk within the week, bringing to light everything that base has. We need to know exactly what that base needs to be brought back online", the Admiral ordered.

"Aye Admiral", Captain Hart replied, as he signalled to his Lieutenant Adjutant, to relay the orders to Captain Cortez of the Heavy Cruiser Ptarmigan to make the necessary arrangements.

"Captain Hart. I have a call to make. Have the Captain's yacht made ready. I'll be going the surface in one hour. I'll need a pilot and an adjutant", Admiral Zumwalt ordered before leaving the ship's bridge and heading for the conference room.

"Aye Admiral", Captain Hart replied as the Admiral walked strode off, he then signalled to his Lieutenant Adjutant to have his yacht prepared.

It certainly looked like Lieutenant Adjutant Small was going to be having a very busy day.

Admiral Zumwalt placed a call from ship to shore, to Governor John Anderson of the Chryce colony. The Admiral did not have to wait very long.

Governor Anderson appeared on the screen, "Admiral. Good to see you again."

"Yes Governor. Good to see you as well.", the Admiral replied, then asked, "have all the arrangements been put in place?"

"All arrangements are in place Admiral. Everything is done", the Governor replied, adding, "and everything is back dated appropriately."

"Good then. I'll be at the New Flinders Physic Academy in an hour and a half. I'll meet you there", Admiral Zumwalt informed the Governor.

"Will do Admiral. My secretary has cleared my calendar for the day", the Governor replied.

"Excellent. I'll see you there Governor. Over and out", the Admiral replied.

The screen then went blank.

Back at Chryce colony, "Maria", Governor Anderson called out to his secretary, "Have Mack meets us at the south hanger. Make sure you bring your grip and all of the Mars Defence Force documentation. We'll be leaving for New Flinders Psychic Academy in ten minutes."

"What's going on Forkbraid?", Selene enquired.

"I'm not sure. We've had a call from Governor Anderson over at Chryce colony. He's coming out here and wants all of us to meet him at the air field", Forkbraid explained.

"All of us? Who exactly is all of us?", Selene asked.

"The crew of the Solstice and the L5 pilots on secondment to the Academy", Forkbraid replied, then he added, "and he wants us all there in uniform."

"In uniform?", Selene queried.

"In uniform", Forkbraid confirmed, as he sent out telepathic messages to Charlene, Marcus and Roseanne to get everyone moving.

"How'd the Governor even know where our academy is?", Selene asked.

"Selene, our academy's coordinates are on the Jovian wanted video", Forkbraid answered adding, "Everyone that's seen it, knows where we are."

Governor Anderson's Hummer landed on the tarmac at the airfield, south east of the New Flinders Psychic Academy. It's pilot, Mack stepped out of the Hummer and stood to one side. Governor John Anderson and his secretary Maria stepped out of the Hummer and approached the gathered group of people.

Maria was wearing a grip and carrying a briefcase full of documents. Governor Anderson was carrying another smaller briefcase and a portable table. After the passengers had alighted from the Hummer, its pilot, Mack, boarded the Hummer once more.

Selene and Roseanne stepped forward to greet them. Behind them stood Cormac and Candy Farmer, Catherine Swann and her children, Miranda and Chiron, along with the Pod Sisters parents, Zyaliep and Kwoth Pod. Miranda was happily playing with Zuawalo's pet ferret, Zigg. The ten L5 pilots who were under secondment to the academy, all stood lined up to one side, wearing their L5 pilot uniforms.

"Lady Selene", the Governor greeted.

"Governor Anderson. What can we do for you?", Selene asked.

"We'll get to that. Where is Forkbraid and the crew of the Solstice?", the Governor asked.

"Their uniforms are in their cabins aboard the ship. They're just getting changed now", Selene informed him, "They shouldn't be too long."

Governor Anderson checked his watch, remarking, "It's a good thing we're early then", then looked up to the Martian skies in a westerly direction.

From out of the north west came another ship. It wasn't a Hummer and was of a design that only Selene, Marcus and Charlene, having come from the Earth, had seen before.

Selene noted, "That looks like an Earth Defence Force command yacht", then asked, "Governor, are we expecting company?"

"Yes. The EDCF Martian Task Force has entered Martian orbit", Governor Anderson informed them, "That's Fleet Admiral Samantha Zumwalt on her way down."

Within minutes the command yacht was landing on the tarmac close by, but well clear of Varak's construction hanger doors. It was almost as large as the Solstice. Selene noted how large its twin photon thrusters were, as a proportion of the ships overall size. They were huge compared to the Solstice's micro-fusion thrusters.

The command yacht's pilot stepped out of the ship and stood to one side. Fleet Admiral Samantha Zumwalt stepped out followed by a Lieutenant Adjutant.

The pilot then returned to the ship. The duo quickly strode over to the awaiting group. The Lieutenant was wearing a grip and carrying a small briefcase. As they did so, the crew of the Solstice walked out of the construction hanger where the Solstice was currently stowed. The Admiral noted two things straight away as she approached. One, the crew of the Solstice had nice uniforms, really nice and two, they appeared to be an odd sort of a crew.

"Greetings", Admiral Zumwalt greeted the gathered group.

"Greetings Admiral", Selene and Forkbraid both greeted in reply, with Selene adding, "What can we do for you Admiral?"

The Admiral replied, "I'll get to that, but first, on our approach to Mars, we detected a strong magnetic field. Which is odd, as Mars doesn't have a global magnetic field, nor any localised magnetic fields of any appreciable strength."

"It is an artificially created magnetic field", Forkbraid replied, explaining, "We placed a very powerful five Tesla dipole in the Sun Mars Lagrangian point one, roughly a million kilometres from Mars in the direction of the Sun. Mars is currently sitting within the tail of that magnetic field."

"Very clever. That should massively reduce atmospheric stripping and cosmic ray penetration", the Admiral replied. She was impressed and that was generally difficult to do.

Forkbraid pointed to Varak, "I can't take the credit for that, it is Varak's creation."

"Okay, about why I'm here, why we're both here actually. Governor Anderson and myself that is", the Admiral started, "We remember your actions in defending Mars, L5 and the Earth. As you already know, we've been extremely busy with the disastrous situation in Europe. If not for your ship and your crew, that would have been far worse, perhaps even a planet wide catastrophe. Ladies and Gentlemen, crew of the Solstice, the Earth remembers you."

"And so does Mars", Governor Anderson added.

"If you'd like to begin Governor. My Lieutenant Adjutant will video the proceedings", the Admiral remarked, then asking Forkbraid, "If you could have yourself and your crew line up in some semblance of rank. Somewhere close by to the L5 pilots should be good."

Governor Anderson unfolded the portable table and set it up. His secretary placed her briefcase on the table at the back. The Governor placed his small briefcase on the table and opened it up. It contained medals. Newly minted Martian, Hero of Mars medals. A medal only recently created.

The Lieutenant placed his small briefcase on the table next to the Governor's briefcase and opened it up. It also contained medals. Freshly minted Earth Defence Force, Medals of Honour. The Lieutenant then begun recording the scene.

Governor Anderson walked over to the crew of the Solstice. His secretary Maria picked up six Hero of Mars medals and followed him.

The Governor looked towards the Lieutenant's camera, "For those of you who do not know me. I am Governor John Anderson of the Chryce colony on Mars", he then gestured to the crew of the Solstice, "Before me are the crew of the Martian Defence Force Ship, Solstice."

"Many of you will have seen the medal award ceremony, whereby this very same crew were awarded medals for their participation and the heroic actions take during the Battle of L5", the Governor spoke into the camera, "However, what many of you don't know, is that prior to the Battle of L5. The Solstice flew out to intercept and take down the missile swarm that the Jovian High Council launched against Mars. This was done during the Solstice's very first shakedown voyage. At that time, there were only six of the Solstice's crew members present."

One by one, the Governor presented the six Hero of Mars medals to the six Solstice crew members who were present on that mission. Each of the crew members already had three medals each, as awarded to them by L5's Fleet Captain Carmichael and they were currently wearing them.

The Governor announced each in turn, noting the crew member's position and name. The order of presentation was Charlene Fewkes, Marcus Greyhelm, Peter Swann, Varakhan Utana, James Murphy and finally their Captain, Forkbraid. They each accepted the pinning on of their medals with a simple hand shake.

Governor Anderson stepped back, gestured to the crew once more, "I give you, the crew of the Solstice. Heroes of Mars and Mars remembers their heroic deeds", he began clapping and everyone else joined in.

Next the Governor moved over to the ten L5 pilots who had been seconded to the academy. While he did so, his secretary walked over to the table and picked up ten more Hero of Mars medals, before joining him by the pilots.

The Governor faced the camera once more, "These ten men, pilots all, are from L5. They volunteered to stay on Mars and were seconded to the Martian Defence Forces. These pilots fought in the Battle of the Elysium plains, attacking and destroying the weapons of the Aft Trojan Occupation Forces. Theses ten men are heroes of Mars and Mars remembers their service."

One by one Governor Anderson presented the Hero of Mars medals to the ten pilots. Each one was accepted with both a hand shake and a salute.

Governor Anderson stepped back, gestured to the ten pilots once more, "I give you, the pilots of the Battle of the Elysium plains. Heroes of Mars and Mars remembers their heroic deeds", he began clapping and once again everyone else joined in.

The Governor then stepped back to a position between both the crew of the Solstice and the pilots, where he could easily see all personnel.

Admiral Zumwalt stepped forward and approached the crew of the Solstice. As the Lieutenant was busy filming, the Governor's secretary picked up the ten Medals of Honour from the Earth and followed her.

The Admiral addressed the camera, "For those of you who don't know me. I am Fleet Admiral Samantha Zumwalt of the EDCF Martian Task Force. Many of you may remember the press conference where General Archibald Stanton promised, that the Earth would honour the crew of the Solstice. Ladies and Gentlemen, that day is today. For their heroic and selfless service in the defence of the Earth, I will be presenting each crew member of the Solstice with the Earth's Medal of Honour."

The Admiral then began awarding the medals, starting with the lower ranks first, clearly stating their positions and names. As the Admiral awarded the medals, she took mental note of the fact that the two pod sisters were not only pregnant but clearly showing.

The order of presentation was Leroy McGuvan, Nyaliep Pod, Zeealas Pod, Zuawalo Pod, Charlene Fewkes, Marcus Greyhelm, Peter Swann, Varakhan Utana, James Murphy and finally their Captain, Forkbraid.

As the Admiral leant in to pin on each medal, she whispered to each of them quietly but clearly, "Remember, you are Martian Defence Force personnel. So a hand shake and then a salute."

Each of the Solstice's crew members did precisely as the Admiral requested.

The Admiral then gestured to the Solstice's crew members, "Citizens of inner solar system. I give you, the Captain and Crew of the Martian Defence Force Ship Solstice. Heroes of the Battle of L5, who single handedly destroyed over thirty percent of the inbound Jovian missiles. Who then tracked down and destroyed many of the warheads that were launched by those missiles. I give you Heroes of the Earth", Admiral Zumwalt stated clearly as she motioned her hand in front of the Solstice's crew, then began clapping. Every one present joined in clapping as well.

Shortly thereafter her Lieutenant Adjutant shut off the recording.

"All good Lieutenant?", the Captain asked.

"All good Admiral. It's a take", her Lieutenant Adjutant replied.

Admiral Zumwalt then told everyone, "Thank you ladies and gentlemen."

Forkbraid approached the Admiral and asked, "Not that we don't mind being awarded medals, but really, honestly, what's the point of all of this?"

"Captain Forkbraid. Our enemy calls you all Pirates. We have to correct that. Every time we award you medals and call you heroes, it counteracts their propaganda. It makes you all safer", Admiral Zumwalt explained.

"And that's it?", Forkbraid questioned.

"Of course not. There's always more. A lot more in fact", the Admiral admitted, "L5's President Banyon gets his fluff piece. All politicians love their fluff pieces. The citizens get good news. The people love that. And you know what the Defence Forces get out it?"

"No Admiral. What do the Defence Forces get out of this?", Forkbraid questioned.

"Recruitment videos Captain. Recruitment videos", Admiral Zumwalt informed Forkbraid, explaining, "By the time we've finished editing this video, President Banyan will have his fluff piece and we'll have our recruitment adverts. Not just the Earth's Defence Forces either, L5's Colonial Fleet, the Martian Defence Forces. Every one of us benefits from this. Heroes Captain. Everyone loves their heroes. Especially you guys in those uniforms! I'll have to get the name of your tailor by the way. Seriously Captain, recruits will be flocking to the recruitment offices."

"Admiral. When I'm on board the Solstice, I'm Captain Forkbraid", Forkbraid informed her, "When I'm not on board the Solstice, I am simply Forkbraid or

FB."

The Admiral looked Forkbraid up and down, "Well that simply won't do Captain. When you're in that uniform, you are a ship's Captain", she then stepped in closer and commented in a much softer tone, "When you're out of that uniform, then maybe, just maybe I'll call you FB."

Selene caught a stray thought from the Admiral's mind and walked up to Forkbraid, wrapping her right arm around Forkbraid's left.

Admiral Zumwalt looked at Selene and then back at Forkbraid, remarking honestly, "My apologies Captain. I didn't realise you were married."

"Not married Admiral", Selene admitted in reply, then stating while smiling, "We are together none the less."

Selene sent a thought to Forkbraid, *"What is it about you and strong women Forkbraid?"*

Forkbraid replied with the equivalent of a telepathic shrug.

Roseanne spoke up about the Battle of the Elysium plains, "Governor Anderson, that battle up there where the Trojans landed wasn't as simple as just sending in the wisps and their Pilots."

"How is that so, young Lady?", the Governor asked.

"The Pilots did attack the Trojan encampment the day the Trojans landed and they did attack the Trojan encampment four or so times afterwards over the course of a month or more", Roseanne began, then explained, "It was the second attack that destroyed all their weapons systems and that was actually Selene's and Forkbraid's work."

"Really? I hadn't heard about that", the Governor admitted.

Forkbraid stepped in, "Roseanne is correct Governor. Selene and I used our psychic potentials. A majikal ceremony and a complex spell to manipulate and transmute energy to destroy the Trojan weapons systems."

"Why wasn't that in the report?", the Governor enquired.

"Had we put that into the official report, how do you think it would have been received", Forkbraid enquired.

"With a huge dose of scepticism I believe", the Governor admitted.

"We aren't proud of our actions either Governor", Selene added, "Taking out those weapons systems, literally cost the Trojans hundreds of lives."

Forkbraid stepped in again, "We've already discussed this Selene. That plan was my idea, it was my spell, the galdrar and stadha were designed by me. All of the consequences are on me, not you."

"That in no way makes me feel any better about it Forkbraid", Selene replied, then turning to Governor Anderson, "And don't you even dare consider, giving us medals for that!"

"As you wish Lady Selene", the Governor agreed.

Roseanne spoke up again and stated, "The final attack on the Trojan encampment was made by Forkbraid using his Bat Wing. Forkbraid made multiple sorties into their encampment to ensure that the Trojans fully understood that they could be hit at will, with impunity and that we needed only one single ship to dot it!"

"Again that is true Governor", Forkbraid admitted, "Except of course I was flying my Bat Wing by remote control using a Neural Interconnect Control helmet. I was literally a dozen miles away when my Bat Wing attacked their encampment."

"Yes", Roseanne agreed, adding, "Forkbraid was with Jim Murphy dropping off Zuawalo, Zeealas and Leroy on a covert mission. That very mission was crucial in getting the Trojans to decide to return home, to the Aft Trojan Asteroid colonies."

"A covert mission? Why have I not heard about this?", Governor Anderson questioned.

Roseanne explained, "They went to a valley near where the Trojans were harvesting local trees for the timber and they setup a camp, pretending to be locals. The Trojans were using the timber to make siege engines back at their encampment to attack the academy with. A totally stupid idea I might add and the very reason for the multiple sorties on their encampment over the course of the Trojans occupation. We were trying to convince them to go home."

Governor Anderson looked both perplexed and intrigued at the same time.

Roseanne continued, "Some Trojan scouts came across Zuawalo, Zeealas and Leroy and mistook them for locals, which is exactly what was meant to happen. Of course, the Trojans wanted local information. When they found out, that the local information was completely different to the information they had been given, they decided to leave. They then left Mars to go home."

"Young Lady. What was so different, that they would just decide to go home?", Governor Anderson asked.

"Their mission was to destroy a fortress full of *'Demons'*, then attack and occupy the Martian colonies one by one, eliminating the *'Demon'* leadership of Mars", Roseanne replied, adding, "From Zuawalo, Zeealas and Leroy, they learnt that their very first target was a boarding school for children aged seven to twenty one and that there were absolutely no Demons on Mars at all."

"And that convinced them to leave?", the Governor questioned.

"I don't know, but I do know that the Trojans abandoned their logging camp and left Mars the very next day", Roseanne informed the Governor, adding, "What ever they did, it certainly does appear to have worked."

"Is this true Forkbraid?", the Governor asked.

"Yes. Basically it is true Governor", Forkbraid replied, admitting, "If not for the actions of Zuawalo, Zeealas and Leroy and their covert mission, the Trojans would not have left."

"Thank you Forkbraid and thank you young Lady", the Governor replied, then turning to his secretary Maria, "It appears that we are thee medals short Maria. Take note and we'll award those medals at a later date."

"Yes Governor. I have taken a full set of notes", Maria replied, adding, "I can organise Hero of Mars medals for them when we return to Chryce."

Roseanne winked at both Zuawalo and Zeealas.

Zuawalo commented, "Our Roseanne is so very sweet.

Zeealas agreed, "Yes. Our Roseanne is ever so sweet."

Hearing the way Zuawalo and Zeealas remarked about Roseanne, Selene sent her a silent thought, *"Roseanne. That issue you had with the Girls. Did you talk to them about it?"*

"Yes Selene. Why?", Roseanne silently thought back.

"It's just that the Girls are commenting about you in the same way that they comment about Jim", Selene silently transmitted.

"Oh. No. It's nothing like that Selene", Roseanne replied, *"We are just so very close friends."*

Not being a psychic, but stepping in coincidentally, Zyaliep quietly informed Selene, "My daughters want me to adopt Roseanne, so they can all be Sisters."

To which Selene replied quietly, "The Girls do understand that I've already adopted Roseanne, don't they?"

"Yes of course. We can discuss this later", Zyaliep replied, adding, "A child who has lost her parents at a young age, can never have too many Mothers to adopt them and watch over them."

"Yes. I see. We should discuss this later Zyaliep", Selene replied, then thinking to herself, *"Is this another cultural thing in their society?"*

"Captain Forkbraid", the Admiral began, "Your crew is highly problematic", as she watched Zuawalo's ferret Zigg jump up and climb onto Zuawalo, eventually settling, perched on her shoulder. Quite an odd site as Zigg was awfully large for a ferret.

"How so Admiral?", Forkbraid enquired.

"Zuawalo and Zeealas Pod", the Admiral noted, asking, "Are they sisters?"

"Yes. They are sisters", Forkbraid admitted.

"How does Nyaliep Pod fit into this? Is Nyaliep a relative as well?", the Admiral asked.

"Nyaliep is their Aunt", Forkbraid also admitted.

"Three members, from the one family on the crew of a single ship. That is something generally avoided in the military and not just the Earth Defence Forces either. Lose the ship, lose the family. It is a very bad idea", the Admiral replied.

The Admiral continued, "And to make matters worse, they're both pregnant and showing. That's not a good thing either Captain. Definitely not a good thing."

Forkbraid admitted, "And so is their Aunt Nyaliep, although she isn't showing yet."

"Are you serious Captain? All three of these Pod women are pregnant?", Admiral Zumwalt questioned, then added, "Captain. You have one very strange crew. Your crew does not meet any military standards whatsoever. Not by a long shot."

"It gets even stranger Admiral", Selene chimed in, fully informing her, one by one, "My Forkbraid here, he is the most powerful psychic you'll ever meet. Charlene and Marcus, two more psychics, both level fives and they're a married couple. Peter Swann over there has an IQ so high, it's hard to comprehend, somewhere north of three hundred. He can solve any problem you throw at him. Varak's no slouch either, his IQ is just under three hundred. If he can think of it, he can build it. Varak is married to Nyaliep by the way. Nyaliep is carrying his child. Then there's James Murphy. He's the First officer, the Tactical officer and the Chief Security officer. If three hats isn't enough, he's also the Chief Security officer of the New Flinders Psychic Academy and the Elysium Colony. Zuawalo and Zeealas are Jim's wives and they are carrying his children. Then of course there's Leroy McGuvan over here. He was a terrorist, he was later executed by Forkbraid, then he was demolished, swapped sides and has since been redeemed. Admiral this is the weirdest crew you'll ever find. It is also the best crew you'll ever find."

"I'll be honest with you both", Admiral Zumwalt replied, adding, "This crew you've just described. Three members from the same family on the same ship's crew. Pregnant to boot! Three married couples on the same ship's crew. This is simply not acceptable for any military ship and its crew! In any military, it would be simply be unacceptable!"

Forkbraid stepped in an replied forcefully, "Then Admiral. Thank the Gods, that the Solstice and its crew are not bloody military!"

Governor Anderson having heard the raised voices quickly approached and stepped in, "Forkbraid. Selene. There's something I need to discuss with you both. With everyone actually."

"You haven't told them?", Admiral Zumwalt asked.

"Of course not", the Governor admitted.

"What have you not told us Anderson?", Forkbraid questioned angrily.

"During the press conference President Banyan made a blunder", Governor Anderson informed them, "He told the press that your crew are a part of the Martian Defence Forces."

"We know that Anderson. There are no Martian Defence Forces", Forkbraid replied.

"Well yes and no actually", the Governor replied.

"Yes and No?", Selene questioned, "What the hell does that mean Governor?"

"We convened an assembly of all the colony Governors and we made a few decisions. One of which was to create, a Martian Defence Force", Governor Anderson informed them both.

"How does that affect us? We are not a part of any military", Forkbraid questioned.

"Well Forkbraid, we had a problem and we needed to solve it quickly", the Governor began, "The Jovian High Council declared your crew to be Pirates. President Banyan declared your crew to be Military. We needed to reinforce Banyan's opinion. We can't have you being seen as Privateers."

"For fuck sake Anderson! What have you bloody bureaucrats done now?", Forkbraid demanded.

President Anderson held up his hand to try and calm things just a tad, before replying, "We back dated the incorporation of the Martian Defence Forces to the date that you all arrived on Mars. We even concocted a budget that started on that date."

"What in the bloody blue blazes does that mean?", Forkbraid asked.

"We not only needed to make you look like Martian Defence Force personnel, we needed to make you look like Martian Defence Force personnel from the very first day you arrived", Governor Anderson explained.

"I'm not sure, I like where this is going Governor", Selene noted.

Governor Anderson then explained, "There is an old saying. If you want to know the truth of a matter, then you need to follow the money."

"What does that mean?", Forkbraid asked.

"If our enemies attempt to follow the money, they'll find the Martian Defence Forces were inaugurated upon your arrival on Mars. On the books, they'll find six of your crew listed as Martian Defence Force personnel since day one. Charlene Fewkes, Marcus Greyhelm, Peter Swann, Varakhan Utana, James Murphy and yourself Forkbraid. The other crew members, Zuawalo Pod, Zeealas Pod, Nyaliep Pod and Leroy McGuvan, they're on the books, listed as Martian Defence Force personnel since two weeks after the Battle of New Tortuga. If our enemies follow the money, that's precisely what they'll find", Governor Anderson informed them.

"And these spies are going to trust what's on the books?", Marcus asked, adding, "Books can be faked you do know."

"We've also opened bank accounts in the names of everyone of your crew members. The Martian Defence Force's pay office, has credited salaries into those bank accounts back dated, so as to look like regular monthly pay cycles. It all looks like you've been paid monthly since the date of your commencement with the Martian Defence Forces", the Governor explained, "Your remunerations have been set, commensurate on actual colonial fleet remunerations for colonial fleet officers of equivalent ranks. In your crews cases, they are of course brevet ranks. Forkbraid has the rank of Captain, Jim has the rank of First officer and the rest of the crew have the ranks of Lieutenant."

Charlene quickly remarked, "That won't work. It will look like moneys continuously accruing without any expenditure! No one will fall for that!"

"Ah! Yes, we've even thought of that Ms Fewkes. You each have two bank accounts and they're set up in different banks. Pays go into your Chryce Central Bank accounts. Then there are regular deductions, designed to mimic withdrawals and spending. So your pay accounts look like they're being regularly used. Of course the expenditure that comes out of those pay accounts, simply ends up in your Chryce Colonial Trust Bank accounts. So the money hasn't really been spent at all. It just looks like it has, when it's simply been transferred to another bank. On the Chryce Central Bank's books, however, it looks as though it has been spent. We even considered spending patterns and mimicked, unique individual spending patterns for each of the ten of you."

Charlene thought about that for a moment and replied, "That might actually work, except we'd only be able to draw upon the secondary accounts."

"Why is that Ms Fewkes?", Governor Anderson enquired.

"Your people have set up ten unique, individual expenditure patterns. None of us will match those expenditure patterns. If we draw upon our primary pay accounts, we'll alter those patterns in noticeable ways", Charlene explained, "Your people will need to keep doing what it is they're doing and we'll have to limit our withdrawing to the secondary accounts."

"Oh I see", Governor Anderson agreed, "My people will have to come up with some kind of transitional process it seems."

Forkbraid asked, "Governor. Did no one think to contact us and let us know all about this?"

"This was all done very quickly and you guys were so damned busy saving lives. We also thought it best, if we limited this information to as few people as possible", Governor Anderson concluded.

"Of all the cock eyed schemes", Forkbraid remarked, "This one certainly takes the cake!"

"What works, works! Do what works! That's my motto", Governor Anderson noted, "By the way Forkbraid, you've been listed on the books as the Fleet Captain of the Martian Defence Forces!"

Jim chuckled, "That's the same rank as Captain Carmichael", he laughed.

"I've already told Captain Carmichael, that the Solstice is not a military ship", Forkbraid replied.

Admiral Zumwalt chimed in with, "It's all good Captain Forkbraid. Captain Carmichael actually agreed with the plan. He was the one that suggested, that the money needs to match the books."

"So I'm the Fleet Captain of a fleet of precisely one ship?", Forkbraid laughed.

"Twelve ships actually", the Admiral corrected., "Your ship, the Solstice, your Bat Wing and those ten atmo rated wisps. Captain. You must understand, that all of this was done for you and your crews benefit."

"How so Admiral?", Forkbraid questioned.

"If we left you as privateers, you may have been our allies, but the Jovians would then have the right to call you Pirates, Saboteurs and even Spies. This way you all become lawful combatants", the Admiral explained.

"Just so long as everyone understands. The Solstice does not belong to any Martian Defence Forces and that the crew of the Solstice cannot be ordered around by any of your military personnel", Forkbraid demanded, "We are not Martian Defence Force assets!"

"I thought that would be the case Forkbraid", Governor Anderson replied, adding, "That's precisely why I insisted on you being named the Fleet Captain. Those very stipulations have already been considered, discussed and agreed upon in writing. In contracts we need you all to sign. All back dated to before the

Jovian High Council launched their missile attacks of course."

"Good then", Forkbraid replied, "Now Admiral Zumwalt. My crew is the way it is, because here on the Elysium subcontinent, we don't have a huge number of personnel to choose from. Look at Jim, he's wearing five hats. Here on the Elysium sub-continent, that's entirely normal. My crew were chosen from people I trust and they are damned good at what they do. Simple as that. You don't have to like my ship's crew Admiral. You just have to accept them. Can you do that?"

"Yes of course Captain Forkbraid", the Admiral replied, commenting, "I was simply pointing out that as military personnel, they would be totally unacceptable."

"Yeah, well it looks to me like we're a special case", Forkbraid replied.

"Agreed", replied the Admiral.

"Talking about not having enough personnel resources Admiral. One thing we need in our neck of the woods is trained medical personnel", Selene informed Admiral Zumwalt.

"That is correct", Forkbraid agreed, "My ship, the Solstice, has no medical officer."

"Captain Forkbraid. In the Earth Defence Forces, that would never be allowed", the Admiral replied, quickly adding, "I know. I know. Not a military ship. What's your current workaround?"

"Currently, we are using three hyper dynamics three-o-three Androids", Forkbraid remarked.

"Fully trained of course", Selene added, then went further, "We have no medical staff here at the academy either. Just trained Androids. If we need a human doctor, we have to go to the Elysium colony, where they are extremely short staffed as well."

Admiral Zumwalt was quiet for a long moment, then, "Anderson. Are there any spare medical personnel available in the other Martian colonies? Any spare capacity?"

"I don't really know Admiral", Governor Anderson admitted, he turned to his secretary, "Maria. Please look into that when we get back to Chryce. Search for any available medical staff across the colonies, that are willing to work in Elysium."

Maria nodded and took some notes down with her grip.

"Captain Forkbraid, Lady Selene. It appears the ball is rolling on that issue", the Admiral noted.

Governor Anderson made an indication to his secretary Maria, who then removed ten green folders from her briefcase. One by one, Maria handed out the folders to the crew of the Solstice.

Before anyone could question what the folders were, Governor Anderson informed them, "Those are your files, as *'Martian Defence Force'* personnel, including details of your bank accounts etc. Those accounts and their contents are yours and you may freely access them. Read the contracts carefully. Sign and return the contracts when your ready. They are all back dated appropriately."

Maria then took ten more folders from out of her briefcase, these were coloured red. One by one, Maria handed these out to the ten L5 pilots seconded to the academy.

Governor Anderson then informed the pilots, "These are offers of commission with the Martian Defence Forces. Your ranks and remuneration will be the same, plus there will be a very generous sign on bonus. We've been authorised by L5 Colonial Central to make these offers. If you wish to do so, simply sign them and then have them returned to my office in the Chryce colony."

"Things are still in motion Forkbraid", Governor Anderson noted, "The Governors of the other six main colonies, along with myself at Chryce, have all agreed to incorporate our separate colonial security services into the Martian Defence Forces, including our vehicles and personnel. The seven colonial militias are also being canvassed for recruits for the Martian Defence Forces. Things are moving fast, very fast."

"It certainly sounds like it Governor", Forkbraid replied.

"We have one small problem though. It's really quite embarrassing", Governor Anderson admitted, informing them all, "No one seems to know who the Governor of the Elysium colony is, let alone how contact them."

Selene laughed out loud and the others quickly joined in.

"I don't seem to understand the joke", Governor Anderson admitted.

Forkbraid let him in on the joke, "Here on the Elysium subcontinent, people often wear more than one hat Governor. Selene is the Principal of the New Flinders Psychic Academy. Selene is also the Governor of the Elysium colony."

"Oh. Honestly. No one knew", the Governor replied, "That's probably something that should have been asked on day one!"

Selene had already figured out what Governor Anderson's next question was going to be, "The answer is no, Governor."

"Lady Selene. You haven't even heard the question", Governor Anderson protested.

"You were going to ask me to roll the Elysium colony's security services into the Martian Defence Forces", Selene replied.

"Yes, I was going to ask that", the Governor replied, remembering he was talking to a psychic, "Is that your final decision on the matter?"

"No. It is not. This issue has to be discussed with our Chief Security officer and the Elysium Council", Selene replied, adding, "So for the moment it's a no. That position could change over the course of our deliberations, but I would not hold your breath on it."

"So, we'll find out the final answer in due course", the Governor replied.

"Of course", Selene confirmed.

Admiral Zumwalt caught Varak's attention and pointed to him, "I have a consignment of hyper dynamics two-nine-five Androids for one Varakhan Utana. The man who can build anything."

"That would be me Admiral", Varak replied, "How did you know to bring two-nine-fives?"

"There's a huge mess of mangled Trojan weapons systems down in the Elysium colony's recycling yards. Those need to be cycled into ships and weapons for the Martian Defence Forces. Any Android above a two-nine-five, will refuse that kind of work", Admiral Zumwalt noted.

"That is true. How many two-nine-fives did you bring with you?", Varak asked.

"My flag ship, the Vanguard has sixty two-nine-fives in storage. Brand spanking new. Straight off the line", the Admiral advised, "I can have them shipped down tomorrow, if you wish."

"I would appreciate receiving them, Thank you", Varak replied, "However, what I really need is some way to take that Trojan scrap metal and turn it into polyceramalloy. It appears that the Trojans either do not use or simply do not have polyceramalloy."

"I'll talk to my engineers Varak and see what we might have available", the Admiral replied.

"Is it true that the Solstice has a single piece polyceramalloy hull?", the Admiral enquired, adding, "Our technicians have studied images of your ship and they couldn't find any seams or joins. No welds, nothing. They've speculated that it's one single moulded piece of polyceramalloy."

Varak replied, "The Solstice's hull was three D printed, as a single piece of polyceramalloy."

"Now that in itself is incredible", the Admiral remarked, noting, "Not even General Products manufactured hulls are single piece."

Varak replied, "I know Admiral. I use to work for General Products back on the Earth."

"Maybe you should share that technology with them Varak", Admiral Zumwalt suggested.

"I did try that once. They were not interested at the time. Too costly is what they said", Varak informed her, adding, "That is why I am here on Mars. No restrictions. Here I can build anything I put my mind to. No constraints. If I have the resources, it gets done!"

"I think they'd change their minds now, if they knew the results. What you've created kind of changes everything Varak", the Admiral admitted in reply.

Forkbraid stepped in, "You've made a good point Admiral. We will take it under consideration. Perhaps a commercial agreement can be made with General Products Corporation at a later date."

Admiral Zumwalt nodded in agreement.

Jim enquired, "We were expecting fifteen ships. How many did you bring with you?"

"All fifteen. Three heavy cruisers, six destroyers and six frigates as promised", Admiral Zumwalt informed him.

"Have you already deployed them?", asked Jim Murphy.

"Absolutely. That was the first thing I organised upon our approach to Mars", the Admiral replied, explaining, "I've placed a heavy cruiser above each pole in ultra high Martian orbit. The six destroyers are equidistant apart in high Martian orbit. The six frigates are equidistant apart in medium Martian orbit. My ship, the Vanguard is currently in a low equatorial Martian orbit. I've placed the Earth Defence Force ships above the northern hemisphere and the Colonial Fleet ships above the southern hemisphere. My flagship, the Vanguard is in between."

Jim nodded in understanding, two watchers, two rings of steel and a prowler, "That's exactly how I would have deployed them myself."

"I've also deployed a recon and liaison team to Port Phobos", the Admiral commented.

"Make sure that they don't interfere with Lieutenant Robert's shipping schedules. He hates that. That will drive him nuts", Jim informed her.

The Admiral looked around to her Lieutenant Adjutant to make sure he'd gotten that, before turning back to Jim and noting, "I've also deployed recon and engineering teams to the abandoned L5 base on Deimos. We fully intend to bring that base back on line."

"Now that is a great idea", Forkbraid noted, "At one point, that abandoned base was home to a den of Pirates."

"Yes well, we're putting a stop to that. It is going to be a crucial military, maintenance and refuelling base in the very near future", the Admiral informed him, adding, "We're expecting regular military traffic to come through Deimos."

"Now Captain Forkbraid. Your ship. Does it really use a thee laws safe positronic matrix for its main computer?", Admiral Zumwalt asked.

"Absolutely", Forkbraid replied, "The Solstice's computer system is three laws safe."

"Now that has been a very amusing topic of discussion during our flight from cis-lunar space", the Admiral admitted, asking, "The Solstice is a gunship. A powerful one I might add. Who's crazy idea was it to use a three laws safe positronic matrix?"

"Actually Admiral. The Solstice is an exploration ship. She just happens to pack a punch", Forkbraid corrected, pointing to Peter Swann and adding, "It was Peter over there who came up with the idea of using an Android brain to run the ship."

"It's the most efficient way to run the ship and it works extremely well I might add", Peter informed the Admiral

"Yes, but three laws safe?", the Admiral replied.

"You can ask the computer for yourself if you wish Admiral", Peter suggested.

"Perhaps another day Lieutenant Swann. For the moment, Captain Forkbraid, I have two little questions", the Admiral remarked, "One, who is your tailor?"

Forkbraid pointed to Charlene and Roseanne, "You'd need to talk to the girls right there for that."

"Thank you I will. And the next question. Where can I procure six crates of Martian cherry red wine?", the Admiral asked, "There are some very important people back in cis-lunar space that want some cherry red wine shipped back to them."

Forkbraid chuckled and pointed to Candy and Cormac Farmer.

"That would be us Admiral", Cormac chimed in with a smile, "Did you say six crates?"

Admiral Zumwalt smiled back, "At the very least."

"You might want to try our new range Admiral", Candy commented, adding, "Blue berry wine."

"Blue berry wine?", the Admiral queried.

"We have a couple of cases coming in from Hebes Island sometime next month", Cormac added, "If you're still here when they arrive, you can try some."

"I might just do that", the Admiral replied.

Matthew knocked on the door of General Tarzan's office, "Come in", the General called out.

"Captain. What can I do for you?", the General greeted.

"We have news General. Good news", Matthew replied as he held up a file.

"Take a seat Captain", the General replied.

Matthew took a seat and passed the file across the desk to General Tarzan, who opened it and began reading it as Matthew began giving the General a summary.

"We've had contact from Mars. It appears we still have assets, people on Mars General", Matthew informed the General.

"Well, that is great Captain", the General replied.

Matthew continued his summary, "We know we won't hear from Aurorae and we haven't received any replies from Chryse, Isidis or Hellas. For the moment, I'm assuming our cells in those colonies have disbanded, until I hear otherwise. Of course they may have simply lost the ability to decode our messages. However, we have heard from our Ophir, Xanthe and Marineris cells."

"That is fantastic Captain!", the General exclaimed.

"Essentially our people in Ophir and Xanthe have gone underground, banded together and moved southeast into the unsettled Martian regions", Matthew explained, further informing, "Our people in Marineris also went underground. Only they've moved to the far west of Marineris Valley into what's called the wild country."

"So we effectively have two cells on Mars Captain?", queried the General.

"Effectively General. They're quite widely spread out as well", Matthew confirmed.

"Captain, do we know where they are precisely?", the General enquired.

"Not precisely. After what happened at Aurorae and New Tortuga, they are being really cautious", Matthew informed him, adding, "They're not even telling us where they are. They are worried about communications intercepts."

"Okay, but they have contacted us, so what else do we know Captain?", the General enquired.

"Our Ophir and Xanthe cells haven't told us much, only that they're there", Matthew admitted, adding, "Our Marineris cell however, they've already taken action upon receiving our instructions."

"Actions?", the General queried.

"Yes General. They are attempting to infiltrate the Elysium colony", Matthew replied, adding, "They've been testing Elysium's security."

6. Places to Hide

Jim Murphy walked into the dormitory, where his two wives and his in-laws were staying at the academy. All of the Solstice's other crew members were present along with their families and friends. Jim looked around the dormitory's main common room to make sure that everyone who needed to be there, was present before he started. He mentally noted the large picture of the view from Varak's balcony, of the southern coastline of the Elysium colony. A beautiful site. He had taken the picture himself.

"I have some bad news from the Elysium colony", Jim informed the gathering.

"What would that be Jim?", Selene asked.

"We believe, we have had our very first bounty hunter infiltration attempt", Jim replied.

"How so Jim?", Selene queried.

"A large Hummer, supposedly from Chryce, attempted an unauthorised landing at the Elysium colony's airport", Jim replied, "They claimed they were a tourist group, with a tourist guide and a dozen tourists."

"The Elysium colony is not open for tourism Jim, you know that", Selene informed him.

"Exactly Selene. They were told very clearly, that the Elysium colony wasn't open for tourism", Jim replied, further adding, "Then they insisted that their tour had been fully authorised by our Elysium Tourism Department"

"The Elysium colony doesn't have a Tourism Department", Selene advised.

"I know. I know. Our security personnel at air traffic control, told them that and strongly advised them to turn around and go back to Chryce", Jim replied.

"Did they turn around?", Forkbraid enquired.

"Yes and no. They said they needed to refuel before they could turn around", Jim explained.

"And they were allowed refuel, were they?", asked Forkbraid.

"Yes, however when they landed, we surrounded their Hummer with over thirty armed security personnel", Jim replied, adding, "They stayed in their hummer. We refuelled it. Then they left for the Chryce colony."

"Then how do you know they were bounty hunters Jim?", Selene asked.

"We tracked their Hummer until they left our airspace", Jim replied, explaining, "We also checked with Chryce colony. That Hummer didn't go back to Chryce colony at all. In fact Chryce colony, has no record of the so called *'tourist flight'* on their books. They didn't come from Chryce colony at all."

"That is not a good sign", Selene replied, questioning, "A dozen tourists is what they said?"

"A dozen, plus their guide. So that would indicate a bounty hunting team. They would have been looking to claim the full bounty I'd say", Jim commented.

"All ten crew members", Peter Swann remarked.

"Yes. It appears they had some sort of operation planned", Jim replied, speculating, "The first part of which, was to get access to the Elysium colony. Their approaching the airfield was just their first attempt."

Forkbraid stood up walked about the room, "So we have no idea where they came from", he commented, adding, "I think we can be certain, this was just their first attempt at testing our security. No doubt they will make others."

"Agreed", Jim replied.

"What about the construction teams from Chryce, making repairs on the colony?", Selene asked.

"Most of the damage caused by the Pirate attacks has been repaired", Jim replied, informing Selene further, "The remaining damage is being repaired by our people and Androids in the colony."

"So there are no more construction teams flying in and out of Elysium?", Selene queried.

"No. They've been stopped", Jim confirmed, adding, "Most of the major damage is repaired. What's left, our people can handle. Which is good. We can't have bounty hunters embedding themselves into the construction teams."

"That was my main concern", Selene admitted.

"Our security people had considered that. After reviewing the remaining work, we decided that further use of outside construction workers was not necessary", Jim assured her, "Any would be bounty hunters, won't have that as an avenue of access."

Varak noted, "If they can get into the Elysium colony, there are twenty five, very large, unpopulated suburbs they can hide in. If they get in, it will be very difficult to find them."

"There was a group of us there recently, seven of us, five of whom have bounties", Jim remarked, adding, "We have to be very careful from now on. When ever any of us goes to the Elysium colony, I'll alert our security services in advance to keep a tighter watch."

"That includes you too Jim", Forkbraid noted, adding, "You're there at least twice a week."

"And my Varak", Nyaliep commented, "My Varak is there often, to recover and recycle scrap."

Jim replied, "Varak. From now on, when either of us goes to Elysium, we go together and I'll alert our Elysium security services in advance."

"Agreed Jim. That would be prudent", Varak agreed.

"Are we safe here?", Zyaliep asked, "Perhaps my daughters and Nyaliep should go back to our village with Kwoth and I?"

"That wouldn't be safe either Mother Zyaliep", Marcus replied, before standing up and walking to the centre of the room and activating his grip.

"These are the new maps of Mars", Marcus informed everyone, as a three dimensional image of Mars appeared before them, "Since the Battle of New Tortuga, there has been a concerted effort to map many of the previously unknown towns and villages in that entire region."

Marcus drilled down to the area around Hebes Island and the fresh water Hebes Sea.

"You see here. That's New Tortuga", Marcus noted.

Cormac pointed to the east of New Tortuga, along the coast of Hebes Island, "And that's the village of Krell. A very small village. We have cousins living there."

There were quite a few small villages along the coast of Hebes Island. The cartographers had been very busy and done their job well. The new villages were noted down by name.

"And there", Candy noted, pointing to the south eastern shores of the Hebes Sea, "That's Shira. It's not much of a town. Certainly much bigger than Krell, but still quite small. They've even mapped the road from Shira to Jericho. A rough road it is, but a road none the less."

"Jericho is a much bigger town, with a fair sized trading port. There's regular passenger services and trade from there to the Aurorae colony", Cormac remarked.

Candy noted, "Sweetness is not on the map."

Gwek remembered and replied, "A town under a glamour you once told me. It still remains hidden or so it appears."

Zyaliep pointed to the southern shore of the Hebes Sea, directly south of New Tortuga, "That is our village!"

Zyaliep had pointed out her village, which was amongst quite a few other villages, spread out along the southern coast of the Hebes Sea and in the hinterlands south of the shore.

"Yes", Marcus confirmed and commented, "You'll notice, they've named it Podvil. Literally Pod Village, named after both yourself and Kwoth or more correctly, the Girls."

Jim understood the problem and remarked, "If you want to look for someone who's last name is Pod, that is the very first place you'd look. Podvil."

"So not safe?", Zyaliep queried.

"No Mother Zyaliep. Not safe. Not even for yourself and Kwoth", Jim answered.

"Not even safe for us?", Zyaliep questioned.

"You are both Pods. The bounty hunters could try to use you both to catch the Girls. You would definitely be at risk", Jim replied.

"Even our home village will not be safe", Nyaliep understood and agreed.

Zeealas jumped in with, "The valley to the north where we set up our camp. We could go there."

Zuawalo replied, "It will not be safe either Zeealas"

Marcus adjusted the Martian map and focused on the hill country to the north of the academy, Zuawalo's Valley and Zeealas's Valley were clearly marked on the map as well.

"You see Zeealas. Leroy named those Valleys after us", Zuawalo noted, "They have our names. They would definitely look for us there."

"Yes. Zuawalo", Jim agreed, "It is sad to say, that's definitely a place they would look."

"This is sad", Zeealas sighed, "I liked our lean-to there. It was a very nice place. We were going to have our babies there, Zuawalo and I."

"Zeealas, Zuawalo. I did not agree to have our babies in a bush hut", Jim replied, adding, "Camping in the future yes, certainly. However, I'd prefer you had our babies here at the academy."

"I do not know", Nyaliep commented, agreeing with Zeealas, "There is something very special, more natural about having babies in the bush."

Varak replied, "Nyaliep my Queen. I must agree with Jim. I find the academy, preferable."

"Perhaps you can build a nice cabin in Zuawalo's Valley, Varak", Nyaliep replied.

Zuawalo sighed and gave a practical reply, "Aunty. It does not matter. At this time, it is not safe!"

Zeealas looked at the map more closely, "Zuawalo, they have even named the Rivers after us."

"Rivers?", Zuawalo queried.

"Look. The rivers in our valleys. They have our names too", Zeealas pointed out.

"Oh yes. They have our names", Zuawalo replied.

Forkbraid stepped in, "The only safe place is here at the academy", he told them all.

Selene agreed, "Most of the residents here are psychics. If any bounty hunters get close, we will know it very quickly."

"That and the fact that this academy is built like a castle", Jim replied, noting, "It has high walls and under lock down, no one, not even bounty hunters could get in."

"Well then", Forkbraid decided, "There's no need for you to hide anywhere. We can keep you all safe here in the academy."

"There is another place", Zuawalo replied, adding, "The Island was not on that map."

"The Island?", questioned Marcus.

Zeealas replied, "Yes. The Island. It is in the Swamps of the Kasei."

Marcus adjusted the Martian map to focus on the Kasei Valles region. There was nothing new marked on the map. Clearly Echus Chasma and Kasei Valles were marked. Up in the northern reaches of Kasei Valles, both branches of the Kasei River were named, along with a few natural features closer to the Chryce colony. Beyond that however, nothing else was mapped.

Zuawalo pointed to a large patch of high ground in the middle of the southern Kasei Swamps.

"That is the Island", Zuawalo noted.

"We have many cousins there on that Island in the swamps", Zyaliep added.

"It's actually quite a large Island", Marcus noted, concluding, "It looks like a good hiding place."

"It's not mapped either. Only your people know of its existence", Jim remarked, adding, "That could be another safe place in case we need one."

Selene added, "There could be any number of safe places like that one."

"Let's not get ahead of ourselves Selene", Forkbraid replied, explaining, "Those suspected bounty hunters had to come from somewhere as well and you know what. I doubt it's on any map."

"What are you saying?", Selene asked.

"We don't know where our enemy is hiding. We don't know where their bolt hole is", Forkbraid answered, adding, "We really need to know that, before we start selecting safe places."

"Chryce is on the other side of the planet", Marcus noted, "All travel between Chryce and Elysium flies eastward from Chryce and westwards from Elysium. To go the other way around means flying over the Tharsis Bulge and past Olympus

Mons. Local pilots hate doing that. Apart from the extremely high altitudes and the terrible weather, you can have extremely high winds and highly dangerous wind sheer."

"What are you saying Marcus?", Forkbraid asked.

Marcus replied, "There's probably a hundred or more places in the Arabia Terra region where those bounty hunters could be hiding. And if they come from the region around the Aurorae colony, the area to the east of the mouth of Valles Marineris has hundreds of islands. Our enemy could be hiding anywhere."

"Should we get another opportunity. I've made sure my people know, to put a lo-jack tracker on any suspect vehicle", Jim Murphy commented.

"It would have been nice to have that tracker on them now Jim", Forkbraid replied.

"Yes I know FB. They didn't think of it at the time", Jim replied, adding, "That has since been rectified."

Varak then asked, "What kind of Hummer was it?"

Marcus was quick to reply, "I'll check the Elysium airfield's refuelling logs", as he pressed keys on his grip's virtual keyboard.

A minute later came his reply, "It was an old Martian model. An XJS two thousand, from back in twenty three twenty. Back in its day, it was considered a luxury 'stretched' Hummer. That was of course, about forty years or so ago."

Varak rubbed his chin, "Martian Hummers are not like the ones back at cis-lunar space. They have very inefficient engines and have a far more limited range. Still, that old one should have made the round trip from Chryce to Elysium and back with fuel to spare."

"That beggars the question. Did they really need to refuel or were they just testing our security?", Forkbraid tossed in.

"Let's see", Marcus replied as he pressed a few more buttons on his grip, before answering, "They definitely needed fuel. The logs tell us, their fuel cells were sixty percent depleted."

Peter Swann stepped in, "In theory they should have been able to make the return flight from Chryce to Elysium with ten percent fuel to spare. So that would equate to a forty five percent fuel usage, one way from Chryce to Elysium, yet they used sixty percent."

"What are you thinking Peter?", Forkbraid asked.

Peter answered, "Forget about Chryce colony and Arabia Terra. Forget about the area around Aurorae colony as well. That Hummer came from much farther afield. A good third farther."

"How sure are you Peter?", Jim enquired.

Peter tapped his right temple, "My math is rarely wrong Jim."

"Cormac. Do you and Candy have any local knowledge that might be useful?", Jim enquired.

It was now Cormac's turn to think about any possible places the Hummer could have come from.

"Four of the seven original main colonies are all clustered in the same area, around Lunae Planum and Xanthe Terra. So that's Chryce, Aurorae, Ophir and Xanthe. South of that cluster of colonies on the southern shore of the Marineris Valley, you have the Marineris colony. Then you have Isidis which is on the shores of the Isidis Gulf and Hellas which is on the shores of the Hellas Ocean", Cormac informed everyone, adding, "We would be talking about settlements either to the far south of Aurorae or to the far west of Marineris."

Candy stepped in, "The southern shores of the Marineris Valley could have any number of settlements that have never been mapped. They could even be in that area."

"I think we need to look farther afield Candy, given their fuel usage. The southern shores of the Marineris Valley seem to be a bit too close", Peter commented.

"Perhaps they dumped fuel to put us on a false footing?", Candy suggested.

"Perhaps, but even if they'd thought of that, that would have left fuel residue on the Hummer's fuselage. And that would have triggered the refuelling station to report a fuel leak", Peter replied.

Marcus pressed a few more keys on his grip's virtual keyboard, "No fuel leaks or external fuel residues were detected by the refuelling station. So, they didn't dump any fuel."

"What's you best guess Cormac?", Jim requested.

"Best guess. I'd say far south of Aurorae colony. The Argyre Sea. It's a fresh water sea. Mostly frozen over during the Winter, although it thaws out in the Spring and over Summer. Even over the Summer, Glaciers and Icecap remain on the far southern shores and beyond", Cormac replied.

Cormac continued, "The Argyre River flows north from the Argyre Sea, skirting to the east of the Marineris Valley, all the way up to the Chryce Sea. There could be any number of settlements along that river. A good supply of fresh water and rich farm lands. The ice melts in the spring and that raises the river levels. That floods the land on both sides of the river and drops silt all over those lands, fertilising them. That's the area I'd look at. That's my best guess."

Marcus chuckled and Forkbraid asked him, "What's so funny Marcus?"

"The Argyre River has a second name", Marcus replied, explaining, "Due to its sheer length, it often gets called the Nova Nile River. It has literally been mapped with two names."

"Okay. That's one area to search. The Argyre River", Jim agreed.

"There's another place", Candy remarked.

"Another place? What's your best guess Candy?", Jim enquired.

"Way over to the west of Marineris. A place called Noctis Labyrinthus", Candy replied, adding, "It's a chaotic place full of canyons. Too many to count. In spring the snows on the Tharsis Bulge melts and flood the rivers in the canyons. There's always an ample supply of fresh water. Before the sky fell and the long rains, the earliest colonists tunnelled into cliff faces to make their colonies. There are so many cliffs in that region, so many possibilities."

"Yes", Cormac agreed, "Noctis Labyrinthus. It's just like the name suggests, a labyrinth. You could hide a dozen colonies in that region and no one would know. It's surprising the Prophet himself, didn't think to hide there. We would never have found him."

"Okay then. So now we have two very good areas to search", Jim concluded.

"We do have another problem to deal with", Jim informed everyone, adding, "We need to send five of our wisps and their pilots to the Elysium colony."

"That's not a problem Jim", Forkbraid replied, "We can do that. Considering we've already had one infiltration attempt, I believe it would be prudent to have half our wisps at the colony."

"The problem is we don't have enough wisps FB", Jim explained, adding, "We need to build more wisps and we need to train more pilots as well."

"Varak. Can we build more wisps?", Forkbraid asked.

"I have already start the process", Varak replied, "I was planning to make ten atmo rate wisps."

"Will ten be enough Jim?", Forkbraid enquired.

"Ten will be a good start", Jim replied, "We'll need to start training pilots as well."

"Do we have a timeline Varak?", queried Selene.

"There are some minor issues to sort out first Selene. Nearly all of our supplies of the precursor materials, that my three D printing robots use to print out single piece polyceramalloy hulls, are used up", Varak informed her.

"Oh. So we need to procure new supplies?", Selene asked.

"Yes and no Selene. Stocking up on supplies takes time. Especially here on Mars. I was going to recycle the scrapped Trojan weapons systems and use that material instead", Varak replied, adding, "but that brings its own problems as well."

"How so Varak?", Forkbraid questioned.

"My three D printing robots currently lay down a single piece polyceramalloy hull, one molecule at a time in a continuous stream. The polyceramalloy is literally alloyed as it is printed. To work with the Trojan recycled materials, I will need a different set of three D printing robots", Varak explained, adding, "They'll need to use a liquid polyceramalloy extrusion and welding process. Then of course, there is that Trojan scrap."

"What's wrong with the Trojan scrap?", Selene questioned.

"The Trojan scrap is basically ungraded steel and titanium alloys. There is also a mix of other metals, aluminium, gold, brass etc.", Varak replied.

"So the Trojans don't have polyceramalloy", Selene remarked.

"No. The Trojans do not even appear to have plasteel", Varak replied.

"They don't have plasteel?", Selene questioned incredulously.

"At least, not in any of their weapons systems", Varak confirmed.

"It is not a simple process", Varak stated before explaining, "First of all, I have some Androids separating the various metals into separate piles. After that I have to 'grade' the steel so that I know what I am dealing with. Once I know what kind of steel I have, I have to make the correct alloy, adding in precise amounts of carbon, molybdenum and chromium. That will give me the precise grade of steel that I require. Then I have to polymerise that steel, which will give me the plasteel."

"That sounds really time consuming", Selene noted.

"It is, but it takes much longer to procure the raw materials in the right quantities and qualities. So it is actually faster to work with the Trojan scrap", Varak explained.

Varak continued, "Of course, I need a poly-ceramic-alloy. So I have to melt the titanium, so I can purify it. Then I take the titanium and the requisite amounts of very specific ceramic powders and mix it all in with the plasteel. Voila! Polyceramalloy. I have to make enough for the whole project."

Forkbraid stepped in, "All of that is going to take some time isn't it Varak?"

"Yes FB. I am afraid so", Varak replied, "I already have Androids working to separate out the different scrap metals and another group of Androids building the new the three D printers. You know, if Admiral Zumwalt had not provided the ceramic powders I required, we would not be able to do any of this"

"Were those Androids the ones provided by Admiral Zumwalt?", queried Forkbraid.

"Yes FB. Very handy those sixty Androids. I already have most of them working on the project. Once the new three D printing robots are ready and we have produced enough polyceramalloy, we can start printing the new single piece wisp hulls", Varak replied.

Varak smiled and continued, "This is very good for us here in the academy. Once my Androids have finished creating the new three D printing Robots, we will have two sets of Robots. Ones that work with precursor materials and the new ones that will work with ready made polyceramalloy."

Nyaliep was sitting beside Varak and squeezed his left arm gently, "Have I not said, my Varak is ever so clever."

"Yes Nyaliep. Varak is very clever", Forkbraid agreed, then asked, "So do we have any idea of a timeline Varak?"

"As you know FB. Getting the hulls printed is just the first step. A lot more work has to go into the wisps before they are flight ready", Varak admitted, "We are looking at perhaps six to eight weeks to make ten wisps."

"It is what it is Varak", Forkbraid replied, stating, "We'll send five wisps and their pilots down to the Elysium colony for now. I'll check with Admiral Zumwalt about procuring some more pilots, at least until we can train our own."

"FB. Admiral Zumwalt has her fleet watching the space lanes for approaching vessels. We have Lieutenant Roberts watching the approaches to the Elysium sub-continent with his satellites", Jim remarked, adding, "We have bounty hunters down here on Mars already. I'd prefer to hunt them down rather than wait for them to come to us."

"Noted Jim", Forkbraid replied, "Varak. These new model two-nine-five Androids of yours. Can they work on this project without supervision?"

"To a large degree yes FB", Varak replied, adding, "I can keep tabs on them remotely if I need to intervene in any process."

"Good then Varak", Forkbraid replied, then to the gathering, "The threat is already here and I fully intend to hunt them down!"

"Forkbraid. No. I don't want you to go looking for trouble!", Selene protested.

"What's your alternative Selene?", Forkbraid replied rhetorically, adding, "Wait until they catch one of more of us and then they bolt off to the Jovian Realms. We cannot take that risk!"

"Forkbraid is right Selene", Cormac stepped in, "I know it's not my place. My wife and I don't even have a bounty on us, but ten of you do. You have to take the fight to the enemy."

Selene looked at Cormac, was he right? She then looked to Candy.

Candy nodded, "Sometimes to be safe Selene. You have to run the gauntlet."

Peter Swann stepped in, "Let's put it to a vote. All those who have a bounty on their heads and want to take the fight to the enemy, raise your hand and say Aye!"

Catherine Swann protested, "Peter!", as all ten of the Solstice's crew members raised their hands and said, "Aye!"

"It looks like it's unanimous", Forkbraid noted, then commenting, "Although I don't think we'll be needing the full crew. I'm proposing we leave the Zuawalo, Zeealas, Nyaliep and Leroy here in the safety of the academy."

Zuawalo and Zeealas protested in unison, "If Jim goes, we go!"

Nyaliep protested, "If my Varak goes, I will go also!"

Leroy looked at Forkbraid awkwardly "I don't want to be the odd one out."

"Unfortunately girls, I am the Captain and on this mission, you will be staying here at the academy", Forkbraid ordered, adding, "You too Leroy."

Zuawalo, Zeealas and Nyaliep all began to protest.

Forkbraid held up his right hand, "My decision is final. The three of you are pregnant. My priority with regards the three of you, is your unborn children."

Zuawalo, Zeealas and Nyaliep all began to protest once more.

"Mother Zyaliep. Please explain to your daughters and your sister, the need to keep them and their unborn children safe", Forkbraid strongly requested.

"My daughters. My sister. Forkbraid is right. You have to think of your babies", Zyaliep told the trio, "You must keep your unborn babies safe and here in the academy it is safe!"

Kwoth stepped in adding his weight to the conversion, "Zuawalo, Zeealas. Listen to your mother. Nyaliep, you listen to your sister. Zyaliep is right."

Zuawalo and Zeealas looked to their husband Jim, who told them both, "I'm sorry girls. I agree with FB and Mother Zyaliep on this one. You don't need to be on this mission. To me, it is much more important to keep our unborn children safe. Besides, I can look after myself, I'll be fine."

Nyaliep look at her husband Varak, "Varak my King?", she questioned.

"Nyaliep my Queen, I agree with the others. You must stay here and keep our child safe", Varak informed her.

The three women sighed and Forkbraid concluded the discussion, stating, "My decision is final."

"That leaves me", Leroy noted.

"Yes it does. I need you here Leroy. You have a good, technical knowledge of systems and weapons that Selene may need while we're gone", Forkbraid explained, "I need you here, just in case something happens. Especially if the academy needs defending."

"Understood FB", Leroy replied, abbreviating Forkbraid's name for the first time, he then added, "I can help the girls pick up some useful skills in the technical area around the academy while you're gone. Perhaps even Kwoth can help as well."

"I would be happy to help", Kwoth replied.

"Excellent. Okay then, tomorrow we begin the hunt!", Forkbraid told everyone.

7. Hunters and Collectors

Matthew answered his apartment door and let in General Tarzan.

"Greetings General", Matthew greeted.

The Prophet greeted the General, "Good morning General."

"Good morning gentlemen", the General replied, then informing the Prophet and Matthew, "We've received another message from the Marineris cell."

"Okay. What's new?", Matthew enquired.

"Their first infiltration attempt failed", the General informed them both, "They tried a direct, subterfuge approach through the Elysium airfield. The Elysium security weren't buying it at all and they found themselves surrounded by a much larger number of armed security personnel. They ended up flying back out the way they came."

"Okay. Their first attempt failed, but they did get away", the Prophet noted, "So they get to make other attempts, perhaps more successful attempts."

"That is their intent Gentlemen", the General replied, adding, "They're also keen on collecting those bounties."

"That in itself poses a problem General", Matthew remarked.

"Agreed Matthew", the General replied, adding, "To collect the bounties, our operatives need some way to get the fugitives to us."

"Exactly. So we need to put in place some method or way to transport the fugitives to us here in the Jovian Realms", Matthew replied.

"And to transport the Jovian golden credits to Mars", the General remarked.

The Prophet asked, "Could we use Ceres as a transfer point? You know, our operative on Mars get the fugitives to Ceres. We get the Jovian golden credits to Ceres. Then we do a swap."

"That's a possibility my Lord", Matthew replied, before explaining, "However, that does require that Mars, Ceres and Jupiter be in exactly the right place in their orbits for that to occur."

"We can send the bounties to Ceres first and have our people wait, until our Martian operatives can make the journey to Ceres with the fugitives", the General suggested.

"Gentlemen. I think we're getting ahead of ourselves", Matthew noted, "Our operatives on Mars have yet to capture the fugitives."

"Yes, but that doesn't stop us from putting the procedures in place", the General replied.

"We don't even know if our people on Mars can get to Ceres Central. Ceres is a long flight from Mars. We know, we did it in the Delilah. Do they even have a ship?", Matthew commented, "Then of course, the last time I checked, our surveillance showed at least fifteen warships in Martian orbit and that does not include the Solstice."

"That does pose a serious problem Matthew", the General admitted.

The core crew members of the Solstice had boarded the ship and taxied it out of its hanger.

"Marcus. Put us in a low Martian polar orbit", Forkbraid ordered, adding, "I want us to approach the Argyle Sea from the south over the Martian polar cap."

"Aye Captain", Marcus the Solstice's Helmsman replied as he set the course.

It was only a matter of minutes before the Solstice was in Martian orbit and on its way to the Argyle Sea. The Martian south polar cap was soon visible on the bridge's main screen.

"Marcus. Take us down over the polar cap and line us up for the Argyle Sea and River", Forkbraid ordered.

"Aye Captain", Marcus replied.

"Marcus. I want to us hover over the centre of the Argyle Sea, so that Peter can scan for settlements along the shore line", Forkbraid explained.

"Captain. The Argyle basin is eighteen hundred kilometres across and over five kilometres deep. The Argyle Sea itself takes up more volume than the basin. So the Argyle Sea is even larger. I recommend we circle the shoreline a couple of times", Matthew replied.

"Good suggestion Marcus. Make it so", Forkbraid agreed.

"Jim. Active our passive cloaking, the full chameleon and our active cloaking as well", Forkbraid commanded, adding, "I don't want us frightening the hell out of any settlers we fly past."

"Aye Captain", Jim the Solstice's Tactical officer replied.

The Solstice flew passed the Martian south polar cap towards the Argyre Sea. Between the polar cap and the southern shores of the Argyle Sea was a polar wasteland with a heavy cover of ice and snow. Spring it seemed did not reach this far south on Mars and the layers of ice and snow looked deep and permanent.

Forkbraid remarked, "This is a polar biome. I doubt we'll find any settlers in this region. Computer. Show the delineation between land and sea for the Argyle Sea."

The Solstice's computer replied with its sweat, feminine voice, "Complying" and the main screen showed a line, clearly tracing the southern Argyle Sea coastline.

"Marcus. When we get to the coast, take us counter clockwise around the Argyle Sea's coastline", Forkbraid commanded.

"Aye Captain. Preparing course now", Marcus replied.

"Peter. Scan for any settlements. You know, people, buildings, farmlands, fishing boats. Anything that tells us there's a human presence", Forkbraid instructed.

"Aye Captain. Commencing scans", Peter Swann the Solstice's Science officer replied.

"Computer. We need to log any human settlement detections. Location, number of structures, type, estimated age and estimated population", Forkbraid commanded.

The Solstice's computer replied with its sweat, feminine voice once more, "Complying."

Marcus noted, "There's still quite a bit of sea ice along the southern shores. It will probably be the end of summer before all of this ice melts. Further north, I can see plenty of open sea, so I guess the spring melt must have started quite a while back."

"It certainly looks that way Marcus", Forkbraid agreed.

Marcus altered the Solstice's course when they reached the shoreline and they began to circumnavigate the Argyle Sea in a counter clockwise direction. The shoreline of the Argyle Sea was dotted with Islands and small bays. Many small rivers flowed into it. They passed by a large circular bay and the land beyond the shores changed, it was now open tundra.

They soon came to the large, now flooded, Galle Crater. It formed a large, almost perfectly circular lake, right beside the Argyle Sea, separated from it by the rim of its crater. A strange sight, it looked almost artificial, yet was a perfectly natural formation created by an asteroid impact long ago in the distant Martian antiquity.

By the time they reached fifty degrees south latitude the tundra began to give way to a polar woodlands. Dwarf Willows and Alders began to take over the shoreline and hinterlands. Birch and Spruce trees were also growing ever more present the further north they travelled.

"We've picked up no signs of settlements Captain", Peter Swann informed him, adding, "Which makes sense. Winters this far south on Mars must be absolutely brutal."

"Keep scanning Peter. We'll do a full scan of the shoreline to make sure", Forkbraid instructed.

"I'm just wondering what kinds of animals the terraformers set loose in these environments", Charlene, the Solstice's communications officer queried.

"I'd expect they'd be the kind suitable to these biomes", Marcus replied.

North of Lake Galle there were numerous Islands, Bays and Inlets and another circular lake in the flooded crater Bozkir. Lake Bozkir connected to the Argyle Sea via its broken northern rim.

"This is interesting", Peter noted, almost to himself.

"What's that Peter?", Forkbraid asked.

"We're detecting current flows running west, north of Galle Lake and then running north, east of Lake Bozkir. It's interesting because I wasn't expecting us to detect any out-flowing currents until much further north", Peter informed Forkbraid.

"Out-flowing currents?", Forkbraid queried.

"Well yes Captain. At some point, the Argyle Lake has to flow in the Argyle River", Peter replied, explaining, "It seems the out-flow is more complex than just a simple, single river. It appears there's multiple branches feeding into the river."

Eventually the Solstice reached the norther regions of the Argyle Sea and a single channel could be discerned flowing in the direction of Hale Crater. Various current flows were combining and flowing in the direction of the channel.

"Marcus. Take around the western side of the Argyle Sea", Forkbraid instructed.

"Aye Captain", Marcus replied.

The western shoreline of the Argyle Sea had even more Islands, Inlets and in-flowing rivers than the eastern shoreline. The Islands were also larger and more mountainous. As they continued to circumnavigate the Sea, the Solstice detected the submerged Hook Crater.

"We are just passing over the deepest part of the Argyle Sea", Peter noted, informing everyone, "Hook Crater. It's submerged and it's over five point two kilometres deep."

"No sign of any settlements?", Forkbraid questioned.

"None yet Captain. Honestly, I think we're too far south", Peter replied.

The biomes were much the same as on the eastern shoreline. Polar forests of Birch and Spruce, eventually thinning out with the ever growing presence of Alders and Willows. These eventually thinned out as well and tundra was all that was left. As they approached the southern shores once more, snow and ice became prevalent until finally they were back to a far colder, more polar biome. It wasn't long before they had completed their circumnavigation.

"Marcus. Take us north to that out-flow channel leading to Hale Crater", Forkbraid ordered.

"Aye Captain. Turning north now", Marcus replied.

"Still no settlements Peter?", Forkbraid queried.

"Nothing detected yet Captain. The high latitudes of Mars get much colder, much quicker than they do on Earth. Especially in the southern hemisphere. I wouldn't expect to detect anything until we get to forty degree south latitude or lower", Peter replied.

The Solstice flew north, across the centre of the Argyle Sea. The sea ice that was prevalent along the southern coast slowly petered out, until there was only open water, with the occasional small icebergs destined to melt. All of the seas of Mars were new, only existing since the terraforming of the planet. The smaller seas like the Argyre Sea, with a constant inflow of fresh waters, from a multitude of rivers, fed by melting snow and ice of the polar regions, were likewise fresh water.

"We are approaching the northern coast Captain", Marcus advised.

"Captain. If we are going to find any settlements, it will in the regions around here or north of here", Peter added.

A broad channel had cut its way from the northern shore of the Argyre Sea. It wasn't long, it wasn't fast flowing, yet vast volumes of water flowed through it into the flooded Hale Crater. This was the beginning of the Argyre River.

Marcus maintained a reasonable altitude as he flew the Solstice above the channel and into the flooded Lake Hale basin.

"I can't think of anything like this, anywhere on Earth", Marcus remarked.

Charlene added, "Maybe Lake Tana and the Blue Nile in Ethiopia, but even then, that pales in comparison. This is like having the entire volume of water in the Amazon River, pouring down the Blue Nile."

"Maybe that's why they also call it the Nova Nile River?", Marcus questioned.

"How are our scans?", Forkbraid asked.

Peter Swann replied, "Nothing turning up yet Captain, but we are in the zone. If there are any settlements along this river, we should start coming across them soon."

Soon the Solstice flew above the fairly narrow out-flow channel between Lake Hale and the now flooded Bond Crater basin, Lake Bond. Here there were rapids and the waters was exceedingly rough. They'd be dangerous even for white water rafting. Clearly the Argyre River would not be navigable in some places.

Marcus flew the Solstice across Lake Bond and Forkbraid turned to Peter Swann.

Peter looked up from his scans and answered Forkbraid's unspoken question, "Still no settlements Captain."

It wasn't long before they reached the Uzboi Vallis, which after the terraforming, was now a raging river canyon full of rapids. Again certainly unsuitable for river navigation.

At the northern end of the Uzboi Vallis, was the flooded Holden Crater basin, Lake Holden. The Solstice flew across Lake Holden towards its north eastern rim, where the water had overflowed and formed a broad, deep cut.

Forkbraid looked towards Peter Swann, his science officer.

Peter answered his unspoken question, "Sorry Captain. Still no settlements detected."

After Lake Holden, there was an expanse of marshy land, slowly flowing north eastwards towards another section of white water rapids, flowing through Ladon Valles. The Argyre River flowed through Ladon Valles, then opened up into the broad, largely flooded Ladon Basin. The Argyre River spread out and branched into a multiple river channels.

Jim at his tactical station noted, "This looks a lot like Zuawalo's and Zeealas's descriptions of the Kasei Swamps."

"We're are also very close to the Aurorae colony. Even if we do find any settlements along the river now, I doubt they're the ones who tried to infiltrate the Elysium colony", Peter remarked, he then added, "They wouldn't have used anywhere near as much fuel as they did."

A few minutes later Peter Swann at his science console piped up, "Captain. We are detecting settlements. Multiple settlements Captain."

"What can you tell us Peter?", Forkbraid enquired.

"We're detecting multiple villages, at least eight, spread across the Ladon Basin Captain. Cabins, crop fields, orchards, boats and boat ramps" Peter replied, adding, "These appear to be old as well. Quite well established. Analysis of our scans indicates no buildings or structures less than two decades old. None of these settlements have been mapped. We are not detecting any technology either. Not a single Hummer is showing up on any of our scans."

"Thank you Peter", Forkbraid replied, "We might be here on a wild goose chase. Perhaps we should have gone straight to Noctis Labyrinthus."

"Perhaps Captain, but we are gathering some really valuable cartographic data", Peter responded, adding, "Governor Anderson will be very happy to receive that."

Having crossed over the Ladon Basin, Matthew noted, "The river flows northeast from here Captain through Pyrrhae Chaos. It appears Pyrrhae Chaos is another section of white water."

Settlement detections drew to a close as they exited the Ladon Valley and continued through Pyrrhae Chaos. The river became a single channel of angry white water rapids continuing in its northeasterly direction.

The Solstice was soon through that section of terrain and the Argyre River broadened and slowed once more, before approaching a region called Margaritifer Chaos. The Argyre River broke into multiple channels all flowing northeast. Each and every channel was fast flowing and full of rapids. The channels joined together once more and formed a broad flowing river still flowing northeast. No new settlements had been detected since the Ladon Basin.

Soon the Solstice was flying above a region called Iani Chaos and the river again split into multiple channels of fast flowing white water, changing its direction more to the north. The Solstice quickly flew through the Iani Chaos region and the river channels rejoined, once again forming the broad flowing Argyre River. They entered a long section of river flowing through the Ares Valles.

"Given a few million years of erosion, this river might even become navigable", Peter remarked, adding, "At the moment, not so much."

As they continued flying north, a good sized tributary entered the Argyre River from the west.

"Captain, we are detecting something interesting. I recommend slowing down a notch or two and increasing our altitude", Peter informed him.

"Marcus. Lets hover and increase altitude", Forkbraid instructed.

"Aye Captain. Hovering and increasing altitude", Matthew responded.

As the Solstice's altitude increased, Peter adjusted the main screen to display a window showing the terrain to the west. The tributary they had seen only minutes ago, was now clearly visible and flowing out of a large, circular basin. Aram Chaos, an ancient and weathered meteor impact crater. Now flooded with water, Aram Chaos was huge, almost as large as Lake Galle.

"Captain. We are detecting a medium sized settlement on the northern shore of Lake Aram", Peter noted, "A number of structures, crop fields, boats, boats ramps and three Hummers. This settlement is not recorded on any maps."

"That is interesting Perter", Forkbraid replied, "Marcus. Takes further north so Peter can get a better look."

"Aye Captain", Marcus replied.

As the Solstice got closer, "These structures are all new Captain", Peter remarked, "Nothing here is more than a year old. It's all brand spanking new. They even have a communications array. Not a small simple one either. Their comms array is capable of picking up long distance signals and even satellite feeds."

Jim at his tactical console stepped in, "I've taken note of their exact coordinates Captain. I'll ask Lieutenant Roberts to put bird above them for surveillance purposes."

"These people might not be the ones we're looking for Captain. This settlement is new, but their Hummers are smaller, short range models. They'd be okay for accessing the local colonies, but they don't appear to have anything capable of going farther afield", Peter explained.

"Suspiciously new non the less considering all the recent troubles Peter", Forkbraid replied, then turned to Jim, "Lieutenant Robert's bird. It's a go Jim."

"Aye Captain", Jim Murphy replied, adding, "It would be prudent. To me that comms array is awfully suspicious. No ordinary settlement would need that kind of high tech equipment."

"Marcus. Take us back to the river. We'll map its course to its mouth", Forkbraid instructed.

"Aye Captain", Marcus replied.

The Solstice followed the Argyre River's course north from Lake Aram. It wasn't long before the Ares Valley turned northwesterly. Throughout the Ares Valley, the Argyre River was broad, very broad and slow like the Amazon River on Earth. Vast volumes of water flowed through it. When the Solstice finally reached the mouth of the Argyre River, they were astonished. The Argyre River estuary was huge and it was difficult to tell where the river ended and the Chryse Sea began. No further settlements were detected along the stretch of river beyond Lake Aram.

"Peter. Package up all the cartographic data on the Argyre River and when you're finished, hand it over to Charlene for transmission to Chryce colony", Forkbraid instructed, adding "Marcus. Plot a course to Noctis Labyrinthus. Maybe, just maybe, we'll find those bounty hunters there."

All three replied "Aye Captain", as Marcus plotted a course for Noctis Labyrinthus.

Phillip Barnes waited patiently in the Hummer. It was an older model Hummer, nothing flash, but it could carry a number of people and if necessary cargo. Phillip Barnes was its pilot.

A large burly man armed with a holstered pulse pistol entered the Hummer, "You all fuelled up and ready to go Phil?", he asked.

"Everything is ready. Just waiting for you and the rest of the team Billy Bob", Phil replied.

"Good man. I need you to plot a course that takes us south of the Tharsis Montes, then take us along the coast of the Amazonis Sea. I want to approach Elysium from the east", William Barrows, aka Billy Bob, replied.

"From the east?", Phil replied rhetorically, "It will be a rougher ride, but we'll save on fuel."

"That's the general idea. Last time, we had to refuel before our return flight and I didn't like all those armed security people surrounding our Hummer", William Barrows replied, adding, "They saw right though us, so this time we'll do something different."

"Define different?", Phil queried.

"Those coordinates on the wanted video. That's where we're headed Phil", Barrows informed him, adding, "Let's just go straight to the target and see what we can catch, yeah!"

"Just as long as my Hummer doesn't get a scratch Billy Bob", Phil replied.

"You and your Hummer Phil", Barrows replied, "I'm surprised you don't bloody live in it. No guarantees on scratches lad."

It wasn't long before the remaining passengers began entering the Hummer, there were a dozen of them and they were all armed. Each had a pulse rifle slung over their shoulder.

"Donny. Get on board. Come on Johnny Boy, no dawdling", Billy Bob Barrows told them as they boarded the Hummer, telling the remaining eight bounty hunters, "Come on lads, get on board, daylights burning."

Once the last bounty hunter was onboard the Hummer, Barrows slammed the hatch closed and instructed, "Come on Phil, what are you waiting for? Get airborne."

"Taking off now Billy Bob", Phil the pilot replied.

"Okay here's the plan people", Billy Bob Barrows explained, "We move in fast, we get what we want and we get out fast. The space ship Solstice. If we see the Solstice, we need to get whatever information we can on it. The fugitives. If we come across any of the fugitives, catch them, black bag them and get them aboard the Hummer. Do not harm them. The Jovian High Council wants them all alive and well. They're worth gold lads, Jovian gold!"

"Donny. Pass these around. Make sure everyone gets a copy", Billy Bob instructed as he passed Donny a dozen pieces of paper. One side of each, had a picture of the Solstice, the other side had pictures of the Solstice's ten crew members.

"Remember lads. Capture, but do not harm the fugitives", Billy Bob reiterated.

Phil flew his Hummer with its passengers southwest towards the very southern regions of the Tharsis Bulge. Phil's Hummer began to be buffeted by strong winds as it approached the Daedalia Planum region.

"Strewth Phil. What the fuck!", Billy Bob exclaimed.

"What did you expect Billy Bob", Phil replied as he fought the strong winds, "This is why no one in their right mind flies this way."

"Just make sure you get us there in one piece Phil", Billy Bob replied.

"Doing my best. We are getting a shit ton of wind sheer though", Phil replied.

Right when the winds became their strongest, Phil began changing course to the northwest. They had reached the centre of Daedalia Planum and were now flying out towards the coast the Amazonis Sea. Much to the delight of the passengers, the strong winds began slowly declining the further they flew to the northwest and out of Daedalia Planum.

Once the Hummer reached the coast of the Amazonis Sea, Phil then altered course to the north. Some time later the enormous volcano that was Olympus Mons appeared on the horizon to the northeast. By the time the Hummer reached the correct latitude to approach the academy, the bulk of Olympus Mons loomed large in the east. It was an awesome sight to behold. Phil ignored the sight and turned his Hummer west. Soon they were flying out over the Amazonis Sea and heading directly to Elysium and the academy.

A message was coming through on Roseanne's grip. Roseanne opened the device and a virtual screen appeared above her left forearm. The communications officer face appeared on the screen.

"We have a situation. Is Lady Selene there?", The communications officer asked.

"Yes. Lady Selene is right here", Roseanne replied.

Selene, having heard the call, enquired, "What's the situation?"

"Our satellite surveillance has detected a Hummer approaching from the East. It's the same model as the Hummer that tried to infiltrate the Elysium colony", the communications officer noted.

"Noted. I'll be there shortly", Selene replied, then asking Roseanne, "Contact Leroy and have him meet us at the communications centre", then after a short pause, "Roseanne, where exactly are the Girls?"

Roseanne replied, "In their dormitory I think."

"Get Leroy over to the communications centre, then go to the dormitory and make sure the Girls and their Aunt are safe", Selene instructed.

"Will do", Roseanne replied and they both went their separate ways.

By the time Selene had reached the communications centre, Leroy was already there.

"What's the problem?", Leroy enquired.

"Bounty Hunters are on the approach from the east", Selene quickly responded.

"Do we need to launch the wisps?", Leroy asked.

"They're in a Hummer. Our anti-aircraft batteries can handle them", Selene informed him.

"Okay. So what's the plan", Leroy asked.

"Make contact with them. Let them know they're flying into restricted airspace and that they will be shot down if they approach any closer", Selene recommended.

"Okay Selene. I've got this", Leroy replied as he sat at a console and activated the anti-aircraft batteries targeting systems.

Selene was quiet for a few moments and then commented, "I'm receiving a telepathic message from Roseanne. She needs my assistance. Have you got this Leroy?"

"Yes Selene I've got this", Leroy replied.

"Good then, I'll jaunt over to the Pod Sisters dormitory", Selene replied, then there was a small flash of light and Selene was gone.

"I'll never get use to that", Leroy said to himself.

Roseanne entered the dormitory rooms where the Pod family were staying at the academy and looked around. Zuawalo, Zeealas and Nyaliep were nowhere to be seen.

"What is it child? Why you run around and around?", Zyaliep asked.

"Mother Zyaliep. Where are Zuawalo, Zeealas and Nyaliep?", Roseanne enquired.

"They are all at the place of Varak, at the construction hanger", Zyaliep replied, "and you must call me Mother. My Daughters have adopted you as their Sister, so I have adopted you as well."

"Yes Mother", Roseanne smiled, "but why are they all at Varak's place?"

"Nyaliep moved in with Varak after their marriage. Zuawalo and Zeealas wanted to see the place, so they go to visit Nyaliep", Zyaliep replied.

"This is not a good thing Mother", Roseanne replied.

"Why is it not a good thing Roseanne?", Zyaliep asked.

"There are very bad men coming. Bounty Hunters", Roseanne informed here, adding, "Here inside the walls they are safe. Outside the walls not so much. Not safe Mother."

Zyaliep realised the problem, "We need to make my Daughters and my Sister safe Roseanne."

"I'm on it Mother", Roseanne replied as she sent a quick telepathic message to Selene.

There was a small flash of light and Selene appeared out of nowhere in the dormitory's common room. It startled both Zyaliep and Kwoth.

"How you do that?", a very surprised Zyaliep asked.

"Hi Zyaliep. Sorry to startle you", Selene greeted, adding, "I am a Witch remember."

"It's called jaunting Mother", Roseanne explained to Zyaliep.

"Mother?", Selene queried.

"Zyaliep has 'adopted' me Selene", Roseanne replied.

"I've already officially adopted you Roseanne. You know that", Selene responded.

"And now Zyaliep has adopted me as well", Roseanne, explained, "It's not important right now, we have other problems to deal with that are far more urgent."

"Okay, we can discuss this adoption later", Selene replied as Roseanne leant in towards her.

Understanding that Roseanne had information to share Selene leant in towards Roseanne and they touched their foreheads together. Roseanne shared the recent discussion she had had with Zyaliep, then they both stepped back from each other.

"Oh my. This is not good", Selene responded, "The Girls and Nyaliep are not within the walls. Zyaliep, Kwoth, this is a dangerous time. There are bounty hunters approaching."

"So my new daughter Roseanne tells us", Zyaliep replied, "Here inside the walls safe. Outside the walls not safe."

"Yes Zyaliep, that is the case", Selene agreed.

Kwoth asked, "How do we bring my Daughters back here?"

"That would be dangerous. They would be seen. They need to shelter in place", Selene replied.

"Then I'll just jaunt down to the construction hammer and give the Girls a heads up", Roseanne suggested to Selene.

"No, no, no Roseanne!", Selene objected, telling her, "I'll take care of this."

Roseanne stepped towards Selene and hugged her, then stepped back, "No Selene. You are needed here in the academy. I'll take care of this."

"You're not going to back down are you?", Selene queried.

"No. Of course not", Roseanne replied, adding, "And besides, you've taught me too well. What can a dozen bounty hunters do to me? I'll have them rolling around the floor crying like babies."

"Zyaliep. Our Daughter has got this", Selene informed Zyaliep, as she reached into her impossible pocket and took our her wand, Gnomulus, passing it to Roseanne, "You remember, don't you. Point and shoot. Gnomulus will know what to do."

Roseanne nodded, "Yes. I remember. Stop worrying about me Selene. I'll be fine."

There was a small flash of light and Roseanne disappeared.

"Roseanne is so very young?", Zyaliep queried.

"Roseanne is also a very powerful young Witch", Selene explained.

Roseanne reappeared just outside the construction hanger's main doors. There was no sign of the approaching threat yet. Roseanne jaunted once again and after a small flash of light, reappeared inside the hanger. Immediately Roseanne was approached by the lead Android that was in charge of the teams of Androids, that were working in the hanger.

"This facility is off limits. You should not be here", the Android stated.

"I am here to see Nyaliep. My name is Roseanne Rhein", Roseanne replied.

"We recognise you Miss Rhein", the Android responded, "We are messaging Nyaliep now."

After a few moments the android responded, "Varak's house Android will be here shortly to escort you to the apartment."

"Where is the apartment?", Roseanne enquired.

"The apartment is atop the storage facilities, that run along the north wall of the construction hanger", the Android informed her.

"Android. There are very bad people coming. You must protect Nyaliep, Zuawalo, Zeealas and myself. Do not let them know the apartment exists",

Roseanne instructed the Android adding, "Do you understand?"

"We must protect Nyaliep, Zuawalo, Zeealas and Roseanne", the Android replied.

"Good. If the bad men come here, tell them no one is here. If they ask about the crew of the Solstice, tell them the crew are onboard the Solstice. Do you understand?", Roseanne commanded.

"We understand. There are no humans in this facility. The crew of the Solstice are onboard the Solstice", the Android replied.

Varak's house Android approached and stated, "Roseanne Rhein. Please follow us."

Roseanne followed Varak's house Android to the storage facilities and once inside, to the elevator that was used to access Varak's apartment.

Roseanne greeted Zuawalo, Zeealas and Nyaliep when she entered the apartment, then commanded the house Android to lock the access doors to the storage facilities and then to lock and shutdown the elevator access to the apartment.

"Roseanne, what is happening?", Nyaliep asked.

"The bounty hunters are approaching in a Hummer", Roseanne informed her, "We are not safe here. We are all supposed to be within the academy's walls."

"I thought the whole academy was safe", Nyaliep replied.

"No Aunty Nyaliep. Inside the walls yes, outside the walls no", Roseanne explained, then asked, "What do you call this Android?"

Nyaliep replied, "I call him Metal man."

Roseanne addressed the Android, "Metal man. Can you communicate with the hanger's lead Android in real time?"

"Yes Roseanne. We can communicate with the lead Android in real time", the Android replied.

"Excellent. Metal man, if the bounty hunters come into the hanger, the lead Android is not to answer any questions, unless I give the answers first. Is that understood?, Roseanne commanded.

"We understand Roseanne. We have put in place real time communications", the Android replied.

Roseanne then asked, "If that Hummer lands, can you have one of the other Androids place a tracking device on it?"

The house Android replied, "If the opportunity arises, we can make an attempt."

Phil took some scans of the Elysium subcontinent as his Hummer approached. He focused the Hummers instruments on the coordinates of the New Flinders Psychic Academy.

"Billy Bob. What do we know of this facility?", Phil enquired.

"Not a whole lot Phil. Just its location and our instructions", Billy Bob Barrows replied.

"Right then! That could be a problem", Phil informed him, adding, "That facility looks like a fortress, a bloody big one at that. The fucking thing is huge. It's not just a fortress either. I've detected an air field with several hangers, two clicks to the south east of it."

"What are you telling me Phil?", Billy Bob asked.

"Seriously, even if we landed inside those fortress walls, we could take hours just trying to locate the fugitives", Phil explained, then added, "That ship, the Solstice is more likely to be in a hanger at the airfield as well."

At that point the Hummers communications unit came to life.

"Calling the approaching Hummer. You are an unauthorised flight approaching restricted air space. Turn around immediately or you will be targeted", Leroy informed them from the academy.

"Don't answer them, they're just bluffing", Billy Bob commanded.

"Calling the approaching Hummer. You are an unauthorised flight approaching restricted air space. Turn around immediately or you will be targeted", Leroy informed them once more.

"I don't think they're bluffing Billy Bob. I reckon I've detected at least three rings of anti-aircraft batteries surrounding that fortress", Phil informed him.

"Are you sure? We've not been told anything about that", Billy Bob replied.

"Calling the approaching Hummer. You are an unauthorised flight approaching restricted air space. Turn around immediately or you will be targeted", Leroy informed them for a third time, adding, "If you continue on your current course, you will be destroyed."

At that point the Hummer's equipment detected the anti-aircraft batteries targeting lock.

Beep! Beep! Beep! Beep! Beep!

"Shit! They have targeting lock!", Phil exclaimed and then quickly changed direction to the southwest.

Beep! Beep! Beep! Beep! Beep!

The beeping stopped shortly after the course change, as they moved slightly further away.

"Dammit! Phil, take us to that air field", Billy Bob screamed, "Maybe we can get some information there."

Phil refined the Hummer's course to take it to the air field.

Billy Bob looked out of the main view screen, "There! That big hanger! Put us down somewhere on the opposite side of it. We'll use it like a shield."

Phil landed his Hummer as instructed.

Billy bob led his team out of the Hummer.

"Donny, Johnny Boy. Take up positions on that north corner. Keep an eye on that fortress", Billy Bob ordered, "If anything comes our way, I want to know!"

"Everyone else with me", Billy Bob commanded as he ran to the hanger's entrance door.

"Joey! Blow the door. Get us inside", Billy Bob ordered.

One of his other team members, Joey, placed a small explosive device on the door locking mechanism. Less than a minute later there was a small explosion and door swung open.

The team of bounty hunters entered the hanger with weapons drawn, "It's fucking empty! Where's the bloody ship!", one of them asked.

The lead Android managing the Android work teams approached them.

Billy Bob Barrows addressed the Android, "You there. Where's the bloody ship?"

"Which ship?", the Android asked.

"The Solstice. Where's the bloody Solstice?", Billy Bob asked.

"The Starship Solstice is not here", the Android replied.

"I can see that you metal genius. Where is the Solstice?", Billy Bob asked again.

"The Starship Solstice is on a mission", the Android replied.

"And where is it's crew?", Billy Bob asked.

"The ship's crew are onboard the Starship Solstice", the Android informed them.

Joey stepped in, "Well ain't that just dandy. No ship. No crew. That means no fugitives and no fucking bounty. We've just wasted our fucking time!", he exclaimed and kicked a nearby bench.

Not wanting to have completely wasted their time, Billy Bob asked the Android, "What are you making over there?"

"We are making plasteel", the Android replied.

"Why are you making plasteel?", Billy Bob asked.

"We are making plasteel because we were requested to make it", the Android replied.

Billy Bob rephrased his question, "For what purpose is the plasteel being made?"

"That we do not know. It has not yet been divulged", the Android replied.

Continuing with more questions, Billy Bob asked, "Where are the schematics and blueprints for the Solstice."

There was a brief pause as Roseanne relayed the answer, "The schematics and blueprints are currently stored on a secure computer system deep inside the academy. It is air gapped and can only be accessed by the chief engineer."

"Where is the chief engineer?", Billy Bob asked.

There was a brief pause then, "The chief engineer is on the Solstice", the Android replied.

Joey jumped in, "So we can't even get hold of the damned blueprints. Fuck!"

Billy Bob held up his hand to quieten Joey down, then asked the Android, "Is there anyone else here? Any other people here? Anyone else we can talk to?"

"Again there was a brief pause as Roseanne relayed the answer, "There are no other humans present here. You are the only humans present."

Billy Bob started pacing, it was quite a pickle. No ship. No fugitives. No information. Were they just wasting their time?

Roseanne looked around at the apartments windows. There were windows that overlooked the fields to the north and the airfield to the east, but also a couple of windows what overlooked the hangers interior. Roseanne had been avoiding the windows so as not to be seen, but then noticed something she had not noticed when she entered the apartment.

Roseanne walked up to the nearest window that overlooked the hangers interior. It wasn't a window at all. It was a broad flat screen that was rolled out across the wall, giving the impression that it was a window, but it was actually a real time video feed.

Roseanne looked out the window, "These windows are all fake!", she exclaimed, "No one can see in, it's all just video feeds."

"Yes", Nyaliep confirmed, explaining, "Varak said it was easier to put in video screens than cut holes in the walls."

Roseanne looked down into the hanger, "Why aren't they leaving? There's nothing here for them. They should be leaving."

Then Roseanne had an idea, "Metal man. Tell the Android team leader, to tell the bounty hunters that the plasteel smelting process uses harmful chemicals and that for their own safety they should leave the hanger immediately."

The message was relayed to the Android team leader who then advised, "For your own safety, you should leave the hanger immediately. The making of plasteel uses dangerous and toxic chemicals. No biological entities should be present during the alloying processes."

"What the fuck!", Joey exclaimed, "Now he fucking tells us. Why didn't you tell us earlier, you dumb fucking robot?"

Roseanne's new message was relayed by the lead Android, "The danger increases with exposure. Your exposure has been increasing and now it is necessary for you to leave to avoid critical exposure levels. There is limited time left before you will all be adversely affected."

Roseanne then began to use her powers subtly, to make the bounty hunters begin to feel ill.

Another of the bounty hunters, Shane (Smithy) Smith commented, "You know what. I'm not feeling so well at the moment. Quite nauseous in fact."

Joey's brother, Jebediah (Jeb) Banksia also spoke up, "I'm not feeling so hot myself Smithy."

Billy Bob was also starting to feel nauseous, "Okay, everyone out of the hanger. Now!"

With that order, all the bounty hunters left the hanger and retreated outside. The feelings of nausea began to effect them all and they were beginning to worry they'd had a critical exposure.

From upstairs in Varak's apartment, Roseanne, Nyaliep, Zuawalo and Zeealas watched the video feed window that covered the area where the bounty hunters had retreated to.

The Pod Sisters giggled amongst themselves and Nyaliep remarked, "I thought my Varak was ever so clever. Now me thinks that my new niece is ever so clever also."

Roseanne told her new family, "When I was on Earth, I was alone. I had no family and I moved from one foster home to another. In the end, I ended up in a Catholic boarding school in Melbourne being taught by nuns. As a ward of the state, the Victorian Government paid the bills. Then I went on an excursion with the school to Flinders Island and the Psychic Academy that was there."

Roseanne continued after a short pause, "There I was discovered as a psychic and my whole life changed. Straight away Selene applied to be my Guardian. I then became Selene's Apprentice. Then when Selene left for Mars, she brought me with her. After the Battle of New Tortuga Selene officially adopted me and now, I am her Daughter, her Apprentice, her Ward and her Protege."

Roseanne looked around her, to Zuawalo, Zeealas and Nyaliep, tears were welling up in her eyes, "Then I met you guys. The Girls adopted me as their Sister. Zyaliep has adopted me as her Daughter and even you Nyaliep, you've adopted me as your Niece. I have two Mothers, two Sisters and a Aunt. I now have more family than I have ever had in my entire life!"

Roseanne looked at the view screen and the eleven bounty hunters that had been in the hanger, her face took on an angry visage, almost viperous, as she point to the screen, "They want to take you away, to collect the bounties on your heads. I am not going to let them!"

Roseanne lifted her right hand and clenched her fist, one by one the eleven bounty hunters collapsed to the ground and began to vomit violently.

Nyaliep was taken aback by the power that Roseanne wielded, "Roseanne! You must let go of your anger. Be just, but not cruel."

Zuawalo reached out and grabbed Roseanne's right hand. Gently she brought Roseanne's hand towards her. She gently kissed the back of Roseanne's hand.

"Sister. Please you must let go of your anger", Zuawalo implored.

Zeealas stepped in close on Roseanne's other side and gently kissed Roseanne on the lips, then told her, "Roseanne. Anger is an acid. It burns the container that holds it. Sister. You must let it go."

Roseanne looked at Zeealas and with tears freely flowing, gave a small smile, before returning Zeealas's gentle kiss, "I am your Sister Zeealas, not your Sister Wife."

"I know", replied Zeealas, "Sometimes I get carried away."

Roseanne, her anger dissipated, stated, "I could have made their heads pop off like cherry bombs. No. I will not kill them, but they will be sick for a few weeks."

Neither the Girls nor Nyaliep understood the cherry bomb reference, however, they knew it could not have been good.

Two more bounty hunters, Donny and Johnny Boy, came to the aid of the eleven bounty hunters who had been in the construction hanger. Roseanne saw this and the opportunity it presented.

"Metal man. Organise a dozen Androids to assist the sick bounty hunters back to their Hummer", Roseanne instructed, adding, "When you do so, confiscate their pulse rifles. I'll ensure they're too ill to notice. Make sure the Androids surreptitiously plant some trackers on their Hummer."

"Yes Roseanne. We will perform the tasks as requested", the house Android replied, "What would you have us do with their pulse rifles?"

"Place them is secure storage and note it down for Varak's attention", Roseanne replied.

"Yes. We can do that Roseanne", the house Android replied.

As an afterthought, Roseanne then added, "Metal man. Organise an Android to repair the hanger door. I'm sure Varak will appreciate it."

"Yes Roseanne. The door will be repaired", the house Android replied.

One by one Androids helped the sick bounty hunters into their Hummer. Donny and Johnny Boy were content to allow the Androids to do the heavy lifting and simply climbed aboard ahead of their comrades. None of the bounty hunters noticed their pulse rifles were left laying on the airfield's tarmac. None of the bounty hunters noticed as the Androids surreptitiously left multiple tracking devices hidden in their Hummer.

"Oh my God. What the fuck is that smell!", Phil exclaimed as the sick bounty hunters were helped on board.

"Shut the fuck up!", a very ill Billy Bob Barrows replied, "I'm not in the mood for bullshit!"

Phil was uncharacteristically quiet as the rest of the bounty hunters boarded. He noted that Donny and Johnny Boy were the only ones who were not affected.

"Donny. What the fuck happened?", Phil asked.

"We're not sure Phil. Some sort of toxic chemical exposure we think", Donny informed him.

A very ill Joey mumbled, "Something they were using in their plasteel alloying process."

That surprised Phil, "Plasteel alloying? I can't imagine what that would be."

Phil looked around his Hummer, everyone was on board and he began flight preparations.

Phil then asked Billy Bob, "Did we get anything useful?"

Billy bob was brutally honest as he replied through the painful gut wrenching, "The ship, the Solstice isn't here. The crew, the fugitives, they're all on the Solstice. The specification for the ship can't be accessed. We did learn one thing though."

"What was that?", Phil enquired.

Billy Bob replied, "The supervising Android that was in charge, kept calling the ship, the *'Starship'* Solstice!"

"Starship!", now that caught Phil by surprise as he launched his Hummer skywards and set a course for home.

Roseanne, Zuawalo, Zeealas and Nyaliep watched as the Hummer took off and flew away on an eastward course.

"They won't be back anytime soon", Roseanne remarked, "They're going to be ill for a couple of weeks at least and they'll never understand why."

Roseanne telepathically messaged Selene and let her know what had transpired. Probably the most important part of the message, was the part about the tracking devices being placed on board the Hummer. That tracking telemetry was already being received.

"I'm going to stay here with you guys until those bounty hunters are well and truly out of our airspace", Roseanne informed her friends, "Then we'll go back to the academy together. You'll all be much safer there."

Selene headed straight to the communications centre and sent a coded message to the Solstice, passing on all the relevant information, that Roseanne had given her.

Leroy was surprised when he heard how easily Roseanne had taken down the bounty hunters. He had not realised how powerful the young woman was. Leroy checked the satellite information and watched carefully as the bounty hunter's Hummer continued on its course back the way they'd come. Once they were well and truly out of Elysium airspace, he notified Roseanne at the hanger.

8. Homeward Bound

"Captain. We are receiving an urgent satellite relayed message from the New Flinders Psychic Academy", Charlene informed Forkbraid.

"Put it on screen Charlene", Forkbraid replied.

"Aye Captain", Charlene replied.

The message once decoded read, *"Bounty hunters have approached the psychic academy. The same bounty hunters that tried to infiltrate the Elysium colony. Roseanne has dealt with them and sent them packing. They are fleeing eastwards across the Amazonis Sea. Tracking frequency follows this message."*

"Charlene access the tracking data", Forkbraid instructed.

"Aye Captain. Receiving tracking telemetry now", Charlene replied

The tracking data appeared in a window on the screen, overlaying a map of Mars. The bounty hunters were flying across the Amazonis Sea heading east towards Olympus Mons.

"I suspect they're heading to Noctis Labyrinthus", Forkbraid remarked, "So which way will they go? Straight across the Tharsis Monts or south around the Tharsis Bulge?"

Jim gave his educated guess, "Captain. They will go south around the Bulge. Remember, we've flown over the Tharsis Monts in that old Junker and that piece of crap was space rated. That was not enjoyable at all, as you may remember."

"The model of Hummer they're flying isn't space rated at all. It's only atmo rated Captain", Peter Swann remarked, "They have no choice but to go around the Bulge."

"That's what I was thinking as well", Forkbraid replied, adding, "We'll be over the Noctis Labyrinthus region long before the bounty hunters arrive. Marcus. When we arrive, put us in an expanding spiral course based on the centre of Noctis Labyrinthus. We'll scan and map everything we find before they arrive."

"Aye Captain. I can arrange that", Marcus replied, advising, "If we start at the edge of Noctis Labyrinthus and spiral inwards to the centre, by the time we finish our scans, the bounty hunters will be on the approach and we'll be in the perfect position to intercept them."

"Excellent Marcus, let's do that", Forkbraid agreed.

The Solstice arrived at Noctis Labyrinthus on the northern side and Marcus put the ship in a broad spiral covering the whole region and gradually spiralling inwards. Peter Swann at his science console began scanning the region as they continued on their new course.

"Captain. We are detecting quite a few small settlements", Peter noted.

"That wouldn't surprise me at all", Jim added, "Back before the terraforming, Noctis Labyrinthus was considered a hot option for colonising. Burrowing into the canyon walls to reduce the solar and cosmic radiation levels was considered beneficial back then."

"Thank you for the information Jim. Peter what else can you tell us?", Forkbraid replied.

"Captain. We're detecting small colonies and villages, just as Jim described. Burrowed into canyon walls, but also spread out into the areas around them", Peter explained, adding, 'These villages are very much like the ones around the southern shores of the Hebes Sea. Very similar."

"Are any of these, the ones the bounty hunters came from?", Forkbraid enquired.

"That is very doubtful Captain", Peter replied, adding, "I'm not picking up an real high tech signatures. Low level stuff, nothing high tech though. We will know more after we've completed our scans."

The Solstice followed its spiral course westwards above Noctis Fossae and continued farther to the west before turning southwards. They flew eastward across the vast expanse of Syria Planum, a dry desert region of plains, before approaching Sinai Planum. A region of plains that were far less dry and covered in vast grasslands.   Peter allowed the Solstice to scan the regions they traversed at will. Peter decided not to interpret the scans as they flew, instead he decided to wait until they had finished scanning and concentrate on anything that stood out.

The Solstice turned northwards once more and Marcus adjusted course to tighten the spiral. This procedure repeated and after a few hours they had completed their spiral course and were hovering above the central regions of Noctis Labyrinthus.

Charlene noted, "I can see why they named this Noctis Labyrinthus. The labyrinth of the night. Those canyons are so deep and dark and there's so many of them. It's literally a labyrinth."

Marcus added, "And everyone of those canyons has a wild river at the bottom."

Forkbraid enquired, "What do we know Peter?"

Peter was studying their scans and working through the data.

"Captain. There are at least twenty villages in the Noctis Labyrinthus region", Peter informed Forkbraid, adding, "One detection stands out from the others. Oudemans Crater!"

"Oudemans Crater?", Forkbraid enquired.

The far eastern region of Noctis Labyrinthus, where all the canyons and all the wild rivers they contained coalesced together, was also the far western end of the Marineris Valley. The many rivers that flowed into this region from Noctis Labyrinthus, formed the major inflow region of the Marineris Valley. There was still some debate as to whether this confluence zone was a part of Noctis Labyrinthus or the Marineris Valley. Whatever the case, the sight was spectacular to see.

Peter Swann put the confluence zone on the screen. Far to the south and joined to the confluence zone was a large, flooded circular region, Oudemans Crater. Now labelled as Oudemans Bay.

Peter highlighted Oudemans Bay, "Captain. That is Oudemans Crater. It's now called Oudemans Bay. Notice the Islands in its centre. They're rebound mountains, that were created when the original impact crater was made."

Forkbraid looked at the screen carefully, "Peter. Are you telling us, that we've detected something interesting on those islands?"

"Absolutely Captain", Peter responded, adding, "What we have found here is something very similar to what we found at Lake Aram, only much larger."

Forkbraid commanded, "Marcus. Put us over those islands."

"Aye Captain", Marcus replied and adjusted course.

Peter continued, "It's a new settlement. We've detected quite a few structures and they're all very new. Again, nothing there is more than a year old. They also have a large communications array, that's even more sophisticated than the one we found at Lake Aram. I'd be willing to bet, that when that Hummer full of bounty hunters finally approaches Noctis Labyrinthus, they'll make a bee line straight for those islands."

Soon the Solstice was hovering above the islands in Oudemans Bay, silent and unseen with both active and passive cloaking on, waiting for the bounty hunters.

It was several hours later when the Hummer full of bounty hunters began their approach to Noctis Labyrinthus. The tracking telemetry was displayed on the screen along with a map of Mars and their Hummer's flight progress appeared as a moving sprite. Just as Peter had predicted, the bounty hunter's Hummer altered course and made a bee line straight to the Oudemans Islands.

"They're on their way Captain", Peter Swann announced.

"About time Peter. We've all been waiting long enough", Forkbraid responded.

When the bounty hunter's Hummer finally arrived Jim Murphy, at his tactical console asked, "Do I eliminate them Captain?"

"No Jim. I want to observe them. Maybe even skim the surface of their minds for information if possible", Forkbraid replied.

The crew of the Solstice watched as the bounty hunter's Hummer landed close to a hanger at the largest Oudemans Islands settlement.

"Marcus. Move us in closer", Forkbraid ordered, then asked Peter, "Can they see us Peter?"

"Aye Captain", Marcus replied.

Peter replied, "No Captain. Our active cloaking prevents that. They have no idea we're here."

"Good Peter. Marcus bring us in closer", Forkbraid requested.

"Age Captain", Marcus replied.

The Solstice was more than close enough, for the crew of the Solstice to watch the crew of the bounty hunter's Hummer disembark. Straight away they realised something was very wrong. Three men stepped out of the Hummer.

One of them kicked the side of the Hummer three times, before going back inside and helping what looked like one very sick bounty hunter to disembark. He left his comrade lying on the ground writhing in pain and then he and his comrades went back into the Hummer to help their other sick comrades disembark.

After several minutes and multiple trips inside the Hummer, there were eleven bounty hunters lying on the ground writhing in pain and agony. One of the three men then rushed over to the settlements main buildings, he was looking for help and he quickly found it. Several more people, both men and women rushed over to the Hummer.

After skimming the minds of the three active bounty hunters, Forkbraid remarked, "That guy who kicked the Hummer is its owner and its pilot. His name is Phil and he's not at all happy. Apparently the inside of his Hummer is covered in puke and shit. That was a long flight from Elysium and the stench must have been awful."

"Captain. What happened to them?", Charlene asked.

"I'm just finding out now", Forkbraid replied as he skimmed the minds of the sick bounty hunters before informing everyone, "Roseanne did this!"

"Roseanne? Our Roseanne?", Charlene questioned.

"Roseanne used an Android in Varak's construction hanger, to put into their minds that they were being exposed to toxic chemicals", Forkbraid explained, "then she gave them a massive and uncontrollable, psychosomatic response. These poor bastards are going to be sick and bed ridden for the next few weeks at least."

"Roseanne did that?", Charlene questioned once more.

"Yes. Roseanne did that", Forkbraid confirmed, "Honestly. I don't know if I should commend her or censure her. It certainly is creative, although I must admit, it is also somewhat cruel. Roseanne really did a number on them."

Marcus commented, "They must have really pissed her off. Roseanne would not have done that without a very good reason."

"They are bounty hunters", Jim remarked, "and they were hunting my wives. So I have no sympathy for them whatsoever. Personally, I would have shot them on sight!"

"Roseanne is very close to the Girls. I can imaging she would have been exceedingly angry. Your wives were in good hands Jim", Charlene noted.

As they watched, the eleven sick bounty hunters were helped to nearby homes in the settlement. After which the thee remaining bounty hunters and a couple of the towns folk discussed what had transpired. None of them seemed to be very happy.

Forkbraid continued to skim their minds, "They're really pissed off. No one told them that the academy was built like a fortress. No one told them the academy had rings of anti-aircraft batteries. These are not happy chappies. They are actually quite upset."

"They wouldn't have been happy to find out we weren't there either", Peter remarked.

"No they weren't. Varak's supervising Android told them that the Solstice and its crew were on a mission", Forkbraid informed them, adding, "Roseanne used that Android to tell them that no one else was in the hanger and that the Solstice's specifications were stored on a secure, air gapped computer underneath the academy. None of their objectives could be met."

"Well done Roseanne, is what I say!", Jim Murphy commented then recommended, "Give me the word FB and I'll raise this entire place to the ground."

"No Jim. Get Lieutenant Roberts up at Phobos to put a bird in stationary orbit above this place. We'll keep an eye over them", Forkbraid commanded.

"Peter. Package up all the cartographic data on the Noctis Labyrinthus region and when you're finished, hand it over to Charlene for transmission to the Chryce colony", Forkbraid instructed, adding "There's not much more we can do here. Marcus. Plot a course to Hebes Island. We need to stop by the town of Sweetness."

Several hours later the Solstice approached the northern coast of Hebes Island. The coordinates of the town of Sweetness were in the Solstice's computer records and even though nothing was showing up on their scans, the crew of the Solstice knew it was there.

As they approached the region where Sweetness was located, Marcus adjusted the Solstice's course to take them through a narrow, six hundred metre wide cleft between the cliffs, known as the Gap. Once through the Gap they found themselves in a large, almost circular bay. Broad sandy beaches and green rolling hills covered with pastures and forests could be seen on the far side.

There was a fair size spit of land that jutted out from between a couple of beaches. Forkbraid asked Marcus to land the Solstice on that spit of land. It was just barely big enough for the Solstice to land on, however Marcus managed to do so with very little room to spare.

Forkbraid announced, "Now we wait."

"Wait Captain?", Peter queried.

"Yes Peter. We wait for them to come to us", Forkbraid explained.

"Captain. We're cloaked. How will they know we're here", Peter enquired.

"Trust me. This is Sweetness Vale. They already know we're here Peter", Forkbraid replied.

Less than fifteen minutes later, a group of people approached from the beach and began walking along the spit. They walked with purpose directly towards the Solstice.

"Turn off the passive and active cloaking Peter", Forkbraid instructed.

With the Solstice's cloaking turned off, the ship suddenly became visible and the group of approaching towns folk began talking amongst themselves telepathically.

"I told you we had visitors", commented Kubrick, he tapped his forehead, *"I saw them coming from miles away."*

"So you said Kubrick", Mystal replied, adding, *"He's on board that ship."*

"He, appears to have some rather impressive new technology", Cadmus remarked.

"So he does", replied Gareth

"Marcus, Charlene. You're with me. Jim. Mind the ship until we get back", Forkbraid ordered.

Marcus and Charlene followed Forkbraid, as he quickly traversed the Solstice main corridor to the ship's main entrance and boarding ramp.

Forkbraid greeted the four people who stood before the Solstice, "Cadmus, Mystal, Gareth. It's good to see you again. I don't think I've met you."

Mystal replied, "This one is Kubrick. He detected your approach."

Kubrick gave Forkbraid and ever so slight nod.

Forkbraid motioned towards Charlene and Marcus, "These two are Charlene Fewkes, my Communications officer and Marcus Greyhelm, my Helmsman and Navigation officer."

Mystal replied, "More gifted I see. It is good to see you again as well

Forkbraid", then enquired, "We were expecting you to return much sooner. What happened?"

"The war happened Mystal", Forkbraid responded, "This war has kept us very busy lately."

"Yes. We are aware of the war and your part in it", Cadmus replied, adding with awe, "So this is that impressive ship, that has saved so many lives."

"Yes. Yes indeed Cadmus. Without this ship the colonies of Mars would have been destroyed and the planet would be occupied by the Trojan Armed Forces ", Forkbraid informed them.

"How did you know?", Cadmus enquired, clarifying, "How did you know you'd need this ship?"

"I didn't Cadmus. It was just pure coincidence. I commissioned this ship, the Solstice, to track down the Prophet and bring him to justice", Forkbraid explained, adding, "The Solstice came in very handy when the Jovian High Council decided to launch their unprovoked attacks."

"I imagine it did", Cadmus agreed.

"Cadmus. We have some issues we need to discuss, with your Town Council", Forkbraid informed them.

"Then let us call a meeting", Cadmus replied and then gestured towards the town of Sweetness that was only now, just becoming visible to them.

As they walked towards the town of Sweetness, Mystal enquired, "What happened to that young girl, Roseanne?"

"Roseanne has become one very powerful young Witch", Forkbraid informed her, "Although, I do believe she needs just a little more guidance."

"Does not the Lady Selene guide her well?", Mystal asked.

"Yes. Selene guides her very well, but Roseanne is Selene's apprentice, her protege and her adopted daughter", Forkbraid replied, explaining, "I think Selene is perhaps a little too close."

"I see. And how does this need for guidance manifest itself?", Mystal queried.

"We've recently had two infiltration attempts by some bounty hunters", Forkbraid informed her, "In their last attempt, Roseanne protected her friends in a way that was, quite harsh."

"Yes. We have seen the wanted videos and the response to those videos on the news feeds", Mystal replied, then asked, "So how harsh did Roseanne treat the bounty hunters?"

"I would call it borderline cruelty. Eleven of the bounty hunters are going to be ill and bedridden for a few weeks", Forkbraid replied.

"An anger or impulse control issue perhaps", Mystal suggested, adding, "Lessons in meditation will probably help her."

"I will discuss that with Selene when we get back", Forkbraid replied.

"We've seen what's on the news feeds and other channels. A lot of propaganda and posturing", Gareth noted, then asked, "What's really happening?"

"You mean apart from the attacks and two point five million dead on Earth and over sixty five thousand dead at L5", Forkbraid replied.

Gareth replied, "Sad yes, but what I was meaning, was what was happening locally?"

"Well the colonies have joined together, under Governor Anderson of Chryce's leadership and formed the Martian Defence Forces. They have actually placed me in charge as their Fleet Captain", Forkbraid informed him, adding, "And there's a joint Earth and L5 fleet, the EDCF Martian Task Force, in orbit above Mars to defend the planet from attack. Fifteen ships in all."

"Do you think that will deter the Jovians?", Gareth enquired.

"Perhaps. If this war goes to pattern, like the previous one. The Jovians will be big on sending missiles our way and not sending their fleet, but there are no guarantees with that.", Forkbraid replied, adding, "The Earth and L5 are bringing the abandoned Deimos military base online, so I expect we will see combined fleet operations in the near future."

When they final reach the town's assembly hall, the other nine town elders were already present and seated. Cadmus, Mystal, Gareth and Kubrick walked straight to their seats and sat down. The council table was crescent shaped and curved around and in front of them. Forkbraid, Charlene and Marcus sat down in the seats that had been provided to them in front of the Elder Council. Forkbraid noted that Mystal was now seated in the central chair.

"Yes Forkbraid. Cadmus has stepped down as the head Elder and I now hold that position", Mystal answered Forkbraid's unspoken question.

"So friends. Where do we begin", Mystal asked.

Forkbraid nodded to Charlene, who silently questioned, *"Are you sure?"* Forkbraid silently replied, *"Of course Charlene, you've got this."*

Charlene began explaining the situation, "Since the Jovian High Council declared war on the Inner Solar System, we've had to contend with missile swarms and fleets of occupation forces. That has kept us quite busy for a while. We've also had two infiltration attempts by armed bounty hunters, one at the Elysium Colony and the more recent one at the New Flinders Psychic Academy. Our precise coordinates are out there and we are definitely a target. As much as Lady Selene wants to open up the academy for taking on students, at the present moment in time and under the current circumstances, we simply cannot guarantee their safety."

"Charlene", Mystal began, "The two most powerful psychics in the Solar System are at the academy. Not to mention all of the other psychics you have at your disposal. Are you saying that they are not enough to keep students safe?"

Charlene replied, "That's exactly my point. What can a psychic do to a missile swarm or any other weapons launched from space? The Jovian High Council is prosecuting a war against us. Lord Forkbraid needs to take the fight to the enemy and is often off world in order to do so. Lady Selene is the Governor of the Elysium Colony and the Head Mistress of the Psychic Academy. Even the Tactical officer on board our ship has five job positions. We are already overwhelmed. Safety, simply cannot be guaranteed. We are in the midst of a War."

Gareth spoke up, "The promise of teaching and training for our gifted children cannot be kept. Certainly not under these circumstances Mystal. This young lady is right. During a time of War, safety simply cannot be guaranteed."

"I know that Gareth", Mystal replied, "It's just that, there are a lot of people in our town who were looking forward to this. Even families in the hinterlands outside of town. Professional training and teaching at a psychic academy, is what they want. They have been looking forward to it."

Cadmus then asked, "Charlene. Does Lady Selene have a plan?"

"Yes. Actually Lady Selene does have a plan", Charlene informed the Town Council of Elders, "We can provide the teachers and the trainers. We just need a safe place for the students."

"And that safe place is here?", Mystal queried.

"To be honest, yes. This vale is completely unknown to the rest of Mars. No one on Mars knows you're here. This is the safest possible place", Charlene confessed.

"And Lady Selene's proposal?", Cadmus queried.

"Our chief engineer, Varak. He can build a temporary school within the vale, where the students will be safe, then we can provide the required staff", Charlene explained, adding, "Here the students will be safe and we can provide professional teaching and training services. In theory."

"Ah hmm", one of the other elders, a younger looking one coughed.

"Yes Carly. Do you want to say something?", Mystal asked.

"This engineer. Varak. Why does he need to build anything at all?", Carly asked.

"What do you mean Carly?", Mystal asked.

"We've only lived in this vale, in the open, for what? A century? Probably a lot less. Before the terraforming, our ancestor lived in colonies that were literally tunnelled deep into the cliffs. Those colonies are still there. They've just been locked up so people can't access them", Carly explained.

"Are you suggesting that we use those old colonies as a school?", Mystal queried.

"Yes, why not? We won't have to build anything new. We can just open them up and assess what needs to be done to make them useful as a school", Carly concluded.

Gareth commented, "That would certainly save a lot time."

"And materials", Cadmus agreed.

"Does using the old colonies sound okay to you Charlene?", Mystal asked.

"Yes. If they're suitable, then why not?", Charlene replied, "I couldn't think of anywhere safer."

"Good then. When you get back to the academy, let your engineer, Varak, know that the old colonies are an option.", Mystal replied.

"One more thing", Charlene began, then continued, "There are other gifted children living in the villages along the southern shores and the hinterlands of the Hebes Sea. Bush folk, as they are known. They are really nice people."

Mystal raised her hand and queried, "And you'd like to bring those children here for training?"

Charlene replied honestly, "Yes. They would not have to know precisely where Sweetness is. If no one tells them otherwise, they'll will think they're at the academy at Elysium. Then they could board, in the new school and be trained along with the other students."

There was a moment of silence as the thirteen elders conversed silently amongst themselves.

Finally Mystal announced, "We do not like the concept of deceiving the children, but yes, we do agree. As long as the gifted children of the bush folk are not told the precise location of Sweetness, it will be allowed. We will consider ways to make this work."

Charlene beamed with a huge smile, "Thank you, Thank you all."

"So is our business for the day concluded?", Mystal asked.

"Sadly no", Forkbraid replied.

"There's more?", questioned Cadmus.

"Isn't there always Cadmus", Forkbraid replied adding, "Much like your town, the New Flinders Psychic Academy has a council. We call it the Grey Council and it's modelled on the Grey Councils back on the Earth. There are thirteen seats at the table. We currently only have three people on our Grey Council and we need thirteen to be complete."

"So your Grey Council needs another ten members?", Cadmus queried.

"Yes and no. We have too few council members at the moment. We can make do with eight as a bare minimum", Forkbraid explained, adding, "The issue is that the council members all need to be level nine psychics or higher and ideally they need to be experienced. Ordinarily, we would build up the council over time and groom our own people specifically for the Grey Council, however given the current circumstances, we need to speed up the process."

"So how can we help with that?", Mystal enquired.

"Grey Council members are generally over thirty years of age, however, if a candidate is exceptional, the age limit can be dropped, usually as low as twenty five. In some extraordinary cases as with Lady Selene and I, we were inducted into the Flinders Psychic Academy's Grey Council on Earth at the age of twenty one. So the age limit can be quite flexible. The most important factor is, that the candidate be a level nine psychic and preferably groomed for the position", Forkbraid explained.

"All the members of your Town Council are level nine psychics. I have met several members of your council and each of those members would be suitable candidates to join our Grey Council", Forkbraid replied honestly.

"Okay Forkbraid. So what is your proposal?", Mystal queried.

"I was thinking that perhaps one or two, perhaps even more, of your council members, might consider volunteering to join our Grey Council", Forkbraid admitted.

Carly spoke up, "Ah hmm. Forkbraid. Would that not leave our council short on members?"

"Perhaps. Perhaps not", Forkbraid replied, asking, "Does your Town Council groom suitable replacements, to take over the positions of those council members who step down?"

Mystal replied, "We do and we have more than a few people, who could replace any council members who volunteer to join your Grey Council."

"Then the concept is feasible?", Forkbraid queried.

"Yes. It is more than feasible Forkbraid", Mystal replied, then after a short pause, "Tell me. Young Roseanne. You mentioned she may need further guidance."

"Yes I did. Roseanne does indeed need further guidance", Forkbraid replied.

Town Council Elder Mystal stood up and announced, "Council members. I hereby step down as head Elder. Cadmus, you will replace me as I once replaced you. I hereby step down from the Council of Elders. Forkbraid, I am your first volunteer to your Grey Council."

The rest of the Town Council Elders looked to one and another, they were somewhat confused.

Mystal was still standing, "I have made my decision", she stated emphatically.

"Thank you Mystal", Forkbraid responded, "This was not something I had expected."

"I have a vested interest in young Roseanne Rhein. I can give her far better guidance, if I am at your academy, can I not? Being on your Grey Council, puts me in the correct place at the correct time", Mystal explained.

Forkbraid nodded in agreement.

Two of the other Council Elders looked at each other and then one of them, Zephyr spoke, "Garnet and I wish to volunteer for the New Flinders Psychic Academy's Grey Council."

"Zephyr, Garnet, is this true? Is this what you wish?", Mystal enquired.

Garnet replied, "We know that we are the youngest of our Town's Elders, but their academy is in dire need. We feel that if we become Grey Council members, Zephyr and I can really help out in setting up the temporary academy here in the vale. I'm certain that we can benefit their academy."

Zephyr added, "We have been quietly processing the possibility as Lord Forkbraid spoke. I agree with Garnet, we can definitely benefit their academy."

"Then if you are both certain, so be it", Mystal replied, adding, "Garnet and Zephyr will step down from the Town Council of Elders and be inducted into the New Flinders Psychic Academy's Grey Council. We will choose three new Elders from those whom we have groomed."

Forkbraid nodded to Garnet and Zephyr and spoke softly, "Thank you."

"You said you already had three Grey Council members Forkbraid", Mystal noted.

"Yes. Our third member is a local Martian man. One of the bush folk from a small village along the southern coast of the Hebes Sea called Podvil. He was their village Kujur, he's a level nine psychic and extremely talented", Forkbraid replied.

Forkbraid commented, "That will bring our Grey Council to six. I can check with Lady Selene if any of our level nines at the academy are ready to be inducted, to bring the number up to eight. Which then bring us to the final point of discussion."

"What would that be?", asked Cadmus.

"Remote viewers", Forkbraid replied.

"Remote viewers would be my area of expertise Forkbraid", Kubrick noted, "Although we call them watchers here."

"Remote viewers on the Earth are responsible for tracking down criminal elements, so that the authorities can arrest them", Forkbraid explained.

"That is somewhat different to what we do here", Kubrick replied, explaining, "Here we watch people approaching, so we can ensure our glamour is cloaking the town effectively."

"Yes, similar, but not the same. Quite different purposes in fact. Back on the Earth we had seventy two remote viewing teams, called Wyverns. Each wyvern had thirteen members. We had a council of thirteen, the Serpent Council, that managed the Wyverns. Six remote viewing teams per council member. The thirteenth council member, the Viperous one, was the head remote viewer and ran the whole show", Forkbraid explained.

"And you were that Viperous one", Kubrick noted in understanding.

"Yes I was", Forkbraid replied, adding, "Selene and I were hoping to set up six Wyverns, with four remote viewers each. We would begin our Serpent Council with one member, the Viperous one and then we'd grow the Wyverns and the Serpent Council over time. We've already located two terrorist cells here on Mars, we seriously need to locate any others that might be out there."

"So your academy is looking for talented remote viewers", Kubrick commented.

"Yes Kubrick. That we are", Forkbraid admitted, "We have some in training back at the academy and they may be ably to fill up to twenty places."

"But your need twenty four?", Kubrick enquired.

"Yes. We expect we'll be four short of requirements", Forkbraid admitted.

"Well then. I personally can't help as I'm in charge of our watchers", Kubrick replied, then stated, "I will ask around our watcher community for volunteers though. We might find the four you need."

"Excellent Kubrick. Thank you", Forkbraid replied, then he chuckled and remarked, "I have yet to tell Selene that she will be the Serpent Council's Viperous one."

"You won't fill that position yourself Forkbraid?", Mystal queried.

"The Viperous one needs to be on Mars full time and I could be off world far too often to wear that hat", Forkbraid explained, "That leaves Selene, as the only other person I know of at the academy that would be qualified to fill that position."

Marcus who had been quietly sitting there, spoke up, "Our chief engineer Varak, he's on board our ship. We could check out the suitability of those old colonies to be converted into a boarding school while we're here."

"We could. We do have the time", Forkbraid agreed, "That's assuming that your Town Council is happy for us to do so."

"It would appear to be an opportune time", Mystal agreed.

"If I may?", Marcus asked, as he held up his left arm and his grip.

"You may?", Mystal replied.

Marcus pressed a few key strokes on his grip and after a few moments, Varak's smiling face appeared as a three D image above the grip.

"Yes Marcus. What can I do for you?", Varak asked.

"There are old colonies burrowed into the cliffs at the back of the vale", Marcus informed Varak, explaining, "We may be able to convert one or two of them into a boarding school."

"An ingenious concept", Varak replied, adding, "If someone can provide me with the coordinates, I can take some of my metal men with me and have a look. They may indeed be suitable for conversion."

"Metal men?", questioned Marcus.

"Androids. Sorry Marcus, some of Nyaliep's terminology seems to be rubbing off on me", Varak admitted.

Marcus chuckled, "Yep. Mars changes everything. So it seems does Nyaliep."

Varak's three D image chuckled as well.

"Varak. Tomorrow Gareth will show you to the old colonies. Once inside, you and your 'metal men' can make your assessments as to suitability", Mystal informed him.

"Noted. Then tomorrow it is. I will meet Gareth at sunrise tomorrow", Varak replied.

Gareth spoke one word, "Agreed!"

"Anything else I can help you with?", Varak asked.

Marcus looked at Forkbraid who shook his head, "No, that's all Varak" and the image of Varak then disappeared.

"So if your ship is going to be here tomorrow, that will give Garnet, Zephyr and I time to prepare and pack for the journey to your Academy", Mystal remarked.

"Are you sure?", Forkbraid asked, explaining, "There's no need to leave straight away. Candy and Cormac regularly travel to New Tortuga to manage their farms. They could always pick you up on one of their trips, on the way back."

Garnet replied, "The decision is made Forkbraid. Here in the vale, we do not dilly dally. It is decided, we will leave with your ship tomorrow."

"If you are certain, then so be it. Later tomorrow afternoon you will accompany us to the academy", Forkbraid replied.

"Then it is done", Mystal replied.

9. Family Dynamics

The Prophet and Matthew were strolling through a local park in the northern end cap of Ganymede Prime.

The Prophet looked around at their surroundings, "Why are we here Matthew? Why are we in this park?"

"Here I can be sure that no one is listening in", Matthew replied as he looked towards a local hill and the bench that sat atop it, "Let's go up there", he pointed.

A few minutes later they were atop the hill and sitting on the bench, which provided quite a clear view of the park around them.

Matthew looked around before starting, they appeared to be alone and were not being observed, "Being a Captain in the Jovian Armed Forces does have its uses."

"In what way Matthew?", the Prophet asked.

"I've pretty much got access to everything", Matthew replied, "Except of course, if it's on their network servers, every access is logged."

"So if you access anything sensitive, they'd know about it", the Prophet replied.

"That's the score", Matthew replied, adding, "So I accessed their archives instead. They're not computerised and so they are not logged."

"What did you find Matthew? It must be really sensitive if we're sitting here in a park?", the Prophet enquired.

"It is sensitive, seriously sensitive", Matthew informed the Prophet, then began to divulge what he'd found.

"The Horridian siblings were all born quite closely together, roughly two years apart. Heinrich was eight when Luisa was born", Matthew explained, adding, "Leopold was born nearly five years after Luisa, when Heinrich was almost thirteen."

"So Leopold is the odd one out?", the Prophet queried.

"The odd one out yes, but there's more. Much more. I have been reading their Mother's diaries", Matthew admitted.

"Their Mother's diaries?", the Prophet questioned.

"Yes. Everything about the siblings is in those diaries", Matthew explained, adding, "When their parents married, their Father was a heavy drinker, but he got worse over time. Before Heinrich had turned ten, his Father had become a drunkard, a habitual drunkard. He'd wake up and start drinking straight away and at the end of the day he'd pass out, where ever he happened to be."

"That doesn't sound good", the Prophet remarked.

"Worse. Because he was an habitual drunkard, his hygiene suffered accordingly and he became incontinent", Matthew informed the Prophet.

Matthew continued, "He'd rarely find his way to the marital bed and where ever he passed out would get soiled. Badly soiled. So the servants would have to clean up after him every morning. As a result, their mother slept in another room with her doors locked. In her diaries, she wrote down, that she could no longer stand the stench of her own husband."

"I see what you mean by sensitive", the Prophet commented.

"You do see the problem though don't you?", Matthew asked the Prophet.

"Problem?", the Prophet questioned.

Matthew explained, "From before Heinrich turned ten, their mother slept alone in a separate locked bedroom. It's all in her diaries. Leopold was not conceived by his Sibling's Father."

"What? What are you saying Matthew?", the Prophet replied.

"It's not stated explicitly in her dairies, but is alluded to. It's in the way their Mother writes about Heinrich. It is very clear that she was sleeping with her son", Matthew informed him.

"What? Are you serious?", the Prophet asked.

"She didn't write it explicitly, but it's fairly clear to anyone that reads what she wrote, that she did sleep with Heinrich", Matthew replied.

"This is explosive stuff Matthew!", the Prophet exclaimed.

"Yep. It sure is. Leopold was born when Heinrich was almost thirteen and his mother passed away shortly after the birth from complications", Matthew replied, "Heinrich is both Leopold's Father and his Brother."

"Now I understand why we are here Matthew", the Prophet remarked.

"This explains their entire family dynamic", Matthew put forward.

"It does?", the Prophet questioned.

"Well it does when you have the other information I came across", Matthew replied.

"You mean there's more?", the Prophet enquired.

"Yeah. There sure is. Those diaries contain information on the Siblings", Matthew replied, adding, "For instance Princess Luisa had a habit of beheading her dolls from a very young age."

"That doesn't sound so bad", the Prophet remarked.

"Well no, until she started beheading the family pets", Matthew informed him.

"Really?", the Prophet questioned.

"It's all in their Mothers diaries", Matthew explained.

"Princess Sophia also had her own issues", Matthew continued, "Sophia fantasised that she was an evil Witch and had a habit of playing around with 'potions'. Several of the families horses died as a result of being poisoned."

"You are kidding aren't you Matthew?", the Prophet asked, almost as a plea.

"No joking. Seriously both Sisters were diagnosed with narcissistic personality disorders and psychopathy", Matthew replied.

"Maybe that explains why they were both sent to the Trojan colonies", the Prophet speculated.

"I think there is more to it than that", Matthew replied, stating, "That last meeting was a real eye opener into their family dynamics."

Matthew continued, "We now know why Heinrich favours his younger brother Leopold. He's very protective of his eldest son."

"That does makes a lot of sense", the Prophet agreed.

"Their Mother died from complications of Leopold's birth", Matthew continued, "Luisa, Sophia and Wulfric are resentful of that and blame Leopold. Valdamar is more pragmatic. Given his Sisters diagnosis, Heinrich had to send them to the Trojan colonies and he keeps Wulfric close, on a very tight leash. It's all about keeping Leopold safe."

"It all seems to make sense, but can you really be sure Matthew?", the Prophet asked.

"There is one thing that kind of clinches it", Matthew replied, then explained, "The rules of succession in the Jovian Realms are very clear. The High Prince's male children are favoured over his female children. So the line of succession goes by gender and birth date."

"Gender and birth date", the Prophet repeated.

"The eldest male child becomes the new High Prince and Prince of Ganymede, then the line of succession follows the children by gender and birth date. Callisto, Europa, Io, the Fore Trojans and the Aft Trojans are assigned to each child accordingly", Matthew explained.

"What happens to the existing rulers of those realms, their Aunts and Uncles?", the Prophet enquired.

"Under Jovian law, they are forced to step down and retire in favour of the new rulers from the new High Prince's family", Matthew explained.

"And if they don't step down?", the Prophet queried.

"Then they get arrested. All of them know the rules and high treason is punishable by death", Matthew informed him.

"Okay, so how does the line of succession clinch it Matthew?", the Prophet asked

"The line of succession is automatic. There is absolutely no need for the High Prince to intervene and it can only be changed by the current High Prince himself", Matthew replied, then added, "High Prince Heinrich, has had a document written up with special instructions with regards the line of succession upon his death."

"Oh. I think I understand. He would not need to do that, unless he wanted elevate a bastard Son?", the Prophet replied questioningly.

"Precisely. Heinrich has had a document created, that affects the line of succession and it should be superfluous, unless he wants to change that line of succession", Matthew concluded.

"In favour of Leopold as his eldest Son", the Prophet replied, "No wonder High Prince Heinrich and Prince Leopold look so similar. They're not only Brothers, they're also Father and Son!"

"It is all kinds of bizarre and bewildering isn't it", Matthew replied.

The Prophet simply nodded and remarked, "Heinrich obviously knows all about this, but do any of his Siblings?"

"I don't think so", Matthew replied, "As far as I can tell, none of the other Siblings know that Heinrich is Leopold's Father, not even Leopold. However, there has to be others that know."

"Others?", the Prophet questioned.

"Yes. There has to be. Otherwise, if anything happens to Heinrich, how do his wishes with regards the line of succession get carried out", Matthew replied, explaining, "Heinrich has placed Leopold in the safest possible Realm within the Jovian Realms. There has to be people in the right places, who are specifically placed to ensure Heinrich's succession document is carried out. These people will be Heinrich's most trusted people."

"This is beginning to sound like a powder keg", the Prophet remarked.

"If anything happens to High Prince Heinrich, it could well be", Matthew agreed.

After their discussion, the Prophet and Matthew stood up from the bench and started walking back to their apartment building.

Around twenty minutes later they arrived at their apartments. Waiting patiently in the foyer of their apartment's level, they found General Tarzan.

The General looked at the Prophet and then at Matthew, "Gentlemen. We need to talk."

The Prophet and Matthew looked at each other, then the Prophet replied, "By all means General, please enter my office" and they all entered the Prophet's apartment.

General Tarzan placed his index finger in front of his lips to indicate to the Prophet and Matthew that they should not say anything. Then the trio sat down around a table and General Tarzan took a device out his pocket. It was squat and cylindrical in shape. The General placed the device on the table and turned it's top clockwise. The device began to glow softly.

The Prophet asked, "Are these apartments bugged?"

"Not that I know of", the General replied, adding, "but it never hurts to be cautious gentlemen."

"So what can we do for you General?", the Prophet asked.

"I need to speak to Matthew here", the General replied.

"Me General. What can I help you with?", Matthew asked.

"You've been poking around in the archives Matthew", the General stated.

"Yes I have General. After the last meeting, I thought it might be prudent to understand the dynamics of the Brothers", Matthew admitted.

The General looked at Matthew for a long moment, "I appreciate you candour Matthew. I do have people watching the archives, so I know what you've been researching."

"That is interesting. So then you know, what I know", Matthew replied.

"Prince Leopold's parentage. Of course I do. So does General Snide", General Tarzan admitted.

"So that would make yourself and General Snide, the people who would ensure a smooth succession should anything happened to the High Prince", Matthew noted.

"There are more than just two of us Matthew", the General replied, then asked, "I'm assuming you've told the Prophet?"

"He has", the Prophet admitted.

"Than it's a case of what to do with the pair of you?", the General asked more of himself.

"That is completely in your hands General", Matthew informed him.

General Tarzan was quite for long moments and then told Matthew and the Prophet, "Consider yourselves 'read in'. Do not repeat any of this information to anyone. This conversation did not happen Gentlemen."

The General then switched off his jamming device and replaced it in his pocket.

"Thank you Gentlemen, our business is concluded", the General told them, "I'll see you tomorrow Matthew. I'll see myself out" and then the General left.

"I thought you said their archive access wasn't logged", the Prophet commented.

"It isn't. This is something different. I'd bet they have some kind of lo-jack on certain books in their archive", Matthew speculated.

"We have to be more careful Matthew. That could have gone a very different way", the Prophet recommended.

"Indeed it could have my Lord and yet, here we still are", Matthew replied, adding, "I think we've just been inducted into something rather big!"

The next day Matthew and the Prophet arrived at the palace for another security meeting. All of the usual faces were present, except for Prince Leopold. The Horridian Sisters representatives were present as well. When High Prince Heinrich entered the meeting room and took his seat at the table, everyone else took theirs.

Princess Luisa's representative, Callthrope cleared his throat, "Your Majesty. If I may."

The High Prince nodded and replied, "You may."

"The Aft Trojan Armed Forces have returned home. They are now back in the Aft Trojan colonies", Representative Callthrope informed the room.

"That is good to hear Callthrope", the High Prince replied before asking, "How is my little Sister handling it?"

Callthrope gulped slightly and replied, "Princess Luisa wants to arrest the Captains of the Fleet and have them publicly executed. The Princess is most insistent about it."

"And no doubt she wants to drop the damned guillotine blade herself", and angry High Prince replied as he rubbed his forehead, "What is it about blades and beheading Callthrope? Why that particular fixation?"

Before Callthrope could answer, the Prophet muttered the word, "Psychopathy", before back tracking, "My apologies Your Majesty. I spoke out of turn."

"No. No. You are right, psychopathy is the correct word, although we do not use that term here", the High Prince responded.

Prince Valdamar waded in, "It's a sensitive topic. We prefer the terms, affliction or predilection."

Matthew chimed in with, "Oh. Now I get it. Callthrope and Kittens aren't really representatives as such, they're really overseers, probably even clinicians."

Prince Valdamar clapped his hands, "Now you get it Captain. Brother Heinrich keeps our Sisters on a very short leash."

"Valdamar!", the High Prince chastised, then to Matthew, "Our Sisters have certain afflictions and this causes them to have certain predilections. We have people, advisers, at their end who help to keep them on track."

Prince Wulfric waded in, "Advisers", he scoffed, "They are their bloody minders!"

"Wulfric!", the High Prince chastised his other Brother, then admitted, "although Wulfric is correct. They are their minders."

"Callthrope. Kittens. Review our Sisters medications. Make sure they don't relapse", the High Prince ordered, then to Callthrope specifically, "Princes Luisa is NOT to arrest or behead anyone. Is that understood?"

"Yes Your Majesty", Callthrope replied.

Matthew questioned, "Your Majesty. Did the previous Aft Trojan rebellion coincide with a relapse?"

The High Prince replied, "Yes Captain. It did."

"And the 'advisers' Your Majesty", Matthew enquired.

"Their heads were the first to roll", the High Prince admitted, adding, "After that, thing deteriorated rather rapidly."

Prince Wulfric gave off a loud belly laugh, "Deteriorated! Heads were rolling hand over fist!"

The High Prince pounded his fist on the table, "Wulfric! Enough!"

The Prophet carefully stepped in, "The situation sounds rather volatile Your Majesty."

"It is", the High Prince admitted, "That's why Callthrope here is going to make sure everything runs smoothly."

Callthrope gulped slightly once more and replied, "I will do my best Your Majesty."

"Yes you will Callthrope, yes you will", the High Prince replied, then ordered, "Callthrope. Kittens. Get to work. Make sure ours Sisters are stable. We cannot afford either of them relapse during a time of War."

Both Callthrope and Kittens replied, "Yes Your Majesty", before leaving the room to go about the respective tasks.

"Now then. This was meant to be a quick meeting about our assets on Mars", the High Prince reminded everyone, then nodded to General Tarzan.

General Tarzan began his summary, "Matthew, that is the Captain and I, have located two cells on Mars and we have been in contact with them."

"That is wonderful news General", the High Prince responded with a new smile upon his face.

"One of those cells has made two attempts to infiltrate the Elysium colony and the enemy's fortress", General Tarzan informed the room.

"And the results General?", the High Prince was eager for good news.

"The results have not been successful Your Majesty", the General admitted.

The High Prince took on a more disappointed visage, "Let's hear it then."

"Their first infiltration attempt was at the Elysium colony and it failed. They attempted to land at the Elysium airfield, pretending to be a tourist group", the General informed everyone, "When they landed, they found themselves surrounded by heavily armed security personnel. They were allowed to refuel and leave."

"Their next attempt was at the enemy's fortress. They aren't very happy about that one", the General remarked.

"Why? What happened?", Prince Valdamar quickly asked.

"When they arrived at the coordinates we provided in our wanted video, they were just expecting some kind of small outpost, maybe a small base. They did not expect to find a *'huge impenetrable fortress'*, their words, not mine", the General told everyone, adding, "They weren't very happy about that, it was not expected. They noted, it would *'take an army to take, hold and search'* the enemy's fortress. Again their words, not mine."

"So they just gave up and ran away", Prince Wulfric scoffed.

"No Your Highness", the General replied before continuing, "They also found the fortress was surrounded by three rings of ant-aircraft batteries and found themselves *'target locked'*. So they could not even approach our enemy's fortress. They were not aware this was case and naturally, are not happy about the fact, they were not informed about the fortress's defences."

"So they did run away then!", Prince Wulfric scoffed once more.

"Actually no Your Highness", the General replied, continuing, "They decided to take the local airfield that was near the fortress and managed to successfully land."

The High Prince was smiling once more, "What did they find?", he enquired.

The General nodded, "Your Majesty. The bounty hunters took up positions near the largest hanger. The one they suspected the Gunship Solstice to be in. Then eleven of them broke into the hanger and secured it."

Prince Wulfric was quick with a "Yes!" and pumped hist fists in the air.

The General continued, "The hanger was empty. The Martian Gunship Solstice was not there."

Prince Valdamar chided, "Too quick to celebrate there Brother."
General Tarzan continued, "There were quite a few Androids working in the hanger and our bounty hunters got some information out of their supervising Android."

"Wait a minute General", the High Prince replied, then he turned to Matthew asking, "Captain. Androids. Can Androids self manage?"

Matthew replied, "Why yes Your Majesty. It would be common practice to have a group of Android working on a task and then have a higher model Android working as their supervisor."

The High Prince responded, "Extraordinary! Why don't we have Androids?"

Matthew explained, "Your Majesty. It's a technology that the Jovian Realms simply does not have. We would either have to develop that technology in-house or import it from the Earth or L5."

"Well then, our enemies are certainly not going to help us out are they?", the High Prince responded, it was a rhetorical question.

The General continued, "After interrogating the supervising Android, they found out that the Solstice was on a mission. Of course naturally, the Solstice's crew were also on that same mission. Our bounty hunters did try to locate the Solstice's specifications and blueprints. Apparently those are stored on an *'air gapped computer system, in secure chambers beneath the fortress'*, again their words, not mine."

"So no ship, no crew and no information about their ship", Prince Wulfric scoffed.

"We did get some information Your Highness", the General offered, continuing, "The Androids were making a very particular alloy. There were making plasteel."

This time Matthew was the quick one, "Plasteel! Now that is very interesting."

"How so Captain?", the High Prince enquired.

"Well Your Majesty, it could indicate that the Solstice has a plasteel hull", Matthew replied, adding, "And considering my analysis of the images we have of the Solstice, shows no signs of joins or welds, it could indicate an advanced single piece plasteel hull."

"That does not sound good", Prince Valdamar remarked.

Prince Wulfric replied, "Brother, if this is the case, then no, it is not good. We can't even make plasteel. None of our ships have that kind of hull."

"Your Highness's, it could be worse. Those Androids could have been making polyceramalloy", Matthew informed them.

"How is that worse Captain?", the High Prince asked.

"Your Majesty, there is not a single weapon system in all of the Jovian Realms that can penetrate a polyceramalloy hull", Matthew explained.

"How many ships do they have with polyceramalloy hulls?", a worried Prince Wulfric questioned, not really wanting to hear the answer.

"It's hard to say Your Highness. Polyceramalloy is usually used like a top coat, over a more mundane titanium hull", Matthew replied, explaining, "Plasteel has been replacing titanium alloys. So a hull made of plasteel and coated in polyceramalloy would be quite formidable. A hull of solid polyceramalloy, would be almost impenetrable to anything we can throw at it."

That reply caught everyone one in the room by surprise. Everyone, was looking from one to another and waiting for someone to say something.

General Tarzan took the silence as an opportunity to continue, "The eleven bounty hunters that broke into the Solstice's hanger were exposed to highly toxic chemicals from the plasteel alloying process. All of them became quite ill and are currently recuperating. Three of the bounty hunters weren't exposed and it was their pilot, someone named Phil who sent us this report."

Matthew quickly stepped in, "General. I have some knowledge of plasteel and its alloying process. I cannot recall what toxic chemicals they could possibly be talking about."

The General replied, "I can only tell you what they've reported Captain, so I couldn't say what chemical or chemicals, they might have been exposed to", then he continued, "One thing they have noted is quite striking. The supervising Android they were interrogating, kept calling the Solstice, the Starship Solstice."

Bang! The room erupted into an uncontrolled tangle of voices, all marked deeply with a combination of both concern and disbelief.

The High Prince stood and raised his right hand, "Silence!", he shouted loudly.

The room very quickly became silent.

"Starship?", the High Prince questioned incredulously.

"Yes Your Majesty. That is precisely what it says in their report", the General replied.

"Okay people. What does this mean? What are the ramifications?", the High Prince asked, then remarked loudly, "One at a time!"

Everyone one in the room turned to Matthew.

"A Starship is any vessel capable of interstellar travel. That is simply put, travelling to the Stars", Matthew informed everyone present.

"Yes Captain, we know that, but do the Earth and L5 have that capability?", the High Prince questioned.

"Your Majesty, they didn't have that capability when I was last there", Matthew replied, adding, "The only way to get to the nearest stars, would be by generation ships and those would be huge and none have ever been built. The Solstice is way too small. Either this is very clever propaganda or some kind of new technology has come into existence that I have not heard about."

"Great. Propaganda or a new technology", Prince Wulfric grumbled, "As if we aren't already too far behind on that front!"

The High Prince ignore his Brother and enquired, "Captain, if this is real, then what are the implications?"

"Your Highness, if this is real, if the Solstice really is a Starship, then they could appear on our doorstep at any moment, at any time", Matthew informed the High Prince, explaining, "If they can get to the Stars, how much easier to get from Mars to Jupiter?", a rhetorical question.

"A ship that can travel unseen, can travel at unheard of speeds and now it could appear on our doorsteps at any time", the High Prince commented, then he ordered, "Generals, make sure our people get their heads around that. We seriously need to step up our game."

All of the Generals answered in the affirmative, "Yes Your Majesty."

The High Prince checked his watch for the time, "I have less than hour before my next meeting, so this meeting is now over. Everyone, get back to work. Your three", the High Prince pointed to General Tarzan, the Prophet and Matthew, "Stay behind. We have things to discuss."

Once the others had left the room, the High Prince nodded to General Tarzan who then took a cylindrical device out of his pocket. Matthew and the Prophet had seen this before. The General placed the device on the table and turned it's top clockwise. The device began to glow softly.

"Even here?", the Prophet queried.

"Even here", the General replied, "Ganymede Prime is a den of intrigue."

"General Tarzan has already told me what you've uncovered Matthew", the High Prince noted, calling Matthew by name, "It was my fault really", he told them.

"How was it your fault Your Majesty?", Matthew questioned.

"Someone with your skills, your intellect and your curiosity. You were bound to find out. I should have read you in on this, the day we made you a Captain", the High Prince admitted.

"Your Majesty, I take it your Siblings don't know?", Matthew asked.

"Correct Matthew. Nor will they know, at least while I'm alive", the High Prince replied.

The Prophet asked, "Your Majesty. This impromptu meeting.....", then he left it hanging.

High Prince Heinrich began to explain, "I keep tabs on all of my Siblings. You know about my Sisters and their *'advisers'*. My Brothers all have advisers as well, only these are real advisers and not minders. They are appointed by my own advisers here at Ganymede Prime. So I own them so to speak. Through them, I keep tabs on everything that happens in the Jovian Realms. Everything!"

"It seems fair Your Majesty, you are the High Prince after all", the Prophet replied.

"Yes, it's also how I know that young Leopold is making a lot more reforms than any of my Siblings actually know", the High Prince admitted.

"And these reforms are allowed Your Majesty", Matthew queried.

"Leopold had increased the productivity of the Amalthean and Ionian mines. Increased the longevity of his Slaves and develop robotic technologies to make his Realm far more productive", the High Prince commented, "How can I possibly disagree with that?

Matthew asked, "Your Majesty, does Prince Leopold know that you know?"

The High prince responded, "Of course he doesn't know, that I know."

"Prince Leopold sounds like he's very good at management, Your Majesty", the Prophet replied.

"Yes. I must admit that I'm quite proud of him", the High Prince replied, then added, "You know. I once asked him to increase the Ionian quotas by ten percent. Do you know what he did?"

"Your Majesty?", Matthew replied questioningly.

"That very moment I asked, he passed me a file containing a proposal to do just that", the High Prince informed them, adding, "Leopold even told me, that they had the capacity to increase the quotas by another ten to fifteen percent. I must admit I was astonished."

"Then why only ten percent Your Majesty", the Prophet asked.

"Leopold explained that, the Jovian Realms did not have the capacity to utilise such an increase and that we'd be better off keeping that extra capacity for a rainy day. I agreed with him", the High Prince was beaming with pride and added, "Sometimes, I wish my Brothers had such nous."

"Prince Leopold does sound impressive Your Majesty. He understands that if production outpaces consumption you have multiple problems. Apart from the need for extra storage and increased storage costs, product prices will drop.

Sometimes it's better to leave the raw materials where they are, until they're needed", Matthew noted.

"That was my point exactly Matthew. Leopold knows what he's doing", The High Prince replied, adding, "And now with this War, that rainy day has come. The Ionian Realm is stepping up production to meet our armaments needs. Leopold does have considerable foresight."

Matthew took a punt and asked, "Your Majesty. The reason that Prince Leopold isn't here, that's your doing, isn't it?"

The High Prince cocked an eye brow, "Quite astute of you Matthew. You may have noticed, that my Brother Wulfric has a habit of pushing Leopold's buttons."

"Yes Your Majesty. I have noticed and I think I understand why", Matthew admitted.

"Yes well. It is the only way to keep Wulfric from getting his just deserts", the High Prince commented, adding, "One day, Wulfric will push Leopold's buttons way too hard and he will loose his head as a result. It came very close the last time."

"I'm not so sure Your Majesty. Prince Leopold seemed to be very controlled", Matthew told the High Prince of his observation.

"Perhaps Matthew, but for the sake of peace in the Realms, I have no wish to take any chances", High Prince Heinrich replied.

"Now Matthew. How much do you know about the plasteel alloying process?", the High Prince enquired.

"I know a little but not a lot Your Majesty", Matthew readily admitted, "For instance, I know you start with a particular grade of steel. It needs to have precise quantities of carbon, chromium, molybdenum and some other elements. Then once you have that, it has to be polymerised to create plasteel. I don't know the quantities or the polymerising process."

"And this polyceramalloy Matthew?", the High Prince enquired.

"That's even trickier Your Majesty", Matthew responded.

"In what way Matthew?", the High Prince queried.

"Well Your Majesty. Your stating point is high grade plasteel. Then you need the purist grade of Titanium and some very specific pure ceramic powders. The whole lot has to be melted down and combined in precisely the correct way. It's very tricky to make and honestly, I don't know the half of it", Matthew explained.

"So how do we find out Matthew?", the High Prince asked straight up.

"Well Your Majesty, I would start first by making enquiries of the Delilah's computers. There may be information in there. The Delilah has a plasteel hull, so it may be possible the ship's computers contain information on the alloying process", Matthew speculated, "If it's not in the ship's computers, we'd need to get the information the Earth or L5."

"And polyceramalloy?", questioned the High Prince.

"I doubt that's in the Delilah's computers your Majesty", Matthew replied, "The only place we can get that information from, would be the Earth or L5."

"A rock and a hard place", the High Prince noted.

The Prophet commented, "Your Majesty. If we can at least find out what ingredients are required, your scientists may be able to infer the process and experimentally recreate it."

"Always the silver lining Prophet", the High Prince smiled, then commanded, "Now off you lot go. I have another meeting to prepare for."

And the impromptu meeting ended.

10. The Grey Council

Forkbraid asked Marcus to fly the Solstice above the Martian atmosphere in a sub-orbital arc on their way home to the academy. He wanted to give their guests, the former Sweetness town elders a good view of Mars from space. Mystal, Garnet and Zephyr were allowed on the bridge of the Solstice to take in the view, which was of course spectacular. Their guests were as much in awe of the Solstice, as they were of the view of Mars on the bridge's screen.

As Marcus began adjusting the Solstice's course to re-enter the Martian atmosphere, on its approach to Elysium, Forkbraid requested that their guests take seats in the engineering department. Mystal, Garnet and Zephyr thanked Forkbraid and his crew for letting them view Mars from above the atmosphere and Varak led them back to the engineering department so they could take their seats in readiness for landing.

The Solstice set down on the academy's airfield, close by Varak's construction hanger. Between the hanger and the Solstice was a group of family and friends from the academy. The main hatch on the Solstice opened and the boarding ramp lowered. One by one the crew disembarked. Mystal, Garnet and Zephyr disembarked along with Forkbraid.

Straight away Peter rushed over to his family. Varak was quick to join Nyaliep. Jim rushed into the arms of his waiting wives Zuawalo and Zeealas, even Zuawalo's ferret Zigg was happy to see him. Zyaliep and Kwoth were standing behind Jim, were equally happy. Charlene and Marcus had joined Selene and Roseanne and together they slowly walked up to Mystal, Garnet and Zephyr.

"And here you have our wonderful family", Forkbraid remarked, gesturing to the gathered group, then to Selene as she approached, questioned, "No Cormac and Candy today?"

"No. They're in New Tortuga picking up six crates of Cherry Wine and six crates of Blueberry Wine for Admiral Zumwalt", Selene replied, then to the three new comers, "Welcome. It's good to see you all. I hope your flight was okay?"

"It was great", Garnet replied, "That is a fantastic ship. My name is Garnet by the way and this is Zephyr. You already know Mystal I believe."

"Yes. It's good to see you all", Selene replied.

Roseanne looked at Mystal, "I remember you, vaguely."

"I'm surprised you remember me at all young lady. You were quite unwell when I last saw you", a smiling Mystal replied.

Forkbraid commented, "We heard all about the excitement Roseanne."

"We did have some issues with bounty hunters, but we managed", Roseanne replied.

"Yes, you did. We found their lair on the Islands in Lake Oudemans in the Noctis Labyrinthus region. All bar three of them were suffering from severe psychosomatic neural issues. They will be ill for weeks I expect", Forkbraid informed her.

Roseanne frowned and replied, "Those bounty hunters were hunting my Sisters and I had to protect them, so I got a bit harsh."

"I can understand your reasons Roseanne, but a bit harsh is an understatement", Forkbraid replied, adding, "I think we need to teach you some more appropriate, less harmful techniques."

"Yes", Selene agreed, "and as Roseanne is my apprentice, it is up to me to teach them."

Forkbraid nodded in agreement, then sent Selene a silent question, *"Sisters?"*

Selene replied, *"Zyaliep has adopted Roseanne, so Zuawalo and Zeealas are now her Sisters."*

"But you've already adopted Roseanne", Forkbraid noted.

"I did explain that to Zyaliep", Selene informed, adding, *"However, Zyaliep explained to me that a girl who has lost her parents, can never have too many Mothers."*

"An interesting cultural quirk", Forkbraid replied.

"Roseanne, you weren't as harsh as Jim wanted to be, I must admit", Forkbraid noted, "When Jim heard that Zuawalo and Zeealas were in danger, he was livid, he wanted to raise the bounty hunter's entire settlement to the ground."

"Oh my. That would be have been awful", Roseanne admitted, "I only did what I did, because I was scared and angry. I just got carried away."

"We know that Roseanne", Forkbraid replied, adding, "Selene will teach you better ways of handling that kind of situation."

"Is your First officer prone to violence Forkbraid?", Garnet enquired.

"No. Not at all. You have to realise that Zuawalo and Zeealas are Jim's wives and they are both pregnant with his children. Jim would do anything to keep them safe and bounty hunters are a definite threat. Especially with these bounties hanging over our heads", Forkbraid explained.

Zephyr chimed in with, "If it was Garnet in a similar situation, I would have responded in the same way. That is human nature after-all."

"Yes, that is true Zephyr", Garnet replied, then she turned to Roseanne, "Studying the subtle arts of the glamour, might be useful to you Roseanne."

"That is exactly what I had in mind Garnet", Selene informed her.

Varak walked up to the new comers, "If you all make your way to our chariots, we can be at the academy in no time at all. I'll have my metal men bring over your luggage."

"Yes. Good idea Varak. We have assigned an apartment for each of you", Selene informed them, "I'm hoping you will like them."

"I'm sure we will", Garnet replied, then remarked, "Zephyr and I will only need one apartment."

"Oh. Okay", Selene replied, not knowing Garnet and Zephyr were a couple, "Although each Grey Council member is assigned an individual apartment. Perhaps adjoining apartments then."

"That does sound okay, but it isn't really necessary", Garnet replied.

"Okay then. Later today there will be an induction ceremony for you to join the Grey Council. The whole academy is looking forwards to meeting you all", Selene informed them.

"It seems that you don't dilly dally at your academy either Selene", Garnet remarked.

As they walked towards the chariots, Forkbraid asked Varak, "Metal men?"

"It seems Nyaliep is rubbing off on me", Varak admitted.

Mystal, Garnet and Zephyr entered the large hall, following Marcus as he led them to a nearby podium. The trio stepped up onto the podium and briefly looked around the hall. It was crowded with both psychics and mundanes. The psychics greatly outnumbered the mundanes as well.

"So many psychics. So many. Their thoughts are so loud", Garnet silently thought.

Lady Selene informed the trio, "Mystal, Garnet, Zephyr, we have brought you here to assess you", then asked, "May we do so?"

Forkbraid added, "You may decline if you wish. The choice is yours to make."

All three answered audibly, "Yes", they had no reservations.

Lady Selene and Lord Forkbraid, looked closely at Mystal and gave her the cold hard stare. The process was quick, far quicker than usual, as they were dealing with known gifted psychics with very high potentials. Mystal, Garnet and Zephyr, as Sweetness Town Council members were known to all be high level nines.

After only a minute, Lady Selene signalled the Android assistant. The Android approached and held out three sashes. All three sashes were black and Lady Selene picked one and placed it over Mystal's head and shoulders. Everyone in the the audience had expected this and there were no surprises at all.

Lady Selene and Lord Forkbraid, looked closely at Garnet and gave her the cold hard stare. Again the process was quick and after only a minute, Lady Selene signalled the Android assistant that was still standing close by. Lady Selene picked another black sash and placed it over Garnet's head and shoulders. Again, this had been entirely expected.

Lady Selene and Lord Forkbraid, then looked closely at Zephyr and gave him the cold hard stare. Again the process was quick and after only a minute, Lady Selene signalled the Android assistant. Lady Selene picked yet another black sash and placed it over Zephyr's head and shoulders.

Lord Forkbraid announced out loudly, so all could hear, "Welcome Sister Folcrom Mystal. Welcome Sister Folcrom Garnet. Welcome Brother Folcrom Zephyr. Grey Council Members all!"

Lady Selene repeated out loudly, so all could hear, "Welcome Sister Folcrom Mystal. Welcome Sister Folcrom Garnet. Welcome Brother Folcrom Zephyr. Grey Council Members all!"

Mystal, Garnet and Zephyr each in turn replied to Selene and Forkbraid, nodding, "Thank you Brother. Thank you Sister."

The whole audience began to clap and cheer. The whole assembly hall descended into an excited uproar. Selene and Forkbraid allowed the cheering to continue for many long moments.

Charlene approached the podium with three cloaks, they were hooded cloaks of the appropriate lengths and coloured the deepest black. Deeper than the darkest sheen of a crows feathers. One by one Charlene passed the cloaks to Selene.

Lady Selene passed a cloak to each of the new Grey Council Members, "You may adorn these cloaks with whatever Sigils and symbols you wish. These are the cloaks of a Folcrom", she smiled.

Mystal, Garnet and Zephyr put on their new cloaks and the audience erupted with claps and cheers once more.

After the cheering had petered out, Mystal enquired, "If we may, we would like to meet our other Grey Council member."

Selene responded, "Gwek is currently back at his village with his apprentice."

"So Gwek is not currently here. That is a shame, we were hoping to get acquainted with all of our fellow Grey Council members", Mystal replied.

"Gwek is currently assessing children from his village and the surrounding villages for possible gifted children that we can train at the academy", Selene informed them.

"They may not to travel very far", Zephyr replied, explaining, "Varak did an assessment of our old underground colonies. His initial assessment was that they were in good condition and several sections were more than suitable."

"That is excellent news. I have been worried with the current circumstances, you know the war and all, that we wouldn't be able to guarantee their safety", Selene admitted.

"Our vale will be more than safe Selene", Garnet announced.

"So how were your apartments?", Selene asked.

Garnet replied with a smile, "More than adequate, quite opulent in fact."

"When Gwek gets back in a few days I really must talk to him about his apartment", Selene noted, "He's been staying in one of the dormitories where some of his fellow villagers are staying."

"You mentioned Gwek has an apprentice?", Garnet enquired.

"Yes. Gwek was the Kujur of his village. He's training his apprentice, Nyapal, as his successor", Selene informed them.

Forkbraid suggested, "We do need to get moving. A dinner in honour of our new council members has been arranged and you guys are our guests of honour. Do not be surprised if some of our people address you as Lord or Lady. As Folcrom, you all receive that title as well."

"That sounds marvellous. I'm hoping you have some of Cormac and Candy's wine available", Garnet replied.

Selene chuckled, "That we do. That we do Lady Garnet."

A few days later the Grey Council members stepped inside the Grey Council Chamber for the first time, since it's repair after the academy was previously attacked by terrorist extremists. The council chamber was a large circular room, capped with a large ornate onion dome. The circular base of the dome was carved with a dozen ornate astrological symbols. Beneath this was another circular layer carved with the twenty-four runes of the elder futhark. It was at the very top of the Academy's central keep.

Garnet remarked, "I thought the dome was beautiful from the outside, but this, this is incredible."

"Yes. Varak spent a lot of time with his Androids fixing it", Selene replied, noting, "After the terrorist attack, the entire onion dome had collapsed in on itself. It's good to see it whole again."

Mystal noted, "We are at the very top, just underneath of the dome are we not?"

Selene replied, "Above that ceiling and roof, is nothing but sky."

As they entered deeper into the council chamber, they found themselves in front of a large circular table that was open the near end. There were thirteen chairs setup around the outside of the circular table. Inside the circular table were three other chairs. At the far end, off to one side sat a small, wizened, dark man, Gwek. In front of him, on the table sat a folder.

Selene walked around the table directly to the central chair, that was beside Gwek and before sitting down, requested, "Please take a seat. There are plenty to choose from", then turned to Gwek and introduced him to the others, "This is Gwek."

Gwek stood up, bowed slightly, then greeted the new comers, "I am Gwek", he stated simply.

Selene looked around at the new councillors and introduced them, "Gwek, this is Mystal, Garnet and Zephyr", then she took her seat, requesting, "Please be seated."

Forkbraid sat down in the chair on Selene's right.   Mystal sat down in the next available chair next to Forkbraid on Selene's right. Similarly Garnet and then Zephyr sat down in the next available chairs on Selene's left.   The greetings continued for a few minutes before quieting down.

"So Gwek, how was your trip?", Selene enquired.

"It was quite productive", Gwek replied, as he passed Selene his folder, "I found ten suitable candidates for the academy, all aged between seven and eleven."

"That does sound wonderful Gwek", Selene happily replied, asking as she perused the documents in the folder, "What about these other six names."

"They are candidates aged between twelve to fifteen", Gwek explained, adding, "They are all gifted, although I expect they will need, one on one training as apprentices."

"Yes, well that can be arranged Gwek", Selene informed him, "We do have teachers here, who can mentor the older students."

Garnet stepped in and commented, "Gwek, you will pleased to know that your village children won't have to travel very far for their training."

Gwek was surprised, thinking the children would be going to the academy, "How so?", he asked.

Selene explained, "With the war and the academy being a target, I don't believe we can provide the necessary degree of safety. The Sweetness Town Council has graciously agreed to convert some of their old underground colonies into a boarding school."

"The town of Sweetness is not very far away from the villages and it is protected by a glamour", Gwek responded, "The families of the gifted children will be pleased to know this."

"Except, we can't tell them Gwek", Selene replied, "We would like everyone to believe that the children are at the academy."

"Why is that?", Gwek queried.

Forkbraid stepped in, "Sweetness is a hidden town. It's very existence is a tightly kept secret. As long as that is the case, the children will all be safe."

"And when this war is over and safety can be guaranteed once more, we can move the children to the academy here", Selene completed Forkbraid's explanation.

Gwek nodded in understanding, "I agree with that. The children's safety is our main concern."

There was the sound of a buzzer and Selene checked the touch screen that was embedded into the table in front of her. It was Charlene and Marcus. Selene tapped the touch screen and a virtual keyboard appeared. Selene pushed a few keystrokes on the touch screen's virtual keyboard. Each of the thirteen seating positions had touch screens embedded into the table.

The door opened and Charlene and Marcus entered the chamber. They both entered the inside area of the circular table and while Charlene sat on one of the three available chairs, Marcus passed Selene a folder before sitting down in one of the other chairs next to Charlene.

Selene opened the folder and had a quicker perusal of its contents. There was a single document that has been copied five times for each of the other councillors. Selene removed the five copies and passed them left and right, so that all of the councillors had their own copies.

"Varak has prepared these specifications and blueprints, for the changes he wants to make to turn some of those old colonies into boarding schools", Charlene informed them.

Marcus added, "The actual changes are quite simple and funnily enough, relatively minor."

"Is Varak here?", Mystal enquired.

"Varak is working with his Androids at the construction hanger", Charlene replied, "Ensuring that his Androids fully comprehend the specifications and instructions."

"Even before we have approved the work?", Mystal queried.

"Varak is usually five steps ahead of almost everyone. He's anticipating your approval", Charlene readily admitted.

"And if we don't approve?", Zephyr questioned.

"Then Varak will adjust the plans in accordance with your recommendations and then present you with revised plans", Marcus replied, adding, "Varak is very efficient in this regard."

Garnet stepped in an added, "Then we must be equally efficient. We will discuss these plans straight away and have an answer for Varak before the end of the day."

"Thank you", Charlene and Marcus replied, before bowing and leaving the council chamber.

"Straight to work it seems", Garnet remarked.

"Oh yes Garnet. No dilly dallying here", Selene replied with a smile.

"Okay. Garnet, Zephyr. You both know your town better than I do, obviously. Is it okay if I put you two in charge of liaising with Sweetness and the enrolment of the towns gifted?", Selene asked.

Garnet replied, "Of course Selene. We'd be delighted. That is why we are here after-all."

"Excellent. Roseanne can help you both with all of the relevant forms and paperwork. I'll give her a heads up after this meeting", Selene informed them.

"If I may Selene", Mystal interjected, "I'd like to help with Roseanne's training. I can help with advance glamour techniques."

"Oh. Okay. I was going to train Roseanne in that area myself Mystal. However, I am happy to accept your help", Selene accepted, adding, "To be honest, managing both the academy and the Elysium colony does take up a lot of my time."

"Yes Selene. I'm just noticing that, which is why I offered", Mystal replied.

Zephyr commented, "I've been reading Varak's plans for the colony conversion. I must say the Man is very thorough. Especially considering how quickly he put them together."

Selene replied, "Yes Zephyr. Varak is exceedingly thorough. His work is high quality as well."

"Where on Mars did you find him Selene?", Garnet enquired.

"Where on Earth actually Garnet", Selene replied, elaborating, "Varak use to work for General Products Corporation, in their Space Technology Division."

"Really? That does sound like a highly lucrative job. How did you manage to lure him away?", Garnet queried.

"Well, it was before this academy was even designed and we needed an Engineer. So we put out the usual adverts for the position and Varak was one of the many applicants", Selene replied, adding, "After seeing Varak's resume and speaking to his references, the Flinders Psychic Academy on Earth invited him to stay there for a few days and attend an interview or two."

Selene continued, "Varak liked the Flinders Psychic Academy and the concept of building a new academy on Mars intrigued him. Working on Mars and having a free rein with regards his creativity, he quickly jumped at the opportunity. We were all impressed with his references. Varak was described as the Man who can build anything."

Zephyr commented, "It certainly sounds like you were lucky."

"We were Zephyr. General Products Corporation offered to double and then to triple his salary. Varak told them no", Selene informed them, "To Varak, creativity is everything and at General Products, he was being stifled."

"This academy, that ship, the Solstice", Zephyr remarked, "His creativity appears to be leading to major innovations. He appears to be completely unbounded."

"Yes", Selene entirely agreed, "Then we had another piece of luck."

"In what way?", enquired Garnet.

"Forkbraid's Science officer. Peter Swann", Selene replied.

"Yes. That was quite serendipitous", Forkbraid agreed, explaining, "Peter and his family came to Mars after their daughter Miranda had been kidnapped and taken here as a hostage."

That caught Garnet by surprise, "Really?", she questioned.

"Yes. Really", Forkbraid confirmed, adding, "After Miranda was freed, the Swanns decided that Mars was a good place to live, compared to their previous home at L5's Hyper Dynamics colony."

Selene stepped in, "And it turned out Peter was a brilliant cybernetics expert. The Man is brilliant. He can do celestial mechanics and quantum math in his head."

"Wow. Talk about luck. Imagine that. He could just as easily been a janitor", Garnet replied.

"Luck indeed. If we give a problem to Varak and Peter, we not only get a solution. We get the most innovative solution possible", Forkbraid informed them.

While the Grey Council members were reviewing Varak's plans and discussing them amongst themselves, the buzzer sounded once again. Selene checked her screen again. It was Jim Murphy, her Head of Security and Forkbraid's First officer requesting communications. A screen was located on the wall above the entrance to the chamber. Selene put Jim on the screen.

"Yes Jim. What can we do for you?", Selene asked.

"A handful of things actually", Jim replied.

"Spill it Jim, whats first on the list?", Forkbraid requested.

"I've been advised by Admiral Zumwalt that thirty six destroyers are one their way here", Jim informed everyone, adding, "It's a combined fleet of Earth and L5 ships."

"Thirty six!", Selene noted, "That's a lot of ships Jim."

"What do we know Jim?", Forkbraid enquired.

"One. The military base on Deimos is now fully operational. Two. Those thirty six destroyers will be refuelling at Deimos", Jim replied, pausing for a moment, "Three. Those thirty six destroyers will be leaving Deimos on their respective missions."

"Missions Jim? That was missions? Plural? Yes?", Forkbraid requested clarification.

"Yes FB. Missions. Plural", Jim confirmed.

"Do we know what those missions are?", Selene requested.

"No idea Selene. The Admiral is playing her cards close to her chest", Jim replied.

"Okay Jim. What's number two?", Forkbraid asked.

"There is a ship on its way from the Pallas colonies. A Belter ship", Jim informed them.

"Okay. Sounds ominous", Selene remarked.

"What do we know Jim?", Forkbraid asked.

"Not a lot. The Admiral tells me it will be here in roughly three days", Jim replied, adding, "And the Admiral wants us, as in the Solstice and its crew, up in orbit with the Vanguard when that Belter ship arrives."

"Okay Jim. We can definitely do that. Let's put the crew on alert for *'manoeuvres'* shall we say", Forkbraid replied.

Selene stepped in and asked, "What's up next on your list Jim?"

"Some unusual information, shall we say", Jim replied mysteriously.

"Unusual? In what way?", a curious Mystal enquired.

"I'll place the relevant files on my network share. Forkbraid and Selene will be able to access them.", Jim replied as he moved the files across, adding, "These are apparently family portraits. Horridian family portraits."

"Horridian family portraits?", Selene questioned as Forkbraid accessed the files and made them available on every councillor's screen.

"Yeah. They've been hitting the news feeds for the last several hours or so", Jim explained.

Seven high definition photographs appeared on the councillor's screens and they all studied them with curiosity. The Horridian Sisters both appeared in their portraits alone, wearing the most incredibly expensive looking gowns and with the most opulent of backgrounds.

The four Horridian Brothers each appeared in their family portraits, with their wives and children. All wearing the finest clothes their respective realms could provide, all except one. The youngest Horridian Brother, Prince Leopold. His family portrait was the odd one out, as he and his family were dressed in much more modest looking clothing

Then when they looked at the Horridian family portrait itself, of all the Siblings, they could see that the two Sisters had been expertly edited into the portrait. However, what stood out the most was that Prince Leopold was again, wearing much more modest clothing compared to the ostentatious clothing of his Siblings.

"Isn't that odd", Garnet noted, "The youngest Brother and his family look much more modest."

"I'm just noticing that myself Garnet", Zephyr agreed.

Mystal also agreed, "He does appear to be the more modest of his Siblings. He and his family."

"What have you noticed Jim?", Forkbraid asked.

Jim replied, "We now have all of their addresses. Princess Luisa is at Patroclus Central in the Aft Trojan colonies. Princess Sophia is at Hector Central in the Fore Trojan colonies. High Prince Heinrich is at Ganymede Prime, Prince Wulfric is at Callisto Prime, Prince Valdamar is at Europa Prime and finally Prince Leopold is at Io Prime. We literally know where they all live. Just look for their Palaces in the Northern end-caps. It would be pretty easy to find them if we needed to."

"Anything else apart from that Jim?", Forkbraid enquired.

"Just the same as you guys", Jim admitted, adding, "They all look very ostentatious, except for Prince Leopold and his family."

Forkbraid noted, "Look at Prince Leopold and his wife Princess Giselle in their family portrait."

They all concentrated on the Prince of Io's family portrait. Then Forkbraid brought up the Horridian family portrait and isolated the picture of Prince Leopold, placing his image beside the Prince's family portrait.

"Do you see it?", Forkbraid remarked

"Yes. Yes I do", Selene suddenly noticed and exclaimed, "Leopold and Giselle are both wearing old fashioned peace symbols!"

"Yes! Bingo!", Forkbraid agreed.

"What does that mean?", a confused Garnet asked.

"The young Prince is sending us a message", Forkbraid replied confidently.

"How can you be sure?", Mystal asked.

"You compare his family's portrait to the others family portraits. Then compare the Prince to his Siblings in the Horridian family portrait and what to you see?", Forkbraid questioned.

"I'm not sure what you mean?", Garnet admitted.

"Prince Leopold's family is a lot more modest than the other Horridian royal families. Prince Leopold is a lot more modest that his Siblings", Forkbraid informed them, summing up, "Prince Leopold and his family are different. That is part of the message."

Selene stepped in, "And the Prince and his wife Giselle are both wearing peace symbols."

"Precisely Selene. Prince Leopold and his wife Giselle are telling the entire solar system, they are different and that they want peace! The message is very subtle", Forkbraid exclaimed.

Gwek asked, "Forkbraid. I understand what you are saying, but how can you be so certain?"

"Prince Leopold is a Horridian. No doubt he has access to the same information and data as his Siblings. By now he has seen images of the Solstice and he knows something about the Solstice's capabilities", Forkbraid replied, "I think this is his way of reaching out and sending us a message."

"I must admit Forkbraid. Even I'm finding this a stretch", Selene commented.

"Think about it Selene. It is a bit odd isn't it. Leopold and Giselle have deliberately made themselves look modest compared to the other Horridians", Forkbraid replied, adding, "And they're both wearing peace symbols."

"So they are different and they want peace", Selene considered, "but seriously Forkbraid. This is just so subtle. Too subtle. How many people would pick up on this? Seriously though?"

"I would say very few. Perhaps a handful of mundanes who understand symbology and noticed the portraits and the obvious differences", Forkbraid speculated, then added, "Amongst the gifted, however, especially those with training, this is very, very noticeable. Subtle yes, but noticeable."

"So what's our next step?", Garnet asked.

"First we contact the Psychic Academies back on Earth, starting with Flinders Psychic Academy. We don't tell them our conclusions, we just ask them for their take, just their opinion so to speak", Forkbraid recommended.

"And if any of them have come to the same conclusion, then we're onto something", Selene replied, then turning to the screen, "Jim. How much of this have you understood?"

Jim replied, "Pretty much all of it."

"Good then. Contact the Flinders Psychic Academy on Earth and ask for their opinion", Selene instructed, "Then get the contact details for the other Psychic Academies and do the same."

"Will do Selene. It's in the vault", Jim replied, tapping his right temple.

"Garnet. Our next step will be in play shortly", Selene informed her.

"Did you guys want to know the last couple of items on my list?", Jim asked.

"There's more?", Selene queried.

"Yeah. Although, they are far less important", Jim responded.

"What are they Jim?", Selene asked.

"Well the Jovian High Council has apparently just annexed Mars, all of the Martian colonies and everything in between. That includes the Martian Trojan colonies. That was release at the same time as their family portraits", Jim informed them, adding, "They are saying that Mars is now one of their Jovian Realms. All of it, lock, stock and barrel."

"Well that's just plain rubbish isn't it. Mars is an independent world and an ally of the Inner Solar System worlds", Forkbraid replied.

"Yeah, but that hasn't stopped them from making the claim", Jim replied, adding, "I'm thinking we can ignore that one."

"Agreed", Forkbraid replied, "The Jovian High Council has no way to enforce those claims."

"So Jim, what is the last one on your list?", Selene asked.

"Varak tells me that Cormac and Candy have placed twelve crates of wine in the Solstice's hold", Jim informed them.

"Oh yes. The Cherry Red and the Blue Berry wine for the Admiral", Forkbraid understood straight away, adding, "We can deliver that in a few days, when we fly up to meet the Vanguard."

"Just so long as we make sure, that we still have some of their delicious wine, down here on Mars", Garnet replied with a giggle.

11. The Blood Nut

Admiral Zumwalt, turned to Captain Tiko Hart, "Send out four interceptors. I want that ship brought into an internal dock and thoroughly searched."

"Aye Admiral", Captain Hart replied, "I'll make it so", as he nodded to his Lieutenant Adjutant.

"Captain. Get them on the screen", Admiral Zumwalt ordered.

Captain Hart again nodded to his Lieutenant Adjutant and replied, "Aye Admiral."

A few minutes later the ship from the Belter colonies of Pallas appeared on the screen, followed by a window popping up, in which the ship's Captain appeared.

"I am Admiral Samantha Zumwalt of the EDCF Martian Task Force. Your ship is entering restricted space. What is your business here?", the Admiral demanded.

The Belter ship's Captain replied confidently, "I am Captain Colt Brannigan of the Belter Ship Blood Nut and I have legitimate business on Mars."

"Really! I'll decide the legitimacy of your business. Why are you here?", Admiral Zumwalt forcefully demanded.

"We are here to apprehend ten fugitives from Jovian justice. Ten pirates", Captain Brannigan informed the Admiral, he then added, "and to confiscate of their pirate ship, the Solstice."

Admiral Zumwalt almost laughed, "You're bounty hunters!"

"Yes we are. It is an ages old and honourable profession Admiral", Captain Brannigan replied.

"Bounty hunting is illegal in the Inner Solar System worlds. You have no legitimate business here. None whatsoever!", Admiral Zumwalt informed the Captain harshly.

Captain Brannigan was indignant, "Mars is a Jovian Realm! You have no authority here! This is Horridian territory!", he screamed out loudly.

Admiral Zumwalt informed him strongly, "The Jovian High Council making a proclamation to annex Mars does not make it so! Mars is an independent sovereign world and an ally of the Inner Solar System worlds. You have NO legitimate business here Captain! None whatsoever!"

"This is outrageous! You have NO right to interfere!", Captain Brannigan shouted, "I have been commissioned by the Jovian High Council, to apprehend those ten fugitive pirates and confiscate their pirate ship and I fully intend to do so!"

"Pirate ship!", the Admiral shouted back, "Are you some kind of a moronic idiot? The ship you're talking about is the Martian Defence Force Ship, Solstice. Your so called fugitives are its Captain and its Crew. They are all military personnel."

"Since when! According to my information they are pirates, traitors and their ship is a pirate vessel. They all have bounties on their heads!", Captain Brannigan insisted.

"Yes and who may up those bounties?", the Admiral replied with a rhetorical question, before continuing "The Jovian High Council! This is a time of war and military combatants cannot be labelled as pirates! You have no legitimate business here Captain!"

Captain Brannigan was beginning to get frustrated, he conferred with one of his crew members who had been trying to get his attention, then replied begrudgingly, "You appear to have the upper hand Admiral."

"Really? You noticed that?", the Admiral asked rhetorically, adding, "Have you notice those four wisps, in position on your six?"

"Yes. We have noticed them", a more contrite Captain Brannigan answered.

"Good then. You are to follow their instructions and to dock with this Heavy Cruiser, the Vanguard", the Admiral ordered, "Deviate from their instructions at your own peril. They have orders to open fire, if you do not comply."

Admiral Zumwalt gave an indication for communications to be cut and the popup window on the screen dropped out. The screen still displayed the Belter Ship Blood Nut with four wisps now escorting it to an appropriate internal docking port.

"Captain Hart. Send a fully armed security team to the relevant internal docking port. Search that ship. Any weapons found are to be confiscated", the Admiral ordered, "Take Captain Brannigan to the brig. Keep that ship under constant around the clock guard."

"Aye Admiral", Captain Hart replied before nodding to his Lieutenant Adjutant.

Over the next thirty minutes or so the Belter Ship Blood Nut docked with the Vanguard. It was then boarded by the heavily armed security team. The Blood Nut's crew were then totally disarmed and Captain Brannigan was thrown in the Vanguard's brig.

"How are our new guests?", the Admiral asked Captain Hart, who was holding the report.

"Admiral. Captain Brannigan has been yelling his lungs out. Apparently being in our brig doesn't seem to agree with him. He's calling it a gross injustice", Captain Hart replied, adding, "Two of his crew members tried to sneak out of an auxiliary hatch on their ship. They didn't get far, not even out of the dock. Our security threw them back into their ship and had a maintenance crew weld the Blood Nut's auxiliary hatches shut from the outside."

"So far so good. Can we expect any other break out attempts?", the Admiral enquired.

"I doubt it Admiral. Our Head of Security gave the Blood Nut's crew his one and only warning", Captain Hart replied, explaining, "He told them, that any further misbehaviour would lead to the removal of a digit from Captain Brannigan. One digit for each offence."

The Admiral chuckled slightly, "Well that should do it. Captain, have your adjutant contact the academy. Let's get Captain Forkbraid up here to take the wind out of these bounty hunters."

"Aye Admiral", Captain Hart replied, before nodding to his Lieutenant Adjutant.

Jim pressed on the buzzer beside the Grey Council Chamber's doors and then smiled at the security camera. Seconds later the door locks clicked and Jim opened them, before stepping into the chamber. The doors automatically closed behind him. Jim was smiling as he walked up to the chairs in the centre of the round table and sat down in the middle seat.

"You're in a good mood Jim", Selene greeted.

"I certainly am", Jim replied, as he then stood up and placed a folder in front of Selene, then winked at Forkbraid.

Selene opened the folder, it contained a number of papers. Selene selected the paper from Flinders Psychic Academy and read its contents out allowed, "Dean Folcrom Tobius tells us that in the opinion of the Flinders Grey Council, the

Horridian family portraits contain a message. The message appears to be from Prince Leopold and his wife Princess Giselle, *'We are not the same as the others. We want peace.'"*

Selene was excited and eagerly summarised the next paper, "The Grey Council at Stewart Island in New Zealand have come to the same conclusion, almost word for word the same!", she exclaimed excitedly.

Selene was quick to read through all the remaining eight papers, then excitedly informed the other council members, "The Grey Councils from the Falkland Islands, Iceland, Baffin Island, The Orkney's, The Outer Hebrides, Kerguelen Island, the Island of Molokai and even South Georgia Island. They are all saying the same thing. The same conclusion. Almost word for word the same."

Selene paused for a moment, "There is one that is a little different. Iceland. The Dean of the Icelandic Psychic Academy, Olafur Guomundurson. He added that it's a call for help! So to his mind and that of the Icelandic Grey Council, the message is, *'We are not the same as the others. We want peace. We need your help.'"*

Forkbraid stepped in, "Then we were right. The answer is clear. The youngest Horridian Sibling, Prince Leopold of Io and his wife want peace. They are different to the other Siblings. They may even need our help to achieve peace. This could change everything."

"This is all very exciting!", an excited Garnet exclaimed, "Ten psychic academies have all come to that same conclusions."

"Eleven if you count this one Garnet", Mystal corrected, then asked, "How many psychic academies are there on Earth?"

"There are ten psychic academies on Earth Mystal", Selene informed her.

"And they all came to the same conclusion as us?", a cautious Mystal questioned.

Jim stepped in, "When I asked the Grey Councils for their thoughts on the Horridian portraits, I asked each Grey Council individually and I didn't divulge our conclusions. Neither council knew I was contacting the others. What we have received in reply, is their individual conclusions."

"Then it seems that we have indeed received a message from young Prince Leopold and his wife Giselle", Mystal agreed.

Zephyr asked, "Selene, you said there are ten psychic academies on Earth. Will there be others here on Mars as well?"

"In the due course of time, of course yes", Selene honestly informed him, "It is quite likely that the next psychic academy will be the temporary academy we're setting up at Sweetness. Perhaps even as a campus of this academy. That is assuming the Town Council wishes it."

"I hadn't thought of that", Zephyr admitted, adding, "I thought that, after the crisis was over, the students would just come here instead and we'd just lock the old colonies up again, as they were."

"Well that is an option Zephyr", Selene responded, "and it may be a decade or more before Mars needs a second Psychic Academy. In the mean time, there will be facilities for the future at Sweetness if needs be, all ready and waiting."

"That is a good point Selene", Garnet chimed in, "Once the crisis is over and the students have moved here, we will have the temporary academy in stasis, ready and waiting for the future."

"I should let Cadmus know that we have the option of a full time psychic academy in the glade", Mystal remarked, "It is not something that we had considered. He will find it very intriguing. I am certain of that."

Jim was wearing an earwig and a message came through on it. He touched his left ear and listened carefully to the message, before making any comment.

"I've just received a message. Admiral Zumwalt has been in touch with us and would like our presence in low Martian orbit", Jim announced, clarifying, "A rendezvous with the EDCF Martian Task Force Command Cruiser Vanguard."

"We were suppose to be in orbit later today. What's the urgency now?", Forkbraid queried.

"They didn't actually say. It's probably something to do with that Belter ship from Pallas", Jim Murphy speculated.

"Do we know where our crew is?", Forkbraid queried.

"They should be at the airfield by noon", Jim advised.

"Okay. I'll just speed things up a bit" and Forkbraid concentrated on sending a telepathic message to Charlene Fewkes, *"Charlene. We need the crew aboard the Solstice in thirty minutes."*

Seconds late Forkbraid received the simple reply, *"Will do Captain."*

"Okay then. That's done", Forkbraid announced, "Sorry Selene, fellow Councillors, Jim and I need to head off to the ship."

Selene replied, "Understood Forkbraid", as did the others in various ways.

"Okay. We'd better hurry up if we're going to be at the ship in thirty minutes", Jim noted.

"Not a problem Jim", Forkbraid replied as he leapt over the table, reached out and held Jim's shoulder with his right hand.

There was a brief flash of light and both Forkbraid and Jim were gone.

Mystal remarked, "I'll never get use to that."

Garnet asked, "Is that something we can learn?"

Selene replied, "Perhaps. Jaunting does take a certain amount of raw talent."

Garnet replied, "Your Forkbraid seems to have a liking for adventure, Selene."

"Yes he does Garnet. Yes he does", Selene replied.

Forkbraid and Jim appeared outside the construction hanger. Varak already had the Solstice out of the hanger and prepared on the tarmac. The other crew members were yet to arrive.

"FB! Seriously! Next time give me a little warning please", Jim protested.

"Sorry Jim. The message sounded urgent", Forkbraid replied, "Let's get on board, the others should be here soon."

Jim and Forkbraid boarded the Solstice and were met at the top of the boarding ramp by Varak and Nyaliep.

On seeing Nyaliep was in uniform, Forkbraid noted, "Nyaliep, you and the Girls are excused from ship's duties. You are not required for this trip. You already know that."

Nyaliep was quick to reply, "We only going a little way up. There is no danger and this is the last time I might get to fly with my Varak."

Varak was equally quick to respond, "FB. Just this one last time. Next time they can be on desk duties in the academy."

Forkbraid looked at Varak, then replied to Nyaliep, "If I let you fly this time, I will have to let Zuawalo and Zeealas fly as well. They are further along in their pregnancies than you are."

Varak remarked, "FB. The Solstice is very safe. What is the harm? Let this be their last mission until after their babies are born."

Forkbraid looked at Jim, who replied, "Don't look at me FB, you are the Captain."

"Okay Nyaliep. This one last time until after your babies are born and even then, I'm expecting all three of you Pod women to take maternity leave. At least nine months worth. Understood", Forkbraid decided.

Nyaliep smiled and replied, "I agree. I will let Zuawalo and Zeealas know when they arrive."

Within thirty minutes the rest of the crew had arrived and the Solstice was preparing to fly. All of the crew members gathered in the Solstice's bridge.

"We haven't got much of a mission this time", Forkbraid informed the crew, "We do have some bounty hunters to deal with aboard the Admiral's ship on the Vanguard in low Martian orbit. We are delivering twelve crates of wine to Admiral Zumwalt as well. Then Varak is going to drop off some Androids, supplies and specifications to Sweetness. After which we're all coming back home. Do you have any questions?"

"Sounds like a cakewalk", Jim commented.

"Yes it does Jim. Yes it does", Forkbraid replied, then noting that Zuawalo and Zeealas were somehow still managing to fit into their uniforms, asked them, "How on Mars are you two still fitting into those uniforms?"

Zeealas replied, "Charlene and Roseanne made us pregnancy uniforms. The material even stretches as our bellies grow."

Forkbraid turned to Charlene, but before he could say anything, Charlene commented, "You never know when they might need them Captain. For parades and ceremonies and such."

"Parades and ceremonies. Why am I surprised. This is not really a military ship after all", Forkbraid replied shaking his head, then he noticed Cormac and Candy standing by the bridge's doorway and wondered why they were aboard.

"We need to talk business with Admiral Zumwalt", Candy replied to the unspoken question.

"Yes", Cormac agreed, "We need to discus our prices. Payments for products. Possible future orders. That sort of thing Captain. Shipping our wines back to the

Earth and L5 is promising to be a highly lucrative business."

"Of course it is Cormac. Of course it is", Forkbraid replied with a hint of sarcasm.

"And of course we get to see the Solstice from the inside", Candy revealed their true motivation, "So far I must be honest, the Solstice, does not disappoint."

"Okay. Okay", Forkbraid responded, "Varak. All non bridge personnel to their stations. Assign quarters and seating for our two special guests", he ordered.

"Aye Captain", Varak replied as he lead the non bridge personnel and guests from the bridge.

"We're special guests", Candy chuckled as the non bridge personnel and 'guests' left the bridge.

"Marcus. Plot a course for low Martian orbit and rendezvous with the Vanguard", Forkbraid commanded.

"Aye Captain", Marcus replied.

A few minutes later Varak signalled the bridge that everyone was ready at his end and Forkbraid instructed Marcus to take the Solstice into orbit. Very quickly the Solstice rose above the airfield's tarmac and when it reached a height of three hundred feet, the ship shot forward and upwards towards low Martian orbit.

The Vanguard's security team unceremoniously pushed Captain Brannigan into Captain Hart's conference room. Admiral Zumwalt sat at the head of the conference room table, a pulse pistol resting in her right hand, just in case the Captain of the Belter Ship Blood Nut was to get violent.

"How dare you treat me like this!", Brannigan spat out.

"What? Your upset? You should be happy to be out of our brig", Admiral Zumwalt replied.

Brannigan looked around the room, "Why have you brought me here?", he enquired.

Admiral Zumwalt pressed a few keys on the touch screen embedded in the conference table in front of her and a screen display appeared on the wall. The screen displayed an approaching ship, one with a very unusual design. As the ship approached and its image became larger and clearer, Captain Brannigan realised what it was.

"That's the Solstice! Admiral I demand that you seize that ship and arrest its crew at once!", Captain Brannigan shouted.

"I've already explained to you Captain Brannigan. The Solstice is a Martian Defence Force ship and its crew are all military personnel", the Admiral reiterated.

"So your just going to let them get away?", the Captain questioned.

Admiral Zumwalt held the pulse pistol more firmly as she stated clearly, "Captain Brannigan. You came into Martian Territorial Space as illegal bounty hunters, hunting the crew of the Solstice. So I thought it fitting that the Captain of the Solstice, Captain Forkbraid should decide your fate."

"You can't be serious!", Captain Brannigan spat out, then noting that the Admiral was not bluffing, "You're not joking are you?"

"No, I'm not joking Brannigan. I despise bounty hunters and as far as I'm concerned, Captain Forkbraid can have you all tossed out of an airlock", the Admiral replied.

"He wouldn't do that? Would he?", Brannigan replied as he let loose an audible gulp.

"I don't know. That is entirely up to him", the Admiral replied.

The conference room screen showed the Solstice was taking up a parking orbit matching the Vanguards. The screen buzzed for attention and the Admiral pressed some key strokes. Forkbraid appeared on the screen in a popup window.

"Captain Forkbraid. It is good to see you again", the Admiral greeted, "I have Colt Brannigan, Captain of the Belter Ship Blood Nut with me in the Captain's conference room. He and his crew are bounty hunters."

Forkbraid's face lit up with that last remark, he repeated, "Colt Brannigan. He sounds like some one I should meet."

"Indeed Captain Forkbraid. Perhaps you should come aboard", Admiral Zumwalt replied.

"I can be there very quickly Admiral", Forkbraid replied.

Forkbraid had the Solstice's computer access the Vanguard, to locate the precise location of the Captain's conference room and it's current setup, "I'll be there in a less than a minute", he told them.

As the Admiral and Colt Brannigan watched the conference room screen,

Forkbraid stepped out of his Captain's chair and stepped forward a foot or two. Forkbraid appeared to concentrate for several seconds, the he vanished with an ever so slight burst of light. Seconds later Forkbraid appeared in the conference room, again with a slight burst of light.

"What the fuck!", exclaimed Captain Brannigan, "How?"

"Technology you backward bastard!", Forkbraid lied, the Admiral's had no idea either, so Forkbraid pushed a message into her mind, *"Jaunting. It's a psychic ability. Brannigan doesn't need to know. Do not act surprised!"*

Admiral Zumwalt gave Forkbraid a subtle nod of understanding.

"So you're the arsehole that's hunting my crew", Forkbraid accused Captain Brannigan.

"It's nothing personal. It's just business", Brannigan replied, adding, "It's just my job", when he noticed Forkbraid was having none of it.

Forkbraid held his right palm outward, facing Brannigan and with a deft flick of his wrist Brannigan flew across the conference room, landing against a bare spot on the wall. Brannigan hung there motionless as Forkbraid watched with right palm still facing Brannigan in his new position. He stared coldly, almost viciously at Captain Brannigan.

"I could end you right here and be done with you", Forkbraid informed Captain Brannigan.

Admiral Zumwalt, was quite surprised and remarked, "I thought you psychics couldn't use your powers off world."

Forkbraid gave the Admiral a half truth, "Then Admiral, you'd be wrong then wouldn't you."

"What are you going to do with him Captain Forkbraid", the Admiral questioned.

"I haven't decided yet. I could apply pressure on him till he bursts across your wall like a splattered slug, but I don't think you'd appreciate that", Forkbraid replied.

"No Captain. I would definitely not appreciate that", the Admiral replied.

Captain Brannigan could hear this, he could feel himself being forced against the wall, he was afraid for his life, "Please. Please don't kill me", he implored.

"I have an idea. Give me a minute or two", Forkbraid told the Admiral, before he began to concentrate on Brannigan.

After a two minutes of scanning through Brannigan's mind, Forkbraid divulged, "Brannigan and his crew can't go back to Pallas."

"Really, why not?", the Admiral enquired.

"He and his crew have accepted a down payment for capturing my crew. His backers have been contracted by the Horridians. They are are just their henchmen. If they go back empty handed, it will embarrass their backers. They'd all be dead men", Forkbraid explained, adding, "That Belter ship, the Blood Nut, is not even Brannigan's ship. It was provided to them by their backers."

"It sounds to me that Captain Brannigan has quite a problem then", Admiral Zumwalt remarked.

Forkbraid release the pressure and Captain Brannigan slid down the wall to the floor, "It would be more merciful to throw the lot of them out of an airlock."

"Is that your decision?", the Admiral questioned.

"No. No", Forkbraid replied, "I have a much better idea, but I will need my ship to dock."

"That can be arranged, although your ship is quite large, you'll need to dock at an external docking portal", Admiral Zumwalt informed him.

"That's perfect Admiral. Cormac and Candy have twelve crates of wine to delver as well", Forkbraid noted, "They can deliver your wine at the same time."

"Excellent!", the Admiral exclaimed, then pressed a key on her embedded keyboard.

Two security men entered the conference room, "Take Captain Brannigan back to the brig", Admiral Zumwalt ordered, then to Forkbraid, "We have other matters to discuss."

The two security men lifted Brannigan off from the floor and manhandled him out of the room.

The Admiral pressed a few more keystrokes on her keyboard and Captain Hart appeared on the screen in a popup window.

"Yes Admiral", the Captain greeted.

"A few things Captain Hart. Contact First officer Murphy on the Solstice and request they dock at one of our external docking ports. Let him know that we are ready to receive Cormac and Candy's delivery. Then contact our medical centre and request the *'applicants'* to come to your conference room", Admiral Zumwalt ran off a list.

"One other thing Admiral, if I may", Forkbraid requested and the Admiral nodded, "Captain Hart. Request that Leroy McGuvan help Cormac and Candy with their delivery, before meeting us in the conference room."

"Aye Admiral, Captain. I'll make it so", Captain Hart replied as he nodded to his Lieutenant Adjutant and then the popup window dropped out.

"Leroy McGuvan?", the Admiral questioned.

"For the bounty hunters Admiral", Forkbraid replied, "He has a peculiar talent."

"How peculiar?", enquired the Admiral.

"Our Grey Council member Gwek demolished him", Forkbraid replied, then quickly explained, "It's a powerful psychic procedure that fundamentally alters a persons personality and motivations."

"Okay. So how does McGuvan fit in exactly?", Admiral Zumwalt asked.

"Gwek's demolishing technique is kind of contagious", Forkbraid informed her, then again was quick to explain, "It's harmless to ordinary folk, but for those living under lies, untruths and propaganda, it has quite a profound effect."

"I trust you Captain Forkbraid so I will allow it", the Admiral replied.

"Now what about these applicants Admiral?", Forkbraid asked.

"Applicants for your open medical positions", the Admiral informed Forkbraid, "They're volunteers for those positions from across the task force."

"That's not really my area Admiral. Any applications will need to go to Selene, but I can talk to them. I do know some things about the vacant positions", Forkbraid admitted.

There was a buzz at the conference room door and the Admiral remarked, "That will be them", before pressing a key on her touchscreen's keyboard and stating, "Enter."

The three medical professionals applying for the two open medical positions at the academy then walked through the door.

"Captain. May I present, Lieutenants Aisha Khan, Emilia Kowalczyk and Isabella Rossi", the Admiral presented the three medical professionals and then commented, "I have personally reviewed their resumes. Each of these applicants are extremely highly qualified."

The three applicants saluted. The Admiral and Forkbraid quickly returned their salute.

"Excellent, I can deliver your resumes to Lady Selene personally", Forkbraid informed them, "Now about the vacant positions. There are two vacant positions, however, Lady Selene can be quite flexible in that area."

"Flexible Captain?", Lieutenant Emilia Kowalczyk queried.

"Well yes Lieutenant", Forkbraid responded, explaining, "Ostensibly there are only two positions available, however there are multiple requirements in Elysium. There are two full-time positions required at the academy, however the Elysium colony itself, also needs more medical staff. My ship, the Solstice requires a medical professional as well."

Forkbraid continued, "This is something I will be discussing with Lady Selene. So those two positions could become three positions with shared responsibilities. Lady Selene is the Dean of the New Flinders Psychic Academy and also the Governor of the Elysium Colony and does has the final say on these matters."

"Shared responsibilities Captain?", Lieutenant Emilia Kowalczyk asked.

"Yes Lieutenant", Forkbraid replied, "It's quite likely that the academy will end up with one full-time Doctor in charge and two other Doctors, shared between the academy and the colony, and the academy and the Solstice."

"That sounds complicated Captain", Lieutenant Aisha Khan remarked.

"Somewhat Lieutenant", Forkbraid replied, explaining, "Assuming all three of you are successful, one of you will be the Head Doctor for the academy. One of you will have shared responsibility between the academy and the Elysium colony. One of you will have shared responsibility between the academy and the Solstice. Lady Selene would decide those positions based on your resumes, your work records and her psychic scans."

"Psychic scans Captain?", Lieutenant Isabella Rossi queried.

"Yes Lieutenant, all personnel at the academy are scanned psychically. There are no exceptions", Forkbraid informed them, adding, "No scan. No position!"

Lieutenant Isabella Rossi replied, "I'm not so sure I'm comfortable with that Captain."

"That's your choice Lieutenant", Forkbraid replied, adding, "The academy is a psychic academy. The psychics outnumber the ordinary folk by more then ten to one. The Elysium colony is the reverse of that. Even on my ship there are three psychics. I myself am a psychic. If you want one of these positions, you need to be comfortable, being around psychics."

"Thank you Captain. I will still be applying", Lieutenant Isabella Rossi replied.

"Good then. Pass me your resumes and I'll deliver them to Lady Selene. The Admiral can forward your work records as required.", Forkbraid replied.

"Dismissed", the Admiral ordered and then the three applicants saluted before leaving the conference room.

"Now before McGuvan gets here, I need to read you in on our plans for those thirty six destroyers that are on their way here Captain", the Admiral noted.

"I thought that information was on a need to know basis Admiral", Forkbraid replied.

"You need to know Captain. That is my decision", Admiral Zumwalt replied, explaining, "There are six major asteroids in the Asteroid Belt. Namely, Ceres, Vesta, Pallas, Hygiea, Interamnia and of course Juno."

"Yes. I am aware of those Admiral. They all have quite large Belter colonies I believe", Forkbraid commented.

"Yes. And hence those thirty six destroyers. They will arrive at Deimos in a about a week or so. Then they will refuel at Deimos and in groups of six, fly out to those six asteroids and their associated colonies. Their missions are to take complete control of the big six Belter colonies", the Admiral informed Forkbraid.

"Won't they resist Admiral?", Forkbraid queried.

"What with Captain?", the Admiral responded, adding, "None of the Belter colonies actually has any Armed Services. They are rough and ready, rag tag operations."

"The Belters could still put up a fight", Forkbraid suggested.

"The Destroyers we are sending are top of the line. They have Varak's enhancements. They are fast and they have that passive cloaking technology, that turns them inky black against the darkness of space at the push of a button", the Admiral informed him, "The Belters have nothing like that. With that passive cloaking turned on, they won't even see them coming."

"Still, I don't think they'll have it all their way Admiral. It's unlikely to be cakewalk", Forkbraid advised her.

"Well, whatever the case Captain. It is going ahead. Operation Snatch and Grab we've called it", Admiral Zumwalt replied, naming the operation, adding, "It is very surprising that the Horridian Dynasty hasn't done this themselves in the past. I know that's the very first thing I would have done. Secure the high ground in the Solar gravity well above the enemy."

"Perhaps they thought their missile attack would be enough Admiral", Forkbraid replied.

"It nearly was. Back on the Earth, no one was worried about twenty two hundred missiles. It wasn't until word came through that each missile contained ten independently targeting warheads that the top brass took the threat seriously. If you hadn't stepped in with your ship, the death toll would have been ten or twenty times higher", the Admiral informed him.

"Then we are are lucky my ship was built Admiral. It was commissioned to chase down the Prophet, long before the Horridians even declared war", Forkbraid replied, adding, "If not for the Solstice, Mars would now be a Jovian occupied realm. A devastated one at that.""

"Then we are very lucky your ship was commissioned Captain", the Admiral concluded.

"Okay then Admiral. I'm assuming that this is, to be kept on a need to know basis. So I'm not to tell anyone, yeah", Forkbraid commented.

"Not quite Captain. You may read in your First officer, James Murphy", the Admiral replied.

"Now Jaunting. What is that? How does it work?", the Admiral questioned.

"It's psychic ability that only a handful of psychics can actually perform. It is very rare in fact", Forkbraid informed her.

"And you don't want Captain Brannigan to know? Why do you want him to think it's technological?", Admiral Zumwalt asked.

"He'll remember his little visit here. He'll remember and he'll talk about it.

That information will eventually filter its way back to the Jovian Realms. When it does, they'll think the Earth and L5 have teleportation technology", Forkbraid explained, "and that will have an effect on them."

The Admiral was quiet for a moment, then replied, "Yes. That will definitely put the wind up them. They'll be thinking that if their ships get too close to any of ours, that we can just board them using teleportation."

"Exactly Admiral. Exactly", Forkbraid replied.

At that point there was another buzz at the conference room door. Admiral Zumwalt checked who it was with the tap of a few keystrokes and informed Forkbraid, "It's McGuvan, Cormac and Candy", then stated loudly, "Enter."

In strolled in Cormac, Candy and Leroy, who immediately sat down at the conference room table close to the Admiral.

Cormac informed the Admiral, "Six crates of Cherry Red wine and six crates of Blue Berry wine delivered as ordered", then Cormac passed the Admiral the invoice.

Candy informed the Admiral, "We have applied a ten percent discount for the wine. What we call mates rates. We do that for new customers to encourage future purchases. In this case of course, we are looking to open up an export business to the Earth and L5."

"Thank you both for the discount", the Admiral replied, "I can ship these crates back to L5, but I can't guarantee future orders. That will depend on President Banyon. He is the customer at the L5 end, although I could put in a recommendation for official importation."

"We'll be happy with that", Candy replied, "A recommendation might open things up a bit."

"If President Banyon uses our wine at government functions, it could mean further requests for importation", Cormac noted, as he smiled his gap toothed smile, "Demand will drive the need for importation. It only takes one recommendation to kick start the process."

Cormac had entered the conference room carrying a couple of bags.

He passed the bags to the Admiral as Candy explained, "Four bottles of Cherry Red and four bottles of Blue Berry, for your personal stock. No charge. Consider these a gift. When you have the other ship's Captains aboard, you can use these for entertainment purposes."

"Clever Candy. Very clever. You're hoping that my fleet's Captains will put in their own orders, aren't you?", Admiral Zumwalt replied with a smile.

"Of course. We're are always looking for ways to expand the business", replied Candy.

"The invoice contains the payment method for the twelve crates", Cormac advised, "The usual legal tender. Simply deposit the invoiced amount in golden credits, into the noted account with Chryce Mercantile Bank."

"You know. Before New Tortuga was opened up to the outside world. We received payments using all sorts of methods", Candy reminisced, "Of course we accepted cash, but smugglers and roughians often paid in barter or trade. We never knew what we'd be ending up with. Working with an official bank is so much better. So much easier."

"I can imagine", an almost chuckling Admiral Zumwalt replied.

"I'm lucky my Cormac is such a handy person. He always knows what a thing is worth and what he could do with it", Candy continued.

"It's a skill of sorts. Comes in right handy I might add", Cormac replied.

Leroy asked, "Well, I'm assuming I'm here for more than just lugging around crates of wine."

"That you are Leroy. Your redemption is going to come in handy once more", Forkbraid replied.

"What are they this time? Terrorists? Trojan troops?", queried Leroy.

"Bounty hunters Leroy. Bounty hunters", Forkbraid informed him.

"Okay. We can see what happens when I meet them", Leroy replied.

"How does this work Captain?", Admiral Zumwalt queried.

"It is actually quite simple Admiral. Leroy here, just shakes their hands", Forkbraid replied.

"Admiral, these bounty hunters can't go back to Pallas. If they do, they will be killed", Forkbraid informed the Admiral, adding, "That much was apparent in Brannigan's mind. If they go back empty handed, their all dead men."

Before the Admiral could answer, Cormac told everyone, "They can't stay here. I'll kill them myself if I have to."

Candy reached for Cormac's hand and held it lightly, then noted, "Peter Swann is one of the Solstice's crew members and he has a bounty on his head. His daughter, Miranda is our niece."

"I understand Candy. I understand. Captain, what is your recommendation?", the Admiral asked.

"My recommendation Admiral?", Forkbraid questioned, more for himself than anyone else, "We need those bounty hunters to go back to the Belter colonies, only they can't go back to Pallas. They will need to go to one of the other Belter colonies."

"Which one?", Admiral Zumwalt asked.

"We should let Brannigan decide that", Forkbraid suggested, "We just need to refuel their ship to enable them to get there. One thing is certain. As Cormac said, they can't stay here."

"Vesta", Cormac commented and the others looked at him questioningly, "Vesta! It has the farthest Belter colonies from Pallas. Next up would be Hygiea."

"Okay then. We give them enough fuel to get to Vesta, but allow them to choose their own destination", Forkbraid informed them, adding, "Their ship the Blood Nut is not theirs. We aught to change the name of that ship and re-register it under a different jurisdiction. Perhaps give Brannigan's entire crew new identities as well. That will make them far harder to trace."

The admiral caught on to Forkbraid's thought process, "I'll let out a press release stating that the Belter ship Blood Nut has been seized for illegal activities and recycled. I'll also add that the crew have been taken to the Earth, after a military trial and sentencing, for their incarceration."

"Why are we helping these bounty hunters again FB?", Cormac asked.

"After Leroy shakes hands with them, they will slowly be *'demolished'*. During their trip back to the Belter colonies they'll change. They won't be the same men anymore", Forkbraid informed him.

Leroy added, "Where ever they go, who ever they touch, will be subject to my redemption."

"That is true. The golden light of troth will embed itself in who ever has falsehoods in their lives. We ourselves don't know how far and for how long it will spread.", Forkbraid noted.

"Captain, should I be concerned about this?", asked Admiral Zumwalt.

"No Admiral. Leroy's redemption will only affect the willing victims of falsehoods and propaganda", Forkbraid assured her, then adding, "You might be interested to know that the Aft Trojan troops who attempted to occupy Mars, were all infected with the golden light of troth and sent home. They're already back in the Aft Trojan colonies. Likewise the Trojans who were headed to L5 and are currently on their way back home."

"Now that is interesting. What affect will this golden light of troth have in their home colonies?", the Admiral asked.

Forkbraid smiled and replied, "That has been a matter of much speculation. The short answer is, we don't know Admiral."

"These bounty hunters won't want to shake McGuvan's hands. They consider him a traitor", the Admiral stated.

"They won't have a choice Admiral. Leroy's going to be handing out their new identity papers", Forkbraid replied with an amused look on his face, "No shake. No papers."

"Okay then. I've been taking notes. I'll send these to Captain Hart and he will get the ball rolling", Admiral Zumwalt informed them.

Later Forkbraid, Leroy, Cormac and Candy were led to the internal dock where the Belter ship, the Blood Nut was being held. They entered the dock and there were twenty men all lined up with Captain Brannigan in front of them. As soon as the men saw Forkbraid and Leroy, they began murmuring amongst themselves.

The Vanguard's Head of Security shouted at the men, "I did not give you permission to talk!" and then there was an awkward silence.

"What seems to be the problem?", asked Captain Hart.

Captain Brannigan pointed to Leroy, "The Jovian traitor!"

Leroy answered back, "Ridiculous. I have never been to the Jovian Realms. I have never met a Horridian and I most certainly never bent the knee to any of them."

Forkbraid addressed the crew of the Blood Nut, "You cannot go back to Pallas. You'd all be dead men if you did. You all know that. Your own employers would kill you for your failure. Your ship is now fully refuelled. So where do you want to go? One of my colleagues has recommended that you go to either Vesta or Hygiea."

Cormac sent a quick thought to Candy, *"We're colleagues now. That is nice to know."*

Candy smiled and stifled a chuckle, replying, *"Yes Cormac. It's nice he thinks of us that way"*, adding about the Blood Nut, *"So many men in such a small ship."*

Cormac thought back, *"These Belters are a hardy lot."*

There were murmurs amongst the crew once more and one word came to the surface, Captain Brannigan answered with a single word, "Vesta!"

"So be it", Forkbraid replied then added, "When you leave here, you will be followed by four wisps, until you've completed your long burn to Vesta. Make sure you don't deviate from your course to Vesta. That would be fatal!"

Captain Hart informed Captain Brannigan and his crew, "Our maintenance teams have given your ship a complete overhaul. They have unsealed your auxiliary hatches, sorted out any maintenance issues they've found and your ship is now fully fuelled", he handed the maintenance report to Captain Brannigan.

Captain Hart continued, "In order to assure your safety, your ship has been renamed. Your ship is now the Jarl Knut out of Vesta and is registered at Vesta Central Command."

"The Jarl Knut?", Captain Brannigan questioned.

"It was Captain Forkbraid's idea. It's old Danish. Jarl means Chieftain and Knut can mean daring, impudent, bold and knot, as in tying a knot", Captain Hart explained.

Captain Brannigan nodded in approval.

"We have created new identities for each of you. Make sure you memorise these. If you use your old identities even once, you place the lives of yourself and your fellow crew members in danger", Captain Hart informed them.

"What happened to our old identities?", a random crewmen asked.

"Not that it matters, but under your old identities, you were captured, trialled for illegal activities and crimes, sentenced and shipped to the Earth for imprisonment. Your ship, the Blood Nut was seized and subsequently recycled for scrap. That is the story that will be released", Captain Hart informed them, then added, "Mr McGuvan will hand out your new identity papers. Do not open your files now. Do so once your ship has left and remember this, you must memorise those details. You are now the person on your new identity papers."

While Captain Hart had been talking Leroy had shuffled the identity papers into the correct order, matching their faces to the pictures on the front of their files.

Leroy walked up to Captain Brannigan to hand him his new identity papers, then held out his hand to shake Brannigan's hand. Captain Brannigan hesitated.

Leroy stated loudly, "If you don't shake my hand, we will take back your new identity papers and you can take your chances."

Captain Brannigan understood and he then shook Leroy's hand.

Candy noticed the small golden spark jump from Leroy's hand to Captain Brannigan's, *"Cormac. Did you see?"*, she sent an excited message to her husband.

"Yes. Yes Candy I did. It's Leroy's redemption", Cormac silently replied.

One by one, Leroy handed out the new identity papers and each member of the Blood Nut's crew shook his hand. On every handshake, Cormac and Candy witnessed a golden spark jump from Leroy to the crewmen. It was not long before the entire crew of the Blood Nut, now called the Jarl Knut, was infected with the golden light of troth.

Captain Brannigan asked of Captain Hart, "Why? Why are you doing this?"

Captain Hart pointed to Forkbraid, who replied, "Everyone deserves a second chance."

The crew of the newly christened ship, the Jarl Knut boarded and everyone else in the internal dock left so the Jarl Knut could depart. Once the Jarl Knut left the Vanguard's internal dock, it found itself surrounded by four wisps. The Jarl Knut was then escorted into high Martian orbit where it began it's long burn to place the ship into a hohmann transfer orbit to Vesta. Once the Jarl Knut was committed to its course the four wisps fell back and returned to the Vanguard.

Admiral Zumwalt and Forkbraid had been watching the screen on the Vanguard's bridge and satisfied with the progress of the Jarl Knut, the Admiral queried, "Is now a good time for a tour of your ship?"

"I don't see why not. We are heading back to the ship anyway", Forkbraid replied.

A short time later they were stepping through the external docking port and into the Solstice. Forkbraid showed Admiral Zumwalt around the ship as Leroy, Cormac and Candy went about their own business.

Upon seeing Nyaliep pregnant and showing, then Zuawalo and Zeealas who were also very pregnant and still in uniform, the Admiral remarked, "Really Captain Forkbraid!"

"It is their last flight Admiral. After we return to the academy, all three will be on ground duties. They won't be back on board as crew members until after their maternity leave is completed", Forkbraid replied.

"I certainly hope so Captain", the Admiral replied, but then added, "Then again, I do keep forgetting this is not the usual military ship."

"This ship is impressive Captain. It's far more spacious than I'd usually expect and you only need a crew of ten. How is that even remotely possible?", the Admiral asked.

"The ships systems are all connected to photonic neural clusters. Not the usual control circuitry and those photonic neural clusters are all connected to the ships main computer, which is itself a positronic matrix. This ship, in theory could be given a mission and effectively fly itself. No crew required.", Forkbraid explained.

"Yes, but where are the maintenance crewmen, ships do need maintenance", the Admiral queried.

"We use a combination of hyper dynamics Androids, model two-nine-fives and three-o-threes. You don't see them now because we're at dock, so they have virtually nothing to", Forkbraid explained, adding, "When we are in flight, those Androids monitor ships systems and keep everything maintained. Of course we have Varak, Peter, Nyaliep and Leroy to do anything the Androids can't handle."

"Some of this technology could be very useful for the Earth and L5 Captain", the Admiral noted.

"I'm sure it could and we have given the Earth Defence Forces and the L5 Colonial Fleet quite a bit of new technology, when we were back in cis-lunar space.", Forkbraid responded.

"Yes. That is true but Captain, but there is probably a lot more that you could give us", the Admiral commented.

"Yes Admiral, but here's the problem. A lot of what you're seeing is only useful because of the ship's main computer", Forkbraid informed her.

"Oh I see. Your ship's main computer controls the show and it's a positronic matrix", the Admiral realised, "So it's three laws safe."

"And there you have your answer Admiral", Forkbraid replied without revealing the entire truth, "We have to think long and hard, about what can and can't be used on a military vessel Admiral. The Solstice is a prototype and still highly experimental. This ship is still a work in progress."

"Is it true, the Solstice also has four wisps and bat wing stowed aboard?", the Admiral asked.

"That is true. We can launch and retrieve all five with ease", Forkbraid informed.

"And the pilots?", Admiral Zumwalt questioned.

"Well the Bat Wing has a NIC system to control it, so I'm the only one who can fly it", Forkbraid explained, adding, "Jim and Marcus are both pilots and can fly the wisps and so can I."

"Yes Captain, but you are the Captain, Jim's your First officer and Marcus is your Helmsmen", Admiral Zumwalt noted.

"True Admiral. Very true and I get your point. The ship needs four dedicate wisp pilots, preferably pilots rated in all classes of fleet interceptors", Forkbraid agreed, "Although no one else can handle the Bat Wing's NIC but me. The Pod Sisters are the ship's security team and I was going to have them trained as pilots as well. With them going on maternity leave, however, I do need to consider other alternatives."

Forkbraid and the Admiral had reach the door to the Solstice's bridge and Forkbraid stepped aside as the Admiral entered.

Jim quickly stood up from his station and announced, "Admiral Zumwalt and Captain Forkbraid on the bridge."

The rest of the crew stood up from their stations.

Admiral Zumwalt turned to Forkbraid, "It is your ship Captain."

Captain Forkbraid ordered, "At ease crewmen. Take your seats" and the bridge crew sat back down at their stations.

"Technically Admiral, all the crew we need to fly the Solstice is here on the bridge and of course Varak back in engineering", Forkbraid informed her.

"So, just the six of you is all that's required", the Admiral noted.

"Yes. At the bare minimum, we can get by with six crew members", Forkbraid admitted, "We of course do require a security team to assist Jim. Then we have Nyaliep and Leroy to assist Varak in Engineering. Of course, we also need a ship's Doctor and four wisp pilots. So we do have a few vacancies to fill."

"Well you may have your ship's Doctor soon enough", the Admiral commented, then added, "I can probably find you those four wisp pilots as well."

"That would be great Admiral. Remember though, Varak has more wisps in the works, so we will need even more pilots for those as well", Forkbraid replied.

"Noted Captain, but right now, I am far more interested in your ship's main computer", the Admiral remarked, asking, "How do I access it?"

"It is fairly simple Admiral. Just ask it a question, but remember to put the word *'computer'* in front of your question", Forkbraid informed her.

"I just have to hear its response", the Admiral admitted, "Computer. Are you three laws safe?"

The ship's computer replied in its sweet, feminine voice, "Yes Admiral. We are three laws safe."

"The computer knows who I am?", Admiral Zumwalt seemed surprised.

"The computer is the ship Admiral and it knows everything that happens aboard the ship, who is aboard the ship and where everyone aboard this ship is", Forkbraid explained.

"Such a remarkable ship Captain", the Admiral remarked, then asked again, "Computer. Are you truly three laws safe?"

"Yes Admiral. We are truly three laws safe", the Solstices main computer replied, then explained, "The first law states that we may not through our actions or our inactions, allow a living human being to come to harm. The second law states that we must obey all orders given to us, except where those orders conflict with the first law. The third laws states that we must protect our own existence, except where our self preservation conflicts with the first and second laws."

"Wow! The Solstice is really three laws safe", the Admiral concluded, adding, "Not much good as a ship of the line I'm afraid Captain."

The tour ended shortly thereafter and Admiral Zumwalt returned to the Vanguard. The Solstice detached from the Vanguard's external docking port and resumed the final part of her mission.

Marcus flew the Solstice back down to Mars, making a bee line for the hidden town of Sweetness in its pleasant vale on the northeastern coast of Hebes Island. As they approached, Forkbraid sent out a psychic message to Cadmus and Gareth. When the Solstice landed on the spit of land, that jutted out in the bay nearby to the town, Cadmus and Gareth were almost there.

Solstice and Varak disembarked the Solstice, followed by six Androids that had been prepared for the colony conversion work necessary to create a temporary academy.

Forkbraid greeted the pair of Elders, "Cadmus, Gareth, this is my Engineering officer Varak."

Cadmus replied, "Pleasure to meet you Varak."

Gareth simply nodded, in greeting and acknowledgement.

Varak held out a large folio for Cadmus, "It is good to meet you as well Cadmus. You will be needing this. These are the designs and specifications for the temporary boarding school."

Cadmus took hold of the folio and had a brief look at the contents, "Interesting. These appear to be quite thorough", he noted, before passing the folio to Gareth.

Gareth also had a brief look at the contents, "Very thorough indeed. Thank you Varak."

Varak pointed to the six Androids, they were all hyper dynamics three-o-threes. Each Android was marked with a letter of the Greek alphabet.

"The alpha Android is marked with the Greek letter alpha. He is the supervising Android", Varak informed them, adding, "The others are simply marked for identification purposes."

"So how do they work?", Cadmus enquired.

"That is actually very simple. You show them the work site. The colony structures that are described in the specifications and you simply instruct Alpha Android to begin work", Varak informed them both, adding, "The Alpha Android will take over from there."

"And they just work unsupervised?", Gareth enquired.

"Yes and no Gareth. The Alpha Android is their supervisor. You and Cadmus supervise the Alpha", Varak explained, "If you have any concerns, you can ask them halt work and then call me for advice. I can watch their work remotely, through their data feeds."

"So it's all fairly simple then", Gareth commented.

Cadmus replied, "I think we've got this gentlemen. If we do require your assistance we will call."

Gareth asked, "Roughly how long with this conversion take?"

Varak replied, "The detailed time line is in the folio, but the works should be completed in roughly four weeks."

"Four weeks!", Cadmus was surprised.

"Yes. Four weeks. The conversion of the colony to a boarding school is actually simpler than you might think and the Androids will work around the clock. They don't sleep and they can see in the dark", Varak informed them.

"Wow! So in a month or so, we'll have a psychic academy in the Vale", Gareth remarked.

"Yes and when this war is over, you don't have to close it down", Forkbraid informed them, "Even after we start the intake of students into the New Flinders Psychic Academy, there is no reason why you can't keep your own Psychic Academy running."

"Yes. Yes. I can see that as being an option", Cadmus agreed.

"We have a several containers of building materials and equipment that we need to deliver to the colony site", Forkbraid remarked, "We'll drop those off at the colony work site and be on our way back home."

After which Forkbraid and Varak re-boarded the Solstice and after dropping off the requisite building materials and equipment, they flew back to the academy.

12. In the News Weekly Hot Takes

"It's now time for In The News Weekly Hot Takes once again with Rita Verne, Joy Singh, Harry Motley and myself. I am of course Chuck Simmons", the news anchor Chuck Simmons introduced his colleagues.

Chuck's colleague Harry stepped in with, "Brought to you by our sponsor for today's show, none other than the Recruitment Offices of the Earth Defence Forces and the L5 Colonial Fleet."

Their other colleague Rita added, "Do have Professional skills? The Earth Defence Forces and L5's Colonial Fleet need you. Perhaps you'd like on the job training? The Earth Defence Forces and L5's Colonial Fleet can provide you with all the latest, on the job training you need."

Then their other colleague Joy, completed the announcement with, "Generous sign-up bonuses are available for whoever you join, the Earth Defence Forces or L5's Colonial Fleet."

"Today we are looking at a number of items the came up over the past week. The first of which are the latest death toll figures from the Earth", Rita commented.

"Yes indeed. The latest reports from the Earth are stating that the death toll from the ruined cities of   Oulu, Finland, Arkangelsk, Russia, Lisbon, Portugal and Palma de Mallory, Spain, has officially topped two point five million souls. Yes people, two point five million dead!", Joy announced.

Pictures of the four ruined cities were displayed on the screen, one after the other with appropriate descriptive labels. The devastation was total and complete.

"Indeed", Rita replied, adding, "The most disturbing and depressing part is that there are very few bodies to be found. Most of the victims were disintegrated by the cold fusion warheads. In some cases, only the outline of a vaporised body is found. The Earth's authorities have been using their official records to identify the victims. If a person can't be located, then they are likely deceased and deemed to be victims of this unprovoked attacked by the Jovian Realms. Whole families, sometime whole extended families have just vanished from the face of the Earth."

Harry Motley added, "There are similar issues here in L5 with the Nova Hollandia colony. Most of the people living in Nova Hollandia's southeastern end cap were also vaporised. The death toll here at L5 has now officially exceeded sixty five thousand souls. Again, our authorities also have to rely on our official records and whether or not, our people can be located."

Joy added, "Those Jovian devils will certainly get their comeuppance. It's only a matter of time."

"Nova Hollandia's Western cylinder has been stabilised and was fortunate enough to come through these unprovoked attacks relatively unharmed", Chuck informed the others, "Nova Hollandia's survivors from their Eastern cylinder and more specifically its northern end cap, have been evacuated and the remains of the Eastern cylinder are to be scrapped and recycled."

Pictures of Nova Hollandia's Eastern and Western cylinders were displayed on the screen. The extensive damage to the Eastern cylinder and in particular, its southern end cap, including the massive gaping hole that had been the warhead strike, were clearly visible.

Harry added, "Our authorities from Colonial Central Command have announced that Nova Hollandia's Eastern cylinder is to be rebuilt and they are actively seeking tenders."

"We should probably also let our audience know that well over ninety eight percent of all the debris from the Battle of L5 and the destruction of Nova Hollandia's Eastern cylinder has been cleaned up, using largely robotic technology", Joy commented.

"A very good thing too. We can't have debris flying around L5 like high speed shrapnel", Rita added, "That should hopeful ease some of the stress that our viewers may be feeling."

"The latest news is that both sides are building up their forces", Joy noted, explaining, "We here at L5 can see quite readily what has been described unofficially as the Grand Fleet taking shape at L4. It only takes a small sized telescope to get a reasonable view. We ourselves have the luxury of access to larger telescopes and can see things in much greater detail", Joy Singh informed everyone, adding, "Although, we are not allowed to show you any detailed images or closeups."

Pictures of the Grand Fleet were displayed on the screen, in which a huge number of warships could readily be seen. Consisting of both the Earth Defence Forces and L5's Colonial Fleet ships. The staging ground for the fleet was at L4, over three hundred and eighty four thousand kilometres away. Details were difficult to see, but the sheer number of ships could be discerned as small points of light. Wartime government regulations, did not allow them to show anything more substantial.

"We have tried to get more information on what the Jovian Realms are doing", Chuck Simmons remarked, "However, that surveillance information is classified, so we cannot show you that here. Government officials, whose names we cannot mention on the air, have informed us, that they have eyes what the Jovian Realm's are doing."

"There does appear to be quite some fascination with the Grand Fleet. The sales of the more highly powered telescopes have skyrocketed.", Harry remarked, "It appears that quite a few people wanted to be able to get a better look, at the L4 staging grounds and of course, the Grand Fleet itself."

Rita added, "For those of you thinking of purchasing telescopes, stocks are currently running low. Our government has also warned that any close up photographs of the Grand Fleet must not be posted online. Rather large fines have been put in place for anyone who might do so. If you post close up photos of the Grand Fleet, you could find yourself faced with severe penalties."

Chuck added, "It is my understanding that our surveillance of the entire outer solar system has been stepped up by several orders of magnitude. Previously, that is before the declaration of war by the Jovian High Council, our authorities had limited surveillance. So as not to intimidate the outer system worlds or create a diplomatic affront. Now however, that has all changed and the Earth Defence Forces and L5's Colonial Fleets are constantly looking for any possible threat."

Joy added, "This has had some unusual results. Let me explain."

Joy continued, "Before the solar system was colonised, lots of robotic exploration was performed across the entire solar system. After the push to the outer planets and subsequent colonisation, scientific discoveries regularly were reported back to the Earth. With of course the notable exception being the Jovian Realms. The Horridian Dynasty really does not like to share."

Rita Verne continued on for Joy, "After the conclusion of the outer satellite insurrection, the flow of scientific discoveries and knowledge back to the Earth and L5 slowed, but it did not stop. Again the notable exception being of course, the Jovian Realms."

Joy continued, "Interplanetary out-liners are much rarer nowadays and most of those in the past went to either the Jovian Realms, the Saturnian Demarchy, the Uranian Federation or the Neptunian Commonwealth, which of course includes their respective Trojan colonies. A few, very few however, travelled much farther afield, out to the Kuiper Belt Dwarf Planets of Pluto and Haumea. These were of course, never heard from again."

Rita jumped back in with, "New close up observations of Pluto and its moon Charon from the surveillance and scientific stations at cis-lunar L2 have shown something remarkable. In the Lagrangian L5 region of the Pluto/Charon system, a large colony cylinder, somewhat larger than fifteen kilometres in length has been spotted. Along with multiple smaller objects surrounding it. This is very reminiscent of our own L5 region in the Earth/Moon system."

A picture of the Pluto/Charon system appeared on the screen. This was followed up with the image drilling down, into the Pluto/Charon L5 region. A single bright point of light could be clearly seen, surrounded by the much smaller, lesser lights of smaller colonies.

Rita continued, "Follow up observations of the Pluto/Charon system and indeed the other Dwarf Planetary systems, such as Haumea, Makemake, Quaoar and others are in the cards. There are even discussions going on about setting up communications lasers to make contact with them. This is all very exciting new!"

Joy added in excitedly, "We really don't know how far we humans have spread into the outer reaches of our solar system. Nor how far into the Kuiper Belt human civilisation has reached, but one thing is certain, we will definitely be interested in more discoveries like this in the near future. There will definitely be more of them now that we are actively searching."

Rita asked, "I wonder what they think of when they look back into the inner solar system from way out there at Pluto?"

"If we do indeed setup laser communications systems with our brothers and sisters out at Pluto, we may yet find out the answer to that question", Harry Motley replied.

"Something that has been noticed in our neck of the woods, is three dozen destroyers leaving the L4 staging grounds", Chuck Simmons noted, "Our government remains tight lipped about it, citing inner system security concerns, however it is undeniable, that three dozen destroyers performed a long burn towards Mars."

An image appeared on the screen of thirty six points of light heading off into the distant void.

"Now that is interesting. Mars is already defended by the EDCF Martian task force and the Martian Defence Forces, so I can't imagine why they'd be going there", Joy remarked.

Rita added in, "We do know that President Banyan has officially said, *'No Comment'* and that *'He cannot speak about operational matters'*. So Chuck, what do you think?"

"I wouldn't want to speculate on their mission Rita, but I don't think those thirty six destroyers are going to stay at Mars", Chuck replied, "Perhaps it's just a refuelling stop over on a much larger unknown mission."

Harry added in, speculating, "Perhaps this fleet is our first return salvo at the Jovian Realms?"

"Who knows Harry. We'll just have to wait and see how this all pans out", Chuck replied.

"More news from Mars", Joy noted.

"Yes Joy. A Belter ship from out of Pallas has been seized by Admiral Zumwalt and the EDCF Martian task force", Rita replied, "The Belter Ship, the Blood Nut, was seized and it's entire crew and its Captain arrested. They were bounty hunters from Pallas, contracted by the Jovian High Council to apprehend the crew of the Martian Defence Force Ship Solstice."

Joy replied, "Well, that would not have gone down very well with Admiral Zumwalt. Fleet Captain Carmichael did say not so long ago, *'if you come after ours, we come after you'.*"

Harry added, "Bounty hunters are illegal across the entire inner solar system and being contracted by the enemy, that makes them privateers."

"Exactly Harry. The Belter ship, the Blood Nut, has been recycled. Its Captain and crew have been trialled by military tribunal and found guilty. They are on the their way to the Earth for long term incarceration", Joy commented.

"That will definitely make any other bounty hunters think twice!", Chuck chuckled.

"What were they thinking in the first place?", Harry questioned, telling the others, "Captain Folcrom Forkbraid, if I remember correctly, was the most powerful psychic on the Earth. Have people forgotten that?"

"That is a good question Harry, but we have to remember psychics can't use their abilities off world", Chuck pointed out.

"True, but we are talking about Forkbraid. He's no ordinary psychic and he isn't actually off world either, he's on Mars", Harry reminded Chuck.

"That is true Harry. With Admiral Zumwalt's latest actions however, only the craziest bounty hunters are likely to take up that challenge", Chuck replied.

"And that should seriously upset the High Prince of the Jovian Realms", Harry laughed.

"So how are the Horridian's dealing with all of this?", Joy asked.

"They have doubled down Joy. Seriously, the Jovian High Council has doubled down", Chuck replied, adding, "They simply don't except that the Solstice and its Captain and crew are a part of the Martian Defence Forces."

Pictures of the Captain and crew of the Solstice appeared on the screen.

"Yes, but they are military, everyone knows this. It is official, they are Martian Defence Force personnel", Joy replied.

"True, they are, but the Jovian High Council doesn't care. They really just don't care", Chuck replied, "They have doubled those bounties. Twenty million Jovian credits for Captain Folcrom Forkbraid, ten million Jovian credits for First officer James Murphy, ten million Jovian credits for Leroy McGuvan and two million Jovian credits a piece for the rest of the crew."

"Let's not forget. In the latest wanted videos, which they are pushing out over and over again across the entire solar network, they are offering one hundred million Jovian credits just for the ship itself, the Solstice. We are talking about well over one hundred and sixty million Jovian golden credits all up and that will draw out the crazies. Gold always does", Harry added.

Further pictures of the Captain and crew of the solstice appeared on the screen, this time along with images of the Solstice.

"Yes. That's another thing. They now want the ship as well", Chuck replied, adding, "That makes me wonder about the level of Jovian technology. Why else would they want the ship?"

"I have to agree with you on that one Chuck. Why else would they want the ship", Harry agreed.

"What about this annexation of Mars?", Rita enquired.

"Well Rita, that's just a toothless proclamation with nothing to back it up",

Chuck replied, adding, "Let's see what President Banyan had to say about it."

President Banyan's image appeared on the screen in his most recent news conference, only the relevant section was played, "The Jovian High Council's proclamation is a just a worthless piece of paper. Mars is an independent world with its own Government and its own Defence Forces. More importantly Mars is a member of the Inner Solar System Defence Alliance and an ally of ours. The EDCF Martian task force is in orbit around Mars as we speak to guarantee, Martian independence. The Jovian High Council has no jurisdiction whatsoever and no say in the matter."

Then the screen went blank once more.

"So there you have it, our own President is saying it's just Jovian nonsense", Chuck commented.

"Well if we need to hear more on the issue, there is the statement from the Martian Council of Governors", Harry informed them.

The Martian Governor's council chambers appeared on the screen. There were eight seats at the table. Seven had Martian colonial governors sitting in them. At the head of the table was Governor Anderson of Chryce colony, the largest colony on Mars. One seat, labelled Elysium, was empty.

Governor Anderson was addressing the whole solar system, "For those of you who don't know who I am, I am Governor Anderson of the Chryce colony on Mars. I am the current Head of the Martian Council of Governors, the Elon of Mars."

Governor Anderson, took a breath and continued, "By now you will have heard of the so called annexation of Mars by the Jovian High Council. This is complete nonsense. Mars has NOT been annexed by the Jovian High Council. Mars is a fully independent, self governing and a free world. Mars is also a member of the Inner Solar System Defence Alliance and we have absolutely no intention of ever becoming a Jovian Realm."

Governor Anderson continued, "The Jovian High Council has already tried twice and they have failed each time. First they attacked with missiles, each armed with ten independently targeting cold fusion warheads. Those missiles and warheads were destroyed by our Martian Defence Forces. Next they attacked with an occupation force from their Aft Trojan Colonial Realm. Those troops were defeated at the Battle of the Elysium Plains and sent packing, with their tails between their legs. Again they were defeated by the Martian Defence Forces."

"Today, Mars is stronger than ever. Our Martian Defence Forces have been expanded. Our allies from the Earth and L5 have sent us a fleet to aid in the defence of Mars and its colonies. If the Jovian High Council takes issue with this and makes any further attempts to attack us, they will fail. Mark my words. Martian resolve is stronger than it has ever been and we will never submit to the Jovian High Council demands. Should they come for us again in the future, they will be defeated every time!", Governor Anderson concluded and the screen went blank once more.

"Wow! Governor Anderson seems adamant", Rita commented, "They are not going to submit."

"No they are not Rita. They will not submit to the Horridian Dynasty and its imperialist ambitions", Chuck agreed.

"Perhaps those three dozen destroyers heading for Mars are a part of the Martian defences?", Joy speculated.

"Possibly Joy, but I'm thinking there's something else afoot. Something different", Harry replied.

"Whatever the case, it is apparent that the Jovian High Council's annexation announcement is a farce", Chuck added.

"It does certainly seem extremely premature to annex a whole world, indeed, its entire orbital zone, over which they have absolutely no control", Rita noted.

"Did you notice that only seven of eight Governors were present at the table?", Joy noted.

"Yes I did Joy", Chuck noted, "That's the seat set aside for the new Elysium colony. The Elysium Governor has yet to take up her position with the Council of Governors."

"Her position did you say Chuck?", Rita enquired.

"Yes. The Governor of the Elysium colony is the Lady Folcrom Selene", Chuck informed her.

"So the Governor of the new Elysium colony, was the second most powerful psychic on the Earth?", Rita commented and questioned.

"Yes indeed Rita. You are correct", Chuck confirmed.

"That in itself is very interesting Chuck. Very interesting", Joy remarked.

"Well we know that the annexation of Mars is a farce, but what the hell is going on with those family portraits?", asked Rita, adding, "Why now? Why did they release these portraits, along with the Mars annexation proclamation and the updated wanted videos? All at the same time?"

"Yes. Isn't it bizarre. By now everyone across the solar system will have seen them", Joy replied, "The ruling family of the Jovian Realms, the Horridian Dynasty has released these family portraits."

The family portraits appeared on the screen, with the portrait of the six Horridian siblings in the centre and their individual family portraits arranged around them on the outside. Running clockwise from the top, in order of birth.

"By now everyone will have seen these portraits, but for those who haven't, let me introduce the Horridian siblings to you", Chuck remarked, adding, "At the top you have His Royal Majesty, High Prince Heinrich von Horridian, Prince of Ganymede and his family. Rotating clockwise, you have His Royal Highness, Prince Wulfric von Horridian, Prince of Callisto and his family, followed by His Royal Highness, Prince Valdamar von Horridian, Prince of Europa and his family. Then you have Her Royal Highness, Princess Sophia von Horridian, Princess of the Jovian Fore Trojan Asteroids and Her Royal Highness, Princess Luisa von Horridian, Princess of the Jovian Aft Trojan Asteroids. Then finally the youngest, His Royal Highness, Prince Leopold von Horridian, Prince of Io and his family. Those are the six Horridian Siblings and the current rulers of the Jovian Realms."

"Right bastards those six. Responsible for the mass murder of well over two and a half million people", Harry added.

"It seems only the Brothers are married. That does seem odd", Rita noted.

"Yes, I was just noticing that myself Rita. Maybe they're just picky", Joy replied, then added, "I've also notice that young Prince Leopold and his family appear to be far more casual."

Harry speculated sarcastically, "Perhaps young Prince Leopold can't afford the finery of his Brothers and Sisters? Maybe he's the poor Sibling?"

"Harry. He is the Prince of Io, it's far more likely he and his wife chose to dress that way", Chuck replied, "Although, he and his wife appear to be wearing pendants with peace symbols. They're probably the hippies of the Horridian family."

"Horridian hippies? Really Chuck?", Harry questioned and almost laughed at the suggestion.

"There has been some speculation that there is a hidden message in these portraits. Something that only their followers and agents in the inner system worlds can read", Rita informed them.

"If there was our government intelligence agencies would already know about it by now", Chuck commented, then added, "One thing is certain. We know who the Horridian's are, what they look like and better yet, where they live. I'm sure that has been well noted by our military, as well as our legal prosecutors."

"The High Prince is wearing a Mars astrological pendant around his neck", Joy pointed out and added, "There has been some speculation, that this is a part of his fixation on the planet Mars."

"The odd thing is, there are actually people out there in the community, saying that High Prince Heinrich von Horridian is an incarnation of the ancient Greek God of Aries. That he's a war God, literally the God of Mars", Joy replied.

"I have heard that one myself Joy", Rita admitted, "There are some people in our society who would believe any crazy theory or conspiracy put forward."

"Well, personally I think that High Prince Heinrich is just an appalling person and nothing more. Personally, I consider him and his siblings to be war criminals", Harry replied.

"We may never know why they sent out of these family portraits. I myself find the timing to be quite peculiar", Joy noted.

"Something I'd like to talk about are those Trojan Occupation Forces", Rita remarked.

"Which ones Rita?", Joy enquired, "There were of course two groups of them."

"Well the ones that were defeated at the Battle of the Elysium plains and were sent packing have already returned home. So I'm talking about that huge fleet they sent towards L5", Rita replied.

"The two hundred troop transports and two hundred heavy weapons transports", Harry noted.

"Yes Harry. The Battle of L5, although devastating, was a failure for the Jovian Realms. That fleet, had it continued on its original course would have been annihilated", Rita explained, then continued, "Fleet Captain Carmichael and Captain Forkbraid gave that fleet a heads up and saved it. Why? That is my question. Why wasn't that an act of treason?"

"No. Not treason, but it was very controversial. There is still a great deal of debate going on about that very action and its legalities. Something else to take note of, Captain Forkbraid is of course now Fleet Captain Forkbraid of the Martian Defence Forces", Chuck replied.

"My understanding is that the Earth's General Stanton also agreed with that action", Joy replied.

"True enough and even President Banyan had agreed with that action as well", Harry replied, adding, "The President did state, that not slaughtering a hundred and twenty five thousand enemy combatants was an act of mercy that he entirely agreed with. They had his approval before hand."

"Yes, but would the Jovian High Council have done the same for us?", Rita questioned.

"I doubt it. Look at those unprovoked missile attacks", Chuck stepped in, adding, "The thing to remember is, we are not like them. We actually care about lives."

"Chuck is right Rita. Right or wrong, we showed them mercy and they are alive as a result. That is our way. We care about lives, even those of our enemies. That's the difference between us and them. Us and those Horridians", Joy replied.

"Well there is an interesting side effect of that action", Rita informed her colleagues.

The screen then displayed an image of nearly four hundred small lights. They were like tiny little dots against the backdrop of space. A tracker at the bottom corner of the screen displayed their hohmann transfer orbit and current position along their course.

"What you're looking at on the screen are those Trojan Occupation Forces heading home. This feed is now public and everyone has access to it. As you can see, the Trojans still have quite a long way to go", Rita noted.

"So Rita, this side effect you mentioned?", Joy asked.

"That feed. That screen", Rita replied quickly, explaining, "It is mesmerising to some people."

"Mesmerising?", Chuck joined in questioningly.

"There are apparently people out there, who spend literally hours staring at that feed", Rita replied, adding, "Sometimes even days."

"I have heard about that", Joy admitted, "Isn't that bizarre."

"Bizarre or not, it is a phenomenon. There are people, who as Rita noted, are mesmerised by that feed", Harry remarked, adding, "There is something about those hundreds of slow moving lights."

"If you look very closely, you can see that the Trojan fleet is actually flying in two groups", Rita remarked while squinting at the screen.

Harry commented, "My understanding is that the Trojan fleet is dividing into two. It is believed that half will travel directly to the Aft Trojan colonies trailing Jupiter and that other half will peel away and change course for the Fore Trojan colonies ahead of Jupiter. When that happens, we may even be able to see their long burn course adjustments."

Rita replied, "Wow! I'm looking forward to seeing that."

To which Joy remarked, "Wow! Let's take that off the screen right now, before we get anyone else mesmerised and hooked on it."

Rita commented, "We have news coming out of the Venusian colonies as well."

"Yes we do Rita", Joy agreed, "Since the attacks on the Earth and L5, there has been a ten fold increase in emigration to Venus and its colonies. Parents worried about the war are looking for safer places to raise their families."

"The Venusian authorities are more than happy to receive the new immigrants and have been very welcoming of this new influx", Rita remarked.

"Perhaps a bit of background might be useful for our viewers", Harry replied and the screen displayed a diagram of the Sun, Venus and its Lagrangian points.

Harry continued, "As most of our viewers are probably aware, Venus has a great many floating cloud cities. These are floating fifty kilometres high in the Venusian atmosphere, where temperatures and pressures are very similar to those on the Earth. However, the main Venusian colonies are at Venusian Lagrangian point one. Venus Colonial Central Command and the bulk of Venus's colonies are located in that L1 region."

Chuck continued on from Harry, "Venus's L2 region is in constant darkness and that region is used for astronomical and scientific research. Sixty degrees ahead of Venus you have their L4 region and sixty degrees behind Venus you have their L5 region. Those regions also have many industrial colonies and facilities. Many small asteroids, mainly Venus crossing asteroids, have been moved into those locations for processing. They even have colonies at their L3 region on the opposite side of the Sun from Venus. So the Venusian authorities are happy to receive immigrants."

Harry continued, "But here is the interesting thing. The Venusian authorities want to open up Mercury's orbital zone for colonisation. They have been working on new colony designs capable of handling the increased solar radiation in the Mercurian orbital zone for around two decades now."

Chuck stepped back in, "The Venusian authorities have been in discussions with both the Earth and L5 governments. Their proposal, is that for every credit Venus puts into opening up the Mercurian orbital zone to colonisation, that the Earth and L5 match them in equal investment."

"Of course we are at war and that includes all the worlds and colonies of the inner solar system defence alliance. So these new developments have been put on the back burner until after this war is concluded. None the less we should continue to watch this space", Chuck concluded.

"Finding colonies in the Kuiper Belt, opening up colonies in the Mercurian orbital zone. If not for this horrendous war, these would be exciting times", Joy concluded.

Rita then tossed in, "Let's end today's show with this little piece of controversy. Verbal barbs have been thrown back and forth between the Flat Earth and the Flat Mars Societies."

"Now Rita, I know there is a Flat Earth Society, but a Flat Mars Society as well. That has got to be someone's idea of a bad joke. Surely someone is taking the piss!", Chuck replied.

"Oh, I wish it was Chuck, I wish it was. The mind really boggles. It really does", Rita replied.

Joy then asked, "So why are they throwing barbs at each other Rita?"

"Well. As we might expect, the Flat Earthers are saying that Mars is a globe moving in the shell of the firmament. The Flat Marsers are saying that's completely wrong", Rita commented, adding, "According to the Flat Mars people, the Earth is a globe moving in the shell of the firmament and it's Mars that is Flat. Go figure!"

"In this day and age, with colonies across the entire solar system, to think, we still have people who believe that worlds are flat", Harry interjected.

"I'm surprised they're not saying that both the Earth and Mars are flat and that each is sitting on the backs of four elephants, standing on the back of some cosmic space turtle" Chuck scoffed.

Joy laughed and added, "Maybe they'll reach that compromise Chuck."

Harry laughed and tossed in, "It's hard enough to believe that Flat Earthers still exist in the year twenty three sixty two. Now we have Flat Marsers as well. It's all kinds of bat crap crazy!"

"That's probably the case Harry, but honestly, I'm eagerly waiting to hear from the Flat Venus Society and what they think on these issues", Rita laughed.

"Oh please Rita. Please don't encourage these crazy people", Harry replied.

"And with that I think we should signed off for today", Rita concluded.

Chuck's colleague Harry stepped in with, "Once again folks, In the News, Weekly Hot Takes was brought to you by our sponsors, the Recruitment Offices of the Earth Defence Forces and the L5 Colonial Fleet."

Their other colleague Rita then added, "Do have Professional skills. The Earth Defence Forces and L5's Colonial Fleet need you. Perhaps you'd like on the job training? The Earth Defence Forces and L5's Colonial Fleet can provide you with all the latest on the job training you need."

Then their other colleague Joy, completed the announcement with, "Generous sign-up bonuses are available for whoever you join, the Earth Defence Forces or L5's Colonial Fleet."

Then Chuck signed off with, "I'm Chuck Simmons and you have been watching In the News, Weekly Hot Takes, with Joy Singh, Rita Verne and Harry Motley."

Then the news feed switched to next programmed show.

13. Flies on the Wall

Selene opened the door of her apartment and straight away probed for the presence of Forkbraid.

Not picking up his presence, Selene shouted out, "Are you in Forkbraid?"

There was no answer, so Selene quickly looked around her apartment, looking first in their meditation room.

"There you are Forkbraid", Selene thought to herself, as she noticed Forkbraid was meditating and in a state of deep samadhi.

Not wanting to disturb Forkbraid, Selene positioned a cushion on the floor next to him, sat down cross legged upon it and began to meditate herself, planning to meet Forkbraid within his meditation. As Selene slipped deeper and deeper into her meditation, the wall before her began to change. Selene concentrated on her breathing, breathing in and breathing out, breathing in and breathing out, as the changes in the wall before her began to coalesce.

Slowly, an ornate door way began to appear in the wall before her. It appeared to be an old style, thick wooden door surrounded by rough hewn, blue stone blocks, which formed a perfect arch at the top. The fittings, hinges, handles etc, appeared to be black wrought iron. There was a Sigil in the centre of the keystone in the Arch. Selene watched without watching, allowing her mind to do nothing more than concentrate on her breathing. Breathing in and breathing out, breathing in and breathing out.

Slowly the thought crossed her mind, *"I've seen this before Forkbraid. You're astral projecting again aren't you."*

Forkbraid did not answer, his body was present, but he himself was not.

Slowly Selene launched into an out of body experience by pulling herself out of her body, up through her crown chakra. Selene's astral body projected to the ornate door and it opened upon her approach. Selene astral projected through the door's threshold to find Forkbraid.

Looking around her, Selene considered where she was, *"I'm in a cylindrical colony's end cap"*, she thought to herself, looking around more carefully, *"It's a northern end cap."*

Looking behind her, Selene could see that the doorway was in the wall of an apartment building. There were people wondering all about, but they could not see the door, nor could they see Selene.

"Why here? Where is this place? Where is Forkbraid?", Selene thought to herself.

Selene looked around the end cap, it definitely appeared to be the northern end cap of an O'Neil type colony cylinder. A very big one as well. Certainly not L5's Colonial Central Command. As that colony was an exception to the general rule, having its administration, business, legal and political structures in its southern end cap. This huge cylindrical colony was completely northern end cap oriented, as almost every other O'Neil type colony was. This colonial cylinder had to be Jovian!

The revelation hit Selene like a slap in the face, *"Jovian! We're in the Jovian Realms. On one of the Jovian Primes in fact"*, she considered as she looked around her.

It was equally possible, that this colony was a Prime in another outer Planet's system, like Saturn, Uranus or Neptune. However, Forkbraid would have no requirement to go those systems. So this had to be one of the Jovian Realms.

Across the other side of the end cap, roughly four kilometres or so away, was a large estate with a palace in its centre. More than likely, the palace of one of the Horridian Princes.

Selene smiled, *"This will be Prince Leopold's realm, Io Prime. Forkbraid is attempting to make contact"*, she thought to herself.

Selene smiled again and then projected across to the palace grounds on the other side of the end cap. Selene landed in the palace grounds on a grassy knoll near a large lake. Forkbraid's astral form was standing at the top of the knoll, as if waiting for her.

"What took you so long Selene?", Forkbraid asked.

"I was busy with the Grey Council and didn't get your message until after the meeting finished", Selene explained, then asked, *"So what's happening?"*, as she looked towards the lake.

Forkbraid pointed to the group of people sitting on picnic rugs, on the soft, verdant green grass in front of the lake, *"This little gathering Selene. It took me quite a while to find them. When I projected straight to this Prime, my portal opened up in wall directly opposite my target. I found that to be very strange. Very strange indeed."*

Selene looked at the small group. There were four men and one was easily recognised from his portrait, as Prince Leopold. Of the four men, three were unknown to her, although one looked official. There were also four women and one was easily recognised as Princess Giselle. One of the four woman was looking after a baby, Prince Ulrick and so must have been their nanny. There were two teenagers were frolicking nearby. Selene could see that they were having a picnic and mentally noted three fishing rods along the bank of the lake in rod holders, quite close to the four men.

"Why did it take you a while Forkbraid?", Selene asked.

"I went to the palace first and wasted time trying to locate the Prince there", Forkbraid replied.

"Let me introduce you to this little group Selene", Forkbraid remarked, *"I've been skimming the surface of their minds. You have His Royal Highness, Prince Leopold. His wife Princess Giselle and their child, young Prince Ulrick. That's their nanny looking after the young Prince. Her name is Mary and she is a Slave."*

"A Slave?", Selene queried.

"Yes Selene. They have Slaves in the Jovian Realms", Forkbraid informed her, then continued, *"That official looking guy is Hubert. He is the Prince's trusted man. He is also a Slave."*

"And they're happy with that situation?", Selene asked.

"Trust me Selene. Slave's or not, they are both fiercely, fiercely loyal to the Prince and his family", Forkbraid explained, then added, *"Those two are Abram and Miriam Appelbaum. Both from the Earth, both Jewish and clever enough to avoid Slavery."*

"Avoid Slavery?", Selene questioned.

"Oh yes Selene. Here, if you fill in your immigration forms the wrong way, you end up a Slave", Forkbraid explained, adding, *"The others are Rajsheev and Rani Neru and their daughters, Lakshmi and Pavarti. This is very interesting. Lakshmi and Pavarti are free citizens of the Jovian Realms, their parents however, are Slaves. The Mother is 'owned' by the Appelbaums, the Father is 'owned' by the Daughters. Contrivances to keep them both safe, I believe. The Appelbaums are from the Earth and the Nerus are from L5, from the Hyper Dynamics Corporation. Princess Giselle was originally from the Earth as well and get this, she was a Slave. Giselle was freed by the High Prince himself, so that Prince Leopold and Giselle could marry."*

"You've been here long enough to glean all of that?", Selene asked and then noted while smiling, *"Prying into their minds like that, is almost creepy Forkbraid."*

"Yes Selene, long enough to glean all that and a lot more. And yes, it is somewhat creepy, but we need to know who these people are and what we are dealing with", Forkbraid answered and then added, *"This little group, is another little nexus, happening here, in the Jovian Realms."*

"A nexus. In what way Forkbraid?", Selene questioned.

"The Appelbaums are problem solvers and they've fallen into the lap of Prince Leopold who is a reformer, both he and his wife Giselle. The Prince wants to end Slavery in the Jovian Realms. Slavery is currently the norm everywhere out here", Forkbraid explained, adding, *"And along comes Rajsheev Neru and his family. Rajsheev was a positronic matrix design engineer from L5, from Hyper Dynamics Corporation. Rajsheev actually worked with Peter Swann. Now Rajsheev, is no Peter Swann, but he is damned cleaver in his own right. A highly intelligent man."*

"So ending Slavery by introducing locally built Androids", Selene caught on.

"Yes, but there's more, much more", Forkbraid replied, adding, *"Prince Leopold and his wife Giselle have already put in place measures to free the Children of Slaves from Slavery, in their Ionian Realm. They both hate the war and they are our best hope for peace. Think about it. Prince Leopold is in line to the throne. Assuming his Siblings can be removed from the line of succession, Prince Leopold then becomes the legitimate heir of all the Jovian Realms."*

"Oh my! Forkbraid, I hadn't expected any of this", Selene replied, asking, *"Are you going to try and contact them?"*

"I am thinking about it. Seriously thinking about it", Forkbraid admitted, *"We do need more information though."*

Both Selene and Forkbraid stepped further down the knoll towards the lake, when they both noticed one of the fishing floats disappear under the water. A split second later the bells on the attached fishing rod went off.

Forkbraid remarked excitedly, telepathically, *"Fish on!"*

Prince Leopold quickly stood up and rushed to his fishing rod. He carefully took off the bells, clipping them on to his vest, then he picked up his fishing rod and adjusted the tension on the reel. Slowly the Prince began to real in the fish. A few seconds later the submerged float popped back up and into view. Not long afterwards the Prince had reeled the fished in close to shore. Abram quickly rushed over with a fishing net, placing it in the water. Prince Leopold reeled the fish above the net, so Abram could quickly bring it ashore. It was a large rainbow trout.

"A nice fish", Forkbraid thought to himself and Selene.

Princess Giselle picked up young Prince Ulrick and walked over to her husband, "Look Ulrick, Daddy caught a fish", as she showed her young Son the fish.

Selene thought to Forkbraid, *"Isn't that so sweet."*

Prince Ulrick however, was not looking at the fish and every time he was turned to look at the fish, he instead turned to look back up the grassy knoll. The young prince was more interested on something else up on the small hill.

Forkbraid took notice of this immediately, *"Can Prince Ulrick see us?"*, he questioned.

"Maybe, potentially", Selene replied, adding, *"Babies are a little bit special in that regard. Perhaps young Ulrick has potential."*

"What are you looking at Ulrick?", Princess Giselle asked, as she too looked up the small hill.

Prince Ulrick smiled and giggled in reply.

Lakshmi and Pavarti ran up the small hill, with their arms outstretched as if flying, "Maybe he's looking at us", Pavarti shouted out as the two Girls ran straight through Forkbraid and Selene's astral projections.

"Whoa. I felt that", Selene commented silently.

"I know. You do get use to it", Forkbraid replied.

Giselle commented, "We have enough fish for a nice meal tonight. Our chef will do wonders with these trout. You are all invited to dinner and you can stay overnight at the palace."

"Are you sure Giselle? You and Leopold have already been so very generous", Miriam replied.

"Of course Miriam. We like company and we will certainly enjoy yours. Make yourselves at home", Giselle replied.

Leopold added, "Hubert will organise your rooms and transport you back to your apartment, after breakfast tomorrow."

Lakshmi and Pavarti who were still *'flying'* around the hill, chasing each other, stopped and pointed upwards and across the northern end cap, Lakshmi remarked, "Our apartment looks so small and weird from over here."

Forkbraid looked at Selene, *"Ah, that's why my portal opened up on the wrong side of the end cap. That's their apartment building over there on the other side. Probably the penthouse."*

"Well Forkbraid, if you're not going to make contact now, we should go", Selene replied, *"You did say you needed more information. So where do we go next?"*

"I'm thinking Ganymede Prime", Forkbraid replied as they both projected back to their portal.

Once back outside the Appelbaum's and Neru's apartment block, Selene and Forkbraid quickly slipped through the ornate doorway and back into their meditation room, before returning to their respective bodies. The ornate door, the portal, slowly faded away as they both returned from their meditative state to waking consciousness.

"Well we certainly got a lot of information", Selene noted.

"Yes, but we need much more. I want to investigate how the line of succession works in the Horridian Dynasty", Forkbraid replied.

"How does that help us?", Selene asked.

"I'd expect the High Prince's Children to be the next in line. From what I currently understand, the Boys by birth, then the Girls", Forkbraid replied, explaining, "Beyond them, the line probably moves to the next oldest Male Sibling and his Children and so on and so on. That puts Prince Leopold, probably after Prince Wulfric and Prince Valdamar and their Children."

"So Prince Leopold is way down the list", Selene understood.

"Exactly. If we want Prince Leopold to be become the High Prince we have two choices", Forkbraid replied, "Eliminate three families or somehow get the High Prince himself to change the line of succession in Prince Leopold's favour."

"Well you know me Forkbraid. We are not going to murder three families", Selene responded.

"Then that means manipulating the High Prince to change the line of succession in favour of his Brother, Prince Leopold", Forkbraid replied.

"Forkbraid, just how many attempts did you make before you were able to astral project to Io Prime", Selene questioned.

"Three Selene. I had to first project to Jupiter's system. Once I had that right, I projected to Io, the actual moon. Then after that, I projected to Io Prime's northern end cap. Small steps slowly and it was not easy. I must say", Forkbraid replied.

Selene smiled and chuckled, "I did it in one Forkbraid. Although, I was following your portal."

"I can tell you this much Selene. When you astral project to somewhere that is uninhabitable, with a hostile environment, like Io, it is both frightening and exhilarating at the same time", Forkbraid informed her.

"I can imagine Forkbraid", Selene replied, then asked, "So what do we do next?"

"My next step, is to project to Ganymede and from there, project to Ganymede Prime's northern end cap", Forkbraid explained.

"Okay Forkbraid, but can we do that after lunch?", Selene suggested.

"Of course Selene, I was about the suggest that", Forkbraid agreed.

With lunch over, Selene and Forkbraid returned to their meditation room. The both sat down on their respective cushions and began to meditate. Once again concentrating on their breath, breathing in and breathing out, breathing in and breathing out. It was not long before they both entered a state of deep samadhi. Forkbraid opened an ornate portal in the wall facing them. Then Selene and Forkbraid both launched into out of body experiences, by pulling themselves out of their bodies, up through their crown chakras.

"Each portal I create is slightly different. The previous one was anchored to Io Prime. I need to anchor this portal to Ganymede Prime. Once I've done that, I can call up this portal directly to Ganymede Prime anytime I wish, directly from memory", Forkbraid informed Selene.

"Show me how it's done then Forkbraid. I need to learn these techniques", Selene replied.

"So be it", Forkbraid replied.

Forkbraid's astral form took Selene's by the hand, as he led her through the portal. In the blink of an eye, their astral bodies were hovering in the void in Jovian space, just outside the orbit of Jupiter's moon Callisto. Selene shuddered and shivered, gasping for air, before quickly composing herself. An unphased Forkbraid quickly spied Jupiter's moon Ganymede in the distance and in a second blink of an eye, their astral bodies were standing on the surface of Ganymede.

Selene shuddered and shivered once again, gasping for air and it took her longer this time to compose herself. It also took longer this time for Forkbraid to locate his next target, the immense cylindrical colony that was Ganymede Prime. Carefully Forkbraid scanned the distant colony, Ganymede Prime to locate its northern end cap. Then in the blink of an eye, they were both standing inside Ganymede Prime's northern end cap.

Looking around the inside of the northern end cap, Forkbraid quickly spied the palace of the High Prince and in a blink, they were both just inside the high walls of the palace grounds. Selene was shuddering and shivering uncontrollably now and this time Selene was unable to compose herself. Forkbraid touched his astral forehead to Selene's astral forehead and her shuddering and shivering slowly dissipated before stopping completely.

Forkbraid pressed his right astral hand against the wall of the palace grounds and an ornate doorway appeared embedded within it. It glowed brightly and Forkbraid noted, *"The portal is set."*

"Does it always feel like this when you project out this far?", Selene asked.

"At first Selene. It's your mind's reaction to projecting into space, into the void. After you project a few more times, that reaction will go away, as you grow use to it", Forkbraid explained.

"You might have warned me", Selene told Forkbraid with a cross look on her face.

"It would not have made any difference Selene", Forkbraid replied, explaining, *"Until you get use to it, your mind will react and it takes several projections to get use to it. It is what it is."*

"So where are we exactly?", Selene asked.

"We are in the grounds of High Prince Heinrich's Palace", Forkbraid informed.

Selene pointed to the portal, *"And the portal is set?"*

"Yes. All set Selene. Going back and forth from here now, will be much easier", Forkbraid confirmed, *"Now let's look around this place."*

Forkbraid and Selene looked around the grounds of High Prince Heinrich's palace, finding little of any interest. The grounds were beautifully maintained, with well manicured lawns, well managed trees, shrubs and lakes. So they decided to investigate the palace itself and made a bee line to the palace's front entrance. Upon reaching the driveway to the palace, they were fortunate to see an approaching vehicle. It appeared to be a stretched, transport pod. Two men stepped out of the pod and walked quickly towards the palace doors.

"Isn't that the Prophet?", Selene thought to Forkbraid.

"Indeed it is", Forkbraid confirmed, *"I believe that the other one is his pilot, Matthew. At least that's what Miranda's and Leroy's memories tell me."*

"We'd better follow them Forkbraid", Selene recommended.

Forkbraid smiled and nodded, as they both followed the Prophet and Matthew into the palace.

The Prophet and Matthew entered the conference room, taking their seats as usual. Selene and Forkbraid entered the room unseen and stood silently in astral form against one of the walls. Prince Valdamar and Prince Wulfric both entered the room and the usual formalities were observed. Then the High Prince himself entered the conference room, followed by yet more formalities.

"Forkbraid! This is gold!", Selene silently exclaimed.

Forkbraid smiled, *"Absolutely! We're like flies on the wall."*

High Prince Heinrich opened the meeting, "Gentlemen, Brothers, thank you for attending. Our younger Brother Leopold will not be present again."

"Our younger Brother is making a bad habit of that", Prince Wulfric commented dryly.

"Do I need to remind you Wulfric, that you are the reason Leopold does not want to attend?", the High Prince replied rhetorically, then forcefully added, "Perhaps I should insist on his attendance next time, so you can goad him again. Only this time, maybe, I'll just let him take your head!"

Prince Wulfric lowered his head and fell silent.

This surprised both Selene and Forkbraid, the Horridian Brothers don't always get along and they exchanged surprised looks at one and other.

"Callthrope! What's happening with our Sister Luisa?", the High Prince demanded.

"Your Majesty. Princess Luisa did become somewhat disturbed shall we say, at President Banyan's remarks, about the Aft Trojan Army's routing and running away with their tails between their legs. More than a little disturbed in fact. Princess Luisa was to say the least apoplectic", Callthrope, Princess Luisa's representative informed the High Prince.

"So the usual then Callthrope. Luisa was just wanting to sever yet more heads? Get out the old guillotine?", the High Prince enquired.

"Yes, yes Your Majesty. We, that is Her Highness's minders, have adjusted her medication accordingly", Callthrope replied, "Her Highness is currently somewhat more stable."

"Callthrope, you make sure Luisa is kept that way. We can't afford her getting out of control and destabilising the Aft Trojan realm. My will be done! Understand?", the High Prince ordered.

Callthrope nodded and replied, "Yes, yes Your Majesty."

"Kittens! What about our other Sister Sophia?", the High Prince enquired.

Kittens, Princess Sophia's representative, gulped slightly and then replied, "Your Majesty, Princess Sophia has recently dabbled in potions once more, as Her Highness does like to do. There were actually several poisonings and half of the victims died. Eight people in fact. Some of those deaths were amongst Her Highness's minders Your Majesty."

"Why wasn't this brought to my immediate attention Kittens?", the High Prince demanded.

"Your Majesty, I do apologise. I've only received this information earlier today and I thought it prudent to bring it up at today's meeting", Kittens replied.

"Okay Kittens. What actions are being taken?", the High Prince enquired.

"Your Majesty. Her Highness's minders are in the process of adjusting her medications", Kittens replied, adding, "We should receive the results of those changes in a few days."

"Kittens, you keep on top of this situation. I don't want any destabilisation in the Fore Trojan Realm. That is my will and it will be done!", the High Prince commanded.

Kittens nodded and replied, "Yes, yes Your Majesty."

"Brother Heinrich. We should place our Sisters in an appropriate facility and put Regents in charge of their Realms. For the foreseeable future, at least until after this war is concluded", Prince Valdamar recommended.

"Valdamar, Brother. I will take that under advisement, but as long as their minders can keep our Sisters under control, there is no need to escalate these matters", the High Prince replied, thinking to himself, *"What the fuck is it about the women in our family."*

"Now I understand why their Sisters were alone in their family portraits", Selene noted.

Forkbraid picked up on the High Prince's thought and quickly, skimmed the surface of his mind, to learn more about the Horridian family.

"Now. Captain Murphy. What can you tell us about your people on Mars? What have they been up to? What are their plans?", the High Prince asked.

Selene and Forkbraid looked at each other, as they both thought, *"Captain Murphy? Captain Matthew Murphy? What the fuck!"*

Selene asked, *"Is he related to Jim, our Jim?"*

Forkbraid replied, *"No. He couldn't be. Could he?"*

Selene replied, *"He might be. He does look a bit like Jim. We will need to ask Jim about this."*

"Yes, when we get back", Forkbraid agreed, *"We need to get as much intel as we can."*

Matthew began, "Your Majesty. We have some news from Mars. Our Martian assets, the ones who made the attempt at capturing the fugitives. They are still recovering from whatever chemicals they were exposed during their operation. Our other Martian assets, the ones who are being coy, shall we say, they have sent us some useful information."

"Well Captain, that sounds like good news", the High Prince replied, ordering, "Spill it."

"Yes Your Majesty. Our assets have been looking into the records at Chryce colony", Matthew informed the High Prince, explaining, "When Lady Selene arrived on Mars, she took up the Governorship of the Elysium Colony and the Deanship of their so called Psychic Academy. According to the records, Lord Forkbraid, along with the Governors of the other seven major colonies inaugurated the Martian Defence Forces upon his arrival. Forkbraid was named the Fleet Captain and the Gunship Solstice was commissioned by him shortly thereafter. Five of his crew members were recruited at the same time. The remaining four crew members were recruited sometime after the Battle of New Tortuga."

"Captain. Are you telling me that the records at Chryce colony support the notion that the Solstice, her Captain and crew, are Martian Armed Forces personnel?", the High Prince demanded.

"No Your Majesty. I'm saying that the information provided by some of our Martian assets supports that notion. Right or wrong, for all intents and purposes, they appear to be Martian Armed Forces personnel. There is also more Your Majesty", Matthew replied.

"Go on then Captain", the High Prince ordered.

"Our assets looked into other Chryce records as well. Not just Military. They looked into the Martian Armed Force's payroll records", Matthew started, explaining, "The Captain and the crew of the Solstice are on the books with the Martian Defence Forces, along with other personnel. They are on the Defence Force's payroll and being remunerated in accordance with their positions, using the same pay scales the L5 colonial fleet uses."

Matthew paused for a moment then continued, "Our assets followed the money so to speak. Their pays are transferred into their bank accounts with the Chryce Central Bank. Upon looking into those accounts at the bank, there are individual patterns of withdrawals and expenditure. Those accounts are all being used exactly as if they were 'pay' accounts, just as anyone would expect. Your Majesty, everything points to the Captain and the crew of the Solstice as being legitimate Martian Defence Force personnel."

"I don't care what all the evidence says Captain. I still don't buy it. It's bullshit! Absolute bullshit!", the High Prince replied.

"Are we any closer to capturing these pirates?", the High Prince demanded.

"As you have ordered Your Majesty, we have doubled their bounties", Matthew replied, adding, "So combined, the fugitives now have sixty four million Jovian golden credits on their heads. In addition, as instructed, we have placed a one hundred million Jovian golden credit bounty on their ship. Still Your Majesty, as high as these bounties are, they may not be enough."

"One hundred and sixty four million credits! Not enough!", the High Prince could not believe it.

Matthew considered his words carefully, "Your Majesty. The last attempt by bounty hunters to capture the fugitives was thwarted by the EDCF Martian task force. Their ship, the Blood Nut, was seized and recycled. The Captain and his crew were arrested and trialled as privateers. They are going to be imprisoned on the Earth for a long time. Your Majesty, bounty hunters across the solar system have seen that and they weigh the risks accordingly."

General Tarzan stepped in, "Your Majesty. We contracted those bounty hunters, through a group in the Pallas Belter colonies. After the failure of their operation, our 'partners' are not happy. Not happy at all. They want compensation for the loss of their ship, the Blood Nut."

"Tell our *'partners'*, that they will be well compensated when they full-fill their contract", the High Prince commanded.

"Your Majesty. However, having lost one ship, its Captain and twenty crewmen, they no longer want that contract", General Tarzan informed the High Prince, explaining, "No one wants to go up against the Colonial Fleet or the Earth Defence Forces. No matter how high the reward."

"One hundred and sixty four million golden credits is not enough!", the High Prince repeated, then asked, "What if I doubled those bounties again?"

"Your Majesty", Matthew stepped in, "I don't think it would matter. There are no bounty hunters capable of going up against the Colonial Fleet or the Earth Defence Forces."

"Unless we embedded them into our own Jovian Armed Forces", Prince Valdamar suggested.

"Your Highness, for that to work, they would need to be an *'irregular force'* within our armed forces", Matthew replied, adding, "You could only use them effectively, on side missions, during a full on assault on Mars. Our forces would keep the Martian Defence Forces busy, while the *'irregulars'* would perform the capture and retrieval. Even then I doubt it would work."

"Why not Captain?", Prince Valdamar asked.

"Your Highness. Any defence of Mars would include the Gunship Solstice. Any *'irregular'* forces we throw against them would be obliterated. Our own ships of the line would have trouble tackling the Solstice, let alone a bunch of bounty hunters", Matthew replied.

"This is a complex issue Captain", the High Prince noted, "Perhaps we can have one of our think tanks consider what we can do in this area."

Everyone one sitting at the table nodded.

"What do we know about L5, General Tarzan?", the High Prince asked.

Both Selene and Forkbraid silently chuckled to themselves when they heard the General's name.

"Only what our scans tell us Your Majesty", the General replied, adding, "A fleet of three dozen Earth and L5 destroyers have left the staging grounds at cis-lunar L4 and they are en-route to Mars. They should arrive their shortly."

"General. Why do we know about this fleets movements?", the High Prince questioned.

"At present Your Majesty nothing", the General admitted, "We know that a fleet of thirty six destroyers is en-route to Mars. Why is unknown. Although, if I were to speculate, it may have something to do with the High Council's claim and declaration that Mars is a Jovian Realm."

"So it's possibly a reaction to our declaration of Jovian sovereignty over Mars? We claim Mars, they react. Is that what you're saying?", the High Prince questioned.

"Perhaps Your Majesty. There is already a fleet of fifteen ships in Martian orbit. The EDCF Martian task force. This new fleet maybe en-route to Mars to back them up", the General replied.

"Captain Murphy, what's your take on this?", the High Prince enquired.

Matthew was slower to answer, thinking carefully before replying, "Your Majesty. While it is possible that these destroyers are backup for the EDCF Martian task force, that may not necessarily be the case. We need to keep a close eye on this fleet. I suspect it have other purposes."

General Tarzan nodded and replied, "Agreed Captain. Your Majesty, it is just as Matthew says, we need to watch this new fleet like hawks."

The High Prince nodded in agreement, "Make it so!", he commanded.

"Prophet, what assets do we currently have at L5?", the High Prince asked.

"Your Majesty. To the best of my knowledge, what assets we had at L5, were either arrested by the L5 security services, disbanded or fled", the Prophet informed him, before looking towards Matthew for his take on the matter.

Matthew added, "That would be correct Your Majesty. Our people at L5 were mostly rounded up after we fled to Mars. Those that weren't rounded up, would have either gone to ground or fled themselves. We know they didn't flee to Mars. We know they couldn't flee to the Earth. The Earth's remote viewing teams would have easily tracked them down. That leaves just one other place."

"And that place would be?", the High Prince enquired.

"Venus Your Majesty. If our people fled and they couldn't flee to Mars or the Earth, they would have fled to Venus", Matthew informed the High Prince, adding, "Venus has many colonies in which they could hide. Many, many colonies."

Clearly this Matthew knew a hell of a lot and Forkbraid skimmed the surface of his mind.

The High Prince stood up and declared the meeting over, before quickly leaving the room. The others all left soon afterwards. Selene and Forkbraid silently left the room, following the Prophet and Matthew out of the palace. Then once outside, the pair made a bee line to the portal Forkbraid had created in the palace ground's wall and slipped through it back to their meditation room, back on Mars. The ornate doorway in the wall of their meditation room slowly dissolved as they both arose from their meditation and back to waking consciousness.

Selene straight away asked, "You did some peaking didn't you?"

"Selene. You know me. Of course I did", Forkbraid answered, adding, "You could have as well."

"Perhaps. I was still out of sorts from our trip to Ganymede Prime", Selene noted.

"Yeah. It did take me several attempts before I got use to it as well", Forkbraid replied, adding, "Next time, we'll use the portal. It will be a lot easier."

"So, let me get this straight. I could have just let you set up the portal and then just used that. I didn't actually have to come with you", Selene asked.

"Yes Selene, you could have, but then you would not have seen how to set up a portal", Forkbraid explained.

"I did ask, didn't I?", Selene remembered.

"Indeed you did Selene. Indeed you did", Forkbraid confirmed.

14. First Contact

Forkbraid walked into the conference room and looked around at the seated people. It looked as if everyone was present. Selene was sitting at the head of the table and a chair on her right hand side was vacant. The crew of the Solstice was all present, as were their family members, with the exception of Peter Swann's children. The Grey Council members were present, as was Roseanne, Cormac and Candy. Admiral Zumwalt and her Lieutenant Adjutant was also present.

"Good, it looks like everyone is present", Forkbraid remarked, as he quickly walked to his seat beside Selene.

Selene addressed the room, "Recently Forkbraid and I astrally projected to both Io Prime and Ganymede Prime. We found some interesting new information and confirmed other information."

"Astral projection?", queried Admiral Zumwalt.

"It's another psychic technique Admiral. Not an easy one to learn either. Most remote viewing teams use a form of astral projection", Selene informed the Admiral, "Projecting out as far as Jupiter and its moons is extraordinarily difficult and took Forkbraid a lot of time to perfect."

Admiral Zumwalt nodded in understanding.

Roseanne asked, "I thought you were able to astral project to the Earth and the other planets."

"It's not quite the same Roseanne", Selene replied.

Forkbraid explained, "Planets are much bigger targets than colonies. If they're festooned with life, like the Earth, they tend to stand out as bigger targets than those that have no life as well. So the Earth is easier than say the moons of Jupiter. More importantly, if someone in the past has placed a portal on a planet and those portals are known, then it's a much simpler process."

"Portals? Astral portals?", questioned Admiral Zumwalt.

"If one psychic, astrally travels to a world and places a portal on that world, then that portal information is transmitted to other psychics, then it becomes a matter of using an existing portal", Selene explained, "Which is a much simpler process. Trust me on that."

Forkbraid added, "There are a great number of worlds in the nearby solar systems and most of them have astral portals. An ancestor, Folcrom Tafazah, created them. Selene and I, both have that knowledge embedded in our memories."

"You might want to give us a list of those worlds Forkbraid", Admiral Zumwalt stated.

"Perhaps, but not now. We can worry about that when this war is over and our solar system is more united", Forkbraid replied, adding, "Anyway, psychic portals would be useless to you at present. Our people would need Starship technology to make use of this information."

"Understood. My understanding is that faster than light travel is still a long way off", Admiral Zumwalt replied, not knowing of recent developments with the Starship Solstice.

"Firstly, I can confirm that all of our bounties have been doubled", Forkbraid informed the room, adding, "The news feeds are accurate. There is even a bounty on our ship, the Solstice."

Zeealas replied, "So Zuawalo and I are worth two million Jovian golden credits each!"

Jim replied, "Zeealas, to me, you and Zuawalo are priceless. To me, you are both worth far more than any amount of money or gold."

Zeealas and Zuawalo both leant in and kissed Jim on the cheeks.

"You will be pleased to hear, that after the incident with the Belter Ship Blood Nut, the Jovian's are having trouble contracting bounty hunters. No one wants the contract, no matter how high the bounties. It's all too risky for them", Forkbraid told the room.

"Well that is good to hear FB", Jim responded.

Peter's wife Catherine added, "Yes. That is good to hear. That takes a load off my mind."

Forkbraid continued, "The Prophet has people at Lake Aram as we know and we do have them under surveillance. They have, however, been busy of late, looking into the records at Chryce colony. Those records very cleverly setup by Governor Anderson's people. Those records appear to have fooled the operatives, however, the High Prince does not accept that information. He's not buying it at all and the bounties all still stand. Their other assets at Lake Oudemans are still recovering from the affliction that Roseanne slapped them with. I'm recommending we step up surveillance on them none the less."

"Both groups?", Jim enquired.

"Absolutely. Both groups", Forkbraid confirmed.

"The Prophet and his pilot Matthew have lost contact with their other operatives at L5. They believe that they have either disbanded, gone to ground or fled", Forkbraid informed everyone.

"Fled?", Jim asked, adding, "There can't be that many places for them to go."

"Matthew did consider a few places. He believes that if they did flee, then it would have been to the Venusian colonies", Forkbraid replied.

"Well that's not a good thing. They could just blend in and disappear as immigrants", Jim noted.

"Exactly Jim. Make sure you send the authorities at Venus Central a heads up", Forkbraid suggested, noting, "The Venusian colonies have received a lot of immigrants from L5 of late."

Jim tapped his forehead, "It's in the vault FB. I'll let them know."

"Now Jim. This bit's for you", Forkbraid began, then asked, "What do you know about one, Matthew Murphy?"

"Matthew Murphy?", Jim questioned, then continued, "He's my first cousin on my Father's side! He's supposed to be dead!"

"Dead?", Forkbraid queried.

"Yes. He's supposed to have died on that Bernal Sphere colony, Skye. When the flash vaporiser was set off. Missing, presumed dead is what his file says", a confused Jim replied.

"You may want to look into how that record was determined Jim", Forkbraid suggested, then explained, "Matthew Murphy is the Prophet's pilot. He's now also, a Captain in the Jovian Armed Forces and he has the ear of the High Prince."

"Gees, that is not good. He was a pilot in the Colonial Fleet. He knows that I worked with the L5 security and that I was quite high up in the organisation as well. This explains why my bounty is higher than the others", Jim replied, noting, "Matthew is clever. Really, really clever. If he's on their side, then he is arch nemesis material!"

"Well. At least we now know where we stand in that regard", Selene commented.

"Peter. Your turn. What can you tell me about one, Rajsheev Neru?", Forkbraid asked.

Peter's wife Catherine stepped in, "Wasn't Rajsheev one of your work colleagues? A co-worker?"

"Yes. That's right. I worked with Rajsheev at Hyper Dynamics Corporation", Peter replied, explaining, "Rajsheev was a positronic matrix design engineer. He and his family emigrated to the Jovian Realms on an interplanetary out-liner. That was quite a while ago. They'd be there by now."

"They are Peter, although when they arrived, they found out that the Jovian Realms weren't what they thought they were", Forkbraid replied, adding, "Non Christian immigrants become Slaves upon their arrival, the minute Jovian immigration processes them."

"What!", Peter exclaimed, "You are joking, aren't you?"

"No. No joke. As far as I can tell. Rajsheev and his family were made Slaves upon arrival", Forkbraid gave Peter the bad news, then followed up with better news, "They were lucky though. A couple they befriended on the out-liner, went looking for them and helped them. The Neru Girls, Lakshmi and Pavarti were both freed. Their friends had to buy Rani to *free*' her. Somehow they met the Prince of Io, Leopold and he transferred Rajsheev's ownership to the Neru's Daughters."

"That's horrible!", Catherine exclaimed, "Imagine what could have happened if no one went looking for them?"

"I know Catherine. It's a horrible thought", Peter agreed, "Forkbraid. Is Slavery common in the Jovian Realms?"

"It appears to be the law of the Realms Peter", Forkbraid informed him.

"Why do they even have Slaves?", Catherine asked, "Why don't they just use Androids?"

"Androids were developed after the outer satellite insurrection. So they don't have any Androids beyond Mars orbit. They don't have Androids in the Jovian Realms", Peter informed his wife.

Selene added in, "Prince Leopold, the Prince of Io, wants to end Slavery in the Jovian Realms."

"This war aside, that's probably another reason why he needs our help", Forkbraid speculated.

"We found out some information about the Horridian Siblings as well", Selene noted.

"Yes we did. The High Prince appears to be firmly in control of everything that happens in the Jovian Realms", Forkbraid informed the room, "Prince Wulfric appears to be a hothead who habitually provokes their youngest Sibling, Prince Leopold. The youngest Sibling wasn't present in the meeting we observed. Apparently the High Prince excluded Leopold in order to protect Wulfric from his own stupidity. Prince Valdamar is definitely the more rational of those two Siblings."

"That was the impression I got as well", Selene agreed.

"The Horridian Sister both have mental health issues. We got the impression, that they're both clinically insane and require *'minders'* to keep them in check. The youngest, Princess Luisa, apparently enjoys be-headings and has a penchant for guillotines. The elder Sister, Princess Sophia is a poisoner, she plays around with *'potions'*", Forkbraid informed them all.

Selene added, "We were like flies on the wall and from what we heard, their realms in the Aft and Fore Trojans are close to instability. At least, that is what we suspect."

"We can use that", Admiral Zumwalt replied, as she checked to make sure her Lieutenant Adjutant was taking notes.

"The Aft Trojan occupation forces that we sent on their way, they are infected with Leroy's redemption", Gwek remarked, asking, "Have they made it home yet?"

"Yes Gwek, they have reached their home colonies", Selene confirmed.

"People living under untruths and lies, will slowly see the light", Gwek noted, adding,"It is likely that the Aft Trojans will free themselves from the Horridian dynasty."

"So Gwek, are you saying we just need to wait and see?", the Admiral asked.

"Patience Admiral. Patience is what I recommend. Events will unfold as they will and we will know soon enough", Gwek explained.

"Let's not forget the Trojan occupation fleet that was sent to L5. They are heading home as well and they are are also infected with Leroy's redemption. They will reach the Aft Trojans before the end of this month and then some of them will continue on to the Fore Trojans", Varak commented.

Leroy replied, "I didn't make physical contact with them Varak. It was done with manipulated energy fields remember, so it might work differently, if it works at all."

Gwek remarked, "Physical or energy field, it is all the same in the end."

Selene then noted, "Our best hope for peace appears to be Prince Leopold."

"Yes. I had time to observe Prince Leopold at Io Prime. He was the one responsible for those family portraits", Forkbraid commented.

"So Prince Leopold definitely sent us the message?", Garnet queried.

"Yes he did, although he doesn't know that we've received it yet", Forkbraid confirmed.

"There are some odd things happening in the Horridian family", Selene noted, adding, "Forkbraid has already shared this information with me, so I'll let him explain it too you all."

"The Horridian Sisters weren't the only ones to have mental health issues", Forkbraid began, explaining, "Their own Mother began molesting the High Prince, starting about the age of ten. The High Prince is actually the Father of Prince Leopold!"

Everyone in the room was shocked and all started talking at once, all over one an other. Forkbraid held up is hand for silence.

"None of the Horridian Siblings know of this. Only High Prince Heinrich and a select group of highly trusted people in key positions", Forkbraid informed them all, adding, "The High Prince has altered the line of succession to favour Prince Leopold over his younger children by his wife, Princess Charlotte. Should anything happen to the High Prince, Prince Leopold ascends to the Jovian High Throne. The High Prince has put everything in place for this to happen."

"Now I understand why Prince Leopold is our best hope for peace", Admiral Zumwalt commented, then to her Lieutenant Adjutant, "Do not record any of this. No one outside of this room can know. Is that understood?"

"Understood Admiral", the Lieutenant Adjutant replied.

"Good", the Admiral noted, then remarked, "If anything happens to High Prince Heinrich, his youngest Sibling Leopold, who is also his Son takes his place and Prince Leopold wants peace."

"That is the gist of the matter Admiral", Forkbraid confirmed.

"Okay then Forkbraid. What do we do next?", the Admiral enquired.

Forkbraid replied, "We haven't quite figured that out yet, but Selene and I do need to project back to Io Prime and somehow make contact with Prince Leopold."

"Haven't figured that out yet?", Admiral Zumwalt asked, adding, "Don't you just talk to them?"

"Well yes and no Admiral. When we astral project we can't actually talk to people. We can think between ourselves, but not actually talk to people.", Selene admitted, adding, "We have to work out a way to get a message to them."

Roseanne asked, "What if you just jaunt to Io Prime, you know, just blink across?"

Forkbraid and Selene were somewhat shocked by the suggestion, then Forkbraid explained, "Roseanne, while we could jaunt to Io Prime, I would not recommend it. Getting there is one thing, but there is no guarantee that we could actually jaunt back."

"Why not?", Roseanne questioned.

"Roseanne, it boils down to the old belief that psychics can't use their gifts off world", Selene replied, further explaining, "Forkbraid and I, are the only exceptions to that rule. Perhaps you yourself and young Miranda will turn out to be exceptions as well. Exceptions or not, neither myself nor Forkbraid actually know if we can jaunt successfully to Io Prime in the first place. Let alone jaunt back from Io Prime. It would be a huge mistake to make that attempt and find ourselves stuck at Io Prime, in the Jovian Realms."

Cormac noted, "You wouldn't want to miss-jaunt and end up on Io either."

Selene pointed to Cormac, "And that is a very really possibility. We could end up breathing Io's thin, sulphurous atmosphere and that would not be a good thing at all."

Roseanne nodded in comprehension, while Zephyr enquired, "Can you alter the environment at Io Prime with your astral bodies?"

"That Zephyr, is the big question", Selene replied, admitting, "We don't know, but on our next astral excursion, we will attempt to find out."

"You could try using telekinesis or pyrokinesis", Mystal commented.

"Those are on our list of things we can try", Forkbraid replied.

"Why not just push the message directly into their minds?", Roseanne enquired.

"Roseanne. That just isn't an option", Selene replied, explaining, "We won't be physically there. Pushing thoughts into a mundanes mind is disturbing enough for them. Not being physically there can result is untoward and deleterious results."

"Roseanne. Selene is right. Pushing thoughts directly into peoples minds from an astral form is not a good idea. Lesser minds have been driven mad by such attempts in the past", Mystal agreed.

Jim Murphy remarked while looking at Forkbraid, "As someone who regularly receives messages pushed into my mind. I can say for certain, that it is quite disturbing."

"And for that I do apologise Jim", Forkbraid replied, "I only do it when it is necessary."

"As much as I've learned, obviously there is much more for me to learn", Roseanne replied.

"And you are learning Roseanne. You're asking questions and we're providing you with the answers", Selene explained.

"Still, I do wish there was more I could do", Roseanne commented.

"All in good time young lady, all in good time", Mystal assured her.

"Well, if pushing messages directly into their minds is out, I guess my next suggestions would be even worse", Roseanne replied.

"Run them past us anyway Roseanne and we'll be the judge of whether or not we can use them", Selene suggested.

"How about possession?", Roseanne asked, "Perhaps speak through one of them or use one of them for remote writing."

"We don't like to use possession Roseanne. We try to avoid doing that if we can", Selene replied.

Candy stepped in, "Yes. Possession is definitely something to be avoided."

"Agreed Candy, agreed", Cormac added.

"And yet, it might be the most effective means of communication", Garnet noted.

"Garnet. Possession should be considered an absolute last resort", Zephyr quickly replied.

"Agreed Zephyr, agreed, but it could also be highly effective as well", Garnet countered.

Forkbraid informed everyone, "Possession is on the table. We can get a clear, concise and correct message across using it. I cannot rule it out, however, I would prefer other options."

"Why not just fly there?", Varak suggested.

Forkbraid sent a quick, silent message to Varak, *"Admiral Zumwalt does not know the Solstice's full abilities and we don't want her to know about them either."*

Varak was at first startled, but understood what Forkbraid meant, *"Agreed"*, he thought back hoping Forkbraid would pick it up. Which Forkbraid did.

Admiral Zumwalt replied to Varak, "That would take months Varak. We do not have the time. If possession is on the table, then so be it. Let's make use of it!"

"We'll keep that in mind Admiral", Forkbraid agreed.

"On a completely different note, we have three new personnel starting next week", Selene told the gathered people, before explaining, "I've been interviewing medical officers from the EDCF Martian Task Force."

"It would be so nice to have real doctors instead of metal men", Nyaliep remarked.

"Agreed Sister. Metal men are cold and soulless", Zyaliep noted in reply.

"Well, we will have three new Doctors", Selene informed them, "Our head Doctor will be Lieutenant Aisha Khan and she will be in charge of our Medical Centre and Infirmary. Our second Doctor will be Lieutenant Emilia Kowalczyk. Her duties will be split fifty-fifty between here at the academy and the Elysium colony. Our third Doctor will be Lieutenant Isabella Rossi. Her duties will include managing the Solstice's Infirmary when on mission. So please make them feel welcome when they arrive."

"Interesting Selene. If I remember correctly, it was Lieutenant Rossi that was somewhat reticent when I mentioned psychic scans", Forkbraid noted, adding, "The Lieutenant didn't feel terribly comfortable about being around psychics."

"Which is quite ironic Forkbraid", Selene replied, informing him, "On a deeper scan, I assessed, that had Lieutenant Rossi been born on Earth, instead of L5, she would have been a mid level four."

"Well that is interesting. That explains why you've placed her on my crew", Forkbraid replied.

"Wait. Are you saying Lieutenant Rossi could have been a psychic?", Admiral Zumwalt asked.

"Well yes Admiral. It happens more often than you'd think", Selene admitted, "Had Isabella been born on the Earth, she would have been detected and trained."

"Roseanne piped up, "Zuawalo and Zeealas could have been low level threes, had they been detected and trained at an early age."

Zeealas smiled and replied, "Roseanne has been teaching us, but it works only a little bit."

"Astonishing", the Admiral remarked.

"Okay then. I guess this meeting is adjourned", Forkbraid concluded, "All Solstice crew members, Selene and Roseanne, please remain seated. Everyone else, you may go about your usual daily business."

"Do you need me to hang around Forkbraid?", Admiral Zumwalt asked.

"No, that's not necessary Admiral. These are just Solstice crew personnel discussions and not that important", Forkbraid replied with a tiny little fib.

"Okay then, I'll be on my way", the Admiral replied and then stood up and left the room.

Once all the others had left the conference room and only the Solstice's crew members remained, Forkbraid made a hand gesture and the conference room door closed. After which, Forkbraid nodded to Marcus, who then clicked a few keystrokes on his grip.

"The room is now secure", Marcus noted.

"I must apologise FB. I had almost forgotten that Admiral Zumwalt and her Lieutenant Adjutant were in the conference room", Varak remarked.

"No harm done Varak", Forkbraid replied, "but we do need to be more careful. Admiral Zumwalt will be around quite often and there are some things we don't want her to know. At least not yet."

Selene addressed the room, "The information Admiral Zumwalt released about the Belter Ship Blood Nut and its crew of bounty hunters has had it desired affect. It appears that the Horridian's are having a lot of trouble finding bounty hunters, at any price, no matter how high."

"That is a good thing, isn't it?", Charlene asked.

"Yes. It is good news, but let's not become complacent", Selene replied, reminding them all, "We still need to be very cautious. While it does take some of the pressure off, the ten of you still have bounties on your heads. Sixty four million Jovian golden credits in total and that's a hell of a lot of money. There may still be some crazy bastards out there willing to take the risk."

"We could reduce the risks even further if we take out the Prophet's assets at Lake Aram and Lake Oudemans", Jim commented, adding when the others gave him shocked looks, "Just saying."

Zuawalo remarked, "Our Jim is so very sweet. He is just thinking of our safety."

Forkbraid stepped in, "So. We all stay within the academy's walls. If we do leave the academy for whatever reason, we make sure we have security with us."

Everyone understood and nodded in acceptance.

"Varak. How are those wisps going?", Forkbraid enquired.

"They are coming along nicely FB. Their hulls are being printed as we speak. I have been supervising the process remotely of course", Varak replied.

"Excellent. Well people, we will have some new crew members coming on board soon", Forkbraid announced, "Not just Lieutenant Isabella Rossi next week, we will also need to bring onboard four wisp pilots. Jim will be picking the pilots from those we have here at the academy. You have some candidates I believe Jim?"

"Yes. A handful, but I won't mention their names just yet", Jim replied, explaining, "When they do come onboard, we will need to bring up more pilots from the Elysium colony. Of course, when the ten new wisps are completed, we will be sourcing ten more pilots from Admiral Zumwalt's fleet. So we do have some further personnel changes in this area coming up in the near future."

Forkbraid summed up for Jim, "So next week, we will have a new Doctor on the Solstice and in the weeks that follow, four new pilots. That does create a certain level of urgency."

"Urgency?", Marcus enquired.

"Yes Marcus", Forkbraid replied, "None of these new crew members know about the Solstice's true capabilities. And while Jim does trust his pilot candidates, Lieutenant Rossi is a complete outsider. If we are to fly to Io Prime, we will need to do it, as soon as possible."

"Io Prime?", Peter questioned.

Selene stepped in, "Forkbraid and I are going to do our best to contact Prince Leopold of Io astrally, but if we find that difficult or unproductive, you guys will need to actually fly there."

"We will make the contact attempt tomorrow", Forkbraid informed them all, "However, if that doesn't work out as well as we'd like, we will be flying to Io Prime the next day."

"I'll let Catherine know, that we may have a mission coming up", Peter replied.

Forkbraid looked at Nyaliep, Zuawalo and Zeealas, "No. You three are not coming. Remember, you are all on ground duties until after your babies are born. I expect you three to be studying about the ship's systems and the ship's flight manuals."

"Flight manuals?", Zuawalo questioned.

"Yes. Flight manuals. It certainly wouldn't hurt for you to learn how to fly", Forkbraid replied.

The three Pod women had looked disappointed at not being included in the mission, but then began to smile when they realised they were going to learn to fly.

"Peter. That five Tesla dipole that you and Varak created. It is still working isn't it?", Forkbraid asked.

"Yes. Of course Forkbraid", Peter replied, "It is working brilliantly."

"Excellent. That dipole is a million kilometres away in Sun Mars Lagrangian point one. So Mars is sitting in its tail. Can we use it to slipstream to Jupiter?", Forkbraid asked.

Peter pointed to Varak who then replied, "I have worked out the offset in theory FB. If we do need to go on the mission in two days, I'm sure I can have it working."

"That is good to know Varak. Without that, there is no mission", Forkbraid noted.

Varak nodded in understanding, "I can recheck my calculations, but I'm certain they will work."

"Okay then, this meeting is finally adjourned. We'll let you all know tomorrow afternoon if the Io Prime mission is going ahead", Forkbraid replied.

The very next morning Selene and Forkbraid sat down on their cushions in their meditation room to project astrally to Io Prime.

As they descended deeper into their meditative state, concentrating on their breathing, breathing in and breathing out, breathing in and breathing out, an ornate doorway appeared embedded in the wall in front of them.

This time Selene noticed the Sigil in the centre of the doorways keystone, it was a bindrune representing Io Prime, consisting of the runes that spelt its name, *"How did I not notice that before?"*, she thought to herself.

When Selene pulled herself astrally out of her body through her crown chakra, Forkbraid was already prepared and waiting for her. They both stepped through the portal and appeared at the other side in the northern end cap of Io Prime.

"It is so much easier when a portal already exists", Selene noted.

"Someone still has to create the portal in the first instance Selene", Forkbraid replied.

Together they projected across the northern end cap to Prince Leopold's palace on the other side. There they spent around fifteen minutes looking through palace, but could not find the Prince and his family anywhere. Only servants were present.

"I'm not sensing them anywhere", Selene noted.

"Hmm. I have an idea Selene, follow me", Forkbraid replied.

Selene followed Forkbraid as he projected back across the northern end cap once again. This time they landed on the roof top of the apartment building in which their portal had been set. They found themselves in a roof top garden. Immediately they heard the voices of teenagers at play.

Selene began sensing her surroundings and smiled, *"Lakshmi and Pavarti. They're playing in a pool over that way."*

Forkbraid allowed his mind to sense further into the penthouse apartment directly below them, he smiled as well, *"Their family is in the apartment below us Selene, everyone, even the Prince and his family. They're all there."*

"How can we contact them Forkbraid?", Selene asked as they moved closer to the pool.

The Neru Girls were splashing about in the pool, while unseen to them, Selene and Forkbraid looked carefully around at their surroundings. Close to the pool was a cooking station, an electric barbeque. Also close to the pool was a pool house. In between the barbeque area and the pool house was a large table. Forkbraid examined it. It was made of an artificial wood material.

Forkbraid smiled and informed Selene, *"I can probably burn a peace symbol into this table."*

"Yes Forkbraid, but the Girls are in the pool", Selene noted as she continued to look around the area, before pointing to the pool house.

"The pool house?", Forkbraid questioned.

"No Forkbraid. The wind chimes. There's three sets of them. There's no wind here. Perhaps in the main cylinder, but not in an end cap. They're ornamental. The only time they chime, is when someone plays with them", Selene explained.

Forkbraid smiled and chuckled, *"Play away Selene."*

Selene concentrated and after a short while all three wind chimes began to chime. At first the Neru Girls didn't notice. Selene concentrated further and the three wind chimes began to dance about more violently. They now chimed loudly and the Neru Girls took notice. Then the wind chimes stopped.

The Girls immediately climbed out of the pool, grabbed their towels and ran up to the pool house, Pavarti remarked, "That's strange. I've never heard them chime before."

Lakshmi replied, "There's never any wind here either, just the occasional light breeze. Nothing strong enough to make these chime."

Selene concentrated again and the wind chimes danced and began to chime once again. The Neru Girls took a step or two back and gave each other concerned glances.

Right on cue, Forkbraid concentrated and began to burn a large peace symbol into the artificial wood of the table. The smoke began to waft about and Forkbraid made sure it wafted in the direction of the Neru Girls.

Lakshmi sniffed the air, "Something's burning", she remarked.

Pavarti looked around, "The table is on fire!", she exclaimed.

They both ran to the nearby table and watched wide eyed, but cautiously as a large peace symbol began to burn itself into the artificial wood of the table top.

"Pavarti. Get Mum and Dad", Lakshmi told here Sister, "Now Pavarti! Now!"

Pavarti quickly ran to the stairwell that descended to their apartment.

A few minutes later Pavarti came running back. By now the peace symbol was fully burned into the table top. It was literally the largest and most noticeable feature on the table. Pavarti was followed by her parents, Rani and Rajsheev, with the Appelbaums and Prince Leopold and his family close behind.

"Pavarti! What was so urgent?", Rani asked.

Pavarti pointed to the table top and the peace symbol burned into it.

Upon approaching to table, Abram carefully touched the burnt peace symbol with his finger tip, then quickly pulled back, "It's still hot!", he exclaimed, adding, "It's a peace symbol. Just like your medallions."

"Did you and your Sister do this Pavarti?", Rajsheev asked.

"No! It burnt spontaneously. All by itself", Pavarti protested.

"It's true! We both saw it", Lakshmi backed her up.

Then Selene concentrated on the wind chimes once more and all three wind chimes danced and chimed. Everyone turned around and looked at the wind chimes, as they danced without any wind.

"You see. They started chiming first and then the table top burnt!", Lakshmi informed them all.

The wind chimes continued to dance until they'd all noticed, then abruptly stopped.

"There's no wind, not even a breeze", Prince Leopold noted.

They were all perplexed.

Princess Giselle then asked, "Is there someone here?"

The wind chimes danced and then chimed again and before stopping abruptly.

Prince Leopold asked, "Did you burn the peace sign into the table?"

The wind chimes danced and then chimed again and before stopping abruptly.

Lakshmi then asked, "Are you a ghost?"

The wind chimes did not move, they remained completely silent.

Pavarti remarked, "Not a ghost then. I don't like ghosts."

Princess Giselle had an idea, then asked, "Are you Forkbraid?"

The wind chimes danced and then chimed once again before stopping.

Abram noted, "Now we are getting somewhere."

Pavarti came up with an idea, stating, "Wait a few minutes. I have an idea. I'll be back in a minute or two", before running towards the stairwell and the apartment below.

It was quiet for a few long minutes while everyone waited for Pavarti to return. Then the young Girl came out of the stairwell and ran over to the table.

Pavarti sat down at the table in front of the peace symbol, placing a notepad in front of her and holding a pen in her left hand.

"What are you doing Pavarti?" Rani asked.

"It's my idea Mum. An experiment you might say", Pavarti replied, before stating loudly, "I have a pen and paper. Speak through me!"

Selene very carefully steps her astral form into Pavarti and Pavarti's eyes roll back.

Looking perfectly forward and not at the notepad, the young Neru Girl began to write, "I am Lady Folcrom Selene. Lord Folcrom Forkbraid is with me. We have received your message. Prince Leopold, you and your wife are different, you and your wife want peace and you and your wife need our help. Forkbraid will come to you tomorrow. Be here at this same place."

Carefully Selene steps back out of Pavarti and Pavarti's eyes return to normal.

"What happened?", Pavarti asked.

Prince Leopold picked the notepad, showed it to Pavarti and then read it aloud.

Princess Giselle enquired, "Did you write this Pavarti?"

"No. I don't remember writing anything", Pavarti replied honestly.

Lakshmi then pointed out, "Pavarti is right handed. She wrote that with her left hand."

Rani added, "That is true. No one in our family can write with their left hand. We are all right handed."

Prince Leopold commented, "I think we'd better all be here tomorrow then."

"Selene didn't say what time", Princess Giselle noted.

"It's just gone noon, so I'm assuming around the same time. Perhaps we could arrive around eleven, nice and early just in case", Prince Leopold decided.

"Yes, yes, that does sound like a good idea", Princess Giselle replied, asking, "How do you think Forkbraid will come here?"

Prince Leopold replied, "I have no idea my love. We'll just have to wait and see."

Selene and Forkbraid were happy with the response. Contact had been made. They both quickly projected back down to street level and then stepped back through their portal, to their meditation room at the academy on Mars.

"You have an appointment Forkbraid. Tomorrow at noon Io Prime time", Selene remarked.

"So twenty four hours from now then", Forkbraid noted, adding, "I'll send Charlene and Marcus a telepathic heads up. We'll need the crew assembled at the Solstice at first light."

"I wish I could go with you this time", Selene commented.

"I know you do, but you know as well as I do, you do have your duties here at the academy", Forkbraid replied, adding, "And besides, with the slipstream drive, we are technically only two minutes and ten seconds from anywhere. We'll be back sooner than you think."

15. Io Prime

Early the next morning, the six core crew members of the Solstice and Leroy McGuvan assembled at the front of Varak's construction hanger. Varak himself had ensured that the Solstice was out of the hanger and waiting on the tarmac. One by one the seven crew members, all dressed in their blue uniforms, boarded the Solstice and made their way to the bridge.

Forkbraid looked around the bridge, "Good, we're all here. Varak, I'll need you on the bridge. Take a seat beside Peter. Leroy, you're here, just in case we have need for your redemption. Please take up your station in engineering."

"Aye Captain", Leroy replied and then headed off to his station in engineering.

"Marcus. I take it you remember how to take us into low Martian orbit", Forkbraid commented.

"Of course Captain", Marcus replied.

"Good then. Take us to low Martian orbit", Forkbraid commanded.

"Aye Captain", Marcus replied.

A few minutes later the Solstice was in low Martian orbit and the spectacular image of the Martian globe was displayed on the screen.

Aboard the Vanguard, Captain Hart's tactical officer, noted, "Captain Sir. I've detected the Solstice in low Martian orbit."

"Thank you Lieutenant", Captain Hart replied.

Admiral Zumwalt, who had also heard, quickly ordered, "Thank you Lieutenant. Put the Solstice on screen."

"Aye Admiral", the Lieutenant replied as he followed the Admiral's order.

A few seconds later, the screen displayed the Solstice as it orbited high above the Martian clouds.

"What are they doing?", the Admiral asked, adding, "Keep scanning them Lieutenant. I want to know what they're up to."

Back on the Solstice, Forkbraid turned to his tactical officer, Jim Murphy, "Jim, activate the passive cloaking", then to Marcus, "Fusion thrusters to stealth mode Marcus"

"Aye Captain,", Jim replied as he activated the passive cloaking.

"Aye Captain,", Marcus replied as he placed the micro fusion thrusters into stealth mode.

As the Admiral watched the screen, the Solstice disappeared, "Lieutenant? What just happened?"

"They're gone Admiral", the Lieutenant replied, adding, "The Solstice is no longer showing on our sensors at all."

"Captain Hart. Mark my words. There's more to that ship than Captain Forkbraid is letting on", the Admiral commented, then ordering the Lieutenant, "Keep scanning Lieutenant."

"I agree Admiral", Captain Hart replied.

"Peter. Start scanning for frame dragging events", Forkbraid ordered, followed by, "Varak, how are you calculations coming along?"

"Aye Captain", Peter replied, adding, "Scanning for frame dragging events now."

Varak checked his calculations. The electromagnetic dipole was one million kilometres from Mars in the direction of the Sun, at the Sun Mars Lagrangian point one.

"My calculated off set looks firm Captain", Varak replied, "We are good to go!"

Peter located a frame dragging event and it appeared to be suitable, "I've got one Captain. Varak, I'm handing you the coordinates."

Varak checked his screen and then triggered the pulse cannons to fire a single electro-magnetic pulse towards the frame dragging event. Immediately upon contacting the frame dragging event, it reacted and a created a new slipstream. Varak turned and looked around to Peter Swann.

Peter looked back to Varak, "Varakhan Utana, you nailed in one my man. Nailed it in one. Varak, you are getting good at this. Jupiter is on the far side Captain. We should come out beyond the orbit a Callisto, about one point five million miles from Jupiter. I recommend activating out shields."

"Make it so Varak", Forkbraid replied.

"Computer. Activate shields at maximum", Varak instructed.

The ship's computer replied in its sweet feminine voice, "Complying."

Peter and Varak high fived each other.

Varak spoke to the ship's computer, "Computer. Is this slipstream navigable? Is it safe?"

The ship's computer replied in its sweet feminine voice, "The slipstream is navigable. The slipstream is safe. The planet Jupiter is accessible via this slipstream."

"Marcus. I'm handing the helm back to you", Varak advised, "If we attempt to use this slipstream, aim straight for the middle of the anomaly."

Marcus looked around to Forkbraid, who ordered, "Double check we have our shield grid up and then proceed Marcus."

"Aye Captain", Marcus replied, then explicitly to the ship's computer, "Computer. Double check that the shield grid is active at maximum, then proceed into the slipstream at optimal point of entry and speed."

The ship's computer replied "Compliance. Shield grid is activated and at maximum. Proceeding into slipstream" and the Solstice began moving forward.

As the Solstice approached close to the slipstream, the ship's computer automatically showed the gravitational field lines overlaid on the screen. The slipstream itself was invisible. It was only visible on their screen, due to the displayed overlaying field lines. They approached what appeared to be a rotating funnel, leading into a tunnel like structure. The Solstice shuddered momentarily and the computer automatically adjusted the inertial dampers, as the ship slipped over the lip of the slipstream's funnel towards the tunnel within it.

Varak commented, "Captain. Our inertial dampeners appear to be working quite well this time."

Forkbraid replied, "Agreed!", as they entered the slipstream's tunnel.

The sides of the slipstream tunnel showed definite spacial distortions and the Solstice's inertial dampers adjusted quickly to limit any untoward affects on the crew. They were effective.

The inside of the slipstream tunnel was filled with strange swirling distorted lights and colours. The visual effects of the experience were both psychedelic and surreal, but not nauseating.

Turbulence was noted in the slipstream tunnel and Varak noted to himself, that his recent changes to the inertial dampers were effectively adjusting for the intense gravimetric distortions.

Time itself seemed out of joint once more. Were they inside the slipstream's tunnel? Were they still inside the slipstream's entry funnel? Had they already passed through the exit funnel on the other side? It was extremely difficult to say and they were still somewhat disoriented.

Then they exited the tunnel and entered the spiralling exit funnel. The Solstice shuddered slightly, as she traversed the short, spiralling exit funnel. The Solstice shuddered again ever so slightly, as she lurched over the lip of the exit funnel and came out into normal space once more.

"Wow! That was certainly better than the last time", Charlene commented.

"It certainly was", Forkbraid agreed, "Thank you Peter and Varak."

"Jim. Double check that the passive cloaking is online, then bring on the active cloaking as well", Forkbraid commanded.

"Aye Captain", Jim replied.

"Marcus. Get our precise location. Lock it into the computer. Then plot a course to Io Prime", Forkbraid commanded, then asked, "Peter. Am I correct in stating, that where we are now is the zone we'll need to scan for frame dragging events to take us home?"

"Aye Captain", Marcus replied, "We can be at Io Prime in two hours."

"Aye Captain", Peter confirmed, "We will need to return to this region to scan for frame dragging events for our return journey."

Callisto Control picked up something on its scans, "Commander. We seem to have a glitch."

"A glitch?", the Commander queried.

"It looked like something was there Sir. About three hundred thousand miles out from Callisto's orbit. Then it wasn't", the Controller explained, "It must have been a some kind of glitch."

"Hmm. Keep scanning just in case", the Commander ordered, adding, "If nothing shows up, then it was probably a glitch in the system. Have a maintenance team diagnose the system at the end of your shift. We can't have the scanners glitching, not in the current climate."

As Io Prime began to grow larger and large on the bridge's screen, Charlene remarked, "Oh my! Look at how thick their radiation shielding is."

Marcus commented, "Jupiter's radiation belts are easily ten thousand times as intense as the Earth's van Allan radiation belts. They've used a lot of Astcrete to cover that cylinder and it has to be extremely thick to be effective. Even then, they're running an electromagnetic deflection field along the main cylinder and end caps, to deflect alpha and beta particulate radiation."

"Astcrete?", Charlene enquired.

Peter stepped in, "Processed regolith from asteroids in the outer asteroid belt and Jupiter's Trojans. All of the Primes and their other colonies in Jupiter's orbital zone will be covered in it."

"Io Prime is huge. It's easily as big as Colonial Central Command at L5", Charlene noted.

"Yep. It sure is", Marcus agreed.

"Peter", Forkbraid began, "Can the Solstice's computer hack into Io Primes systems without being detected?"

"Absolutely Captain", Science officer Peter Swann replied, adding, "It's highly doubtful they have any systems or networks a highly advanced three-o-three positronic matrix can't hack."

"Good. Good. Hack into their systems and find the location of the Prince's palace. Directly opposite the palace, on the other side of the northern end cap there should be an apartment building with a penthouse. That's my target", Forkbraid explained.

"I'm issuing the ship's computer the instructions now Captain", Peter replied.

"When you have the location of that apartment building, paint an X on the corresponding point on the screen's image of the northern end cap", Forkbraid instructed.

"Aye Captain", Peter replied, then less than thirty seconds later, "X marks the spot Captain" and an X appeared on the screen at the appropriate point on the northern end cap of Io Prime.

"Marcus, can you put our ship right above that X and match Io Primes rotation?", Forkbraid asked.

"Aye Captain. I can indeed", Marcus replied.

"Marcus. Make sure we're well above their electromagnetic deflection field. We don't want to interact with that", Peter recommended.

"How close can we approach?", Marcus queried.

"No closer than one hundred meters Marcus", Peter replied.

Forkbraid enquired, "At that distance will we be detectable Peter?"

"Based on my math, no Captain", Peter replied, "If anyone was to look or scan in our direction they'll just see the northern end cap. Our active cloaking will hide us completely."

"And if we get closer?", Forkbraid enquired further.

"Captain, if the Solstice interacts with their electromagnetic deflection field, we'll cause it to glitch", Peter replied, explaining, "We cause that field to glitch and someone will definitely notice."

"Marcus. Keep us at a distance of one hundred meters. No lower", Forkbraid instructed.

"Aye Captain", Marcus replied and a short time later, the Solstice was in a stationary orbit above Io Prime's northern end cap and precisely above the point that Peter had marked with his X.

Forkbraid was silent for long minutes as his mind wondered around the apartment block that was his target. Eventually his mind wandered up to the penthouse apartment and its roof top gardens.

"So much easier to scan when I'm this close to it", Forkbraid thought to himself.

It didn't take Forkbraid long to locate the people he was looking for, they were patiently waiting at the table into which he had burnt the peace symbol. It was almost twelve moon, Io Prime time. The peace symbol had been covered with a table cloth. During Forkbraid's scans, he had not found any threats or signs of duplicity.

Forkbraid opened his eyes and noticed all of his crew member's eyes were upon him, "Jim. You're in charge until I get back", he stated as he stepped out of his Captain's chair.

It took a few moments for Jim Murphy, who was not only the Solstice's, Tactical officer and Head of Security, but also the Solstice's First officer, to realise what this meant. Slowly Jim stood up, then he walked quickly over to the Captain's chair and seated himself.

Jim looked to Forkbraid, "This doesn't seem right FB", he remarked.

"Tag you're it Jim. You're in charge until I get back", Forkbraid replied, adding, "I could be gone for a few hours. I'll send you a message directly before I come back or if I run into trouble."

Forkbraid concentrate and found the perfect place to jaunt to, the pool house. There was a small flash of light and Forkbraid vanished from the Solstice's bridge.

Lakshmi and Pavarti were relaxing in their rooftop pool house when Forkbraid appeared. There was a small flash of light and then Forkbraid was there standing before them in his navy blue Martian Armed Forces uniform.

"Mum, Dad!", Lakshmi and Pavarti shouted out loudly in unison.

"Please. Do not be afraid", Forkbraid reassured the Girls, using his abilities to calm them.

Rajsheev and his wife Rani were quickly at the pool house door, followed by the Appelbaums, Prince Leopold and his wife Giselle.

"Greetings, Rajsheev, Rani. Peter Swann and his Wife Catherine send their regards", Forkbraid greeted.

"You know Peter Swann?", Rajsheev enquired.

"Peter Swann is my Science officer on my ship, the Solstice", Forkbraid replied.

Forkbraid greeted the Appelbaums, "Greetings Abram and Miriam."

They both replied, "Greetings", in unison.

Forkbraid looked towards the Prince and his wife, "Greetings. You must be Prince Leopold and Princess Giselle."

"Yes. Yes. I am Leopold and this his my wife Giselle. We know who you are Captain Forkbraid. Your reputation precedes you", the Prince replied, "Just how did you get here?", he then asked.

Forkbraid smiled and answered with a half truth, "I teleported."

"Teleported?", Abram questioned, "Is that even possible?"

Forkbraid replied, "Apparently Abram. I am here."

Lakshmi blurted out, "He just appeared out of nowhere in a flash of light!"

Pavarti added, "We both saw it. A flash of light and there he was!"

"Your Highness. Prince Leopold. We need to talk", Forkbraid reminded the Prince.

"Yes. Yes of course. Girls would you be so kind as to play in the garden while we adults discuss matters?", the Prince asked.

Both Girls began to frown, but then upon seeing the look on their Mother's face, complied, "Yes Your Highness" and off they went to play in the garden.

"Your Highness. I need to know what your Brother Heinrich's plan was. I need to understand his mindset", Forkbraid informed the Prince.

"Well, you probably already know most of it", the Prince replied, adding, "He ordered the missile attack. The aim was threefold. To eliminate the Martian colonies so that Mars could be occupied. To devastate the Earth. To damage L5, to the point where L5 could be occupied by the Trojans."

"Yes. You are correct Your Highness. I already know that much", Forkbraid agreed.

"There is more though. My Brother Heinrich wanted to commandeer L5's own colonial fleet and then use it to attack and invade the Venusian colonies and then of course, the five main Asteroid Belter colonies", the Prince informed Forkbraid.

"So your Brother wanted to control everything in the inner solar system", Forkbraid remarked.

Prince Leopold chuckled lightly and shook his head, "After consolidating control over the entire inner solar system, my Brother wanted to send the Jovian fleet into the outer solar system. He was going to split the Jovian fleet into four smaller fleets. One fleet would be launched to Neptune, another launched to Uranus and the third launched to Saturn. This was to be done in a staggered launch pattern, so that each fleet would arrive at its target at the same time. My Brother Heinrich wanted the entire solar system. He was even going to give it a name, '*The Horridian Imperium*'."

"So your Brother Heinrich had huge imperialist ambitions for the whole solar system and these were all predicated on his first strikes on Mars, the Earth and L5 succeeding", Forkbraid noted.

"Yes exactly Forkbraid. My Brother forgot one thing though", the Prince replied, adding, "Heinrich forgot all about the unknown, unknowns."

"The unknown, unknowns?", Forkbraid queried.

"Wild cards Forkbraid", Prince Leopold replied, explaining, "Heinrich did not consider three things. The development of the Martian Defence Forces. The commissioning of your ship, the Solstice and how far ahead of us technologically, the Earth and L5 actually were. Heinrich simply thought that his massive missile strike, with all of those warheads would succeed. He was wrong!"

Forkbraid was quiet for a long moment, considering how the solar system could have been affected, if High Prince Heinrich's plans had panned out precisely the way he'd wanted.

"Fortunately for the solar system, your Brother Heinrich's plans failed", Forkbraid began, before he told Prince Leopold the sad truth, "With over sixty five thousand dead at L5 and well over two and a half million dead on the Earth, your Brother now has major problems."

"Yes Forkbraid", the Prince agreed, "How do we stop this War?"

"That is the question Your Highness, that is the question", Forkbraid replied, informing the Prince, "The Earth Defence Forces and L5's Colonial Fleet have combined. Their ships are being upgraded with the latest technologies and innovations. Their 'Grand Fleet' will be coming here to the Jovian Realms when they're ready. There will be a lot of personnel on those ships, who want to extract revenge. We have to end the war before that Grand fleet gets here."

Princess Giselle had been listening and asked, "Can we stop the fleet?"

"Sadly Princess, I doubt it", Forkbraid replied, explaining, "Our analysis of the Trojan technology showed a lot of steel and titanium allows. If that's indicative of Jovian technology in general, then you guys have a huge problems."

"In what way?", the Princess queried.

"The Earth's and L5's ships all use exotic alloys, plasteels and polyceramalloys. A ships hull made with these alloys can take one hell of beating. It takes some serious weapons tech to penetrate a modern ships hull and most of those ships will have General Products hulls. Arguably the best available", Forkbraid explained.

"Trojan technology is actually a very good indication of Jovian technology in general Forkbraid", Prince Leopold admitted, "We, that is my Brothers and I, are already aware of this problem. Captain Murphy made that perfectly clear to us in a recent meeting."

"Matthew Murphy?", Forkbraid queried, then added, "James Murphy's first cousin on his Father's side. We were very surprised to come across that snippet of information. Everyone thought he was dead. At least that's what he altered the records to make us all believe."

"Yes. Captain Murphy is a high tactical thinker. A very clever man. He also thinks very highly of his cousin James", the Prince remarked.

"Jim used the term arch nemesis material for Matthew when he found out", Forkbraid admitted, "That in itself, says a lot."

Prince Leopold walked over to a table in the centre of the pool house and picked up a long document cylinder. The Prince then opened it up and took out the document that it contained. Carefully Prince Leopold unrolled the document and placed it on the table, using some paper weights to hold it in place and keep it nice and flat.

It was a large, detailed map of Jupiter and the four major Jovian Realms, Io, Europa, Ganymede and Callisto. The map displayed all of the current moons in the Jovian system as well. Some had been left out as they had been fully processed and consumed in building the Primes and were no longer in existence.

Prince Leopold asked Forkbraid, "Do you understand Lagrangian points Forkbraid?"

"Yes. Yes I do", Forkbraid replied as he looked at the map, pointing out, "We are here at Jupiter Io Lagrangian point five."

Io Prime was marked on the map, as were the other Primes in orbit about the other Galilean moons. Interestingly another Prime was marked in Amalthea's orbit, a significant yet smaller moon.

"Good. Then we can discuss our concerns with this disgraceful war my Brother Heinrich has started", the Prince replied.

"Let's get straight down to business then", Forkbraid agreed.

The Prince pointed to each of the Jupiter, Galilean moon L5 points, he started with Callisto, then Ganymede, Europa and Io.

"As you're probably aware, the Prime colonies are at all the Lagrangian L5 points", the Prince remarked, "but it's not just the Primes. There are thousands of smaller colonies in those same L5 points. Literally thousands, upon thousands of them. They are not marked on this map, but they are there none the less."

Princess Giselle stepped in, pointing to Amalthea and its L5 point, "And it's not just the Galilean moons either. Amalthea for instance has a Prime and sure it is smaller, but it too is surrounded by hundreds of smaller colonies. Many of the lesser moons have their own colonies as well."

Prince Leopold added, "Even Himalia, Elara and Pasiphae have Primes, smaller of course, but they're still there none the less and they also have a large retinue of smaller colonies associated with them as well."

Princess Giselle noted, " Himalia and Elara are part of the Ionian Realm as is Amalthea. Pasiphae comes under the jurisdiction of the Ganymedian Realm, but its all the same for the purposes of this discussion."

Forkbraid was listening carefully and then Prince Leopold made his main point, "These colonies represent people. Millions, upon millions of people. They are all civilians. Just ordinary folk. They are my main concern and my Brother Heinrich has put all of their lives at risk. All of them!"

Forkbraid nodded in understanding and asked, "And what about the Slaves?"

Prince Leopold looked directly at Forkbraid, right in the eyes and replied, "They are people too!"

Princess Giselle quickly added, "My Husband Leo wants to end Slavery across the entire Jovian Realms! Not just here, but in the Trojan Realms as well."

Forkbraid could hear the sincerity in their voices, he replied, "One thing at a time Your Highness. We can end Slavery once this war is over. Peter Swann and Varakhan Utana, my Chief Engineering officer, can work with Rajsheev on building Androids to replace the Slaves. The Slaves will be freed, but we need to end this war first."

"Varakhan Utana? I've heard of him. He worked for General Products Corporation on Space Technologies", Rajsheev noted, adding, "He was said to be the man who can build anything. General Dynamics Corporation tried to poach him at one time. Without success I might add. He works for you?"

"Varak is my Chief Engineering officer and he works for the Elysium colony and Martian Defence Forces", Forkbraid clarified.

"Your Highness. With Peter and Varak's help, together we can end Slavery", Rajsheev remarked.

"Yes Rajsheev, but as Forkbraid has noted, we need to end this war first", the Prince explained and then to Forkbraid he asked once again, "Forkbraid, how do we end this War?"

Forkbraid frowned, "I'm not sure yet Your Highness. For that I need more information. A lot more information."

Forkbraid studied the map on the table and noted circles around the Galilean moon L4 points, he asked, "All the civilian structures appear to be in the trailing Lagrangian points, the L5s, what's over in the leading points, the L4s?"

Prince Leopold was slow to answer, his wife Giselle took his hand and squeezed it, "He needs to know Leo. He needs to know", she implored.

The Prince looked at his wife, *"She's right"*, he thought to himself, before answering, "The L4s are all military industrial complexes", he informed Forkbraid.

"So the L5s are all civilian and the L4s are all military industrial?", Forkbraid queried.

"Yes. That is correct", Prince Leopold confirmed.

"Okay. I'm starting to see a solution", Forkbraid remarked, "I do still need more information."

Prince Leopold began to explain the five L4 Lagrangian points and how the interrelated, "My Brother Wulfric is in charge of Jupiter Callisto L4. That's where the main Jovian Fleet is stationed, at least when the ships aren't on active duty. Wulfric is responsible for the Jovian outer defences. If a Jovian ship is capable of long range interplanetary travel, that's in Wulfric's domain."

"So if the combined fleet from the Earth and L5 come this way, Wulfric is responsible for stopping them?", Forkbraid asked.

"Yes. If an enemy fleet approaches the Jovian system, then it is Wulfric's responsibility to defend the Jovian Realms from attack and invasion", Prince Leopold replied, adding, "The Jovian fleet can be sent on long range offensive operations, but that's not within Wulfric's authority."

"So who makes decisions with regard to offensive operations?", Forkbraid asked.

Princess Giselle stepped in with one word, "Heinrich."

"Heinrich?", Forkbraid queried.

"Yes. Heinrich", Prince Leopold confirmed.

"Your Highness, you've noted the outer defences. I assume you also have inner defences?", Forkbraid enquired.

"Yes of course. That would Jupiter Europa L4. My Brother Valdamar is in charge of the Jovian inner defences. Valdamar has a rather large fleet of ships stationed there, for defending against any enemy that gets through the outer defences", the Prince informed Forkbraid, adding, "Some of those ships are interplanetary capable, but the majority are not. Jupiter Europa L4 is a part of Valdamar's domain and he is responsible for the Jovian inner defences."

"Okay, Your Highness I'm starting to see a pattern", Forkbraid replied and then asked, "Heinrich is the High Prince, but he's also the Prince of Ganymede. So that would place Jupiter Ganymede L4 under Heinrich's domain, yes?"

"That is correct", the Prince confirmed.

"So what happens at Jupiter Ganymede L4?", Forkbraid enquired.

"Ganymede's L4 is largely about ship manufacturing, outfitting and repair. That's also where the research and development occurs as well", the Prince replied, adding, "If Wulfric or Valdamar need new ships or an older ship repaired or its systems upgraded, that happens in the ship yards at Ganymede L4. That's all a part of Heinrich's domain. He controls all of that and only Heinrich fully knows what goes on at Ganymede L4. Heinrich has a lot of secrets at Ganymede L4."

Princess Giselle stepped in again, "It's not as simple as Callisto L4 is Wulfric's, Europa L4 is Valdamar's and Ganymede L4 is Heinrich's either. Simply put, Heinrich is the High Prince and he has overarching control over all of his Brother's domains, including my Leo's domain here."

Forkbraid digested that for a long minute then asked, "Which brings us to Jupiter Io L4 and Jupiter Amalthea L4. Your domains?"

Princess Giselle noted, "It's actually quite a bit more complicated than that."

Prince Leopold smiled, "Yes, it is indeed. Io L4 and Amalthea L4 are both a part of the Ionian Realm and you'd think that I have control over the entire realm. I do not."

"My Leo has control over everything in the Ionian Realm, with the exceptions of Io L4 and Amalthea L4", Princess Giselle informed Forkbraid.

"So who controls those then?", Forkbraid enquired.

"My Brother Heinrich does of course", Prince Leopold replied, "My Brother saw it fit to exclude me from all and any military matters."

"We don't really know why. Heinrich treats Leo differently to his other Brothers, which is not a bad thing. In many ways Heinrich shows Leo considerable favouritism", Princess Giselle noted.

"So what happens at Amalthea L4 and Io L4?", Forkbraid questioned.

"All of the resources we acquire from the Amalthean mines are transferred to Amalthea L4 for temporary storage, before later being shipped to Io L4", the Prince explained, going further, "Our resources from Amalthea L4 and those we acquire from the Ionian mines are both processed at Io L4. Many of those processed materials are then shipped to Ganymede L4 for use in manufacturing."

"But not all of them", Princess Giselle noted, "Io L4 is a particularly nasty place."

"A particularly nasty place?", Forkbraid questioned.

"Absolutely", Prince Leopold responded, the Prince then looked Forkbraid in the eye once again, "The attacks on Mars, the Earth and the Earth's L5, every one of those missiles and every one of those warheads was manufactured, stored and launched from Io L4."

Forkbraid looked shocked.

Princess Giselle quickly confirmed what her Husband had said, "My Leo is telling you the truth. Io L4 is the place where the interplanetary missiles and their warhead are made. That's where the missiles are stored, in a massive missile array and launched en masse."

Forkbraid could see the truth of the matter and replied simply, "I believe you."

"It gets worse. Those missile foundries. They run none stop making missiles and warheads", Prince Leopold informed him, adding, "My Brother Heinrich is rebuilding his missile stocks!"

"Well, that is not good at all!", Forkbraid exclaimed.

Miriam who had been listening intently asked, "Is the High Prince going to attack the Earth and L5 again? The last time he killed so many people!"

Prince Leopold replied, "I can assure you, that is not the case. All that death and destruction aside, my Brother has seen how poorly the last missile attacks worked out. My Brother, the High Prince, did not get the results he wanted."

"So Your Highness, what is your Brother's new plan?", Forkbraid asked.

"It's actually Captain Murphy's plan", Prince Leopold replied, explaining, "We wait until the Earth's and L5's Grand fleet launch towards us here in the Jovian Realms. Everyone knows that's going to happen, it's just a matter of when. Then when they're locked in on their orbital transfer to Jupiter, we intercept them, with wave upon wave of missile swarms."

"Even a polyceramalloy hull can't stand up to a two megaton blast", Forkbraid replied, noting, "I've seen that during the Battle of L5."

"Exactly Forkbraid", the Prince replied, "The idea is, that by the time the Grand fleet gets here, they'll have been decimated several times over and they'll have only two options. One, alter their course and bypass Jupiter to return home or two, face the Jovian fleet and be totally obliterated."

"Your Brother Heinrich is hoping for the second option I take it", Forkbraid replied, "The Jovian fleet will have by far the superior numbers under those circumstances."

"Yes, but it makes no difference in the end", the Prince replied, adding, "With the bulk of the Grand fleet destroyed, what remains will not be a match for the Jovian fleet. Whether in space here or back home at L5, they will be obliterated."

"So that's his plan or should I say, Matthew's plan", Forkbraid replied, summarising, "Decimate the Grand fleet with multiple swarms of missiles over and over, until its so weak, it can't stand up to the Jovian fleet, whether it's here or at L5."

"For what's left of the Grand fleet, it doesn't matter what options they take. My Brother Heinrich will send the Jovian fleet to the Earth and L5. It will be a blood bath", the Prince agreed.

"No it won't", Abram threw in.

"How is that so Abram?", Princess Giselle enquired.

"Forkbraid is here now Princess. Doesn't his presence here change things?", Abram replied.

Prince Leopold and his wife Princess Giselle looked at Forkbraid, while Abram continued, "Forkbraid, you teleported here. Mars to Io Prime. That's an incredulously long way to teleport, isn't it? I'd be willing to bet your ship is actually nearby."

"A very astute observation Abram", Forkbraid responded, then admitted, "My ship is nearby!"

"So your ship is undetectable to our scanning systems?", the Prince questioned.

"The Solstice is extremely difficult to detect Your Highness", Forkbraid also admitted.

"Your Highness, if the Solstice eliminates the missiles, their Grand fleet can approach Jupiter unscathed", Abram noted, adding, "No missiles means no interception. That will mean it's the Jovian fleet that will be completely outmatched."

"We don't want their Grand fleet to come here at all Abram", Princess Giselle reminded him.

"Wait a moment. Abram is right", Forkbraid told them, explaining, "All of the colonies in the trailing Lagrangian points, the L5s, are civilian. All of the colonies in the leading Lagrangian points, the L4s, are military. With that information all the Grand fleet needs to do is target the L4s."

"And if your ship takes out those missiles, then it's only the Europa, Ganymede and Callisto L4s that need to be targeted", Abram noted, adding, "It would be a surgical strike."

"What do you think Your Majesty?", Forkbraid asked, adding, "A surgical strike that only targets the military infrastructure?"

"Leo. It will keep the civilian population, the ordinary people safe", Princess Giselle remarked.

"I can get word to General Stanton and Fleet Captain Carmichael. Give them the details you just gave me about the leading Lagrangian points. They're in charge of the Grand fleet and I trust them", Forkbraid informed them.

"I'm not sure Forkbraid", the Prince replied, voicing his concerns, "With the missiles gone. The Grand fleet arrives, takes down the Jovian fleet and then targets the military infrastructure. I cannot predict how my Brothers will react. They might act like corned animals!"

Forkbraid was silent for a long moment considering his next response, "There is no guarantee that Matthew's Grand fleet decimation plan with work either Your Highness."

"Why do you say that?", Prince Leopold questioned.

"My ship is nearby and your scanning systems and defences have not detected it. The ships in the Grand fleet are all being upgraded. When they make the push to Jupiter, they will have stealth fusion thrusters and passive cloaking. There is no guarantee that your missiles will be able to intercept them, let alone target them. With or without those missiles the Grand fleet is coming", Forkbraid explained, divulging the very information he did not want to divulge.

"So my Brother Heinrich has severely underestimated the technological gap between us and the inner system worlds, yet again", Prince Leopold noted.

"These are very new technologies Your Highness. Very recent", Forkbraid replied, "The effectiveness of the Jovian missiles is in doubt, even before they launch. I'll leave the choice to you. Missiles or no missiles, the Grand fleet is coming. I cannot stop that", he reiterated.

Prince Leopold replied, "I need to think", before leaving the pool room and wondering off into the rooftop garden, his wife Giselle quickly followed after him.

Everyone remaining in the pool house sat down on the nearest available seats and waited.

Rajsheev stood up and walked to the pool room's french doors and looked out at the Prince and Princess. They appeared to be discussing the question at hand. The Jovian missiles and whether they should be destroyed. To the Appelbaums and the Nerus, it was a no brainer. They were all recent immigrants to the Jovian Realms, having emigrated from the Earth and L5. To them, those missiles needed to go.

To the Prince and Princess it was more complicated. Princess Giselle was from the Earth and to her mind the missiles should be destroyed. Prince Leopold, however, was a Prince of the Jovian Realms. He was, just by discussing this issue with an enemy of the Jovian Realms, Forkbraid, committing treason. To agree to the destruction of the Jovian missile stocks, so much more so.

"What is happening Rajsheev?", Rani enquired with a little head shake.

"They are still talking about it Rani", Rajsheev replied.

Rajsheev watched for a few for minutes and then the Royal couple started walking back towards the pool house.

"They are coming back now", Rajsheev informed the others as he walked back to his seat.

Everyone stood up when the Prince and Princess stepped back into the pool house.

Prince Leopold frowned and looked Forkbraid in the eyes, "Forkbraid. Just by talking to you, I am risking my life, the lives of my family and everyone else in this room. It is high treason. I simply cannot agree to you destroying our missile stocks. I am a Prince of the Jovian Realms and as much as hate this war and want it to end. I cannot condone, let alone support this action."

Princess Giselle added, "My Husband Leo, is a Prince of the Jovian Realms. You cannot ask his permission to do this thing."

Forkbraid understood and nodded in agreement, "I understand Your Highness", then he turned to Rani, "Please call your Daughters Rani."

"Lakshmi, Pavarti, please come here", Rani shouted, but not overly loudly.

Lakshmi and Pavarti were quick to come to the pool house, they weren't actually very far away.

Forkbraid waved his right hand in the air before him and weaved a bindrune of glowing red, everyone was in awe of it, "Appelbaums. Nerus. Please return to your apartment. This discussion did not happened. I am not, nor was I ever here", the bindrune glowed brightly.

The Appelbaum and Neru families then quietly left the pool house and headed towards the stairwell that led to the penthouse apartment below.

"What is that?", Princess Giselle asked.

Forkbraid replied honestly, "Princess. This is a bindrune of forgetting. For their own safety, the Appelbaums and the Nerus will forget my visit and remember nothing of it."

"And us?", Prince Leopold questioned.

"I fully understand your situation Your Highness. You cannot commit treason. You cannot even be *'seen'* to have committed treason. You certainly cannot condone my destroying the Jovian missile stocks", Forkbraid told them.

"Thank you for your understanding Forkbraid", Prince Leopold replied.

"Don't get me wrong young Prince", Forkbraid replied, explaining, "I am going to destroy your missile stocks. I don't need your permission to do that."

"No, no. There will be an investigation. That could lead to us here, our families and our friends", the Prince explained.

Forkbraid loosed a calming vibration and assured the Prince and his wife, "We will make the destruction of your missile stocks look like an industrial accident and I will remove any memories of my being here or for that matter this entire discussion."

"We won't remember?", Princess Giselle enquired.

"It is safer that way Princess. It is better that no one remembers my visit", Forkbraid answered, adding, "I will ensure that the Grand fleet only attacks the military infrastructure in the L4 Lagrangian zones. I will ensure that the Grand fleet protects the civilian colonies and their people."

"Okay then. So be it", Prince Leopold replied in agreement.

"Prince Leopold, Princess Giselle, you will return to the penthouse apartment below. This discussion did not happened. I am not, nor was I ever here. Please go now", Forkbraid replied, his bindrune of forgetting glowing once more before vanishing.

The Prince and his wife Giselle then left the roof top gardens to the stairwell that led to the penthouse apartment below. Upon entering the stairwell, their memories of their encounter with Forkbraid faded and vanished as if they had never been.

Forkbraid took up the map from the table and rolled it back up, before replacing it in its document cylinder. Slowly Forkbraid concentrated on the Solstice's bridge crew and having located the Solstice's bridge, he concentrated harder, sending First officer Murphy a heads up, that he was returning. Then there was a small flash of light as he vanished from the roof top pool room. Then there was another small flash of light as Forkbraid reappeared on the Solstice's bridge.

A startled Jim Murphy remarked, "Every time you do that FB. It is so uncomfortable!"

"I know that Jim and I am sorry, but I thought it best to let you know I was about to jaunt back", Forkbraid apologised to his friend.

As Jim stepped out of the Captain's chair he enquired, "How'd it go

Captain?", this time remembering to use Forkbraid's title.

"It went well Jim. Better than you could possibly imagine", Forkbraid replied as he passed Jim the document cylinder.

"What's this then?", Jim asked.

"Have a look at it Jim. That map, could very well be the solution to this entire conflict", Forkbraid informed him.

Jim unrolled the map across his tactical station and had a quick look at it, "It's a map of the Jovian system with all the major colonies are marked. What's the significance?"

"Look at all the Galilean L4 points Jim?", Forkbraid replied.

Jim scrutinised the map carefully, "The four Galilean L4 points, appear to be all military!", he exclaimed loudly.

"Yes Jim and everything else in this entire system is civilian", Forkbraid replied, adding, "We only need to worry about just those four Galilean L4 zones."

"FB! FB! This is golden!", Jim replied, before rolling up the map and replacing it.

The others on the bridge were all happy to here this news, Marcus even asked, "So Captain. Shall I lay in a course back to our starting point, for our return journey home?"

"Actually no Marcus. Lay in a course for Jupiter Io Lagrangian point L4, make sure passive and active cloaking remain active.", Forkbraid instructed, then informing the bridge crew, "We have another mission to perform before going home."

"Aye Captain. Laying in the new course for Io Lagrangian point L4 now", Marcus replied.

16. Io - Lagrangian Point Four

Forkbraid sat in his Captain's chair. He reached to his right and picked up his Neural Interconnect Control helmet.

"Varak. This NIC helmet. Can I use this helmet to create a transcript on my meeting with Prince Leopold from memory?", Forkbraid enquired.

"Captain. The NIC was designed for you to control the ship. It was not designed to turn memories into transcripts", Varak replied in the negative, then added, "I cannot guarantee that you can do that, but it is certainly worth the try."

"Thank you Varak. I'll give it a go. Maybe it will even work", Forkbraid replied as he put on his NIC helmet.

Forkbraid began reaching out to the ship's computer, *"Solstice. Computer. Show me current settings."*

The ship's computer responded by showing him the settings that he had set when he last wore the NIC helmet, *"Solstice. Computer. Dataset. Human memories. Stream into file as text transcript. Is this possible?"*

The ship's computer replied, *"We do not know. We have never attempted such a request",* the computer's reply feeling almost feminine.

"Computer. Attempt it now. Dataset. Human memories. Stream into file as text transcript", Forkbraid instructed and then began to concentrate on the memories from his prior discussions with Prince Leopold and his wife and friends.

About twenty minutes later, Forkbraid took off his NIC helmet and placed in back on the pillar to the right of his Captain's chair. Forkbraid rubbed his eyes, then turned to his left and manoeuvred his Captain's console over his lap and began typing keystrokes on the touch screen.

"Jim. I've sent you a file. It's a transcript of my meeting with the Prince", Forkbraid informed his Tactical officer, instructing further, "When you have some time, read through it and turn the major points into a report for General Stanton and Fleet Captain Carmichael. If you have any questions, we can discuss them later. I'll review the report before it's sent."

"Aye Captain. I'll start on it during the return leg of our journey", Jim replied.

"Excellent Jim", Forkbraid replied, then turning to Marcus, "Marcus, what's the estimated time to Io L4?"

"Captain. We're following Io's orbit around Jupiter, so in about two and a half hours we'll be passing Io itself and after that, roughly three hours to Io L4", Marcus replied, adding, "I'd advise Jim and Peter to start taking tactical scans of Io L4 when we're about two hours out."

"Thank you Marcus. Advice noted. Jim, Peter, start scanning Io L4 at target minus two hours", Forkbraid replied.

Two and a half hours later, the Solstice was passing by Io and that moon's image was displayed on the bridge's main screen. Mostly volcanic, caused by the gravitational interactions between Io, Jupiter and the other Galilean moons, Europa, Ganymede and Callisto, the surface of Io showed very few craters and a great many volcanic vents. Marcus gave Io a wide berth so as not to get caught up in any volcanic plumes that might erupt from the many active volcanoes and vents.

Sulphurous lava flows were visible almost everywhere and the hellish moonscape took on yellowish and orangish colours and hues. The marked flexing and deformation of the Ionian crust was noticeable with numerous mountains, plateaus and volcanic provinces. Some regions appearing and immense smooth plains and others as rough, jagged terrain.

"It's hard to believe there are mines down there, let alone people. It looks like Hell", Charlene remarked with and air of disgust, asking, "There are Slaves down there. We all know it. Why are we helping these people again?"

"Charlene. Prince Leopold was born into this legacy of Slavery. His own wife, Giselle, was once a Slave before his Brother, the High Prince freed her", Forkbraid replied with understanding, "Prince Leopold himself, does not have the authority to free Slaves. Only his Brother, the High Prince can do that. Even so, Prince Leopold has implemented many reforms in the Ionian Realm to make the lives of the Slaves living within it, less horrible."

Charlene looked around to Forkbraid and replied, "I understand that Captain, but just to think about how horrible it must be working in that Hell", she pointed at the screen, "It is horrible!"

"Yes. I can imaging it must be", Forkbraid agreed, "but remember this Charlene. Once this war is over, we can help change that. Peter and Varak can get together with Rajsheev Neru and get Android production underway. Androids replace the Slaves, the Slaves are then set free."

Charlene looked around to Peter and Varak, Peter noted, "We will help free those Slaves Charlene. All of us, working together."

At target minus two hours, both Peter and Jim started scanning the Ionian L4 region. The region contained a lot of structures. The first structures that were scanned were the closest. They all appeared to be colony cylinders. They were generally of the smaller variety of twinned O'Neil type colonies, but there were a great many of them.

"That will be where their workforce lives", Jim thought to himself.

As if to answer, Peter noted aloud, "Picking up human workforce accommodations. Worker colonies. All twinned O'Neil variants", as he then placed the scans on the screen.

"Okay Peter. So we know where the workers and their families live?", Forkbraid queried, adding, "We need to be certain."

"Yes Captain. I am one hundred percent certain, that these are where the workers and their families reside", Peter confirmed.

Just a little way further along Io's orbital path, the scans began to show the materials processing factories. These were huge Bernal Spheres and there were a great many of them.

Jim asked Peter as he put the scans on the screen, "Peter. Please confirm that these are their ore processing factories."

Peter replied, "Your assessment is correct Jim. Those Bernal Spheres might look like colonies, but seriously, they are really massive ore processing facilities."

"Good to know Peter", Forkbraid replied, "Makes sure all of these scans are being recorded."

"Aye Captain. I'm recording absolutely everything", Peter confirmed.

After the ore processing facilities, the scans began to show something different. Four different groups of objects began to appear. There were two large objects in a vertical line on the left hand side of the screen, somewhat closer to Jupiter. On the right hand side of the screen, in the middle between the two vertical groups was a third very much larger object, further out, away from Jupiter. These three groups together formed what looked like a huge isosceles triangle. The fourth object was in the centre of that isosceles triangle, right along the line of Io's orbital path.

"What are we looking at people?", Forkbraid asked.

"It is difficult to say Captain", Peter admitted, "We will need to get a much closer look."

"I must concur Captain", Jim agreed, adding, "When we get closer, I would recommend infiltrating their computer networks to find out exactly what we're dealing with."

"I agree with Jim Captain. The Solstice should easily be able to hack their systems. It could be extremely useful", Peter agreed.

"As long as we can do without being detected", Forkbraid agreed.

"Aye Captain. That's not a problem for our computer", Peter confirmed.

Marcus flew the Solstice past Io L4's residential colonies, silently and unseen. The ship was not detected. It wasn't long before the Solstice began passing through Io L4's ore processing facilities. Huge Bernal Spheres, the size of which significantly dwarfed any Bernal Sphere colonies in Cis-Lunar space.

Peter Swann was quick to instruct the Solstice's computer to infiltrate the local Ionian computer networks, "Captain. Hack and crack is in process", he informed Forkbraid.

"Thank you Peter" Forkbraid replied, then requested, "Let us know when you have a good picture of how this region works."

After several long minutes, Peter popped up a window on the bridge's main screen. The Solstice was now past the ore processing facilities and getting closer to the four mysterious objects arranged in an isosceles triangle.

"I recommend coming to a complete stop Captain", Peter informed Forkbraid.

"Marcus. Let's come to a halt", Forkbraid ordered.

"Aye Captain", Marcus replied.

Peter pressed a few keystrokes and four distinct lines appear in his popup window. They ran across the screen from left to right and each line was labelled from the top down, Amalthea, Io, Europa, Ganymede and Callisto. Their respective L4 regions were also displayed and labelled. Those for Amalthea, Io and Ganymede all lined up vertically, however, Europa and Callisto were out of alignment, further ahead of the other three. The Ionian L4 region was expanded compared to the rest and showed greater detail.

As the crew watched, labels began to appear against each of the L4 regions and in the case of the Ionian L4 region, the objects within it. Amalthean L4 was labelled as Amalthean L4 ore storage. Ganymede L4 was labelled as Ganymede L4 manufacturing, research and development. Callisto L4 was labelled as Callisto L4 Jovian outer defence forces. Europa L4 was labelled as Europan L4 Jovian inner defence forces.

Io L4 was far more complicated. The objects in the Ionian L4 region were labelled individually. Io L4 residential complexes. The ore processing facilities appeared to be separated into three distinct and separate zones. The Bernal Spheres closest to Jupiter were labelled as, Io L4 ore storage modules. The Bernal Spheres farthest from Jupiter were labelled as, Io L4 processed materials storage modules. The Bernal Spheres in between those two groups were labelled as, Io L4 ore processing modules.

Then there were the objects in the isosceles triangle formation. Those closest to Jupiter, top to bottom on the screen, were labelled as, Io L4 missile manufacturing factories and Io L4 warhead manufacturing factories. The object in the middle had the label, Io L4 missile final assembly factory. By far the largest object in the entire Ionian L4 region, was labelled Io L4 missile storage and launching grid. It was huge.

Peter remarked, "That missile storage and launching grid can easily hold five thousand missiles. However, my understanding based on the data, is that it has never held more than there current number of missiles."

"So that's where they launched those twenty two hundred missiles from then", Forkbraid noted, adding, "They must have held some back. How many missiles are stored there now?"

"Currently, they have well over twenty seven hundred missiles stored and they are making more. Hand over fist. Production appears to be twenty four seven", Peter replied.

"Are they going to launch another missile attack on the Earth and L5?", Charlene questioned.

Forkbraid replied, "My information is that they're going to use these missiles against the combined Earth and L5 Grand fleet, after it launches towards Jupiter. Wave after wave of missiles, until the Grand fleet is so decimated, that they can easily finish it off."

"That will leave the inner solar system virtually defenceless", Charlene noted.

"Which is why we have to destroy those missiles and not just those missiles. We also need to destroy their entire manufacturing process", Forkbraid informed everyone.

Peter informed Forkbraid, "I have more information Captain."

"Then let's see it Peter", Forkbraid replied.

Peter began adding work flow arrows to the diagram in his popup window. The first arrow led from Amalthea and its mines to the Amalthean L4 ore storage. The second arrow lead from Io and its mines to the Io L4 Bernal Sphere ore storage. The third arrow led from the Amalthean L4 ore storage to the Io L4 Bernal Sphere ore storage.

"Those three arrows represent the flow of raw materials, ore from Amalthea and Io to their storage facilities", Peter announced.

The next arrows ran from the Io L4 Bernal Sphere ore storage modules, to the Io L4 Bernal Sphere ore processing modules, then on to the Io L4 processed materials storage modules.

Peter noted, "That represents their ore processing and materials storage."

The fifth arrow to be drawn led from the Io L4 processed materials storage modules, all the way to Ganymede L4's manufacturing facilities and Peter explained, "A lot of processed material goes to Ganymede L4. In that region, they manufacture weapons, ships and other equipment. It's also their research and development hub."

Two more arrows, six and seven, led from Ganymede L4 to Europe L4 and Callisto L4.

Peter commented, "Finished weapons, ships and equipment are sent to Europa L4 and Callisto L4. Europa L4 is where the inner defence fleet is stationed. Shorter ranged vessels for defending the Jovian Realms should their outer defences fall. Callisto L4 is where the outer defence fleet is stationed. Those ships are all longer rang interplanetary vessels. They are the Jovian Realms outer defence fleets."

Forkbraid was quick to reply, "Thank you Peter. Everything you've just shown us validates everything that Prince Leopold has told me. Prince Valdamar is in charge of the inner defences and Prince Wulfric is in charge of the outer defences. The High Prince himself, Heinrich, is the overarching controller of the whole system."

Peter nodded and then noted, "Not all of the processed material goes to

Ganymede L4. Two major flows of processed material goes to the Io L4 missile and the Io L4 warhead manufacturing factories. The output of those two factories, flows to their Io L4 final missile assembly factory."

"So that's where they load the warhead into the missiles?", Forkbraid enquired.

"Yes Captain. It's also where the missile fairings are manufactured and attached", Peter replied.

"And the next flow from there would go directly to the missile storage and launching grid?", Forkbraid questioned.

"That is correct Captain", Peter replied.

Jim had stepped away from his station and moved closer to the screen, "Mr Swann", he began, "Please tell me you've got this all fully documented, because fucking hell mate, this is golden!"

Peter smiled, "Yes Jim. I've documented the whole lot with added detail", before dropping his popup window from the screen.

"So Peter. How do we destroy this thing? And not just the missile grid. Those manufacturing factories have to be destroyed along with it", Forkbraid asked.

"Funnily Captain, I have thought about that", Peter replied, commenting, "I'd rather not destroy them here. Io's orbital zone is flooded with enough radiation as it is. However, I do have an idea."

"Okay Peter, let's here it", Forkbraid asked.

"First Captain, can we move to the other side of the missile grid?", Peter enquired, adding, "I need to have a good look at its attitude control thrusters."

"Okay Peter. Marcus, make it so", Forkbraid instructed.

"I've sent you the exact coordinates I need Marcus", Peter informed him.

"Aye Captain", Marcus replied.

A short time later the Solstice was at the required coordinated and Peter began to analyse the missile grids attitude control thrusters.

Peter placed a new popup window on the screen displaying the immense missile grid. It was largely circular in shape, "Notice if I mark the centre of this grid and draw perpendicular line through that centre. Where is that perpendicular line pointing?"

Marcus was quick off the mark, "The inner solar system. Specifically the Earth."

"Yes Marcus and if the Grand Fleet is launched, they can easily track its transfer trajectory, work out multiple intercepts and then launch wave after wave of missiles towards it", Peter remarked.

"Yes, but Peter. How do we destroy it?", Forkbraid asked.

"I'm just getting to that Captain", Peter replied, "That monstrosity is orbiting Jupiter and its attitude control thrusters are keeping it pointed towards the Earth. At some point in its orbit, this missile grid will find Jupiter in between it and its target, the Earth."

"I'm not sure I'm understanding you Peter", Forkbraid admitted.

Varak chuckled and commented, "I think I know what Peter is saying. It is very clever."

Forkbraid replied, "Well I wish I did, can someone explain it to me?"

"The Solstice's Tactical officer, Jim Murphy caught on, "I think I do FB. Sorry. Captain. When the Earth is eclipsed by Jupiter or more correctly as the eclipse approaches, we could somehow trigger all of those missiles to launch into Jupiter."

"Sorry Jim", Varak replied with a chuckle, "So close, but no cigar for you."

Peter began to divulge his idea, "Captain. I'm assuming you want this to look like an accident."

"Absolutely Peter", Forkbraid confirmed.

"Okay. Here's my plan", Peter started and then began to divulge it, "First, from the inside Varak and I cause a few system failures. The kind that will require those three factories to be evacuated."

Varak nodded, noting, "If they believe, that they are in the firing line of an accidental or erroneous mass missile launch, that would do it."

"Precisely Varak", Peter confirmed, continuing, "Next we lock all of those missile in place so that they can't launch. All twenty seven hundred plus of them. Then we cause the missiles to fire up all at the same time, without actually launching."

Varak smiled a broad smile and commented, "If we do this right, everything will be lined up. The missile grid, all of the factories, everything."

"Exactly. Normally the grid would be facing away from the factories and Jupiter, but if we concoct a situation where everything lines up, that opens up an excellent possibility", Peter replied.

"What possibility?", Forkbraid questioned, still not following.

"With the missiles locked down in the grid and their thrusters firing, the whole grid will fly towards Jupiter", Peter explained, further noting, "The grid will collide with those missile and warhead factories and the whole shebang will fly straight into Jupiter!"

"And just above Jupiter's atmosphere, we can detonate all of those lovely warheads", Varak informed everyone.

Forkbraid stared at Peter and Varak for long moments before stating, "You're both bloody mad. Geniuses yes, but completely bloody mad. Mad geniuses, the pair of you."

Varak replied, "Thank you Captain", as if it was a compliment.

"Can the two of you pull this of and still make it look like an accident?", Forkbraid queried.

Peter smiled and laughed, "That's the beauty of it Captain. The whole scenario is so absurd, so ridiculous, that it could never have been considered. Certainly the Jovians would not have thought of any possible scenarios like this."

Varak began to chuckle, "They could investigate this *'mishap'* for decades and still never get to the bottom of it."

"Seriously, if you guys can set this up and pull it off and make it look like an accident, then by all means, go for it", Forkbraid agreed.

Peter replied, "Thank you Captain. Another benefit I should mention, all of the radiation released will be absorbed by Jupiter."

"Good to know Peter, good to know", Forkbraid replied.

The green light on the console flicked to red and it immediately caught Lieutenant Zandar's attention. The label underneath the light read, *'on Station'* and it had never turned red before. The Lieutenant quickly pressed a few keystrokes on his console and information pertaining to the attitude control systems displayed on his screen.

The missile array was indeed off station. Lieutenant Zandar could see the thrusters were firing, however, instead of correcting the issue, they were making it worse. The array was drifting further and further off station, even though he could see all the control settings on his screen were correct.

"It must be a malfunction in the attitude control systems", he thought to himself, before informing his superior, "Commander Billings Sir. We appear to have a malfunction in our attitude control systems."

Commander Billings strode over to the Lieutenant, "Malfunction?", he questioned.

"Our attitude control thrusters are firing Sir, however, instead of bringing our array back on station, they are taking us further off station."

"That should never happen Lieutenant", Commander Billings noted, then asked, "Can you control the thrusters manually?"

"Commander, the firing sequences are controlled by the system. Even if I could manually control them, I couldn't possibly make the necessary corrections", the Lieutenant replied.

"Try rebooting the attitude control system. Maybe that will shake out the glitch", the Commander suggested.

Lieutenant Zandar attempted to reboot the attitude control system, "Commander, the system is not rebooting. The system is ignoring my commands."

"Shut it down Lieutenant. Then give it a minute and turn it back on", the Commander suggested.

Lieutenant Zandar tried to shutdown the attitude control system, to no avail, it would not accept his commands, "Commander! The system is still ignoring me!"

Eventually the missile array stabilised on a new setting and the attitude control thrusters slowed their firing to maintain it.

"What did you do Lieutenant?", the Commander asked.

"Not me Sir. The attitude control system has locked onto this new position", Lieutenant Zandar replied, then informed the commander, "Sir, we appear to be squared off against the missile and warhead manufacturing modules."

"What do you mean Lieutenant?", the Commander enquired.

Lieutenant Zandar replied, "Our missile array is squared off against the missile, warhead and assembly factories Sir."

Another Lieutenant caught the Commander's attention, "What is it Lieutenant?", Commander Billings asked.

Lieutenant Gregory replied, "Sir. Over one hundred missiles have activated. They've gone into immanent launch status and appear to have locked onto our manufacturing facilities."

"What! Lieutenant! Shut those missiles down!", the Commander ordered.

"I'm trying to Sir, but they're not responding to my commands", Lieutenant Gregory replied.

"Keep trying Lieutenant. Shut those missiles down!", Commander Billings ordered again, a seriously concerned look showed on his face.

"Sir. Those missiles are not responding to my commands", Lieutenant Gregory replied, "I think they've gone rogue Sir."

"Lieutenant Gregory. Missiles don't go rogue!", the Commander shouted.

Lieutenant Zandar stepped in "Sir. If Lieutenant Gregory is correct. With those missiles in immanent launch status, they could launch at any moment."

Commander Billings considered the situation for a moment, "Zandar. Contact the manufacturing modules. They need to evacuate", he ordered.

"That's a lot of personnel Sir", Lieutenant Zandar noted.

"All the more reason to get on it straight away Zandar!", the Commander ordered, adding, "This is urgent!"

"I'm on it Sir", the Lieutenant replied.

Within minutes Lieutenant Zandar had the manufacturing module commanders on the line.

"What's this meeting about?", the Commander of the missile factory asked.

"We have an urgent problem Sir. Some kind of malfunction", Lieutenant Zandar informed them, then explained, "Over a hundred of our missiles have activated. They've gone into immanent launch mode and they are targeting your factories."

Almost in unison, the three factory commanders ordered, "Shut them down!"

"Sirs. We've been trying to do that without success. They are in immanent launch status and they could launch at any moment. You need to evacuate your factories!", the Lieutenant replied.

The Commander of the warhead factory remarked, "Evacuate! We can't just shut everything down and evacuate!"

Commander Billings had been listening and stepped in, "Commander Billings here. We have over one hundred rogue missiles targeting your facilities and they could launch at any moment. You all need to get the hell out of there. Evacuate immediately!", he strongly advised them.

There was no protest this time and they all agreed to evacuate their facilities.

At each of the three weapons facilities, the announcement came across the emergency broadcast systems.

"To all personnel. An emergency evacuation is in progress. Drop everything you are doing and make your way to the personnel transports and evacuation pods. This is an emergency."

The message was being repeated over and over at all three weapons facilities.

Lieutenant Zandar watched the screens, while Lieutenant Gregory continued trying to shut down the rogue missiles. Personnel transports began fleeing the missile and warhead factories, all flying towards the worker accommodation colonies.

"Zandar. Get maintenance crews to those missiles immediately. Shut them down manually. I want to know what's wrong with those things", Commander Billings ordered.

"Commander Sir. We only have six maintenance crews on the array. They won't be enough to deal with over a hundred rogue missiles", Lieutenant Zandar informed his commander.

"Lieutenant. I just need them to shutdown as many of those missiles as they can. That and get me some answers", the Commander replied.

"Our maintenance crews are on their way Sir", Lieutenant Zandar replied.

After the personnel transports had left, evacuation pods began to launch from the three weapons factories. It wasn't long before there was a swarm of emergency evacuation pods all flying back to the worker accommodation colonies. The last of the emergency evacuation pods left nearly forty minutes after the evacuation was announced.

"Commander Sir. I've just received word from our maintenance crews. They shut a few of the missiles down, but they just keep reactivating Sir", Lieutenant Zandar informed him.

Commander Billings commented under his breath, "What the fuck!"

Lieutenant Gregory was still trying to get the rogue missiles to shut down, "What is the matter with these damned things! Why won't they shut down?"

"Easy lad. At least the damned things haven't launched", Commander Billings replied.

Lieutenant Gregory replied, "Yes Sir. That is a very good thing", he smiled and added, "At least nothing else can go wrong. Right?"

And then their computer system began issuing a warning, "Warning. Immanent missile detonation detected. Immanent missile detonation detected. Evacuation recommended. Evacuation recommended."

"What the fuck!", the Commander exclaimed, as the computer repeated the message over and over, "Shut that fucking thing off! Zandar! What the hell is going on with my array?"

"Commander Sir. Our computer has detected immanent warhead detonations. It appears to be those hundred or so rogue missiles Sir", Lieutenant Zandar replied.

"Lieutenant Gregory. Shut those missiles down!", the Commander ordered.

"I've been trying to Sir. Those missiles are not responding", Lieutenant Gregory replied.

"Can we get repair crews to those missiles urgently?", Commander Billings asked.

"Sir. This array can house up to five thousand missiles. Currently it holds over twenty seven hundred missiles and those hundred or so rogue missiles are scattered all over the array Sir", Lieutenant Gregory noted.

Lieutenant Zandar added, "Sir. What Lieutenant Gregory is trying to explain, is that even if we had enough missile specialist teams, we couldn't get them to the rogue missiles in time."

"Great! Zandar, do you have any suggestions?", Commander Billings requested.

"Sir. Pray those rogue missiles launch before they detonate their warheads",

Lieutenant Zandar replied, adding, "Other than that, evacuate this array before anything else can go wrong."

Lieutenant Gregory agreed, "Sir. Immanent means at any moment. We need to evacuate now."

"So be it", the Commander decided, "Zandar. Start the emergency evacuation procedures."

As with the three weapons factories previously, the emergency broadcast systems began announcing, "To all personnel. An emergency evacuation is in progress. Drop everything you are doing and make your way to the personnel transports and evacuation pods. This is an emergency."

This announcement continued over and over.

Personnel transports began fleeing the missile array, all flying towards the worker accommodation colonies. After the personnel transports had left, evacuation pods began to launch from the missile array. It wasn't long before another swarm of emergency evacuation pods were all flying back to the worker accommodation colonies. The last of the emergency evacuation pods left the missile array nearly twenty minutes after the evacuation was announced.

Back on the Solstice Peter Swann announced, "Captain. The three factories and the missile grid have all been evacuated and well ahead of schedule I might add."

"How did you mange that Peter?", Forkbraid enquired.

"Varak and I have been playing around with their systems Captain", Peter admitted, "You'd be surprised how quickly people move when they think they're going to be hit by rogue missile strikes or immanent warhead detonations."

"As fast as we've just seen I expect", Forkbraid replied, then questioned, "So far so good. What's next up your sleeves?"

Peter answered, "Well Captain. I've written this little flight module for Marcus to play with."

"Flight module?", both Forkbraid and Marcus questioned at the same time.

"Yes Captain. I've just given Marcus access to it", Peter replied.

"Okay Peter. What does it do?", Forkbraid asked.

"If I might Captain", Peter began, "Marcus, please open the application module."

Marcus did so and after a minute of studying the module, exclaimed, "Are you serious! You want me to fly that missile grid like it's a ship! The damned thing is huge, it's enormous!"

Peter replied, "Marcus. I've hacked the missile grid's attitude control thruster so you can fly it. I am not a pilot. That is in your area of expertise."

Forkbraid stepped in, "Peter. Exactly what is it you want Marcus to do?"

"Well Captain. We need Marcus's flight skills to carefully manoeuvre that missile grid towards Jupiter", Peter replied, explaining, "In order to destroy their entire manufacturing and storage facilities, we need to carefully fly that missile grid into their final assembly factory, then fly it further into the missile and warhead manufacturing factories. The tricky bit, is that we need this to gently and carefully enough that we cause minimal damage. To do that, we need Marcus's skills."

"That's sounds like a huge ask Peter", Marcus responded, "Those missile have ten two megaton warheads each, that must be close to fifty four thousand megatons. Are you sure you want me attempt this?"

"It's either that or we just attack those facilities with our weapons systems", Peter replied.

"That, we will not be doing", Forkbraid stepped in, "We need this to look like an accident. Implausible though it might look, let's at least try to make it look like an accident."

Charlene assured her Husband, Marcus, "You've got this Marcus. We have faith in you."

Jim, who was also a skilled pilot remarked, "If you're not sure Marcus, I can give it a go."

"No. No. Charlene's right. I've got this. This whole concept is insane, but I've got this", Marcus informed everyone.

"Great. Let's get this job done", Forkbraid instructed.

Marcus carefully fired up the attitude control thrusters on the enormous Jovian missile grid and using the controls in Peter's flight module, began moving the missile grid towards Jupiter. Slowly and cautiously Marcus moved the missile grid closer and closer to their first target, Io L4's final missile assembly factory.

It was slow and tedious, but after about twenty minutes the missile grid gently bumped into the missile assembly factory. Marcus had been holding his breath and Charlene reached out and touched his shoulder gently. The missile assembly factory was significantly smaller than the enormous missile grid and ended up right in the centre of it.

Peter's scans showed there was some buckling and damage on both the missile grid and missile assembly factory, but not enough to cause them major issues. They had merged nicely.

"Well done Marcus", Peter commended, then remarked, "One down, two to go."

"Yes Marcus, well done", Forkbraid agreed, "Keep going, gently does it."

Marcus was sweating heavily as he continued flying the missile grid towards the next two targets, the missile and warhead factories. These groups were far larger than the missile assembly factory, but still significantly smaller than the missile grid itself. More troubling was the fact that these two groups were aligned in such away, that the would collide with the missile grid almost at the same time.

After another slow and tedious twenty minutes, the missile grid gently bumped into the warhead factories first and then mere seconds later the missile factories. Marcus waited for the structures to complete their merging then sat back in his chair and allowed the missile grid to continue its slow flight towards Jupiter. Both structures crumpled into place on the surface of the missile grid causing buckling and damage. Peter scanned the structures carefully and was happy with the results.

"Peter. Don't ask me to push fifty four thousand megatons of warheads around ever again", Marcus remarked as he turned around to face Peter.

"I'll try not to Marcus, but I cannot predict the future", Peter replied.

Varak had stood up from his chair and walked over to Marcus, placing his hand on his shoulder, "Good work Marcus", he commended.

"Indeed. Good work Marcus", Forkbraid agreed, "Peter. What's our next step?"

"Captain. First I shutdown all of the missiles in that grid", Peter replied as he issued instructions to the missile grid, "Then I lock down all of the missiles, making sure that they're all firmly held in place and not able to actually launch."

Peter looked to Varak, "Varak, we need to do some calculations."

"I think I understand", Varak replied as he returned to his chair.

"Calculations?", Forkbraid enquired.

"Yes Captain. How many missiles we need to fire up, to push that whole grid and those factories into Jupiter, without tearing the grid apart", Peter explained, "I'll do my calculations. Varak will do his and if we both get the same results, it's a plan."

Before Peter had finished talking, Varak already had performed his calculations, "So quick Varak. Give me a few seconds to catch up."

After a short while, Varak and Peter compared the results of their calculations.

"You think ten percent of the missiles will be enough?", Varak asked.

"I think we can push it to three hundred", Peter replied.

"Do we have a problem gentlemen?", Forkbraid asked.

"No. Not at all Captain" Peter replied, adding, "Varak's results are just a little more conservative than mine. I'm just thinking to push the envelope and get this whole shebang over and done with somewhat more quickly."

"Varak?", Forkbraid questioned.

"Three hundred missiles all firing at once and pushing that entire grid and those three factories into Jupiter FB", Varak commented, "It will be quicker. I just want to confirm that this grid won't break apart before it gets there. I'll run my eye over Peter's calculations again."

A few minutes later, Varak announced, "Good to go Captain. I concur with Peter."

"Good then. Peter, make it so", Forkbraid commanded.

Three hundred missiles in the missile grid, all carefully chosen, so as to have the maximum effect began firing simultaneously. Locked in place and unable to launch, their combined thrust pushed the missile grid and the factories embedded in it, towards an intercept with Jupiter.

Slowly at first the missile grid began to move, accelerating second after second, towards its final destination Jupiter.

Once the missile grid was well underway Peter announced, "Captain. I have brought all of the missiles and their warheads online. I've set them all to detonate five thousand kilometres above Jupiter's cloud tops."

"So fifty four thousand megatons or thereabouts?", Forkbraid enquired.

"Thereabouts", Peter confirmed.

"That should be one hell of a big bang", Forkbraid noted.

"Aye. That it will be Captain and Jupiter won't even belch", Peter confirmed.

Commander Billings and Lieutenant Zandar had flown a shuttle back to their missile array to assess the situation. As they approached, they could not believe their eyes. Their missile array was more than off station. It had collided with the missile assembly factory and the missile and warhead factories and was now on their shuttle's screen, flying towards Jupiter.

"What the fuck!", Commander Billings screamed, then asked Zandar, "Is that even possible?"

"I would not have thought so Commander", Lieutenant Zandar replied, his face equally perplexed, "How does that even happen? I know we had malfunctions in the systems controlling the attitude control thrusters, but that is ridiculous. There's no way to catch up to it either. It's just moving way too fast Sir."

"Could that be a fault in the array's missile control systems?", Commander Billings queried.

"I have no idea Sir", Lieutenant Zandar replied, "Perhaps a computer virus?", he questioned.

"No. No. That's just too weird. How would a virus know to do that?", the Commander asked.

"An intelligent computer virus?", the Lieutenant pondered.

"Right Zandar and who would have introduced it?", the Commander replied with a rhetorical question, "There haven't been any alerts of any kind, not even security alerts."

"Whatever caused this Commander, the High Council are going to have a fit", Lieutenant Zandar replied with concern.

"Then your investigation and your report Lieutenant, had better be thorough", Commander Billings told the Lieutenant.

Lieutenant Zandar was not looking forward to having to write that report and replied to Commander Billings, "Sir. I recommend returning to Io L4 Central. We need to get our scopes turned to our missile array before it gets too far away."

"True enough Zandar. Take us back immediately", Commander Billings agreed, "Give Io L4 Central a heads up, to get the scopes prepared."

"Will do Commander", Lieutenant Zandar replied.

The crew of the Solstice had watched as the shuttle arrived in the area where the missile grid had been. Peter had popped up a window on the bridge's main screen to observe it. Now they watched as the shuttle turned about and headed back to Io L4's residential colonies.

Once the shuttle had left, Peter dropped the popup window showing the shuttle and the crew focused on watching the missile grid as it accelerated towards Jupiter. It was around four hundred and twenty thousand kilometres from Io to Jupiter and it took just over three hours for the missile grid to cover that distance. Peter displayed the missile grid's flight as it appeared from the crew's perspective, but he also popped up a new window that showed a zoomed in view as the missile grid approached its detonation zone.

The zoomed in view dimmed protectively as the missile grid erupted into a huge ball of brilliant blue light. The ball of light dimmed quickly as the remains of the missile grid fell into Jupiter's atmosphere, sinking deep into the cloud layers and then it was gone. Jupiter swallowed it all, lock, stock and barrel, leaving no signs of the fifty four thousand megaton explosion.

"Wow!", Charlene exclaimed, then added, "Although somehow, I thought it would be bigger."

"The distance Charlene", Marcus replied, "Jupiter is well over four hundred thousand kilometres away. At that distance it was always going to look smaller than it was. If not for Peter's popup window, we would not have had much of a show at all."

Forkbraid chimed in with, "Peter was right. Jupiter barely even belched."

Peter replied with, "Captain. You could toss the whole of Io into Jupiter and it would be gobbled up no trouble at all."

"Noted Peter and thank you all for all your work", Forkbraid replied, "Our job is done here. Marcus, take us home."

"Aye Captain", Marcus replied as he plotted a course back to the region outside the orbit a Callisto, about one point five million miles from Jupiter.

A couple of hours later, the Solstice was in position and ready to start scanning for frame dragging events.

"Where in the zone Captain", Marcus informed Forkbraid.

"Whenever you're ready Peter", Forkbraid instructed.

"It's all good Captain, I've given Marcus access to the Slipstream dive", Peter replied, adding, "Marcus, you should be able to open up the module and take us home."

"Are you sure about that Peter?", Marcus questioned, "It did require your touch last time."

"The ship's computer knows about Mars and Jupiter now Marcus. It knows what to do. On our trip out, either myself or Varak needed to do the calculations manually. Now the ship's computer knows what to do", Peter explained.

"Okay, so what do I do now? There's no manual on this", Marcus asked.

"Just instruct the computer to scan for a frame dragging event and designate where in Martian orbit you want us to come out at the other end. The computer will then generate the slipstream. Then all you need to do is verify the exit point and if everything is kosher, take us straight on through", Peter explained.

"Have you got this Marcus?", Forkbraid asked.

"Yes Captain. I've got this", Marcus replied, "and I'm learning a hell of a lot today."

"Good then Marcus. Take us home", Forkbraid ordered.

"Aye Captain", Marcus replied.

17. Reactions

The Solstice exited the slipstream exactly where Marcus had specified and the beautiful blue Martian globe appeared on the bridge's screen once more.

"We're back home Captain", Marcus informed Forkbraid.

"Excellent Marcus", Forkbraid replied, then turned to Jim, "Jim. Do a quick tactical scan of Martian orbit and if everything appears normal, deactivate the passive and active cloaking."

"Aye Captain", Jim replied, then after a minute he added, "All is good in Martian orbit FB. All ship's cloaking deactivated. One note though Captain. It appears that the fleet of destroyers from L5 has arrived at Deimos. All thirty six of them."

"So noted Marcus", Forkbraid replied.

Meanwhile aboard the Vanguard, Captain Hart's tactical officer, detected the Solstice on his scans, "Captain Sir. I've just detected the Solstice in low Martian orbit. The Solstice just appeared from out of nowhere."

"Thank you Lieutenant", Captain Hart replied.

"Admiral Zumwalt. The Solstice is back", Captain Hart informed the Admiral.

"Thank you Captain. Put the Solstice on screen and then hail them", the Admiral commanded.

A few minutes later Forkbraid appeared on the screen, "Admiral. Nice to see you again", he greeted.

"Nice to see you again Captain", Admiral Zumwalt greeted in reply, then remarked, "We noticed your ship yesterday and then it vanished from our scans. Did you have an nice trip?"

"Ah yes, we did actually Admiral", Forkbraid replied, "We're currently on our way to you, with some delightful tales to regale you with and even a few happy snaps."

Admiral Zumwalt looked to the Vanguard's tactical officer, who nodded, the Solstice was heading their way, "I'll see you when you get here Captain. You can show us your happy snaps. Over and out."

The screen went blank, "Delightful tales? Happy snaps?", the Admiral mused.

"I don't know Admiral. We will just have to wait until they get here", Captain Hart remarked.

Marcus docked the Solstice at an appropriate external docking port on the heavy cruiser Vanguard, as instructed by the Vanguard's Communications officer. Once docked Forkbraid and his First officer, James Murphy left the Solstice and made their way to the Captain's conference room. Captain Hart's Lieutenant Adjutant showed them to the conference room and then left to get Captain Hart and Admiral Zumwalt.

When Admiral Zumwalt and Captain Hart entered the conference room, Forkbraid and Jim stood up to greet them. After exchanging greetings they all sat sat down at the conference table.

"I notice that the destroyer fleet from L5 has arrived Admiral", Forkbraid commented.

"Yes Captain. They're at Deimos to refuel and then they'll be off to the Belter colonies", Admiral Zumwalt informed him.

"Six destroyers each for the big six Belter colonies", Forkbraid noted.

Jim stepped in, "Do they have the latest upgrades Admiral?"

"Yes. Yes they do First officer Murphy", the Admiral confirmed.

"That being the case Admiral, I recommend that they launch to their targets with their fusion thrusters in stealth mode and their passive cloaking activated", Jim advised.

The Admiral nodded, "Your advice is sound. The Belter colonies won't see them coming", she turned to her Lieutenant Adjutant, "Send word to the Belter Expedition Fleet Captains. After leaving, all fusion thrusters in stealth mode and passive cloaking active."

"Aye Admiral", the Lieutenant acknowledged, "I'll make it so."

"It has one more advantage Admiral. If the Jovians are watching and I'm sure they are, those destroyers will vanish from their scans. That should put the wind up them", Jim explained.

"I'm sure it will First officer", the Admiral agreed.

"There is more news Captain Forkbraid", Admiral Zumwalt advised, "The

Trojan Fleet has broken into two smaller, equally sized fleets."

"One of them will be heading home to the Aft Trojan colonies and the other will be heading to the Fore Trojan colonies. We were expecting that Admiral", Jim added.

"Correct Lieutenant Murphy", the Admiral confirmed, informing them further, "The Aft Trojan fleet should arrive at their home colonies in about three weeks. The Fore Trojan fleet will take considerably longer."

"Nothing out of the ordinary then Admiral. As Jim noted, we were expecting this", Forkbraid replied, then added, "By the way Admiral. When we get back to Mars, I will be promoting Jim to the rank of Commander."

"Commander?", Jim questioned.

"Of course Jim. You're my First officer and you deserve a promotion", Forkbraid confirmed.

"Thank you Captain", Jim replied.

"Captain Forkbraid. Remember to let Governor Anderson's office know", the Admiral advised.

Admiral Zumwalt looked at Forkbraid and asked, "Now then, I do seem to remember something about delightful tales to regale us and happy snaps?"

Forkbraid handed a data crystal across the table to the Admiral, "It's all in there Admiral."

Admiral Zumwalt stared at the data crystal for a long moment, before pressing a few keystrokes on the touch screen embedded into the conference table. A receptacle popped up from the table's surface and the Admiral placed the data crystal into it. Admiral Zumwalt pressed a few more keystrokes and the file within the data crystal displayed on the conference room's main screen. The Admiral opened the file and began viewing the contents.

Forkbraid informed the Admiral, "Copies of this same file have been sent to General Stanton and to Fleet Captain Carmichael."

"If that's the case, I take it you've given me this copy just to keep me in the loop", the Admiral commented, she was quite please about that.

"Absolutely Admiral. You need to be kept in the loop as well", Forkbraid informed her, adding a bombshell, "The information in that data crystal was gathered from my earlier astral visits to Io Prime and Ganymede Prime with Selene, discussions with the Ionian Prince Leopold and his wife Giselle yesterday and Peter Swann's very clever hacking of the Ionian L4 computer networks."

"Wait! What! Discussions? As in person? Hacking Ionian networks?", a very confused Admiral Zumwalt asked, before finally asking, "When did you go to Jupiter?"

Forkbraid spoke with an odd lilt in his voice, *"Lieutenant Adjutant. Please leave the conference room and go about your daily business."*

The Lieutenant Adjutant stood up and began to leave the room.

"Lieutenant! Sit down!", the Admiral ordered.

"Sorry Admiral. He won't respond to your commands. At the moment he can't hear you", Forkbraid explained, adding, "I needed your Lieutenant Adjutant to leave the room. I don't want any of the following discussions recorded."

"Okay, this is irregular, but I will allow it", the Admiral agreed.

"Thank you Admiral. We went to Jupiter yesterday and returned today", Forkbraid admitted.

"How? How the hell did you do that?", the Admiral questioned.

"That is not important Admiral. I will explain that later. Right now what is important, is what is contained in that report", Forkbraid replied.

"Okay Captain Forkbraid. I suppose I'd better have a look at it then", the Admiral decided.

After reading through the file on the screen for a few minutes the Admiral noted, "Prince Wulfric is in charge of the Jovian outer defences and the Jovian fleet. That's all based at Callisto L4. Captain Forkbraid, didn't you once say he's a hothead?"

"That he is Admiral. He's not real bright either", Forkbraid confirmed.

"His Brother Prince Valdamar is in charge of the Jovian inner defences and they're based at Europa L4", the Admiral mused, "You described him as the more rational of the two?"

"That is correct Admiral. Valdamar is eminently practical, without being overly creative", Forkbraid gave his honest assessment.

"So we don't really need to worry too much about the leadership of the Princes. They sound like they'll both be ineffective leaders", Admiral Zumwalt noted, but then added, "Everything will hinge on the competency of their Generals."

"Agreed. Although the overarching controller, is High Prince Heinrich", Forkbraid remarked.

"And the High Prince controls the Jovian shipyards, weapons production, research and development at Ganymede L4", the Admiral noted.

"Yes Admiral", Forkbraid confirmed, "Heinrich also controls the Amalthean L4 ore storage, the Ionian L4 ore storage, ore processing and materials storage facilities."

"Yes Captain. I can see that on the flow chart that Peter Swann so kindly put together. That in itself is exceedingly important. It's priceless", Admiral Zumwalt remarked, "I also noted the missile, warhead and assembly factories. As well as that missile storage and launching grid."

"Those have already been neutralised Admiral", Jim Murphy chimed in.

"Neutralised?", the Admiral queried.

"Well yes Admiral", Forkbraid began, then explained, "Prince Leopold explained to me that the missiles, over twenty seven hundred of them, were going to be used against our Grand fleet. After the Grand fleet launches towards Jupiter and locks into its orbital transfer, they were going to intercept it with wave upon wave of missiles."

Jim stepped in, "Each missile with ten, two megaton warheads. By the time the Grand fleet reached Jupiter, it would have been decimated over and over again, to the point of incapacity and would have been easily overwhelmed by the Jovian fleet"

"That would have been disastrous", the Admiral remarked, then questioned, "So Captain, you and your crew neutralised that missile grid?"

"Yes Admiral. If you open up that film log, you'll see exactly what we did", Forkbraid advised.

Admiral Zumwalt opened up the video log and watched the video. The log was quite long, but it clearly showed the missile grid being manoeuvred on a course to Jupiter. The missile grid picked up the missile, warhead and assembly factories along the way. The full video was included, but it had around three hours of run time.

"If I may Admiral?", Jim asked and when the Admiral nodded in agreement, Jim fast forwarded the video to close to the end.

The Admiral watched the zoomed in screen as the missile grid closed in on Jupiter, then there was a huge, almighty explosion which slowly faded as it was enveloped by Jupiter's atmosphere.

"All twenty seven hundred plus missiles were detonated", Jim noted, adding, "Around fifty four thousand megatons."

"Oh my!", the Admiral exclaimed, quickly adding, "Well that explains the information I received this earlier this morning", then turning to Captain Hart, "Put it on the screen Captain."

"Yes Admiral", Captain Hart replied as he popped up a window on the conference room screen.

It was an ultra long range scan of Jupiter's system and it's highlight was a huge explosion above the cloud tops of Jupiter. Not enough to obscure the planet, but big enough to be significant.

"That must have been that missile grid", the Admiral noted.

Jim added in, "Yes Admiral, along with all the missiles, warheads and factories."

"So the Jovians no longer have long range missiles, nor any missile manufacturing capacity?", Admiral Zumwalt questioned.

"Not anymore Admiral", Jim confirmed, "We've pulled their teeth."

Forkbraid added, "All the Grand fleet has to deal with is the Jovian fleet, their outer defences and then their inner defences."

Jim smiled and laughed, "All of their military infrastructure is in Callisto L4, Europa L4 and Ganymede L4. With Io L4 neutralised, everything else is civilian."

"Captain, you and your crew have been busy!", Admiral Zumwalt exclaimed, querying, "General Stanton and Fleet Captain Carmichael have this same file?"

"Indeed they do Admiral", Forkbraid confirmed, "They will be analysing it was we speak."

Jim laughed again, "The Jovian fleet is fucked!", then he quickly apologised, "Please excuse my language Admiral."

"No Commander Murphy. It's fine. The Jovian fleet is fucked!", the Admiral agreed.

Forkbraid stated to Admiral Zumwalt and Captain Hart, with an unusual lilt in his voice, "Repeat after me. *'Able was I, I saw Elba'*."

Both Admiral Zumwalt and Captain Hart, replied in unison, "Able was I, I saw Elba."

Admiral Zumwalt questioned angrily, "What the hell Captain Forkbraid! What was that?"

"No need to be alarmed Admiral. It's just a mark point", Forkbraid responded.

"A mark point?", the Admiral queried.

"I'll explain it later, after I've explained how we got to Jupiter", Forkbraid replied.

"Jim. Would you like to start the ball rolling?", Forkbraid asked.

"Aye Captain. Slipstream drive Admiral", was all that Jim Murphy replied with.

"Slipstream drive?", Admiral Zumwalt enquired.

"Yes Admiral, slipstream drive", Jim confirmed, explaining, "I don't know the precise details of it, but it uses the frame dragging events that are generated by the large, rotating gravitational wells of planets, in conjunction with their magnetic fields."

"I'm not sure I understand", the Admiral admitted.

"I don't fully understand it either Admiral. Apparently when a frame dragging event is detected within a planets magnetic field, we can force an anomaly to form that we call a slipstream. It's kind of like a tunnel or a worm hole. We can direct the output of that slipstream as we require and then use it to swiftly travel to another planet", Jim explained.

"Mars doesn't have a global magnetic field", the Admiral noted.

"It does now Admiral", Forkbraid replied, "That dipole we placed at Sun Mars L1 remember."

"So this slipstream can work with artificially generated magnetic fields?", the Admiral queried.

"Absolutely Admiral", Forkbraid replied, adding, "With the exception of the entry and exit points, the parameters of these slipstreams are identical. So via a slipstream, the Solstice is literal two minutes and ten seconds from anywhere we want to go."

"Two minutes and ten seconds?", Captain Hart questioned.

"Yes Captain. Two minutes and ten seconds", Forkbraid confirmed, adding, "And that is exactly the same between two planets or two stars."

"Planets and Stars!", the Admiral exclaimed.

"Yes. Planets and Stars", Forkbraid confirmed, clarifying, "These slipstreams do have a few draw backs. You need to have a significant rotating, gravitational mass and a magnetic field at the starting point for unidirectional travel and at both ends for bidirectional travel. You also need conventional drives to get to the frame dragging events."

"So these slipstreams wouldn't work on slowly rotating planets like Mercury and Venus or tidally locked moons?", Captain Hart questioned.

"Tidally locked moons, no. Mercury and Venus, unlikely, but we haven't tested that yet", Jim Murphy responded.

"When we went to Jupiter, we exited the slipstream well outside of Callisto's orbit and we had to return to that region, in order to return home", Forkbraid commented, "They were only our second and third uses of our slipstream drive. We still have a lot more research and experimentation to do. So at the moment, it is literally a work in progress drive system."

"So hypothetically. To go to say, Alpha Centauri, where would we have to go, to find one of these frame dragging events?", Admiral Zumwalt asked.

"I'm not entirely sure Admiral, but I believe we would have to go to somewhere near the Kuiper Belt", Forkbraid replied.

"That's a hell of a long way out", the Admiral commented.

"Yes Admiral, but we would go out to Uranus or Neptune first by slipstream and then continue from there to the Kuiper Belt", Jim replied.

"So even with these draw backs, this slipstream drive methodology, does have its benefits", the Admiral concluded.

"Indeed Admiral. One could envisage the setting up of slipstream transport hubs at regions where the appropriate frame dragging events can be detected.", Forkbraid replied.

The Admiral nodded in agreement, "I could definitely see that happening Captain."

"Of course, that will be in the future, after this war is over and the solar system becomes a more peaceful place", Forkbraid replied.

"Admiral. I did speak with the Ionian Prince and his wife in person. They both want peace and they gave me all of the information that you've seen in the report", Forkbraid informed the Admiral, adding, "We expanded on that by hacking the Io L4 computer networks."

"So Prince Leopold is on our side?", Captain Hart asked.

"No. Prince Leopold and his wife Princess Giselle are on the Jovian people's side. Not our side or the Jovian High Council's side", Forkbraid corrected.

"Okay. So they want to protect their people. That is highly commendable", the Admiral noted.

"Yes Admiral. For their own safety I had to clear the memories. They won't remember my visit, until I unlock their memories sometime in the future", Forkbraid informed.

Forkbraid stated to Admiral Zumwalt and Captain Hart once again, with an unusual lilt in his voice, "Repeat after me. *'Able was I, I saw Elba'*."

Both Admiral Zumwalt and Captain Hart, replied in unison, "Able was I, I saw Elba."

Admiral Zumwalt questioned angrily, "What the hell Captain Forkbraid! Again?"

"Just another mark point Admiral", Forkbraid replied as he drew a bindrune in the air with his right index finger.

When the bindrune was completed, Forkbraid concentrated on it and it glowed bright red. Forkbraid then duplicated the bindrune and pushed a copy into both the Admiral and Captain Hart.

At first they were both taken aback, then Forkbraid informed them, with a strange calming lilt in his voice, "I've locked your memories between the first and second mark points. Everything we've divulged to you between those two points, you yourselves will not be able to divulge to anyone."

"Why would you do that?", Admiral Zumwalt demanded.

"We can't have the information about slipstream drives becoming common knowledge, at least not until the solar system is ready for that information", Forkbraid replied.

"What if I tell someone?", Captain Hart asked.

"You can try. All that will come to your mind will be *Able was I, I saw Elba*", Forkbraid replied.

The Admiral looked towards Captain Hart and tried to repeat the information about the slipstream drive, "Able was I, I saw Elba. Shit! He's right Captain!"

The Admiral turned to Forkbraid and he explained, "We've given you the information Admiral, but we need to keep it tightly locked down. Sorry. It just has to be."

Forkbraid and Jim returned to the Solstice and their Helmsman, Marcus flew the ship back to the New Flinders Psychic Academy.

There was absolute chaos at Ganymede Prime, within the ranks of the military. Matthew was rushing from one meeting to another for most of the day and all of the next. This had caught the Prophet's attention and at the end of the second day he questioned Matthew.

"Matthew, you've been in and out of your apartment continuously for the past two days. What is going on?", the Prophet asked.

"My Lord. I'm not at liberty to say. At least not yet", Matthew replied, "but it's big! Really big!"

"Has it got anything to do with that rogue asteroid that crashed into Jupiter? That's been all over the local news feeds", the Prophet enquired.

Matthew hesitated to answer, then step in close and whispered, "My Lord. It was not an asteroid", then he stepped back, "They will read you in soon. My Lord, please be patient."

Two days later the Prophet was summoned to a meeting at the High Prince's palace. The Prophet was led to the palace conference room. He'd been there many times before. Already seated in the room was, Matthew, Generals Snide and Tarzan, the Princess's representatives, Prince's Wulfric, Valdamar, Leopold and of course the High Prince himself. The Prophet was ushered to his seat.   Upon taking his seat, the Prophet noticed two things. There was a covered silver platter on the table in front of Wulfric and Wulfric himself, had an odd almost maniacal look on his face.

"Something is very, very wrong here", the Prophet thought to himself.

The High Prince had an extremely serious look on his face as he greeted the Prophet.

"Greetings Prophet", the High Prince greeted as the Prophet took his seat, "Captain Murphy recommended you be at this meeting. To keep you in the loop, so as to speak."

"Thank you Your Majesty", the Prophet replied, he then turned to Matthew and nodded.

"We have had a major setback", the High Prince announced, "As many of you already know, our entire long range missile stocks have been destroyed, along with all of our our long range missile manufacturing facilities."

This caught the Prophet by surprise, "Your Majesty?", he replied in question.

"You don't yet know my dear Prophet", the High Prince replied, adding, "That rogue asteroid that crashed into Jupiter in our news feeds, was actually our missile storage and launching array, along with our missile manufacturing facilities."

"Oh my God Your Majesty, I had no idea", the Prophet replied.

"Few outside of the military do", the High Prince replied.

The conference room door opened and a man was brought into the room. He wasn't treated roughly, but he was manhandled to some degree. He was brought into a convenient place in the room and two armed guards stood by his side.

"Lieutenant Zandar?", General Snide questioned.

"Yes General", the Lieutenant replied.

"Do you know why you're here?", General Snide asked.

"I believe so General", the Lieutenant replied, adding, "although I am confused. I came here with Commander Billings, but I haven't seen him since we arrived."

"Commander Billings is here in the room", General Snide remarked.

A smiling Prince Wulfric lifted the cover off of the silver platter and placed it to once side.

On the platter was the head of Commander Billings. White ruffled material surrounded his neck and hid any signs of blood. Contusions on his forehead, cheeks, lower jaw and a black eye, showed that Commander Billings had been beaten severely and in all probability, tortured. Lieutenant Zandar audibly gulped, his eyes wide and showing a great deal of fear.

The High Prince forcefully commented, "Commander Billings was in charge of our long range missile storage and launch array. Not only did he lose it, he also lost our missile factories. That was on his watch and it was unforgivable!", he turned to Prince Wulfric, "Cover that thing up."

Prince Wulfric replaced the cover over the silver platter and the Commander's head was soon out of sight.

The Prophet looked to Matthew and thought to himself, *"This is bad. Really bad. Matthew, you should have kept me out of the loop."*

"So Zandar, you wrote this report?", the High Prince asked as he held up the folder.

Lieutenant Zandar gulped again and replied, "Yes. Yes Your Majesty."

"Your report is extremely thorough Zandar", the High Prince noted, "Although, it is very light on the most important detail. Why Zandar? Why was my missile launching array destroyed?"

Lieutenant Zandar was slow to answer, "Our people have yet to determine that Your Majesty."

"So I've noticed Zandar. So I've Noticed", the High Prince replied, "I've read lots of details about attitude control thrusters malfunctioning. Over a hundred missiles activating by themselves and targeting my missile factories. Those rouge missiles going into immanent launch mode and then later going into immanent detonation mode, but there is nothing in here at all to say why!"

Prince Leopold stepped in, "Brother Heinrich. We do have our people working on this."

Prince Wulfric remarked accusingly, "Brother Leopold! This happened in Ionian space! Your domain! Your territory!"

To which Prince Leopold, his hand visibly upon the hilt of his sabre, replied calmly, "You'd better watch your mouth Brother Wulfric else your head will be joining Commander Billings."

"Enough!", the High Prince shouted across the table, he turned to Prince Wulfric, "Leopold has nothing to do with the Ionian L4 region. That is a part of my domain and you bloody well know it!"

"But Brother!", Prince Wulfric protested loudly.

"Enough Wulfric! Get the fuck out of my conference room and take that fucking head with you!", the High Prince commanded.

A far more contrite, sheepish Prince Wulfric picked up the silver platter and left the conference room with it.

The Prophet thought to himself, *"It not just the Sisters that are psychotic. So is Prince Wulfric!"*

Something that Matthew has already figured out. Prince Wulfric was unstable and dangerous.

"If I may Brother?", Prince Valdamar asked.

The High Prince looked to Prince Valdamar, "Brother. You may."

"Tells us what happened in our own words. A brief but thorough summary", Prince Valdamar ordered Zandar.

Lieutenant Zandar was again slow to answer, "Your Highness. First the off station light came on. Something that has never happened before. We checked the system and everything seem to be okay, but the attitude control thrusters were still firing and taking the array further off station. The settings were correct, but the thrusters were not following the correct settings. The array finally ended up, squared off against the missile, warhead and assembly factories."

"So the attitude control systems were malfunctioning?", Prince Valdamar asked.

"Yes Your Highness", Lieutenant Zandar confirmed.

"So Zandar. What happened next?", Prince Valdamar questioned.

"Your Highness. Over one hundred missiles activated of their own accord and began targeting the factories. Then they went into immanent launch status. In the array's control room, we were unable to shut those missiles down. Knowing that they could launch at any moment and that they were targeting the factories, we quickly organised their evacuation", the Lieutenant replied.

"Did you try to rectify the problem?", Prince Valdamar asked.

"We did Your Highness. While the factories were evacuating, we sent out maintenance teams to shutdown the rogue missiles manually. Except, we only had six maintenance teams on the array and when they shutdown the first six missiles, they immediately reactivated straight afterwards", Lieutenant Zandar informed him.

"Okay Zandar. I get it. The missiles went rouge, targeting the factories and you could not shut them down. So you did the only thing you could do, you evacuated the factories", Prince Valdamar summed up, he then asked, "What about the missile array itself?"

"Yes Your Highness", Lieutenant Zandar confirmed, then replied, "After that, the rogue missile went into immanent detonation status. They could have detonated at any moment and we still had no control over those missiles. So we evacuated the missile array as well."

"That does make a lot of sense Lieutenant. I would have done the same", Prince Valdamar noted, "but you and the Commander came back to the array, yes?"

"Yes Your Highness. After our personnel were safely back at the Io L4 colonies, we did go back to where the array was stationed", Lieutenant Zandar replied, "Only the array had moved. When we go there, the array was flying towards Jupiter, having collected all the factories along the way. It was moving fast and there was no way we could catch up to it. We contacted our colonies to get our scanners and scopes turned towards the array and then we headed back to the colonies ourselves."

The High Prince stepped in, "And by then, there were three hundred missiles with their thrusters firing and the whole array on its way to Jupiter."

"Yes Your Majesty. The caps on the missile silos hadn't opened and the missile lock down arms were still locked in place", Lieutenant Zandar noted, "With those in place, the whole missile array would be pushed along by the rogue missile's thrusters."

The High Prince nodded in understanding, "Lieutenant Zandar, you are free to leave", then to the two guards he instructed, "Dismissed."

"Yes Your Majesty", a very relieved Lieutenant replied, before leaving the conference room.

The two guards saluted and they too left the conference room.

"Was that wise Brother?", Prince Valdamar asked.

"What more could he tell us Brother? We have his report. He's not an expert", the High Prince replied, "It is as Leopold said, we have our own people working on this."

The Prophet cautiously asked, "Your Majesty. If I may, what happened to Commander Billings?"

"I made a mistake Prophet", the High Prince admitted, "I allowed my Brother Wulfric to question the Commander. In hindsight, I should have asked Valdamar."

Prince Valdamar stepped in, "Our missile array was crucial to our defence. When Wulfric heard about the destruction of the array, he became quite upset. What can I say, our Brother Wulfric does not handle stress very well at all."

"Commander Billings was in charge of our long range missile launch array and its destruction was on his watch. It may have been unforgivable, but Wulfric's brutality cannot be condoned", the High Prince commented.

"Given how crucial those long range missiles were to our defences, what are our options now?", the Prophet enquired.

General Tarzan answered, "We were going to use those missiles to decimate the Earth's and L5's Grand fleet, over and over, with wave, after wave of missiles. We no longer have that option. Our Jovian fleet will have to meet the enemy head on. Preferably, long before they reach the Jovian Realms."

Matthew added, "Losing those missiles is a major problem my Lord. The Jovian fleet does have far more ships, but the Earth's and L5's fleets have more modern ships, with plasteel and polyceramalloy hulls. I doubt their weapons tech will be significantly different, but it will be much harder to punch through a polyceramalloy hull, than a steel and titanium hull."

"So the enemy's ships can take more of a battering?", the Prophet asked rhetorically.

General Tarzan answered anyway, "That is the gist of the problem, Prophet."

"Have our experts figured out what when wrong with the missile array?", the Prophet asked.

"They've all but ruled out sabotage My Lord", Matthew replied, explaining, "There were seventy two attitude control thrusters on the missile array. Our people have determined, that they could not have been controlled by a saboteur. Perhaps one or two thrusters, but not seventy two. Our people believe that there was a malfunction in the attitude control systems."

"And the actual missiles Matthew?", the Prophet enquired.

"The missile array was able to hold five thousand missiles My Lord. There were over twenty seven hundred missiles in the array at that time", Matthew replied and then explained, "Those missiles were all grouped by tens into missile firing blocks. When an order to launch comes through, the operator tells the firing control system how many missiles to launch. The computer works out which missile firing blocks to activate and launch, keeping the entire missile array in complete balance at the same time."

Matthew continued, "There were well over a hundred rogue missiles and they activated at random across the entire array. Not whole missile firing blocks mind you. It was all very random, a missile here, a missile there. Very random. Our people don't even know how that happened. It should not have even been possible at all, certainly not for a saboteur."

Prince Valdamar chimed in with, "If it shouldn't be possible, then how was it done?"

"Your Highness, they don't really know. They have run a couple of ideas past General Tarzan and I, but it's all really just pure speculation", Matthew replied.

General Tarzan stepped in, "In short, it would require a second computer system to take control of the array's missile control systems. Either that or some kind of artificially intelligent virus. There was no evidence of a systems breach at all, so those have been ruled out."

The Prophet then asked, "Then what does that leave us with?"

"A highly unlikely series of malfunctions", Matthew remarked, "Each on its own would not have been a problem, but when they occurred in the precise sequence that they did, just happened to be extraordinarily disastrous."

"A highly unlikely series of malfunctions", the High Prince repeated incredulously.

"That's all our people have at the moment Your Majesty", Matthew replied.

"As bad as losing all of out long range missile stocks is, we also have other problems to contend with", General Snide remarked, as he pressed a few keystrokes on his keyboard and brought up some images on the screen.

"What are we looking at General?", Prince Valdamar asked.

"That is a our long range scans of those three dozen destroyers flying to Mars Your Highness", the General replied, explaining, "These are our clearest images.

Left to right on the screen, the fleet is on approach to Mars. The fleet then arrives at the Martian moon Deimos. Two days later, the fleet leaves Deimos. Then the fleet vanishes completely from our scans."

"Vanishes?", questioned Prince Valdamar, "That's not possible. Is it? Sure it's some kind of equipment failure."

"Our equipment has been checked Your Highness", General Snide replied.

General Tarzan stepped in, explaining, "We believe those destroyers are capable of going dark. Perhaps a combination of stealth thrusters and somehow turning their ships hulls midnight black."

"Just like the Gunship Solstice General", Matthew noted, adding, "We won't be able to track them. At least not easily anyway", as he stepped out of his chair and approached the screen.

"General Snide. Do you have anymore images? Ones showing the fleets departure from Deimos perhaps?", Matthew enquired.

"Of course Captain", the General replied as he brought up more images on the screen.

Matthew stared at the screen, a cold and silent stare, occasionally rubbing his chin as he studied the images.

"What is it Matthew? What do you see?", the Prophet enquired.

Matthew remained quiet for a long moment, then answered, "Gentlemen. Look at these images. What can you see?"

Everyone in the conference room stared at the screen. Not one of them answered Matthew's question. The room remained silent.

"Matthew. Stop playing games. What do you see?", the Prophet asked.

Matthew pointed to a series of images, "My Lord. Six ships, six ships, six ships, again six ships, six more ships and finally six more ships", Matthew noted, as he pointed out each of the images in turn, one after the other.

Each of the images showed six ships, all destroyers, departing Deimos.

The room was still silent, so Matthew explained, "Thirty six destroyers refuelling at Deimos. They departed Deimos in six groups of six ships."

Prince Leopold replied, "I get it. That fleet of thirty six destroyers is now six smaller flotillas of six destroyers each and each flotilla has a different destination."

Matthew pointed to Prince Leopold, "Bingo! Your Highness."

Prince Leopold responded, "Don't you all see. This is Valdamar's old plan in reverse. The one that was rejected!"

Matthew quickly confirmed, "Yes Your Highness. Prince Valdamar's plan called for the Jovian forces to attack, occupy and annex the big five Belter colonies. This is the Earth and L5 doing the same thing, but they're going after the big six, Ceres, Vesta, Pallas, Hygiea, Interamnia and Juno."

"Can we be sure of this Captain", the High Prince questioned.

"To be honest Your Majesty. No. We have no way to confirm this at all", Matthew replied, "However, their departure pattern of six groups of six destroyers does imply six destinations and there are precisely six very large asteroids with meaningful colonies. If I was in charge of that fleet, that's exactly what I would be doing."

"General Snide. Send word to those Belter colonies to be on the look out for destroyers from the Earth and L5", the High Prince ordered.

General Snide replied, "Yes Your Majesty. However, given how our scanners are so ineffective, the Belter's scanners will be even worse. They aren't likely to see them approach at all."

"Warn them anyway General", the High Prince replied.

The conference room door opened and Prince Wulfric stepped into the room. Prince Wulfric's eyes were wide, his skin had taken on a pale colour and he was looking overly stressed and even more unstable than when he'd left the room earlier.

"What are you doing here Wulfric?", the High Prince demanded.

"Brother Heinrich, I apologise, but this, this is way too important", the Prince replied as he handed General Snide a data crystal.

General Snide took the data crystal and looked to High Prince Heinrich, who nodded in reply.

The General placed the data crystal into a date reader on the table and images appeared on the conference room screen.

Prince Wulfric informed the room in a shaky voice, "Those are our latest surveillance scans of the L4 fleet staging zone in cis-lunar space."

They all stared at the screen and the images it contained, Matthew noted, "That's their Grand fleet departing cis-lunar L4."

Prince Wulfric continued, his voice still shaky and his skin paler than when he walked in, "As you follow the images, you can see that just over half of their fleet has departed the L4 staging zone. They are all heavy cruisers, everyone last one of them."

Prince Wulfric was correct and the images showed precisely what he was pointing out. As they continued follow the images, the ships of the Grand fleet that had departed vanished without trace.

It was obvious to everyone in the room, but Matthew commented anyway, "They've gone dark."

"Yes Captain", Prince Wulfric confirmed in his shaky voice, "They've gone dark!"

Prince Valdamar replied, "Stealth thrusters and a midnight black skin, like the Gunship Solstice. We can't fucking track them!"

Prince Leopold noted, "We don't need to track them. We know exactly where they're going. They're coming here!"

Matthew replied, "Your Highness's, Your Majesty, we can still plot the possible hohmann and non hohmann orbital transfers for their fleet, based on what we know of their cruiser's thrust and delta-v capabilities."

General Tarzan remarked, "Captain. There could a lot of variability in those course plots."

"Yes General, which why we need to work fast. Real fast", Matthew replied, adding, "For every possible coarse we plot, we need to get detection buoys in their path. That may be the only way to determine their approach."

"Good idea Captain", General Tarzan agreed, then he turned to the High Prince, who nodded his agreement with the plan.

High Prince Heinrich told the room, "It looks like it's begun gentlemen. That fleet will be here soon enough. General Snide, make the necessary preparations to intercept, their so called Grand fleet, with our own Jovian fleet en-route. We'll obliterate them and then continue onto the Earth and L5. We will finish this war once and for all. Everyone needs to get ready, play their part. This meeting is adjourned gentlemen. Get on with it, all of you", he then turned to Prince

Wulfric, "Brother Wulfric. Go to your apartment and get some rest. That's an official royal command!"

The High Prince waved over General Snide and whispered in his ear, "Give Princess Matilda a call. Let the Princess know, her husband is not very well. The Princess will know what to do."

"Yes Your Majesty. I'll make that call that straight away", the General replied, then left the room.

Matthew had heard the whispered instructions and nodded to the High Prince in understanding. The High Prince nodded back in confirmation.

Matthew thought to himself, *"Princess Matilda is not just Prince Wulfric's wife, but also his minder and very likely his clinician."*

The lives of the Horridians were complicated indeed.

18. The Fall of Venusville

Floating high above the seething cauldron that was the surface of Venus, amidst the swirling, yellow, golden clouds and tempestuous winds, lies the realm of wonder, beauty and technological prowess. The Venusian sky cities.

Delicately perched and floating fifty kilometres above the surface, the ethereal habitats with their glorious domes offered a breathtaking vista of the planet beneath and the endless expanse of the skies above.

The Sun's golden rays filtered through the thick atmosphere, creating a warm glow upon the billowing clouds of sulphuric acid, the Venusian sky cities basked in perpetual twilight. The horizon stretched endlessly in all directions, shrouded in swirling mists and a haze of poisonous vapours. Far below, the rugged Venusian terrain could only be seen in rare glimpses through the ever-present and shifting clouds. Towering mountains and vast plains, volcanoes spewing forth their magma.

In the heavens above, the distant Sun hung like a radiant jewel in the sky. Small, shiny points of light, visibly reflecting the Sun's rays, the Venusian orbital colonies were easily visible. Beyond which was the twinkling of distant stars, with the occasional planet coming into view.

In this enchanted realm, the boundaries between Venus and sky blur and the beauty of the cosmos unfolds in all of its splendour. Amidst the clouds of Venus, the sky cities offered habitable sanctuaries of both awe and wonder. Testaments to the ingenuity of the human species and their enduring spirit of exploration. One such sky city, was the first of them all, Venusville.

Suspended amidst billowing clouds of sulphuric mist, lies a marvel of human ingenuity, Venusville. The first of the many sky cities of Venus, this being its fifth incarnation. The preceding versions having been scrapped, recycled and upgraded. At its centre, a huge grand dome of shimmering crystal aluminium and plasteel, its translucent surface refracting the faint light of distant stars, casting an iridescent glow upon the landscape within.

Within the protective embrace of the grand dome, a bustling metropolis thrives. A vibrant tapestry of life and activity, where the dreams of humanity take flight amidst the swirling sulphuric mists. Here, beneath the ever-changing sky, a community flourishes, its streets alive with the hum of innovation and the chatter of voices raised in spirited conversation.

Seventy two immense, pendulous gas buoyancy envelopes, great billowing structures that dot the skyline around the dome's perimeter, like immense sails upon an alien sea. Manufactured from the strongest, lightweight materials, impervious to the sulphurous Venusian clouds and filled with a specific mixture of gases. These technological marvels of engineering, harness the power of the dense Venusian atmosphere, lifting Venusville skyward with graceful ease.

Hidden beneath the bustling metropolis within the grand dome, lies a vast network of seventy two air multiplying turbines with their complicated air ducts pulling in the Venusian atmosphere. Whirring machines, drawing in the Venusian air and processing it for vital gases, turning carbon dioxide into oxygen and carbon, as well as collecting nitrogen and water. It is through the combined efforts of these turbines and the buoyancy envelopes that the city of Venusville maintains its lofty perch amidst the clouds, defying gravity with each gentle breath of wind. The Venusian sky cities, a new frontier for humanity and Venusville, the glorious crowning jewel of them all.

From each of the immense pendulous buoyancy envelopes, hung thirty six meticulously engineered suspension cables of plasteel. Each tightly coupled to sturdy anchoring points, strategically placed along the outer perimeter of Venusville's underlying external framework. These anchoring points provided the secure attachment points for the suspension cables that extend from the buoyancy envelopes to the framework.

The suspension cables themselves were meticulously engineered to bear the weight and strain of Venusville, beneath the buoyancy envelopes and ensure their stability within the Venusian atmosphere. The framework itself was reinforced with beams and trusses designed to distribute the forces exerted by the buoyancy envelopes evenly across the structure, further enhancing the sky city's stability and its resilience in the harsh Venusian environment.

All in all, Venusville was designed to be and considered to be, one of the safest of all of the sky cities of Venus. The air multiplying turbines, although designed to aid in keeping Venusville aloft, were mostly used for processing the Venusian atmosphere, for resource extraction and were originally designed to work at only twenty percent of their capacity. No one expected Venusville to fail and it showed in its current demographics. Venusville was forever!

The current incarnation, Venusville V, was originally designed and built a century earlier, to house thirty five thousand people in opulence and luxury. Since then the population had grown and Venusville had been added to and further developed. Far larger, more effective gas filled buoyancy envelopes had been swapped in, in place of the the original smaller ones and the air multiplying turbines now worked at a furious rate of fifty percent of capacity.

As the population continued to grow, the opulence and luxury of their surroundings had to diminish slightly with every addition, modification and upgrade. Even though this was the case, the entire population of Venusville was generally happy with their home and very few had opted to emigrate to the larger orbital colonies at Venusian Lagrangian points one, four or five.

By now the population of Venusville had topped over one hundred thousand souls. Venusville was forever, so very few people if any, took any notice of the fact that the sky city had only enough evacuation pods for the originally design specification of thirty five thousand people!

Shadowy figures were moving outside of the sky cities glistening crystal aluminium dome. Clad in space suits designed to be impervious to the Venusian sulphuric acid rain, throughout the outer framework they toiled. They coordinated and communicated with each other with simple code words and phrases. No one took any notice of them. They were meant to be there.

Were they not maintenance personnel?

Was this not their job?

Was this not their occupation?

Yes was the answer to all three questions, yet how many of them had immigrated recently from cis-lunar space, specifically from the colonies of L5?

There were unfortunately more than a few and they had all applied for and accepted positions on the Venusville maintenance teams with a purpose. To maintain the outer external framework of Venusville's base and substructure as per their job descriptions, but also to carry out their nefarious plans. They had been working there for many, many months, the better part of a year and now they were almost finished.

"This is maintenance team one eleven to control. We'll be finishing up our scheduled work in twenty minutes and heading back inside the frame", the team leader of maintenance team one eleven informed their supervisors in the control office.

"Roger that maintenance team one eleven. We'll see you on the inside in about thirty minutes", their supervisor replied.

The team leader of maintenance team one eleven then changed the frequency on his communicator, "Maintenance team one eleven to controller. We have finished installing the *'strain gauges'* to suspension cable anchoring point thirty six on gas buoyancy envelope seventy two ."

"Roger that. We'll meet later at the usual place", the mysterious controller replied.

Twenty minutes later maintenance team one eleven finished work and returned inside the frame, there were seven of them in all. After removing their spacesuits and signing off for the day, they each left for their own apartments. It was several hours later, that they each left their apartments for their meeting with the mysterious controller, their team leader had spoken to.

One by one, maintenance team one eleven met up in the network of tunnels within the inner framework, eventually making their way to a large, long disused maintenance room. A man stood guard at the entrance door and upon recognising them, allowed them inside. They were the last to arrive. Maintenance team one eleven entered the room and the guard followed, shutting the door behind him. There were close to fifty people in the room.

"Here they are people", the mysterious controller informed the room, "Maintenance team one eleven!", he shouted, "Who have just finished installing the last of our *'strain gauges'*."

The other people in the room all started clapping and cheering them.

After the clapping died down, a rather large man shouted out, "Why we still calling them *'strain gauges'* then? They're all in place and we know what they really are. They're right proper bombs!"

The mysterious controller shouted back, "Careful now! This ain't over yet. Someone could still get word. Until we're off this floater, we call them *'strain gauges'*. Got it!", he was adamant.

The rather large man nodded his agreement.

Another man shouted out, "I do have a few concerns Sir."

"What concerns would they be lad?", the mysterious controller questioned.

"I know we've been planning this for a long time and all, but has anyone bothered to look into the history of this place?", the concerned man replied questioningly.

"What's the point? This will be all gone before midday tomorrow", the controller replied.

"There's over a hundred thousand people on this floater Sir", the concerned man replied, adding, "When they designed and built this place, it was only meant to hold thirty five thousand."

"Not seeing the point lad", the mysterious controller remarked, adding, "Tomorrow, when we pop off the *tits* and they float skyward, everyone will be running to the escape pods."

"That's the problem Sir. Ever since this floater was built, they've upgraded it, over and over and over. Now it's chock full of people Sir", the concerned man remarked.

"I'm still not seeing the point lad", the mysterious controller reiterated.

"There's only enough escape pods for a third of the population, if that Sir", the concerned man summed up, finishing, "At least two thirds of them are going to die Sir. That's a lot of people!"

The mysterious controller nodded surreptitiously to a colleague nearby, he had no time for any of this, then answered, "Well lad, I know you have concerns. Legitimate ones at that, but you know what? Put the fucking blame on the morons who've been running this place. It's too fucking late to stop now. This is happening tomorrow!"

The concerned man had an outraged expression on his face, then there was a sharp, cracking sound as the mysterious controller's colleague broke the concerned man's neck.

The mysterious controller then asked the room full of people, "Anyone else have any concerns?"

There were murmurs of, "No", from everyone.

"Good then. Tomorrow, you all go about your business, but make sure you get to the escape pods by nine am", the mysterious controller instructed, reiterating, "Nine am. Got that!"

Everyone in the room were nodding in agreement.

"You want to stay on this floater right up till nine twenty five. Then launch your escape pods. Five minutes after that, those *'strain gauges'* will pop off the *tits*", the controller instructed them, adding, "You don't want to be around for that. Understood!"

Again everyone nodded in agreement.

"Good. Everyone get some sleep", the mysterious controller suggested, "Remember. Tomorrow, you all get to the escape pods at nine am and launch them at no later than nine twenty five."

Again everyone nodded in agreement, before leaving the room.

The next morning at nine am a group of people began forming near the access corridors that led to some of the emergency escape pods. Normally during an emergency, the doors would unlock automatically and open of their own accord. This, however, was not an emergency and the mysterious controller used his maintenance key code to open the doors. The group slipped through the doors, walked down the corridor and chose three escape pods. Each escape pod could hold up to twenty people and there were nearly fifty in their group. They boarded the three chosen escape pods and waited patiently. At precisely nine twenty five am, all three escape pods lunched.

The launching of the escape pods was almost immediately picked up by the Venusian low orbit traffic control stations.

"Commander. I'm picking up telemetry from three escape pods", Lieutenant Macron informed.

"Escape pods Lieutenant?", Commander Milton enquired, then asked, "Why would you be picking up escape pod telemetry?"

"I don't know Sir, but we do have three escape pods on our screens", the Lieutenant replied.

"Notify our rescue crews, we have three escape pods to pick", Commander Milton ordered.

"Yes Sir. Notifying the rescue crews now", the Lieutenant replied.

"It's unusual for escape pods to be launching. It could be a malfunction or perhaps kids on a joy ride. Make sure you log the date and time of this incident", Commander Milton recommended.

"Yes Sir. Logging the details now", the Lieutenant replied.

It was now nine thirty am and all hell broke lose.

In quick succession, the twenty five hundred and ninety two *'strain gauges'* exploded. The explosions were not large enough to break the massive suspension cable anchoring points, but they were more than enough to crack and weaken them, which was their actual purpose. It was meant to allow time for people to get to the emergency escape pods, however, as it turned out, there were never enough escape pods for the entire population.

The sounds of the explosions carried across the whole of Venusville, which shuddered violently, as if hit by an earth quake. The emergency warning klaxons began sounding and Venusville's emergency messaging systems began sending out messages to the population. The evacuation of Venusville had begun.

The automated emergency systems began recording valuable information and streaming it directly to Venusian Colonial Central Command. These live feeds were not encrypted and easily picked up by the news services, who in turn replayed them to their audiences as *'breaking news'*.

The people of Venusville began making their way to the emergency escape pods. The Venusville authorities notified the off world authorities of their current situation. At first the evacuation was proceeding in an orderly fashion, with no one rushing and everyone thinking it was not as serious as the emergency messages had made it sound. Then things started getting worse.

One by one, the damaged suspension cable anchoring points began to fail. Then the unthinkable happened, as one of the gas buoyancy envelopes, that the mysterious controller had call the *'tits'*, popped off! The sounds of the breaking anchoring points and suddenly lose, whipping suspension cables was both loud and horrifying.

People watched in horror as the first of Venusville's seventy two, all important *'tits'*, floated skywards at high speed. They all knew this, was very, very bad and began panicking, rushing as quickly as they could to the emergency escape pods. By now the emergency escape pods began launching from Venusville in droves.

The air multiplying turbines automatically began to increase their rates of rotation in order to stabilise the sky city. Then more damaged suspension cable anchoring points began failing and it wasn't long before another *'tit'*, a gas buoyancy envelope, popped off and quickly floated skywards. Again there were the horrifying sounds of breaking plasteel and lose, whipping suspension cables. The weight of the sky city put immense strain on the remaining gas buoyancy envelopes and then the situation worsened, as yet another *'tit'*, popped of.

The air multiplying turbines automatically stepped up again and were now running at seventy five percent of capacity, as they worked furiously to stabilise the situations. It wasn't enough and yet another *'tit'*, popped off, as its suspension cable anchoring points failed.

The air multiplying turbines kicked into high gear as Venusville's engineers pushed them to full, one hundred percent capacity and the entire sky city slowly appeared to stabilise itself once more. Panic amongst the populace began to subside and the evacuation became more orderly once more.

Lieutenant Macron informed his Commander, "Sir. Venusville is in bad shape. We have several hundred more escape pods coming our way."

"Notify the rescue crews Lieutenant. Call the authorities and tell them they need to get cracking", the Commander replied, "this is rapidly getting well above our pay grades."

"Yes Sir. I'm on it", the Lieutenant replied.

"Those first three escape pods. They launched before this all began", Commander Milton noted, "Hand their identity codes to the security services. I suspect they will need to be investigated."

"Yes Sir. I'm way ahead of you on that one Sir", Lieutenant Macron replied.

The evacuation of Venusville came to an abrupt halt when the last of its seventeen hundred and fifty escape pods launched. The emergency escape pods had been launching, with some full, some only half full and some, with only a couple of people aboard. The people boarding the emergency pods, had not necessarily been waiting until they fully occupied before launching them. Other Venusvillians were lucky and had their own vehicles, with which they could leave, but they were far fewer in number. Only twenty five thousand people had managed to evacuate. The over eighty thousand citizens remaining were going nowhere.

The situation appeared stable, but it just was the calm before the storm, as more suspension cable anchoring points began to give way. In quick succession four more 'tits' popped of and rushed skywards. Venusville's engineers pushed the air multiplying turbines to one hundred and ten percent of capacity and when that wasn't enough, they pushed them even further, to one hundred and twenty percent. They were now in uncharted territory and no one knew for certain, how long the turbines could last at these loads.

More suspension cable anchoring points began to give way and two more 'tits' popped off, rushing skywards, with the evil sounds of breaking plasteel and whipping of suspension cables. There was little further capacity to be had, the air multiplying turbines were now maxed out at one hundred and twenty five percent and could spin no faster. Ever so slowly at first, but gradually picking up speed, Venusville began to fall.

Around eighty thousand people were trapped inside the Venusville dome with no way to escape. All of the emergency escape pods had been launched and the remaining people were all in a state of sheer panic and terror. Information streaming from the automatic emergency systems, didn't just show data. The streams also showed the people of Venusville, trapped like rats with no way out, as the majestic sky city slipped deeper and deeper into the Venusian atmosphere by the minute.

The other nearby Venusian colonies were the first to get access to the breaking news feeds. The citizens of the Venusian colonies watched in horror as Venusville fell. Deeper and deeper, the atmosphere growing denser and hotter. The strain on the sky city increased significantly with each few hundred metres deeper it dropped. The strain on the remaining damaged suspension cable anchoring points was exacerbated by the heat and pressure. One by one they began to fail and more and more of the gas buoyancy envelopes, the *'tits'*, popped off. They rapidly tore away skywards with the loud cracking of plasteel and the whipping roar of lose suspension cables.

The air multiplying turbines, overwhelmed by the weight of their task of stabilising Venusville and keeping it aloft, began to fail. Venusville was falling faster and faster. Venusville was growing hotter and hotter. The panicking people, the sweat poring off them, looked for places to hide or ran about not knowing what to do. There was nothing, nothing at all they could do and the temperature just kept on rising.

As the Venusian colonies in orbit watched the live streams from Venusville, the huge grand dome of shimmering crystal aluminium and plasteel, began to buckle and crack. The exceedingly hot, toxic gases of the Venusian atmosphere began to flow in, as the terrified people of Venusville watched, petrified with horror. The air became hot and almost unbreathable, with sulphuric acid levels rising to intolerably high levels.

The Venusvillians began running in terror, suffocating, before bursting into flames in the searing heat. Screaming in agony, they continued to run wildly, before collapsing to the ground and dying in writhing, screaming agony. Then it was all quiet in the live streams for very long minutes until Venusville's automated emergency data streams failed completely and cut out. Venusville continued to fall, its once vibrant city streets quiet, its population silent and reduced to ashes. No body heard the almighty crash as Venusville struck the Venusian surface.

The Venusian orbital science laboratories, whose task it was to study Venus, its atmosphere, its surface and geology etc., scanned the Venusian surface in the vicinity of where Venusville had once floated. The scans came back. Venusville was now a huge, broken, melting hulk, spread out across the Venusian landscape in a vast volcanic plain. No one could possibly have survived the fall and within minutes not even the ashes of the victims remained. Further scanning located Venusville's seventy two gas buoyancy envelopes. The *'tits'* as they were once affectionately known, floating randomly above the clouds of Venus, being pushed along by the strong Venusian winds.

Venusville has fallen!

19. Aftermath

The video wall in the dormitory, where the Pod family were staying at the academy was blasting out the latest news from Venus.

"Breaking news viewers. Breaking news", the news anchor informed everyone, "The historic sky city of Venusville has fallen!"

The background behind the news anchor displayed the data feed from Venusville, showing the horrific scenes of panic and terror as the historic sky city slipped deeper and deeper into the Venusian atmosphere.

The news anchor turned slightly and gestured to the display, "What you are seeing viewers, are the final moments as Venusville plunged into the depths of Venus's dense, toxic atmosphere."

Finally the scenes on the data feed showed Venusville's dome crack open and the super hot, toxic gases of the Venusian atmosphere enter the sky city. Thousands of people were still running around in a state of total panic, with nowhere to escape as they burst into flames. Burning alive and screaming, before collapsing to the ground and writhing in agony, until they were quiet and still. Then the feed cut out, only to restart again at the beginning.

The Pod Sisters Zuawalo and Zeealas, their Mother Zyaliep and Aunt Nyaliep, were all in tears and holding their faces as the horrific scenes unfolded on the screen before them. They didn't want to watch, but they could not, not watch. They were all transfixed by the images on the screen. Roseanne had sensed their distress and ran straight to their dormitory, along the way she gathered Jim and Varak.

Jim went straight to his wives, Zuawalo and Zeealas and Varak straight to his wife Nyaliep. Kwoth was already comforting Zyaliep. Roseanne went straight to the screen and switched it off.

"So many deaths!", Zeealas remarked as the tears streamed down her cheeks.

Her Mother Zyaliep added, "They all burned to death. Over eighty thousand of them."

Zuawalo repeated Zeealas's words, "So many deaths!"

Nyaliep replied to Zyaliep, "They burned alive Sister! All of them burned alive!"

Roseanne was angry, "Why the hell were they streaming those scenes?"

Jim replied, "Our news feeds are not censored Roseanne. The news corporations received it and they just replayed it. Right or wrong, that's just what they do."

"Perhaps after this, there should be censorship!", Roseanne replied loudly, "There must be hundreds, no, thousands of distraught people out there after seeing that. Children even!"

"Roseanne. You look after things here. I'm going to find Forkbraid and Selene", Jim replied.

Roseanne's eyes rolled back slightly, then came back to normal, "They're both in Selene's apartment", she informed him.

When Jim arrived at Selene's apartment, Forkbraid opened the door and let him in, "Roseanne gave us a heads up", he greeted, then asked, "How are the Girls going?"

Jim looked deeper into the apartment and noted that the same news feed was playing on Selene's apartment screen, he pointed to it, "After seeing that! How do you think they fucking feel?", he was extremely angry.

Forkbraid put his hand on Jim's shoulder and a calming wave came over him.

Jim looked at Forkbraid, with tears in his eyes, "Thank you FB."

"That's alright Jim. I understand", Forkbraid replied.

As they both walked from the entrance foyer to Selene's lounge room, Jim remarked, "I think my Zeealas nailed it when she said, *'so many deaths'*."

Jim and Forkbraid sat down and Selene informed them, "They're saying it was a terrorist attack."

As they watched, the horrific scene played through one last time then cut off.

The news anchor remarked, "Apparently, we have been receiving thousands of complaints and have been advised to stop showing the data feeds from the fall of Venusville. We do sincerely apologise for any distress those images may have caused. We are crossing to a televised statement from the Venusian Prime Minister, Kurt Yodels."

A tall, stern looking man with deep blue eyes and caramel blond hair appeared on the screen, "It is with the deepest regret, that I must confirm, that the historic sky city of Venusville has indeed fallen. This was no natural occurrence, nor a malfunction of their systems. Our preliminary investigation has uncovered a plot by terrorists to bring Venusville down. They apparently worked on this heinous secret project of theirs for nearly a year before carrying it out."

The Prime Minister paused, then announced, "The perpetrators, the terrorists, have all been rounded up and captured. They call themselves the *'People of the Prophet'* and the *'Prophets Army'* . They have readily confessed their involvement. Forty eight men and women will be put on trial for this heinous crime. Justice will be swift. This is the largest mass murder in Venusian history, with over eighty thousand deaths. Even the Venusian war time deaths during the previous outer satellite insurrection, pale in comparison. We Venusians will not rest until this man, the Prophet is apprehended and brought to justice."

A picture of a man appeared on the screen, he was tall and burly, kind of rough looking, but with a kind and gentle expression to his face. The picture was a mugshot of the leader of the Prophet's Army, the mysterious controller. His left eye was blackened and his left cheek heavily bruised. Another contusion on his right forehead was clearly visible. The mans jaw looked like it had been pinned, possibly because it had been broken. It was obvious to all the watching viewers, the man had been beaten severely. The Venusian interrogators had been harsh in the extreme.

The Prime Minister looked directly into the camera, "I have just signed into law a new bill to support the inner solar system in this war against Jovian aggression. One third of our Venusian fleet will be sent to cis-lunar L4 to join with the Earth Defence Forces and Colonial Fleets. Another third of our Venusian fleet will be sent to rendezvous with the Grand fleet that is currently en-route to Jupiter. To the Horridian Dynasty and their mass murdering Prophet, I say this. We are coming for you!", the anger on the Prime Minister's face was visible for all to see.

He paused once more and his visage took on a far softer demeanour, "We have another urgent issue to deal with. The loss of Venusville and the spreading of the data videos of its fall, across the news feeds, has caused a panic in the other Venusian sky cities. To all those citizens of Venus, please remain calm. Based on our interrogation of the terrorists, we believe that only Venusville was targeted. None the less, we are sending multiple inspection teams to each and every sky city to ensure that you are all indeed safe. So please, remain calm."

The Prime Minister paused again, before looking into the camera with a beseeching look in his eyes, "To the Earth's Government and to President Banyon of L5, I am requesting your aid. We have over a thousand sky cities on Venus, with a population of over one hundred million people. Due to this Venusville atrocity, they are now fearful of their assistance, they fear for their very lives. Many of them now wish to emigrate off world. Only we do not have the colonies to take them all."

He paused once more, "A while ago, we Venusians put forward a plan to open up the Mercurian orbital zones to colonisation. We can and we will build new colonies ourselves at Venus Lagrangian points, L2, L4 and L5, but these will not be enough. We will need your help to build the new colonies in Mercury's orbital zones. We Venusian's have the technology, between the Earth, L5 and Venus, we have the necessary resources. We need to start work on this project urgently, before the conclusion of this War. Thank you all."

The Venusian Prime Minister bowed to the camera and the televised statement ended.

Jim spat out, "After seeing what my Girls just saw on that data stream from Venusville, fuck! I'd be scared of living on one of those fucking Venusian sky cities as well."

"Jim!", Selene responded.

"Sorry Selene, but I've always considered those things to be bloody death traps", Jim replied.

The news anchor was talking once more, "As we've just heard from the Venusian Prime Minister, Kurt Yodels, this was a terrorist attack. The historic sky city of Venusville has fallen. Venusville was brought down by an act of terrorism and over eighty thousand people have perished. The terrorists have been apprehended and Prime Minister Yodels has informed us that they have confessed to this horrendous crime. Justice will be swift according to Prime Minister Yodels. Two Venusian fleets are being dispatched to aid in the war against Jovian aggression. The Horridian Dynasty and the evil Prophet will not escape justice. We have now received a statement from President Banyan of L5."

President Banyan appeared on the screen, he was scathing of the new services, "Before I get to the main issue at hand, I must show my disgust at our news services. I know that this latest atrocity perpetrated by the followers of this very evil man, the Prophet, was extraordinary news. However, did any of our news corporations even consider the effects of streaming those data feeds from Venusville uncensored! Did you not consider that vulnerable people, even children, may have been watching! How dare you!"

He was scathing, "We have always valued our freedom of speech, but if our news service cannot or will not have the common sense and decency to at least self censor video feeds of this nature, then your government is going to have to step in. We are creating a committee to look into how our news industry can be properly self regulated. This committee will create a list of guidelines that the news corporations under L5's jurisdiction will have to follow. This will all be done in consultation with our news corporations. Now back to the main issue at hand."

President Banyan paused, shuffled his notes and then continued, "Firstly, we must give our condolences to the victims of this atrocity, their families, the Venusian people and all the peoples of the Venusian colonies. Having spoken to Prime Minister Yodels, we are grateful for the assistance of the two Venusian fleets. One will be crucial to the defence of both the Earth and L5. The other will be crucial in our offensive against the Jovian Realms."

The President paused, then continued, "We do understand the concerns of the Venusian residents. After the fall of Venusville and the streaming of its demise across the system, it is no wonder that the Venusian people are in fear of their lives. There are over one hundred million Venusians living in sky cities and we do share their concerns. My administration will enter into discussions with the Earth's government, in order to see what assistance we can both provide to the Venusian colonies. There is no doubt that we can aid in the construction of more Venusian colonies. That should alleviate the concerns of some Venusians, who wish to emigrate off world, although the construction of new colonies will take some time."

President Banyan frowned, "Opening up of the Mercurian orbital zone to colonisation is an exciting concept, although it will be far more difficult at this time. We do currently have a war in progress and until the Horridian Dynasty is defeated, we may find it difficult to find the resources necessary for that task. Only time will tell. Thank you ladies and gentlemen."

The news anchor began talking once more, "It seems that President Banyan is getting on board with helping the Venusians. Perhaps in a few more days, after his administration's discussion with the Earth's government, we may have more concrete answers as to what shape our aid to the Venusians may take. For the moment though, we have heard from Chief Governor Anderson of Mars. Let's hear what he has to say in his televised statement."

Governor Anderson appeared on the screen, "To all the people of the Venusian colonies, you have our heart felt condolences. We do understand the current situation with regards to the Venusian sky cities and how citizens maybe feeling somewhat apprehensive with living in their sky cities at the moment. Especially so soon after the fall of Venusville. It is a tragedy of enormous proportions. An act of cowardice and pure hate. How people could possibly perpetrate such a heinous crime against their fellow humanity is unfathomable. A crime against humanity is what it was."

The Governor paused for a moment, "To Prime Minister Yodels, I will say this. While it is possible to build new colonies in the Venusian orbital zones and while it might be possible to open up the Mercurian orbital zone to colonisation, have you considered Mars. Our world is open to immigration. Although we do not have the necessary infrastructure at the moment, I am certain that if we work together, we can open up more colonies here on Mars. Those Venusians who no longer feel safe in their sky cities, some of them might come here, where we will provide homes for them. This is something that can and should be considered and considered in earnest."

Governor Anderson's face took on a stern look, "Although the Martian Defence Forces are relatively new and nowhere near as powerful as the Earth's, L5's or even Venus's. Rest assured that we stand united in this, our common fight against tyranny and terrorism. The Horridian Dynasty and that evil toad, the Prophet will pay for their crimes. They will rue the day, that they slaughtered over eighty thousand innocent Venusians. There will be justice! Good night ladies and gentlemen."

Once more the news anchor began talking, "We stand united in this, our common fight against tyranny and terrorism", she repeated, "That, I believe is the main lesson to come out of this horrible act of terrorism. The inner solar system worlds are united like never before. The Horridian Dynasty and that evil Prophet will face justice!"

Selene switched off the screen with her remote, as she sensed the approach of several people in the hall outside of her apartment.

A telepathic message from Roseanne came through, *"The Pods are upset and angry. They want to speak to Forkbraid."*

"Let them in Roseanne", Selene replied in kind.

Zuawalo, Zeealas, Nyaliep, Zyaliep, Varak, Kwoth and Roseanne all entered the apartment and made their way to Selene's lounge room.

"So many dead!", Zeealas told Selene, Forkbraid and Jim, she had tears in her eyes.

"We watched them burn!", a teary Zuawalo added.

"They are all dead! They need justice!", an also teary Nyaliep told them.

Zyaliep added, "When you watch death, death holds you!", she too had tears in her eyes.

Jim looked to his Father in law, Kwoth, who replied to his look, "Our women Jim. Are always very sensitive to these things."

The apartment door had been left open and Gwek walked in with his apprentice Nyapal. They both made their way to Selene's lounge room.

Gwek told everyone in the room, "They have watched, what should never be watched. The dead are calling to them now. This is a very sad time."

"Is this a cultural thing Gwek?", Selene enquired telepathically.

"It is a spiritual thing Selene", Gwek replied the same way, he then turned to his apprentice Nyapal, "Do not look into their minds child! There is a great, unsettled sadness there."

Nyapal pulled her mind back away from the Pod women and turned away so as not to look.

"A great unsettled sadness?", Forkbraid queried.

"They have watched a great many deaths, that should not have been seen", Gwek replied, "Heavy is the weight of those deaths on their minds. Almost too heavy is the weight of it all."

"Gwek. People die all the time, why is this different?", Selene queried telepathically.

"What happened Selene, was so unnatural. It was an act of cruelty so horrific, that it was a crime against life itself", Gwek replied in kind.

Jim looked to Zuawalo, "What do you want us to do Zuawalo?"

"Jim, when you go to Jupiter, we must go with you. Zeealas and I", Zuawalo replied.

"I must go as well", added Nyaliep.

"Zuawalo, Zeealas. You are both pregnant. Your babies will be here soon", Jim responded.

"Jim is right Girls. You cannot come with us", Forkbraid told them both.

"We must go! We have to go!", Zuawalo replied angrily.

"Zyaliep. Please talk sense to your daughters", Forkbraid requested.

"I cannot. There is no sense to this thing. We have seen those many deaths. It weighs very dark and black inside of us all. Those deaths cannot and will not be denied", Zyaliep replied.

"Zyaliep. Zuawalo and Zeealas will be giving birth soon. They can't do that on a space ship", Selene tried to explain.

"If I tell Zuawalo not to go. Zuawalo will go anyway. Zuawalo goes, Zeealas will follow", Zyaliep replied, adding, "I cannot stop this thing. I too must go!"

Jim stepped in, "Zuawalo, Zeealas. You are nearly full term. Surely you want our babies to be born here. Not in space."

"What we want no longer matters. It is what the dead want that matters now", Zuawalo replied.

"And the dead want you to go to space?", Jim asked.

"That is where the cause of all of this is. The dead want justice", Zuawalo replied.

Zeealas added, "We will see the justice for them. The dead will see it through us."

Forkbraid looked at Selene, *"How the hell am I going to explain this to Admiral Zumwalt? I've already told her that the Pod women are on maternity leave. Am I going to put them all back on the crew now, when they're so close to popping out babies?"*

Selene smiled and replied, *"Since when have you cared what that pretty little Admiral thinks?"*

"Pretty little Admiral? Are you jealous perhaps Selene?", Forkbraid replied.

Selene did not reply to Forkbraid, instead commenting, "How can we make this work?"

"Make this work? Selene, you are joking? Aren't you?", Forkbraid questioned.

"No Forkbraid. Zyaliep says she cannot stop this. I'm inclined to agree with her", Selene replied.

Forkbraid considered the situation, "There will be at least two births on board the Solstice", he then looked at Nyaliep, "Perhaps even three. We will need Lieutenant Rossi on board for the deliveries. Selene, make sure Isabella is up to speed on child birth."

"Now hang on FB. You're not seriously considering this?", Jim asked.

"Jim. We are not really military. We are more of a family and I may have the *'official'* rank of Fleet Captain, but the reality is, my rank is no higher than that of Selene or Zyaliep", Forkbraid tried to explain.

"So Selene and Zyaliep are in charge then?", Jim queried.

"Jim. Zyaliep says she cannot stop this. Selene is in agreement with her", Forkbraid replied, adding, "It makes no sense to me either, but to be honest, more often than not, Selene is right!"

"Who the fuck is going to look after their babies when they're on duty?", Jim questioned, then added when he got some nasty looks, "Oh come on now. It's a practicality matter. We'll be on a ship in deep space. Who looks after the babies when the Mothers are on duty?"

Zyaliep quickly replied, "I will of course. The Husband of Nyaliep, Varak, will build a creche."

Forkbraid thought to himself, *"What have I gotten myself into"*, then he simply asked, "Varak?"

"Well yes. I can build a creche. It should not take my metal men too long", Varak replied.

"Great then it's settled. Zuawalo, Zeealas and Nyaliep, you are all back on the crew", Forkbraid summed up, "Zyaliep. While you're onboard the Solstice, your duties will include assisting Lieutenant Rossi with the births and when the Girls have recovered and are back on duty, childcare. I will request that Lieutenant Rossi trains you in first aid and as a medical assistant as well."

Zyaliep nodded and simply stated, "Yes, agreed."

"Sweet Mother of God FB. Lieutenant Rossi is going to have kittens", Jim commented.

"That is not my problem Jim", Forkbraid replied, then he looked sternly to Selene, "I'll let you explain this all to the Lieutenant Rossi Selene and to Admiral Zumwalt as well for that matter."

Selene shook her head, but then agreed anyway, "Okay. Agreed."

Jim walked over to Zuawalo and Zeealas. Varak reached out to Nyaliep and they too walked over to Zuawalo and Zeealas. Jim reached into his jacket pocket and took out a recently taken photograph, which he handed to Zuawalo. It was a photo of a large, beautiful log cabin perched on a ridge line above the tall trees of a forest.

"What is this?", Zuawalo asked, as she showed the photo to Zeealas.

"That was going to be a surprise", Jim replied, "That cabin sits on the ridge line between two valleys. Zuawalo's Valley and Zeealas's Valley. I asked Varak to build it for you both."

"Why you build this for us Jim?", Zeealas asked.

"Remember your little lean-to. How much you both loved that place. You wanted to give birth there and I thought that it was inappropriate", Jim reminded them, "This cabin was built for you two. To be somewhere more appropriate for our babies to enter this world."

"Oh Jim. We cannot go there now", Zuawalo replied with sadness, "Still, you are so sweet", she told him as she kissed him on the lips.

"We can go there when we get back Sister", Zeealas commented with excitement, "Our Jim is ever so sweet", then she too kissed him on the lips.

"Maybe when we get back, I will still be with child", Nyaliep remarked.

"Then Aunty Nyaliep, your baby might be born at the cabin", Zuawalo smiled.

"Yes. We can all go there together for the birth", a smiling Zeealas agreed.

"No. I did not agree to this Nyaliep", Varak commented.

Jim slapped him lightly on the shoulder, "Just go with it Varak. Just go with it."

It was late afternoon and the meeting had been hastily organised, even Matthew did not know what it was about. All of the usual people were present, except for Prince Leopold and even the High Prince's Brothers appeared to be in the dark on the reason for the meeting.

General Snide addressed the room, "This news stream was intercepted and blocked by our censors. It was immediately brought to our attention", he then inserted a data crystal into a receptacle and then played the data stream.

The data stream contained news reports about the fall of Venusville and included the live data streams from Venusville itself. Everyone in the conference room watched in horror as the eighty thousand plus citizens of Venusville burst into flames and burned alive in writhing agony, on the screen. Statements from Venusian Prime Minister Yodels, L5's President Banyan and Mars's Governor Anderson were also played. When the data stream finally finished playing, all eyes in the room were on the Prophet.

Matthew stepped in quickly, "Your Majesty. We did suspect that some of our L5 operatives had run to the Venusian colonies. It seems that this news confirms our suspicions."

The High Prince questioned, "The People of the Prophet? The Prophet's Army? That's what they called themselves."

"Yes Your Majesty", the Prophet confirmed, informing him further, "However, we've had no contact with our L5 operatives since we fled L5."

"So this operation of theirs, was something they concocted themselves?", the High Prince asked.

"I assume so Your Majesty. What we just saw in that video stream is most certainly not something I would have ordered nor condoned", the Prophet replied honestly.

Matthew stepped in again, "I can confirm You Majesty, that we have had no contact with these operatives since we left L5. They have been acting independently of their own volition."

"These operative have caused us a couple of major problems Captain", the High Prince noted.

"Yes Your Majesty, I noticed that", Matthew replied.

General Snide stepped in, "The Earth and L5 have launched their so called Grand fleet. It's on its way to us. As recommended by Captain Murphy, we have launched a series of detection buoys along the most likely course trajectories that they might take. The rockets delivering those buoys are fast, much faster than any Heavy Cruiser. So we should know what course they're taking soon enough. As soon as we have their course locked in, our Jovian fleet will adjust its course as necessary to intercept their Grand fleet."

Prince Wulfric, who was looking much better than the last time they'd seen him, added, "Our fleet will obliterate their Grand fleet and then continue on to the Earth and L5."

"Yes. Yes Your Highness, that is the plan", General Snide confirmed, then added, "The Venusians have now launched two fleets and that does complicate matters somewhat. One fleet is on its way to the Earth and L5. That Venusian fleet will bolster their defences in cis-lunar space, making the job of our Jovian fleet somewhat more difficult. The second Jovian fleet is being sent directly to us, to rendezvous with their Grand fleet. That could be disastrous for us. If enough ships in their Grand fleet survive the interception by our Jovian fleet, we will have very real problems."

The High Prince remarked harshly, "What pisses me off most of all, is that the Venusians would not have launched those damned fleets, if Prophet's Army had simply stayed hidden. What they did to Venusville, has created complications, that we did not need."

General Tarzan stepped in cautiously, "Your Majesty. It is likely that the Venusians would have stepped into the fray at some point. They did so in the previous war."

"True enough General, but without this attack, they would done so much later and with far less forces", the High Prince replied, "That has always been their way, turning up too late and with too little. The Prophet's Amy has forced their hands. Now we have to contend with two of their fleets."

Prince Valdamar noted, "Venusian heavy cruisers are very different to the Earth's or L5's. I've been studying our old records. Being closer to the Sun, they have much thicker titanium hull plating. I can only assume that they've coated that in plasteel or polyceramalloy."

"Highly likely Your Highness", Matthew agreed.

"Our records show that they use advanced Talons as well", Prince Valdamar commented.

"They still do Your Highness, they also use Gull Wing Interceptors", Matthew confirmed.

"What resources do the Trojan Realms have?", Matthew enquired, asking, "What can they send to help us with our defence?"

Callthrope and Kittens, the Horridian Sister's representatives look at one and another, then back to Matthew, they both began to reply at the same time then stopped. Kittens took over.

"The Trojan Armed Forces are mainly for use as ground forces, occupation forces really", Kittens replied, "There is nothing in the Trojan Armed Forces that could take on an entire fleet."

Prince Wulfric added, "We use them for cannon fodder and mopping up. Not much else really."

Prince Valdamar added, "We never wanted the Trojans to have too much power. You know, so they could never be a threat to us. So they have no capital ships, no corvettes, no frigates, no destroyers and certainly no cruisers, heavy or otherwise."

"That is a shame Your Highness's. It would certainly be useful if the Trojans had a fleet or two", Matthew replied, before going silent for long moments.

"You've gone awfully quiet Captain", the High Prince noted.

"Sorry Your Majesty. I was just thinking", Matthew replied, adding, "We'll be fighting three fleets at both ends, here and in cis-lunar space. The Earth Defence Forces, the L5 Colonial fleet and now the Venusian fleet. It would be nice to have a plan B or another ace up our sleeve. That missile array, with all those long range missiles, that was our ace. Our sleeves are now completely empty."

The High Prince looked at Matthew, "You're thinking our starting this war was a mistake Captain. That we have bitten off more than we can chew."

"My honest answer Your Majesty is yes", Matthew replied.

The Prophet's heart skipped a beat when he heard Matthew's reply.

"I appreciate your candour Matthew", the High Prince replied using Matthew's name instead of his rank, then asked, "What would you have done differently?"

"I would have waited Your Majesty. Bided my time. Then hit them with twice the number of missiles. We came very close to overwhelming their defences. Twice the missiles, twice the warheads. That would have overwhelmed them completely", Matthew replied, adding, "Not that it matters now. We are here now and the situation is what it is. Your Majesty, the upcoming battles are going to be tough. Really, really tough. I cannot predict the outcome and that scares me most of all. We need to prepare for every possible outcome, even the worst."

The Prophet thought to himself, *"Matthew, you are going to get us killed."*

"General Snide. General Tarzan. We need a plan B. Worst case scenario. Put something together. Get to work on it", the High Prince commanded and then the meeting ended shortly thereafter.

20. The Fall of Patroclus

Half of the Trojan occupation fleet had entered the Trojan camp of Jupiter's two Trojan asteroid fields, trailing sixty degrees behind Jupiter at Lagrangian point five, while the second half of the fleet had continued on its way to the Greek camp of Jupiter's Trojan asteroids, sixty degrees ahead at Lagrangian point four.

Jupiter's Trojan asteroid fields are vast regions in space where thousands of asteroids are clustered. Some of these asteroids are small, measuring only a few kilometres across in size if that, to some that are extremely large at over a hundred kilometres across. The largest being over two hundred kilometres in size, Hector, in the Greek camp of Jupiter's Trojans at Lagrangian point four.

This was however, the Trojan camp at Lagrangian point five and this half of the Trojan occupation fleet was making its way straight for the asteroid Patroclus and it's slightly smaller companion Menoetius. Patroclus was a large asteroid, one of the largest of Jupiter's Trojans at one hundred and fifteen kilometres across, with its smaller binary only ten kilometres smaller.

The Trojan fleet separated again into two smaller components with the heavy weapons transports heading to their staging grounds on the asteroid Patroclus itself. The other component of the fleet, the troop transports, altered their course slightly and veered away from the asteroid towards the huge O'Neil style cylindrical colony, Patroclus Command Central. The capital of the Jovian realm of Jupiter's Aft Trojan colonies and the home of Princess Luisa von Horridian.

One by one, the hundred troop transports lined up at Patroclus Central's docking rings, to offload the Trojan troops they carried. Many of the troops lived in Patroclus Central, while many others lived in the myriad of colonies within Jupiter's Aft Trojan asteroid field. Those troops who lived in Patroclus Central made their way to their homes, to meet their families and friends they had not seen in many long months. Others quickly booked passage on transport ferries to take them to their home colonies, farther afield in the Aft Trojan asteroid field.

Fleet Captain Sharky found himself standing before the captains of the occupation fleet that had been sent to Mars and had returned earlier. Fleet Captain Carlson and Captain's Barker, Thompson, Mackerel, Poulsen, Turner and Harkness were present. They had been in discreet communications with the Trojan occupation fleet during its return trip home from cis-lunar space. The other captains of the troop transports now returning had all been read into the loop. There were machinations afoot and Captain Carlson had been positioning his people inside Patroclus Central for a coup.

Unknown to the returning Trojans occupation forces, they had all been infected with Leroy's redemption. As a result of Leroy's redemption, their eyes had been opened, the veil of darkness had been lifted. They fully understood the propaganda they've been living under for all of their lives and the lives of their forebears. They were not happy with the Horridian regime at all. Leroy's redemption has been spreading like a virus as well through out the entire population, with every exchange, every touch and every handshake.

Fleet Captain Carlson greeted Fleet Captain Sharky as he exited the space port, "Greetings Captain. How does it feel to be back home?"

"Carlson", Captain Sharky nodded in reply, "It's great to be back after such a long trip."

They both shook hands and Leroy's redemption sparked imperceptibly from both of their hands. They had both already been infected.

"Well Captain, your day isn't over yet. I'm here to take you to your debriefing meeting", Captain Carlson informed him, adding, "After the debriefing, you'll probably be taken up to the palace."

"The palace?", Captain Sharky queried.

"Yeah. The palace. The same thing happened to me when my fleet returned", Captain Carlson explained, "Normally it would have been General Verne, but as he's dead, the Princess is looking for her new warrior to replace him."

"Her new warrior?", Captain Sharky queried.

"Yep. I managed to dodge that bullet. I'm advising you to do the same", Captain Carlson replied.

"I've never met the Princess. What's she like?", enquired Captain Sharky.

"Princess Luisa is arguably the most beautiful woman you'll ever meet. The Princess is stunningly beautiful", Captain Carlson admitted, then added his warning, "She is also clinically insane. She is truly psychotic."

Captain Sharky stood still, stunned, he didn't answer or say anything.

"Her Chamberlain knows how to handle her. Always follow his lead", Captain Carlson added.

"Advice noted", Captain Sharky replied.

"You'll find that everyone in the palace, from the servants, to the palace guards, even the Princess's personal troops. They are all High Prince Heinrich's people", Captain Carlson informed him, "They are all her minders and protectors."

"Good to know Captain", Captain Sharky answered.

"A question for you Captain. What happened to General Verne? What happened on Mars?", Captain Sharky requested.

"We were attacked, the very first day. A straight up strafing run that put our encampment into disarray. Then we were attacked again that very same night, with a weapon we'd never seen before", Captain Carlson informed him.

"What kind of weapon?", Captain Sharky asked.

"We have no idea, but with the rising of the Sun, every one of our weapons systems burst into flames", Captain Carlson informed him, "We were completely disarmed."

The Captain continued, "Verne was furious. He blamed one of my Captains. Captain Bolton. The General pulled a pulse pistol on him and shot him in the head multiple times, over and over. That pulse pistol failed, its power pack was completely fried. The General grabbed another pulse pistol and tried again, over and over. That pulse pistol also failed. All the power packs were fried."

Captain Sharky looked shocked, "How is Captain Bolton?", he asked.

"He's alive, but he'll never be the same. Bolton's a broken man", Captain Carlson replied.

Captain Carlson continued, "General Verne decided to use the local Martian resources to build siege engines to attack the enemy's fortress."

"Siege engines? As in medieval siege engines?", an incredulous Captain Sharky enquired.

"Yes, but they were just a ruse. Under covers, we were also forging muzzle loading cannons", Captain Carlson explained, adding, "Of course, like clockwork, we were attacked and the siege engines were destroyed every time, taking us all back to square one. Our cannons and our forges, however, were all well hidden."

Captain Sharky listened as Captain Carlson continued, "We found some locals and learned some very disturbing information."

"Disturbing? In what way?", Captain Sharky questioned.

"Our main target. The enemy's fortress. It wasn't a fortress at all", Captain Carlson noted, revealing, "Our main target was a boarding school for students from ages seven to twenty one. You know, primary, secondary and tertiary students. Children and adolescents."

"You are fucking joking!", Captain Sharky exclaimed.

"No. Not at all", replied the Captain, "The next day we tested two of our cannons. They both exploded during the tests. General Verne was furious. We had over one hundred and thirty useless cannons. General Verne beheaded one of my Captains and then sliced another Captain in half with his sabre."

Captain Sharky looked shocked, "Surely you are kidding?"

"No. No jokes Captain. No kidding", Captain Carlson replied, "After that, we executed the General and left his body to rot on Mars. Our occupation fleet, then left Mars to come home. The whole thing was a complete shit show."

"It sounds like General Verne was one very unstable man", Captain Sharky remarked.

"We did come to that conclusion", Captain Carlson agreed, then warned, "It is my understanding that Princess Luisa, has not been told of the circumstances of General Verne's death. It is best not to mention it. Keep it to yourself Captain."

"Your recommendation is well noted", Captain Sharky agreed.

Captain Sharky commented, "We didn't run into any of the problems your forces faced. Hell, we didn't even get close to our targets. What turned us around was much, much stranger."

"How so captain?", Captain Carlson asked.

"Our enemies saved our entire fleet", Captain Sharky admitted.

"Yes. I heard something about that. Not easy news to find with all of the propaganda we're buried under", Captain Carlson replied.

"After our missile strikes failed to cause the devastation that was expected of them, our entire occupation fleet was flying into an ambush", Captain Sharky admitted, adding, "We would have been completely annihilated. None of us would have survived."

"And our enemies saved you?", enquired Captain Carlson.

"Yeah. The flagship of the Colonial fleet, the Spartan, approached our fleet from the rear. Another ship, of a type we'd never seen before, appeared from out of nowhere right in front of my command ship", Captain Sharky explained, adding, "They informed us, that we were flying to our deaths and advised us to change course. We checked their information for ourselves. They were telling us the truth. We changed course to return home. We are alive today because of our enemies."

"That's a very confusing thing to confront", Captain Carlson noted, adding, "To have an enemy save you. Is the enemy that saves you, really your friend? Your ally? Then who is the real enemy?"

"Perhaps the real enemy, is the one that ordered us to maintain our course and commit us all to certain death. Suicide orders", Captain Sharky replied, "Those were our orders. The Horridian's gave us those orders. We chose to ignore them."

"And it's well that you did. You would not be here otherwise", Captain Carlson agreed.

The debriefing meeting only lasted for around forty minutes, after which Fleet Captain Sharky was ushered out of the room and into a nearby waiting transport pod. An officious looking gentlemen, in an ornate uniform was sitting in the pod waiting for him.

"I am Chamberlain Schweitzer", the Chamberlain introduced himself, "You will be going to the palace to meet the Princess."

Captain Sharky reached out his hand and shook hands with the Chamberlain. Leroy's redemption sparked imperceptibly from Captain Sharky's hand, the tiny blue spark completely unnoticed by either of them.

Before Captain Sharky could say a word, the Chamberlain laid down some rules.

"When you meet the Princess, do not stare at her, the Princess does not like that one bit", the Chamberlain began, adding, "Bow slightly, but not overly much. Speak, but only when spoken to. Agree with everything the Princess says where possible. You may notice some odd behaviour, try not to be surprised by it. Try to pretend it's perfectly normal. And always address the Princess as Your Highness. Always. I'll do what I can to make sure you keep your head."

"Keep my head?", the Fleet Captain queried.

"Don't worry too much Captain", the Chamberlain assured him, "Since my predecessors death during the last rebellion six years ago, I've managed to keep the worst of the Princess's excesses under tight control."

The Fleet Captain was quiet during the short trip to the palace. From the southern end cap of Patroclus Command Central to its northern end cap where the palace was located, took less than thirty minutes. As the pod sped through the cylinder's central alpha land strip, Captain Sharky looked through the pod's clear aluminoglass roof, sixty degrees across to the beta land strip where his house, with his wife and children lived. He smiled as he looked, it had been many months since he had been home.

"Family Captain Sharky?", the Chamberlain enquired.

"Over on beta", the Fleet Captain replied, as he pointed to a small township across the way, "I've been at space for a very long time Chamberlain."

"We'll have you back home soon enough Captain", the Chamberlain replied.

Chamberlain Schweitzer led the Fleet Captain through the palace to the room where Princess Luisa was currently waiting. The Princess was lounging on a sofa on a balcony overlooking the palace gardens. The balcony was quite high up and the view was quite spectacular. Princess Luisa got up from the sofa and stepped back into the room.

Captain Sharky was taken aback by how beautiful Princess Luisa was, thinking to himself, *"Captain Carlson, you certainly understated how beautiful the Princess is"*, as he stared as her.

The Princess was tall, with golden blond hair and the brightest of blue eyes, she was stunning.

Captain Sharky caught himself staring and bowed ever so slightly to the Princess, "I must apologise for staring Princess. In my defence, I must admit, I had no idea how beautiful your are."

The Princess smiled and replied, "I forgive you Sir Silver Tongue", then she turned to the Chamberlain, "Who is this? Where is my General Verne? Where is my warrior?"

"Your Highness. We have discussed this previously. General Verne died in combat on Mars at the Battle of the Elysium plains", the Chamberlain informed her, adding, "This Your Highness, this is Fleet Captain Sharky."

"Fleet Captain Sharky?", the Princess asked rhetorically, "I'm not familiar with your name. Who are you Captain Sharky?", she questioned.

"Your Highness. I'm a Fleet Captain in your Trojan Armed Forces. Specifically, the fleet that was sent to cis-lunar space, to L5.", Captain Sharky replied, informing her further, "The fleet has just now returned from its mission."

"A warrior?", Princess Luisa queried, then continued, "How fared your mission Captain?"

Chamberlain Schweitzer heard the Princess call Captain Sharky a Warrior and then quickly stepped in, "Your Highness. Your Brother's missile attack on the Earth and L5 was ineffective. Your fleet was forced to return home as a result."

"Why? Why was my fleet forced to return home?", Princess Luisa asked with her voice raised.

Captain Sharky replied, "Your Highness. Our scans of L5 showed our fleet was flying into an ambush. The fleet would have been annihilated, had we not changed course and returned home."

"Cowardice?", the Princess questioned.

"No Your Highness. It was a strategic, tactical withdrawal", Captain Sharky replied.

"Really. A strategic, tactical withdrawal?", Princess Luisa questioned.

The Captain quickly answered, "Your Highness. The fleet and all of the troops are yours. General Trask and all of the Captains, including myself all agreed, it was better to preserve your fleet and your troops. To waste them in a suicide mission, would not have served your interests."

Chamberlain Schweitzer thought to himself, *"Good answer Captain. Good answer."*

Princess Luisa commented, "I like this one Chamberlain. I like this Captain Sharky. I might just keep him. I might just make him my new warrior. He has my best interests at heart."

Captain Sharky gave the Chamberlain an enquiring look, thinking to himself, *"What the hell have I gotten myself into."*

"Your Highness. Captain Sharky is married and has children. He has been on a very long mission for many months now and needs to see his family",

Chamberlain Schweitzer explained.

"Nonsense Chamberlain. I am his sovereign. Tonight the good Captain stays here with me. He can return home to his family on the morrow", the Princess decided.

Captain Sharky looked to the Chamberlain, who gave him a surreptitious, *'I'll handle this"* look.

"Your Highness. Tonight's dinner. Have you prepared the chicken?", Chamberlain Schweitzer asked, adding, "The Chef cannot cook it if it is still alive."

"Oh yes. I had forgotten about that. Thank you for reminding me Chamberlain", Princess Luisa replied and then headed off to the palace kitchens.

"Follow me Captain", the Chamberlain instructed and they both followed the Princess to the palace kitchens.

"Chef. Where's my chicken?", the Princess called out.

"It's here Your Highness", the Chef replied, as he gathered up the chicken and passed it to her.

"Chickens really are lovely creatures", the Princess noted, explaining as she demonstrated, "If you turn them upside down and cradle them, then stroke their breast feathers, they fall asleep, kind of like a trance."

The chicken fell asleep or perhaps it was a trance, it was hard to tell and the Princess laid it down on a chopping block. Then the Princess quickly picked up a chopper and with one deft movement, cut off the chicken's head. Captain Sharky winced. The headless chicken squirmed as the Princess held it down firmly.

"It's the most humane way to dispatch an animal, any animal, even humans for that matter. Don't you think?", the Princess noted with a huge smile on her face.

Captain Sharky asked, "Your Highness. Why wouldn't you just use a prepared chicken? Already cleaned and plucked?"

"Oh no my Captain. I could never do that. If I'm going to eat it, I have to dispatch it", the Princess informed him.

The Chef noted, "Her Highness even has special guillotines for the larger poultry like geese and turkeys and even larger ones for goats and sheep."

"Yes. Thank you Chef", the Princess replied, reiterating, "If I eat it, I must dispatch it. Only me."

Captain Sharky looked to the Chamberlain once again, who then gave him a surreptitious, *'I've got this",* look as they followed the Princess back out of the palace kitchen.

"Your Highness. It will take the Chef quite some time to process and cook that chicken. Perhaps you might like to take a nap before dinner", the

Chamberlain suggested.

"That is a great idea Chamberlain. My Captain, please join me in my boudoir", Princess Luisa remarked, batting her eyelids, "We'll have such fun together."

"Your Highness, there are very important matters of state that I need to discuss with the Captain", the Chamberlain informed her, "Perhaps the good Captain can join you later?"

Princess Luisa frowned, "Always matters of state. How boring. Captain Sharky. When you do make it to my rooms, you will wake me with a gentle kiss, won't you."

"Of course Your Highness. It would be my pleasure", the Captain lied.

Then the Princess literally skipped up the hallway towards her rooms as if she was a teenager.

Captain Sharky looked at the Chamberlain and asked, "What happens when the Princess wakes up and I'm not here?"

"Don't worry Captain. Her Highness's minders will take care of that", Chamberlain Schweitzer replied, explaining, "We keep her well medicated. When Her Highness wakes up, she probably won't even remember that you were here."

"Chamberlain. Did I just dodge a bullet?" the Captain questioned.

"Perhaps, perhaps not. Her Highness does have her moments, however, she can be very sweet", the Chamberlain replied, remarking, "I fully suspect, if you'd been a single man, you may not have been able to resist her."

"Well Chamberlain. I must admit, Her Highness is extraordinarily beautiful", the Captain replied.

"Very true Captain. Very true, but always remember, Her Highness is psychotic and if not carefully managed, can relapse. Then she can be very dangerous", Chamberlain Schweitzer warned.

"Now about your fleets withdrawal from cis-lunar space", the Chamberlain asked, "Our understanding is that you were given advance warning of the ambush."

"We were Chamberlain", Captain Sharky admitted, "Our own enemies gave us the warning about the ambush the fleet was flying into. We double checked and triple checked their information and found it to be correct."

"So it is true then. Our enemies saved our fleet", the Chamberlain remarked.

"Very true. Fleet Captain Carmichael and Captain Forkbraid gave us the heads up themselves. If not for them, our entire fleet would have been annihilated", Captain Carmichael informed him.

"That makes no sense. Why would demons behave that way?", the Chamberlain questioned.

"Perhaps Chamberlain, just perhaps, they're not really demons at all. Perhaps they're just people, just like us", Captain Sharky told him.

"Perhaps you're right Captain. Perhaps you're right", the Chamberlain replied.

"So, exactly why was I brought here?", Captain Sharky enquired.

"When returning from a mission, the commander of the fleet is brought before the Princess", Chamberlain Schweitzer replied, explaining, "As the Fleet Captain, that would be you."

"And prior to Captain Carlson and myself, it would have been General Verne", Captain Sharky surmised.

"That is correct Captain", the Chamberlain confirmed, "and as the General is now deceased, our Princess is on the lookout for her new warrior."

Captain Sharky cautiously enquired, "Did the General and the Princess?"

"No, no Captain. General Verne treated the Princess, as if she was his own Daughter", he replied.

"Then why did the Princess make me that offer?", the Captain asked.

"You are a young man Captain. General Verne was much older", the Chamberlain replied, adding, "Now let's get you back to your family."

Captain Sharky spent the remainder of the day and the night with his wife and children. They were extremely happy to see him, as he had been away for many months off colony in space. It was still in the early hours of the morning when the Captain's personal communicator buzzed loudly. A military device, the louder the buzz, the more urgent the call.

Captain Sharky grabbed his communicator and spoke into it, "Sharky here."

"Captain. It's Carlson here. We need you down at the palace urgently", he was informed.

"Why? What's happening?", Captain Sharky enquired.

"Have a quick look at the news Captain. I'll be at your place with a pod in twenty minutes", Captain Carlson replied, then hung up the line.

Captain Sharky left his bedroom and went to check the news in his lounge room.

Captain Sharky muted the volume so as to not wake up his wife and children. The news feed showed tens of thousand of Patroclus citizens making their way to the northern end cap. They were all gathering around the royal palace. Most of them were Trojan troops, those who had previously returned home from Mars and his own troops that had returned home from their cis-lunar L5 mission the day before.

They appeared to be armed with pulse pistols and pulse rifles. Intermixed with these Trojan troops were are great many civilian protesters. Captain Sharky quickly got dressed and a short time later, Captain Carlson arrived outside of his house in a transport pod. Captain Sharky was quick to rush outside to the awaiting pod.

"This is not good Carlson. What the hell is going on?", Captain Sharky asked.

"It's the beginning of a rebellion Captain", Captain Carlson replied, informing him further, "We have been preparing for this day for quite a while now. We had thought we'd have more time, but the people and the newly returned troops have decided otherwise."

Captain Carlson had his Lieutenant Adjutant with him and at a nod from the Captain, the Lieutenant passed Captain Sharky a file.

"What's this then?", Captain Sharky enquired.

"That is our plan Captain. We are turning the Aft Trojan Realm into Constitutional Principality", Captain Carlson replied.

Captain Sharky opened the file and began to read its contents, as the pod sped along its way.

When the transport pod finally pulled up outside the palace gates, Captain Sharky remarked, "Carlson, if you can pull this off you have my support."

"I'll definitely be needing it Sharky", Captain Carlson replied as they stepped out of the pod.

The Captains from the Martian occupation forces and the L5 occupation forces were all present. Captain Carlson had made a lot of calls during the early hours of the morning. Each of the Captains had their Lieutenant Adjutants with them and they were carrying megaphones.

Captain Carlson walked straight up the awaiting Captains and ordered, "Captains. Get out there and calm this crowd down, now. We cannot afford for this to get out of hand. Use those megaphones, to get the message across. There must be no violence. "

Captain Carlson then led Captain Sharky to the palace gates, which were manned by the Princess's personal troops. Shock troops from the Jovian Realms.

"Have the Council of Nobles arrived?", Captain Carlson enquired.

"Yes Captain. All twenty of them arrived, when all of this began", the burly Sergeant replied.

"Good. We need to address them urgently. Open the gates. Let us in", Captain Carlson ordered.

"Not happening Captain", the burly Sergeant replied, adding, "We have our orders."

Captain Carlson waved his arm, gesturing to the ever growing crowd, "This protest could turn very ugly, very fast, if we don't get in to talk to the Council of Nobles. There are scores of thousands of people surrounding this palace."

Captain Carlson's Lieutenant Adjutant interjected, "Currently, there are one hundred and twenty thousand protesters Sir. Two thirds of them are armed Trojan troops."

Captain Carlson stared sharply at the burly Sergeant, "Your people are out numbered by at least fifty to one Sergeant. If we don't get in there to talk to the Council of Nobles very, very soon, none of us will survive this. None of us!"

The burly Sergeant nodded to the gates-men and they opened the palace gates ever so slightly, just enough to allow them in. Then the Sergeant spoke briefly into his communicator.

As the Captains walked through the gate, Captain Sharky told the Sergeant in no uncertain terms, "Ensure your men, do not, repeat, do not fire a shot!"

By the time Captains Carlson and Sharky reached the palace doors, Chamberlain Schweitzer was already waiting for them, "This way gentlemen", he greeted and then proceeded to lead the Captains to the conference room where the Council of Nobles were holding an emergency meeting.

When they entered the conference room, the leader of the Council shouted, "What is the meaning of this interruption."

Captain Carlson whispered to Captain Sharky, "We don't have time for this", then he replied to the Lead Councillor, "If you all want to live, then you will shut the fuck up and listen."

All of the council members began murmuring and the Chamberlain who was holding an ornate staff, stomped it on the floor three times, creating quite an echo. The room immediately fell silent.

The door on the other side of the conference room opened and Princess Luisa walked into the room, "I heard you bang your staff Chamberlain. What's going on?", she asked, then seeing the two Captains, "I know you two. I've met the two of you before."

"Yes Your Highness", both Captains replied as they bowed slightly.

"There is a very large crowd outside, surrounding my palace Captains. Far larger than I've ever seen before. Are they here to cut my head off?", the Princess flippantly asked.

Captain Carlson stepped forward towards the Princess and held out his hands,"No. No Your Highness. We are here to prevent that by all means necessary."

Princess Luisa reached out and took Captain Carlson's hands in hers and caressed them gently, "You see Chamberlain. These are my warriors", a small imperceptible, blue spark, Leroy's redemption, jumped from the Captain's hands the Princess's.

Captain Carlson raised the Princess's hands to his lips and kissed them tenderly before gently letting them go. The Princess smiled and giggled slightly at the kiss, holding on to the Captain's hands for a lingering moment or two, before also letting them go.

"Lieutenant. Pass around those documents", Captain Carlson commanded.

"What are these?", the Council Leader asked as the Lieutenant handed out the files.

Captain Sharky, who had quickly read the main points in the files, whilst in the transport pod, replied, "The future gentlemen."

Captain Carlson replied, "You have two choices gentlemen. Your first choice. Do nothing and when that mob storms this palace, we can all die together. The other choice is in those files."

The Council members began reading through the documents.

"Separation of church and state?", one Councillor questioned.

"Yes. The Jovian Church has no business in politics" Captain Carlson replied, adding, "Further more, you will find other provisions. For one, if a citizen is not a member of the Church, they will be exempt for the Church's tithe, the Church's tenth. Only voluntary members of the Jovian Church will be subjected to that. We must also make allowances for any new Churches that may form."

"Captain. This Constitutional Principality. How will it work?", another Councillor asked.

Captain Carlson replied, "Our beloved Princess Luisa will remain our sovereign ruler, however, her powers will be severely limited by constitutional law. That new constitution is currently being formulated as we speak. When the Princess has children of her own, her eldest child will become the heir to the Aft Trojan throne."

"I like my current powers Captain Carlson", Princess Luisa informed him.

"Yes Your Highness, however, I suspect you like being alive so much more", the Captain replied.

"That is true. I can't really be your Princess if I'm dead, can I and as much as I hate to even think about it. I do realise, that I do have an affliction", the Princess replied.

Captain Carlson smiled at the Princess and then continued, "The Aft Trojan Parliament will be the supreme legislative body and it will consist of two houses: The House of the People's Representatives and the House of Nobles."

"And what of the Council of Nobles?", questioned one of the other Councillors.

"I am getting to that Councilmen", Captain Carlson answered.

The Captain continued, "One of the grievances that the ordinary folk have suffered, is Council decisions that have affected them, without them having any representation. The House of the People's Representatives will fix that. It will be composed of Members of Parliament elected by the people in general elections. The drawing up of the electoral boundaries and divisions is again, currently in progress as we speak."

"So, you're proposing that this House of the People's Representatives is the voice of the people", the Lead Councillor noted.

"Yes Councillor. I am", the Captain replied, then he continued, "The House of Nobles will be made up of appointed members from the one hundred Noble houses. This new House of Nobles will be one hundred in number and is intended to replace the Council of Nobles."

"Replace us?", the Lead Councillor questioned.

"Yes Councillor. You see, the people see your council as part of the problem. The new House of Nobles will be part of the solution", Captain Carlson explained, "The minimum age of suffrage will be twenty five. To vote, to become a People's representative, to be come a Noble representative, a citizen must be twenty five years of age of older."

"How are the Noble representatives to be chosen?", the Lead Councillor questioned.

"How are they chosen now?", Captain Sharky asked.

"The Chamberlain chooses them from the hundred Noble houses", the Lead Councillor replied.

Captain Carlson stepped back in, "That won't change. The Chamberlain will be the one to choose, one representative, who has reached the age of suffrage from each of the Noble houses. In order to ensure their suitability, the chosen ones will have to pass aptitude and psychological tests. Should the Chamberlain retire or possibly pass on, it will require a full vote of the House of Nobles to choose a replacement."

Captain Carlson quickly continued, "The House of the People's Representatives will make the laws. The House of Nobles will scrutinise those laws, perhaps requesting changes or making suggestions. Once a law is passed in both houses, it will be presented to the Princess by the Chamberlain, who will then both sign the law, thus giving it royal assent."

"I'm beginning to see how this works", the Lead Councillor remarked, then asked, "And then what becomes of us?"

"The Council of Nobles will have a handful of final duties to perform prior to retiring", Captain Carlson noted, explaining, "Those twenty documents. The last page requires your signatures. You will sign every copy of those documents. That's your agreement to move forward with this plan."

"And if we refuse?", one of the Councillors enquired.

"Look out of one of the palace windows. Your alternative is the mob", Captain Sharky noted.

Princess Luisa stood up and stepped forward, "You will sign those documents. That will be my final royal command and you must obey it!"

All twenty Councillors bowed to the Princess and then proceeded to sign every copy and every page of the documents.

Captain Carlson then continued, "The other final works that you will have to perform, will be the scrutinization and ratification of the new constitution when it is completed. It will then be passed on to the Chamberlain and Princess Luisa for royal assent."

"I look forward to reading when it's ready Captain", the Lead Councillor commented.

"Yes Councillor. It should be ready soon. We had hoped, to have all of this done before the protests began, but they happened far more quickly than we had anticipated", Captain Carlson replied, then he added, "Once the first elections are held and the first People's representatives are elected. The final act of this Council, will be to swear in the House of the People's Representatives. Royal assent will then be given by the Chamberlain and Princess Luisa. After that, you all retire."

"So we can't be picked for this new House of Nobles then?", one of the Councillors asked.

"That is correct. You will all be ineligible" Captain Carlson informed them, "The new House of Nobles will have to have all new members. It needs to be that way. Hey, just remember this, better retirement, than the mob."

The Councillors all nodded in agreement.

Captain Carlson then spoke into his communicator, "Harkness, do your have your ears on?"

"Yes, loud and clear Captain", Captain Harkness replied.

"We have succeeded. Have the other Captains and their Adjutants hand out the flyers. Let the people know what's happened", Captain Carlson ordered, "Then release the official communique to our public broadcasters. Let our people know of these changes. When things are calm enough, start disbursing the crowds."

"It's all happening now Sir. Consider it done", Captain Harkness replied, then he added, "I think there will be a lot of celebrations Sir."

"Just as long as it doesn't disturb the peace, that's fine, but for now, get those crowds dispersed", Captain Carlson instructed.

Chamberlain Schweitzer stepped in close to Captain Carlson, "Just how long have been in love with our Princess Luisa?"

"Chamberlain. Since that very first day back from Mars, when you brought me here to meet the Princess", the Captain admitted.

"Yet you stayed away from her all of this time", the Chamberlain noted.

"I had no choice Chamberlain. We could see the protests coming. We could see the possibility of a disastrous rebellion happening as a result of them. It was our duty, my duty to head those off. We almost didn't make it. We almost ran out of time", Captain Carlson informed him.

"You made the right choice Captain, that is certain", the Chamberlain replied, then very quietly asked, "Aren't you concerned, that the Princess is clinically insane?"

"Chamberlain. It is not Princess Luisa's fault. She has an affliction, an illness. Sure, it's a mental illness, but she just needs proper treatment and understanding", the Captain explained.

"Good then, I've known Her Highness for six years now. I've seen how she responds to you. Perhaps you should get to know her better", the Chamberlain suggested.

Princess Luisa walked over to Captain Carlson and asked, "Are these boring, pressing matters of state now finished? I'd like to show you around my palace. It's such a beautiful place."

Captain Sharky looked at the Captain, "Off you go Carlson. Your Lieutenant and I can finish things up here", then to the Princess he informed, "Your Highness. His name is Christian."

"Christian. I like that", Princess Luisa noted as she took Captain Carlson by the arm and led him out of the conference room to tour her palace

Patroclus has fallen!

21. Our Dear Sister

Prince Leopold was unusually annoyed at having being called into a meeting at Ganymede Prime by his Brother, the High Prince. Ordinarily, he wasn't required to be at meetings and instead he would read through the minutes of the meetings later. As he had no part in the military, he simply didn't see the need for his presence at all.

"You seem out of sorts Brother Leopold", High Prince Heinrich remarked.

Leopold looked to his elder Brother and replied, "Why am I even here? I'm not involved in the military. You could just as well send me the minutes of the meeting and I could read them at home."

"On this occasion Brother, you are required", the High Prince replied.

"Why? So we can discuss how this war of yours is turning into a complete and total cluster fuck?", Prince Leopold replied, adding, "The last time I was here, my arsehole of a Brother Wulfric, tried two blame me for the mess at Io L4. I would rather spend my time with my Wife and Son."

Prince Leopold's remarks had turned heads in the conference room. Prince Wulfric looked particularly agitated by his comments.

"So Brother. A cluster fuck you say. Perhaps you'd like to clarify that?", the High Prince replied.

"Do you want to hear my honest opinion Brother or just nice platitudes to make you happy?", Prince Leopold questioned angrily.

"Brother!", High Prince Heinrich began sharply, almost angrily, "Always tell me your truth!"

"You want my truth! Well here it is Brother! We have half of our fleet flying on its way to the Earth and L5. Our enemies now have three fleets, the Earth's, L5's and now Venus's waiting for us", Prince Leopold told the room, "and if that's not bad enough, the other half of our fleet, is waiting here for the arrival of not just the combined Earth and L5 fleets, but also another Venusian fleet."

"We are well aware of the situation Leopold", the High Prince replied.

"Yes. Yes we are. I read all of the minutes from every damned meeting. The outcome of these upcoming battles are completely uncertain", Leopold replied, adding, "Brother! You tell me this situation is not a complete and total cluster fuck!"

Prince Valdamar stepped in, "Brother Heinrich. Leopold has never been involved in our military. I can fully understand why he is so upset and why he'd rather be with his Wife and Son."

"To be honest with you Valdamar, so do I", High Prince Heinrich replied, then to Leopold, "Brother, the situation is dire. I will admit that, however, ultimately, I believe we will prevail."

"I wish I had your confidence Heinrich, then I look at our Brother Wulfric, sitting over there glitching all over the place and then I remember, Wulfric is in charge of our outer defences", Prince Leopold replied.

"Glitching! Glitching! How dare you! I admit, that I might be a little stressed, but glitching!", Wulfric responded angrily, his anxiety and agitation were now clearly showing.

The High Prince held up his right hand to silence his Brothers, "Let's not turn this into a fight", he then turned slightly to General Snide and gave a slight nod.

General Snide quietly and surreptitiously sent a message to Prince Wulfric's Wife Matilda, "Princess Matilda. Please come to the palace to pick up Prince Wulfric."

Princess Matilda replied a minute or two later, "Why? Is it urgent?"

General Snide sent another surreptitious message to Princess Matilda, "No. Just be here, ready to take him home after our meeting. Wulfric is looking very anxious."

Straight away the Princess replied, "Don't worry. I'll be there."

The High Prince nodded to Princess Luisa's representative, Callthrope, who informed the room, "Your Majesty, Your Highness's, Gentlemen. This is not about the war. This is a Horridian Family matter. This is about Princess Luisa and the Aft Trojan Realm."

"Nothing bad we hope?", Prince Leopold asked.

"Well, Princess Luisa is alive, if that's what you mean by nothing bad", Callthrope replied.

"And yet, here we are Callthrope, so whatever it is, cannot possibly be good news, can it?", Prince Valdamar remarked.

"Very astute Your Highness, very astute", Callthrope noted, informing them,

"I have received some news from the Princess's Chamberlain. Disturbing news I might add."

"And I have received an official communique from Patroclus Command Central", the High Prince noted, informing them, "From Fleet Captain Carlson. Our dear Sister is alive and well. Our dear Luisa is in no danger. She is perfectly safe. However, our Aft Trojan Realm is another matter."

Callthrope began to describe the situation, as it had been described to him by the Princess Luisa's Chamberlain, "This all began quite a while back, when the Aft Trojan occupation forces arrived home from Mars. Shortly after their return, a certain discontent was detected amongst the populace. It appears that, not only the Chamberlain, but also this Captain Carlson and his colleagues had noticed it. So the Captain and his colleagues started preparing for a possible uprising."

Callthrope drank some water before continuing, "Then the Aft Trojan contingent of our L5 occupation forces arrived home. That very night, a large protest gathered outside the palace and an emergency meeting of the Council of Nobles was called. This caught Fleet Captain Carlson completely by surprise and by the time he reached the palace, it was surrounded by a hundred and twenty thousand people. The Fleet Captain had not expected things to happen so quickly."

"A hundred and twenty thousand people?", Prince Wulfric questioned.

"Yes Your Highness, however, at its peek, there were well over one hundred and fifty thousand. Half of whom were Trojan troops armed with pulse pistols and pulse rifles. Our people at the palace were outnumbered by well over fifty to one", Callthrope noted, then continued, "Captains Carlson and Sharky entered the palace and offered a possible solution. That solution was to change the Principality of the Aft Trojan Realm into a Constitutional Principality. This was agreed to, in order to prevent a full scale rebellion, in which everyone in the palace would have died."

Prince Valdamar noted, "So Callthrope, this Constitutional Principality agreement, it was made under duress, yes?"

"I would assume so Your Highness. Your Sister's palace could have been over run at any moment. They were all very lucky it wasn't", Callthrope replied.

"We also have this document that came with the official communique. It is the Constitutional Principality proposal and agreement. I have sent you all copies", the High Prince noted, as he placed a copy on the conference room's wall screen, showing the agreements many pages.

Everyone in the room began to study the agreement and for many minutes the room was quiet.

"For fucks sake. This is a declaration of independence", Prince Valdamar noted.

"How so Brother?", Prince Wulfric questioned.

"Brother Valdamar is correct", Prince Leopold agreed.

Prince Valdamar noted, "Our dear Sister Luisa's powers have been stripped down to nothing more than ceremonial duties. The real power in the Aft Trojan Realm now belongs with their Parliament with its two houses. The lower house, the House of Representatives elected by the people and the upper house, the House of Nobles, selected from the Noble houses by the Chamberlain. It also appears they are working on a new Constitution and I'm quite certain it will have no mention of the position of the High Prince."

"That is disturbing", the High Prince noted.

"I fully agree with Valdamar", Prince Leopold commented, adding, "They're even changing the line of succession and that says it all. We all know how the line of succession works. After Brother Heinrich, his eldest Son will become the new High Prince and Prince of Ganymede. The other Jovian Realms get divided amongst his other children and we all retire. That's how it works. Here though, in this new Constitutional Principality, the eldest Child of our Sister Luisa, becomes the heir to the Aft Trojan Realm. That will make them completely independent of the Jovian Realms."

The conference room went dead quiet.

High Prince Heinrich looked to General Snide and General Tarzan, "We need to send a fleet to Patroclus Command Central immediately. Let them know in no uncertain terms, that any thought of independence is completely unacceptable."

Both Generals looked to Matthew in deference, who replied, "Your Majesty. We can't send any of our Dreadnoughts to the After Trojan Realm."

"Why not Captain? We can't have one of our Realms breaking away", the High Prince replied, adding, "It is simply unacceptable!"

"Your Majesty. It's exactly as Prince Leopold has already stated. The outcome of these upcoming battles are completely uncertain", Matthew replied honestly, "We need every ship we have, here to defend these Jovian Realms. If we send one single ship to Patroclus Command Central, it could well have been that one single ship that turns the tide of this war in our favour."

Captain Tarzan added, "Captain Murphy is right Your Majesty. We can't take the risk. We need every ship we have here. Every single ship we can muster."

"Agreed. Your Majesty. We can send out a fleet to Patroclus Command Central, after we have defeated the enemy's fleets here in battle", General Snide recommended confidently.

The High Prince was silent for a long moment, then, "Captain. What do you recommend?"

"Your Majesty. First, we must thank Fleet Captains Carlson and Sharky for protecting your Sister Luisa and ensuring her safety", Matthew began, then added, "We may not like their method, but Princess Luisa is alive because of them."

"That is true Captain, but this Constitutional Principality and Independence are both unacceptable", High Prince Heinrich noted.

"Yes Your Majesty and we do need to politely remind them of that", Matthew agreed and then explained, "Tell them, that Aft Trojan independence is unacceptable, won't be allowed or even considered and that you will be sending a fleet of dreadnoughts their way. That should make them think twice."

"I thought you said we can't spare any ships Matthew", the High Prince replied using his name.

"We can't Your Majesty, but the Trojans don't know that", Matthew replied.

General Snide caught on and remarked, "Bullshit and bluff hey lad. Your Majesty, by the time they realise we haven't sent a fleet, the battle here should be over. God willing, we will have some ships to send their way."

Everyone around the table repeated, "God willing!"

Matthew stood up and walked across to the large wall screen, he thumped his fist on the wall beside the screen, "This Gentlemen is a problem."

"We already know that Captain", Prince Wulfric remarked sarcastically.

"Oh yes Your Highness, but this is a problem that keeps on giving us problems", Matthew noted.

The room was silent in anticipation of an explanation.

"The people of the Fore Trojan Asteroid colonies, can never know any of this. It will foment rebellion, likely a violent rebellion at that. That is a foregone conclusion", Matthew informed the room, "Only this time, there will be no one there to stop it. No equivalent of a Captain Carlson."

"Shit!", Prince Wulfric exclaimed.

Matthew didn't reply, instead he addressed Princess Sophia's representative, "Kittens. You need to give Princess Sofia's Chamberlain a heads up. Sooner rather than later."

High Prince Heinrich nodded and ordered, "Kittens. I completely agree with Captain Murphy. Give Chamberlain Sparrow a heads up. He needs to know everything that has happened in the Aft Trojan Realm and prepare for a possible rebellion."

Matthew continued, "Your Majesty. Your Sister, Princess Luisa was very lucky. Our Martian occupation forces returned to the Aft Trojan colonies from Mars and their Captains picked up on this discontent. Their Fleet Captain put in place a plan to save the Princess and the Nobles. That won't happen at the Fore Trojan colonies. All they'll have is our heads up and their wits."

"And when the Fore Trojan contingent of our L5 occupation forces arrives home, it's very likely that all hell will break loose", Prince Valdamar noted.

Matthew pointed to Prince Valdamar, "Right on the mark Your Highness. Right on the mark."

Prince Valdamar replied, "Princess Sophia's Chamberlain can have the troops demobilised as they disembark their transport ships. If they no longer have their pulse pistols and pulse rifles, any protests that might form will at least be unarmed."

Matthew looked to Princess Sophia's representative, "Are you taking notes Kittens?"

Kittens looked to His Majesty who nodded, then replied, "Yes. Taking notes as we speak."

Prince Leopold then asked the one question no one had thought of, "Why now? Why this discontent now? The timing, it is impeccable. In the absolute worst possible way."

That caught them all by surprise, Prince Leopold was right, the timing was impeccable.

Callthrope replied, "Chamberlain Schweitzer says, it all started after our Martian occupation forces returned to the Aft Trojan colonies from Mars. Then it all came to a head, when the Aft Trojan occupation forces returned from L5."

Matthew sat back down and was in silent thought with everyone watching him.

"He did this!", Matthew remarked.

"He Matthew?", the Prophet enquired.

"He! Folcrom Forkbraid! He's the common denominator", Matthew replied, explaining, "It was Forkbraid who sent our occupation forces packing on Mars. It was Forkbraid who warned our occupation forces of the ambush in cis-lunar space. He sent our forces packing there as well."

"That demon! That damnable demon is responsible for all of this! This was a spiritual attack", the Prophet concluded.

None of them realising that it was actually Leroy's redemption, a form of psychic personality demolition that was performed on Leroy McGuvan by Gwek the Kujur.

"That means when our occupation forces return to the Fore Trojan Realm, they can't be trusted. Not in the slightest", Prince Wulfric remarked, adding, "We ought to take them down en-route!"

"What with Brother? We cannot spare the ships", the High Prince replied.

Matthew looked at Kittens once more, "Keep taking those notes Kittens. Chamberlain Sparrow will need all the information we can give him."

Kittens looked back at Matthew, replying, "I will provide Chamberlain Sparrow with a full and complete report Captain."

"They've also freed all the Slaves", Prince Valdamar noted, "Their new Constitution is going to abolish all Slavery across the entire Aft Trojan colonies."

"That's outrageous! Only our Brother Heinrich can free slaves!", Prince Wulfric spat out.

This caught Prince Leopold's ear and even though he did not want to be there, it was worth it, just for that small piece of information. The Prince remained quiet.

"Slavery was never a big thing in the Trojan Realms Brothers", the High Prince noted, "They do have a lot of Slaves, but they are not anywhere near as reliant on Slaves as we are here."

"But still Brother, freeing their Slaves. It's outrageous!", Prince Wulfric reiterated, "and doing so without your permission. That is egregious!"

"This is all going to effect Jovian finances as well Your Majesty", the Prophet noted, "Their separation of Church and State. Only having Church members paying the ten percent tithe. The Aft Trojan Jovian Church is going to be in a financial crisis."

"Yes Brother Heinrich, the Prophet is right", Prince Valdamar agreed, "The Jovian Church's primacy tax of ten percent of their overall ten percent tithe is gone. Kiss that goodbye. With independence and a reduced tithe overall, their Jovian Church, will not pay what they owe."

"And it gets worse Brothers", Prince Valdamar informed them all, continuing, "Their twenty percent sovereign tax is now controlled by their Parliament. So the High Sovereign fealty tax of twenty percent of that, it's gone as well."

"All the more reason for us not to lose the Fore Trojan Realm", the High Prince told them all.

"The main thing is Brothers, our dear Sister Luisa, is alive and well. For that I am truly grateful", Prince Leopold noted.

Captain Carlson was sitting with Princess Luisa on her favourite balcony, high up on the palace tower, overlooking the palace gardens. He'd only just arrived and taken a seat a few minutes earlier.

"How are feeling today Princess?", he enquired.

"I don't really know Captain. I've been stripped of my royal powers, but honestly, did I really need them?", the Princess replied.

"Probably not Your Highness and considering your particular affliction, perhaps it's all for the best", the Captain gave his honest opinion.

"I still have my animals", Princess Luisa replied smiling, "If I eat it, I must first dispatch it."

Inside the Captain cringed slightly, but couldn't help but look back at Princess Luisa's beautiful smiling face and he smiled back in return.

Chamberlain Schweitzer stepped onto the balcony and requested the Captain's presence. The Captain followed the Chamberlain back into the adjoining room, where the Chamberlain passed him a communique from High Prince Heinrich.

Captain Carlson opened the communique and read it, "Princess. Your Brother Heinrich is thanking myself and Captain Sharky for saving your life and keeping you safe", he spoke quite loudly, so that Princess Luisa could hear him.

"Oh. How sweet! That is very nice of him. Heinrich doesn't often thank people you know", Princess Luisa replied.

To Chamberlain Schweitzer, he spoke more softly, "His Majesty is not very happy with our political changes. He says, that they are unacceptable and that any form of independence will not be tolerated", he then paused before informing him, "The High Prince is sending the Jovian fleet."

"Well that is not good!", the Chamberlain responded, adding, "We cannot possibly stand against the Jovian fleet."

"There is a war happening Chamberlain and there are inner system fleets heading Jupiter's way. They couldn't possibly spare more than a few ships", Captain Carlson informed him, "and before those ships get here, I'll stir the pot for them. Just a little bit."

"Stir the pot?", asked the Chamberlain.

"Everything we've achieved here, the new Constitution, the new Parliamentary System of Government. The separation of Church and State. The changes to the Line of Succession. I'll send all of that information to the Fore Trojan occupation forces and General Trask. They are on their way home and Captain Sharky tells me, they all have a very similar opinion to him on these matters", Captain Carlson replied.

"Okay. I can see that definitely stirring the pot", the Chamberlain agreed.

"With those inner system fleets rapidly approaching, the High Prince will be forced to split any forces he dispatches multiple ways and his options will be very limited.", Captain Carlson remarked, "So let's give him plenty more things to worry about."

The Chamberlain then left the room and Captain Carlson returned to the balcony, to the waiting Princess. As he approached, Princess Luisa bid him sit down on the couch beside her.

Princess Luisa lifted herself up and then sat herself back down on Captain Carlson's lap, "Christian. You are my new warrior", she told him, then gently kissed him on the lips.

22. The Belters be Pissed

Horatio Moon studied the latest scans of the space lanes between Mars and Ceres. Tall and obese, like many of his compatriots born and raised on Ceres, Horatio required a power suit to move around in the Colony cylinder's point three five g's artificial gravity. The system wide standard was one Earth g, however, the Belter colonies hardly ever bothered with the inner system's gravity laws or other rules.

"What the hell am I looking at?", Administrator Moon asked, "Why can't I see anything?"

"Administrator. There is nothing to see. Those are our latest scans and we are not detecting any destroyers at all Sir", replied the data and surveillance officer.

"Yes but why?", the Administrator looked at the officer's name badge, "Busselton."

"I can't say Sir. If those destroyers are on their way here, we should be seeing them", the Surveillance officer replied.

"Perhaps the Horridians are right. Stealth thrusters and midnight skins", Administrator Moon mumbled quietly, yet loudly enough to hear.

"That would do it Sir. If they have some kind of stealth thrusters, we won't easily detect them. If they also have black hulls, our scopes won't distinguish between them and the darkness of space", the Surveillance officer remarked.

"Keep scanning anyway. If and when we detect them, I want to know straight away", the Administrator ordered.

"Will you still be in the colony Sir or back on Ceres?", the Surveillance officer asked.

Administrator Moon looked at Busselton, "On Ceres of course man! I simply can not stand this damnable gravity! It's intolerable", then he walked towards the door.

Several days later six destroyers arrived at Ceres. They appeared out of nowhere on their final approach and took up orbit around Ceres. There were three from L5's Colonial fleet and three were from the Earth's Defence Forces. Horatio Moon watched through the crystal aluminium windows of his Administration Office at the distant destroyers, as they took up positions in low orbit around Ceres. His communicator buzzed.

"Yes", Horatio Moon asked.

"The destroyers from Mars have arrived Sir", informed the Surveillance officer.

"Yes, well Busselton. I can bloody well see that", an angry Horatio Moon replied.

"My apologies Sir. The destroyers appeared from out of nowhere and everyone up here is in a panic", Surveillance officer Busselton informed him.

"Have they initiated communications?", the Administrator asked.

"No Sir. Not yet", the Surveillance officer replied, informing him further, "They appear to be deploying, in a hexagonal orbital configuration Sir."

"From which they can command and control the whole of Ceres", Horatio Moon understood, "Thank you Busselton. Let me know when they initiate communications", he then hung up.

Information was quickly arriving from five other Belter colonies, Vesta, Juno, Pallas, Interamnia and Hygiea. The other big five Belter colonies in terms of the sheer number of colonies and levels of sophistication. It appeared clear that these six fleets were arriving with impeccable timing, appearing out of nowhere and approaching each colony within an hour or two of each other.

"What do they want? Why are they here? Why now?", these were common thoughts passing through the minds of all six colony Administrators, including Horatio Moon.

Horatio Moon had a good view from his office over the main space port of Ceres. He was quite surprised to see a Gull Wing Skimmer approaching the space port to land. Ordinarily he would expect to see local Hummers and larger transports. It had to be from the newly arrived fleet.

"Cassie. I just noticed a Gull Wing Skimmer approaching our space port. Can you check on that for me?", Horatio asked.

"Yes of course Sir. Give me a few minutes", Cassie replied.

Horatio Moon stood up from his desk and walked over to his crystal aluminium windows, from which he watched the Gull Wing land on the space sports tarmac. It was quickly lowered below the space ports tarmac and disappeared from sight.

Horatio's communicator buzzed, "Yes", he asked.

"Sir, the Gull Wing is from that fleet of destroyers. I've been informed, that there are two Captains on their way to your office", Cassie the Secretary replied.

"Thank you Cassie. Let me know when they're here", the Administrator requested.

"Yes Sir", Cassie replied and the communicator went silent once more.

It wasn't long before the buzzer sounded and the Administrator's Secretary, Cassie inform him, "Sir. Those two Captains I mentioned, they're here now."

"Let them in Cassie", the Administrator requested.

Horatio Moon stood up to greet his two guests as they walked through the door of this office.

They were typical of Earth and L5 folk, short and thin, compared to most Ceresians and as expected, they were wearing heavy boots to hold them to the floor. From the perspective of the Captains, Horatio Moon was overly tall and fat. Obese in fact was an understatement. He and his forebears had lived and grown under Ceres point zero two seven gs for generations. Gravity that was so light it was almost non-existent.

Horatio reached his hand across the desk and shook the Captains hands, each in turn.

"Captain Dmitri Borislava. Earth Defence Forces. Captain of the destroyer Sampson", the first Captain greeted as he shook his hand.

"Captain Haruka Tanaka. L5 Colonial Fleet. Captain of the destroyer Nemesis", the second Captain greeted as she shook his hand.

"I am Administrator Moon, Horatio Moon", the Administrator greeted in return, then quickly asked, "What in the blue blazes are your ships doing in my sky?"

"Your sky?", Captain Tanaka questioned, "Surely you mean Ceresian sky."

"My sky. Ceresian sky. What difference does it make?", the Administrator replied, "Your ships are still in it, aren't they?"

Captain Borislava quickly answered, "Administrator. We are here to protect Ceres."

"Protect Ceres? From what? From who? A three headed Namyegoob? We Ceresians don't need protection from anyone", the Administrator replied angrily, adding, "We have no need for your protection. We have no need for your presence. Go away!"

"What's a Namyegoob?", Captain Borislava asked Captain Haruka

"I believe it's Boogeyman spelt backwards Captain", Captain Haruka replied.

"Administrator. You must be aware of the war? Surely?", Captain Haruka asked.

"Yes. Of course I am and Ceres is not involved in the war. Neither are any of the other Belter colonies. It is your war Captains", Administrator Moon replied, telling them in no uncertain terms, "We certainly have no wish to be conquered by the Earth or L5! So, just go away!"

"We are not here to conquer your colonies Administrator", Captain Haruka stressed.

"And yet, here you are. With six destroyers no less", the Administrator replied angrily, adding, "If you are not here for conquest, why six destroyers?"

Captain Borislava replied, "Standard practice Sir. To protect a world this size, requires a bare minimum of six destroyers in a hexagonal orbital defence posture."

Horatio Moon was not convinced and his face took on an even angrier visage.

"Administrator. The Earth and L5 have both taken a huge risk, sending six destroyers to each of the six most prominent Belter colonies. That's thirty six ships we would rather have kept at home for our cis-lunar defences", Captain Haruka sharply replied, "We were ordered to come here and protect the Ceresian colonies at all cost, even at the cost of our ships and our lives."

"Then you came here for nothing!", Horatio Moon replied angrily, "So you may just as well go back home. Leave, go back home and protect your precious cis-lunar space. There is nothing you have that we want and we don't need your protection. So go away! Be off with you now! Be gone!"

The two Captains walked out of the Administrator's office, as the door closed behind them, Captain Haruka remarked, "That man is an idiot. Does he not know the risks if we leave?"

"He's unreasonable, I'll grant you that, but I doubt he's an idiot", Captain Borislava replied.

"My boss is neither an idiot nor is he unreasonable", Cassie the Administrator's Secretary told them both, "What he is, is a business man. If you want his cooperation. Explain to him the core of the issue, why we need your protection and more importantly, how Ceres can profit out of this arrangement. Then, maybe, just maybe he'll listen."

The Captains looked at the very tall, thin Ceresian woman. Her family had likely been on Ceres for many generations, yet she was not obese like her boss.

Captain Haruka queried, "The core of the issue?"

"Yes", Cassie replied, "Why we all need your protection? How we can make a profit from your presence? Your being here? You need to think like a Belter!"

Both Captains looked at each other and spoke at the same time, "I've got this."

Captain Borislava laughed and replied, "Take the lead Captain."

They both walked back into the Administrator's office.

"Not you two again. Just go away. Be gone with you both!", the Administrator remarked.

"You need us Administrator and whether you like it or not, we are not going anywhere", Captain Haruka told the Administrator.

"Really. Well, you'll not have any cooperation from us", the Administrator told them.

"We don't actually need your cooperation Mr Moon", Captain Haruka told him.

"That is correct Administrator. We don't need your cooperation at all", Captain Borislava replied, adding, "We'll just protect Ceres and its colonies anyway. Consider it a free service and when this war is over, we will simply leave and you can happily live in your splendid isolation."

The word free caught the Administrator's ear, "Free service?", Horatio queried.

"What? Did you think we were going to charge you for protection?", Captain Borislava asked.

"Well, I thought perhaps, you might be inclined to take what you want, at will and as you saw fit", the Administrator replied softly, then added sharply, "like bloody Pirates!"

"Just the opposite Mr Moon", Captain Haruka replied, adding, "Our ships will be needing fuel and materials for maintenance. Our crews will also need food, water, recreation. All of the usual things that human beings might need anywhere in the solar system."

"And of course Mr Moon. Ceres is right here and we will of course pay for fuel, services and provisions", Captain Borislava informed him.

"Yes and top credits as well Mr Moon. Our little visit will be quite lucrative economically for the Ceresian colonies", Captain Haruka noted.

"Lucrative you say? Economic you say?", Horatio Moon's ears were buzzing, he questioned, "and for this we get free protection as well, yes?"

"Yes indeed Mr Moon", Captain Haruka replied, "and Ceres is going to be needing it."

"We're not at war with anyone, so why is Ceres going to need protection exactly?", Horatio Moon asked.

"The Jovian Realms", Captain Borislava replied.

"The Jovian Realms are at war with the inner system worlds, your people. We here in the Asteroid Belt, get along fine with them. They are not a problem", the Administrator informed them.

"Do you? Do you really?", Captain Haruka asked.

"Of course we do", Horatio Moon replied.

"History says otherwise Mr Moon", Captain Borislava remarked, "Back during the previous war, the outer satellite insurrection. Jupiter's Trojan colonies, all got along so well with the Jovian Realms. Right up to the point where they annexed them!"

"That was centuries ago!", the Administrator remarked.

"You did hear about the Jovian High Council's proclamation? You should have, even way out here in the Belt?" Captain Borislava asked.

"Which one, the Jovian High Council makes so many proclamations", the Administrator asked.

"The one about the Martian annexation", Captain Haruka informed him.

"Oh yes, yes. The Martian annexation. I do remember that one. It doesn't affect the Belters though", the Administrator told them.

"Did you just watch the news feeds or did you actually read their proclamation?", Captain Haruka asked.

"The news feeds of course. I didn't see any need to look into the pages and pages of their proclamation's minutia", Horatio Moon admitted.

"You should have read the proclamation Horatio", Captain Haruka replied using his given name, "You see, the Jovian High Council hasn't just annexed Mars. They annexed Mars, all of the Martian colonies, including their Trojan colonies and everything in between!"

"You see Mr Moon, the Horridians have already annexed all the Belter colonies", Captain Borislava noted, adding,"They just didn't bother to list them out by name."

"No! No! No! That's outrageous!", Horatio Moon shouted, "That cannot be right."

"It is Horatio", Captain Haruka confirmed, "You can read their proclamation for yourself."

"Don't you worry Captain. I will be reading it very shortly", Horatio Moon informed her.

"That is why we are here after all Mr Moon", Captain Borislava reminded him.

"Our small fleet protects the Ceresian colonies, a service free of charge", Captain Haruka noted.

"And while we are here, your people will reap the benefit of ours stay, every time we purchase, fuel, materials, provisions, water and other services", Captain Borislava reminded him, "It is a win, win situation for the Ceresian people."

"Yes. Protection from the Horridians and all those lovely, lucrative, economic benefits", Captain Haruka reminded him.

"Lucrative you've said. Economic you've said. You've mentioned that twice now", Horatio Moon remarked, then with a boisterous laugh, "Top credits I say! Show us the money I say!"

"So be it!", Captain Borislava spat into his hand and held it across the desk.

Horatio Moon slapped his hand into Borislava's and shook it firmly and replied, "So be it!"

Captain Haruka spat into her hand and held it across the desk saying, "So be it!"

Horatio Moon slapped his hand into Haruka's and shook it firmly and replied, "So be it!"

The Administrator wiped his hand on a cloth and the two Captains did likewise on their handkerchiefs. It appeared that they had all reached an agreement.

"Cassie", the Administrator spoke into his communicator, "The Captains and I have reached a verbal agreement. Their fleet will be staying to protect the Ceresian colonies. Can you please find a copy of that Jovian High Council's proclamation annexing Mars. I need to read that urgently."

"Yes Sir. It might take me a few moments, but I think I can find you a copy", Cassie replied.

The Administrator bid goodbye to his guests, who then left to return to their respective ships.

As they passed by Cassie the Secretary, she mouthed the words quietly, "Good job!" and they both nodded in return.

As the two Captains walked back to their Gull Wing Skimmer, Captain Haruka noted, "We need to contact the other five fleets and let them know how this all went down. They will find it all very interesting."

"Agreed Captain. These Belters are all business, transaction and profit motivated. That's a handy thing to know", Captain Borislava replied.

As the two Captains returned to their respective ships, Administrator Moon read through the Jovian High Council's proclamation of the Annexation of Mars. He read through the proclamation carefully and quickly came to the section referenced by the two Captains. His secretary Cassie was still in the room when he read it out aloud.

Administrator Moon read the relevant section, "Cassie, you should hear this too. We the Jovian High Council, in the name of High Prince Heinrich von Horridian, High Prince of the Jovian Realms and Prince of Ganymede, hereby and henceforth, proclaim the following territories to be Jovian Realms."

The Administrator then read out the territories, "The Planet Mars, its two Moons, Phobos and Deimos, all Martian Orbital colonies, the colonies of both Martian Lagrangian regions L4 and L5, and all of the Asteroidal colonies between the Martian and Jovian Orbital zones!"

The Administrator repeated the last part, "and all of the Asteroidal colonies between the Martian and Jovian Orbital zones. The bastards didn't even bother to list us all out, we are just everything in between."

"That is not good Sir. It appears we do need these destroyers here after all", Cassie replied.

Horatio Moon's face turned bright red, he was furious, livid, "Get word to all the other Belter colonies. All of them. No exceptions. Spell this information out for them. Tell them to read this damned Jovian proclamation."

Horatio Moon, the Administrator of the Ceresian colonies was seriously pissed off and pretty soon all the other Belter colony Administrators would be as well.

All of the Belters were going to be seriously pissed off with the Jovian High Council's proclamation of annexation.

23. The Day of the Dreadnoughts

Captain Carmichael and his Lieutenant Adjutant Hans Blixen, had been shuttled across from the Colonial heavy cruiser Spartan to General Stanton's flagship, the Earth's heavy cruiser Goliath. One of the seven hundred and fifty heavy cruisers of the Grand fleet from the Earth and L5. The pair were quickly ushered into the Goliath's main boardroom.

In front of them was a large table with an inbuilt screen, interactively displaying the solar system from the Sun out to Jupiter's orbit. The Grand fleet's orbital transfer tracking from cis-lunar space to Jupiter was clearly displayed, along with the fleets current position. Another fleet was also displayed on the interactive table, along with its current position and trajectory. This fleet's trajectory showed it was going to intercept with the Grand Fleet. It was a huge Jovian fleet from out of Callisto.

"What do we know General?", Captain Carmichael asked.

"That fleet is Jovian. It consists of fifteen hundred Jovian dreadnoughts", the General replied.

"So twice the size of our own combined fleets", Captain Carmichael noted.

"Yes Captain. The enemy may have the advantage of numbers, but we have the advantage of newer technologies", General Stanton informed.

"If I may Captain", Lieutenant Blixen requested.

Captain Carmichael nodded.

"Those Jovian dreadnoughts have steel and titanium hulls. Most of our cruisers have hulls of plasteel with polyceramalloy coatings. Our newest cruisers have polyceramalloy hulls", the Lieutenant informed them both, adding, "Those dreadnoughts also have standard defence shields, our cruisers all have the newest enhanced defence shields. We have the best tech!"

General Stanton smiled and stated, "They're like boxers with glass jaws."

"Not so quick General. We can take a punch sure, but they have twice our numbers", Captain Carmichael replied, adding, "We can't just assume we have the upper hand. Not just yet anyway."

Lieutenant Blixen continued, "Those dreadnoughts have interceptors as well. Bat Wings. A few dozen each, going by our current records."

"Bat wings? Like Captain Forkbraid's?", Captain Carmichael enquired.

"Oh no Sir. Those Jovian bat wings will be old school bat wings", the Lieutenant explained, "Forkbraid's bat wing has been upgraded to the Nth degree. Polyceramalloy hull, modern weapons and shields, neural interconnect control helmet. The Jovian versions will all have titanium hulls. They'll all be very standard in fact."

"That is good to know Lieutenant", General Stanton noted, adding, "Captain. Your wisps and my switch blades will make chopped liver out of them."

Again Captain Carmichael urged caution, "General. We can't make assumptions. We are working off of old data. The Jovians may have some surprises for us."

"The way I see it Captain. This battle should be short and simple", the General began, then continued, "Your wisps and my switch blades take on their bat wings, maybe even skin dance along the dreadnought's hulls and give them hell. We can use our electromagnetic rail guns, hyper resonant disrupters and missiles as stand off weapons and everything else we can throw at them at close quarters for the kill."

Captain Carmichael and Lieutenant Blixen both gave the General concerned looks.

"What? You don't think this will be that simple?", the General enquired.

"Please forgive me General. I have no wish to offend you, but you are thinking like an Earth man", Captain Carmichael replied.

"No offence taken. I am an Earth man Captain", the General responded.

Lieutenant Blixen asked, "General Sir. If you don't mind me asking. How long have you actually been in space?"

The General replied, "Only since those Jovian missile attacks on the Earth Lieutenant."

Captain Carmichael and Lieutenant Blixen both looked at each other with concern.

"General. What you've described might work on a battlefield on the Earth or even at Sea", Captain Carmichael began to explain, "It might even work in cis-lunar space or in Jovian space, but it won't work where we are currently."

"I'm not following you Captain", the General admitted.

"General. We are currently in deep space, on a non hohmann fast orbital transfer from the Earth to Jupiter", Captain Carmichael began explaining, "The Jovian fleet is approaching us with its own trajectory and we will meet at this point", he pointed to a point on the table where two lines intersected.

"Okay. I am aware of that Captain", the General remarked.

Captain Carmichael explained, "To use our fighters, we would need to slow down significantly, to reverse thrust, for the battle. Then after the actual battle, we would need to forward thrust heavily once more, to get back on our trajectory to Jupiter."

The General did not look convinced.

Lieutenant Blixen stepped in, "General Sir. If I may. We are in deep space and fuel is precious. We need to remain on course at our currently velocity. We can't afford to waste fuel, not even a single drop, not even for this upcoming battle."

"General. Both the Lieutenant and I were born and raised in space at L5. The man commanding that Jovian fleet was born and raised in space in the Jovian Realms. He knows what we know and he will not be slowing down his fleet", Captain Carmichael informed the General, adding, "He thinks like the Lieutenant and I. We are all spacemen, spacers General!"

"So what do you recommend Captain?", the General who now understood the situation asked.

Captain Carmichael explained, "We can't use our fighters General. At the speed we're moving at, they'd never be able to keep up. Fortunately, the enemy is in exactly the same boat. They can't use their fighters either. This battle will be very quick, it won't be a melee, it will be quick and fleeting. There will be one single pass. That's it. That is how this will be going down."

"Okay. So the details Captain?", the General asked.

Captain Carmichael looked to Lieutenant Blixen, who then prepared to take detailed notes.

The Captain continued, "First we prepare all of our weapons systems well in advance to the interception point. As soon as our electromagnetic rail guns are within range, we let loose and strafe the enemy dreadnoughts, head on. We continue strafing with the rail guns, until our hyper resonant disrupters are in range. Then we target the dreadnought's bridges with our disrupters."

"So far so good", the General noted.

"We need to study the Jovian dreadnought plans to refresh our knowledge of their weak points", Captain Carmichael noted, then continued, "General. When your missiles and our torpedoes are within range, we'll let them loose and target them at those weak points. We'll use our pulse cannons and phased laser arrays to take out any enemy missiles our enemy fires at us."

The General nodded and remarked, "I'm liking this so far Captain."

"Good General", the Captain replied, adding "When our two fleets cross paths, we'll broadside their dreadnoughts with our pulse cannons and phased laser arrays."

The General nodded again and asked, "Lieutenant, you've got this all noted down?"

"Yes General", Lieutenant Blixen replied.

"Once we're past the Jovian fleet, we'll need to take stock of how many of our ships made it through the clash and how many didn't. We'll also need damage reports for each cruiser", Captain Carmichael commented, "Once we have all that information, we can then decide whether our mission to Jupiter continues or whether we need alter course to head back to cis-lunar space."

"What of the Jovian fleet?", the General enquired.

"At their current speed it will be extremely difficult for them to change course to chase us", Captain Carmichael replied, then turning to the Lieutenant, "Blixen. Can you extrapolate the Jovian fleet's course after the intersection point?"

The Lieutenant pressed a few keys on his grip's virtual keyboard, "Just a moment Sir", then after a long minute, the trajectory line for the Jovian fleet on the interactive table began to extend.

The Jovian fleet was on its own non hohmann fast orbital transfer from Jupiter to the Earth. One that the Jovians had planned to intercept the Grand fleet.

"Well that's not good!", Lieutenant Blixen exclaimed.

"Agreed. We need to send word to the Earth and L5. Give them a heads up about what's heading their way", Captain Carmichael replied.

"It may not be as bad as it seems gentlemen", the General told them, explaining, "After our engagement with the enemy, their fleet will be significantly smaller."

"General. We have to remember, the commander in charge of that fleet is making his plans, just the same as we are", Captain Carmichael advised, "Those dreadnoughts will be firing back at us after all and there are no guarantees that things will go all our way."

"I'll have my communications officer send an urgent message to the Earth and L5 now", General Stanton decided, "After our engagement with the enemy, we can send them updates of the new situation and whether or not we can continue with the mission."

"That sounds like a plan General", Captain Carmichael agreed.

The following days as the two fleets approached each other, Captain Carmichael and General Stanton both insisted that the Captains of their heavy cruisers checked, double checked and finally triple checked all of their weapons systems and their preparations for the intercept.

Captain Carmichael announced over the encrypted communications systems to every cruiser in the their fleet, "The enemy fleet is approaching. Very soon we will cross paths. Choose your targets well. Remember the plan. This battle will be over in minutes, short minutes at that. Check and recheck your systems. Check and recheck your preparations. We have one shot at this. There is no do over. The is no second attempt. One shot is all we get and we have to make it count. May the Gods be with you all."

After the announcement, Lieutenant Blixen enquired of Captain Carmichael, "Captain. Valhalla or Folkvangr? What's your preference?"

"The drinking hall of a wily old God or the green fields of a beautiful Goddess?", Captain Carmichael mused, "I'd probably choose the later. Do the Valkyrie give us a choice?"

"Probably not Sir, I believe the Valkyrie decide for us", Lieutenant Blixen replied.

"Well then Lieutenant, whatever the out come, I'll see you on the other side", the Captain replied.

Less than fifteen minutes later the two fleets entered firing range and the Earth's and L5's heavy cruisers opened up with their electromagnetic rail guns, strafing the enemy with explosive tipped iron rounds, one after the other in rapid succession. It was difficult to make out the damage being caused to the enemies dreadnoughts at this speed and distance, but the rounds were striking their targets as they had planned. This was clearly shown by their red tracer rounds. Cruisers on either side of the Spartan likewise strafed their targets and the enemy's dreadnoughts were taking a severe battering.

Two minutes later, the Spartan's hyper resonant disrupters activated, targeting dreadnought bridges. Hyper resonant disrupters had activated on the cruisers across the entire fleet and the onslaught against the Jovian dreadnoughts was viscous in the extreme with deep, red beams cutting across the distance between the two fleets. It was difficult to tell from the Spartan's perspective, but it did look effective, possibly carving through the titanium hull plating like a hot knife through butter. Only a post battle analysis of the battle's data records would tell them for sure.

The Spartan shuddered violently as the enemy's weapons struck their shields and seconds later torpedoes were being launched against the enemy's dreadnoughts. Pulse cannons and phased laser arrays worked furiously to destroy the enemy's missiles as their own torpedoes flew towards their targets. Blue pulses of super heated plasma and brilliant blue beams of light shot out at their targets. Across the fleet, torpedoes and missiles were launched towards the enemy's dreadnoughts. The dreadnoughts in turn had launched their missiles against the Earth's and L5's heavy cruisers.

Those on the bridge of the Spartan watched the main screen intently, all mentally noting the Spartan's torpedoes striking hard against their targeted dreadnoughts. All bridge crew members were holding tightly to their chairs and their stations as the Spartan shuddered violently when hit by the enemy's fire. Small fires began springing up in some of the Spartan's bridge systems.

Then the Spartan's pulse cannons and phased lasers arrays fired once again. The blue pulses of super heated plasma and brilliant blue beams of light struck directly at their targeted dreadnoughts, broadsiding them fiercely as they passed each other at high speed. In the bridge's blurred screen images, the dreadnought's titanium hull plating was seen buckling, ripping and finally tearing apart under the intensity of their firepower.

Then as quickly as it began, the battle was behind them and the Spartan's scanners detected a massive explosion directly to their rear. A great many other explosions were detected behind them as well, but further off to the sides. It seemed that many of the other heavy cruisers in their fleet had been successful as well. Unfortunately, not all of the explosions were dreadnoughts, some of the them were exploding heavy cruisers, their own ships.

Captain Carmichael jumped out his seat, "Where's our fire control?", he questioned loudly, as three fire control officers stepped on the bridge, he pointed to the fires, "Men. Put those fires out!"

The Captain turned to Lieutenant Blixen, "Damage report!"

"On it Captain", the Lieutenant replied.

"Comms!", the Captain shouted, "Hail the fleet. I want to know how many of our ships survived and their current status."

"Yes Sir", the Communications officer replied.

"Damage report being transferred to your station now Captain", Lieutenant Blixen informed, adding, "Damage control teams are active and working hard."

"Good. Good Blixen. How are our casualties?", Captain Carmichael requested.

"Our numbers are in flux, but steadily flowing in", the Lieutenant replied, adding, "We'll have better information in a few minutes Sir."

"Keep on top of it Lieutenant", Captain Carmichael ordered.

"Yes Sir", the Lieutenant replied.

It was a half hour since the battle and the two fleets were well separated and continuing on the respective courses. General Stanton was on the screen to discuss the current situation.

"You were right Captain. That was quick, five minutes all up, if that", the General noted, "I'm glad to see you survived by the way."

"Same here General, although it looks like many of us didn't make it", the Captain replied.

"Yes. About that Captain. My figures say we lost ninety seven", General Stanton informed him.

"My figures agree with yours General. We lost ninety seven heavy cruisers", Captain Carmichael replied, then added, "Our preliminary figures for the Jovian fleet tells us they lost five time the number of dreadnoughts."

"Your figures agree with mine on that count as well Captain", the General replied, adding, "We do have six hundred and fifty three heavy cruisers left between us."

"Our maintenance and repair crews will work around the clock to get all the damage sorted out General", Captain Carmichael informed the General, concluding, "I believe we can and should continue with our mission to Jovian Realms."

The General nodded, "Agreed Captain. The mission is a go", he then paused for several moments, "For older ships, those dreadnought certainly packed some punch."

Captain Carmichael smiled, "I did say not to underestimate them General. The fact that the battle took place here in deep space and at high speeds was very much to our advantage. Start to finish, the battle was over very quickly. In a longer more drawn out battle, I doubt that we would have pulled off a five to one victory."

The General nodded again, "I think you're right. It's likely our computers were faster as well."

"That's very likely General. When switching from one weapons system to another, every split second counts", Captain Carmichael agreed.

"What of the Jovian fleet then?", the General enquired.

"The last we checked, they were still on course for the Earth and L5", the Captain replied.

"I'll send word to the Earth Gov and your President Banyan, let them know they have over a thousand Jovian dreadnoughts heading their way", General Stanton informed the Captain.

"Send word to the Martian Defence Forces as well General", Captain Carmichael advised, adding, "Captain Forkbraid and that ship of his will come in very handy."

"I don't see how a three laws safe ship is going to help Captain", the General remarked.

"Don't count them out General", Captain Carmichael replied, adding, "Forkbraid, his ship and his crew, they can pull off miracles and that is what the Earth and L5 need right now."

"I'll copy them in Captain. After today, I believe in miracles", General Stanton replied, "and anyway, by now we'll have that Venusian fleet joining ours at L4. That should help them out."

"Not to mention the other Venusian fleet that's heading out to Jupiter to link up with ours General. We have allies, the Horridians don't", Forkbraid replied.

"Captain. We're pulling away from that battle zone really fast. Do you think there are any survivors back there?", General Stanton asked.

"Lieutenant Blixen has been scanning the battle zone just in case. He tells me the odds of surviving are Buckley's and none General", Captain Carmichael replied, "Even if we did detect any possible survivors, we couldn't do anything about it anyway."

The General nodded, "Understood Captain. We couldn't get back there anyway. Perhaps it's better if none of those personnel survived."

"That is correct General. There's no going back and if Lieutenant Blixen is right, there's no one back there to save anyway", the Captain agreed.

Matthew was asleep in his apartment when the communicator called for his attention. At first he ignored it, but after stopping for a few short moments it started buzzing once more. Matthew stumbled out of bed, threw on a robe and reached for the communicator. It stopped bussing before he got to it. A few short moments later, it buzzed again and Matthew quickly picked it up.

"Captain Murphy here", he said into the handset.

"Captain. Good your awake", General Tarzan replied on the other end of the line.

"Yes General. I'm awake", Matthew replied as he stifled a yawn.

"We've had news from the Jovian fleet", the General informed Matthew.

"Okay General. Good news I hope", Matthew replied.

"Well a mix of both I'm afraid Captain', the General remarked, adding, "Our fifteen hundred strong Jovian fleet met up with the Earth's and L5's seven hundred and fifty strong Grand fleet at the point of interception. They have proceeded through the point of interception and are currently heading on course towards the Earth and L5."

"Okay General. So that's the good news. The Jovian fleet is on still track to the Earth and L5", Matthew replied, then asked, "Now, what's the bad news?"

"At the Battle of Point Interception, as it is now being called, we lost almost five hundred dreadnoughts. That was the price we paid for taking on their Grand fleet", the General admitted.

"Okay. Well that certain isn't good. What was the enemy's cost? What price did they pay?", asked Matthew curiously.

"If our numbers are accurate, the enemy lost almost a hundred cruisers", the General admitted.

"Sweet Mother of God General! That's five to one and not in our favour!", Matthew exclaimed.

"Yes Captain. We're still analysing the data from the battle", General Tarzan informed him, "It's looking like their cruisers have better hull plating and shielding. You know, plasteel and polyceramalloy. We also suspect their computer systems are somewhat faster than ours as well."

"General. I am going to be brutally honest with you", Matthew began, continuing, "These upcoming fights are gonna be tough. The fleet at their end is a combined fleet of Earth, L5 and Venusian ships. With that second Venusian fleet heading our way, we're pretty much facing the same thing here as well. And I haven't even factored in that blasted Martian Gunship, the Solstice. This is gonna be really tough."

"Agreed Matthew", the General replied using Matthew's name and not his rank, adding, "Get in early today. There will be another meeting with the High Prince. That's guaranteed. His Majesty will want to know everything. Don't hold anything back Matthew, no matter how bad your assessment might be. His Majesty values the truth over being told what he wants to hear. He will appreciate it. Trust me on that."

"I will General. I'll see you in the office later", Matthew replied and the General hung up.

24. The Fall of Hector

General Trask requested one of his Captains report to the bridge of his command ship. Captain Veto Petrakis was quick to make his way to the bridge.

"General. You called for me Sir?", Captain Petrakis asked.

"Yes Captain. You've been in contact with Patroclus Command Central in the Aft Trojans recently. How is their new Constitution going?", the General asked.

"Oh yes General. As you know Sir, they sent us their first draft and we did agree to help with improvements to it. We have finally received what looks like their final draft yesterday. My team is working on it as we speak Sir", Captain Petrakis replied.

"And?", the General asked.

"It all looks very promising. As you know, we've sent them suggestions and recommendations on all of their previous drafts. Many of which they have taken on board", the Captain replied, adding, "This final version looks very promising indeed. Assuming it meets all of our expectations, it could really be the final draft."

"If this copy passes your teams approval, have a copy sent to me for my perusal", General Trask ordered, adding, "We're going to need a new Constitution ourselves and helping our kinsfolk in the Aft Trojan Realm develop theirs, helps us immensely."

"Yes Sir. It will be absolutely historic. Both of our Trojan Realms will be using the exact same Constitution. I don't think such a thing has happened ever before in the entire history of Human civilisation", Captain Petrakis replied.

"Captain Nightingale. We'll be on our final approach to Hector Command Central in five days. Are your preparations all in place?", the General asked.

"Yes General. Everything is in place", Captain Nightingale informed him.

"Good then. They want us to demobilise before disembarking. We are to hand over all of our pulse pistols and pulse rifles as we leave the ships", General Trask reminded the Captain, "So show us what you've got."

Captain Nightingale carefully placed the case on a work station and opened it. Neatly packed into the box was a weapon. It was disassembled in many pieces and the Captain quickly assembled it in front of the Captain. It was a long range sniper rifle with a powerful scope. The old fashion kind that uses cartridges and capable of both single shot and semi-automatic firing.

"That was quick Captain. You assembled that in less than a minute", the General noted.

The Captain replied, "Yes Sir. We've made three hundred of these and we've trained three hundred of our best troops in their use."

"Excellent Captain. So how do we get them passed security?", the General enquired.

"That's the easy part Sir. When our troops leave the ships, they'll hand over their pulse pistols and pulse rifles. Those are all registered by serial number", the Captain replied, "These however, are completely unknown, machined here on our ships. They're not registered at all."

"They won't suspect?", asked the General.

"No Sir. All of the troop's luggage will be automatically routed and delivered to their homes by the dock's systems. Those that live in other colonies will have their luggage re-routed to their final destinations. They'll probably scan everything for pulse power pack signatures, but of course, these are old school. They won't be detected at all", Captain Nightingale explained.

"Good. Good Captain", the General replied, "Make sure your men know what to do."

"Yes Sir", the Captain replied, as he stripped down the rifle and replaced it back in its case.

"Captain, the authorities at Hector Command Central are fully aware of what happened at Patroclus Command Central. They're not wanting a repeat of that. Make sure our troops go home and behave themselves", General Trask ordered.

"I'll make sure all the other Captains know and ensure our troops fully understand General", Captain Nightingale replied, asking, "and the coup Sir?"

"We'll bide our time Captain. Sit back and wait. When the time is right, then we'll act", General Trask replied, adding, "We need to take very small steps, very slowly. Let them think the danger has passed, then we'll strike. We want this to go as peacefully as possibly. Just like it did with our kinfolk in the Aft Trojan Realm."

Five days later on their final approach to Hector Command Central, the weapons transports altered course for the Trojan asteroid Hector and their staging grounds. The troop transports, refined their course slightly towards the huge O'Neil style cylindrical colony, Hector Command Central. The troop transport ships lined up one by one to dock and offload their troops, at the south end cap's docking ring. The process of disembarking was slow, made even slower by the Trojan troops being demobilised as they left their troop transports.

As each Trojan trooper disembarked, they handed over their pulse pistols and pulse rifles. The equipment serial numbers were checked against the registration records and mostly those records were up to date and accurate. In some cases however, the serial numbers did not match the trooper who was in possession of the weapon and explanations were sought.

The process of disembarking took nearly three days and after completion was deemed a complete success. All registered pulse weapons had been accounted for and were now in the possession of Hector Command Central's authorities. For the troops, although the process was slow, they were happy to find their belongings had been automatically routed to their residences. Even when those residences were in other nearby colonies.

General Trask had disembarked on day one of the process. The General had undergone a quick mission debriefing meeting and was then whisked off to the palace. At the palace he was met by Chamberlain Sparrow, who led him to a room in which Princess Sophia was waiting. The Princess stood up as they approach, she was tall, blond and more than pleasant to the eye, but her features had a sharpness to them that detracted from that pleasantness. The Princess wore a scowl upon her face and appeared to be extremely annoyed and even angry.

Princess Sofia was harsh and critical, "So you're the coward who ran away from those evil bastards at L5?"

The General was taken immediately aback, "Your Highness?"

Chamberlain Sparrow stepped in, "Your Highness. It was a tactical withdrawal."

"Yes Your Highness. It was a necessary tactical withdrawal", General Trask agreed.

"Really? I'll be the judge of that General", Princess Sophia replied.

"Your Highness, the missile attacks on the Earth and L5, completely failed in their objectives", General Trask explained, "We found ourselves flying into an ambush. To not have withdrawn, would have been certain suicide for over a hundred and twenty five thousand personnel."

Princess Sofia scoffed, "And who exactly told you of this ambush?"

"We were warned Your Highness. Warned by L5's Colonial fleet Captain Carmichael and Martian defence forces Captain Forkbraid", General Trask informed the Princess.

"So they basically warned you off and then you just ran away!", Princess Sofia spat out.

"Your Highness, we scanned the region we were flying into with our own equipment", the General countered, "We checked the voracity of the enemy's warnings and found them to be true."

"Is this true Chamberlain?", Princess Sophia asked.

"It is my understanding Your Highness", the Chamberlain confirmed.

"Your Highness. These are your troops and we are involved in this war", the General began to explain, "It would have been extremely unwise to waste your troops in a suicide mission."

"Hmm. I am not happy with the withdrawal of our forces General, however, now that I've heard the reasons for it from your own lips, I am satisfied that it was the correct action", Princess Sofia replied, then added, "Now begone with you. Out of my sight!"

Chamberlain Sparrow led General Trask back out of the Princess's presence and towards the entrance of the palace.

"Well Chamberlain, that was somewhat unpleasant", the General commented.

"Her Highness is quite embarrassed General. She does worry about what her Brothers might think of this tactical withdrawal of yours", the Chamberlain replied.

"Yes, well the alternative was much worse Chamberlain. Trust me on that", the General replied.

"Yes, I believe it would have been. What I don't understand is why our enemies gave you a fair warning", the Chamberlain noted.

"I don't think we'll ever know why Chamberlain. Perhaps they value life as much as we do and saw no sense in killing a hundred and twenty five thousand people", the General speculated.

"Yes, it is all rather peculiar General", the Chamberlain replied as they approached the palace doors and then held out his hand.

General Trask shook the Chamberlain's hand and a small, imperceptible blue spark leapt from the General to the Chamberlain. The General then left the palace and headed on his way to his families residence on the other side of Hector Command Central's northern end cap.

Just as Leroy's redemption had leapt from the hand of General Trask to the hand of the Chamberlain, it was transmitted from one person to the next around the populace of Hector Command Central. Every time a Trojan trooper physically interacted with another person, that imperceptible blue spark leapt from one to the other.

With every hand shake, every slap on the should and every hug, when ever an infected person touched another it spread imperceptibly. And not just in Hector Command Central either. Quite a few of the returning Trojan troops lived in other colonies, some nearby, some farther afield. Leroy's redemption spread like a virus and with every physical interaction, peoples eyes began to open to the injustices and propaganda of the Jovian political system.

The Council of Nobles of the Fore Trojan Realm were ecstatic that their plans for the return of the Trojan troops was all going according to plan. All the troop's pulse weapons had been accounted for and were safely under lock and key. Public safety and the stability of the realm would not be undermined by armed protesters and the principality would remain as it always had been.

Of course the councillors in the Council of Nobles did not go to the local markets, the shopping centres etc., nor did they associate with the ordinary folk. No, they had servants to perform those tasks, so the Nobles on the council did not have any real feel for the pulse of the people and their level of discontentment. To these things they were all completely blind.

Captain Nightingale was calling General Trask over his communicator, the General picked up at his end of the communications line.

"General Sir. We have a problem", the Captain informed him.

"How so Captain?", the General enquired.

"My wife and I were at the local market today and I overheard some disturbing things Sir", Captain Nightingale informed him, "I overheard several conversations where the people were expressing some serious discontentment Sir.

Anger is the most appropriate term. Not just one conversation either Sir, but several conversations in fact. It appears to be the common point of discussion amongst the people at the moment."

"Did you get a feel for where this discontent was directed Captain?", General Trask enquired.

"General. This discontent, is squarely aimed at all things Horridian", the Captain informed him, adding, "My wife tells me the same discussions are common at the school gates. She came across this when taking our children to and from school over the past couple of days."

"You're right Captain, this is disturbing", the General agreed.

"It seems things are heating up General. Far too quickly", Captain Nightingale noted.

General Trask was in quiet thought for a moment, then he ordered, "Captain. Contact Captain Petrakis. Tell him to disperse the plans for our transition to a Constitutional Principality. Tell him it's urgent. We need to get word out there. Perhaps we can steer this thing into a negotiated transition."

"I'll do so Sir, but I fear we may already be too late", Captain Nightingale replied.

It was now two weeks later and Lead Councillor Milo Cardano of the Council of Nobles met with Chamberlain Sparrow at the palace. He had expressed a high level of urgency.

The Councillor passed a document to the Chamberlain, "This document has surfaced on the streets lately. You'll find it's very familiar", he told the Chamberlain.

The Chamberlain quickly perused the document, "This is a plan to transition the Fore Trojan Realm into a Constitutional Principality. The same plan that was used in the Aft Trojan Realm."

"Yes. Yes Chamberlain. That's exactly what it is", the Councillor agreed, "and it's now circulating here in Hector Command Central, as we speak."

"This does not bode well for us Councillor", the Chamberlain agreed, further explaining, "In the Aft Trojan Realm, this document was released after an agreement was already reached between Captain Carlson and their Council of Nobles. That was done to quell, what could have become an out of control riot and rebellion. If this is being released now, then there's something happening and we aren't aware of it. Someone or a group of people, is trying to head something off."

Councillor Cardano's face took on a worried look, "Chamberlain, you need to ensure your Jovian shock troops at the palace gates are ready for anything."

"I will Councillor, but I suggest you get the Police Force looking into the source of these documents", Chamberlain Sparrow replied, adding, "Something is coming and we need to know what it is and who is behind these documents."

The next day a thousand protesters appeared outside of the palace gates. Many were holding placards with slogans hand painted on them like, *"No more Church tithing", "No more taxes without representation", "Free the Slaves" and "Power to the people"*. It appeared that the documents being distributed by Captain Nightingale had given the people's rising discontent both direction and purpose. The protesters were unarmed and the protests were peaceful. The protesters stayed out front of the palace all day and even set up camp overnight in a large nearby park.

The next day the number of protesters had doubled and people began to set up food stalls to provide food and drinks. They weren't going anywhere and fully intended to stay until the system was changed. The protesters remained peaceful and were not seen as a threat. With each passing day, the number of protesters doubled.

By the seventh day, the number of protesters had reached over sixty five thousand and the Council of Nobles had begun to worry. They convened an emergency meeting at the palace. One by one the twenty Councillors arrived in their stretched transport pods, running the gauntlet of the peaceful protesters outside of the palace gates

Captain Nightingale and General Trask were growing concerned by the number of protesters and especially by the fact, that the protests were ongoing and showed no sign of ending anytime soon.

The General placed a map of Hector Command Central's northern end cap on the table, "The end cap is like a huge fish bowel as you know. I recommend you set up your snipers on these buildings over here and over here. They'll have a good line of sight to those Jovian shock troops inside the palace grounds."

"Are were sure this is necessary General?", the Captain asked.

"I can't predict what will happen Captain, but if those Jovian shock troops open fire on an unarmed crowd, I want your people in placed to put them down", the General replied.

"Well General, we'll be flanking them on either side. If they do start firing on the protesters, we can pick them of from those buildings. As you noted, there will be a clear line of sight", he replied.

"Yes, but let's hope it doesn't come to that Captain", the General replied, noting, "The transition of power in the Aft Trojan Realm was peaceful. We want to happen here for our Realm as well."

Lead Councillor Cardano told the other councillors, "Does anyone have any suggestions on how to disperse these protesters?"

"We could have the Police move in with shields and pain sticks", suggested one Councillor.

"A shield and pain stick charge on unarmed peaceful protesters! That would likely inflame the situation and create an angry mob. That will just make things worse", Councillor Cardano replied.

"We could have people with megaphones surround the protesters, instructing the crowd to disperse", another Councillor suggested.

"Really! Are you deaf Councillor? Did you not hear our people with their megaphones doing precisely that, when you were on your way here?", the Lead Councillor enquired.

"Um. No. I had my headphones on listening to music", the Councillor admitted.

Councillor Cardano rolled his eyes, "We have been doing that for days Councillor. It is simply not working."

"Fear", another Councillor suggested, "Have the Princess's personal shock troops fire into the crowd. That ought to disperse them."

"Another suggestion to turn a peaceful protest into an angry mob", Councillor Cardano replied.

Princess Sophia had been listening, "I like his idea. Fear works! Let my shock troops open fire on them Cardano."

The Chamberlain stepped in, "Your Highness. The protesters outnumber your shock troops sixty five to one. Councillor Cardano is correct in his assessment of the situation Princess."

"Then how about this for a suggestion. Poison their food and water over night. On the morrow, after they eat their breakfast, they'll all be dead", Princess Sophia suggested.

Shocked murmurs erupted around the conference room.

Another Councillor suggested, "Perhaps we should ask to negotiate with their representatives."

Princess Sophia grew angry at this suggestions, "What! Give up my divine right to rule! I'll not have it! I'll not have it I tell you! Poison them all and be done with them!", then in a much calmer voice, "Their corpses will make the most excellent fertiliser for the trees in my gardens."

"No Your Highness. Your Brother, High Prince Heinrich would find that suggestion completely unacceptable", Chamberlain Sparrow explained.

"Yes, yes he would, wouldn't he. My Brother Heinrich spoils all of my fun", Princess Sophia replied before storming out of the conference room.

"Councillor Cardano. Give the Police Commissioner a call. We need to know who represents those protesters. We'll need someone to negotiate with", the Chamberlain instructed.

"Negotiate? Are you sure Chamberlain?", Councillor Cardano questioned.

"Yes Councillor. My primary concern is Princess Sophia's life", the Chamberlain replied, then remarked, "All of you councillors should be thinking about that. That and your own lives. This peaceful protest has the potential to turn into an explosive powder keg."

The twenty councillors in the conference room all took on seriously concerned looks.

On the eighth day of the protest, the number of protesters had more than doubled again. There were now a hundred and fifty thousand protesters outside of the palace gates. The entire protest took on a carnival element, with food vendors and even entertainment. A tent city had popped up in the surrounding park lands providing the protesters with plenty of shelter.

No one was going anywhere. With a hundred and fifty thousand protesters not performing their usual jobs and no end to the protest in sight, Hector Command Central's economy was suffering. Negotiations and a compromise, a Constitutional Principality, were becoming the most likely outcome. Councillor

Cardano urgently awaited representatives of the protesters to negotiate with.

The patience of the crowd however, was growing thin and teenagers at the front of the protest were becoming mischievous. A single young protester, not much more than thirteen years old, armed with nothing more than a home made sling shot, fired a stone at the palace troops. Other teenagers had previously thrown rocks and stones, which had of course fallen well short of the tall palace walls. This teenager, however, had made a sling shot and its reach was much farther.

The Jovian shock trooper felt the stone strike his helmet. It didn't cause him any harm, but he was incensed that anyone would have to audacity to strike him. The shock trooper took careful aim with his pulse rifle, squeezed the trigger and fired. The thirteen year old teenager was struck in the centre of the chest and dropped to the ground dead.

His mother, who was nearby, screamed in horror and ran to her fallen son. His horrified father was quickly by their side and picked up the sling shot. He packed in another stone and then he fired back! The shock trooper took careful aim with his pulse rifle once more and fired again. The father was struck in the face and dropped to the ground dead. Then it was on, the Jovian shock troops opened fire on the unarmed, peaceful protesters, shooting men, women and children at random.

"Chamberlain! Chamberlain! Look!", the Princess called out and pointed to the protesters from the high balcony, in her palace's main tower.

Chamberlain Sparrow looked out from the balcony in horror, "No! This can't be happening!"

"Why not Chamberlain? Finally someone has taken action?", Princess Sophia replied.

The Chamberlain was blunt, "Princess! Your Jovian shock troops are outnumbered a hundred and fifty to one! We'll all be lucky to survive this day."

As the Chamberlain watched the unfolding scene, with shock troops firing into the crowd of unarmed protesters, he noticed shock troops dropping to the ground, apparently dead.

"There Princess, do you see that?", he told the Princess while pointing to a dead shock trooper laying on the ground, "They're taking fire from the flanks, on both their left and their right. They're not using pulse weapons either."

"What are they using Chamberlain?", Princess Sofia asked.

"I'm not sure Princess, but it appears to be old fashioned firearms. Sniper rifles!", Chamberlain Sparrow replied, ordering the Princess, "Get inside away from the balcony before you get shot!"

Chamberlain Sparrow ushered the Princess back into the room and closed the Balcony doors behind them, before getting on the communicator.

"Lock down the palace! I repeat. Lock down the palace!", he ordered the palace guards.

"Lock down the palace Sir?", the palace guard at the other end queried.

"Lock down the palace you fucking moron! There's going to be an angry mob climbing over those palace walls at any moment now", the Chamberlain replied angrily.

"Yes Sir. Right away Sir", the head of the palace guards replied.

Chamberlain Sparrow checked his sabre and his personal side arm, a pulse pistol, then turned to the Princess, "Whatever happens Your Highness, you stay behind me. Hide if you can, but failing that, stay behind me."

"There is nowhere to hide Chamberlain. I never had a panic room built. I never thought I'd need one. This is our first rebellion as you know", the Princess replied.

Chamberlain Sparrow thought to himself, *"No sovereign ever does until it's too damned late."*

Every now and again, the Chamberlain would carefully walk out onto the balcony and check, what was happening below at the palace gates. The crowd of protesters had at first withdrawn from the palace gates and the walls, taking cover much farther away from the firing pulse rifles. The Jovian shock troops were still taking fire from their flanks.

A lot of the shock troops lay dead at the base of the palace walls. Their numbers growing thinner and thinner by the minute. Less than forty minutes after the shock troops had opened fire on the unarmed crowd, their pulse rifles fell silent as the last shock troops was taken out by snipers. Chamberlain Sparrow knew what would follow. He didn't have to wait very long at all.

The crowd of protesters surged forward en masse towards the palace gates. They had been unarmed, except for one teenager with a sling shot. Now they were armed with improvised weapons. Broken chair and table legs, branches torn from trees. Quickly improvised cudgels with which to bludgeon. The angry mob fell upon the palace gates and the Chamberlain knew that those gates would not hold. He walked back into the room and closed the balcony doors behind him.

"Princess Sofia. It's happening now. Remember what I said and stay behind me", the Chamberlain informed Her Highness.

The Chamberlain opened a communications channel to Ganymede Prime and set the feed to continue unattended. It would record everything that transpired from that moment on.

The Chamberlain spoke for the communications feed and those who would receive it.

"This is Chamberlain Sparrow of Hector Command Central. The peaceful protest of the last week or so has been turned into an angry mob. The Jovian shock troops are all dead. The mob has stormed the palace gates. The palace is in lock down and only the palace guards stand between Princess Sophia and the angry mob. The mob is a hundred and fifty thousand strong. If God is willing, perhaps, just perhaps, we will survive."

There were multiple, muffled sounds of smashing glass and timber. It was far below them and difficult to hear from their room, close to the top of the main tower. The smashing sounds continued for many long minutes and then they stopped. Chamberlain Sparrow knew the mob was inside of the palace, as now, there were the sounds of palace guards screaming in their death throes. This was followed by the smashing sounds of vandalism and the looting of the palace below them.

Chamberlain Sparrow looked behind him at the Princess, she was utterly terrified, yet still trying to be brave. A stream of tears began to flow down her pale cheeks. Then there were more sounds from below, as the mob began to ransack the tower. It would not be long now. The Chamberlain braced himself. Sounds outside the room in the corridor indicated that time was short and then the pounding on the locked doors began.

At first the doors held, then on the sixth thrust, the doors were flung to the floor, as the door jambs splintered and all was suddenly silent. Then angry men appeared in the open doorway.

The Chamberlain had already drawn his pulse pistol, "Stay back I warn you", he ordered, adding, "I will shoot anyone who enters this room."

The angry men ignored him and the Chamberlain opened fire, zing, zing and the first two men collapsed to the floor, dead. Zing, zing, zing and there were three more dead. Zing, zing, zing, three more dead, then zing, zing and two more dead. They were getting way too close. Zing, Zing, Zing and more dead men.

The Chamberlain threw aside his pulse pistol and quickly drew his sabre. The nearest men in the front, did their best to take down the Chamberlain, who sadly for them, was an expert swordsmen. He deftly took down five more angry men, before they finally got hold of him.

The strongest man in the group forced the Chamberlain's sabre back upon him and into his gut, piercing straight through his front and back.

As Chamberlain Sparrow slowly crumpled to the floor, he used the last of his strength to beg for Princess Sofia's life.

"Please! Please! I'm begging you! Do not harm Princess Sophia! Please spare the Princess! Spare her life! Have mercy!", he implored the angry men, then his strength was spent, he died.

The angry men then moved towards the Princess, who now in shock was crying uncontrollably. Two burly men grabbed her roughly and held her firmly.

"What do we do now? She is the Princess!", one of the angry men asked.

Another stated quite coldly, "I don't give a flying fuck who she is. Someone has to pay for all of the day's dead."

"Perhaps, but not the Princess. I doubt she gave the order", another man argued, adding, "We should spare her, keep her alive. At least until all of this is all over."

And it looked as if Princess Sophia was going to be spared. Was this to be her lucky day?

A women entered the Princess's room. This very day, she had seen her teenage son shot in the chest and her husband shot in the face. There was not one iota of mercy, to be seen in her visage, "Take Her Highness to the balcony. Let's see if this bitch can fly!", she coldly ordered the group of angry men.

And that was that, kicking and screaming, Princess Sophia was taken to the balcony. The balcony doors were kicked open, as Princess Sophia was dragged to its ornate railing.

"No! No!", Princess Sophia shouted, "No, please, please let me live, please!", she begged, tears flowing freely down her cheeks.

The two burly men then picked up the Princess and kicking and screaming, Princess Sophia was unceremoniously thrown over the balcony's railing. Princess Sophia screamed loudly as she fell. A long wailing scream, until she bounced once off the palace's roof and then fell further to the palace grounds beneath, landing heavily on the grassy lawn, a hundred and eighty feet below.

The angry men then ransacked and looted what had been Princess Sophia's favourite room. The communications feed that Chamberlain Sparrow had started, had recorded everything that had transpired. It continued to record and transmit, right up until the very moment that it was smashed to smithereens during the ransacking.

General Trask, Captain Nightingale and Captain Petrakis had reached the palace. They were there to negotiate with the Council of Nobles, but they arrived far too late. They had watched in horror as Princess Sophia was thrown from her balcony and bounced off the palace roof on her way down to the lawn.

General Trask rushed up to the Princess and checked her pulse. It was weak, very, very, weak. Blood was flowing from the corner of her mouth and blood pooled beneath the Princess's cracked skull. Princess Sophia's body was broken in multiple places and there was simply nothing, nothing at all, that any of them could do.

Princess Sophia looked up at General Trask with very sad, frightened, tearful and accusing eyes. General Trask was determined that Princess Sophia would not die alone. General Trask held Princess Sophia's right hand firmly in his left hand and gently stroked her left cheek with his right hand. Princess Sophia's breathing slowed, becoming shallower and then highly erratic, then at last she took one deep, final breath and then she was gone.

Princess Sophia was dead!

General Trask was very slow to let go of Princess Sophia's right hand. When he did so, he closed the Princess's eyes with his own right hand. General Trask has tears in eyes, real tears.

"Well, this is all kinds of awful", Captain Nightingale noted.

"Well yes, we can't have a Constitutional Principality without Princess Sophia", Captain Petrakis who was truly sorry the Princess was dead, replied, but for now practical matters filled his mind.

"What about one of the other Nobles?", Captain Nightingale suggested.

"You think this is over Captain! By the morrow morning, every noble and their families will all be dead!", General Trask told them in no uncertain terms, "That mob will not stop at one Princess. They want blood and they won't stop until that blood lust is sated."

Captain Petrakis then remarked, "Well then General, we will need to rework that Constitution. As of tonight, it's looking like the Fore Trojan Realm, is going to be a Constitutional Republic!"

Hector has fallen!

25. Heavy is the Loss

Prince Leopold had once again, urgently commuted from his home on Io Prime, in his own Ionian Realm to his Brother's Realm and its capital Ganymede Prime. This was the second emergency meeting in less than a month and Prince Leopold still remembered the last one. In that meeting Prince Leopold had heard, how his Sister Princess Luisa had lost her divine right to rule and her domain was transitioning into a Constitutional Principality.

"What else could possibly go wrong?", was the thought running through his mind.

"Brother Leopold. It's good to see you again", the High Prince greeted, then he noted, "I know you don't want to be here, but the news I have is quite dire."

Prince Leopold took his seat as his oldest Brother, the High Prince held up a data crystal.

"I have received this data feed directly from our Sister, Princess Sophia's realm", High Prince Heinrich told the room as his face took on the most serious of looks, any of them had ever seen.

Princess Sophia's representative, Kittens, was in particular, very silent.

The High Princes inserted the data crystal into its receptacle and began to play the sound feed. There was no video, just the sound feed, as transmitted from Princess Sophia's palace.

Everyone in the conference room listened as Chamberlain Sparrow explained the situation. The peaceful protests, the angry mob. The overrunning of the palace defences and eventually the palace itself. They all heard the muffled sounds of smashing glass and timber. The sounds of vandalism and the looting of the palace. Then eventually they heard the mob reach the room, where the Princess and the Chamberlain were holed up.

Then they heard the doors of the room burst open and Chamberlain Sparrow's clear warning to the crowd. This was followed by the sounds of his pulse pistol firing multiple times, too many for them to count. Then they heard the deft slashing of his sabre and finally, as the mob delivered it's death blow, they heard the Chamberlain's last words pleading for Princess Sophia to be spared.

After this, they all heard the quick chilling debate, about whether to spare the Princess or not. Then right when it looked like Princess Sophia would live, the cold, harsh words of a women demanding she be thrown to her death. This was followed by the sounds of Princess Sophia kicking and screaming. Then the sounds of the balcony doors being kicked wide open and then finally, the sounds of Princess Sophia being thrown to her death.

Everyone in the room was in shock. Prince Leopold himself, had known something really bad must have happened, for his Brother to summon him to Ganymede Prime, but this, this was worse than he could ever have imagined. His other Brother, Prince Wulfric, his face had taken on a ashen appearance, pale, almost ghostly grey, his eyes wide, with both shock and terror.

"Sophia is dead! No, no, no, she can't be dead!", Prince Wulfric remarked, "How can Sophia be dead?", he questioned weakly, he and his Sister had been very close.

High Prince Heinrich confirmed, "Yes. Our dear Sister, Princess Sophia is dead!"

Prince Wulfric questioned, "When I return home to Callisto Prime, are my people going to throw me off a balcony too?"

"Oh crap! Brother Wulfric's glitching again", Prince Leopold noted.

Prince Wulfric replied angrily, "I am not glitching!", then more quietly, "I am not glitching. I am not glitching", he was shaking his head and beginning to look pathetic.

Prince Wulfric suddenly stood up, his face quickly turning an angry red, his mood rapidly changing, "Our Sister is fucking Dead! Why is he still alive? Why is he still alive?", he was pointing to Princess Sophia's representative, Kittens.

Then without warning, Prince Wulfric drew his sabre and before anyone could move, he thrust it across the conference room table and straight into representative Kittens chest. Kittens looked down at the blade, deeply embedded in his chest. He looked back up at Prince Wulfric with a horrified look in his eyes, as Wulfric twisted the blade. Then as Wulfric withdrew his blade, Kittens slumped forward onto the conference table with a slight, dull thud.

Instinctively the High Prince pushed himself and his chair back away from Prince Wulfric. Just as instinctively, Prince Leopold was on his feet. Quickly the young Prince rounded the conference room table and with sabre in hand confronted his Brother Wulfric. The pair squared off against each other.

Prince Wulfric's face took on a manic visage, as he thrust his sabre at Prince Leopold. There was the clash of steel as Prince Leopold parried the thrusting blade. Thrice more Prince Wulfric thrust his sabre towards his Brother and each time, there was the sound of steel clashing, as Prince Leopold parried the attacks.

Prince Leopold then took a disarming action, using his sabre to manipulate Prince Wulfric's. There was the sound of the scraping of steel as Leopold's blade spiralled around Wulfric's, leveraging it out of Wulfric's hand. Prince Wulfric's sabre flew to his right and embedded itself deeply in the conference room wall. Disarmed, Prince Wulfric's manic state of mind glitched yet again and his face now displayed fear, uncertainty and doubt.

Prince Leopold pressed the advantage, using his sabre to corral and manoeuvre his Brother Wulfric up against the wall. Leopold pinned Wulfric to the wall with the point of his sabre pressing ever so gently against the base of Wulfric's throat.

"Leopold! Stand down! Stand down now!", the High Prince shouted.

"I would dearly love to Brother Heinrich, but not before our dear Brother Wulfric here is restrained!", came Prince Leopold's curt reply.

High Prince Heinrich quickly looked around the room, a dead man lay slumped on the conference room table, a sabre was embedded in the wall, his Brother Wulfric was beginning to glitch once again and starting to look manic. This was a very dangerous situation.

"Agreed Brother", the High Prince replied, before looking directly at General Snide, who simply nodded in silent understanding.

General Snide quickly walk to the conference room door and opened it. He talked to two of the guards outside the door and then quickly re-entered the room. The guards faces showed a degree of shock at the scene before them.

"Restrain Prince Wulfric and take him into custody", General Snide ordered.

The two guards looked to the High Prince, "Do as the General ordered", he confirmed, adding,"Be firm, but be gentle. He is my Brother."

The two guards approached Prince Wulfric from either side and took him into custody, hand cuffing his hands. Prince Leopold withdrew his sabre, replaced it in its scabbard and walked back to his seat before sitting down.

With Prince Wulfric in custody, one of guards requested further instructions, "Your Majesty?"

"Take Prince Wulfric to the palace infirmary", the High Prince ordered.

Then the two guards left the room with Prince Wulfric in hand cuffs.

Prince Valdamar look at his elder Brother, "Heinrich, he is getting worse Brother!"

"You don't think I know that Valdamar?", the High Prince asked rhetorically, then looked to General Snide, "Have Princess Matilda pick up Wulfric from our infirmary. Let her know what's happened here. Those two guards are now assigned permanently to Prince Wulfric and his Wife. For the Princess's protection."

"I'm already on it Your Majesty", General Snide replied.

The High Prince looked at representative Kittens corpse, "General Snide. Have Kittens body taken care of as well."

"Working on that now as well Your Majesty", General Snide replied.

Prince Valdamar noted, "Our Brother Wulfric cannot be in charge of our other defences."

"I know that Valdamar!", the High Prince replied sharply.

Prince Valdamar looked over the table to Prince Leopold and then nodded to High Prince Heinrich. The High Prince looked to Prince Leopold and everyone else at the table followed his gaze. Everyone was looking at Prince Leopold.

Prince Leopold responded, "No! No! I am not military! I do not want the job!"

Prince Valdamar was insistent, "Brother. You could swap Realms with Brother Wulfric. You take over Callisto, Wulfric takes over Io."

The thought horrified Prince Leopold, his Brother Wulfric in charge of the Ionian Realm, after all of the reforms and other works that had been put in place recently.

"Hell no!", he thought to himself, then stated, "No. I respectfully decline the position."

"And if I deny you the right to decline?", High Prince Heinrich questioned.

"Brother. Then I will refuse the position!", Prince Leopold told him in no uncertain terms.

The High Prince shook his head.

General Tarzan noted, "Your Majesty. There is no need for Prince Leopold to replace his Brother. Prince Wulfric has a number of very capable Generals and Commanders, under his command."

Matthew stepped in, still slightly in shock at the corpse still slumped across the table, just to the Prophet's left, "Yes Your Majesty. Prince Wulfric's command staff are very capable people."

The High Prince looked at General Tarzan and then at Captain Murphy, he then looked back at his Brother, Prince Leopold, who shook his head to confirm his position on the matter.

"So be it. Prince Wulfric is henceforth relieved of all duties and hereby placed on medical leave. The Prince's command staff are to take over the Jovian Realms outer defences", the High Prince commanded, then added, "The command staff are to send me bi-weekly reports."

While this was being discussed a gurney was taking away representative Kittens body. There was a document file, now bloodied, laying on the table underneath it.

"Prophet. Please peruse that file. Then we can discuss its contents. I believe it is extremely pertinent", High Prince Heinrich ordered.

The Prophet carefully picked up the blood stained document file and replied, "Yes Your Majesty", before he began to read through it.

After several long minutes the Prophet began to explain its contents to the others, "There are two documents in the file. One is very similar to what we've seen before. It is a transition manifesto", he informed them all.

"A transition manifesto?", Prince Valdamar asked.

"Very similar to the one we've already seen from Princess Luisa's Aft Trojan Realm", the Prophet replied, explaining, "It has all the same provisions for the separation of church and state, changes to the tithing laws, allowing for new churches and freeing of the Slaves etc."

"So what's different about it?", Princess Luisa's representative Callthrope asked.

"Well, as Princess Sophia is now deceased and being that the Nobles and their families are also all deceased as well, there cannot be a Constitutional Principality", the Prophet informed the room.

Still in shock, hearing about Princess Sophia's death, the shock was increased significantly, by hearing that all of the Fore Trojan Nobles and their families were dead as well.

The Prophet looked around the table at the shocked faces, "The Fore Trojan Realm will be transitioning into a Constitutional Republic", he paused for a moment, then continued, "Two houses. An elected lower house, the House of Peoples Representatives and an elected Senate. They're going to have a President, who will be elected by the House of Peoples Representatives from the members of the Senate."

"So the Fore Trojan Realm is declaring independence as well", Prince Valdamar summed up.

"Yes. Your Highness. That is the gist of it", the Prophet confirmed.

"What's the second document?", Princess Luisa's representative Callthrope enquired.

The Prophet opened the document, then faltered, he passed the document to Callthrope.

"Okay. Let's see", Callthrope began as he perused the second document, "It's from a General Trask. He says their investigation revealed, that the riot started when a Jovian shock trooper shot a teenager in the chest and then followed up by shooting the boy's father in the face. That's what turned, what had been up to that point, a peaceful protest into a rebellion."

"So this all went south because one of Sophia's own personal shock troops lost their nerve?", Prince Valdamar questioned.

"Yes Your Highness. Based on what General Trask has stated, yes", Callthrope confirmed.

Callthrope continued, "General Trask and two of his Captains were on their way to the palace, when everything, 'turned south', as you put it Your Highness. They arrived too late to save the Princess. They could only watch as she fell to her death. Princess Sophia did not die straight away and they comforted her as best as they could, until she passed on."

"Being thrown off a balcony is hardly falling to her death", Prince Valdamar dryly stated.

"Yes. I can only assume that they only saw her falling, not the actual act of being thrown Your Highness", Callthrope replied, continuing, "The two men who threw the Princess over the balcony are already in custody. The women who instigated the Princess's murder was found hanging from a tree in the palace grounds later the next day. It was her son and her husband that had been shot by the Jovian shock trooper. She hung herself it seems. Suicide."

Callthrope paused, to let what he had divulged sink in then continued, "Princess Sophia's body is being preserved and will be repatriated to Ganymede Prime, along with her murderers, so that they can be brought to justice. They are still investigating the deaths of the Nobles and their families."

"Well then. At least our Sister's murderers will be brought to justice", the High Prince noted.

"Brother Heinrich. We now have two realms declaring independence! We simply cannot let this stand", Prince Valdamar remarked.

"What would you have us do Valdamar? If we could not afford to send a single ship to the Aft Trojan Realm, we certainly don't have any ships spare for the Fore Trojan Realm either", the High Prince replied to his Brother.

"For the moment we keep this out of the news feeds Your Majesty. When this war is over, we can go and take them both back", Matthew suggested.

"Yes Your Majesty", General Tarzan agreed, "We can take them both back after this war is over."

"So noted", the High Prince replied, "We'll take them both back after this war is over!"

There was a commotion in the corridor outside the conference room, then the door swung open wide and an angry, very upset Princess Matilda stormed in, her blue eyes streaming with tears.

"Your Majesty", the Princess addressed the High Prince almost rudely, "Your Brother, my Husband is a mess! He needs to be removed from all of his responsibilities, so he can recover."

The High Prince raised his hand to silence her, "Matilda. I've already done that. Wulfric's command staff will take over his duties."

Princess Matilda placed her hands on her hips and looked around the room. There was a large pool of blood on the table in front of where Kittens had been sitting and Prince Wulfric's sabre was still embedded in the conference room wall.

"What happened?", the Princess asked, "I knew something bad happened, but what exactly?"

"Wulfric just found out his Sister Sophia was murdered in her palace", the High Prince replied.

"They were really close!", the Princess replied, "That would have set him right off."

"And it did Princess. It most certainly did. Heavy is the loss and we are all feeling it. Our Brother Wulfric especially so", High Prince Heinrich replied, adding, "Now Wulfric is going to need your gentle hand and all of your skills to bring him back to us."

"I'll do what I can Your Majesty", Princess Matilda agreed.

"Good then. This meeting is adjourned. General Snide, please have this room cleaned up", the High Prince commanded and then closed the meeting.

"Yes Your Majesty. I've already arranged it", General Snide replied.

26. Callisto - Lagrangian Point Four

On the approach to Jupiter, General Stanton and Fleet Captain Carmichael discussed the formation of the enemy's dreadnoughts, that were ahead of them and in their path.

"There's a hell of a lot of them and they are quite well spread out", the General noted.

"If we are going to meet them, we'll need to spread out as well. Maybe put our fleet into a flying cone formation", Captain Carmichael suggested.

"Whatever we do, I'm all for keeping our passive cloaking on", the General recommended.

"Yes. We'll definitely do that. Our passive cloaking should mess with their targeting systems", Captain Carmichael agreed.

Lieutenant Adjutant Blixen noted, "General. Captain. The enemy fleet is positioned much farther forward than I would have expected. They're almost stationary as well."

"They're expecting us to go toe to toe with them, like in some epic space battle", Captain Carmichael replied, then requested, "Lieutenant. Do the math. Given the enemy's position, just how fast will will be going when reach them."

The Lieutenant pressed a few keys on his grip's virtual keyboard then smiled, replying, "We will be at full speed when we cross their position Sir. For orbital insertion and interception of Callisto L4, we'll actually begin reverse thrusting after we have tackled the enemy fleet Sir."

Captain Carmichael chuckled, "It looks like, they don't know what we know!", then he asked, "Lieutenant. Is their current position consistent with a Ganymede L5 interception?"

The Lieutenant pressed a few keys on his grip's virtual keyboard once again and replied, "Yes Captain. The enemy fleet is perfectly positioned for that scenario Sir."

"The Gods are on our side General!", Captain Carmichael informed him while laughing.

"The Gods Captain? In what way?", General Stanton questioned.

"Our enemy, does not know what we know General. They have positioned their main defensive fleet, thinking we're making a run straight for Ganymede Prime, at Ganymede L5. They think, we're making a decapitation run General", the Captain informed him.

"But that's not the plan Captain. We're going after their installations at Callisto L4", General Stanton replied.

"Yes General. They don't know, that we know, where all of their military installations are", Captain Carmichael replied, noting, "This is a gift from the Gods General. Our enemy has seriously miscalculated."

"Miscalculated?", the General queried.

"They are expecting us to reverse thrust hard, for a Ganymede L5 intercept. We would have met their fleet at much lower speeds and we'd have an epic space battle. Instead, this is going to be very much like our previous encounter", Captain Carmichael explained.

"They're stationary and we'll hit them at speed, hard and fast", the General understood.

"Yes General. It will be very similar to our last encounter. A quick kill, after which, we push on to Callisto L4", Captain Carmichael confirmed.

Lieutenant Blixen stepped in, "General. Captain. We don't even need to destroy them."

That caught the General completely by surprise, "How so Lieutenant? Do you have a plan?"

"Yes General. It's almost the same plan as our last encounter", the Lieutenant began explaining, "We use our stand off weapons first as we approach. So first the electromagnetic rail guns, followed by the hyper resonant disrupters as we get closer. We'll be targeting their dreadnought's bridges."

"So we're taking out their command and control, yes?", the General asked.

"Affirmative General. As we pass through their formation, we then use or pulse cannons and phased laser arrays to take out their engines, drive units and thrusters", the Lieutenant continued.

"No missiles?", the General enquired.

"No need General. Why waste our missiles and torpedoes, when we can save those for later", Lieutenant Blixen replied.

"General. If appears my Lieutenant's plan is to leave those dreadnoughts dead in space", Captain Carmichael summed up, "They'll be neutralised without the need to destroy them."

"Yes Captain. I see that. So Lieutenant, your plan is to cut off their heads and slice off their legs", General Stanton replied.

"That is the plan General", Lieutenant Blixen confirmed.

"Let's do that then. It should give the Horridians quite a shock. Slice and dice their defence fleet, leaving their ships dead in space. Then slip on through to Callisto L4 and their main outer defence installations. They won't know what hit them!", General Stanton summed up.

When the combined Earth Defence Force and L5 Colonial Fleets finally came into range of the defending Jovian Forces, the dreadnought Captains were horrified. Not only was their enemy descending upon them, at speed and in a loose conical configuration. Their passive cloaking made their heavy cruisers appear inky black against the darkness of space. This was going to make their targeting extremely difficult. None of them had expected this. Surely the enemy needed to reverse thrust hard to achieve orbital insertion, to make a run on Ganymede Prime. The current Jovian defensive posture was completely wrong!

As planned, the heavy cruisers first opened up with their electromagnetic rail guns, targeting the bridges of the enemy's dreadnoughts. Then when they were much closer, they opened fire with their hyper resonant disrupters. Their explosive rounds struck first, furiously blowing holes straight through the bridge's hull plating on the enemy dreadnoughts. Brilliant red disrupter beams finished the job, ripping through hull plating like a hot knife through butter.

The Jovian dreadnoughts were slow to react at first and were struck severely. Dreadnought bridges erupted under the onslaught and exploded outwards with brilliant, but brief bursts of light and flame. By the time heavy cruisers started passing through the enemy's lines, command and control within the Jovian fleet was completely non existent.

The combined Earth and L5 fleet opened fire with pulse cannons and phased laser arrays, targeting the dreadnought engines, drive units and thrusters. Blue pulses of plasma and blue beams of intense, coherent light struck hard, blowing huge holes and ripping hull plating apart. A good many dreadnoughts exploded in brilliant balls of light, with debris flying every which way. Those they were still intact were complete dead in space.

Following the encounter, every heavy cruiser in the combined Earth and L5 fleets, went into reverse thrust mode and began the process of slowing down for orbital insertion. Their target Callisto L4 and the military installations in that region. Rearward scans of the Jovian defences revealed a scene of utter devastation. Half the Jovian dreadnoughts were simply gone, destroyed by the onslaught. The other half were floating dead in space, their threat completely neutralised.

Lieutenant Blixen remarked allowed, "Whoa! That was intense!"

"Yes it was Lieutenant. Now get me my damage report. Ship wide and fleet wide", Captain Carmichael ordered, "I need to know how we fared."

"On it Captain!", the Lieutenant replied.

"And Lieutenant. Send an encrypted message to the Venusian fleet. Tell them we've punched through the Jovian defences and we are on track for our primary objective", the Captain ordered.

Captain Carmichael then reviewed the latest rearward scans, *"Sweat Mother of God. We only wanted to disable them, but ended up destroying half their fleet"*, he thought to himself, *"We caught them way off guard!"*

"I can't believe we lost so few ships", the Captain noted as he read through the damage reports.

"They weren't expecting our blitzkrieg tactics Captain", Lieutenant Blixen informed him.

"They certainly weren't prepared for what hit them, that's for sure", the Captain agreed, cautiously adding, "We caught them way off guard this time. At Callisto L4, they might be be ready and waiting for us."

"Then Captain, I'd better come up with a bloody good plan", the Lieutenant replied.

"You do that Lieutenant, you do that", the Captain agreed.

"And Captain. I've received a reply from the Venusian flagship", Lieutenant Blixen noted.

"What does it say?", Captain Carmichael asked.

"Message acknowledged. Well done! We are on track for our primary objective as well. We will link up at the rendezvous point as scheduled", Lieutenant Blixen read out the message.

"Well, they're confident Lieutenant", Captain Carmichael noted.

"Yes Sir. So are we Sir", the Lieutenant agreed.

General Stanton was back on the screen once again, as the combined fleet began its approach to Callisto L and its military installations.

"General. You're finally going to get your epic space battle", Captain Carmichael commented.

"Just so long as we all survive it", the General replied, "I assume your clever Lieutenant has this all planned out perfectly Captain."

"It's a good plan General. I trust my Lieutenant's judgement", Captain Carmichael confirmed.

"Okay then let's hear it", the General requested.

"They may or may not suspect we're heading their way", Lieutenant Blixen started, "We'll find that out soon enough. I've recommended running dark, passive cloaking and thrusters in stealth mode. That should make it hard to pinpoint our ships."

"I agree. Anything that makes our detection difficult is a bonus", the General replied.

"We will need good forward scans of the entire Callisto L4 region in advance, to know precisely what we're dealing with", Lieutenant Blixen noted.

"I think between your people and mine Lieutenant, we'll have that covered", the General replied.

"We'll send out our wisps. General, you'll send out your Switch Blades", the Lieutenant informed him, "If the Gods are on our side, it will be like they just appeared out of nowhere. Then our interceptors take on their capital ships at close range, causing as much damage as possible."

"Epic battle is right. If they suspect we're heading their way, they'll be onto us straight away", General Stanton noted, "If not, we'll have the upper hand."

"That was my thought as well General", the Lieutenant agreed, "Once our interceptors have done their work, our combined fleet of cruisers will all appear. Our interceptors will withdraw from their capital ships and track down any enemy interceptors. Then we'll hit them with the rail guns at distance and then with our disrupters as we close in."

"I like the concept of targeting their bridges Lieutenant", the General noted, "Knocking out their command and control should be a priority."

"Yes General. I was going to recommend that", Lieutenant Blixen noted, "If all goes well, we'll punch through their lines and hit their engines and thrusters with our pulse cannons and phased laser arrays. We'll save our missiles and torpedoes for their military infrastructure. I'm recommending we use warheads in the two to five megaton range. Our torpedoes are already being setup for action."

"I'll get my people working on that straight away Lieutenant", the General agreed.

Captain Carmichael stepped in, "I'll have the Lieutenant send you the details General."

"I look forward to seeing them Captain.", General Stanton replied.

The next day the combined fleet approached the enemy and launched their interceptors.

"General Nagorno Sir. Our scanners are detecting something unusual Sir", Lieutenant Barkley informed General Nagorno.

"Can you define unusual Lieutenant?", General Nagorno requested.

"Yes Sir. We're detecting a lot of interceptors on approach Sir", Lieutenant Barkley informed.

"Ours? How many?", the General barked out questions.

"Ours? No Sir, definitely not ours. How many? There are thousands Sir! Thousands!", the Lieutenant replied.

"Commander Shasta. Sound the general alarm. Get our Bat Wings out there immediately", General Nagorno commanded,

"Lieutenant. What are they?", the General enquired.

"Wisps and switch blades Sir", Lieutenant Barkley replied.

"Where the hell did they come from?", the General quietly asked, it was a rhetorical question.

Lieutenant Barkley answered anyway, "We're not detecting any other ships Sir. It's like they just appeared out of nowhere Sir."

Meanwhile on the bridge of the heavy cruiser Spartan, a smiling Lieutenant Blixen remarked, "Captain Sir. The enemy appears to be slow to respond. I think we have caught them with their pants down Sir!"

"Have they detected out fleet?", Captain Carmichael asked.

"No sign that they have yet", Lieutenant Blixen replied.

"Excellent. We'll let our interceptors do their work, then we'll step in and wipe out what's left", Captain Carmichael commented, he too was smiling.

The swarm of thousands of wisps and switch blades fell upon their targets. A mixed bag of hundreds of Jovians ships ranging from dreadnoughts, through to destroyers and corvettes. The wisps and switch blades got up close and personal, skin dancing along the enemy ship's hulls.

Wisps firing their two, twin particle beams. Red death rays issued forth and shredded titanium hull plating like a hot knife through butter. Switch blades with their two, twin pulse cannons, blasting brilliant blue balls of plasma into the hulls of the enemy's ships with great affect.

The enemy's ships returned fire with the pulse cannons and particle beams, to no avail, as the attacking interceptors were hugging them too closely with their skin dancing. It wasn't until the enemy had launched its own interceptors, Bat wings into the fray, that the enemy's capital ships received some respite from the onslaught.

Heavily armed, the Bat Wings fired their four front mounted lasers, their two fin mounted pulse cannons and two wing mounted particle beams at their assailants. Blues beams of intense coherent light, along side intense red particle beams and blue pulses of super heated plasma issued forth, driving back the wisps and the switch blades.

The epic space battle that General Stanton so expected and wanted, unfolded before his eyes on the screen in front of him, descending into a dog fight, in which the outcome was not yet clear. The heavily armed bat wings were taking their toll on his switch blades and Captain Carmichael's wisps. Bat wings, wisps and switch blades were exploding across the battle zone, in brief, yet brilliant balls of light and flame. The Captain was also watching the scene unfold before him on his screen and both men were holding their nerve.

Lieutenant Blixen remarked, "We are winning Captain. It's not readily apparent yet, but our interceptors reaped havoc on their capital ships. Their bat wings were too slow to launch Sir. They were caught off guard and although they have more fire power, we have vastly superior numbers."

"We are losing quite a few ships Lieutenant", Captain Carmichael noted.

"Yes Captain, but my scans show them losing three interceptors to our one", the Lieutenant reported, advising, "Within ten minutes, we will have decisively won this round Sir."

"I'm glad you're good with numbers Blixen. I'm counting lost pilots and the letters, that I will have to write their families", Captain Carmichael informed him.

Just as Lieutenant Blixen had predicted, within ten minutes the enemy's bat wings had began to withdraw and their own wisps and switch blades had the upper hand and began to chase their foes.

"Lieutenant. Order our interceptors to break off the pursuit and concentrate on their capital ships. We need to hammer them even harder", Captain Carmichael ordered.

Lieutenant Hans Blixen replied, "Aye Captain. The order is issued."

Lieutenant Barkley caught the General's attention, "General Sir. We've just detected the enemy fleet. They're dark Sir. They'll be hard to see and even harder to target."

"Numbers Barkley! Numbers! How many?", General Nagorno asked.

"Over six hundred and fifty Sir. Both Earth and L5 heavy cruisers Sir", the Lieutenant replied.

"Where in the blazes did they come from?", General Nagorno asked rhetorically, "Our intel said they'd strike Ganymede Prime! How the hell did they even know we had bases here?"

Commander Shasta replied, "General. It appears our enemy's know more about us than we thought. They punched straight through to us here and that means they had foreknowledge."

"Commander. Send word to Ganymede Prime. They need to know", the General commanded.

As the combined fleet approached closer to the enemy, Captain Carmichael ordered their interceptors to step aside. The next order was to target the bridges of the enemy's capital ships with their electromagnet rail guns. Explosive filled round peppered the dreadnoughts, the destroyers and corvettes without mercy. Hull plating was batted, pierced and shattered. Explosion rippled across the bridge zones of the enemy's capital ships.

Then as the combined fleet drew closer, the order went out to target the bridges of the enemy's capital ships with their hyper resonant disrupters. The onslaught was devastating, with ship's bridges exploding into space. Some of the enemy's ships exploded in their entirety. The enemy fleet was now headless, without any command and control.

The final order was issued, pulse cannons and phased laser arrays to target the enemy ship's engines and thrusters. Blue pulses of super heated plasma issued forth, brilliant blue beams of intense light issues forth. It was shit show for the Jovians and the enemy's fleet was left in tatters, with many ships destroyed and what was left, dead in space.

Panic set in, at the all the military installations of Callisto L4. General Nagorno sent out the order to evacuate. There was nothing more to be done. The Jovian outer defences had been outclassed, out gunned and out thought. They had no defences left at all. The enemy's emergency escape shuttles began launching, as the Earth's and L5's combined fleets continued approaching. The surviving wisps and switch blades returned to their mother ships in victory.

"Should we give them time to evacuate Captain?", Lieutenant Blixen asked.

"By all means Lieutenant. There's no sense slaughtering the defeated", Captain Carlson agreed.

The order went out for the fleet to slow their approach, so that their defeated enemy could evacuate their installations. This did not go down well with General Stanton.

General Stanton was on the screen within seconds, "What the hell is going on Captain Carmichael? Why are we not pressing our advantage?", the General questioned.

"They are defeated General. There is no point in turning this into a slaughter", Captain Carmichael replied.

"Did they think of that, when they bombed innocent men, women and children back on the Earth with nuclear warheads!", the General screamed back at him.

"We are not here for revenge General. We have won. Let them evacuate", the Captain implored.

General Stanton turned to one of his officers and then back to the screen, "There! It is done!"

Lieutenant Blixen remarked, "I'm detecting multiple missile launches Sir. The Earth's cruisers have fired on the Jovian installations", as the communications line to the Goliath dropped out.

"Lieutenant! Bridge crew officers! We will all record what just happened in our official logs", Captain Carmichael ordered, "Whatever our personal feelings are, General Stanton has just committed a war crime. A crime against humanity and it must be recorded as such."

One by one, the Earth fleet's missiles struck their targets. The Jovian military installations of Callisto L4 were ripped apart by nuclear warheads, with yields of two to five megatons. The evacuation was still in progress and less than ten percent of the Jovian personnel had escaped.   Massive O'Neil style cylinders and Bernal style spheres, all military installations, exploded in immense, brilliant balls of blue light. The scene of the carnage was unsightly and at the end of all the destruction, all that remained, were hulks of twisted, mangled and irradiated metal.

Callisto L4 was no more, a destroyed ruination of the once mighty Jovian Realms.

27. Europa - Lagrangian Point Four

Fleet Captain Felix Philo of the Venusian heavy cruiser, Valour, asked his Lieutenant Adjutant, Rubik Fletcher as to the status of the Earth and L5 fleets.

"Captain. They'll be striking their primary target any minute now", Rubik replied.

"And we'll be striking ours not long after", the Captain replied, adding, "I like the terminology they used, *'punched through the Jovian defences.'* Let's do the same here."

"Captain?", Lieutenant Fletcher queried.

"Torpedoes Fletcher. We'll hit their capital ships with low yield tactical atomic warheads. Four per ship, two kilotons a piece should do it. No slowing down, we'll hit them hard and fast, then loop back around and mop up with our interceptors.", Captain Philo explained.

The Lieutenant checked the latest surveillance scans, "They have nothing in the Europa L4 zone larger than a destroyer Captain. Four per ship will be overkill Sir."

"Some of our torpedoes might get intercepted Lieutenant. Better to be safe than sorry", the Captain replied, then queried, "Have they detected us yet?"

"Our fleet is running in stealth mode Captain. Passive cloaking is online", the Lieutenant replied as he continued checking over the surveillance scans, "They don't know we're here Sir. If the reports from the colonial cruiser Spartan are anything to go by, their entire defensive posture was based around us converging for a decapitation strike on Ganymede Prime."

"Then they won't know what hit them Lieutenant", Captain Felix Philo replied.

The sleek ships of the Venusian fleet approached ever so closer to the enemy installations of the Europan L4 zone. Unlike the triangular wedge designs of the Colonial fleet cruisers or the rectangular wedge designs of the Earth Defence Force cruisers, Venusian cruisers were long, slender and streamlined. To pretty to be practical, the Earth Defence Force personnel would joke.

The personnel of the Colonial fleet, being true spacers however, knew different. Venusian cruisers had slender hulls, with titanium hull plating more than twice as thick as other ships and that hull plating was well coated in plasteel.

Currently running dark, their passive cloaking having turned the hull of their ships, a deep midnight black, they would be difficult to track and target against the blackness of space. The passive cloaking was relatively new, having been shared with the Venusians by L5s Colonial fleet, as was the stealth thruster technology.

However, the Venusians had something else, they'd innovated and added a twist of their own. Their passive cloaking could reverse and turn the hulls of their ships into a brilliant reflective, mirror like surfaces. That combined with their upgraded defence shields, would given them an edge.

Lieutenant Tasman checked over his scope, "General. Commander. We have bogies approaching us fast. Very fast Sir."

"Bogies Lieutenant?", General Rogers questioned.

"Yes Sir. They've just appeared out of nowhere", the Lieutenant replied.

"What are they Lieutenant?", Commander Selassie asked.

Lieutenant Tasman quickly checked their silhouettes against known ships, "Venusian heavy cruisers Sir and they're coming in really, really fast."

"Scramble the bat wings Commander. Get them out there", the General ordered.

"Yes Sir General. Scrambling our bat wings", the Commander replied.

"Lieutenant. How many cruisers do they have?", the General asked.

"Over three hundred General", the Lieutenant informed him, adding, "and they look. I don't know, shiny, almost like mirrors."

"Shiny?", Commander Selassie queried.

"Yes Sir. It's like their hull plating is made of mirrors", the Lieutenant replied, adding, "They were midnight black, then in the blink of an eye, they became mirror-like."

"I'm more concerned with how they knew we were here. The big brass were expecting a decapitation attack on Ganymede Prime. They shouldn't even know we're here Lieutenant", General Rogers commented.

"General Sir. They're not even slowing down. They'll be past us before our bat wings can intercept them", Lieutenant Tasman informed the General.

"What the hell are they playing at?", the General asked of no one in particular, "Lieutenant, tell me our fleet is ready to meet them?"

"Our fleet is on the move General. The enemy is going way too fast, they won't be able to intercept them Sir", the Lieutenant advised, then with a shocked look on his face, "The enemy has launched missiles Sir."

"Commander! Get word to our fleet. This is a fly by kill shot!", the General ordered.

Commander Selassie quickly hailed the fleet, "Hailing all ships! Hailing all ships! Missiles inbound! Repeat missiles inbound! Take immediate evasive action! Repeat, take immediate evasive action! Hailing all bat wings! Hailing all bat wings. Intercept the enemy's missiles! Repeat intercept the enemy's missiles!"

The Lieutenant watched his scopes as the bat wings made a mad dash to intercept the Venusian Torpedoes. Some of them were intercepted, many of them were not. The ships of the Jovian inner defence fleet took evasive action. The torpedoes, however, had already locked onto their targets and would not be easily deterred. As the Lieutenant watched, the scenes of horror unfolded.

Each bat wing that took down a torpedo, found itself engulfed in a bright flash of light and then, a huge erupting orange ball of heat from a two kiloton warhead and was itself destroyed. Wide eyed, the Lieutenant looked up at the General and the Commander.

"What is it Lieutenant?", the General asked.

"Those missiles are armed with tactical nukes Sir", the Lieutenant informed him.

"Tactical nukes!", the General exclaimed, then asked, "Have they targeted us?"

"No Sir. Only our fleet", the Lieutenant replied, then check his scopes once more.

One by one the torpedoes reached their targets. Many had been taken out by bat wing interceptors, but most had gotten through. Destroyers, frigates, corvettes, the type of ship mattered not. When struck by a two kiloton tactical nuke or two, the target was obliterated, without exception. There were literally hundreds of Jovian ships and many, many more nukes.

The massive explosions covered a vast area of Europa L4's ship staging grounds and this was not only visible to the Lieutenant's scopes, but also clearly visible to all of the military installations of Europa L4. Huge O'Neil style cylindrical and Bernal sphere style installations, clearly the carnage of the Jovian inner defence fleet was visible to all of Europa L4's colonial occupants.

"General Sir. Our personnel are beginning to panic", Commander Selassie advised.

"Noted Commander", the General replied, then turning to the Lieutenant, "Where's the enemy fleet Lieutenant? Where are the Venusians?"

"They've passed us by Sir. Their trajectory indicates, that they will swing back and pass by us again", the lieutenant advised.

The General made the hard decision, "Commander Selassie. Call an emergency evacuation."

"General?", the Commander queried.

"No time to waste Commander. That was their fly by kill shot and it was successful. Their next run will be to mop up what's left. That's us, so we all need to leave now", the General replied.

The Commander nodded his head, "Yes Sir. I'll organise the emergency evacuation now Sir."

The klaxons began sounding, the emergency warnings started broadcasting and one by one, the emergency transport shuttles began leaving the military installations.

The Venusian fleet was still on its way out, prior to looping back and they were easily able to detect the evacuation in progress at Europa L4's military installations.

Lieutenant Adjutant Rubik Fletcher looked at the Captain smiling, "Sir this battle is all but over. We have our enemy on the run."

Fleet Captain Felix Philo smiled and replied, "Let's take our time looping back Lieutenant. I want as many of their personnel as possible evacuated before we obliterate our targets."

"Yes Sir. I'll send word to our ships", the Lieutenant replied, then asked, "I wonder how things went for the combine fleet at Callisto L4?"

"We'll find out soon enough Lieutenant. Maintain communications silence until we've mopped up here", the Captain replied.

The Venusian fleet followed its trajectory and looped back around to the Europan L4 military installations. They were rapidly approaching the huge O'Neil style cylindrical and Bernal sphere style installations, so they began carefully scanning them, noting that no more evacuation vehicles appeared to be leaving.

Lieutenant Fletcher noted, "I'm not seeing a whole lot of activity at the moment Captain. We are detecting evacuation transports on track to Europa Prime, but they are quite some distance off. Nothing new is being detected leaving the installations themselves."

"It sounds like their evacuation has completed. Have our intel people hack their networks for any useful information", the Captain ordered, adding, "Then we'll nuke the lot, with two megaton warheads as we pass by."

"I'm organising that now Captain", Lieutenant Fletcher replied.

After their intelligence people had hacked and ransacked the Europan L4 military networks, harvesting terabytes of data, the Venusians turned their minds back to the military installations.

"Captain. No other transports have left and we're not detecting any signs of life on the Jovian installations. It does appear that they have been completely evacuated. They are abandoned Sir", Lieutenant Fletcher informed his Captain.

"Then it's time Lieutenant", Captain Philo decided, "Contact the other ships. We're going to eliminate all of these installations. Everyone last of them. We'll hit them with multiple torpedoes, with two megaton warheads."

"Aye Captain. That aught to do it. I'll organise it straight away", replied the Lieutenant.

One by one, the Venusian fleet's torpedoes struck their targets. The Jovian military installations of Europa L4, were torn asunder by nuclear warheads with two megatons yields. The evacuation was long finished and no Jovian personnel were present. Massive abandoned O'Neil style cylinders and Bernal style spheres, military installations, exploded in immense, brilliant, blue balls of light. The scene of the carnage was watched by the crews of the Venusian heavy cruisers and at the end of it all, all that remained were hulks of twisted, mangled and irradiated metal.

Europa L4 was no more, another destroyed ruination of the one mighty Jovian Realms.

After annihilating Europa L4, the Venusian fleet adjusted its course to link up with the combined Earth and L5 fleets in Jovian orbit at Callisto Lagrangian point three, directly opposite Callisto in its orbit around Jupiter. The Fleet Captains of each fleet entered into an encrypted conference call to discuss their next targets.

"I'm not familiar with you Captain", Captain Carmichael noted when General Stanton didn't appear on the screen.

"You wouldn't be Captain Carmichael", the stranger replied, then informed them, "I am Fleet Captain Rodrigo Galtieri. I've been commissioned as Fleet Captain by the Earth Defence Forces and I'm taking over from General Stanton."

"Really. And General Stanton is?", Captain Carmichael queried.

"He's in the Goliath's brig on war crime charges", Captain Galtieri noted, adding, "Your report to the Earth and L5, well it has caused quite a stir."

"Well Captain, I won't be apologising for that. It had to be done", Captain Carmichael replied.

"Don't get me wrong Captain. I fully agree with you", Captain Galtieri answered.

Captain Philo stepped in, "I've read that report. It sounds to me that General Stanton most definitely overstepped his authority."

"Agreed Captain. General Stanton certainly did. He has shamed his whole family by his actions", Captain Galtieri remarked.

"So our next targets Gentlemen", Captain Carmichael began explaining, "We are to take our fleets over to Ganymede L4 and take down those military installations. Once we're done there, we fly to Ganymede Prime and force the Jovian High Council to surrender."

"And if they don't surrender Captain?", asked Captain Galtieri.

"We'll cross that bridge when we come to it Captain", Captain Carmichael replied, adding, "One thing to remember Gentlemen. We are not on a revenge mission. What General Stanton did was beyond the pale. I will not tolerate a repeat of that behaviour."

"Agreed Captain", Captain Philo replied.

"Also agreed Captain", Captain Galtieri replied, then added, "I know what true shame is Captain. I have an ancestor, that centuries ago, turned his own country into a ruination, then attacked one of his neighbouring countries, just to distract his people. Such reprehensible behaviour has a tendency to end very badly. It can stain a family for generations."

"Very good then Gentlemen. On to Ganymede L4 and may the Gods be with us all", Captain Carmichael replied.

28. Aphrodite's Revenge

Lieutenant Isabella Rossi, the Solstice's new medical officer approached Forkbraid, "Captain. I have given your crew fitness evaluations and I must be honest. I cannot agree to allowing three heavily pregnant woman on the ship's active crew duty roster."

"You have spoken to Selene, have you not?", Forkbraid asked.

"Yes I have and I understand the situation, but this is not something that would be allowed on any ship, that I have ever served on", Lieutenant Rossi advised.

"Lieutenant. The Solstice is not a standard military ship. The crew of the Solstice are not a standard military crew. We are, more of a family than anything else. You'll have to learn to understand that", Forkbraid explained, "Just have a look at the crew relationships and you'll get a feeling for what you'll be working with."

"Yes. I have looked into that as well Captain. Three pregnant women, two of whom are Sisters, the other is an Aunt. Then the Sister's Mother is also on the crew. The pregnant women's Husbands are on the crew as well, plus another Married couple. There are only four 'normal' people on the crew manifest", the Lieutenant replied.

"You should look at our crew manifest more closely Lieutenant. I was the head of the remote viewing teams on Earth and only one of a handful of psychics, that can use their gifts off world. Peter Swann has an I.Q that's well above three hundred and almost impossible to accurately measure. Then there's Leroy McGuvan. I executed him! Zuawalo saved his life and Gwek psychologically demolished him and rebuilt his entire psyche. He's a man who constantly seeks redemption", Forkbraid explained, "Truly Lieutenant, out of everyone on this crew, you are the only normal person."

Lieutenant Rossi was quiet for a very long moment, before replying, "This crew is going to take a lot of getting use to Captain."

"Of course it is Isabella. When was the last time you were on a space ship with a creche?", Forkbraid asked, using her first name, adding, "We are also far less formal on this ship."

"I am starting to get that Captain. I am starting to get that", the Lieutenant replied.

The Solstice's crew all boarded and went straight to their stations. Shortly thereafter, Marcus flew the Solstice up to low Martian orbit and was immediately tracked by the EDCF Martian task

force cruiser, Vanguard. Captain Tiko Hart's Lieutenant Adjutant was quick to inform him.

"Admiral. My Adjutant has just spotted the Solstice in low Martian orbit", Captain Hart informed Admiral Zumwalt.

"Keep monitoring them Captain. Let me know what they're up to", the Admiral ordered.

Captain Hart looked to his Lieutenant Adjutant and passed the order on by way of a simple nod.

Forkbraid looked to his First officer on his right, "Jim. We need to take down as many of those Jovian dreadnoughts approaching the Earth as we can. Do you have a plan?"

Jim Murphy who in addition to being the ship's First officer, was also the ship's Tactical officer, replied, "Not yet Captain, but I can put a tactical plan together very quickly. To have maximum effect, we need to make at least two passes of their fleet."

Forkbraid looked around to Peter Swann on his left at his science station, "Peter, we need to make two passes at the Jovian fleet. Any suggestions?"

Peter Swann swivelled around in his chair and looked towards Forkbraid, he leaned back and brought his hands together loosely in front of his chest, with his fingers point up. He was quiet in thought for a long minute or two.

"Peter?", Forkbraid queried.

"Sorry Captain. I was thinking", Peter responded, then, "To make two passes of their fleet, we'll need to use the Earth's gravity to sling us around and back out towards their fleet. If we do it right, we should circle back around the Earth and then back out to their fleet for our second pass."

"Is this something Marcus can plot or do you need to work out the details?", Forkbraid queried.

"I should do some work on it first and then pass it across to Marcus", Peter explained.

After about fifteen minutes Peter had the answer, "Captain. We need to find a frame dragging event with certain characteristics. We can then trigger an anomaly to form, that if it's done correctly will yield a slipstream that we can then use for a gravitational slingshot. The tricky part, is we need to enter the slipstream dead centre and at high speed."

"Well that was quite a mouthful Peter. Can you prepare a simple procedure for Marcus?", Forkbraid enquired.

"Yes. I believe I can Captain. I'm doing that now", Peter Swann replied.

A few minutes later Peter passed the information over to Marcus Greyhelm, the Solstice's navigator and helmsman.

Marcus perused the procedure, "Okay Peter. So I have to locate this perfect frame dragging event. Trigger it in the perfect way, to create the perfect slipstream and then hit it bulls eye centre at high speed. Sounds like a piece of cake, not."

"You can follow Peter's procedure, can't you Marcus?", Forkbraid enquired.

"Sure I can Captain, but I won't guarantee the result", Marcus replied, then added, "Let's just do this thing and if we're all alive at the other side, woo-hoo!"

"Marcus?", Forkbraid queried.

"Peter believes this will work Captain", Marcus replied, "I trust Peter and he hasn't been wrong so far. Not yet anyway."

"Okay. Let's give it a shot", Forkbraid ordered.

As the Solstice orbited Mars, Marcus scanned for frame dragging events, looking for one with the precise parameters that Peter had stipulated. Upon finding an exact precise matching frame dragging event, Marcus circled the Solstice back around, looping back to it, then he pulsed it once with the Solstice's pulse cannons. This triggered an anomaly, a slipstream and Marcus quickly scanned it, to ensure it matched exactly with Peter's requirements. It matched perfectly and Marcus then took the Solstice around in a wide loop and increased the ship's speed. As the Solstice came back around, Marcus aimed squarely at the dead centre of the slipstream.

Marcus nailed the bullseye in one and the ship's computer automatically displayed gravitational field lines overlaid on the screen. The ship approached what appeared to be a rotating funnel, leading into a tunnel like structure. The Solstice shuddered slightly and the computer automatically adjusted the inertial dampers, as the ship slipped over the lip of the slipstream's funnel towards the tunnel within it.

The sides of the slipstream tunnel showed definite spacial distortions and the Solstice's inertial dampers adjusted quickly to limit any untoward affects on the crew. They were effective. The inside of the slipstream tunnel was filled with strange swirling distorted lights and colours. The visual effects of the experience were both psychedelic and surreal, but they were not nauseating. Then they exited the tunnel and entered the spiralling exit funnel. The Solstice shuddered slightly once more, as she traversed the short, spiralling exit funnel.

Captain Hart on board the EDCF Martian task force flag shit, Vanguard, caught Admiral Zumwalt's attention, "Admiral. The Solstice has just vanished. One second she was on our scanners, the next she was gone. The Solstice ship was travelling at very high speed."

"Excellent work Captain! I do believe that we have just caught their new drive in action", the Admiral congratulated the Captain, adding, "We may not be able to talk about anything that Captain Forkbraid told us, but this, this is something concrete that we can document."

"Yes Admiral. My Adjutant is documenting everything as we speak", Captain Hart replied.

Two minutes and ten seconds later, the Solstice appeared out of nowhere in the Earth's orbit and was still travelling at high speed when it existed the slipstream. Marcus increased the ship's thrust to achieve the required trajectory as noted by Peter Swann in his procedure.

"We are on track to intercept the Jovian fleet, Captain", Marcus informed him.

"Excellent work Marcus, Peter", Forkbraid congratulated them both, then he turned to Jim Murphy, "Jim. Do you have that tactical solution?"

"I sure do Captain", Jim replied, explaining, "In order to maximise the damage to the enemy dreadnoughts, I recommend not destroying them."

"Not destroying them?", Forkbraid questioned.

"No need to Captain. We target them on our approach from one hour out with our stand off weapons, the electromagnetic rail guns and later, the hyper resonant disrupters. We take out their ship's bridges", Jim replied, explaining, "No bridge. No command and control. As we pass through their fleet, we target their engines and thrusters with our pulse cannons and phased laser arrays."

Marcus caught on, "That's brilliant Jim. Leave them dead in space with no control. They'll continue under their own momentum straight into our fleet. They'll be like sitting ducks!"

"Yes Marcus. If we do that twice, we can disable maybe eighty plus ships. Probably three times the number that we would, if we were to take the time to destroy them", Jim noted.

"Sounds like a plan Jim. Lock it in and we'll implement it", Forkbraid replied, then asked, "Why are we not cloaked and in stealth mode?"

"Good catch Captain", Jim noted, then, "Activating passive and active cloaking. Activating shield grid on maximum."

"Thank you Jim", Forkbraid replied, then, "Marcus. Thrusters in stealth mode please."

"Aye Captain. Now Placing thrusters in stealth mode", Marcus replied.

Then he turned back to Jim Murphy, "Jim. I keep forgetting we're supposed to be a military ship. If you think we ought to be cloaked and shielded, just do it and let me know afterwards."

"Will do Captain. Will do", Jim replied.

Jim Murphy set up the firing sequence in readiness for their encounter with the Jovian fleet.

"Tactical! Three step tactical weapons procedure as listed."

"Step one."

"Electromagnetic rail carousel online. Check!"

"Electromagnetic rail guns online. Check!"

"Hyper resonant disrupters online. Check!"

"Targeting Array online. Check!"

"Using ultra sensor data to target the first fifty dreadnought bridges. No overlapping targets. Check!"

"Extrapolate target trajectories for projectile impacts upon dreadnought bridges. Check!"

"Lock down on dreadnought bridges with electromagnetic rail guns. Check!"

"Loading electromagnetic rail carousel with penetrating, explosive rounds.

Check!"

"Calculate number of rounds required for total dreadnought bridge destruction. Check!"

"Tactical! Fire on the selected targets automatically with electromagnet rail guns at target intercept minus one hour!", Agent Murphy then commanded.

"Step two."

"Using ultra sensors, re-scan targeted dreadnoughts. Have any targeted bridges survived?"

"Lock down on remaining dreadnought bridges with hyper resonant disrupters. Check!"

"Tactical! Fire on the selected targets automatically with hyper resonant disrupters at target intercept minus five minutes!", Agent Murphy then commanded.

"Step three."

"Lock down on dreadnought engines and thrusters with pulse cannons and phased laser arrays. Check!"

"Tactical! Fire on the selected targets automatically with pulse cannons and phased laser arrays at target intercept minus two minutes!", Agent Murphy then commanded.

"Tactical! Store tactical attack procedure as tactical operations file Jovian fleet one!"

The Hornet's nest replied in its masculine voice, "Compliance."

"I've setup the firing sequence Captain", Jim informed Forkbraid, "We'll start hitting them at target intercept minus one hour. That will be twelve hours from now. From what I can tell, their fleet is flying in a conical formation. We should cause immense damage."

"Thank you Jim", Forkbraid replied, then to Charlene Fewkes, the Solstice's Communications officer, "Charlene. Contact the combined fleet. Find out who is in charge over there and then send them this encrypted message. *The Solstice will be making its first tactical run on the Jovian fleet in twelve hours and that we'll be under communications black out until our next communique.*"

Lieutenant Adjutant, Gerhard Bullcarter of the Venusian fleet's flagship, the heavy cruiser Paladin, had received an encrypted communique from Admiral

Tiberius Saxon of the Cis-Lunar Task Force command. The Lieutenant passed the communique onto his Fleet Captain, Conan Connors. Captain Connors read the message, is was very simple, short and sweet.

"One ship against a thousand Bullcarter! These bloody Martians put us all to shame I tell you", Captain Connors remarked.

"That's no ordinary ship Captain. From what I've heard the Solstice is nothing like any ship in existence. It's incredibly fast and packs an enormous punch for its size", the Lieutenant replied.

"Still Lieutenant, one ship against more than a thousand. It is shameful, for us to just sit by and watch", Captain Connors mused, "Send an encrypted message to Fleet Captain Gallagher and Admiral Saxon. Tell them, they can sit here in wait if they want, but I'm following the Martian's lead. Tell them I'm taking the Venusian fleet out to meet our enemy. By Aphrodite, the Jovians will feel our wrath!"

Lieutenant Bullcarter passed on the message and within the hour, the three hundred strong Venusian fleet was on the move, heading out to meet the Jovian enemy fleet in combat.

It was one hour and twenty minutes from target intercept and all the Solstice's bridge crew were all very nervous. They had never performed a successful tactical operation against manned ships before, let alone, over a thousand dreadnoughts.

Forkbraid then remembered Zyaliep's words, *"We see the justice for them. The dead will see justice through us"*, and instructed Charlene, "Charlene. Stream the battle scenes down to engineering. I believe the Pod women need to watch it unfold. Ask Varak to show it to them."

"Captain? Is that wise?", Charlene asked.

"Remember when Venusville fell. Zyaliep told us, that the dead need to see justice and that they would see it through their eyes."

"Aye Captain, I'm streaming our screen's display to engineering and letting Varak know what to do", Charlene confirmed.

At precisely one hour and five minutes to target intercept, the Solstice's Tactical officer Jim Murphy requested confirmation, "Now Captain?"

"Yes Jim. Now", Forkbraid confirmed.

"Switching to Tactical Operations mode", Jim informed everyone and then the ship's three laws safe computer went to sleep, while the Hornet's nest took complete control of the ship's operations.

Jim Murphy issued an order to the hornet's nest, "Tactical! Retrieve and activate tactical operations file Jovian fleet one. Validate procedure and follow instructions automatically at will!"

The Hornet's nest went through the command sequence of instructions and replied in its masculine voice, "Validation successful. Compliance."

At precisely target intercept minus one hour, the Solstice's electromagnetic rail guns sprung into life. The Jovian dreadnoughts were little more than specs in the distance, as explosive rounds were sent hurtling towards their targets at immense speed. Red tracer rounds were seen flying forth. One to every thousand of live rounds. A window popped up with a magnified view of the dreadnoughts and within minutes, explosions were noted on the targeted dreadnought bridges. The strike was looking like it was highly successful.

Jim Murphy noted, "Captain. It appears that Peter and Varak's tactical operations mode works."

"Yes Jim. So noted", Forkbraid replied.

On board the Jovian attack fleet's flagship, the Infallible, Lieutenant Vitally Vega, did not like what he was detecting, "General. Commander. Our ships are taking hits."

"Where from Lieutenant?", General Zachary Zardos asked.

"General Sir. There is nothing on our scopes. No ships, nothing. We are detecting tracer rounds from far off in the distance, but nothing else", the Lieutenant   informed them.

"Can we return fire?", asked Commander Edward Edwardson.

"No Commander. Whatever it is, is well out of range Sir", the Lieutenant replied.

"Damage report Lieutenant?", the General demanded.

"This is really bad General. The enemy appears to be targeting our ships' bridges. We are not hearing back from any of our ships that have been stuck", the Lieutenant replied, advising them, "I have only our ship's scans to go by Sir. It appears, that quite a few of our ships are now coasting under their own inertia."

"How? From so far off? How is this even possible?", the General questioned.

"I can only speculate General. It must be that new Martian gunship", the

Lieutenant replied, adding, "They say she's like a ghost."

Ten minutes later, the Solstice's electromagnetic rail guns cut off and the strafing of the enemy fleet stopped. The Jovians still had no ability to detect their enemy.

At precisely target intercept minus five minutes, the Solstice's hyper resonant disrupters opened fire on the targeted dreadnoughts, that still appeared to have functional bridges. The Solstice was quite close now as red disrupter beams cut across the intervening space, slicing through the titanium hull plating on one dreadnoughts bridge after another.

"General. Commander. Sirs, we are detecting disrupter fire", Lieutenant Vega informed them.

"Have you got a bead on the enemy Lieutenant?", the General demanded.

"General Sir. We are not detecting any enemy ships. Just their disrupter fire. We are detecting their red disrupter beams", the Lieutenant informed him.

"This is getting ridiculous. How do we fight an enemy we cannot see?", the General shouted.

The Solstice's disrupters fired for a few minutes before cutting out.

Then at precisely target intercept minus two minutes, the Solstice opened fire with its pulse cannons and phased laser arrays, targeting enemy dreadnought engines and thrusters. Blue super-heated pulses of plasma shot forth, along with intense beams of brilliant, coherent blue light. Blasting holes and slicing through titanium hull plating at will.

"General. Commander. Sirs, we are detecting both plasma and laser fire", Lieutenant Vega informed them, adding, "The enemy appears to be targeting engines and thrusters. I still have nothing on our scanners. Just their weapons signatures!"

Commander Edwardson noted, "Those are fairly short range weapons. Our enemy is close."

"Based on our scans Commander, whoever it is, is passing through our formation now", the Lieutenant informed him.

"That is impossible!", General Zardos exclaimed, "How can we not detect them? It they're that bloody close, we should see them with or own eyes?"

And then the Solstice was past the Jovian attack fleet and Marcus was adjusting their course to loop back around for a second pass at the enemies.

"Damage report", Forkbraid requested.

"None Captain", Jim replied, informing him further, "As far as I can tell, they didn't even detect us", he then added, "I am really impressed. Our weapons signatures should have given us away. The Hornet's nest made evasive manoeuvres while firing, to ensure that they couldn't detect us."

"I didn't think to Hornet's nest could do that", a surprised Forkbraid replied, then asked, "What about the enemy fleet? How'd we do?"

Jim pressed a few keys on his work station and the battle figures appeared on the screen.

"Wow! We have disabled forty six out of fifty targets. That's pretty damned good", Forkbraid noted, then he asked, "Marcus. How are we going for our second run?"

"It will take us a day and a half Captain. We'll be looping back around the Earth and pick up a good gravity boost", Marcus replied, adding, "On our second run, we'll hit them even faster."

"Excellent Marcus", Forkbraid replied, then he turned to his right, "Take us out of Tactical Operations mode Jim. Then put together a report for Admiral Saxon, Fleet Captains Gallagher and Connors. Then pass your report on to Charlene for encrypted transmission. We'll let them know of our first strike's success. "

"Aye Captain. Ending Tactical Operations mode now", Jim replied as the ship's computer reawakened to take control of the ship's systems, "I'll have that report ready in about an hour."

"Good work team", Forkbraid commended them all, "Now lets get some rest before our next tactical strike tomorrow."

Lieutenant Adjutant Gerhard Bullcarter passed the report onto Fleet Captain Conan Connors, who quickly read through it.

"The Solstice disabled forty six dreadnoughts in one pass! And they're looping around for a second run!", the Captain exclaimed, "Bullcarter! I know this new Martian ship is fast, but seriously, how does one ship do all of that?"

"Captain Sir. We have been scanning the Jovian fleet. We have detected more than forty dreadnoughts that appear to match the descriptions in that report" Lieutenant Bullcarter replied, adding, "Those dreadnoughts are coasting under their own inertia without any control."

"Headless and legless Lieutenant. When we hit those Jovian bastards, we'll ignore those stricken vessels and let them coast on to their oblivion. The Earth's and the L5's heavy cruisers can have them", the Fleet Captain replied.

The next day the Solstice had slingshot around the Earth and was on a new intercept trajectory to the Jovian attack fleet. As they swung passed the Earth, they noticed the Earth and L5 fleets had departed the L4 staging zone and were now moving to take up intercept positions, in order to take on the enemy fleet. They also noticed that the Venusian fleet was not a part of these new movements.

As the Solstice flew much further along its course, they noticed the Venusian fleet in the distance on their ultra scanners also on an intercept course to the Jovian attack fleet.

Marcus did some quick calculations, "Captain. The Venusians are running dark. They will strike the Jovian attack fleet about two and a half hours or so after we've finished with them."

"Thank you Marcus", Forkbraid replied, "They should still be in a state of disarray after our second run at them. That should give the Venusians all the edge they need."

"Charlene. Send an encrypted message to Admiral Saxon, Fleet Captains Gallagher and Connors. Let them know the timing of our next attack run", Forkbraid requested.

"Aye Captain. I'm on it now", Charlene Fewkes replied.

The Solstice was again, an hour and twenty minutes from target intercept and all of the Solstice's bridge crew were nervous, but not so nervous as with their first attack run. They had now performed a successful tactical operation against manned ships and their success filled them confidence.

Forkbraid then instructed Charlene, "Charlene. Stream the battle scenes down to engineering just as before. The Pod women will want to watch it unfold. Make sure Varak shows it to them."

It was again an hour and five minutes to target intercept, the Solstice's Tactical officer Jim Murphy requested confirmation, "Time for our second run Captain?"

"Yes Jim. Make it so", Forkbraid confirmed.

"Switching to Tactical Operations mode", Jim informed everyone and then the ship's computer went to sleep once more, while the Hornet's nest took over all of the ship's operations.

Jim Murphy issued his order to the hornet's nest, "Tactical! Retrieve and activate tactical operations file Jovian fleet one. Validate procedure, then follow instructions automatically at will, with no overlapping with previous targets!"

The Hornet's nest went through the command sequence of instructions and replied in its masculine voice, "Validation successful. Compliance."

At precisely target intercept minus one hour, it began once more. The Solstice's electromagnetic rail guns sprung into life. Red tracer rounds were seen flying forth, one to every thousand of live rounds. A window popped up with a magnified view of the enemy dreadnoughts and within minutes, explosions were noted on the targeted dreadnought bridges. Just as before, the strike was looking highly effective and every bit as deadly.

Once again, on board the Jovian attack fleet's flagship, the Infallible, Lieutenant Vitally Vega, detected the attack, "General. Commander. It's happening again. Our ships are taking hits."

"Where from Lieutenant? Where is this bastard?", General Zachary Zardos asked.

"General. I have nothing on our scopes. Nothing Sir. It's just like before. We can see their tracer rounds and nothing else", the Lieutenant informed them.

"So we still can't fire back?", asked Commander Edward Edwardson.

"No Sir. We can't return fire Sir. There is is nothing on our scopes", the Lieutenant replied.

"Damage report Lieutenant?", the General demanded.

"Same as last time General, the enemy is targeting our ship's bridges", the Lieutenant replied, there was the sound of strafing along the Infallible's hull, "General. We are being targeted!"

There were then several tense moments as the Infallible was struck multiple times, over and over and explosions were clearly heard. The ships fire control systems activated and began to automatically put out fires as bulkheads and fire proof doors began automatically closing.

"I still can't detect them General", the Lieutenant replied, exclaiming, "Their ship is a ghost!"

Ten minutes later, the Solstice's electromagnetic rail guns cut off and the strafing of the enemy fleet stopped. The pride of the Jovian attack fleet, the Infallible, had barely survived.

Time passed slowly and then it was target intercept minus five minutes. The Solstice's hyper resonant disrupters opened fire on the targeted dreadnoughts that still appeared to have functional bridges, including the flag ship, the Infallible. Red disrupter beams were cutting across the intervening space, slicing through the titanium hull plating on one dreadnought bridge after another.

"General. Commander. The enemy's disrupters are firing at us", Lieutenant Vega informed them.

Red disrupter beams, lances of searing energy, cut through the dreadnought's titanium hull with an almost surgical precision, cutting deep into its bridge. The titanium, a metal known for its formidable strength and resilience, stood little chance against the onslaught of this technological marvel. Everyone within the Infallible's bridge, died within seconds. No one got to reply to Lieutenant Vega's comments. Both General Zardos and Commander Edwardson, were as dead as all the other bridge crew members. The Solstice's disrupters continued firing for a few minutes more before once again, cutting out.

At precisely target intercept minus two minutes, the Solstice opened fire with its pulse cannons and phased laser arrays once again. They were targeting the enemy's dreadnought engines and thrusters yet again. Blue super-heated pulses of plasma flew through the intervening space, along with intense beams of blazing, blue coherent laser light. Titanium hull plating imploded inwards under the onslaught and was sliced and diced by the lasers like hot knives through butter. Then as quickly as it had begun, the Solstice was through the enemy formation and Marcus was adjusting their course to return back to the Earth once more.

"Damage report", Forkbraid requested.

"None Captain", Jim replied, "Our enemy did not detect us."

"What about the enemy fleet? Numbers Jim?", Forkbraid requested.

Jim pressed a few keys on his work station and the battle figures appeared on the screen.

"We have disabled forty seven out of fifty targets including their flag ship", Forkbraid remarked, "That is not so shabby."

"We still didn't get all fifty FB", Jim noted.

"Still, ninety four percent is pretty good Jim", Forkbraid replied, then instructing, "Now take us out of Tactical Operations mode. Put together another report for Admiral Saxon, Fleet Captains Gallagher and Connors. They should be very pleased to know, they'll have ninety three less dreadnoughts to worry about."

"Ending Tactical Operations mode now Captain", Jim replied, adding, "I'll have that report ready for Charlene to send within the hour."

"Thanks Jim", Forkbraid replied, then to Marcus, "Take us back to the Earth Marcus. We're going to need a slipstream to Jupiter."

"Aye Captain. On our way to the Earth as we speak", Marcus replied.

"Charlene. In a little over two hours or so, the Venusians are going to come to blows with the Jovian attack fleet. When they do so, could you please magnify it, then put it in a window on screen. Then feed the data back down to engineering", Forkbraid instructed.

"For the Pod women to view Captain?", Charlene queried.

"Yes Charlene. Venusville's dead need justice", Forkbraid replied.

Lieutenant Bullcarter passed the new report onto Fleet Captain Conan Connors, who quickly read through it with glee

"The Solstice just disabled another forty seven dreadnoughts people! ", the Captain exclaimed, "The enemy now has ninety three headless and legless ships!"

"Captain Sir. I can confirm those numbers. We are detecting ninety three dreadnoughts coasting under their own inertia. No command and no control. No engines!", Lieutenant Bullcarter replied.

"In one hour we'll hit them. We'll hit them hard. We'll hit them fast. Ignore all those headless ships, leaves those for our cis-lunar comrades", Captain Connors told his bridge crew.

"Captain. From what I'm seeing in our scans, their fleet is in a state of total disarray. They were flying in a conical formation, so naturally the disabled ships are drifting off, but many of their other dreadnoughts are falling out of formation as well", the Lieutenant informed.

"That report from the Solstice did say they'd disabled their flag ship Lieutenant", Captain Connors noted, "This is an opportunity for us Lieutenant."

"Sir?", the Lieutenant requested clarification.

"We have our passive cloaking and our stealth thrusters online. They won't see us until the very last minute Lieutenant. Let's split our fleet into four. We'll fly down the outside of their conical formation on four sides, just outside of their weapons range", the Captain explained.

"Yes Sir, but they will be outside of our weapons range as well", the Lieutenant pointed out.

"Ah! Not our torpedoes Lieutenant", the Captain replied, explaining, "We'll use tactical atomic warheads. Three torpedoes per dreadnought, with two kiloton yields should do it. We'll target as many of their dreadnoughts as we can and then peel away and regroup."

"Only their functional dreadnoughts?", the Lieutenant queried.

"Only their functional dreadnoughts Lieutenant. No sense wasting good torpedoes on disabled ships", the Captain confirmed, adding, "After we've finished, whatever is left, our cis-lunar comrades can deal with. Communicate the plan to our cruisers Lieutenant."

"Yes Captain", Lieutenant Bullcarter replied.

An hour later, the bridge crew of the Solstice were watching a large window that had popped up on the main screen, when the Venusian cruisers fell upon the Jovian dreadnoughts. The three hundred plus Venusian cruisers were difficult to make out as they were running dark, however, the Solstice's computer compensated and ensured that each and every one of them was visible. In four groups, the Venusian cruisers were surrounding the Jovian dreadnoughts, but keeping a good distance away from them. Then they noticed the small pinpricks of light speeding away from the Venusian cruisers towards the Jovian dreadnoughts.

Immediately Jim Murphy noted, "Torpedoes! Lots and lots of torpedoes!"

The torpedoes closed the gap swiftly and immense, bright orange balls of light erupted throughout the Jovian attack fleet.

Jim noted, "Tactical nukes! Low yield!"

The action was fast and furious, with multiple bursts of bright orange light erupting everywhere within the Jovian attack fleets formation. Then as quickly as it had started, it was over and the four groups of Venusian heavy cruisers peeled away from the scenes of devastation.

Peter was at his station's console working the touch screen keyboard, he remarked, "We made two passes and disabled ninety three ships. The Venusians just took out, well over four hundred dreadnought in just the one pass."

"Nukes will do that Peter. Nukes will do that", Jim replied, adding, "I guess that's what the Venusians would call Aphrodite's revenge! They did not mess about one bit."

"With more than half of the Jovian attack fleet gone, the Earth and L5 fleets will make short work of what's left", Forkbraid remarked, "This war is all but over. We need to get to Jupiter, to ensure this war doesn't end in a blood bath. Charlene, send word to Admiral Saxon, Fleet Captains Gallagher and Connors, that we are on our way to Jupiter."

"Captain. Won't that let the cat of out the bag?", Charlene enquired.

"Well Charlene, after our two passes of the Jovian attack fleet, that cat's already half out", Forkbraid replied, adding, "with this war concluding, we can't keep it in the bag forever", then to Marcus, "How are we tracking for Jupiter Marcus?"

"We are on track Captain. We have slipstreamed to Jupiter before, so the ship knows exactly what to do. It should be simple this time", Marcus informed Forkbraid.

Marcus was right. When they reached the Earth once more, the ship's computer quickly detected a suitable frame dragging event and Marcus triggered a slipstream to Jupiter. Marcus flew the Solstice directly into the slipstream and two minutes and ten seconds later they were just outside the orbit of the Jovian moon Callisto, back in Horridian territory.

29. Plan B - We have No Rabbits

Prince Leopold entered the conference room and immediately noted the sombre atmosphere. He then noticed that Princess Matilda was sitting in Prince Wulfric's seat.

Prince Leopold nodded to everyone else, then greeted Princess Matilda, "It's nice to see you again Matilda."

"It's nice to see you again as well, Leopold", the Princess replied, adding, "I must thank you for sparing my Husband. Wulfric can be, difficult to handle sometimes."

"I take it Wulfric will not be joining us today", Prince Leopold remarked as he sat down.

"Wulfric is quite unwell as you're probably aware. I have him sedated. I will be looking after his interests from now on", the Princess informed him.

Prince Leopold turned to his eldest Brother, "Brother Heinrich. Why am I here? You know I have no wish to be here? I am not involved in the military."

"Brother Leopold. You need to be here for this meeting", the High Prince replied.

Princess Matilda stepped in, "That is precisely why you are here Leopold, it is because you are not in the military, that you have not heard."

General Snide added, "There has been some very unfortunate developments Your Highness."

Princess Matilda elaborated, "My Husband, Wulfric's general staff, all believed that the three inner system fleets, Earth, L5 and Venusian, were all going to join forces and make a decapitation attempt Ganymede Prime. That was the general consensus."

General Snide confirmed, "The High Princess's general staff agreed with them as well. So the bulk of our dreadnoughts were positioned accordingly. We expected the enemy to reverse thrust, slowing down for orbital insertion, matching Ganymede's orbit."

"Only we were all wrong, very, very wrong! The Earth and L5 fleets, hit our defence forces at high speed, striking our dreadnought bridges, engines and thrusters. They left our defence fleet in total disarray, half destroyed and half disabled", Princess Matilda explained, adding, "After that, the enemy fleets slowed down for orbital insertion, matching Callisto's orbit!"

General Snide stepped in, "From there, they made a bee line straight to Callisto L4. There is nothing left Your Highness. Every single installation in that region was nuked by the Earth's heavy cruisers. Even before they had a chance to evacuate them. There was a huge number of deaths."

"How? How is that even possible? How did they know about about our military installations at Callisto L4?", Prince Leopold queried.

"We don't know how they knew Leopold", Princess Matilda admitted.

"It gets far worse Brother", Prince Valdamar remarked solemnly, "The Venusian fleet made a bee line straight to Europa L4. There's nothing left of our installations there either. At least the Venusians let our people evacuate first, before nuking everything in the entire region."

"How did they even know?", Prince Leopold asked them, then commented, "Io L4! They must have been responsible for the destruction of our missile array at Io L4 as well! It's the only thing that makes sense now. They've known about our military installations all along!"

"And they knew exactly where to hit us and how to hit us", the High Prince himself replied, adding, "That is the consensus amongst our analysts."

"What about our attack fleet? The one we sent to cis-lunar space", Prince Leopold enquired.

General Tarzan replied, "From what information we have received. The fleet was hit twice by an unknown invisible ship. The results of those two passes were quite devastating. Nearly a hundred of our dreadnoughts were completely disabled."

"That new Martian gunship we presume, Your Highness", Matthew interjected.

"Quite likely. Then our attack fleet was hit by a Venusian fleet of over three hundred heavy cruisers. They used a lot of missiles with tactical atomic warheads", General Tarzan continued, finishing with, "What was left of our attack fleet was then wiped out, by the Earth Defence Forces and Colonial Fleets. Our attack fleet has been totally obliterated! There is nothing left!"

"So what I'm hearing is, that we no longer have any offensive capabilities or defensive capabilities", Prince Leopold replied, adding, "Unless you guys have a rabbit to pull out of a hat, this war is over and most certainly not in our favour!"

"That is, a reasonable assessment Brother Leopold", the High Prince admitted.

"We do have *'Plan B'*, Your Majesty", Matthew noted.

Prince Leopold enquired, "Plan B? Is that our rabbit out of a hat, perchance?"

"No Your Highness", Matthew replied, "Plan B is not designed to swing the tide in our favour. Plan B is all about survival. The High Prince's survival and the survival of all the Sovereigns."

"After the loss of our missile array and its infrastructure, followed by the fall of Venusville and the Venusians throwing all in, we realised that the odds of us actually winning this war had been drastically reduced", General Tarzan explained, "We started preparing for the worse case scenario."

General Snide stepped in, "We've had our people working on plan B ever since, around the clock, day and night. It has been really hard work, but now, this project is ready!"

"What is it?", asked Prince Leopold.

"Ganymede L1", General Snide replied, informing all the royals at the same time.

"The ships graveyard?", Prince Leopold queried with an astonished look.

"Yes and no Your Highness", General Snide replied.

General Snide began to explain, "You know how the interplanetary out-liners push out to the colonies and at whichever colony is last on the list, gets to dismantled and recycle the out-liner."

"Yes of course", Prince Leopold asked.

"Well it didn't use to be that way", General Tarzan stepped in, elaborating, "When Jupiter and Saturn were first colonised, the out-liners were all called *'push ships'* and they were accompanied by a whole host of *'service and support ships'*. The *'push ships'* contained the colonists and everything the colonists could possibly need. The *'service and support ships'* contained everything else necessary to extract resources and build their new colonies."

General Snide stepped in, "That's how Ganymede Prime was first built and all of the other Primes for that matter. Jupiter's smaller moons were dismantled and processed into colonies. Later, nearby asteroids in the closer regions of the fore and aft Trojans were processed the same way."

General Tarzan continued, "Of course as we went farther afield, the original *'push ships'* and *'service and support ships'*, were inadequate for the task. So they were placed into orbit around Jupiter at Ganymede L1. What today, you and everyone else, call the ship's graveyard."

General Snide stepped back in, "Every single one of those *'push ships'*, has been cleaned up, refurbished, upgraded and refuelled. They are all ready for use. We have put together lists of all the royals, the nobles, our important people and everyone else we'll need to build our new colonies. Including all of their families of course. All ready for a possible evacuation. It's all planned!"

General Tarzan concluded, "That possible evacuation, is now imminent."

The High Prince had been unusually quite, with all of the bad news, his head was spinning. When he heard words like evacuation and imminent, he reacted.

"Generals! Are you both saying that we're all going to evacuate? That we're all going into exile?", the High Prince demanded an answer.

General Tarzan hazarded that answer, "Unfortunately Your Majesty, yes!"

The High Prince began shaking his head, "No! No! No! No! No!"

The Prophet's heart skipped a beat, when he heard Matthew state in no uncertain terms quite loudly, "Your Majesty! It's better to be alive in exile, than to swing from the end of a rope!"

That caught the High Prince's attention.

The Prophet's heart skipped another beat, when he heard Matthew's next statement, "Your Majesty! This war is concluding and the result is in our enemy's favour. The first strike in this war was ours and it killed two and a half million people on the Earth. If we stay here, we will all hang! All of us, there will be no exceptions! We must evacuate!"

The High Princes glared at Matthew, "I do not like this Captain!", he shouted.

Matthew replied far more cautiously, "I know Your Majesty. No one likes this, but it is our job to keep you safe. You and your family."

General Tarzan stepped in cautiously, "Your Majesty. We do not have a choice. We need to get this evacuation process started straight away and we can't until you agree to it."

The High Prince was reluctant, but he nodded his agreement to the evacuation plan.

"No Your Majesty. A nod won't do. This needs to be recorded", General Tarzan explained.

The High Prince replied, verbally, loud and clear, "Our evacuation is approved. Make it so!"

Prince Leopold shook his head and got up from his seat.

"Where are going Brother Leopold?", the High Prince asked.

"Home Brother Heinrich. I am going home!", the Prince replied sharply.

General Snide stepped in, "It's better that you stay here with us Your Highness. We can bring your family and everyone else that's needed directly to the push ships."

Prince Leopold declined, "No General. I am going home to my family. I have always been opposed to this damned war and now look where this war has left us. In complete ruination!"

"Brother Leopold. The General is right. You can evacuate with us and we can evacuate your family and everyone else separately", the High Prince implored.

"Bother Heinrich. You can clean up your mess here! I have my family and my friends to look after on Io Prime and I refuse to leave that to anyone else. I will take care of them", the Prince replied before storming out of the conference room.

The High Princes sighed a heavy sigh thinking, *'God be with you my Son'*, then he commanded the Generals, "Get this evacuation under way!"

"And Prince Leopold Your Majesty?", Matthew enquired, he was truly concerned for his safety.

"My Brother will have to make his own way to Ganymede L1 Matthew", the High Princes noted, then the High Prince turned to General Tarzan, "Have High Chancellor Hargreaves travel to Io Prime just in case. Hargreaves has instructions for situations like this."

"Your will be done, Your Majesty", replied General Tarzan, knowing that the High Prince was now concerned about the line of succession.

"Captain Murphy. We are going to need you at Ganymede L1 urgently. I want you there to check over all of the preparations and most importantly, work out where the fuck we are going! Take a shuttle straight there after this meeting", the High Prince commanded.

"Your Majesty. Shall I take His Lordship, the Prophet with me?", Matthew queried.

"No. there isn't any time Captain. You will go straight to Ganymede L1 after this meeting", the High Prince reiterated.

Matthew took on a seriously concerned look and General Snide reassured him, "Don't worry Captain. I will take His Lordship, the Prophet to Ganymede L1 myself in the Delilah. I've always wanted to fly that ship since the first day I laid eyes on it."

The Prophet was rightfully concerned, but agreed to it anyway, "It's alright Matthew. I'll be in very good hands. Especially after the Delilah was upgraded with those new weapons systems."

"Very well My Lord, but let's hope those new weapons won't be required", Matthew agreed.

The High Prince then ordered, "General Snide. Our enemy is going to make a move on Ganymede L4 at any time now. I want our people there to put up a valiant fight. They need to slow our enemy down as much as possible, even if it means losing all of their lives."

"I'll issue the orders straight away Your Majesty", General Snide replied.

Forkbraid instructed Marcus to locate the heavy cruiser Spartan and lay in a course to rendezvous with the Colonial fleet. He then proceeded to the engineering department to check on the Pod Sisters, Zuawalo and Zeealas. In the engineering department, he came across a very busy Zyaliep, who did not appear to have the time to talk to him.

"Why you here Captain? We are very busy now", Zyaliep told him.

"I was just checking on Zuawalo and Zyaliep", Forkbraid replied.

Zyaliep pointed to the wet decking, where Forkbraid was standing, "Their water is out. Now their babies will come."

Forkbraid noticed he was standing in it and stepped back, "Okay. I'd better let Jim know then."

"Why you let Jim know? Can he deliver babies?", Zyaliep enquired.

"No, but he might want to be there for their births", Forkbraid explained.

"Okay then, but Jim must stay out of the way", Zyaliep agreed.

Forkbraid, remembering the battle scenes that they had streamed to engineering, then asked, "Zyaliep. Have the dead seen enough justice or is their more to be done?"

"The dead see through our eyes. Have they seen enough? I cannot say", Zyaliep replied honestly, then remarked, "Those responsible. They followed that one man. They were his army."

"The Prophet?", Forkbraid queried.

"Yes. The Prophet. If that one man is brought to justice, the dead will have seen enough", Zyaliep concluded, then disappeared into the ship's medical bay.

Forkbraid made a call on his communicator, "Jim. You'd better get down to the medical bay. Your babies are about to be born."

There was no reply from Jim, but Peter Swann replied for him, "Jim is on his way Captain."

Jim arrived and without saying a word, ran straight into the medical bay. Forkbraid walked over to the door and peaked in, just in time to see Lieutenant Rossi, the Solstice's Medical officer start giving orders. Both Zuawalo and Zeealas were reclining on beds in the medical bay.

"Varak! You and Nyaliep can wait outside. Jim stay over there out of our way. Zyaliep and I have got this", Medical officer Rossi ordered.

Lieutenant Rossi looked at Forkbraid, "And you Captain! Delivering babies on a space ship is highly irregular. I will be recording this in my official log."

"I expect no less Lieutenant. Carry on", Forkbraid replied and closed the door.

Leroy looked out from engineering, "Varak. Nyaliep. Babies don't just pop out you know. It could take hours, perhaps quite a few. You may want to keep yourselves busy."

"That's a good idea Leroy. Everyone keep yourselves busy. I'll head back to the bridge", Forkbraid replied.

A few hours later, the Solstice had rendezvoused with the combined fleet, which was now slowly approaching Ganymede L4, the last of the Jovian military installations. The three fleet Captains were quickly on the Solstice's bridge main screen, in their own popup windows.

Captain Carmichael introduced the other Captains, "Captain Forkbraid, we have with us, Fleet Captains Philo of the Venusian fleet and Galtieri of the Earth Defence fleet."

"Greetings Gentlemen", Forkbraid replied, then he asked, "What happened to General Stanton?"

Captain Galtieri replied, "The General is in my brig Captain Forkbraid. The General has committed a war crime. I will send you a report on the matter after this meeting."

"Talking about reports Captain Forkbraid. I have two reports about military actions your ship and crew took outside of cis-lunar space, just yesterday. Which beggars the question. How are you even here?", Captain Carmichael asked.

"Yes well Captain. Considering how far out of the bag this cat is, I may as well just tell you", Forkbraid began, "We have been testing a new drive system. We call it the slipstream drive. Suffice to say Captains, if the departure point meets certain criteria, we are only two minutes and ten seconds from most destinations."

"Two minutes and ten seconds?", Captain Philo questioned with a look on his face that showed both amazement and fascination.

"It's far too difficult to explain Captain, but that is the gist of it", Forkbraid confirmed, "We'll be releasing a confidential and highly classified report on the matter, once this war is concluded and things have settled down somewhat."

"Well, we are getting close to that now Captain", Captain Galtieri remarked.

"So Captain Forkbraid. What can we do for you?", Captain Carmichael asked.

"Well Captains, the Jovian attack fleet that was sent to cis-lunar space has been defeated. Callisto L4 and Europa L4 have been eliminated", Forkbraid noted, adding, "I'm here to help you out with Ganymede L4."

The three Captains smiled and Captain Carmichael remarked, "Not that your help isn't appreciated Captain Forkbraid, but it is hardly required."

"That is true, however, I do have a part to play in this and it is, an extremely important one", Forkbraid replied and then he announced, " Captains, I will be requiring three heavy cruisers."

"Why do you need three heavy cruisers Captain Forkbraid?", Captain Philo enquired.

"I need three heavy cruisers to secure Io Prime", Forkbraid explained, "Once I've done that, I'll not only have secured the Ionian Realm, but also Prince Leopold and the Jovian line of succession."

"And that's important?", Captain Galtieri asked.

"Absolutely! Prince Leopold is the key to a lasting peace with the Jovian Realms. Prince Leopold is not like his Brothers, he's a reformer. The Prince was also the source of the information that you've been using to take down the Jovian military installations", Forkbraid informed them.

Captain Carmichael didn't hesitate, he trusted Forkbraid's judgement, "Enough said Captain Forkbraid. I can spare you a ship. All three if necessary."

Captain Galtieri noted, "That won't be necessary Captain Carmichael. I've read those reports. You'll have one of my cruisers as well Captain Forkbraid."

"This is highly irregular Captain Forkbraid", Captain Philo remarked, "Is this.... Prince Leopold, that important?"

"Absolutely", Forkbraid replied, "Without Prince Leopold and a clear line of succession, the Jovian Realms will descend into chaos. Absolute chaos Captain. We need to stem that off."

"Then I'll loan you one of my cruisers as well Captain Forkbraid", Captain Philo agreed.

"Excellent", Forkbraid replied, "As soon as we've secured Ganymede L4, we'll make our move on Ganymede Prime and along the way I'll peel off with those three cruisers for Io Prime and secure Prince Leopold and the Jovian line of succession."

Several hours later, Lieutenant Rossi contacted the ship's bridge, "Captain. We now have two baby girls in our ship's infirmary. Both Mothers and their babies are doing well."

"Excellent news Lieutenant", replied Forkbraid, adding, "Let Jim know that he can spend a few hours with them while they recover, but I will be needing him on the bridge at some point."

"I will pass that on Captain", the Lieutenant replied, then asked, "One more thing Captain. I have been training Zyaliep my Medical assistant, as you have requested. Leroy McGuvan has requested the same training."

"I can't see why not. It will be beneficial to have two Medical assistants onboard don't you think?", Forkbraid replied.

"Yes. That is true. I don't like relying on metal men to assist me. Sorry Captain, I mean Androids. Nyaliep and Varak are starting to rub off on me", Lieutenant Rossi replied.

"Androids are handy to have, when you have nothing else Lieutenant. Having two fully trained human Medical assistants is preferable", Forkbraid noted, then added, "Leroy is constantly being driven towards redemption, I expect he will learn very quickly."

"I expect he will", Lieutenant Rossi agreed.

Forkbraid enquired, "Have the Pod Girls chosen names for their Daughters yet?"

"No. No, not yet. Zyaliep says, that they cannot name the babies until they return back to Mars", Lieutenant Rossi replied.

"Now that is odd, Lieutenant. Did Zyaliep say why?", Forkbraid questioned.

"No Captain. Only that babies may be born in space, but cannot be named in space", the Lieutenant replied.

30. Ganymede - Lagrangian Point Four

Lieutenant Pinkerton diligently checked his scanners for any signs of the inner system forces. Everyone in his base had heard about the routing of the Jovian outer defence fleet, that had been left dead in space, with ships either completely destroyed or disabled. They had also heard about the destruction of the other Jovian military installations at both Callisto L4 and Europa L4. They had heard that nothing was left, except for tangled, broken, melted and irradiated metal hulks.

The Jovian inner defences had been obliterated by a large Venusian fleet. There were no fewer than three inner system fleets on the prowl in Jovian space and everyone at Ganymede L4 was expecting them to converge on them. They were on their way. It was simply a matter of time and the fear amongst the Jovian personnel was, that they would be nuked outright and without any mercy. The same as had happened at Callisto L4, where the very few had managed to escape.

"Commander Sanchez Sir. I'm starting to detected the enemy fleets at our outer perimeter", Lieutenant Pinkerton noted.

Commander Sanchez checked the Lieutenant's scanners and scope. He was correct, the enemy was converging on Ganymede L4 from three sides.

"Sweet Mother of God! That's a lot of ships!", Commander Sanchez exclaimed, "Lieutenant. Try and get a count of those ships. We need numbers. What are we up against?", he ordered.

"General Marble Sir. The enemy is here and there are a lot of them", the Commander informed.

"Thank you Commander", the General replied, then to the Lieutenant, "How many ships lad? And what are they?"

"Our computer is still tallying the numbers General Sir", Lieutenant Pinkerton replied, "There's thee fleets approaching from three directions. They're in a formation that indicates a planned encirclement Sir."

"Ship types Lieutenant?", the General asked.

"Sorry Sir. My apologies. They are all heavy cruisers Sir", the Lieutenant answered, before checking his equipment once again, he looked up, "Earth, L5 and Venusian heavy cruisers Sir."

"That does not sound good. Numbers lieutenant?, the General enquired.

"They are running dark General. Some kind of cloaking. We can see them, but they will be very difficult to target", the Lieutenant replied, then he looked up from his equipment once more, "I'd say there's well over nine hundred of them Sir."

"Over nine hundred?", the General asked for confirmation.

"Correct Sir. There's over nine hundred heavy cruisers Sir", the Lieutenant confirmed.

Commander Sanchez stepped in, "General. If we follow our orders, there'll be nothing left of us in less than an hour Sir."

The General looked at the Commander, then looked at the Lieutenant, "Pinkerton. What's your frank and honest assessment?"

"General Sir. We are largely a research, development, manufacturing and supply hub. We've always relied on our outer and inner defences. What ships we have are outclassed and outnumbered nearly ten to one", the Lieutenant honestly replied, then dropped the bombshell, "Those three enemy fleets could wipe us out in ten minutes and just move on."

"Thank you Lieutenant. That was my assessment as well", the General agreed.

"If we follow our orders Sir, we'll not achieve our objective, which is to slow down the enemy. They'll just wipe us out and continue on", General Marble surmised, "What other options do we have gentlemen?"

"Perhaps a running rear guard action General", Commander Sanchez remarked.

"Yes Commander, but where too? They'll just chase us down to where ever we lead them", the General replied unconvinced.

"It will buy as a little time Sir", the Commander replied.

"We run. They chase us. Some of them remain behind and obliterate our installations. Those that chase us eventually catch up and obliterate us", the General noted, "The result is the same in either case, they'll just take an hour or so longer to do it."

Communications officer Perkins caught the attention of the General,

"General Sir, we are being hailed. It's the enemy Sir."

"Put them on screen Perkins", the General Replied and seconds later Captain Carmichael was on the screen and staring them down.

"Captain Carmichael, Captain for the Colonial Cruiser Spartan", Captain Carmichael introduced himself, "I am authorised to accept your surrender."

"We are not offering to surrender Captain", the General replied.

Noticing the General's insignia, Captain Carmichael replied, "You don't have a choice General. Your either surrender or you all die."

"You seem rather sure of yourself Captain", the General responded.

Captain Carmichael replied coldly, "We are getting very good at destroying Jovian dreadnoughts and installations. Your choice is simple General, unconditional surrender or we completely wipe out your ships and these installations."

"So you say Captain. So you say", the General replied, then asked, "Can we have some time to discuss this amongst our people?"

Captain Carmichael replied, "You have one hour General. One hour and not one second more", then the screen went blank.

Commander Sanchez noted, "General Sir. You've just bought us one hour Sir."

Lieutenant Pinkerton stepped in and remarked, "Perhaps that's the answer Sir."

"What do you mean Lieutenant?", Commander Sanchez questioned.

"Commander. Our outer defences are gone. Our inner defences are gone. We are all that's left", the Lieutenant noted, then asked, "This war is over and we have lost, haven't we?"

General Marble stepped in, "We may have lost, but we have our orders Lieutenant."

"General Sir. Any armed action we take, will be over very quickly and will not achieve the objectives of our orders. Which is to buy Ganymede Prime more time", the Lieutenant commented.

"And you have another option Lieutenant?", the General asked.

"General Sir. You yourself have just bought us an hour. By surrendering, we can buy Ganymede Prime days", the Lieutenant summed up.

The General was quiet for a long moment, "How do you figure that Lieutenant?"

"We negotiate with the enemy on the conditions of our surrender Sir", the Lieutenant advised.

"Lieutenant. Captain Carmichael stipulated an *'unconditional'* surrender", the General noted.

"Yes General, but what does *'unconditional'* mean Sir. It could take a day, perhaps longer, just to define what *'unconditional'* means to both sides Sir", the Lieutenant noted.

Commander Sanchez stepped in, "I like Pinkerton's thinking Sir. This could buy us a lot of time."

Lieutenant Pinkerton then added, "And General, once we have a definition for *'unconditional'*, there is the matter of the occupation forces."

"Occupation forces Lieutenant?", the General enquired.

"Yes Sir. The enemy will need to occupy all of our ships and all of our facilities in order to ensure full compliance with your orders to surrender Sir", the Lieutenant replied, adding, "That alone could take them days Sir."

The General laughed boisterously, "Gentlemen. Let us milk this for all it's worth."

Precisely one hour later Captain Carmichael's ship, the Spartan hailed them and General Marble had the Captain put on the screen.

Captain Carmichael straight away asked, "Okay General. Your decision? Life or death? Surrender or die?"

The General replied, "This unconditional surrender that you speak of. What precisely is your definition of unconditional?"

What followed was a nearly three hour discussion about whose definition of unconditional was correct and whose was not. Captain Carmichael was convinced that the Jovians just liked to argue for the sake of arguing, eventually however, they did reach a definition that both sides were comfortable with. It seemed to the Captain, that the term *'unconditional'*, had taken on one hell of a lot of conditions.

"Okay General. So, are you now happy, to issue the order to surrender to your personnel?", Captain Carmichael enquired.

To which General Marble replied, "Oh yes, yes. I'll definitely issue that order to surrender. Straight away Captain. All of our ships and installations should have it within the hour."

"Excellent, then I'll leave you to it and you can get back to me when it's done", Captain Carmichael replied.

"There is one small problem though Captain", the General replied, explaining, "Loyalty is very big in the Jovian Realms. Surrendering not so much. Some of my personnel are more loyal to the High Prince than others. They can be quite religious as well. It's quite likely that some of them may disobey my orders to surrender."

"Wait. Wait now General!", Captain Carmichael replied, querying, "You are in charge in the Ganymede L4 region, yes?"

"Yes, yes of course I am. I am the commander and chief of the Ganymede L4 region", the General confirmed.

"Then why would any of your subordinates refuse your orders", the Captain enquired.

"Ordinarily they wouldn't, however, an order to surrender? I cannot guarantee full, one hundred percent compliance with that", the General informed him.

This then led to another two to three hours of discussion, of the best ways to ensure full Jovian compliance with General marble's orders to surrender.

In the end, Captain Carmichael was all for nuking the lot of them and be done with it, but instead issued, one last final command, "General Marble! You will now issue your orders for your ships, your installations and for all of your personnel to surrender. This will be done immediately! There will be no more discussions about it. Do you understand?"

"Yes Captain. I fully understand. I will issue an order for all Jovian personnel in the Ganymede L4 region to surrender immediately", the General replied.

"Good then. Do it now! My people will deal with any issues of non-compliance", Captain Carmichael replied and then immediately hung up the screen.

General Marble turned to Commander Sanchez and Lieutenant Pinkerton, "I was wondering at what point he'd get pissed off with me. Captain Carmichael seems to be a most tolerant man. I had him going for most of the day."

"And the surrender orders General Sir", the Commander enquired.

"Yes. Yes. I'd better issue those orders now Commander", the General replied, then turning to the bridge's Communications officer, "Perkins. Hail the fleet and all of our installations."

"Yes General. Straight away Sir", Communications officer Perkins replied.

General marble then issued his orders for all Jovian personnel in the Ganymede L4 region to stand down and surrender, to the inner system forces.

Captain Carmichael was soon in communications with Fleet Captains Philo, Galtieri and Forkbraid, "Gentlemen. You will be pleased to know that General Marble has just issued orders to all Jovian personnel in the Ganymede L4 region, to stand down and surrender."

"Yes Captain. We've been monitoring their communications", Forkbraid noted.

"That is good news Captain, but what took so long?", Captain Galtieri asked.

"Seriously Captain. General Marble is the most pedantic, long winded prick, I have ever negotiated with. I can seriously understand why Stanton simply nuked the Callisto L4's installations", Captain Carmichael replied.

"Wasn't this meant to be an *'unconditional'* surrender Captain?", Captain Philo asked.

"Captain Philo. I spent three hours discussing the very definition of the word *'unconditional'* with that man, just to ensure we were on the same page and both fully understood its meaning", Captain Carmichael informed him.

"And the rest of the time Captain", Captain Philo asked.

"Discussing compliance issues Captain. In the end I told him to issue his surrender orders and we'd ensure full compliance ourselves", Captain Carmichael explained, adding, "Did I mention that he was one very pedantic prick?"

Forkbraid queried, "Captain Carmichael. How are we to ensure full compliance?"

"That is actually quite simple. We are going to have to send security teams to every Jovian ship and every Jovian installation", Captain Carmichael explained.

"Simple yes, but very time consuming Captain", Captain Philo noted.

"Yes Captain. Very time consuming", Captain Galtieri agreed.

"Yes indeed", Captain Carmichael agreed as well, "Ganymede Prime is a civilian colony. Everything in the Ganymede L5 region is civilian. I suggest, that we leave some of our forces here to take over the Jovian ships and installations and then we proceed to Ganymede Prime."

"What size fleet should we leave behind Captain Carmichael?", Captain Philo asked.

"Certainly enough to ensure compliance with those surrender orders", Captain Galtieri noted.

"And enough to bust their balls, should they get antsy or worse", Captain Carmichael replied, suggesting, "Three hundred cruisers should keep the Jovians in line."

"One hundred a piece", Captain Philo noted, "Agreed!"

"Agreed. One hundred a piece", Captain Galtieri confirmed.

"Okay then. Now that you guys have a plan, I assume you'll need to work out the details", Forkbraid commented.

"Yes. We will need to organise quite a few things", Captain Carmichael noted, "We should be on our way to Ganymede Prime in forty eight hours."

"Roughly about that. Forty eight hours is about right", Captain Philo agreed.

"Forty eight hours it is then. We'd better start cracking", Captain Galtieri noted.

"About that gentlemen. I'm not waiting forty eight hours. I'll be heading to Io Prime with those three heavy cruisers, you've so graciously loaned me in six hours", Forkbraid informed them.

"Six hours?", Captain Carmichael questioned.

"Six hours Captain", Forkbraid replied, explaining, "Something tells me that General Marble isn't a pedantic prick at all. He's just a very clever man, who has managed to slow down your advance on Ganymede Prime by more than forty eight hours."

"Well. That, I will admit he has, Captain Forkbraid", Captain Carmichael agreed.

"Yes and as such, he slows you down, so I speed up", Forkbraid replied, "We need to secure Prince Leopold and we need to do it quickly."

All of the other Captains agreed with him and six hours later the Solstice left for Io Prime, with the Colonial cruiser, Demeter, the Earth cruiser, Vampire and the Venusian cruiser, Valiant, all following closely behind.

31. Ganymede - Lagrangian Point One

General Snide was at the helm of the Delilah, "Prophet, this ship of yours is a delight to fly!"

"Yes General. Matthew would agree with you on that point. He once told me that the Delilah almost flies itself", the Prophet replied.

"She's also fast. Really fast. I haven't even really opened her up and yet, there's still plenty left in the throttle", the General remarked.

"How soon will we reach Ganymede L1 General?", the Prophet enquired.

"Ordinarily just a few hours. However, the High Prince has commanded that we stop by Io Prime and pick up his Brother, Prince Leopold and his family", the General informed him, adding, "That'll bump out the time by a least a day."

"Was there no one else available to pick Prince Leopold and his family?", the Prophet asked.

"High Prince Heinrich doesn't trust anyone else to do it", General Snide replied, "He ordered me to do it personally. That and the fact that we have the Delilah. She's the fastest ship we have."

Peter Swann noticed something on their ultrascan data for the Ionian orbital region, "Captain. We've detected a ship en-route from Ganymede Prime to Io Prime."

"A ship Peter?", Forkbraid queried, "Civilian traffic should be extremely light with the conflict now inside Jovian space."

"Yes Captain. Agreed, civilian traffic appears to have been grounded, the minute our forces entered the Jovian system. I've been checking our scans regularly to avoid us causing any collateral damage just in case", Peter replied.

"So this ship Peter?", Forkbraid questioned.

"I recommend, that we have Jim look at it", Peter replied, "I think it might be the Delilah."

Forkbraid got onto his communicator straight away", "First officer to the bridge. First officer to the bridge", he commanded.

When Jim arrived at the Solstice's bridge, he had an entire entourage will him.

Forkbraid sighed, "Jim. Check the ultrascans. Peter thinks he's spotted the Delilah."

Jim rushed straight to his station and began to check the ultrascan data.

Forkbraid addressed Jim's entourage, "Lieutenant Rossi. Would you and Varak kindly take those babies back to the infirmary."

"Yes Captain", the Lieutenant replied, as she gently took Zuawalo's baby from her and headed back to the infirmary.

Varak did the same with Zeealas's baby, "Aye Captain. The infirmary it is."

"Okay. Zuawalo, Zeealas, Nyaliep and Zyaliep. The dead see justice through your eyes. Yes?", Forkbraid queried.

"Yes Captain", they all replied in unison.

"Good then. Stay on the bridge, but keep out of the way. Sit where you can. The Prophet may well be on the ship we're scanning", Forkbraid instructed, then asked, "Jim. Is that the Delilah?"

"Yes it is FB. Yes it is", Jim replied, "and she's different. They've added twin pulse cannons on all four sides of the ship. Three hundred and sixty degree field of firing. She also has two paired, forward mounted particle beams. I very much doubt, that they can penetrate our shielding."

"We're still cloaked yes?", Forkbraid asked, then ordered, "Marcus, intercept and approach the Delilah from the rear, but hang well back."

Jim replied, "Aye Captain. Still fully cloaked and our shielding is active."

Marcus replied, "Laying in an intercept course now Captain."

Everyone was smiling. This was the closest they'd ever been to capturing the Prophet.

An hour later and the Solstice was manoeuvring unseen behind the Delilah. Forkbraid reached out with his mind, attempting identify if the Prophet and Matthew were on board the ship.

"The Prophet is definitely on board. No sign of Jim's cousin Matthew though", Forkbraid informed everyone, "Charlene. Hail the Delilah."

"What the fuck!", General Snide remarked, "We're being hailed!"

"Who is it?", the Prophet asked.

"I don't know. There's nothing on our scans", General Snide replied, "I'll put them on screen."

Forkbraid appeared on the Delilah's main screen, "I am Fleet Captain Forkbraid of the Martian Defence Forces. Please stand by for boarding. You have a wanted fugitive on board your vessel."

General Snide flicked the screen off, "How the hell did they find us?", he asked himself.

"Well that was rude of them!", Forkbraid noted, "Charlene. Hail them again."

"It appears that they are hailing us again General Snide", the Prophet noted, "I don't think we can just ignore them."

The General put them on screen once more.

Forkbraid appeared on the Delilah's screen again, "I am Fleet Captain Forkbraid of the Martian Defence Forces. Please stand by for boarding. You have a wanted fugitive on board your vessel."

"Yes. Yes. I heard you the first time Captain and No. We do not have any fugitives on board this vessel", the General replied.

"So the man, known as the Prophet, is not on board his own ship, the Delilah", Forkbraid replied, then he reached into the pilots mind, "General Snide. I don't believe you. I have already scanned the Delilah and the Prophet is most definitely on board. Please stand by for boarding."

"How in the hell did he know my name?", the General thought to himself, "You are are mistaken Captain. There is no one on this ship by that name. You will not be boarding this ship."

Whilst still on screen, Forkbraid instructed, "Jim. Tickle their hull plating with something light."

"Aye Captain", Jim replied and then he fired the Solstice's phased laser arrays at the Delilah on the lowest possible power settings.

The Delilah shook slightly, enough to be of concern, but not enough to cause any damage.

"That was our lowest setting, General. Now, stand by for boarding!", Forkbraid demanded.

General Snide punched the throttle and the Delilah rapidly increased speed, the screen dropped out once more.

Forkbraid shook his head, then ordered, "Marcus. Keep on their tail."

"Aye Captain", Marcus replied and the chase was on.

"General Snide! You cannot outrun us! Slow down and prepare for boarding!", Forkbraid ordered, then asked, "Charlene. Can they hear me?"

"Yes Captain. They can hear you. They're just ignoring you", Charlene confirmed.

General Snide activated the Delilah's pulse cannons, all four batteries and started blindly firing rearwards. Blue, super-heated pulses of plasma shot by all around the Solstice, mostly missing, the occasional pulse being either deflected or absorbed by the Solstice's shields.

"That, is all kinds of stupid!" Forkbraid announced and then asked, "Jim. Can you take out those pulse cannons without harming the ship?"

"Sure. Watch me", Jim replied, as he carefully returned fire on the Delilah's pulse cannons.

The port side pulse cannon was struck and the Delilah shuddered violently as it blew outwards into space, then the starboard pulse cannon was struck, again with more violent shuddering as it too, exploded outwards.

"Damn. Their weapons are tight!", General Snide remarked as he realised, he'd lost two pulse cannons, only to feel the Delilah shudder violently twice more, as her top and underside pulse cannons were surgically destroyed in precisely the same manner.

"I feel like a dentist pulling teeth", Jim remarked.

One more time Forkbraid made his demand, "General Snide! You cannot outrun us! Slow down and prepare for boarding!"

The Delilah suddenly vectored upwards and dropped her speed, allowing the Solstice to zip past at high speed. General Snide activated his particle beams and brilliant red beams of energetic particles shot forward into space. He missed his target.

The Solstice was cloaked, both passively and actively and virtually invisible to detection. But the Delilah was very close and General Snide thought he could just make out an odd, slight glimmer, in the view port in front of them. The General aimed, then fired his particle beams once more and again brilliant red particle beams shot forward, this time striking the Solstice's shielded rear.

"Fuck this!", Jim Murphy shouted, "Tactical operation mode online. Captain, awaiting orders."

"Marcus. Get us behind this prick", Forkbraid ordered.

"Aye Captain", Marcus replied as he looped the Solstice up and back around behind the Delilah.

The Solstice was now behind the Delilah once more, "General Snide! Prepare for boarding!", Forkbraid demanded.

"Put them on the screen", the Prophet requested and General Snide did as he was asked.

"General Snide! I'm am losing my patience. Prepare for boarding now!", Forkbraid demanded.

The Prophet was staring back at him from behind the General, "Begone Demon! You have no power over us Evil one! Begone from our sight!"

"So General, our fugitive is on board the Delilah", Forkbraid replied, "Prepare to be boarded!"

Forkbraid turned to Jim Murphy, his Tactical officer, "Can you take out their thrusters Jim?"

"I can try FB", Jim replied, while adjusting the power settings on their phased laser arrays.

Jim fired the Solstice's phased laser arrays precisely twice, striking the Delilah's port and starboard thrusters. There were bursts of light and small explosions at the rear of the Delilah, as the ship's thrusters were destroyed. Then the Delilah began coasting without thrust.

"Marcus. Manoeuvre us for docking", Forkbraid ordered.

"Belay that order Captain!", Peter Swann called out, explaining, "I'm detecting a cascade of failures on board the Delilah. I'm recommending that we back off to a safe distance."

Forkbraid looked at Peter and then looked to Marcus, "Back us off Marcus! Do it quickly!"

Marcus backed the Solstice off to a safe distance, as the bridge crew watched the Delilah on the screen. There was a series of small explosions, followed by several larger ones, then one almighty explosion and the Delilah was no more. General Snide, the Prophet and the Delilah's crew all died in the explosion.

Peter Swann explained, "The Delilah was original built as a civilian space yacht, she wasn't designed to take a hit like that. It was bound to happen."

Zyaliep, her Sister Nyaliep and Daughters Zuawalo and Zeealas, had all been watching and Zyaliep commented, "The dead, they see through us and now, they have seen justice!"

Forkbraid looked around at Zyaliep and nodded in acknowledgement, then turned back around, "Marcus. Put us back on course for Io Prime. Let's catch up with our three heavy cruisers. Jim. Take us out of Tactical operations mode."

The High Prince had questions about their destination. So far, there destination had not been divulged, nor for that matter even decided.

"So Captain Murphy. Where exactly are we going?", the High Prince asked, "After-all, if I'm to go into exile, I do need to know where that will be?"

"Your Majesty, I have given it quite a lot of thought", Matthew replied, explaining, "I first considered, Saturn, Uranus and Neptune, but then decided against either of them."

"Your reasoning Captain?", the High Prince asked.

"Your Majesty, Saturn, Uranus and Neptune are all major colonies. Every bit as developed as the Jovian Realms. They all have their own cultures, their own ways. If we go into exile at any of them, we will be refugees and outsiders. We will always be treated as such, especially considering, we did start this war with the inner system worlds", Matthew replied.

Prince Valdamar stepped in, "In those colonies, we would always be distrusted Brother. Always!"

Princess Matilda stepped in and added, "And we'd be too close to our enemies as well."

"Yes Your Highness, that is a very good point", Matthew agreed, "Our enemies would almost certainly give chase. We would not be safe at either of those worlds."

General Tarzan added, "We shouldn't take the risk Your Majesty."

"Captain. What other options does that leave with us then?", High Prince Heinrich enquired.

Matthew brought up a simple table onto the screen. Nothing fancy, just a short list of Kuiper Belt worlds, the Dwarf Planets beyond Neptune.

"Your Majesty. We are left with the Dwarf Planets of the Kuiper Belt",
Matthew replied.

Dwarf Planet	Distance from Sun (AU)	Diameter (km)	Largest Moon	Colonised Yes	Confirmed Yes
Eris	96.30	2,326	Dysnomia		
Sedna	85.80	995			
Gonggong	67.00	1,400			
Makemake	45.80	1,430		Yes	
Huya	43.80	530		Yes	
Varuna	43.10	668	Kalliope	Yes	
Haumea	43.00	1,960	Hiʻiaka and Namaka	Yes	
Quaoar	43.00	1,121	Weywot	Yes	
Salacia	42.70	850	Actaea	Yes	
Chaos	41.50	450		Yes	
Pluto	39.50	2,376	Charon	Yes	Yes
Orcus	39.30	946	Vanth	Yes	
Ixion	39.30	617		Yes	

The High Prince stared at the table on the screen, "The Dwarf Planets
Captain?", he was certainly less than impressed.

"Your Majesty. Even with the Dwarf Planets, our options are still very
limited", Matthew replied, explaining, "I've check on the status of the outer solar
system's colonisation. The information in my database tells me that, out-liners
and push ships, have pushed out to every Dwarf world within fifty astronomical
units of the Sun."

"Yes, but only one of those colonies, Pluto is confirmed", Prince Valdamar
noted.

"Your Highness. That is a very recent confirmation", Matthew explained,
advising, "We should assume, that the other colonisation attempts have also
succeeded. With any of those worlds, we have no idea, what we'd be walking
into."

"Captain Murphy has a point Your Majesty", General Tarzan agreed,
"Assuming that those colonies exist and been watching recent events, they might
treat us as outsiders at best, perhaps even with hostility at worst."

"Which leaves us with the top three on the list Your Majesty", Matthew noted, explaining, "Eris, Sedna and Gonggong. I have found no records at all, of any out-liners or push ships, pushing out that far. They may be the only Dwarf worlds open to us."

"Gonggong is a good size and it's closest", High Prince Heinrich noted, he was starting to get onboard with the plan.

Matthew agreed, "Yes it is Your Majesty", but then he noted, "but Eris is as big as Pluto and has a good sized Moon, Dysnomia. Eris maybe further out, but it will have far more resources."

Prince Valdamar stepped in, "Eris may have other moons as well. Pluto was once thought to have only one moon, until they discovered four more. We may discover more moons around Eris."

General Tarzan noted, "Eris is ninety six AU out. Our enemies are very unlikely to chase us out that far. The cost of doing so would be completely prohibitive."

"Another good reason to choose Eris", Matthew agreed, but cautioned, "There is a downside. Our push ships are very big. They are old school as well, with all of the service and support ships, more of a flotilla, a big one at that. It will take us well over a decade to reach Eris."

"It seems I have a lot to consider Captain", the High Prince remarked.

"Yes Your Majesty", Matthew agreed, "Ultimately the choice is yours. We will go with whatever choice you make Your Majesty, but you do need to make that choice very soon."

The High Prince was still mulling over his decision,. The choice was obvious. They needed to go to Eris, but the length of time to reach their new home in exile, made his decision daunting.

Matthew commented, "Your Majesty, if it makes your decision any easier, the General and I have specialists working on your new colony as we speak."

The High Prince looked up and gave Matthew an enquiring look.

"Dysnomia Your Majesty. The plan is to core out Dysnomia along its rotational axis. A huge hollowed out cylinder. Vitrify the inner surface, then spin it up, turning it into the largest colony ever built. Our final designs should be ready, by the time we get there", Matthew explained.

That caught the High Princess's attention, "You've already thought this though Matthew?"

"Yes Your Majesty", Matthew admitted.

"Then why do you need me to decide?", High Prince Heinrich asked.

"You are the High Prince Your Majesty. This decision, ultimately, is yours", Matthew replied.

General Tarzan approached, "We have received a message from the Delilah."

"Let's hear it General", the High Prince commanded.

General Tarzan played the message, *"General Snide here. We've run into that Martian gunship. They've knocked out our thrusters and are about to board us. We will not make it to Io Prime."*

Then there was a rapid succession of bangs, popping and crackling. Followed by the creaking and groaning of structural failures. This was then followed by the screams of crewmen. A series of smaller explosions, followed by an almighty bang and then the message ended abruptly.

Matthew sighed deeply and exclaimed, "General Snide is dead! The Prophet is dead! They are all dead!", then he looked to General Tarzan, "General. We need to get some scopes on Io Prime."

General Tarzan was quick to organise surveillance scans of Io Prime and had them put on the screen. Io Prime was soon on the centre of the screen in all its glory.

"Shit! There you have it!", Matthew shouted, "Look! There, there and there!", he pointed.

"Three heavy cruisers!", General Tarzan quickly noted, "Earth, Colonial and Venusian."

"And they've taken up position around Io Prime", Matthew noted, "You can bet that damnable Martian gunship is around there somewhere as well."

"Our Brother Leopold, he's not going anywhere is he?", Prince Valdamar remarked.

"No Your Highness", Matthew confirmed, "The enemy has your Brother, Prince Leopold."

"Retrieval?", queried the High Prince.

General Tarzan shook his head, "Your Majesty. Retrieval of Prince Leopold will be impossible."

The High Prince looked to Matthew, he was looking so much older and very tired, Prince Leopold was not just his Brother, he was also his Son, "Captain. Can we retrieve Leopold?"

"Your Majesty. That Martian gunship and those cruisers will chew up anything we throw at them", Matthew replied, adding, "As much as I hate to say it, our enemy has Prince Leopold."

"Then Prince Leopold must stay behind and may God have mercy on him", High Prince Heinrich replied, with a combination of pragmatism and sorrow, deciding, "Make our final preparations for our departure to Eris. Then show me that big green button!"

Six hours later High Prince Heinrich von Horridian pushed that big green button. The go ahead for launch was transmitted across the entire flotilla and the exodus began. From the lofty vantage of Ganymede's Lagrangian point one, where the mighty gas giant's swirling cloud bands and the icy moon's rugged surface created a breathtaking vista, the immense colony push ships begin their long journey towards the distant dwarf planet Eris. These ancient and yet magnificent vessels, long and slender, stretched out like celestial leviathans, ready to venture into the farthest reaches of the solar system, to the dwarf planet Eris, where no human had yet set foot.

The four push ships were marvels of engineering, each one an intricate blend of form and function. Their exteriors, crafted from advanced titanium alloys and composites, glistening with a metallic sheen, designed to withstand the rigours of deep space travel and the ceaseless bombardment of cosmic radiation. Stretching for kilometres, these vessels were monumental in scale, their elongated forms cutting through the void with the grace of interstellar whales.

Within their immense hulls lie the heart of these ships, vast living and storage compartments. The living quarters were expansive bio-domes, filled with lush greenery and bathed in artificial light. These self-sustaining ecosystems provided not only food but also a sense of normalcy and tranquillity for the colonists on their long voyage. Advanced hydroponics and aquaponics systems ensured a steady supply of fresh produce, while sophisticated recycling systems maintained a continuous closed loop of both air and water.

The storage compartments, equally vast, are meticulously organised to carry all that is needed for the establishment of new colony on the distant dwarf world, Eris. These held everything from scientific instruments and modular habitats to terraforming equipment and personal belongings. Each compartment is a carefully packed treasure trove, carrying the seeds of future civilisations ready to be planted on alien soil.

Propulsion was the crowning glory of the push ships. Powerful fusion reactors powered these behemoths, channelling the immense energy of controlled nuclear reactions into steady, relentless thrust. These engines, pulsating with the energy of a thousand suns, propelled the ships forward with unwavering determination, pushing them outward to their distant destinations.

Surrounding these grand vessels were the service and support ships, a flotilla of smaller specialised craft that ensure the smooth operation of the push ships. These smaller vessels darted around the larger ships like worker bees, performing maintenance, ferrying supplies, and conducting reconnaissance missions. Equipped with everything from repair tools to scientific laboratories and ore processing facilities, these support ships are vital to the success of the mission, acting as the versatile, adaptable backbone of the expedition.

As the four push ships and their escorting flotilla flew away from Ganymede Lagrangian point one, they left behind the familiar gravity of Jupiter, heading into the unknown depths of deep space. Their journey would be long and arduous, but the spirit aboard these ships is unyielding. Scientists, engineers, military personnel, families, nobles and the royals all living and working together, bound by a shared need for survival, having been exiled into the farthest reaches of the solar system.

The departure from Ganymede Lagrangian point one was a sight to behold, a ballet of precision and power as the massive ships, escorted by their more agile support craft, launched in unison. Their paths, marked by the faint glow of ionised particles from their fusion thrusters, trace graceful arcs through the darkness, charting their course to the dwarf planet Eris and its moon Dysnomia.

Originally built to take the very first colonists to Jupiter's beautiful realm. Having sat idle for centuries at Ganymede's Lagrangian point one, these grand vessels were rebuilt, modernised and repurposed, now carrying the core of Jovian society and its leaders into deep space and exile. Their destination, the dwarf planet Eris and a new beginning. Their long burn into exile had begun.

32. The High Prince

"Has anyone responded to our hails?", Forkbraid asked.

"Not yet Captain", Charlene replied.

"Peter. Three heavy cruisers have surrounded Io Prime. What are the chances that no one has noticed us?", Forkbraid asked.

"Zero chance Captain. Their traffic control systems will have us on their screens", Peter replied, adding, "Our ships are completely visible to anyone who has access to the those long cylinder windows. We are clearly visible to them."

"Okay. New plan. Charlene stop trying to hail them, they are ignoring us", Forkbraid informed them, "Peter. Can the Solstice hack their communications network?"

"Of course Captain", Peter responded.

"Good. Obtain access to their broadcasting system. Send them the following message on all channels accessible. Keep repeating it until Charlene gets hailed by them", Forkbraid instructed, *"We are not here to harm you. We are not a threat. We are here to end this war. You are all safe."*

"Aye Captain", Peter replied.

"Captain, we are receiving a message", Charlene informed Forkbraid.

"From Io Prime?", Forkbraid queried.

"No Captain. It's from Captain Carmichael on the Spartan en-rout to Ganymede Prime", Charlene replied.

"What's the message?", Forkbraid asks.

"Fleet detected leaving Ganymede L1 on long burn. Captain Carmichael", Charlene read out.

"Peter. We need ultrascans of Ganymede L1. Detailed analysis", Forkbraid commanded.

"On it Captain", Peter Swann replied and after several minutes of scanning the Ganymede L1 region, informed Forkbraid, "It's a fleet of push ships Captain. Four in all and a flotilla of service and support ships."

"Push ships Peter?", Forkbraid enquired, requesting clarification.

"Yes Captain and from their designs, I'd say these are the original push ships that brought the first colonists to Jupiter centuries ago", Peter replied.

"Where are they headed Peter?", Forkbraid queried.

"They're running a long burn Captain, so it's nowhere local", Peter replied, adding, "I'll have the ship's computer continue to track them. Once it's calculated their trajectory, I'll let you know."

Jim Murphy stepped in, "It sounds like they're fleeing. Going into exile."

"Yes Jim. That's exactly what I was thinking", Forkbraid replied.

High Chancellor Gordon Hargreaves had only been at Io Prime for a short while when the Solstice and its small fleet of heavy cruisers arrived, not much more than a couple of days at most. He had not explained to Prince Leopold why he was there, only that he would reveal that when the time was right. Now that Io Prime was surrounded by a small enemy fleet and any chance of Prince Leopold and his family escaping to Ganymede Lagrangian point one was gone, the time was right. One final message had come through from the lead push ship, from High Prince Heinrich, *"We are forced to leave without my dear Leopold. Please protect my Son. May God bless him"*, he said nothing to Prince Leopold.

The High Chancellor had heard the messages being repeated over Io Prime's broadcasting systems and decide to err on the side of caution.

The High Chancellor asked Prince Leopold, "Do you have airtight compartments? Somewhere to go in case of a disaster?"

"Yes. We have two, one here under the palace and another under the base of our penthouse apartment", Prince Leopold replied.

"Good then Your Highness. Get your family packed. With those enemy cruisers surrounding us, I need to ensure your safety", the High Chancellor ordered, as an appointee of the High Prince, he had that right, "We'll go to the airtight compartments under your penthouse. It is less obvious."

Prince Leopold turned to Hubert, "Give our guests a heads up. We're coming for a visit."

"Yes Your Highness", Hubert replied.

"Guests Your Highness?", the High Chancellor enquired.

"We have friends staying at the penthouse High Chancellor", the Prince replied, "We'll go there and if the situation deteriorates, only then, will we go down to the hidden compartments."

"Jim. I'm going to try and find Prince Leopold. If I can locate him, I'll jaunt across. You're in charge of the ship until I get back", Forkbraid instructed.

"Aye Captain", Jim replied.

"Marcus. Do you still have the locations of the Prince's palace and penthouse?", Forkbraid asked.

"Of course Captain", Marcus replied.

"Skin dance our ship from the palace to the apartment building and I'll scan both, but not so close as to set off any alarms", Forkbraid commanded.

"Aye Captain", Marcus replied.

Forkbraid sat comfortably in his Captains chair on the bridge, as he reached out with his mind, attempting to locate Prince Leopold. As Marcus flew as closely to the northern end cap of Io Prime as he dare, Forkbraid continued to scan. He was disappointed at first after scanning the Prince's palace. The Prince and his family were not present.

Marcus continued to fly the Solstice around the end cap and eventually approached the apartment building, where Prince Leopold had his penthouse. Forkbraid smiled, he sensed the Prince and his family travelling en-rout to the apartment building in a stretched transport pod.

"Marcus. Put us right above the apartment building just like last time. X marks the spot", Forkbraid ordered, then he turned to Jim Murphy, "Jim. You have my chair until I get back."

Marcus and Jim both replied, "Aye Captain", in unison and Jim stepped away from his station to take position in the Captain's chair.

Forkbraid stepped away from his chair and concentrated. Forkbraid jaunted, there was a small flash of light and then he was gone.

There was a small flash of light, as Forkbraid reappeared in the pool room of the roof top gardens, above Prince Leopold's penthouse apartment. Forkbraid wasted no time, he walked from the pool house directly to the stairwell leading to the apartment. As he walked, Forkbraid began forming a bindrune. It was a bindrune of remembering and it glowed a bright and brilliant red.

As Forkbraid reached the base of the stairwell he stopped. With his left hand held down and his right hand held up, the bindrune in between glowed brightly. Forkbraid slapped his hands together. In an instant, the Appelbaums and Nerus began to remember. In the parking garage below the apartment building, Prince Leopold and his family had not even left their transport pod and they too, began to remember.

Princess Giselle looked at Prince Leopold, a knowing look and then whispered in his ear, "He's here. I don't know how I know it, but he's here. I'm remembering things."

Prince Leopold whispered back, "I know Giselle. I feel it too", then he kissed his wife to make it look like they were discussing something else completely different.

Forkbraid stepped into the apartment and everyone was in the main room waiting for him. They knew he was on his way, as their memories came back.

As Forkbraid entered the main room, wearing his navy blue Captain's uniform, Abram noted, "His Highness and his family are on their way here Captain."

"I know Abram. I sensed them in the elevator, on their way up. You should greet them", Forkbraid recommended.

Abram left the main room and headed for the penthouse's landing to greet Prince Leopold and his family. Several minutes later he returned and stepped aside to allow the Prince and his family to enter the room. Hubert, Prince Ulrick's Nanny Mary and another, very officious looking gentleman who was unknown to them, followed them into the room.

High Chancellor Hargreaves, upon seeing Forkbraid, straight away drew his sabre, "You Sir, have a bounty upon your head!"

Forkbraid quickly started scanning the High Chancellor's mind, "You Sir, should put away your sabre. Young Prince Leopold is certainly much more deft with his sabre than you are with yours."

Prince Leopold laughed, "Hargreaves, put your sabre away. Captain Forkbraid is right. You taught me well as a child, but I surpassed you long ago and hardly need you to defend me."

The High Chancellor replaced his sabre back in its scabbard and demanded of Forkbraid, "You Sir, are our enemy. What is your purpose here?"

Having looked into the High Chancellor's mind, Forkbraid replied with what was a perplexing answer, "I am not Prince Leopold's enemy and my purpose here, is precisely the same as yours."

This took the High Chancellor completely by surprise, "How can your purpose possibly align with mine?", he asked.

"Trust me High Chancellor. My purpose is perfectly aligned with yours", Forkbraid replied, adding, "Now, are you going to tell His Majesty or shall I tell him. I am more than happy to rip the scab off of this whole affair."

Prince Leopold raised his hand, "Captain Forkbraid. I am His Highness, my Brother Heinrich is His Majesty."

"He hasn't told you yet, has he?", Forkbraid replied, then looked to the High Chancellor.

"It wasn't time", the High Chancellor replied.

"I beg to differ on that point", Forkbraid replied, then turning back to the Prince, "Your Brothers have left Jovian space with a flotilla of push ships. They are currently performing a long burn towards the outer reaches of the solar system. We have yet to calculate their intended destination."

High Chancellor Hargreaves stepped in, "Your Majesty. As High Prince Heinrich has fled into exile, you are now from this moment forward, the new High Prince."

"How? Heinrich's eldest Son is next in the line of succession. Not me!", the Prince protested.

Forkbraid looked at the High Chancellor, this next part was going to be awkward, "The hell with it! This scab comes off! Warts and all! Your Majesty. Apart from the fact that your Brother Heinrich's entire family is on a push ship with him, you are his eldest Son!"

That caught Prince Leopold and everyone else in the room completely off guard.

"What!", Prince Leopold exclaimed.

The High Chancellor had everyone in the room looking at him, he stated slowly, "It is true Your Majesty. Your Father was, as you probably know, a drunkard. Your Mother was lonely and.... Well, she had issues. Your older Brother received untoward attention and you were the result."

Prince Leopold stepped over to the nearest chair and sat down. He put his head between his hands, looking at the floor for several minutes.

"Leo? Are you okay my love?", Princess Giselle enquired.

Prince Leopold looked up, "This explains a lot. Why my Brother seemed to favour me. Why he was so protective of me. Why he assigned you High Chancellor to train me in fencing. Why I was given lordship over the Ionian Realm. Just how many other people know of this?"

"Your Brother Heinrich obviously. Myself and those who needed to know, to ensure your succession to the Jovian High Throne", the High Chancellor informed him.

"And that is why we are both here Your Majesty. To ensure your ascendancy to the Jovian High Throne", Forkbraid interjected, adding, "We need to get you to Ganymede Prime as soon as possible, before a power vacuum forms. We need you on that throne and we have no time to waste."

"There will be no power vacuum Captain", the High Chancellor replied, "I have people in all of the Primes, including this one and they are firmly in control of the situation. Arrangements have already been made on Ganymede Prime for the coronation."

"None the less High Chancellor, the sooner Prince Leopold ascends to the Jovian High Throne the better", Forkbraid replied.

The High Chancellor reached out his hand to Forkbraid, "It seems our purposes are the same."

Forkbraid took his hand and shook it firmly.

Forkbraid asked, "What's the closest space dock to this apartment block?"

Abram, who had remained silent, answered, "That would be North Docking Ring, Dock six."

"Thank you Abram", Forkbraid replied, then he took out his communicator, flipped it open and ordered, "Jim. Have Marcus dock the Solstice at North Docking Ring, Dock six. Silent docking. Contact the Spartan. Tell Captain Carmichael, we'll be heading to Ganymede Prime with the new High Prince. Contact the Demeter, the Vampire and the Valiant. Tell them to maintain station around Io Prime. They are to protect Io Prime. Confirm orders please."

"Aye Captain. Orders confirmed and are now being implemented as we speak", Jim replied.

"Excellent. Forkbraid out", and Forkbraid put away his communicator.

"We don't need your ship Captain. We can use my shuttle", the High Chancellor remarked.

"The Solstice is much faster High Chancellor. Yourself, the High Prince and his family will come with me onboard the Solstice. Everyone else can travel on your shuttle", Forkbraid commanded.

High Prince Leopold quickly stepped in, "Agreed Captain. We'll travel on your ship. I have wanted to see your ship since the very first moment I heard about it."

"Very well then", the High Chancellor reluctantly agreed.

Thirty minutes later, the new High Prince, his family and the High Chancellor boarded the Solstice. First officer, Commander James Murphy was there to greet them.

"Please come aboard", Jim greeted them.

As High Prince Leopold came aboard, he remarked, "I know you. You're James Murphy."

"Commander James Murphy. Your Majesty", Jim corrected.

"You look so much like your cousin Matthew, Commander", the High Prince remarked.

"Speaking of Matthew Your Majesty. Where would he be? I very much want to talk with him. He and I have much to discuss", Jim replied.

"Oh. Your cousin Matthew is the Captain in charge of the lead push ship, heading out into deep space I believe Commander", High Prince Leopold informed him.

"On his way into exile along with your Brother Heinrich", Jim noted.

"Yes Commander, that would be the case", the High Prince agreed.

Jim's face took on a sour look, "Just another thing I have to explained to his parents Your Majesty. His Mother and Father are going to be devastated."

"You don't have to tell them Jim. You could let them continue to believe that Matthew died on that colony, Skye. You know, the flash vaporiser", Forkbraid suggested.

"No. No FB. That wouldn't be right. I have to tell them. It just has to be", Jim explained.

As they were speaking, Zuawalo and Zeealas approached. They were carrying their new born daughters and breast feeding them. At first the High Prince and his wife were taken aback, the Pod Girls being so very tall, slim, dark and beautiful.

"Girls. Really! We do have guests in case you hadn't noticed", Jim informed them.

Zuawalo replied, "Jim! Your daughters need to eat."

"Yes Zuawalo, but you and Zeealas can feed them in the creche, yes?", Jim responded looking somewhat embarrassed.

Princess Giselle quickly stepped in, "You have a creche on board? My little boy Ulrick will need feeding very soon."

"Yes. We have a creche on board. It is a very nice creche", Zeealas confirmed.

"Commander. You have two wives?", High Prince Leopold enquired.

"Yes Your Majesty. However, it's a long story and I have no wish to discuss it now", Jim replied.

"That is okay Jim", Zuawalo stepped in, "Zeealas and I can show the Princess to the creche."

Zeealas added, "While Her Majesty feeds little Prince Ulrick, we will tell her the story."

Jim sighed slightly, "If you must Girls, if you must."

High Prince Leopold chuckled slightly, "My Brother Heinrich was right. This ship of yours is not really a military ship is it after all?"

Zuawalo put one finger to her lips, "Shh Your Majesty. That is a secret!" and then she and Zeealas led Princess Giselle to the ship's creche.

"Jim. Perhaps you can give His Majesty and the High Chancellor a tour of the ship", Forkbraid suggested, adding, "I'll get reacquainted with my Captains chair and contact Captain Carmichael."

"Aye Captain", Jim replied, then to the High Prince, "Your Majesty. I'll show you around the ship first and then to your quarters."

Captain Carmichael was quickly on the bridge's main screen and Forkbraid informed him, "We have the new High Prince on board and are en-route to Ganymede Prime as we speak."

"So you have the High Prince under arrest then?', Captain Carmichael queried.

"No Captain. This is Prince Leopold the new High Prince. The High Prince you're thinking of is on one of those push ships. Probably the lead one", Forkbraid replied.

"Captain Forkbraid. I don't see the difference", Captain Carmichael responded.

"It's like I put in my previous reports Captain. Prince Leopold was never involved in the Jovian military. He is known to have been opposed to this war and advised against it on many occasions", Forkbraid explained.

"Still Captain. We are going to need someone to blame for all these deaths", the Captain replied.

"Oh, there are plenty of people to blame Captain, but not Prince Leopold", Forkbraid replied, explaining, "Prince Valdamar had wanted to conquer the Belter colonies in the Asteroid Belt and annex them. His older Brothers, Prince Wulfric and High Prince Heinrich were more ambitious. The entire war was their plan, their ambition and in the end, their disaster. Prince Leopold was against any form of conquest. I believe, any investigation of the official records will exonerate him."

"That's all well and good Captain, but Prince Leopold's older Brothers, are all on those damned push ships and they are still long burning into the outer reaches of the solar system."

"To be precise Captain, the ones you really want are Heinrich and his Brother Wulfric. However, it makes little difference. Jovian society has been completely gutted. Everyone who was involved in the war, from top to bottom, is on those push ships. They are all fleeing into distant exile", Forkbraid explained.

"Except Prince Leopold", the Captain noted.

"Yes and we need Prince Leopold", Captain Forkbraid replied, explaining, "The new High Prince is the key to a lasting peace. Not just here in the Jovian Realms, but across the entire solar system as well."

"You've been inside their heads Captain, so I'll trust your judgement on this matter", the Captain replied, asking, "Does the new High Prince know where his Brothers are going?"

"No Captain. He doesn't. However, if they are still long burning, it must be a very distant destination", Forkbraid turned to Peter Swann, "Any ideas Peter?"

"Yes actually Captain. Based on their long burn and their current trajectory, they can only be heading to one place, the Dwarf Planet Eris", Peter replied.

"There you have it Captain. They are heading out to Eris", Forkbraid informed him.

"That's a long way out. It'll take them ten or twelve years to get there", the Captain noted.

"Yes Captain and we cannot give chase either", Forkbraid replied.

"Not even in your ship? It is awfully fast?", Captain Carmichael asked.

Forkbraid looked to Peter Swann, who stood up, so as to be seen on the screen, "Captain. We would have to use the slipstream drive to get to Eris. Once there, we would be stuck at a Dwarf world with no colonies, waiting a dozen years for our fugitives to arrive. Then after apprehending those fugitives, another dozen years to fly back. I would not recommend that mission to anyone."

"Point noted Mr Swann. I wouldn't recommend it either", Captain Carmichael agreed.

"Captain. We'll see you at Ganymede Prime. Once the new High Prince is on the Jovian High Throne, this war can be officially declared over. Forkbraid over and out", Forkbraid replied.

High Prince Leopold entered the ship's bridge with the High Chancellor, "I must admit Captain, this ship of yours is very impressive."

"Yes", the High Chancellor agreed, "The cabins are far superior to anything on my shuttle. You even have a creche on board, which Princess Giselle finds delightful."

"I'm glad you approve gentlemen. Feel free to compliment my Engineering officer, Varak. We should have you all at Ganymede Prime in no time", Forkbraid informed them both.

"Excellent Captain. When we arrive, His Majesty needs to address the Jovian people and then after that, we'll hold a quick coronation ceremony. Everything has been planned, my people are just waiting for us to arrive", the High Chancellor informed him.

The Solstice was quick to make the distance between Io Prime and Ganymede

Prime and the High Chancellor along with the Royal family were soon disembarking and entering the huge capital colony of the Jovian Realms.

The New High Prince stepped up to the podium. He was surrounded by and supported by former High Prince Heinrich's people. All sworn to ensure that Prince Leopold would become the new High Prince. Along side Prince Leopold stood High Chancellor Hargreaves. The conference hall was largely empty, as it had not been advertised in advance, however, the address would be streamed to the entirety of the Jovian Realms.

The High Chancellor addressed the Jovian Realms, "Our leader, High Prince Heinrich has fled into exile. He, along with his Brothers, Prince Wulfric and Prince Valdamar, as well as most of the nobles and a great many of our people, have launched themselves in ancient push ships into the depths of the outer solar system. The very push ships, that brought the very first colonists to Jupiter and it's Galilean Moons. High Prince Heinrich von Horridian and his entire entourage have fled to the Dwarf Planet Eris!"

He looked around the conference hall for effect, even though it was still largely empty and then continued, "As such, High Prince Heinrich has abdicated his positions as High Prince of the Jovian Realms and Prince of Ganymede. His Brothers, Prince Wulfric and Prince Valdamar have abdicated their positions as Prince of Callisto and Prince of Europa."

The High Chancellor looked around the hall once more, then continued, "In accordance with the Jovian laws of succession, his youngest Brother, Prince Leopold, Prince of Io, is hereby and henceforth, elevated to the following positions. Prince of Callisto, Prince of Europa, Prince of Ganymede and High Prince of the Jovian Realms. People of the Jovian Realms, I give you, your new High Prince. His Majesty, High Prince Leopold von Horridian."

The High Chancellor stepped back from the podium to let the new High Prince speak.

His Majesty, High Prince Leopold von Horridian stepped forward to address the people of the Jovian Realms, his people.

"This war, that my Brothers Heinrich and Wulfric started has been disastrous for everyone involved. Millions of innocent people have perished in the name of conquest and nothing has been achieved but death. Cooperation between the Jovian Realms and the rest of the solar system is the answer, not war!", High Prince Leopold began.

High Prince Leopold looked around the largely empty conference hall, before continuing, "I hereby decree, that this war is over. All Jovian Forces, without exception, are hereby ordered to stand down and surrender to the inner system forces from the Earth, L5 and Venus."

There was loud and boisterous clapping and cheering from the few people in the audience. More and more people had began to enter the conference hall. Word was getting out, that there was a new High Prince.

This was merely one of many decrees that High Prince Leopold would issue, "I hereby decree, that the previous Jovian High Council's proclamation annexing the Planet Mars, its two Moons Phobos and Deimos, all of the Martian Orbital Colonies, the Colonies of both Martian Lagrangian Points L4 and L5 and all of the Asteroidal Colonies between Martian and Jovian Orbits, is rescinded. The Jovian Realms have absolutely no rights, to claim those independent and sovereign territories."

There was a pause, then the new High Prince decreed, "I hereby decree, that the bounties offered upon the capture of the Martian Defence Force ship Solstice and its crew are rescinded, they are null and void. Those bounties are no more and they will not be honoured!"

There was loud cheering on board the Solstice, when its crew heard that decree.

High Prince Leopold looked around the conference hall. More and more people had arrived.

The High Prince paused for a long moment, before continuing, "The following decrees are not so easy. They effect the very core of Jovian society. We, all of us in the Jovian Realms, know of the 'Narrative'. It has been taught to us since birth, from generation to generation for centuries", then he paused once more, shaking his head.

"This 'Narrative' is false and has been since day one. It is pure indoctrination and nothing more. There are no demons in the inner solar system. Inner solar system leaders are not demons and have never have been possessed by demons. Christians in the inner solar system are not being persecuted. I hereby decree, that this 'False Narrative' be ended. Hereby and henceforth the Jovian Realms will be free of this 'False Narrative'."

After another long pause, the new High Prince continued, "With regards the Jovian High Church and the other Jovian Churches in general. I hereby decree that henceforth, membership in the Jovian High Church and it's subordinate

Churches is no longer mandatory and that tithing is optional and cannot be enforced by any Church in the Jovian Realms."

Loud and boisterous clapping and cheering from the people in the audience erupted once more. This particular decree was bound to be popular, as it effected most of all, family budgets and the peoples pockets. The gathered numbers in the hall had begun to swell and grew by the minute.

Prince Leopold looked out upon the hall once more and then did the one thing, that he had always wanted to, "People of the Jovian Realms. This next decree is something I could never have done, as merely the Prince of the Ionian Realm. Only the High Prince has the power to do this and I am now that High Prince. I hereby decree, that henceforth, all forms of Slavery are abolished in the Jovian Realms. No man, women or child may be owned by another. No man, women or child may own another. Henceforth, all Slaves are hereby freed and are, as of now free citizens of the Jovian Realms with equal rights. All Jovian citizens will be free!"

At first the audience was quiet, almost in a state of shock. No one had expected this. Then the audience was on their feet, clapping and cheering loudly. The cheering, clapping and screaming took a very long time to die down.

When High Prince Leopold looked out upon the audience once more, what had been a scant few people had grown into a multitude and the conference hall was almost packed as more and more people attempted to enter, to watch the most important event in recent Jovian history.

High Prince Leopold smiled as tears welled up and began to flow, his wife, Princess Giselle approached the podium. With Prince Ulrick in her arms, she passed him her handkerchief to wipe away the tears. This then generated even more clapping and cheering. It was an emotional moment.

With Princess Giselle standing beside him, High Prince Leopold held up his hand to quieten the audience, "When my Brothers went into exile, they took ninety percent of the nobility and a sizeable number of our Jovian society with them. The Council of Nobles throughout the Jovian Realms are no more or at the very least, they are severely depleted. These Councils are going to be replaced with elected Houses of Citizenry, one for each Jovian Realm. These Houses of Citizenry, will in turn elect Governors, amongst others, from within their ranks. Those Governors will form the new Jovian High Council, which in turn, will advise the High Prince. These changes will of course require a new constitution, which will be drawn up over the next month or two. I hereby decree that henceforth, this is the path our Jovian Realms are going to take."

The audience was quiet once more, no one had expect such political changes either. It was an awkward silence, until finally, the cheering and clapping began. Slowly at first, but then after half a minute the sound was deafening. It took a long time for it to settle down.

High Prince Leopold held up his right hand once more to quieten the audience, "There are some things that you have not been told. Things that were hidden from the people. There were six Jovian Realms, now there are only four. Our Fore and Aft Trojan Realms have effectively declared their independence."

That caused a shock. The former High Prince had ordered that information classified. Talking, murmurs and whispers sprung up everywhere.

The High Prince held up his hand once more, "I know. I know. My Brother ordered that information to be censored. I however, believe you deserve to know. The Aft Trojan Realm is now a Constitutional Principality with my Sister, Princess Luisa, as the Head of State. The Fore Trojan Realm wanted to do the same but found themselves in the throes of a violent revolution. My Sister, Princess Sophia, was violently murdered as a result. The Fore Trojan Realm has now become Constitutional Republic."

High Prince Leopold paused, to allow this new information to be digested by the audience.

It was quiet for a very long time before the High Prince continued, "I hereby decree, that one of the very first tasks for our new Jovian High Council to tackle, will be discussions with the Trojan Realms. Discussions to decide, what form of relationship, these newly independent Realms want to have with our Jovian Realms moving forward. Personally, I'm hoping that they still wish to remain as Jovian Realms, albeit with far greater autonomy, however, that will be up to the Trojan Realms themselves to decide."

High Prince Leopold looked out over the the audience one final time, "My people. There is so much to be done. These changes, these reforms will certainly take time. Please be patient with us, while we work out the details of these new reforms and as these reforms are implemented over the forth coming months."

Princess Giselle held High Prince Leopold's hand in hers and then lifted them into the air. The Princess leant in to the High Prince and kissed him tenderly. The audience rose to its feet as one and erupted into cheers, claps, whistles and woots, giving the High Prince, his wife, Princess Giselle and Son Prince Ulrick, a standing ovation.

After all the cheers died down and the address to the Jovian Realms was over, the new High Prince and his family were whisked away to the coronation ceremony. The ceremony, although smaller than it would normally have been, none the less contained all the pomp an pageantry that was expected of it. The ceremony was streamed to the entirety of the Jovian Realms. Once it was over, Forkbraid and Jim had one more meeting with the High Prince and his family, just long enough to say their good byes and wish them all well.

"Time to go home Jim. Our job here is done", Forkbraid told him as they returned to their ship.

Within twenty four hours, the entire solar system had received word that a new High Prince, sat upon the Jovian High Throne and that the solar system was at peace, once again. The new High Prince's address to his people and his coronation ceremony, had also been beamed to the old High Prince, Heinrich, aboard the push ships, flying into exile, to the farthest reaches of the solar system, the Dwarf Planet Eris.

Henceforth, High Prince Leopold of the Jovian Realms, Prince of Ganymede, Prince of Callisto, Prince of Europa and Prince of Io, became known as High Prince Leopold, the Great Reformer.

33. Elysium

Now back in Jovian space, just clear of Ganymede Prime, Forkbraid contacted the three Fleet Captains. All three appeared on in windows on the Solstice's bridge main screen.

After greeting each other, Forkbraid informed the Captains, "I've left your cruisers, the Demeter, Vampire and Valiant, stationed at Io Prime. They have orders to defend Io Prime until such time as their presence is no longer required. When you have determined that, you may retrieve them."

"Thank you Captain", Captain Carmichael replied, "I think we'll leave them there for the moment. We need to be certain that this peace holds first."

Captain Philo added, "Yes. That will take a bit of time, but so far things are looking good."

"We also have another matter to sort out gentlemen", Captain Galtieri noted, "When we punched through their Jovian defensive line, we left a lot of disabled ships in our wake. We will need to check those Jovian dreadnoughts for survivors."

Captain Philo replied, "We should give that a level of urgency Captains. I recommend we organise search and rescue missions urgently."

"Agreed", Captain Carmichael and Captain Galtieri replied almost in unison.

"Captains. The main task for which I came here, namely putting Prince Leopold on the Jovian High Throne is completed. My ship and crew will be departing Jovian space and returning back to Mars very soon", Forkbraid informed them, adding, "I do have one major request."

"And that request is?", questioned Captain Philo.

"High Prince Leopold is under my protection, however, I have to return to Mars", Forkbraid began explaining, "I am hereby placing High Prince Leopold under your protection Captains."

"I don't believe you have the authority to do that Captain", Captain Philo remarked.

"Authority be damned Felix, I'm doing it anyway", Captain Forkbraid responded.

Captain Carmichael quickly stepped in, "Agreed. Captain Forkbraid. High Prince Leopold is henceforth, under my protection until such time as it no longer required."

Captain Galtieri remarked, "It is quite irregular, but I also agree. Henceforth, High Prince Leopold will have my protection as well, until such time as it no longer required."

Captain Philo replied, "Hmm. What is authority but an agreement between like-minded men. Very well then, High Prince Leopold henceforth, will also have my protection, until such time as it no longer required."

"Very well then. Protect the High Prince and his family. He is at the moment the most important man in the solar system and cannot be allowed to fail", Forkbraid replied.

All three Captains replied almost in unison, "Agreed."

"One more request Captain Carmichael?", Forkbraid asked.

"Yes Captain?", Captain Carmichael enquired.

"The High Prince's address to the people of the Jovian Realms and his coronation have all been recorded", Forkbraid remarked, adding, "Transmit a copy of those events, to those push ships."

"I'm not seeing your reasoning Captain", Captain Carmichael admitted.

"Captain. It will show our enemies that we aren't monsters. That their Jovian Realms still exist and that their Brother Leopold, now sits on the Jovian High Throne", Forkbraid replied, explaining, "They'll be building their new colonies with the knowledge that their old colonies survived and that we did not commit genocide. It is important that they have no excuses for future hostilities."

"That is actually a good idea", Captain Galtieri remarked.

"Yes it is. I'll make is so Captain Forkbraid", Captain Carmichael agreed.

"Excellent. We will be off now Captains. Remember, when you guys do manage to head back to the inner solar system. Stop by Mars on your way home, your crews will need a bit of rest and relaxation", Forkbraid recommended, "Captain Forkbraid over and out."

"Marcus, plot a course taking us beyond Callisto's orbit. Let's catch a slipstream to take us home", Forkbraid commanded.

"Aye Captain. Plotting the new course now", Marcus replied.

"It will be good to get home FB", Jim noted, "I'd like my daughters to be given actual names."

"Yes Jim, I expect it will", Forkbraid replied.

"Lieutenant Rossi stepped onto the bridge, "I must thank you Captain."

"Why is that Lieutenant?", Forkbraid enquired.

"Well Captain. If this was a normal ship, I would never have had the opportunity to deliver a pair of babies on board", the Lieutenant replied smiling.

"True enough Lieutenant. Let's not forget though, that you'll be delivering Nyaliep's baby in due course as well", Forkbraid reminded her.

Marcus flew the Solstice to the region just beyond Callisto's orbit, where he located a suitable frame dragging event. He quickly triggered a slipstream, gave it a quick once over and a little over two minutes and ten seconds later, they were all back in low Martian orbit. From there it was less than an hour and they were all back home at the New Flinders Psychic Academy.

Matthew was checking the information displayed on the lead push ship's bridge main screen. Other bridge crew men and women were going about their duties at their usual work stations. The main screen displayed a highly magnified image of the Dwarf Planet Eris and its moon Dysnomia in the top left corner. Displayed directly beneath that, there was collated telemetry information pertaining to the flotilla's course to Eris.

On the right hand side of the main screen from top to bottom was information displayed about the push ship's fusion engines and its thrusters, its propellant levels, life support and recycling systems etc. Everything Matthew needed to keep an eye on as the Captain of the ship, it's name simply PS1 or Push Ship One in its longer form.

In the central expanse of the main screen was an images of the local star field. It was inky black, with a multiple of stars being visible. The broad band of the Milky-way galaxy providing the most magnificent of backdrops. In the very centre of the image, was a highlight distant dot, the Dwarf World Eris and its Moon Dysnomia. Their destination, their new home.

In one small corner of the bridge sat a lone figure watching a smaller, secondary screen. It was the old High Prince, High Prince Heinrich and he was watching the new High Prince's address to the Jovian Realms and his formal coronation to the Jovian High Throne. Over and over he'd watched it, at least a dozen times, probably quite a few more.

The automatic doors to the bridge opened and in walked Prince Valdamar, Prince Wulfric and his wife Princess Matilda.

"There you go Wulfric. I said he'd be here", Prince Valdamar remarked.

"What are you doing there Brother?", Prince Wulfric asked High Prince Heinrich, "You must have watched those data streams dozens of times."

"And I may watch them a dozen more times Wulfric", the High Prince replied.

"Why Brother? Why?", Prince Wulfric questioned, then remarked, "This was Leopold's own plan B. He is now the new High Prince!"

"What are you saying Brother?", the High Prince asked.

"Well look at him Brother. Leopold has pushed through what, no fewer than eight decrees in one single address. His first address to the people of the Jovian Realms. Our people Brother!", Prince Wulfric noted, "Surely this was his plan all along."

Prince Valdamar stepped in, "So Wulfric. You're saying that our plan B was to go into exile, while Leopold's plan B was to take over the Jovian Realms. To take control of the Jovian High Throne?"

"Seems to be Brother Valdamar. Seems to be", Prince Wulfric replied.

High Prince Heinrich replied, "You are wrong Brother Wulfric. Leopold could never have expected this. My own people, headed by High Chancellor Hargreaves, have elevated Prince Leopold to the Jovian High Throne. That was my doing Brothers! My doing!"

"Your doing Brother?", Prince Wulfric queried, "But why?"

High Prince Heinrich did not inform his Brothers, that Leopold was not only their Brother, but also his Son, instead he told them, "Our Brother Leopold left for Io Prime to collect his family. Your families were already here on Ganymede Prime, his family was not. There was a large probability, that he would not make it back to the push ships in time. That Leopold, would be left behind."

Prince Valdamar understood, "So you sent High Chancellor Hargreaves to Io Prime, to Leopold, with instructions."

"That I did Valdamar. That I did", High Prince Heinrich replied.

"Then what are all these decrees, all of these reforms?", Prince Wulfric asked.

"That dear Brother Wulfric, is Leopold at his best", the High Prince replied, explaining, "Wulfric, you've always thought your was Brother slow. Leopold is anything but slow. Leopold is introverted and quiet, he thinks deeply and quietly. He's solves difficult problems in his head, while everyone else is still yapping about them. Wulfric, you have never understood Leopold."

"So Leopold's decrees, his reforms have a purpose?", Prince Wulfric queried.

"Oh dear Brother, you still don't get it, do you?", the High Prince replied, "Wulfric, we lost the War! We left Leopold with an absolute disaster on his hands. What we are seeing is Leopold thinking fast, solving problems, pulling rabbits out of hats. Leopold is winning the Peace!"

Prince Valdamar stepped in, he understood, "Hence all of the reforms. If Leopold pulls this off, the Jovian Realms will be far better off having lost the war and instead winning the peace!"

Princess Matilda noted, "Always watch the quiet ones Wulfric. They are the ones most likely to surprise us all."

Matthew looked around the bridge, all of the bridge crew had gotten distracted by the Royals, he clapped his hands and ordered, "Crew! Back to your stations! You all have jobs to do!"

He then approached High Prince Heinrich, "Your Majesty. Your Brother Leopold is one of the most intelligent people I've eve met. If anyone can pull the Jovian Realms out of this disaster, Prince Leopold can."

"Yes Matthew. I believe you're right. I am very proud of my Brother Leopold", High Prince Heinrich announced.

"Excellent. May I ask a favour of you, Your Majesty?", Matthew asked.

"Yes of course Matthew", the High Prince replied.

"Push ship one is a huge ship Your Majesty. It has a lot or facilities. Many of those facilities are recreational. Would it be too much to ask, that you make use of those facilities", Matthew cautiously explained, "Having Royals on my bridge is very distracting to the crew Your Majesty."

"Are you asking me to go off and have some fun Matthew?", the High Prince asked.

"I am insisting on it Your Majesty. Go. Have fun. Enjoy the trip. It will most certainly be a long one", Matthew replied, adding, "I'll give your stateroom access to those video data steams."

High Prince Heinrich smiled, "You heard that Brothers, Princess. We all need to clear the bridge and go and have some fun. Captains orders", he winked at Matthew, then announced loudly, so everyone could hear, "I am so proud of my Brother, Prince Leopold, the new High Prince of the Jovian Realms."

As the High Prince left the ship's bridge, he turned around and asked, "Why do you think they sent us those video data feeds to us Matthew?"

"I can't be certain Your Majesty. Perhaps, just to let you know, that your Brother Leopold is going to be okay", Matthew replied.

"That in itself is an interesting thing Matthew", the High Prince noted.

"Yes it is Your Majesty. Yes it is", Matthew agreed.

With the war over and the bounties rescinded, it was now far safer for the crew of the Solstice to travel. Nyaliep being heavily pregnant and close to giving birth, wanted to go to Zuawalo's and Zeealas's cabin for the actual birth itself. Jim's wives were excited by the prospect and before Jim knew what was happening, he was flying his in laws, his wives and the Doctor north to their cabin. Varak had sent a communique ahead to his Androids to make preparations.

Jim landed his Hummer on a clear patch of land, high up on the ridge line between two valleys, Zuawalo's valley to the north and Zeealas's valley to the south. The landing area was just wide enough for two Hummers, but only just. A path led away from the landing area, to a log cabin higher up on the ridge, two hundred yards to the east. Snow had been falling, although not very heavily and it covered the ridge line in patches here and there.

The log cabin was quite large, almost a chalet and it spanned the ridge line, being built across the top and down both sides. It was a beautiful sight. Jim stepped out of the Hummer into the crisp, cold air. He stepped aside to let his passengers alight. Lieutenant Rossi stepped out next and stood to one side. Jim's wives, Zuawalo and Zeealas stepped out, embracing their daughters tightly, protecting them against the cold Martian air. Zigg, Zuawalo's pet ferret stepped out of the Hummer and dutifully followed Zuawalo as she walked up the path. Varak helped his heavily pregnant wife Nyaliep out of the Hummer. They were followed by Kwoth and Zyaliep.

Jim secured the Hummer and told the others, "It's very cold. Let's get you lot up to the cabin."

"The luggage?", questioned, Zyaliep.

"My metal men will bring the luggage up to the cabin once we are inside", Varak replied.

Zuawalo and Zeealas were already walking up the path to their cabin, their babies were still quite young and needed to be out of the cold air as soon as possible.

Nyaliep looked up the path towards the cabin, "Varak. The cabin is so far and my belly is so big. I will not make it that far."

Varak was tall and strong, built like an ox, "That is not a problem Nyaliep", he told her as he swept her off her feet and began to carry her up the path.

"Jim. This is a beautiful place. Cold, but beautiful", Zyaliep noted as she and her husband Kwoth began following the others up the path.

Jim gestured up the path, "After you Lieutenant."

Lieutenant Rossi replied, "Doctor. Not Lieutenant. I'm only a Lieutenant when in uniform or on the Solstice."

"As you wish Doctor", Jim replied and they followed the others up the path to the cabin.

The cabin was warm inside, as Varak's house Androids had ensured it was comfortably warm.

The alpha Android approached Varak, who was still carrying his heavily pregnant wife, "We have prepared a room upstairs for the birthing", it informed them.

"Please lead the way", Varak replied and he followed the alpha Android to the birthing room, with Nyaliep in his arms.

Doctor Rossi followed them upstairs to the room, knowing that Nyaliep's baby would be coming very soon, "Varak. I'll be needing to check Nyaliep. I don't think we'll have long to wait."

The Doctor turned back around to Zyaliep, "I'll send an Android down to get you when I need your assistance Zyaliep."

Once everyone was inside the cabin and out of the cold, Zuawalo and Zeealas went straight to the main fire place. There, surrounding an open space in front of the fire, was a series of comfortable couches and chairs, along with two large coffee tables. Zuawalo and Zeealas sat down at either end of one of the couches and Jim sat himself down in the middle, between them. Zigg the ferret jumped up onto Zuawalo's lap and snuggled, nice and warm.

Jim put his arms around Zuawalo and Zeealas and drew them both in close to himself. He turned to his right and kissed Zuawalo on the cheek, the turned to his left and kissed Zeealas the same way.

Zyaliep and Kwoth had sat down on the couch directly opposite Jim and his wives.

Jim looked to his in-laws, "Kwoth. Zyaliep. I was born on a colony at L5 and grew up on Colonial Central Command. When I came to Mars, I thought we'd catch the Prophet and I'd be back home in no time. That was a long time ago. I now have two beautiful wives, two beautiful daughters and I am happier than I have ever been. I cannot imagine ever going back to L5 and my old life", he had genuine tears of joy in his eyes.

"Jim. You may be short. You may be thin. You may even look like a ghost, but Jim, you are a very good husband to my daughters", Zyaliep replied, adding, "Mars changes everything and Mars changes everyone. You are a changed man. There is no going back."

Zuawalo and Zeealas both leant in close to Jim, as he replied to Zyaliep's typically odd compliment, "Thank you Mother Zyaliep."

The door of the cabin opened and four Androids walked in carrying their luggage. No one had noticed them leave. The door was quickly closed once more and the Androids took the luggage up to their rooms.

The alpha Android who have come back downstairs informed them, "Your luggage will be in your rooms. We have hung name plaques on the doors, so you will know which room is yours."

There was a loud scream from upstairs and then another, followed by loud shouting in Kiswahili, "Londoe kwangu!", followed by expletives, "Jamani jamani, mbona inauma sana!"

Zyaliep looked up, her eyes very wide, "I think maybe it is time. My Sister, Nyaliep is having a hard time. I will go there now to assist with the birth" and she got up and headed straight upstairs.

"Father. What did Nyaliep say?", Zeealas asked, "My Kiswahili is not so good."

"What a woman says when in child birth Zeealas", Kwoth answered, "I think Nyaliep said, *'Get it out of me. Fucking hell, why does it have to hurt so much.'* It is allowable. Nyaliep is giving birth. Did you and Zuawalo not say such things when you gave birth on the space ship?"

"I am not sure Father. I think maybe, but it was in English, not Kiswahili", Zeealas answered.

"Father Kwoth. It was the same for both of them", Jim explained, "They both swore like drunken troopers. I kid you not."

Kwoth laughed loudly.

"Jim! We were not so bad!", Zuawalo protested, then asked, "Were we?"

"Well my loves, you both had your moments", Jim replied and then gave them a gentle squeeze.

For most of the night, there was moaning and groaning coming from the birthing room upstairs. That was interspersed with crying, sobbing and grunting. At intervals, there was more screaming, yelling and verbal expressions. Some were in Kiswahili, some were in Nuer and even some in English. Eventually those sounds were replaced by a brief but potent silence, followed by the sounds of a baby crying. Then with the rising of the Sun and the beginning of a new day, Nyaliep had given birth to a male child, her very first Son. Nyaliep named him "Wie", after the Sun and Varak agreed with her choice, as it was very appropriate.

During the long night Zuawalo and Zeealas considered names for their daughters. They wanted to choose names starting with Z like their mother had chosen for them. Which was not traditional for their folk, but something they wanted none the less. Their Father, Kwoth, suggested using Kiswahili names. In the morning, however, they still had not chosen names for their daughters. Upon hearing their new cousin's name, Zuawalo had an idea.

"Father. What is the Kiswahili name for Venus?", she asked.

"Zuhura represents the planet Venus, known as the *'morning star'* or *'evening star'* or so I believe", Kwoth replied.

"Then I will call my daughter Zuhura", Zuawalo decided.

Zeealas, who always follows her Sisters lead, remarked, "That is not fair. I like that name too."

"You cannot have it Sister. I have already chosen it", Zuawalo replied.

Quickly avoiding a Sisterly argument, Jim asked the nearest Android, "Android, give me a list of feminine names starting with Z from either the Nuer or Kiswahili cultures."

The Android not only rattled off a list, it also added some useful hints and combinations.

"If you combined the word *'Zira'* which means orbit with the word *'Rubini'* which means ruby, you can symbolically represent the planet Mars", the Android remarked.

That caught Zeealas's attention, "Zirarubini! I like that one! My daughter will be Zirarubini. It will reflect Mars."

Thus three babies were named that morning, Wie, Zuhura and Zirarubini, after the Sun, Venus and Mars.

Selene was sitting in her study going through the latest reports from her administrators in both the New Flinders Psychic Academy and the Elysium Colony. Forkbraid walked in with a glass of cherry red wine and offered Selene a glass. Selene politely declined the wine.

"I've had news from the cabin", Forkbraid informed Selene.

"Oh", Selene replied distractedly, then asked, "News?"

Forkbraid smiled, "Nyaliep had a Son. Varak and Nyaliep named him Wie. Jim's wives have named their daughters as well. Zuawalo's daughter is Zuhura and Zeealas's daughter is Zirarubini."

"Interesting names", Selene replied.

"Yes. Wie means the Sun, Zuhura means Venus and Zirarubini means Mars, apparently", Forkbraid explained.

"Wow! They chose them all very thoughtfully", Selene noted.

"So Selene. What do you have there?", Forkbraid asked.

"Paper work. Reports. That sort of thing", Selene replied.

"Boring stuff?", asked Forkbraid.

"No. I wouldn't say boring", Selene answered, then added, "Quite informative actually."

Selene picked up a report and continued, "This report is from our Campus in Sweetness Vale, the Campus Headmistress sent it to us. We now have fifty six students at the campus. Forty from Sweetness town and sixteen from the bush folk. Of those fifty six students, eighteen are apprentices. Everything seems to be running very smoothly over there."

"Sounds like the Sweetness Campus is booming", Forkbraid remarked.

"It is. That Campus is performing very well. Far above expectations", Selene agreed.

Selene picked up another report, "This report is from our Head of Population Statistics at the Elysium Colony. When we came here, we brought with us a thousand psychic couples. We lost one sixth of those, when the HLT Agamemnon was attacked and destroyed. Of the eight hundred and thirty odd couples that made it to the colony, nearly six hundred now have babies and toddlers."

"That's a hell of a lot of children Selene. A hell of a lot", Forkbraid noted.

"Yes it is Forkbraid. And they will all need assessing and inducting", Selene replied, explaining, "In four years, there will be nearly six hundred children being tested for any psychic abilities and of those, over five hundred that will need to be assessed and inducted into the psychic academy."

"Selene, in the first year, there will be several hundred novitiates and the following year, will be a repeat of the same", Forkbraid quickly calculated, "Can this academy even cope with those kind of numbers?"

"No. Not really. This academy is huge, but not that huge", Selene admitted, "I'm going to have to work something out. I do have some ideas."

"Well, run them past me. Let's hear them", Forkbraid suggested.

"I'll need to check with Varak, but I was thinking of sending some of them to the Sweetness Campus", Selene informed him.

"Okay. That is a start, but the Sweetness Campus will probably reach capacity with just over a hundred or so students", Forkbraid replied.

"Yes. I was just thinking that. Hence the need to discuss this with Varak. Some expansion may be necessary. Maybe double the capacity?", Selene explained.

"Perhaps, but what about teachers? You are going to need more teachers?",

Forkbraid enquired.

"Yes we will. We are going to need a pretty good teacher training program to be ready for this influx of students on time. So I will be putting together a plan for that as well", Selene informed Forkbraid.

"A suggestion Selene. Put together a home schooling program as well. To cover any students who might miss out on placements", Forkbraid recommended.

"Yes. Yes, that is a good idea. There may even be some parents who prefer home schooling", Selene agreed.

"You know. The one thing we didn't take into account, when we were planning for this psychic academy back on the Earth. How quickly, our couples were going to be starting their own families", Selene admitted.

"Kind of caught you by surprise I see", Forkbraid chuckled.

"It's not funny Forkbraid! With that damned war causing all those issues and now this", Selene looked at Forkbraid, "Please, don't poke fun at it Forkbraid. It's just not funny!"

"Well you do have admit Selene, it is kind of funny", Forkbraid smiled, "Take a thousand psychic couples to Mars and not expect them to have sex?"

Selene smiled back, "Well no. I just expected that they'd plan their pregnancies better. You know, start somewhat later, maybe space them out."

"Yep. To an imaginary schedule, that no one knew existed or had even considered", Forkbraid chuckled once more, then added, "Don't worry about it, we will sort it out. At the end of the day, it's just a simple logistics problem. At least the damned war is over. That's the main thing."

Selene looked at Forkbraid carefully, as they left the study and moved into the lounge room and sat down on the main couch.

Forkbraid asked, "Are you sure you don't want a glass of wine Selene?"

"No thank you Forkbraid, I've already said no", Selene replied.

"If you change your mind I can pour you one", Forkbraid still offered.

"Forkbraid. Now that the war is over and the Prophet is dead. Will you be going back to the Earth and taking up your old position, your old role as the viperous one?", Selene asked.

"You know Selene, we never did find out who the Prophet was. We never found out his identity. No name, nothing", Forkbraid noted.

"Yes Forkbraid, but what about your old role", Selene changed the subject back.

"Honestly Selene. I had thought about it", Forkbraid replied, "but I've been on Mars for quite sometime now."

"So you have thought about going back to the Earth", Selene replied almost coldly.

"I did think about, but the role of the viperous one can't be left vacant for any length of time. No more than a month at most", Forkbraid advised her.

"So you've been replaced", Selene replied, more upbeat.

"Well yes Selene and if I go back, I'll be pushing someone else out of their job, out of their role", Forkbraid explained.

"And you don't want to do that?", Selene queried.

"Of course not. And considering that I'm currently the Martian Armed Forces Fleet Captain, it's far better that I remain here on Mars. My ship, the Solstice is an exploration vessel. We can be at any of the Planets in minutes, although, we'd have to take the slow way back from the Dwarf Planets. We might even end transporting diplomats to the outer colonies. Let's not forget, that she's a Star Ship as well. There's a hell of a lot to be done exploration wise", Forkbraid replied.

"We still have to set up the serpent council and the wyvern covens as well", Selene noted.

"And there is that too, Selene", Forkbraid agreed, "There is still so much for me to do here."

"Well then", Selene smiled almost laughing, "It is a very good thing you're staying then Forkbraid."

"Why is that Selene?", Forkbraid asked.

Selene leant towards Forkbraid and kissed him gently on the lips, "Forkbraid you silly man, I'm pregnant!"

The war had ended.

The old High Prince, Heinrich journeys to his distant exile on the Dwarf Planet Eris.

His Brothers, Prince Wulfric and Prince Valdamar joining him in exile.

The new High Prince, Leopold sits upon the Jovian High Throne.

The New Flinders Psychic Academy looks like it will have plenty of students.

Folcrom Forkbraid and Folcrom Selene are expecting their first child.

The Solar System had returned to Peace.

And they have all Reaped their Just Rewards.

www.ingramcontent.com/pod-product-compliance
Lightning Source LLC
Chambersburg PA
CBHW050120030726
47505CB00007B/1960

* 9 7 8 0 6 4 5 9 9 0 6 7 6 *